FRAG

INI

'The tension builds to a gripping, unputdownable read. So haunting, the story became my own experience – I suffered the isolation and wilted during those hot Indian days and nights. Brilliantly realised, vividly written and meticulously researched. This enthralling novel engages the reader in a stimulating exploration of the perennial themes of sexual, social and political power.'

Ruth Mannion-Daniels *The Patrick O'Brian Society*

'Engaging and very thrilling. Richly evocative of life in Guernsey and India in early Victorian times. A splendid book. It was a wrench to leave that world.' Gwen Ritter

'*Fragments of Indigo* gives a compelling and seductive voice to the European pioneers in the early nineteenth century who made Bengal their home. I read it twice.'

Rex Valentine *BRLSI*

'I sense that *Fragments of Indigo* is set to become one of our favourite novels from this period. The character of Francina from small, abandoned child to young lady searching for love and self-fulfilment is as sensitively portrayed as Brontë's Jane Eyre.'

Olivia Lybbe-Simms

Marie-Louise Luxemburg was born in Ceylon and spent the first thirteen years of her life growing up in India and Malaysia.

She studied graphic design in London, English and Cultural Studies at Warwick University, and worked in several London publishing houses before becoming a freelance designer and writer. She lives with her partner in South West France, and Bath in Somerset.

Her family connections in Guernsey stretch back two hundred and fifty years to a French Huguenot preacher who settled on the Island and married into a local Guernsey family.

Her family connections in India stretch back to a young Breton who went out to India in 1755 and rose to become Commander of the Troops in the French Colony of Pondichéry. His daughter, who was born in Pondichéry, married a Tuscan surgeon who was doctor to the local rajahs. They settled in Bengal and began a new venture – planting indigo.

The indigo plant
Indigofera tinctoria

FRAGMENTS *of* INDIGO

Marie-Louise Luxemburg

little tower press

First published in 2016 by
Little Tower Press
35 Green Park, Bath BA1 1HZ
littletower.press@yahoo.com

ISBN 978-0-9929262-0-5

For

Martin, Toby, and Adam

Author's Note

The inspiration for this novel was a letter discovered in an old tin trunk. The letter, written in 1855, was sent from a mother to her daughter, and between its lines I sensed intrigue and scandal, events too delicate to divulge in respectable Victorian society. *Fragments of Indigo* is my interpretation of the story behind the letter. My characters, although created from clues gleaned in the scant references I uncovered, are fictitious and in no way profess to be portraits of the originals.

Most of events described really happened, but the timescale may have altered. All other characters are pure invention – but they could so easily have existed.

Glossary Note

At the time of this novel Britons living in India referred to themselves as 'Indians' and to the Indians as 'natives'. So an 'Indian Civilian' was a Briton in the Indian Civil Service, and Francina's 'Indian Aunt' was a lady of European stock living in India. Later in the nineteenth century Britons began to call themselves 'Anglo-Indian'. It was not until the twentieth century that 'Anglo-Indian' came to describe a person of mixed race, and 'native' was dropped in favour of 'Indian'.

Nineteenth century transliterations of Indian words such as Calcutta (now known as Kolkata), Cawnpore (now known as Kanpur), the Hoogly River (now known as the Hugli) or suttee (sati) have been retained.

CONTENTS

All night I dream you love me well,
All day I dream that you are cold;
Which is the dream? Ah, who can tell,
Ah, would that it were told.

Christina Rossetti *Untitled* 1853

FRANCINA'S
Paternal
Family
in St Pierre,
GUERNSEY
May 1855

- GRAND-PÈRE
  The Very Rev. Daniel Duquesne
  Dean of Guernsey
  m.
  GRAND-MÈRE
  - **AUNT MARQUAND**
    née **Mary Duquesne**
    widow
    - **Mrs McCREA**
      wife of **Colonel McCrea**
    - **Mrs BONAMY**
      wife of **Rev. Bonamy**
    - **COUSIN MATTIE**
      Matilda Marquand
      unmarried
    - **COUSIN ALEX**
      Alex Marquand
      Coffee planter, Ceylon
  - **AUNT SABONIÈRE**
    née **Sophia Duquesne**
    widow
  - UNCLE DUQUESNE
    Rev Havilland Duquesne
    m.
    AUNT DUQUESNE
    née Charlotte Maingay
    widow
    living at Haute House
    - COUSIN WILLIAM
      William Duquesne
      Coffee planter, died Ceylon
    - **COUSIN ANTHONY**
      Anthony Duquesne
      Lieutenant Bengal Artillery
    - **COUSIN JULIA**
      Julia Duquesne
  - **AUNT DORÉ**
    née **Louisa Duquesne**
    m.
    UNCLE DORÉ
    John Saumarez Doré
    Commissary General of Guernsey Militia
    living at Elm House
    - HORATIO
      died in India
    - **COUSIN CHARLIE**
      Charles Doré
      Midshipman, in Crimea
    - **COUSIN LULU**
      Louisa Doré
    - **COUSIN SAMMY**
      Saumarez Doré
  - **PAPA**
    Frank Duquesne
    Indigo planter, Bengal
    1826-1842
    Wine Exporter, London
    m. *Bengal*
    MAMMA
    vanished in India
    - **ANGELO**
      Angelo Duquesne
    - **FRANCINA**
      Francina Duquesne
    - BABY ALBERT
      Albert Duquesne
      died in India

FRANCINA'S Maternal Family in INDIA
July 1856

GRAND-PÈRE
Gaston Angelo Savi
from Elba
Indigo Planter
Bengal
m.
GRAND-MÈRE SAVI
born Pondichéry
French India
Living with the Bartons in Russel Street, Calcutta

- **AUNT BARTON**
  née **Maria Savi**
  b. Bengal
  m.
  UNCLE BARTON
  Robert Barton
  Partner, 'Crawley & Son' Merchants & Agents, Calcutta
  living Russel Street, Calcutta
  - **COUSIN JANE**
    (granddaughter of Aunt Barton
    m.
    FREDERICK BULPITT
    Indigo planter, Nudinapur, Kandria
    - **ALICE** age 6
    - **FREDDIE** age 5
- **JULES SAVI**
  b. Bengal
  Indigo Planter,
  Koxically,
  Burdwan
- **AUNT CECILIA**
  née **Cecilia Savi**
  born & m. Bengal
  UNCLE VAULOUÉ
  Bernard Vauloué
  Indigo planter
  living Middleton Street, Calcutta
  - **COUSIN JACQUES**
    Jacques Vauloué
    Indigo planter
    Moisgunge,
    Kishnaghur
    m.
    EVANGELINA
    b. Chandernagore, French Bengal
    - **VICTOR** age 5
    - **AURELIA** age 3
    - **PHILIPPE** age 1
  - **COUSIN CISSIE**
    Cissie Vauloué
    born Bengal
    m.
    ARCHIE BALFOUR
    Indian Civil Service
    Magistrate & Collector
    Tirhgunj
    - **LIONEL** age 4
    - **BABY MAUD**
- MAMMA
  Theresa Elizabeth Savi
  born & m. Bengal
  vanished 1842
  PAPA
  Francis William Duquesne
  b. Guernsey
  indigo planter
  Moisgunge,
  Kishnaghur
  1830-1842.
  now living London
  - **ANGELO**
    Angelo Duquesne
    born Bengal
    Coffee Planter, Ceylon
  - **FRANCINA**
    Francina Duquesne
    born Guernsey
  - BABY ALBERT
    Albert Duquesne
    born & died in Moisgunge,Bengal

Prologue

She is sipping tea near the rose garden. Sunlight has patterned her bell-shaped skirts and brushed the back of her cane chair, so she appears to have sprouted a pair of wings. Her sunhat has become a halo. She looks like the angel painted on the wall of the shrine, sailing across the Heavens on a golden cloud.

The angel inclines her head and beckons.

The child stumbles down the steps between lines of potted chrysanthemums, across the sea of grass and boards the island carpet to reach her. Then she hesitates. To kiss the beautiful apparition, a hill of muslin and lace must be negotiated. Standing on tiptoe she puts out fat little arms. The angel leans forward. The child feels under silky curls for the angel's neck and hoists herself up the white frothy slope. The angel's face is lost in shadow but the child knows she is smiling. She nestles close, pressing her belly against the softness above the whalebone. Burrowing under the sunhat, the child plants a wet kiss on each cheek and inhales deeply. The ambrosia of almond, sweat and jasmine makes her shiver. She is drowning, drowning in a tide of contentment.

The angel takes her hand and together they ascend a beam of shimmering light. The child has become the cherub in the fresco. She has discarded petticoats and pantalettes and is soaring naked across plump feathery clouds. The angel, too, has thrown off mortal clothing. Her gossamer shift twists and billows in dramatic sweeps to outline shapely limbs beneath. Faint musical notes ebb and flow on the wind, composing a melody sweeter than any the child has heard before. She grips the angel's hand. She will never let go. She will stay with the angel for ever.

But a distant sound, a thin shrill wail, distracts the angel and they plummet to earth.

'Dearest,' whispers Mamma, lifting the child off her lap, 'you are creasing my skirts.'

The child races across the grass. A swallowtail butterfly darts across a hedge of plumbago and skirts the line of hot red poinsettias. She chases it between overflowing flowerbeds of verbena, pansy and mignonette, until the heat makes her wilt and give up the chase. Sweat trickles down her temples. Her straw hat itches and the backs of her knees prickle. Slowing her pace, she gravitates towards the shade of the great banyan tree and finds the swing that the *mali* has made for her.

'Mamma, Mamma! Watch me!'

The child clutches the rough hemp ropes, leans back and thrusts out her feet. Slowly the swing begins to move and gain momentum. Back and forth, back and forth. Hugely proud, she glances round.

But Mamma is not looking. Mamma takes a lace bundle from the ayah's arms and smothers it with kisses. Her face is obscured by the sunhat but the child knows she is singing: her soft voice floats across the garden like cottonseed on a sultry day.

The child turns away and uses all her strength to propel her sturdy little legs back and forth. She looks up. Flashes of brilliant sunlight penetrate the canopy and momentarily dazzle her. She shuts her eyes. Behind her closed lids the flashes have turned green, glowing in her mind's eye like Mamma's emerald earrings. The motion of the swing seems more intense when her eyes are closed. Back and forth, back and forth.

It is hot, so very hot.

The steady rhythm stirs up a faint current of air to cool her cheeks. This is how Baby must feel when ayah rocks his cradle. In her darkness she becomes aware of the river noises that rumble quietly beyond the garden wall. The sounds are so constant she hardly notices them. But now, with her eyes shut, she hears coolies splashing in the shallows, bullocks bellowing, the steady pound-pounding as women beat clothes clean on rocks at the water's edge. She can picture the huge flat indigo barges; the small boats covered in wickerwork cowls that ferry them across the river; the fishermen casting nets from rickety crescent boats. Somewhere, a pariah dog is barking. Then a parakeet screeches in the treetops.

'I'll push you!'

'Please Angelo. As high as the cookhouse roof!'

Her brother shoves his hands into the small of her back. The child shrieks and grips the rope with white knuckles. Each time her brother pushes, she rises higher. Higher and higher. Until she can see over the garden wall and glimpse the wide muddy river meandering across the flat landscape. She sees the thatched roofs of the native village and the wisps of smoke rising from dung fires.

'Angelo, be careful! She's only little.'

'I'm four - a big girl, Mamma!'

She is laughing now.

'Push me higher, Angelo!'

She is flying like a bird, across a patchwork of blue and green; gliding over the mud walls of the paddy fields and across the endless fields of indigo - so high that she can see the yellow eyes of the crows perched in the cork trees. Vultures flap their enormous wings in surprise and leave their high lookout posts.

She follows the course of the sluggish river. Crocodiles slip silently into the brown water. Circling kites scatter. Far off her mother is calling: 'Careful, child, be careful!'

'I'm safe, Mamma!'

Jackal and wild boar scamper into the jungle. A cobra slithers into a hole.

Baby starts to wail.

She loses her balance, hits the ground with a thud and lies motionless. Her starched dress is torn; her white stockings are laddered and streaked with blood. She has lost a shoe. She lies in the red dust sobbing; waiting to be scooped up, kissed and caressed, comforted and reassured - but no one seems to notice her.

'Mamma, Mamma!'

Mamma does not come.

The child dabs her grazes with the hem of her skirt as she has seen Mamma do with a handkerchief. She tries to put on her shoe, but she cannot fasten the buckle. She feels helpless and anxious, frightened of the hollow growing inside her. Two big tears slide down her cheeks and splat in the dust.

Limping into the house, she finds Mamma's room. She scrabbles under the mosquito net and lies on her bed, perfectly still. She feels safer now, safe and small in this cage of netting. The sheets are clean and stretched tight. They smell of sun and grass and river water, but not of Mamma. She buries her head under the pillow, muffling the sounds of the river, the crows, and Baby's cries.

Of course! She knows exactly where Mamma is. Why did she not think of it before? She licks her tears and wipes her nose across the pillow. Her knees have painted long red streaks across the sheet, she notices, as she scrambles out of bed.

Now she is skipping across the garden. All the hurt has gone. A squirrel scampers across her path and darts up a tree trunk, twitching its tail.

The little shrine stands beyond the plantain grove, near the riverbank. To reach it she must skirt the stable block and follow the path through the vegetable garden.

She likes coming in here. It is cool and dark, for the candles are not alight. She can just make out the tiny altar, and the embroidered cushion on which Mamma kneels to pray to the Lady in Blue.

In the semi-darkness, the waxy camellias in the vase stand out like full moons; their scent so strong, it makes her dizzy.

The fresco behind the altar is growing clearer . . . She sees the cherub cradled in a billowing cloud; the smiling, half-dressed angel dancing on a beam of light. The child balances on the cushion then scrambles on to the altar. The angel watches with her head inclined. If the child stands on tiptoe, she can just touch the angel's face.

'Mamma?' she whispers.

But her cheek is cold and hard.

PART ONE

I watched and waited with a steadfast will:
And though the object seemed to flee away
That I so longed for, day by day,
I watched and waited still.

Christina Rossetti *Three Stages* 1854

GUERNSEY
May 1855

If only she could remember what really happened, but after all these years, imaginings mixed with memory and now it was impossible to distinguish between them. She hugged herself into a tight ball. The pain was still there; it was always there, bubbling inside her. Some days it grew so large that it rose into her throat and choked her. She remembered Papa's despair, Baby's inconsolable screams. She was told he had died of a broken heart. His little coffin was taken by boat to Kishnaghur, buried so far away. There was nothing left of him; no likeness, no teething ring, not even a lock of his hair. It was as if he had never existed.

A dog was barking. The noise echoed through the sleeping Town with the dull persistence of a steam hammer. Then a cock crowed in some far off place, and was challenged by the cock at Castle Carey. But the deep boom across the water checked everything. It was the cannon of Castle Cornet announcing sunrise, such a familiar sound that she usually slept through it - a safe comforting sound, reminding her that her Island was protected, watched over by the Artillery. Today, it was the spur to get up.

She slipped out of bed and drew back the curtains. In the dawn light the small grey Town looked enchanting. All down to the harbour rooftops glinted with moisture and the smoke from the brewery chimney was touched with pink.

The post-steamer was cutting an arc of foam through the water as it headed towards St Pierre. She used to dream that one day the steamer would bring her a letter. Now, of course, she knows better.

She pulled off her nightgown and eyed her reflection in the glass. She looked oddly vulnerable, clutching herself like that bowed figure in the painting: *Adam and Eve expelled from the Garden of Eden.* She drew her hands away and stood tall, striking the pose of the chained *Greek Slave* (the statue that was so admired at the Great

Exhibition), and turned her head defiantly to one side. If the slave was the ideal of feminine beauty, then she was not a bad specimen. Does she look like Mamma? How can she tell? Papa destroyed everything that had belonged to her. There was no letter or portrait, no tiny memento to keep in a locket near her heart. Mamma's face had faded from her memory. She knew nothing about her. Papa would not speak of her.

She poured cold water from the heavy jug into the bowl and washed herself. Refreshed, she put on her stockings, her lace-trimmed pantalettes and chemise, tied on three stiff petticoats, the heavy horsehair crinoline and her skirts. She hooked up her corset, buttoned her bodice and stared at herself in the glass. Trussed and constrained, the slave girl was now Miss Francina Duquesne, a picture of propriety.

After Mamma vanished, Papa sold his interest in the indigo concern and they left India. That year, Papa told her, the market collapsed. It was a bad time to sell. But she remembered little of those dark days. Angelo, being older, could recall them more clearly. Some months later, two stunned children and their grief-stricken father had stepped ashore at Southampton in a cold grey mist. Papa took lodgings in London and began a new venture. Much of his time was taken up travelling, and as he had no wish to leave his motherless children alone in a strange smoke-filled city, he asked his sister in Guernsey to take them in.

Francina untied the plait that fell down her back. Without Louisa's help it was difficult to dress her hair, so she resorted to a simple snood at the nape of her neck and two braids that she wound over the crown of her head. Her hair was so straight and heavy that she had given up the idea of copying Louisa's fashionable ringlets.

She was four years old when she had arrived in Guernsey. But Aunt Doré was nothing like the mother she had lost. Aunt never took her in her arms or sang her nursery songs. Aunt preferred the Bible to the company of children. She was more interested in the welfare of the Unfortunates than in the wellbeing of the children under her roof.

It was hard to adjust to life at Elm House. She was used to roaming free in that rambling garden in Bengal. She was used to being cosseted by an army of servants; running barefoot across cold stone floors, and sleeping beneath the stars under thin white gauze. Only Nurse had understood. Mrs Grieves, the large comfortable nurse who had come to look after little Saumarez, gave her the love and affection she had craved. For months she clung to her skirts, too frightened to let go.

Louisa murmured in her sleep. Francina watched her as she slept, her pink mouth puckered. A flaxen ringlet tightly wound in curl-papers had escaped from under her nightcap. Even in sleep, her cousin was beautiful.

Francina crept out of the bedroom and down the back-stairs, pausing by the towering mahogany cupboard that Aunt unlocked each morning to apportion the daily stores, methodically recording in her red accounts book each item that she handed to Cook.

She could hear Cook bustling in the kitchens. She was working here long before Francina had arrived. She had come as a widow with her young son, Baptiste, from the low-lying northern part of Guernsey, which was an island in Grand-mère's time (before the marshes were drained during the French Wars). Cook spoke Guernésiais with the dialect of the Vale and brought with her many of the superstitions that persist there. Francina suspected that she was *une quéraude,* a white witch.

Tying on her bonnet, she slipped outside. She loved this time of day, when few people were about. The air was clear and fresh. She climbed the steps and crunched across the gravel to the coach house.

Baptiste was sitting on a step brushing mud off Uncle's top boots, whistling softly to himself. He never treated her with suspicion. He had just accepted the little foreigner. He was short, sturdy like his mother, and had absorbed her vast store of country knowledge. He knew all the plants that grew on the Island, their good and bad effects. Sometimes at first light before the household was awake, he would roam the damp green lanes for herbs, berries or mushrooms, which he would sell to the Town herbalists. He could name the birds that hunted over the wet gorse and point out where their nests were hidden. As children they had all played together. They had lain on springy tufts of heather at the cliff's edge, the wind tugging at their hair, and watched in awe as he had edged down fearlessly between crags and cleft-rocks in search of gulls' eggs.

Things were different now. They had grown up. Baptiste was the footman. He looked up as she approached

'You're early, La Missie.'

'I could not sleep - I shall get some air. It is such a beautiful morning.' She could hear the dogs whining. 'Untie the dogs, Baptiste; I shall take them with me.'

He unlocked the kennels and the spaniels sprang out, wagging their docked tails and jumping up at her.

'They're frisky first thing,' he said, holding their collars.

He opened the little iron gate for her and the dogs bounded out, pulling at their leashes.

In front of the house was an area of open ground, the only public promenade of St Pierre. In an hour or two it would be seething with townspeople walking their dogs, or nursemaids airing their charges. Sometimes the Militia entertained them with loud, spirited music. On fête days the place choked with painted stalls and fluttering flags.

Now it was quiet. The rising sun had cast long shadows and ground mist covered the grass. She walked along a path shaded by elm trees that skirted the open space and sat on a bench on the far side. Blackbirds hopped about, inspecting the ground for morsels.

Here, she had an excellent view of the houses built on the ridge above Town. Elm House was the last and grandest in the row. It was a square house of white stucco with large airy windows - too plain for fashionable taste, but it suited Aunt's temperament. Only three storeys were visible, but on the garden side there was a lower floor, for the ground sloped down to the lane behind Mr Priaulx's garden.

She unleashed the dogs and they raced off to chase the birds

She stifled a yawn. She had slept fitfully, disturbed by a dream and had woken, struck by a curious sensation that Mamma was standing at the foot of her bed. What did it mean? She had feigned sleep, kept a watchful vigil through her lashes, but nothing had re-appeared. She had heard rumours that old Mère Falliot had 'table-turning' sessions in her cottage and could summon up spirits beyond the grave. If only she could find an excuse to speak to the old woman without Aunt finding out.

A slight girl dressed in black was walking towards the house. It was Ellie. When the dogs saw her, they raced over, barking. Ellie opened the little gate and disappeared down the steps to the kitchen.

The dogs followed, hoping to be fed.

Francina stood up and brushed her skirts. She, too, must return indoors. Aunt would not approve of her sitting here at this hour unaccompanied.

A whiff of Uncle's tobacco infused the library. It was the only room where he was allowed to smoke, for Aunt detested the weed. The smell reminded Francina of him - his sparkling eyes, his mottled nose, and the tickly moustache that hid his smile. In her mind's eye she saw Uncle lean back in his leather chair, waistcoat buttons straining across his paunch. She saw him draw on his pipe and watch spirals of smoke rise to the ceiling. Sometimes, she would prepare his pipe for him. She treasured those moments, feeling his eyes on her as she pulled strands of umber out of the tobacco box to stuff into his pipe.

She could spend all day amongst these shelves, helping Uncle to catalogue his books, but Aunt disapproved of her being in here, so it was only when Aunt was on some charitable errand or otherwise distracted that she dared to venture here.

'Too much knowledge causes discontentment,' Aunt would say, but Francina knew that Miss Chesterton thought that 'Knowledge can set a girl free'.

She raised the blind. Sunlight had transformed the garden terraces into patterns of light and shade, accentuated the tops of the high granite walls and thrown deep shadows in their wake. It streamed through the panes, catching motes of dust and casting diamond patterns on the boards. It reflected off the sea, the glare so brilliant that the islands of Herm and Sark appeared as ghostly shadows. Rooftops obscured the encircling walls of the little harbour she knew so well, but across the glittering water she could just make out the massive walls of Castle Cornet, rising like an old worn volcano from the sea.

Standing on the library steps, she extracted the volume from its hiding place. She had recently found this tiny book (such that a lady might conceal in her pocket) and knew instinctively that Aunt would forbid her to read it, so she had taken the precaution of hiding it on the top shelf, and was reading snatches when it seemed safe to do so.

She perched on the window seat, spread her skirts and found the page she had marked. The stark chapter on *Infidelity in Love* was followed by a chapter on *Monstrous Births*. She caught her breath as she studied the engravings of children born with two heads, or four arms. Does Infidelity breed Monsters? The author was unclear.

Ellie appeared at the door.

'Missie, I have been looking all over for you. Did you not hear the bell for petit déjeuner?'

Francina glanced at the clock, returned the little book to the top shelf and ran down the stairs. They were waiting for her.

The servants were huddled by the buffet, the Dorés stood around the table. Aunt's glare followed her to her chair. Uncle snapped his hunter shut and they bowed their heads for Morning Prayers, just as the cherub on the old French clock struck the hour with his tiny baton. She was ten minutes late.

When the servants had filed out, Aunt asked for an explanation.

Francina muttered an apology as she sat down. 'I was in the library, Aunt,' she whispered. 'I lost sight of the time.'

Aunt shook out her napkin with a practiced flick of the wrist. She was dressed as usual in a black gown and plain white cap. The only decorations she allowed herself were the chatelaine at her waist and the pince-nez pinned to her chest.

'See me in the parlour after breakfast.'

This was Aunt's way of saying that her hand would feel the cut of the little riding-crop kept in a drawer of her escritoire. It was what she expected. But nothing had prepared her for the first time it had happened. No one had ever deliberately hurt her before. Later, she discovered that she had not been singled out; her cousins were just as susceptible to the whip.

This was the way of life at Elm House.

Baptiste entered with a steaming dish, which he set ceremoniously on the table. Uncle Doré removed the silver cover and a wisp of steam rose to the ceiling. Francina buttered her *pain* as Uncle spooned bacon and devilled kidneys onto his plate. This was not for her. This was never for her. She was obliged to follow Aunt's frugal diet.

✸

The girls ran down the garden steps, through the door set in the high wall and into the lane behind Mr Priaulx's garden. Francina tripped, strewing books everywhere.

'Hurry up! Don't make us even later!' cried Louisa.

Francina picked up her books carefully. Her hand smarted.

They dashed past Candie and caught up with old Père Le Page transporting a box across Town. Louisa stopped the cart with a beguiling smile and addressed the carrier in Guernésiais. Aunt would have been horrified to hear her speak the language of the country people. When the Dorés spoke French, it was Parisian French.

The carrier muttered through pipe-clenched teeth. Taking this as consent, Louisa scrambled into the back of the cart.

'Come up, Ina. It will be quicker.'

Francina climbed up after her. They perched on an old trunk, tucked in their skirts and waited. The carrier cracked the whip across the old mule's back and they set off at a snail's pace. A woman, balancing a basket of laundry on her head, eyed them curiously.

Soon the cart reached tree-lined Grange Road and stopped by a pair of heavy gates opened just enough to allow pupils to enter in single-file. A paved path, constricted on both sides by a low clipped hedge, led to the front steps of a large square house. The house was smothered in ivy, which made it look as though it was being squeezed by the tentacles of a giant octopus. A maîtresse stood at the entrance ringing the old iron bell. Above her head, just visible through the ivy, was a sign announcing in bold black letters:

MADAME LE BROCQ'S ACADEMY FOR YOUNG LADIES

They clambered out of the cart, ignored the smirks of the girls who had arrived by more conventional means, and followed the shoal of blue dresses into the cavern.

After assembly, they changed into their satin slippers for a dancing lesson in the hall with Monsieur Lasource, whose grandfather (it was said) had instructed the French aristocracy of the *ancien régime* to dance at Versailles. Monsieur Lasource was hot headed and particular, and if one of his pupils did not carry out the steps correctly, he spluttered a torrent of incomprehensible French, and banged his ebony cane so hard on the boards that little pitted scars followed him about the hall.

Francina loved dancing and was often asked to demonstrate. Today, she realised, catching the dancing master's eyes upon her, would be no exception. Monsieur Lasource placed his hand on the small of her back and signalled to Mademoiselle Tissot, who was hard of hearing and awaiting instructions at the pianoforte.

Mademoiselle pounded the keys, and dancing master and pupil launched into a spirited polka past a line of blurred girls.

One-two-three - hop! One-two-three - hop!

What an absurd couple we make, she thought, removing her gaze from his glistening pate, she was at least two inches taller. She caught sight of Mary Lihou standing apart from the other girls, sullen and forlorn. She longs to be in my place, Francina thought with a little rush of triumph, for she knew (all the girls knew) of Mary's *pash* for the dancing master.

Monsieur threw his head back. 'See, Mademoiselles,' he shouted. 'Now, find partners and copy the steps. In - time - to - the music!'

Skirts whirled in all directions. Suppressed giggles rippled above the notes. Mary Lihou was dancing with Hettie Tupper. The thinnest with the fattest. Another incongruous pair.

The next lesson was with Miss Chesterton. Their English teacher, new to the Academy, was spiriting novel ideas into their lessons. Instead of teaching them poems by rote, she urged them to understand the meaning behind the poet's words.

'To reach his soul, his *raison d'être!'* proclaimed Miss Chesterton, thumping her breastbone with a clenched fist.

It was a daring concept - especially with a wicked poet such as Lord Byron. Madame Le Brocq would certainly not approve if she knew, and that made their lessons all the more thrilling. They studied his poetry carefully, looking for clues that would uncover his dark secrets.

Does Miss Chesterton also have dark secrets? Francina wondered. What circumstances had made her accept a post at Madame Le Brocq's? Was she fleeing from an impossible romance? Perhaps she had been governess at a rambling country mansion and had fallen hopelessly in love with the Master, who, she discovered one dreadful rainy day, was betrothed to Another:

'It is known that Mr Rochester is to be married?'

'Yes; and to the beautiful Miss Ingram.'

She could picture him: *strong, with an impressive chest, stern-featured, with a heavy brow; long past youth but not yet middle-aged . . .*

But fancy Miss Chesterton fleeing to *Guernsey!* She must feel lonely on an Island where foreigners are treated with suspicion. Why, lodging at the Academy and overseeing the dormitory of boarders, Miss Chesterton had few opportunities to meet any eligible gentlemen.

'Read next, if you please, Miss Gosselin.'

Sophie Gosselin stood up and recited in her timid voice:

> 'Tis melancholy, and a fearful sign
> of Human frailty, folly, also crime,
> That love and marriage rarely can combine
> Although they both are born in the same clime;
> Marriage from love, like vinegar from wine -
> A sad, sour, sober beverage - by time
> is sharpen'd from its high celestial flavour,
> Down to a very homely household savour.'

'What do you understand by: *love and marriage rarely can combine,* Miss Gosselin?'

'Could it be that a marriage starts with promise then turns sour?' she whispered. 'As wine becomes vinegar, Miss Chesterton?'

'Good. But do you know why that should happen, girls?'

'No, Miss Chesterton,' chorused the girls, sitting up with interest.

'Marriage changes the participants. A woman before marriage is idolised, courted and wooed - but after marriage she becomes nothing more than her husband's property. In short, she becomes his *slave*. - What is a slave, Miss du Frocq?'

'A person who belongs to another, Miss Chesterton?'

'Exactly, Miss du Frocq. Lord Byron was lamenting the fact - as indeed do *I* – that marriage is not a union of mutual respect and understanding, but one of master and slave.' Miss Chesterton pivoted around and wrote in large letters on the blackboard:

'*That* is the lot of the married woman, girls,' she said, striking the words with a pointer. 'She has no rights. She must forfeit her property, stifle her aspirations and be at the complete mercy of her husband. Even her children do not belong to her. Her opinions count for nothing. So, girls, she ceases to express opinions and *as surely as night follows day* she sinks into ennui. - What is *ennui*, Miss Doré?'

'Listlessness, Miss Chesterton.'

'And . . ?'

'Fatigue?'

'You must pay attention, Miss Doré, I have told you often enough!' Miss Chesterton's eyes searched impatiently round the room. 'Does anyone remember?'

'The scourge of Society?'

'Indeed, Miss Duquesne,' beamed Miss Chesterton. 'Ennui is the scourge of Society.'

Tinkling keys were advancing down the corridor. Madame Le Brocq was on the prowl. A hush fell over the classroom as they waited, still and silent, for the footsteps to pass . . .

Instead, the door burst open and Madame swept into the room.

Benches grated. The girls stood up and curtsied. Madame stood motionless beside Miss Chesterton, small, compact and acute; her neck swivelling like an oystercatcher's ready to peck anything that moved. Her sharp eyes darted back and forth - then rested for a moment on the blackboard. There was a collective intake of breath. Would Madame realise that they were studying the work of a poet with unspeakable passions and forbidden loves?

But this time she was out-smarted. She looked away again, her eyes registering nothing.

'May I be of assistance, Madame Le Brocq?'

'Miss Chesterton, I wish to have a word with one of your girls.'

Francina followed Madame Le Brocq's tapping footsteps down the corridor. Me? Why me? Has something happened to Papa?

Madame ushered her into her parlour. This was the first time Francina had stepped into this hallowed sanctuary. It was dark and close. Ashes smouldered in the grate and the windows were tightly shut. Around the walls, engraved heads of noble personages stared disdainfully down at her. Madame positioned herself between Her Gracious Majesty and the Prince Consort, and sat down behind her desk. She studied her pupil carefully, as if seeing her for the first time.

'Miss Duquesne, reports have just come to my attention. Mrs Doré is your aunt, I believe?'

'Indeed, Madame.'

'Your legal guardian?'

'Yes, Madame.'

'But how can that be? Your mother is alive, is she not?'

'I do not know, Madame.'

'You do not know if your mother is alive!' Madame stiffened behind her desk. 'Why the mystery, Miss Duquesne? - Did you ever ask yourself that?'

Madame produced a handkerchief from the folds of her skirts and held it to her nose, as if to block an unpleasant smell.

'I also understood that your father was a gentleman,' she sniffed. 'Now I hear he is in trade!'

If Papa was found to have leprosy or committed murder, Madame Le Brocq and the Noble Heads could not have been more horrified.

'I might have been prepared to make an exception for a *tradesman's* daughter, not only out of respect for the Doré name, but also out of regard for that charitable lady, your aunt, who has the goodness to keep you under her roof. I accepted you as a pupil at this school in good faith, Miss Duquesne, but I have been deceived, woefully deceived. This is a highly respectable establishment. The faintest hint of scandal cannot be allowed to tarnish our good name. - Miss Louisa Doré leaves at the end of the semester, does she not?'

'Yes, Madame. She is to attend the Conservatoire in Brussels.'

'An exemplary pupil. Now that young lady is a fitting credit to the Academy. You will leave with Miss Doré. I shall write to inform your aunt of my decision. I do not wish to distress the good lady more than necessary, so I shall allow you to remain a pupil until the end of the semester. That will cause minimum disruption, and - I hope - no hint of scandal.'

*

When the noon cannon sounded from Castle Cornet, the girls hurried home for déjeuner. Madame Le Brocq's letter burned in her pocket. For a moment she thought of ripping it into pieces and throwing it in the ditch, but Aunt would learn of Madame's decision eventually, so the sooner the ordeal was over the better. She slipped the letter amongst the pile on the hall salver as they filed into the dining room and mentally prepared herself for the eruption.

'I had a word with the Dean this morning,' said Uncle Doré to his wife as he sprinkled chunks of stale bread over his *potage*. 'He made some very favourable remarks about the Charity Fair. He is fully aware that without your unstinting hard work, my dear, the Fair would not have raised a fraction of the amount for the War Fund.'

Aunt gave a faint smile.

Baptiste brought in the English newspapers and the mail that he had collected from the Post Office. He handed the newspapers to Uncle and the letters to Aunt, who distributed them at the table.

'I have a letter from Charlie,' cried Louisa.

And *I* have one from Angelo, thought Francina. She put it in her pocket. She would read it later, away from prying eyes.

'*Her Majesty* passed in the Royal Yacht on her way to Osborne, so close that Charlie had an excellent view of her,' Louisa said, skimming through her letter. 'And when the fleet gave the Royal Salute, there was much cheering. – Oh, if only we could have been there!'

Charlie's portrait hung above the buffet. He was the elder son. The artist had captured his sturdy physique, his brown curls, his high forehead, but had enhanced his mouth, so he stared down at them with a crooked smile.

'Charlie is on his way to the *war*.' Louisa's eyes brimmed with tears. 'Hateful war! Why should we care about the silly Turks!'

It was Charlie's greatest wish to join the Royal Navy. He loved the sea and was always asking the fishermen to take him out in their boats. Sometimes, when he was late home, he was found at St Sampson watching the brigs and schooners under construction in the boatyard. All the caulkers and riggers knew him by name. In the evenings he would make tiny replicas of the sailing ships he had observed. One graced a shelf in the library. Uncle was particularly impressed by the rigging simulated in fine silver wire.

Francina glanced across the table. Aunt's expression told her that she had reached Madame's letter.

'I understand that you spoke to Madame Le Brocq this morning?'

'Yes, Aunt.'

'Did she give you an explanation for your dismissal?'

'Madame has discovered that my father is in trade.' Francina took a deep breath. 'She also asked . . . about Mamma.'

Silence descended, muffling the clatter of silver on porcelain, the tick of the clock. Baptiste left the room and closed the door.

Uncle looked at his wife, enquiringly.

Aunt passed him the letter. When he had finished reading, he removed his spectacles and raised his eyebrows. 'And how do you feel about this, Francina?'

'I am resigned to it, Uncle.'

2

My dearest Sister –

There is so much Society in the City that I can scarce find a moment to pick up my pen. I am staying with my old friend de Jersey, who has been showing me the sights. We have been to Epsom, the Gardens at Vauxhall, and have dined sumptuously at his Club with several chums from Elizabeth College. I even had the good fortune to win at cards.

And now for the important news: I am going to Ceylon! I have booked my passage on the Queen, *which sails from Gosport on 30th July. I have even ordered my cabin furniture, which I trust will be fitted in time.*

Father seems more at ease now that my plans are settled, and so, I treated him to a night at the Opera. By the bye, at the end of the performance, we were accosted by a curious couple who recognised Father from Indian days. Mrs Barton, it transpires, is our Mother's sister! We dined with them the following night and were entertained in the most lavish way. The Bartons mentioned that they would be spending some weeks in Guernsey, so Father suggested that they pay you a visit. (I am warning you in advance, for you may receive a letter from them soon.) I have had a pressing invitation to stay with them in Calcutta - which I think I will accept. The Bartons are a capital introduction to Indian Society. They have been there for so long - they must know a great many people.

I must now tear myself away from de Jersey's influence, return to Father's lodgings and immerse myself in dreary studies. I plan to return to Guernsey for a short holiday before I leave.

Pray for me to do well in my examinations!

- Your loving brother, Angelo

Mamma's sister? She did not know Mamma had a sister. Francina re-read the letter. After all these years of silence, all this secrecy, should she welcome or dread a visit from a person who must have known Mamma intimately? She stuffed the letter in her pocket as the hand bell marked the end of lessons. Feelings tumbled inside her. All those questions she had tried to ask Papa - could Mrs Barton answer them, or would she be as evasive as everyone else?

They stopped at the open ground behind Elizabeth College on the way home. They used to play in the field by the old l'Hyvreuse Mill, before the Victoria Tower was built, but now it was fenced off and used by the Arsenal. The recent spate of sun had forced wild flowers to burst into colour, and insects were flitting from bloom to bloom in a frenzy of activity.

Louisa sat in the shade on a tuft of springy grass. A nanny goat, tethered nearby, was tearing at the new leaves.

Francina untied her bonnet and flopped beside her.

'Only a few more weeks at that beastly place.'

Now that she had got over the affront, she was delighted to be leaving. Why, she had learned more in a month from the books in Uncle's library than from five years at Madame Le Brocq's. She saw herself flinging her school books out of the carriage like Miss Becky Sharp and shouting, 'Good riddance. That is what I think of your Academy, Madame!'

She lay in the grass and watched leaves quiver overhead.

'All the years we have wasted listening to Madame prattle on about nothing. If only we could have had an education like the boys - an education that would have prepared us -'

'Don't be absurd, Ina. How could a smattering of Latin or Greek possibly help us to become better wives and mothers?'

'But what about those who do not become wives or mothers?'

Louisa ignored this question.

'I shall be sorry to leave,' she said.

'Of course you will,' snorted Francina. 'You're Madame's *pet*.'

'Madame might have been more charitable towards you, if you were not always so obstinate in your manner.'

Louisa sprang up and marched up the lane, but it was blocked by a farmer driving his oxen across the open ground. He shouted and struck the animals across their rumps. They bellowed, but did not budge.

Francina ran after her. 'I only want to be useful. Perhaps I could become a nurse like Miss Nightingale.'

Louisa was tired of this conversation. She had heard it many times before. 'You know Mamma would not approve of you taking up nursing and mixing with common soldiers and sailors. If you want to be useful, you must help Mamma with her charity work.'

'Giving the poor food or clothing when times are hard eases their condition for a while - but nothing changes. Why, Lulu? Why - despite all Aunt's efforts and the good works of others like her - does it never get better for them?'

'How can you dismiss Mamma's good works so glibly. You, of all people! Where would you be without Mamma's charity? You would be *nothing*.'

Francina bit her lip. 'You are right, Lulu. I am nothing.'

The oxen were moving at last.

They strode silently up the lane and climbed the steps to the New Cemetery. Eyeing a fresh mound of earth topped with a wreath of wilting flowers that had appeared since their last visit, they made their way to a stone tomb sited in the far corner of the cemetery and sat in the long grass under a cypress tree. They often came to this peaceful spot. Louisa's brother and sister lay at rest in this tomb. They had died within days of each other during the cholera epidemic that had struck the Island before Louisa was born.

Insects rose into the air and settled on their laps to investigate the blue fabric of their dresses. The air was hot and sultry, vibrating with the hum of bees. Francina untied her bonnet and shook out her hair.

Louisa brushed a fly from her face. 'You were reading a letter in Madame's lesson. Who was it from?'

'Angelo. He has booked his passage to Ceylon. He will be leaving soon.'

They fell silent, their eyes drawn towards a grave-digger working near the entrance. Shovelfuls of earth flew out of the hole as rhythmically as a pendulum.

'I shall not see him for years and years.'

'Be brave, Ina. We must be happy for Angelo. Why, the country must have changed since William went out. Alex Marquand would never have taken out his bride if the place were still uncivilised.'

They fell silent again.

Angelo was going; Lulu would soon be gone . . . How would she fill the void that stretched ahead?

Francina picked some sweet-scented violets and placed them on the tomb. No one would marry her without a dowry. She would become one of those countless old maids who filled their lives with meaningless activity, pitied and ridiculed by society. She glanced at Louisa. Her future shone like a beacon before her. After a year at the Conservatoire and a season in London, she would have poise and manners to conquer any level of society. Louisa would have sophisticated friends and worldly conversations, while she would know nothing of life beyond this Island.

'May I see Angelo's letter?'

Francina stared at her. She wanted to keep Mrs Barton to herself, to mull over the questions she would put to her. But she knew that Louisa would not rest until she had prised the letter from her.

Louisa read in silence. Her bonnet lay on the grass. Sunlight had transformed the pollen above her head into an aura, and her curls to a golden tangle.

She belongs here, thought Francina. Kneeling with her head bowed, she looks like an angel watching over this tomb.

Louisa looked up, her eyebrows perfectly arched. 'Fancy, your mother's sister!'

'Please don't mention this letter, Lulu,' Francina said, knowing how free she was with her tongue. 'Not until Mrs Barton writes, of course. I don't want to trouble Aunt needlessly.'

'I shall not say a word,' said Louisa. She loved secrets.

3

'You were seen alighting from a carrier's cart outside the Academy,' frowned Aunt Doré. 'What induced you to do such a thing?'

The girls stared at the strawberry hulls on their dessert plates.

'Today, I called on Mrs Hawtrey – who has improved since my last visit – unfortunately however, Mrs Lihou was also there. It was *she* who saw you riding in the cart.'

It had to be Mrs Lihou - the most pernicious gossip in Town.

'I will not have my family ridiculed by the likes of Mrs Lihou. On a small Island such as this - as you both know full well - every lapse of decorum is noticed and commented upon.' Aunt swept out of the room. 'See me in the parlour immediately!'

An hour later, sitting in her high-backed chair, Aunt Doré was still smarting with indignation. 'Louisa. If your posture does not improve, you will have to use a backboard.'

Louisa sat up. She had been lolling on the sofa, nursing her sore hand and feeling utterly wretched. Prince, who had sensed her mood, rested his muzzle on her lap.

It was hard to believe that the smiling woman in the miniature hanging above the fireplace and the frowning one in the flesh studying the Bible were the same person. The miniature was painted when Aunt was about Louisa's age. Curls peep out from her lace cap and frame her bonny face. Louisa, sitting there with her fair tumbling curls, was the image of her mother at that age.

Francina returned to her novel. With her dark hair, close-set brows and long straight nose, she did not resemble anyone in the family. She turned the page, feeling irresistibly drawn to the misunderstood orphan in the story. *Castaway, interloper, alien*, Mr Brocklehurst had called her.

'Francina, could you not occupy your time more usefully?'

She had placed her volume inside a work of poetry as a

precaution. But nothing, it seemed, ever escaped Aunt's sharp eyes.

Slipping the volume behind the curtains, she sprang up to fetch her workbox. Returning to the window seat, she made a great show of unfolding the canvas and threading the needle. She pulled the crimson wool in and out of the petal of a blown rose with much exaggeration and little enthusiasm. It was infuriating. She had reached an interesting point in the story and longed to know what would follow. But at least it was better to embroider hideous pictures than to be sent to a miserable Institution.

It was cool and dark in Church, and Francina felt oddly mollified, cocooned in the Doré family pew. It was a change of scene, a chance to quell the racking boredom. Whispers and coughs gradually subsided, and the Service began.

She preferred the English services in St James, but out of loyalty to Grand-père they came here. (Grand-père had been Dean of Guernsey for nearly forty years. Older members of the congregation still spoke of his fiery sermons from this very pulpit.) His memorial was mounted on the nave wall close to the family pew. It was a marble relief depicting Grand-père on his deathbed. The shapely young woman in the memorial kneeling devoutly before him had to be his wife, but she was nothing like the Grand-mère Francina had known. She remembered a formidable old lady, dressed in black, sitting in her north-facing parlour that overlooked the Cimetière des Frères. Grand-mère took a morbid pleasure in that little grassy cemetery with its array of lichen-spattered tombs. She would stare at Grand-père's tomb as though engaged in some secret telepathic conversation with him. Sometimes a smile crossed her face, as though Grand-père had whispered something amusing in her ear. Once, Grand-mère had restrained her with a claw-like hand of surprising strength as she had walked past the chair. She had tried not to cry. Grand-mère smelled of fish and looked like a witch. Little grey hairs twitched at the corners of her mouth.

'Child, do you see Grand-père's tomb?'

'Oui, Grand-mère.'

'Soon I shall be united with Grand-père in that tomb. Be sure to visit us.'

'Oui, Grand-mère.'

'Keep it tidy. Free from weeds.'

When Grand-mère died, she left Francina a small bequest, which helped Papa to finance her education. Papa came back for the funeral. It was the last time he had set foot on the Island. He looked so distraught, hunched in a huge black cloak as he led the long cortège to the cemetery that he had frightened her.

Close to Grand-père's memorial was a family plaque commemorating the life of her cousin Horatio. She remembered him as an intimidating youth with large hands. He left for India shortly after she arrived, and she never saw him again. He died, the plaque informed her, *carrying the colours of his regiment in the memorial victory of Moodkee in the Punjab War.*

The Dean's voice rumbled down the nave, and skittered over the heads of the congregation. It was growing hot and oppressive, and it was hard to keep her eyes open . . . She had slept badly, her mind confused by fragments of dreams . . .

Someone comes into the coach-house. She holds her breath and crawls to the hatchway, carefully avoiding the creaking floorboard. The pocket of her pinafore catches on a nail and she loosens it carefully. Aunt will whip her if it tears. A cobweb brushes across her face but she keeps quiet. They must not know she is up here . . . Horatio and Polly are playing a rough and tumble game by the tackle. Polly's cap comes off. Her hair unravels. She giggles and tells him to stop but he just laughs and pushes his face into hers. Polly loses her balance. She slips down the wall and her skirts scrunch up. Horatio has grabbed her wrists. Polly's cheeks are red; her eyes as bright as a cornered rabbit. Polly's giggles have become choking sobs. Polly is her friend. She wants to climb down the ladder and push him away. But Horatio is big. He will hurt her again. She shrinks into her Secret Place. She must stay here until . . . until they leave. The cat wafts her tail across her arm. They're only playing a game, Kitty, she whispers. She buries her face in the soft fur as the sickening hurt grows inside. She draws the old sacking over her head. It is hot and itchy, and smells of mildew. Her head is pounding so hard she can hardly hear Kitty's purrs. Hush Baby hush don't make a sound.

'Wake up, Ina, the Service is over.'

Francina picked up her prayer book and followed Louisa down the aisle. Aunt and Uncle and the rest of the congregation were outside, blinking in the sunlight. Old Grand-mère Doré enveloped in her black silk calash was being helped into her sedan chair. That old chair emblazoned with the Doré arms was a familiar sight about Town, for the old lady was carried everywhere down narrow winding lanes and up precarious flights of steps.

The girls followed the Dorés and the sedan chair up High Street.

'Lulu, do you remember Polly?'

'Polly? Whatever made you think of her?' Louisa flicked her curls at two boys from Elizabeth College who were sauntering past.

'What became of her?'

'Nurse said she deserved what she had coming to her.'

'What did she have coming to her?'

'How should I know, Ina? It was so long ago.'

It was strange to think of Polly after all this time . . . or was it Polly? There were moments when she had the impression that it was not Polly in her dream, but Mamma – and not Horatio, but someone else.

Aunt and Uncle were out, so Francina was enjoying an evening of uninterrupted reading, and she had reached an astonishing point in the story: Mr Rochester had just asked Jane to marry him. To have such a proposal, such a declaration of love! A penniless governess to become mistress of such a grand house. If only such things really happened.

The door opened and Louise appeared with her work basket.

'Miss Hobson must be in love,' she announced. 'She is so agreeable these days.'

'But with whom?'

'Shall we try and find out?'

Louise rang the bell and ordered Baptiste to fetch Aunt's maid from the attic bedroom. A few minutes later Miss Hobson stood shyly at the door, carrying a bundle of stockings. She was dressed in her simple grey gown. She was neither beautiful nor plain but pleasantly agreeable. Her skin was pale and freckled, and her unruly red hair was scraped into a chignon.

'We thought you might sit with us, Miss Hobson. It must lonely in that little room of yours.'

Miss Hobson looked surprised and rather touched.

In Aunt's high-backed chair, Miss Hobson looked younger than her supposed twenty-eight years. She eased a black stocking over a wooden mushroom and began to darn.

Humming to herself, Louisa took out the patience cards from the walnut box and dealt them in a circle on the small round table.

Francina looked up from her book and studied Miss Hobson. She knew little about her except that her last mistress had come to Guernsey hoping the sea air would improve her health, but she had died soon afterwards leaving Miss Hobson alone and in distressed circumstances. Aunt heard of her plight and found her a position at Elm House.

'Tell us about your time at the orphanage, Miss Hobson,' said Louisa.

Francina pictured her standing on a stool like poor Jane Eyre.

'I shall always be beholden to the charity for providing me with a roof over my head, Miss Louise, but I cannot say that I was happy.' Miss Hobson placed the darning on her lap and gazed out of the window. 'We were always cold and hungry, and our education was poor. If it had not been for a kind lady who taught us needlework, I do not know what would have become of me.'

'Were you always at the orphanage?' probed Louisa.

'Indeed no!' Miss Hobson said with surprising passion. 'When I was born, my father was curate in a country parish. When he died, Mother became housekeeper at Levison Hall, a fine country house in Hampshire. We were happy there, for the mistress was kind to us.'

Louisa transposed a king to the bottom of the pack.

'Yes, but did Levison Hall accommodate as many servants as Beau Sejour? A *butler*, perhaps?'

Louisa slapped down the last king.

'I was young, Miss Louise. I cannot remember.' Frowning, Miss Hobson tied a knot and cut the wool with her sissors.

Perhaps Louise was opening old memories that were best forgotten, thought Francina. She hoped Louisa would lose interest and stop questioning Miss Hobson, for she wanted to return to her book.

Jane Eyre had just discovered the identity of the mad woman. Poor Miss Eyre, so heartlessly deceived by Mr Rochester! Of course she must leave him - for how could she live as his wife without the sanctity of marriage? And how could she trust a man who had so grievously deceived her by denying the existence of his wife, the mad woman in the attic?

The maniac bellowed; she parted her shaggy locks from her visage, and gazed wildly at her visitors. I recognised well that purple face -

Numbness crept over her. Had Mamma been sent away? Was that the truth behind her disappearance? Was Mamma a lunatic, a mad demon locked up in an Institution and hidden from sight? A blight on the family name?

The lunatic sprang and grappled his throat viciously; and laid her teeth to his cheek.

She tried desperately to remember . . . to see them clearly . . . those distant images, those hazy memories.

'That is my wife,' said he. 'Such is the sole conjugal embrace I am ever to know!'

Now she understood why Papa refused to speak. He was protecting her from the truth.

4

'You have turned the wrong way,' shouted the dancing master. 'What is the matter with you this afternoon?'

'I feel a little hot, Monsieur,' whispered Francina. She was so pleased to have been chosen to dance at the end of term concert, but how could she remember the steps while her mind churned with images of Mamma locked in a sunless cell and surrounded by lunatics?

Monsieur Lasource looked at her closely, and added a little more kindly, 'Perhaps I am working you too hard. Sit quietly in the vestibule for a few minutes, Mademoiselle, and try to regain your composure.'

Dismissing her with a wave of his hand, he turned and clapped. 'The rest of you, face the piano and raise the tambourines in your right hands. *Right* hand, ignorant girl!'

Francina slipped out of the hall and sat in a dejected heap on the windowsill. The sash was raised, and the faint breeze blowing in revived her a little. Behind the sound of Mademoiselle Tissot pounding the keys, and the dancing master shouting at his pupils, she could hear girls practising their instruments in other parts of the building. Bedlam must sound like this, she thought. Poor Mama. To endure this cacophony day and night.

She put her head in her hands. She was at a loss as to know what to do. If only there was someone she could consult, someone she could trust . . .

Catching sight of a figure strolling alone in the garden, Francina climbed out of the window and ran to join her.

'Miss Chesterton, may I ask you something hypothetical?'

The English mistress raised her eyebrows. 'Of course, child.'

They sat on the bench in the arbour. Unable to contain herself any longer, Francina burst out, 'Miss Chesterton, a friend of mine has asked for my advice.'

'Indeed?'

'You see, a friend of hers - a loving wife and mother - has disappeared. And my friend was struck by the idea that the poor lady might have been incarcerated against her will. What she was wondering - and what I am asking is – do you think it possible that someone, who has previously shown no signs of madness, could be wrongly imprisoned in a lunatic asylum?'

Miss Chesterton looked towards the sea.

Eventually she said, 'Regrettably, it is perfectly possible. Stories do circulate from time to time – I am sure you must have heard some of them - of women who have been tricked into signing forms they do not understand, forms that commit themselves unwittingly to the asylum. Once there, of course, surrounded by all the distressing manifestations of madness -'

'But why should anyone do such a wicked thing?'

'To trick a woman out of her inheritance – or to silence her.'

'To silence her?' Francina's pulse began to race.

'I know of a woman who was branded 'mad' because she spoke her mind and aired her views. Does that constitute madness? In the opinion of her husband it did – for a wife has no opinions, especially if they should differ from his own. There is no law in this land, Miss Duquesne, which says a husband cannot incarcerate his wife, either in his home or in an asylum - if he wishes to silence her.'

'The practice is not readily acknowledged,' continued Miss Chesterton, unaware that Madame Le Brocq was watching them through an upstairs window, 'but I believe it is an insidious custom that festers through society. Of course it is the fear of such consequences that stifles all but the bravest woman from engaging in serious open debate. Single women, especially if they have financial independence, do have some autonomy to speak their minds. But, as I have stressed many times, Miss Duquesne, when a woman marries, she forfeits all her rights of independence – and that includes the right to express herself.'

Madame Le Brocq now stood framed portentously in a window that opened to the terrace. This time, Miss Chesterton had also noticed her.

'Take my handkerchief, child, and dry your tears. I am sure there is a perfectly reasonable explanation in your friend's case. Now quickly return indoor for your lesson.'

Madame Le Brocq met her at the window. 'Miss Duquesne, why are you not dancing? Are you not one of Monsieur Lasource's girls?'

'Yes, Madame, but I was feeling unwell,' said Francina. 'Monsieur suggested that I should rest for a few moments.'

Madame Le Brocq narrowed her eyes in contempt. 'Just because I have allowed you to stay until the end of the semester, does not mean that you can try my patience. If you continue to flout the rules of this Establishment, Miss Duquesne, I shall be forced to dismiss you immediately.'

Francina curtsied and returned to the hall. What a blow it would be to the reputation of your precious Establishment, Madame, if you should discover that one of your pupils was not only the daughter of a tradesman, but of an incarcerated lunatic as well.

'Papa, you haven't listened to a word I've said,' pouted Louisa. 'I was saying that Signor Bandini has asked me to play *two* pieces at the end of term concert.'

Uncle Doré grunted behind his newspaper.

'Papa!'

Uncle Doré looked up. 'Did you say something, my dear?'

Louisa frowned. 'What are you reading, Papa, that is so important?'

She leaned over his shoulder.

'*Heavy English and French losses at Sebastopol. Names of officers fallen will be forwarded immediately,*' she read.

'Oh Papa, might that be Charlie?'

'Dearest pet, Charlie's ship is nowhere near Sebastopol.' Uncle patted her hand. 'By my calculations, if the weather has been favourable, the fleet will have just reached Constantinople.'

'Are you sure, Papa?' whimpered Louisa, her eyes full of tears. She had no idea where Constantinople was.

'I am more than certain, pet,' Uncle said, stroking her hair. 'Besides, in this particular campaign, it was the Army and not the Royal Navy that was involved. Come, girls! We will go to the library, and I shall show you just where Charlie's ship is.'

The little group trudged up to the library. Uncle spun the globe and pin-pointed the position of his ship with a set of dividers. Then he spread out a large-scale map of the region across his desk on which he had been plotting the daily position of Charlie's ship. By his calculations Charlie would reach the Crimea in a week's time.

They peered at the rugged ink lines accentuated by a light-blue wash, demarcating land from sea; the grid lines of longitude and latitude; the wiggly rivers and the hatch marks denoting mountains. Fanning words with swirling serifs proclaimed: *SEA OF MARMARA, BOSPHORUS, SEA OF AZO, GULF OF KARKINITE.* They followed Uncle's neat pencil painstakingly charting the long slow course, and realised how many hours he had pored over this map, how anxious he really was. The ship looked dangerously close to the conflict.

For the first time since Charlie had left, they understood the gravity of the situation. Through their minds passed the daily reports that filtered out from the Crimea to swamp the newspapers; the long published lists of casualties that Uncle regularly scanned. There seemed no end to the numbers of men being lost through battle or disease. If only they could rub out the little pencilled cross and place Charlie's ship somewhere else. If only they could screw up the map and pretend the Crimea did not exist.

5

There must be another explanation. She did not believe that Papa would lock up Mamma for expressing opinions. She took up the volume again and skimmed down the lines for the answer . . .

At last she has it. Bad blood.

But surely there were warning signs?

'Francina, it is time you began to occupy your days more profitably,' said Aunt. 'Instead of filling your head with paltry romances, I would like you to start taking an interest in my charity work. I shall appoint you my Assistant, and we shall begin your training forthwith. Tomorrow you will accompany me to the House of Correction.'

What was Aunt implying?

'Don't look so startled, Francina. They are harmless souls. You know full well that the more violent are safely confined behind bars.'

So here she was, listening to Aunt Doré preach to the Unfortunates. Of course, she had encountered these silent shuffling creatures before, for Uncle Doré, in his role as President of the Poor-Law Board, was fond of escorting visitors around the House of Correction, and sometimes she would accompany him. But this afternoon she felt an empathy with these pitiful beings that she had never felt before. How many of these bewildered souls had been incarcerated for expressing opinions? How many were just eccentric old women imprisoned by relatives who wanted them out of the way, or girls who had refused to marry against their will?

As the wife of the President of the Poor-Law Board, Aunt was politely welcomed and allowed to practise her form of admonition, for she firmly believed that these creatures had brought misfortune on themselves through their own wickedness, and it was her duty to help them renounce their evil ways. But as most of them were unable to read, Aunt would inspire them with His Holy Words. But could they follow Aunt's Parisian French, when Guernésiais was the only language they spoke? Somewhere, in another Institution, Mamma might be listening to a similar sermon.

Francina studied the row of faces across the table. Ten shifting forms, aged from fifteen to forty, darkening against the fading light. They wore identical brown gowns, black aprons and white caps. Sluggishness had blunted their features, apathy dulled their eyes. She was told that they suffered from epilepsy, hysteria or mental confusion, but were said to be harmless. Nevertheless, she was pleased that a heavy deal table and a large expanse of floor separated them from her. She glanced for reassurance at the able-bodied wards-woman who sat in a chair by the grated fire; her jaw set, her arms folded, and her eyes surveying her line of charges for unruly behaviour.

The one called Kate unsettled Francina most. She was the youngest refractory in the House of Correction. Small and slight, she was constantly rocking, either on the bench or crouched in a corner. Today, rocking as usual with her head down, she picked frantically at the fibres of the rope, producing a mound of oakum far exceeding that of her fellows.

'Pitiful sinners!' announced Aunt Doré. 'You - the meek, the humble and the afflicted - I bring you good news, joyous news!'

Mystified, her captive audience blinked and coughed, shuffling their feet under the table.

'Repent, I beseech you! The Lord has not forsaken you. You are all God's children.'

'God's childer!' squeaked an inmate. Her fellows sniggered behind the oakum.

'Silence,' bellowed the wards-woman. 'Where's yer manners!'

In unison the inmates bowed their heads and continued to work.

Hardly conscious of the interruption, Aunt continued: 'Fly from temptation! Cast out your sins and follow the True Path of Righteousness!'

Francina's eyes wandered. It was a clean room, surprisingly free of foul air. The flag-stones were scrubbed daily and the windowpanes gleamed. There was little furniture (save the long narrow table and benches, the chairs reserved for visitors, and a framed quotation from the Scriptures hanging above the fireplace) but it was the model of order, cleanliness and industry. Uncle Doré was proud of the Town's Hospitals, and pleased to show visitors from London or Paris who came to observe their humane methods.

A noise interrupted Aunt's address. Kate, having exhausted her portion of rope, jumped up and snatched her neighbour's. With a howl of protest her neighbour, a fat red-faced creature, slapped the thief across the face. '*Petite voleresse*!' she screamed.

'*Fainéant*!' spat little Kate.

The wards-woman sprang into action. Ringing the bell at her feet, she pounced on little Kate, restraining her with an iron grip. Matron flew into the ward, keys jangling at her waist.

'What is the meaning of this commotion?' she demanded.

The red-faced refractory threw her apron over her head. She would be punished now. 'T'warn't me,' she sobbed under the apron, 't'war 'er!'

Little Kate's eyes registered fear.

'Beg pardon, Ma'am,' said the wards-woman tightening her grip, 'but t'were 'er! She's a bad 'un and no mistake!'

'Kate, you again?' Matron said in a gentle but exasperated tone. She turned to Aunt. 'I apologise, Mrs Doré, for this unseemly disruption. Kate has a child's mind -'

'All the more reason to be firm, Matron. If she has a child's mind then she must be instructed as a child. Children are disciplined, are they not? Taught to respect authority, to know right from wrong?'

'Indeed, Mrs Doré.'

'It is one thing to interrupt a lesson, but to obstruct the Word of the Lord? Surely such behaviour must be reprimanded?'

'Most certainly,' said Matron. One did not contradict the wife of the President of the Poor-Law Board, and a major fundraiser for the Establishment.

'One must set standards, Matron.'

During this exchange the refractories cowered in their seats, snuffling and twisting the corners of their aprons. Little Kate stood locked in the wards-woman's grasp, her eyes wide with fright.

'Come with me,' snapped Matron, knowing she was no match for the President's wife and not wishing to prolong a scene in which those in her custody would witness her humiliation. 'It's time you were taught a lesson, my girl.'

Matron and the wards-woman pulled Kate towards the door. She began to cry. The sound was pitiful.

'Kate meant no harm, I 'm sure!' Francina burst out.

Aunt looked at her in surprise. 'Explain yourself, Francina.'

'Kate is so hard working. Look at the amount of oakum she has made. Her over-enthusiasm caused that momentary lapse.'

Aunt Doré inspected the piles of oakum.

'Kate is our most *diligent* worker,' said Matron.

This disclosure put new light on the offence. Aunt mulled over the dilemma.

'One should not be seen to punish diligence . . . Matron, we have been a little hasty! We should show mercy, be forgiving - as our Lord forgave those who betrayed him.'

'Indeed, industry should be applauded.' Matron loosened hold of Kate's arm. She did not quite have the courage to let go until she was quite sure of Aunt's change of heart.

'You will be a great help in my work, Francina,' said Aunt Doré as they strolled the short distance from the House of Correction to Elm House. A wind had got up. It funnelled down the narrow lane between the high stone walls, spinning dust across their path.

'Today we instructed the Unfortunates on an important Christian doctrine,' continued Aunt, as branches swayed above their heads, 'namely the principle of *Forgiveness*. Not through the Scriptures, which has been my way, but by a clear demonstration in a manner appropriate to their simple understanding. It is an aspect of the Lord's moral teachings, which I have overlooked. But you, Francina, have properly set me right.'

During the night a storm arose. Rain lashed against the panes with such force that the frames shook. The wind whistled and howled. Icy blasts seeped through cracks in the mortar and found their way under Francina's coverlet, chilling her to the bone. On such a night, Cook told her, the *King of Auxcriniers* would lie in wait for unsuspecting mariners. As a child, the image of that hideous dwarf with unearthly features, who rose above the waves, wrecked ships and sent sailors to a watery grave, petrified her. Whenever the fog bell tolled, those childish images returned to haunt her.

Half-waking, half-dreaming, she finds herself in the House of Correction. Only this time she is sitting with the refractories, dressed in a rude gown, and cowering behind a mound of oakum. Aunt stands on a dais. She is preaching; shouting to make herself heard above the storm. Her words tumble over the oakum and press on her shoulders. It is difficult to keep upright under the weight.

One creature topples off the bench and falls to her knees on the flagstones. 'Enough, enough,' she sobs. 'I cannot bear it any longer!'

But Aunt Doré will have none of it. From her great height, she overpowers the crouching woman. '*Indian Messalina*!'

'Mamma?' cries Francina in her dream. 'Mamma, is it you?'

'Yes, my dearest!'

'Oh, Mamma, I did not know you!' She clasps the kneeling woman in her arms. Tears stream down her cheeks. At last she has found her. She will hold her forever.

6

The day of the Concert began close and sultry, sapping the energy of everyone at home. Miss Hobson washed their hair, added a little pomatum and carefully set it in curl papers. They lay on their beds in their chemises and fanned their curls dry. The hours passed excruciatingly slowly.

At five o'clock, the brougham carrying the Dorés set off. Francina and Miss Hobson followed in a hired gig.

The Academy had been transformed. Workmen had assembled a stage in the hall and arranged the chairs in regimented rows. Floors shone, windows sparkled, furniture gleamed; window sashes were raised and the doors flung open. The scent of flowers wafted through the rooms.

The Dorés joined the other guests on the terrace. Mrs Lihou came over with Mary and another lady, whom she presented as her sister-in-law from Derbyshire. Mrs Hervey acknowledged them with a friendly nod, and singled Francina out to admire her costume.

Francina blushed at her blue satin slippers. She loved this costume: the soft white fichu; the georgette apron edged in pink ribbon; the sky-blue skirt, just short enough to expose the flurry of petticoats when she twirled. She had helped Miss Hobson sew on the pink satin streamers that tickled her cheeks.

'It is a peasant dress from Tuscany, Mrs Hervey. I shall perform dances from that country with some other girls this evening.'

'I look forward to seeing you dance,' smiled Mrs Hervey.

'Mary will be reciting poetry,' Mrs Lihou added, fanning herself with a large black fan (which like her outfit was excessively laced and beribboned), 'which I have always thought is far more taxing than dancing or singing. I have great difficulty in remembering poems, so I am full of admiration for the dedication Mary has shown to learn the lines.'

Everyone smiled politely.

The bell rang for the guests to take their places in the hall, and

Mrs Lihou led her party to the front row of chairs reserved for distinguished guests.

The Concert opened with a song performed by the youngest girls prettily attired in white dresses with blue sashes.

Soon it was Louisa's turn on stage. She drew up the piano stool and arranged her flounced skirt into a perfect bell about her. Signor Bandini (his wayward locks for once controlled by copious amounts of oil) stood anxiously in the wings . . . But as Louisa played, she surpassed even his high expectations. Music coursed through the hall as fluidly as water in a bubbling brook; and when she sang, each note rang out as clear as tinkling glass.

It was Mary Lihou's misfortune to follow such a performance. Francina heard her voice wavering through the curtains as she slipped backstage to take up her position on the stage with her fellow dancers. The porters shifted the pianoforte to the side, while the dancers waited for their cue. Monsieur Lasource stood in the wings, mouthing last minute words of encouragement.

The applause for Mary's effort died down. The curtains opened, and Mademoiselle Tissot pounded the keys.

They skipped and pirouetted in all the combinations they had perfected during the long rehearsals; beating their tambourines with all the fire of the peasant girls of Tuscany.

The next dance was of a different tempo - slow and rhythmical. The girls linked arms and glided across the stage as effortlessly as ice-skaters, while the tremulous sound of their tambourines rose and fell around them. The tempo changed and they broke away, tapping their heels across the boards. Faster and faster in time to the music, until the sound reached a crescendo - and it was over.

The girls sank into a deep curtsy.

People mouthed compliments as they returned to their seats. Francina sat down as Hettie Rynd began to play her guitar. But she was not listening; she was still on stage . . . still whirling and twirling, and shaking the tambourine above her head.

Guests and pupils elbowed their way towards the refreshments. The desks were pushed together, hidden under crisp linen tablecloths. Hams, tongues, veal pies and sandwiches, jostled with rainbow jellies and custards in small glasses. Francina went in search of some cordial. When she returned, Louisa was surrounded by a dizzy set of girls who only talked of fashion and romance.

Having no desire to join them, Francina slipped outside.

The sun was sinking, casting diagonal shadows across the garden. She leaned against the wall, rolled the cool tumbler across her hot forehead and shut her eyes. The babble in the schoolroom drifted out through the open windows . . . she heard ripples of laughter, and caught snatches of conversation.

'I am most impressed with the performances this evening,' she heard someone say. 'Miss Doré's playing was exceptional. She is a very talented young lady.'

'The Dorés are a charming family.' (She recognized Mrs Lihou's voice immediately.) 'I have always admired Mrs Doré for bringing up her brother's children - in very difficult circumstances.'

'Indeed?' Now Francina realised that the first voice belonged to Mrs Hervey.

'I'm talking, of course, of Miss Duquesne – the gypsy dancer.'

Francina flattened herself against the wall.

'Her mother was a planter's daughter, born and bred in the jungle, with a touch of the tar brush, if I'm not mistaken,' whispered Mrs Lihou. 'Whatever was Mr Duquesne thinking, marrying such a creature! Madame Le Brocq was most obliged when I informed her, for such people can quickly ruin the good name of the Academy. Miss Duquesne's departure is long overdue, in my opinion.'

'I know nothing about her background, of course, but she danced with flair.'

'It was shameless, wanton!' hissed Mrs Lihou. 'Are you familiar with the saying: *Like mother, like daughter*? We saw her in her true colours this evening. Gypsy colours.'

'You are being rather uncharitable, Elizabeth,' whispered Mrs Hervey. 'All the dancers looked like gypsies. It was the nature of the costume.'

'But my dear,' persisted Mrs Lihou, 'I was at the harbour when her mother came to Guernsey. Imagine my astonishment at seeing a *foreign* woman in the most *outré* costume step ashore on Mr Duquesne's arm - followed, no less, by a *black* servant in native dress. It was the talk of Town for months. It traumatized the old

Dean to discover that his son had not only married a foreigner, but a Roman Catholic! Of course, Mr Duquesne was bewitched. She was striking, in a feral sort of way. But - to add to the affront - cool as you please, Mrs Duquesne suddenly vanished, leaving her poor babies motherless and quite alone in the world!' (Mrs Lihou lowered her voice.) 'Rumours flew across Town. She *ruined* poor Mr Duquesne. I don't believe he has ever got over the disgrace. Some say he is too ashamed to show his face on the Island again -'

Francina heard no more, for their conversation was drowned by other voices. She stood on the terrace unable to move. Mamma destroy Papa? She covered her face in her hands. She saw it all so clearly now: that intemperate, unchaste exhibition on the stage. How could she have behaved so *wantonly*!

When she was sure that Mrs Lihou had moved away from the window, Francina crept inside. Bodies shifted to let her pass, and she fancied them thinking: 'Make way for the little gypsy!'

She hung her head. She would never shake off Mamma's stamp. If she had the words, *the true daughter of an infamous mother* etched across her forehead, she could not have felt more conspicuous. She hated this costume. When she got home she would tear it to pieces.

She found Louisa spooning jelly into her mouth. 'Where have you been? I was looking for you.'

But Francina could not speak. She fancied everyone pressing round her, sniggering: *Little gypsy! Little gypsy!*

Aunt removed a white glove and placed a cool finger against her forehead. 'Are you ill, Francina? You look very pale.'

'I should - I should very much like to go home.'

'Louisa, ask Miss Hobson to summon the gig. Francina is unwell.'

'Pretty as a picture you looked in your costume,' Miss Hobson said, as she helped her undress for bed.

Francina stared in the glass while Miss Hobson brushed her hair.

'Do I look like a gypsy?'

'You certainly danced like a gypsy.' Miss Hobson smiled at her in the glass. Her lashes and brows were so fair they were almost invisible, and she had to be extra vigilant with her pale complexion in the sun. Francina had seen her trying to remove freckles off her face with a mixture of lemon juice and borax powder. Next to Miss Hobson, she looked dark and foreign.

'But do you think I have gypsy blood?'

'Whoever suggested such a thing!'

'Mrs Lihou said I had gypsy blood.'

'Take no notice of what Mrs Lihou says - her tongue's as sharp as a viper's,' Miss Hobson said, as she plaited her hair for bed. 'Miss Francina, you have beautiful hair - blue-black, the colour of a raven's wing.'

'Gypsies have black hair,' she retorted.

She slept little that night and was conscious of rain beating against the sash for several hours. She tried to empty her mind, but it was impossible. She could not shake off the chill that ran through her bones. Dozing fitfully, she dreamed of angels, gypsies and purple-faced lunatics until daylight seeped through the curtains. She should have risen elated - for it was Prize Day, the very last day she need ever attend Madame Le Brocq's Academy, but she just lay there with her eyes closed, her thoughts returning again and again to Mrs Lihou's remarks. The shadowy memory of Mamma; the angel that had nursed Baby. That image had shattered into a thousand fragments, and in its void stood a wild gypsy that had bewitched and ruined Papa. Poor Papa! To have lived with such a siren - a planter's daughter like Bertha Mason. Am I really the daughter of such a creature?

'Ina, please get up. I don't want to be late - not today, of all days. I am sure to receive a prize, Madame Le Brocq hinted as much.'

'I am unwell, Lulu.'

'You can't be, Ina. Surely you want to say good-bye to everyone?'

But she could not move. She could not face Madame Le Brocq or any of them again.

Louisa ran to fetch her mother.

7

Doyle House, Pyke Yard, London

My beloved Daughter,

I took a nap after dinner, but slept longer than I should have done and consequently have not much time for letter-writing. I am a little better, but still do not have the strength to perform as many tasks as I would wish. And since my illness, several business concerns have arisen that need my attention, so I cannot, after all, come to Guernsey this summer.

For too long now Angelo has been wasting time in the company of those whose sole purpose appears to be the pursuit of pleasure. It will be a great relief when he departs for the East and leaves those bad influences behind. But now, at last, he is beginning to understand the importance of his studies, and to realise how fortunate he is to have this opening in Ceylon. We must thank God and your Aunts for their overwhelming generosity in assisting him - but it breaks my heart that I, your Father, am unable to provide for my two poor Children.

Soon you will receive a letter from Mrs Barton. It is my wish that when the Bartons arrive in Guernsey, you will receive them in a courteous and respectful manner. I have given Mrs Barton leave to answer any questions you may pose regarding your Mother, for I confess, the whole sorry business has made me weary.

I do not wish to read of your amusements and dancing, Francina. What is of greater interest to me is to learn that you are assisting your Aunt in all her duties, complying with her wishes, and saying your Prayers. Your conduct and virtue are your greatest assets - indeed, they are your only assets - and the key to securing your future.

If I am to catch the mail, I must now conclude this letter.

I remain as ever, your affectionate father,

Frank Duquesne

Wherever she went, Francina was conscious of people turning away. Why had she never noticed their whispers before? If Mrs Lihou kept spreading rumours, she would soon have no standing on the Island. She had been asked to leave the Academy - how many other places would soon exclude her? She had nothing to look forward to except Angelo's arrival, and that anticipated his departure. Now, she dreaded meeting Mrs Barton. Whatever there was to know about Mamma, it was bound to be disagreeable.

But at home, at least, everyone was too preoccupied to notice her unhappiness. Saumarez was due home for the summer holidays, and decorators were putting the finishing touches to the old nursery. The faded yellow wallpaper had been replaced by a bolder blue pattern; in place of the nursery furniture was a solid mahogany bed, and all the accoutrements that make up a young man's room. On the landing stood Dobbin, the old rocking horse, whose grey mane she had loved to plait; the treasured doll's house; the Noah's Ark; the nursery books and the old torn chapbooks, crudely illustrated. Each stirred childhood memories and now all awaited storage.

In her mind's eye she saw the nursery of her childhood: the five children perched in their little chairs. She saw herself and Louisa working at their samplers under the omnipotent eye painted with the words: PREPARE TO MEET THY GOD on the plaque above the door; she saw them seated at Nurse's feet while she read them *Robinson Crusoe* or *The Sorrows of Yamba*. She saw embers glowing in the grate; steam rising from freshly laundered baby clothes airing on the clothes horse; Sammy's little cot, and the old iron bed huddled in the corner where Nurse found time to rest her weary head.

Memories of her old nurse brought pangs of sadness - she missed her comforting embrace in times of distress, her sympathy and her unbiased love. Sometimes in the night when feelings of loss had overwhelmed her, she would creep barefoot from the bedroom she shared with Louisa and climb into Nurse's narrow bed. She would snuggle between the rough linen sheets, nestle in her arms and rest her head against her capacious bosom. She could still recall the balmy smell of her soft warm skin. When Saumarez was sent to school, Nurse was dismissed, and found a new position in England. She never saw her again.

The weather turned cold the day Saumarez was due home. The sun was hidden behind billowing clouds, and a blustery wind threw up crests on a murky sea. Miss Hobson had an errand to run in Town, and as it looked as though it might rain later, Francina asked to accompany her. There was just enough time to change her library book before they were due to meet Sammy off the steamer.

Hugging their mantles, they scurried under the tossing branches of the trees on Candie Road, through narrow Anne's Place, and across the square to Mrs Barbet's Establishment in Smith Street; thankful at last to climb the narrow stairs to the small Circulating Library upstairs.

The room was warm and close, and unusually crowded; the air stale from the burning gas lamps. She resented the arrival of the summer visitors - they seized all the new additions, especially those in the English language. Only when they had left at the end of the season did she ever manage to find a new novel, by which time it was dog-eared and marked. But at least they were all strangers here today. No one in here knew her.

Miss Hobson (who had no time for novel-reading) was happy to wait for her by the window, where she could watch the passers-by in the street below. Francina placed her umbrella in the stand and stood back to survey the shelves. She loved this place of learning: the hushed tones, the musty books, the learned scholars propped in the corners. Being in no mood for History or Geography, Topography or Zoology – indeed, for any serious topic today - she squeezed past a monocled gentleman to reach the romances. She would continue her quest to read all the romances from A to Z. She had reached B for *Brontë*.

She found a novel by Miss Emily Brontë - it was new, some of the pages still uncut. She held the book up to inhale the faint odour of printing ink, a smell that she had always found intoxicating.

Stepping back, she collided with the library steps. The young man on them lost his balance and jumped down, dropping his book with a loud thud on the boards.

Francina muttered apologetically.

'Mademoiselle, I should have known better than to over-balance on those steps,' smiled the young man, retrieving the volume from the floor. 'But this is hardly the way to treat a fine work of poetry. Are you familiar with the poems of John Keats, Mademoiselle?'

He opened the volume and turned the pages. His movements were slow, his expression grave, but she sensed him teasing her. He stopped at a poem:

'I met a Lady by the Meads
Full beautiful, a faery's child
Her hair was long, her foot was light
And her eyes were wild –'

His voice was hardly more than a whisper but she was sure everyone was listening.

'. . . She found me roots of relish sweet
And honey wild and manna dew
And sure in language strange she said
"I love thee true." '

'She took me to her elfin grot
And there she wept and sigh'd full sore
And there I shut her wild wild eyes
with kisses four . . .'

He raised his eyes. He was waiting for her to respond. She stared at his shoes. They were of fine leather, highly polished. What could she possibly say?

'Did you not feel it?'

'Monsieur?'

'The passion, the intensity? An attraction that is fated?'

Turning away, she fumbled in her purse for tuppence to hand to the librarian for the privilege of borrowing a book. The young man returned to his volume of poetry.

'What a curious young man,' said Miss Hobson, as they left the library.

Despite the disagreeable weather, the Town was full of country folk who had travelled across the Island to visit the Saturday market. They jostled along High Street, squeezing past black-garbed women balancing baskets on their heads; lads leading donkeys laden with panniers of shellfish; farmers driving wagons piled high with cages of fattened rabbits and poultry. In that thronging cobbled street, the howl of the wind was drowned by the clatter of heavy nailed boots, hooves and iron-shod wheels. Shop signs swung and creaked above their heads. They passed the *Umbrella & Parasol Maker*, the *Silk Mercer*, the *Cheese-Monger*, the *French Glove & Boot Deposit*, the *China Depository*, the *Milliner & Straw Hat Manufacturer*. Two shining bow-windows caught Francina's eye; it was the stylish façade of the *Ladies' Dressmaker & Haberdasher*.

'Have you visited Monsieur Le Boutillier's new shop yet, Miss Hobson?'

Miss Hobson admitted to having done so.

But for a moment Francina did not see the beautiful gowns in the windows. She saw a shadowy figure reflected in the glass; a still figure dressed from head to foot in deepest black, remote and detached from the vibrating street behind.

They made their way behind the Town Church to a dim lane off Fountain Street where Miss Hobson had to deposit a pair of Aunt's boots for repair. The streets in this part of Town were narrow, gloomy and damp, and the abundance of cats and dogs did little to improve the ambience. The buildings here were old, some jutting out so precariously that folk in upper rooms could touch hands with those living opposite.

The cobbler's shop was dark, impregnated with the smell of oiled hides hanging from nails along the walls. The cobbler sat on a high stool surrounded by scraps of leather, and was working by the light filtering through the small dusty window. He was old, and had spent so much time bent over the workbench that his back had become permanently stooped.

While Miss Hobson spoke to the cobbler, Francina gazed at the display of fancy boots in the window.

Suddenly the light was obscured by a figure peering in and she shrank into the shadows of the shop . . . but the young man from the library was more interested in examining the boots than to gaze further in. Unobserved, she studied him. He was fairly tall, perhaps in his early twenties. His eyes were deep-set under dark brows, keenly observant. His nose was too long, his mouth too wide, his cheek-bones too distinct - yet together they made a fascinating face. Then, as abruptly as he had appeared, he vanished from sight, and by the time they had left the shop he was nowhere to be seen.

Market Square was a hive of bustle. They stepped over straw and poultry feathers scattered and swirling on the cobblestones. Island women, huddled in thick woollen shawls, blinked sleepily at them as they passed their stalls. They saw flowers bunched in every hue, baskets of fresh brown eggs, tubs of creamy butter and pots of Island honey - and paused for a moment to watch a lady haggle over the price of a capon. A hungry urchin followed the pie man, begging for a hot meat pie.

They stopped at Mère Falliot's sweetmeat stall. The old woman's face creased like a wrung sheet as she coaxed them to buy. When Francina was young, a visit to this stall was a treat on her birthday. Nurse would let her choose as many jujubes as would fill a square of brown paper. Choosing the sugary concoctions was an agonizing but pleasurable task: should she have the hard boiled sweets that cut the roof of her mouth, the soft jellies coated with powdered sugar, or the black strands of liquorice? Dotted amongst the jars of sweets were the small wooden toys that Mère Falliot's sons carved when their fishing boats were grounded in rough weather. She saw the same peg dolls with round red cheeks, the straight-legged animals that always toppled over, the fishing-boats, bird scarers, catapults and whistles that she remembered from her childhood.

A crash of thunder shook the Square. Rain poured down in torrents, and everyone ran to seek shelter.

'Good people, please squeeze up a little more,' called a voice. 'These two ladies are still exposed to the elements!'

It was the young man from the library waving his cane, orchestrating the crowd like a conductor.

Surprisingly, the crowd shuffled closer to make room for them. It happened so quickly - but here she was, pressed under the arches of Les Halles with the young man from the library. They were now protected, but he was not. Soon he would be wet through. Francina gave him her umbrella, but it was small and offered little cover. He pushed closer, trying to seek protection from the building; so close she could feel his breath flutter across her cheek.

'It is a long time since I have seen such a downpour,' he said, cheerfully commenting on the weather, as if to stand pressed against a stranger in the rain was the most natural thing in the world. If only she had the *savoir faire* to behave as if it meant nothing to her.

To avoid his eyes, she looked over his shoulder and prayed for the rain to stop.

The Square was deserted. Water cascaded over the stalls which were draped in sheets of oiled cloth. Standing in awful solitude and now clearly visible at the far end of the Square were the sinister tools of punishment: the flogging post, the stocks and the great basket cage. As a child that cage had terrified her. She could still see that poor soul cramped inside, as a barrage of rotten eggs was thrown at him. The cage was Nurse's final recourse when the boys were being particularly tiresome. 'I shall see that the Bailiff puts you in the cage,' she would threaten, 'if you don't do as I say!'

The rain stopped as quickly as it had started, and the crowd began to disperse.

He returned her umbrella. The handle was still warm. She longed to ask his name. Instead, she took her leave and departed. There was no reason for her to stay.

Some minutes later, a noise made her turn round.

It was the young gentleman from the library again. He held up her mud-spattered book.

She blushed. 'It must have fallen out of my basket in the commotion.'

He flicked playfully through the pages. He was not reading her journal, yet she felt as though her secret thoughts were exposed in big black letters on the pages.

Then he dropped the book into her outstretched hand and bowed. '*Wuthering Heights*. It is a wild and passionate tale of love and revenge. You will enjoy it, Mademoiselle, I have no doubt.'

Oh, for the sophistication to thank him with a witty quip. Instead, she inclined her head and walked away.

8

Saumarez was playing with the dogs along the wide sweep of the sandy shore. He threw a stick and the dogs bounded through the foam after it. Everyone liked Sammy. He was a genial fellow, who sailed through life with little to disturb or provoke him. Neither dunce nor scholar, he was shrewd enough to do the minimum required to pass examinations or escape a flogging. Aunt's reserve had melted now he was home. Misdemeanours were going unnoticed and unpunished. Louisa did not resent the boys' privileged places in their mother's heart. Boys are a race apart. They are indulged, favoured. That is the way of the world.

Francina wished she had his energy. But in this searing heat she had just enough to keep awake. Just in case . . . just in case the stranger from the library should saunter by. It was impossible to concentrate on anything. She could not work or paint (although she had read *Wuthering Heights* in view of his remarks), and had used every excuse to walk to Town in the hope of seeing him again. But he had vanished. He must have been a visitor after all, for no one of consequence could exist for so long on the Island without being seen.

Louisa was snoozing in the shade of an overhanging rock.

Francina yawned. The sluggish motion of the tide had lulled her into a half-dreaming stupor. There was hardly a breath of wind. In the distance, children were building a sandcastle; across a shimmering haze of sand, a couple strolled at the water's edge. Through half-closed eyes she saw herself and the stranger from the library. Every so often she would examine something thrown up by the tide - a bleached shell, perhaps, or a strand of seaweed. She would take his arm again, and they would walk on a little, until something else caught her eye. While high above them, sea birds soared on currents of air.

✸

As she withdrew from the table that evening, Aunt called her back.

'Angelo arrives soon, I believe?'

'He arrives on Thursday, Aunt.'

'Ask Ellie to see that his room is prepared.'

'I will do so, Aunt.'

Aunt frowned over her pince-nez. 'Francina, you seem restless these days. Is something troubling you?'

Francina traced the pattern on the damask tablecloth with her finger. Should she tell Aunt that her mother had turned out to be a pernicious witch, or that it was Mrs Lihou who had urged Madame Le Brocq to expel her before her presence sullied the good name of the Academy?

'I am unhappy because Angelo is going away.'

'You must not be selfish. Your brother has a chance to make a success of his life. A great future in Ceylon is opening up for him.'

'- and there is Papa. I had hoped he might visit us this summer.'

'You know how often I have asked him to visit us, Francina. But if my brother sets his mind on a plan, nothing will make him change it.'

Baptiste came in to remove the dishes from the buffet. When he had gone, Aunt held up a lilac envelope. 'There is another point I wish to raise: the arrival of the Bartons.'

Francina held her breath.

'It seems,' said Aunt Doré, skimming through the letter, 'that Mrs Barton is a relative of your mother's. Her husband is to have an operation in London, and Mrs Rolichon has invited them to Guernsey to stay at La Colline until he recovers.'

Aunt pronounced the name 'Rolichon' with distaste. Francina had heard of the Rolichons, but they were not of Aunt's circle, and she had never been to La Colline - the villa was hidden behind high walls on the outskirts of Town and rumoured to be haunted.

'Mrs Barton wishes to see you when she is in Guernsey.' Aunt frowned over her pince-nez. 'How do you feel about this, Francina?'

It would please Aunt Doré if she confessed to having no desire to see Mrs Barton.

'When your aunt arrives, Francina, it will only be a matter of days before it becomes common knowledge that Mrs Barton is your mother's sister, This Town is full of tittle-tattle; folk are only too eager to spread malicious gossip. This is precisely why I am so particular about your conduct. Gossipmongers must find no cause to compare you to others.'

Aunt had no need to point out the obvious. She carried Mamma's legacy like a millstone on her shoulders. That beautiful gypsy, that siren; she was still tainting the lives of everyone in her wake.

'However, it is my brother's desire that you meet Mrs Barton, so we must carry out his wishes.' Aunt folded up the letter and swept out of the room. The subject was closed.

Francina wandered outside and sat on the bench under the cherry tree. Louisa found her in the garden and sat beside her. In silence they listened to the blackbird trilling his complex song in the branches above their head.

When her tears had dried, they ambled arm-in-arm around the New Ground. The sky was a mass of cloud, the sun nowhere to be seen. They sat on the grass and gazed at the line of houses that increased in width and grandeur, terminating at Elm House. Smoke meandered into the air from kitchen chimneys. Beyond the coach house, just visible above its perimeter wall and through a clump of trees, were the reddish battlements of Castle Carey.

After a while, they continued their walk. A cricket match was in progress at the far end of the Ground. Intermittently, hearty clapping would ring through the air as a cricketer raced across the grass after the ball. The dogs pulled at their leashes to join in the chase.

A threesome was strolling towards them. A young lady dressed in pink was walking between two young gentlemen. Francina held her breath. The dark-haired gentleman looked like the stranger from the library. But Mary Lihou was on his arm – was he *Mary's* beau?

They passed each other on the gravel path. The stranger touched his hat. It really was him!

'Do you know those young ladies, Mary?' she heard him ask. 'Would you introduce us?'

'Of course, Gilbert.' There was a spark of irritation in Mary's voice. 'Louisa, Francina . . . may I present Mr Henry Fetherstone, and my brother Mr Gilbert Lihou? - Miss Louisa Doré and Miss Francina Duquesne are fellow pupils at the Academy.'

He was Mary's *brother*.

'May we accompany you?' he smiled, raising his hat.

Mr Fetherstone strolled between Louisa and Mary; Francina followed with Gilbert Lihou.

'So you are at the Academy with Mary?'

'We were - but we left this summer. My cousin is shortly to study music in Brussels.'

'You are not going with her?'

She shook her head. She could hardly explain that Papa could not afford to send her abroad.

'Brussels is a fine place,' he said. 'Fetherstone and I passed through on our way to Paris. We have just spent two glorious weeks in Paris.'

Paris. That was why she did not see him again. 'I have never been to Paris, but I have read so much about the place: the Champs-Élysées, the Arc de Triomphe, the Louvre. I should love to see the picture galleries.'

'Are you are fond of painting?'

'I dabble a little in watercolour.'

As they circled the New Ground, he described the paintings he had seen in Paris. Although not an artist himself, he was very knowledgeable on the Arts (she suspected that he was knowledgeable on most subjects). She also learned that he and Mr Fetherstone were at Haileybury College preparing to enter the Indian Civil Service.

'India seems such a mysterious place. I should love to know more about India.'

He laughed. 'Oh, India is hardly mentioned. It is considered bad form to acknowledge that the sole purpose of College is to prepare for India. Apart from one or two, most of the Professors take a very lenient view of our studies - if we scrape through our exams, it is conceded that we have a brilliant career before us.'

'And do you?'

'Perhaps I exaggerate. But even the study of Oriental languages, the chief feature of the College, is conducted as if we have no particular interest in the country. Everything I know of India is from reading the letters Fetherstone has received from his family. But I have made an effort to study the languages: Persian and Sanskrit -'

He broke from what he was saying to shout: 'Bravo, sir, an excellent catch!' (He was watching the cricket from the corner of his eye.)

'I lived in India as a child, but I remember little of it,' she said, to catch his attention again. 'Everything I know about the country I have learned from my uncle's travel books.'

'I believe you like reading, Miss Duquesne. One does not often meet pretty girls in the library. Young ladies are more interested in fashion or society - at least those, I believe, are Mary's interests.'

He altered his direction, so that he faced her. 'I am delighted to find you again, Miss Duquesne, and to discover that you are a friend of Mary's.'

She looked down at the sprigs printed on her white muslin dress. He was sweet-talking, she knew he was sweet-talking. But would he be so civil if he knew who she really was: a creature so despicable that his mother had persuaded Madame Le Brocq to expel her?

'You were reading *Wuthering Heights* when we last met. How did you find it?'

She took a deep breath. 'I had never conceived of such a world before - a world of wrath and savagery. It is hard to believe that Miss Charlotte Brontë and Miss Emily Brontë were sisters - one sister so restrained, the other so passionate.'

'And which sister do you prefer, Miss Duquesne? The restrained or the passionate?'

'I like them both equally.'

He flashed a smile. 'Perhaps that is because you are both restrained and passionate. Are you, Miss Duquesne? Do you think it possible for an individual to be fashioned of conflicting characteristics?'

'Quite often the conflicting characteristics - as you call them, Mr Lihou - are nothing more than the restraints society has placed on the individual.' She had not intended to regurgitate Miss Chesterton's words.

'Miss Duquesne, I believe you are a romantic!'

She bit her lip, frustrated at not understanding him.

'Are you familiar with the writings of Monsieur Rousseau?'

She shook her head. It was all very well for him, he had been properly educated. It was not because she was stupid that she could not converse at his level.

'Monsieur Rousseau asserted that Man is born a *noble savage*, whose perfect nature is corrupted by society. He pleaded for naturalness and freedom from constraint.'

'I have often wanted to live in a wild, lonely place - and to have the freedom to run barefoot across the moors!' She blushed. The thought had not crossed her mind before. A hobgoblin was whispering in her ear, filling her head with soporific nonsense.

'I could picture you in such a landscape – free and elusive as a young doe. Miss Duquesne, you are indeed a child of nature!'

She liked that. A child of nature

'Nowadays, however,' he added seriously, 'Monsieur Rousseau's theories are considered fanciful. The constraints of society have set us far above the *noble savage*. How could we have gained authority in India, for instance, if we behaved no better than the natives?'

He, obviously, was no romantic.

'No, Miss Duquesne, to gain respect in the Colonies, we have to stand above the natives by demonstrating our superiority not only in the way we behave, but by setting into place some of the remarkable advances that have been made by science this century. Did you see the Great Exhibition?'

At last he had stumbled across a subject on which she could speak with some knowledge.

'It was the most remarkable experience of my life!'

Uncle Doré had taken them to see the Great Exhibition shortly after Horatio had died. Aunt, still in mourning, had stayed behind. They had caught the steamer to Southampton, travelled by train to London and stayed in lodgings in Kensington. That summer Papa was the happiest she had ever known him.

'I remember looking up at the roof of the Crystal Palace, amazed at how such an enormous glass structure could be supported!'

'Indeed. No finer example could there be, Miss Duquesne, to demonstrate to the world of the excellence and superiority of British engineering and manufacturing.'

'And so many astonishing exhibits. Did you see the Guernsey Section? The De La Rue paper and envelope-making machine?'

But he would not stray from his point. 'Miss Duquesne, I am sure you will agree - in The Great Exhibition we had a perfect example of how far the Civilized Nations have advanced above the native.'

She had never had a conversation like this. She did not know how to answer, and she was frightened of saying the wrong thing and exposing her ignorance.

They walked in silence. Ahead, Louisa was giggling at a remark of Mr Fetherstone's.

Night after night, she had danced across the misty moors with the stranger from the library. Now here he was in the flesh talking about Civilized Nations and British manufacturing. This was not the poet who had flashed his eyes and seduced her with talk of faeries and wild kisses. This was Mrs Lihou's son, who was interested in cricket and intimidating her with his superior knowledge. They had reached Elm House and without thinking she announced that it was time to return home.

Mr Lihou raised his hat. She inclined her head. Her dreams had shattered.

Mary, smiling now, resumed her rightful position as the threesome continued on their way.

'Why did you insist that we return home?' hissed Louisa, as she opened the small iron gate. 'I was having such a divine conversation with Mr Fetherstone.'

'I'm sorry, Lulu, but I felt rather uncomfortable talking to Mr Lihou.'

'Ina, forgive me. From the snippets I overheard, he sounded such a pompous bore. Poor you, trapped with that *lizard,* while I was captivating Mr Fetherstone. Is he not the handsomest man you ever saw?'

9

The tide was out when they arrived at the harbour to meet Angelo off the steamer. All the way to Castle Cornet outcrops of seaweed-covered rocks lay exposed amongst the harbour construction muddle, and along the foreshore, stranded fishing boats lay helplessly on their sides. Between a line of casks, boys were shouting and waving sticks at a herd of oxen that had emerged through the tunnel at Rue des Vaches and stood huddled on the beach, awaiting transportation to France.

The vriac season had begun. The sands were littered with Islanders and their children scrabbling amongst rocks to collect the brown seaweed, which they were heaping onto ox-drawn carts or stuffing into mule panniers. The more determined had followed the ebbing tide in boats to distant rocky outcrops, and were sending vriac by the boatload to the beach. There was no time to lose. Vriac was so prized as a winter fuel and crop improver, that there were strict laws regarding its times of collection.

They picked their way between the crab pots, barrels and boxes of produce piled on the quay side, clambered down the slippery steps of the North Pier and found a route between the rocks and pungent heaps of vriac to the water's edge. Crabs and sand insects scampered away; seagulls mewed above their heads.

The vriac-gathers, with sleeves rolled up to expose their brown muscular arms, took no notice of them. Shouting to each other in Guernésiais, they ripped vriac off the rocks with their billhooks. They took even less interest in the steamer anchored in the roads, or the small boats busily ferrying passengers ashore. A great number of visitors had arrived by this steamer, and as the milling crowd grew on the beach so did the profusion of carpet bags, bed rolls, hat boxes and packages. Ragged boys, watching this latest invasion of foreigners, laughing at their strange manners and pulling faces behind their backs, had congregated on the shore amidst the host of beseeching porters jostling for trade.

It took a moment to realise that the young man helping two ladies alight from a boat on the far side of the beach was Angelo. He looked so much the fashionable man-about-town that he took their breath away. Turning, he saw them and hurried over with outstretched arms. Saumarez ran up to him, shouting and calling. The girls followed in a more lady-like fashion. After the usual kisses and handshakes, Francina and Louisa linked arms with him, and laughing, they all made their way back to the North Pier.

In that moment St Pierre looked beautiful. The tall drab houses, climbing the steep hillside in muddled disorder above the wharf, were suddenly spirited into life as sun glinted across the windowpanes. It was a picture unchanged since Francina was a child, and its timelessness instilled in her a wonderful sense of peace and belonging. She watched Angelo scan the old familiar scene, inhale the distinctive tang of the Island - that amalgam of salt, fish and vriac overlying the gentle ambrosia of heather and furze - and smiled. Yes, she thought, he feels it too.

No one could call Angelo good-looking, but he had a charm that drew others to him. His blue eyes, shaded by thick brows, displayed a keen intelligence. He was of medium height and athletic build. His long nose and light brown hair, falling in unruly curls either side of his temples, gave him an aristocratic air, which suited his flamboyant attire.

Angelo escorted them up the barnacle-encrusted North Steps. A red-coated sentry patrolling the quay intercepted them, asked his business on the Island, then let him proceed.

Angelo let out a cry and broke away from them. Waving his stick, he darted after a porter who was loading his baggage onto the wrong vehicle. He returned a few moments later with the disgruntled fellow following behind, carrying his heavy bags.

'Dratted porters,' he muttered under his breath. 'They have fewer brains than a monkey. Ah, Martel - take my bags, if you would.'

The coachman loaded Angelo's baggage onto Uncle's carriage. A disagreement broke out. Angelo accused the porter of incompetence and refused to tip him for carrying his bags up the beach. Francina rested her hand lightly on his arm. Angelo caught her meaning and checked himself. Parting with a penny, he laughed dismissively.

As it was a fine day, Angelo declined the carriage and decided to walk home. He wished to familiarise himself with the Town again and asked Francina to accompany him. She smiled. For a short time at least she would have him all to herself.

They strolled past the Town Church and into High Street. She clutched his arm, hoping everyone would notice her distinguished brother. He looked down at her and smiled, a warm benevolent smile.

The sun was quite intense now, so they edged to the shady side and ambled along the flagged pavement to narrow cobbled Pollet Street. At one time, leading Island families lived in these towering buildings, but now the coats of arms carved in the lintels of the doorways were the only clues to the opulence that had once flourished behind these granite walls. They passed the baker's shop and caught the aroma of hot bread wafting out of the open door. The baker's wife, filling the window with a fresh batch of rolls, nodded in greeting.

A middle-aged gentleman with swarthy cheeks and a dishevelled appearance hurried past. Angelo's face must have registered in some forgotten recess of his mind, for he turned and said, 'Delighted to see you again, young fellow!'

Angelo introduced his sister to Mr Collins, a master from Elizabeth College. Master and ex-pupil then exchanged scraps of news until Mr Collins extricated a hand from under his pile of books, raised his hat and hurried on his way.

'I think he must have mistaken me for some other boy,' muttered Angelo. 'The only attention I ever received from him was to be incarcerated in the lock-ups.'

The last house in the street jutted out at an angle, and having edged round it, they encountered the wide expanse of the Esplanade and the full heat of the sun. Francina lifted her face to catch the breeze blowing off the sea.

The seafront was busy. Angelo steered her through the crowds returning home with their donkeys weighed down with over-flowing panniers of vriac.

'I wish Papa would come to Guernsey.' She nestled close. 'How did you find him, Angelo?'

'At first my arrival was a welcome diversion for him,' he said, avoiding a group of children playing marbles in the dust. 'I even persuaded him to venture into society on occasions. But he soon lapsed into one of his debilitating moods. Time has not treated Father kindly.'

Mamma had so much to answer for! Was this the moment to bring up the subject? Later. She would broach the subject later. This moment was too special to spoil.

Turning into a narrow lane that led steeply up to the New Ground, they caught a glimpse of the tangle of ropes, blocks and tackle, hanging from the rafters in the chandler's shop. The lane was overgrown. It was difficult to walk abreast, so she released her hand and drew her skirts in close. The incline soon became a precarious flight of crooked steps, and they braced themselves to begin the ascent. Lichen-spattered walls on either side hid the cottages that nestled behind them.

'During the months I stayed with Father, I remember only two callers, and those, I believe, were business acquaintances. He has lost contact with all his friends. He is too ashamed to let them see his true circumstances. So he has few distractions to lift his spirits.'

'I gather from Papa's letters that he has an accommodating landlady,' she said over her shoulder as she picked her way round thistles and sprawling stems of dog rose.

'Mrs Hills treats Father kindly. He is fortunate in that respect. I hate to admit it, Ina, but I found his lodgings so oppressive, that I spent as little time there as possible. And my absence seemed to irritate Father even more than my presence.'

The rise was now so precipitous, they could scarcely find breath to speak, so they stopped to rest. Far below, the steamer had weighed anchor and was turning direction for Jersey, leaving a trailing white gash in the water. Even at this height above the sea, they could feel the vibrations of the great paddle-wheels.

They continued the ascent. The lane gradually widened. Tender green ferns, pink-edged daisies, forget-me-nots and wild parsley grew in the crevices of the sun-baked stone. A blue butterfly fluttered across their path and settled on a clump of red valerian. They came upon a wooden door hidden under cascades of honeysuckle, and through a chink in a worm-eaten panel, glimpsed a secret, tumble-down garden.

'I was glad to leave Father's lodgings - but not London. If only I could have found a position in the City, instead of having to travel half way round the world to end up in some godforsaken backwater!' He spoke with such passion that her heart went out to him, but she did not remind him of the many openings he had turned down in London.

The granite walls were lower here, almost hidden under knots of hart's tongue fern and twisted branches of wild myrtle. A lizard darted behind a clump of foxgloves.

At the summit of Les Escaliers des Corbins, they stopped to catch their breath and enjoy the breeze blowing off the sea. The sun was shimmering across the water. They followed the green-blue lines of the coastline and watched sea birds soar and dip near the rock cliffs. The islands of Herm, Jethou, Sark and Jersey appeared as diminishing blue shadows ending at the coast of Normandy, just visible on the horizon.

Visitors often remarked on the transparency of the waters surrounding the Islands, and today Francina agreed with them. An artist would find it difficult to capture this blue without it seeming unnatural. Even Castle Cornet looked enchanting: the sun reflected off the battlements and pantiled roofs like a series of glittering mirrors.

'That could still be your goal, Angelo,' she said, breaking the silence. 'When you have made a fortune in Ceylon, you could still return to London.'

'It will be years before I have the means to return. By the time I have paid off my debts I shall be a decrepit old man, shrivelled by the sun and worn down by disease.'

'How can you say that, Angelo! Think of the success cousin Alex has made of his life.'

'Alex Marquand was born into luxury. He did not start his career saddled with debt!'

'But the family has made such sacrifices to enable you to go to Ceylon,' she whispered.

He kissed her hand. 'Little sister, I go for your sake. I shall send you the finest silks, and make you a handsome allowance. You will have your own maid -'

'Stop it, Angelo!' She hated it when he was insincere.

He picked some forget-me-nots, bound them with rye grass, and presented them to her. 'You deserve so much more, little sister.'

She took his arm, and they walked in silence, through the tree-lined track between Castle Carey and Les Côtiles to Elm House.

After dinner they settled in the parlour to hear more of Angelo's stories. Francina sat on a stool by his feet. Uncle leaned against the chimneypiece, a hand resting on his satiated stomach. It was his habit to retire to the library after dinner and smoke his pipe, but he had delayed that pleasure tonight. He could not refrain, however, from sucking on his pipe unlit.

The setting sun had cast yellow patches across the walls. The décor in this room must be as old as the house, Francina thought. As old as Aunt and Uncle's marriage. The room had hardly changed since the day she and Angelo had first walked in here. The same grey drugget covered the carpet; the same ivy pattern (fading now in parts) twined up the walls - only nowadays, the upholstery was protected by green slipcovers, and Horatio's portrait dominated the room.

Angelo waved theatrically as he described a visit to Mr Wyld's Monster Globe. London had changed him. He had acquired the mannerisms of a young aristocrat. He might be an actor performing on stage, Francina thought, as he opened an exquisite little box and conveyed snuff to his nostrils with an exaggerated flourish. Aunt regarded snuff-taking with as much contempt as she did smoking, but so far she said nothing.

'You have a very handsome jacket,' Louisa said, fingering the cloth of his sleeve.

'I have invested in outfits over here. They should see me out.' He gave a dry laugh. 'After all, there can be little opportunity to dress up in the jungle.'

'You must be mindful of spending what you do not have, Angelo,' Aunt said without looking up from her work. 'Only when it has been gainfully earned can you claim the right to impress people.'

A flush rose on Angelo's cheek.

'Presents! Come girls. Help me distribute them. The names are written on the labels.'

Saumarez was delighted with his paper kite that resembled the Royal Vauxhall balloon, Aunt unwrapped a pair of kid gloves; Uncle, a box of fine Manilla cigars. Louisa found an ivory fan in her parcel, meticulously painted with a panorama of London.

Francina's parcel contained two small embossed leather cases. She unclasped one. It was a daguerreotype, a perfect likeness of her brother. He was leaning against a secretaire toying with a quill, staring into space, as if he were a poet seeking Divine Inspiration. 'I shall cherish it always, Angelo!' she whispered.

It took a few seconds for her to realise that the figure in the second daguerreotype was Papa. He was leaning by a small table on which rested his hat and gloves. His hair had grown quite white, and his shoulders were hunched, as if the weight of life stood on them. Papa looked so old and weary.

Some days later, they hired sturdy ponies from the livery stables in Anne's Place for an expedition across the Island. Aunt had other plans for Louisa: they were to go to Town to order outfits for their trip abroad. Poring over the fashion magazines in Monsieur Le Boutillier's shop - choosing fabrics from his extensive range of velvets, silks, satins, organdies and fine chambrays, and selecting the trimmings and buttons to go with them - was Louisa's idea of heaven. In a rash and happy moment, she offered to lend Francina her riding habit.

They set off early. It was a perfect day for an excursion: warm with a light breeze and hazy cloud to defuse the sun's glare. Francina was conscious that the skirt of the riding habit was too short, but as long as she remained in the saddle she was adequately covered. The problem would arise if she were obliged to dismount.

They rode northwards along the military road that skirted the Bay, passing the stone quarries around St Sampson where, they noted sadly, new workings were scarring the landscape. The open harbour of St Sampson vibrated with activity. They stopped to admire a new schooner secured on stocks in the shipyard, almost ready for launching. Workmen were fixing the figurehead: a poupée of a sea nymph with flowing tresses and pert white breasts. The tide had not quite risen, so they could cross dry-footed behind a line of up-turned hulls waiting for repair. Caulkers stopped hammering and touched their hats. It was not a place to linger. Caustic smoke from fires of burning pitch stung their eyes and clung to the backs of their throats.

They cantered by some pretty northern bays. Francina slowed to a trot to catch her breath and patted the pony's velvety neck. She had grown fond of this good-natured little mare with her blond mane that flew back in the wind. Ahead, flocks of sea birds rose in waves as the boys raced through them.

Saumarez reined in his pony and waited for her to catch up.

'I confess, Ina, that I have absolutely no desire to return to College,' he said, when she reached him. Exhilarated, he glowed pink with health.

'I thought you liked College, Sammy.'

'Tolerably. I have a prefect who is not such an ogre with the stick if I am behind with my Greek essays - unlike old Brassey. He is regularly thrashed black and blue, poor fellow.'

'For what reason?' Her eyes followed a skylark flitting over bushes of furze, tripping and tumbling in the air.

'No particular reason - except for poverty and the inability to pay his way out of trouble.'

'Is that what you do, Sammy, pay your way out of trouble?'

'I have no need,' he said lightly.

They galloped off to join Angelo. In her imagination, she transformed Saumarez with his tousled hair and boyish grin into Gilbert Lihou, whose dark eyes were enticing her to break free. She was Catherine riding with Heathcliff across the moors.

They passed through the gates to L'Ancresse Common. Francina always felt uneasy on the Common; the place was steeped in superstition, and dotted with mystical carved monuments of great antiquity. A scraggy sheep, restricted by a rope that attached her hind to her foreleg, stumbled out of her way, bleating urgently for her lamb to follow. The sun was rising. The riding-habit was restricting. She had tied her stays tighter than usual to fit into it. Twisted at this awkward angle, her whale-bone was pinching, and perspiration was trickling down between her shoulder-blades. She must slow down.

They passed a circle of huts made of rock and twigs. Smoke

seeped out of bracken roofs. Children with dirt-engrained faces and matted hair hid behind their mothers' skirts and glowered at them. Francina had no desire to approach too closely. She had heard of these folk - half-gypsy and half-beggar - who inhabited this corner of the Common, spoke in a strange dialect and dabbled in magic. They gathered herbs at midnight, cast sinister looks upon the cattle and bewitched people.

It was a relief to reach the weather-beaten Vale Church perched on a hillock near the exit gate and leave those glares behind. They rode through hamlets of white-washed cottages. Women washing clothes at a pump eyed them curiously. In cottage gardens, protected from the winds by stalwart walls overgrown with ivy and honeysuckle, they glimpsed neat vegetable plots and plaited beehives under stunted, leaning fruit trees.

They cantered across the sandy flats where, every so often, their view was arrested by a stark defence tower built on a craggy shore-line spur. The rocky bays were alive with wading birds that flew off in all directions as they approached. The causeway to Lihou Island was still visible, but quickly becoming submerged by the incoming tide, and from the clouds of acrid smoke drifting towards them, they realised great quantities of vriac were being burned to make iodine.

They zigzagged up the hill to Pleinmount. Skirting the high cliffs, they watched the Atlantic waves pound this southern, wild extremity of Guernsey. Then, overcome by hunger, they made their way to the farmhouse perched on the headland. Their arrival startled a brood of hens pecking in the dirt, which squawked and darted in all directions. The farmer's wife was milking a goat in the yard. Nodding courteously at their request, she left her milking and disappeared inside the farmhouse. Unperturbed, the goat ripped at the bale of straw above her head and stared at them with wide unblinking eyes. As they waited for the woman by the *hecq*, Francina peered into the darkness of her simple living-quarters: the floor of compacted earth, the fire of vriac smouldering in a vast blackened fireplace; the pots and pans and salted hams hanging from hooks in the rafters; the great *jonquière* box-bed stuffed with ferns nestling in the corner.

A few minutes later, the woman brought out a basket containing a loaf, a goat's cheese wrapped in a red chequered cloth and a pitcher of warm milk. Thanking her, they followed a small path overgrown with heather to the cliff's edge, and found a spot to eat their picnic.

Narrowing her eyes against the glare, Francina sat on a tussock and stared out to sea as she tore at a chunk of bread and sipped milk from a cracked thick-rimmed mug. She was eight years old again, holding her breath as the boys dared each other to edge down the cliff face to steal eggs. The gulls were never deterred by this intrusion. They returned to the same nesting spots, year after year. They were there now, keeping up a battery of screams, deep in a gorge below her feet. She never found the noise grating. It was the music of the Island.

She fell back in the thyme-scented grass and shut her eyes, engulfed by a drowning sensation. Was it possible to be happy and sad at the same time? These were Angelo's last days on the Island. This day must be fixed in her memory like a daguerreotype. Next year, Angelo would be on the other side of the world. And Louisa? Who knows where she will be. Saumarez will follow . . . while she will remain, alone with her memories . . .

The sun was now high in a cloudless sky. Returning the empty basket to the farmer's wife and pressing a franc on her for her trouble, they headed home via the dark shady water lanes.

The contrast between the hot open expanses and the damp dark tunnels could not have been more welcoming. The horses pricked up their ears at the sound of tinkling water and increased their pace. Overhanging trees choked with ivy blocked out the sun and formed an arch above their heads. Guided by splashes of sunlight, they followed the course of the gurgling stream.

Francina lowered her veil, for the tunnel was alive with insects.

10

'Do you think the sash is an improvement?'

Louisa jumped out of bed and ran across the room in her chemise and bare feet. Taking her ball-gown off the hook, she clutched it in front of her and studied herself in the glass.

'The blue brings out the colour of your eyes,' Francina said, without looking up.

Louisa peered closely to examine her eyes. 'Yes, it does rather.'

Ellie knocked at the door. 'Mesdemoiselles, beautiful flowers are come for you.'

Louisa snatched the posies. 'Aren't they exquisite! I wonder who sent them?' She tore open the little envelope. 'Oh - they're from Angelo.' She tossed hers on the bed in disappointment.

Francina ran her fingers over the tight rosebuds, the pink satin ribbon and fine ecru lace. Dear Angelo. They looked very costly.

At eight o'clock they were dressed and waiting in the drawing-room for the Doré carriage to return. Aunt, who was on the Organising Committee, had departed earlier with Uncle to welcome guests to the Assembly Rooms. They had helped each other dress. Francina was instructed to pull Louisa's stays tighter than ever before. She wanted a waist measurement as small as the Empress Eugénie's. Ellie hovered in the doorway as Miss Hobson teased a curl here, and adjusted a flower there.

Louisa pulled Francina towards the glass. 'Are we not the most *ravishing* creatures you ever saw?'

Two flushed girls stared back at them. Were they really cousins? They looked so different. Lulu was a concoction of lace, flounces and ribbon - the epitome of a Breton beauty. Francina's raven hair was sleeked into waves at the nape of her neck and secured by a band of rosebuds. She loved this cream gown of antique moiré silk with its little sleeves. Dear Miss Hobson. It was her skill with the needle that had transformed the gypsy into the stunning creature that smiled at her in the glass.

Angelo burst into the room, immaculate in evening dress. 'No lady in the whole of London, could possibly compare with these two delectable beauties!'

'Don't exaggerate, Angelo,' gigged Louisa. 'But thank you for the posies.'

Saumarez appeared, and strutted round the room like a peacock. His hair was flattened with scented oils, and his dress for once was spotless. 'Well, how do I look?'

'Almost presentable,' said Louisa. 'I might even agree to dance with you.'

'If I ask you,' he retorted.

A short time later, they had squeezed into the brougham and were clattering down the winding streets to join the line of vehicles threading their way towards Market Square. A fine rain was falling on the cobbles, spraying off the wheel rims and splattering the windows with muddy droplets. But the weather could not stifle their spirits, the smallest incident seen from the carriage windows caused them all excessive amusement.

Eventually the carriage found a space to draw up outside Les Halles. Angelo jumped out, pushed aside the children who had come to see the society folk in their finery, and the ragamuffin who had hoped to earn a few doubles by sweeping away the puddles, and with a flourish of his new London manners, helped Francina and Louisa out of the carriage.

The girls lifted their skirts and tripped over the gleaming cobbles, trying not to stain their satin shoes. The shrill of voices grew louder as they climbed the stairs. They removed their capes in the ladies' room and tidied their hair in the glass. Someone passed Francina a programme. Clutching the tiny swinging pencil, she quickly wrote down Angelo's name for the last dance in her programme as she had promised.

Aunt and Uncle, and stately Mrs Le Marchant blocked the entrance to the Assembly Rooms, delaying them with frivolous chatter. Uncle pulled the girls to one side. 'My dears, every young blade in the place is certain to fall madly in love with you,' he beamed with fatherly pride, 'but if either of you should be in the lamentable position of finding a space on your programme, I should be delighted to step into the breach and take a turn around the floor.'

'Silly, Papa,' giggled Louisa, standing on tip-toe to kiss him. 'It would be a pleasure.'

The place seethed with people who turned their heads to observe the latest arrivals. The conversation was so loud that they could hardly hear the musicians tuning their instruments. Officers in dress-uniforms of scarlet and gold vied for attention with ladies in billowing silks or frothing lace. The Assembly Rooms had been transformed by the festoons of garlands pinned around the pale green walls.

Two elderly gentlemen accosted them. Encouraged by Louisa's smile, the Colonel, whose nose was as scarlet as his jacket, began his campaign in earnest: peppering his talk with compliments which he fancied was the stratagem to conquer the fairer sex. The reedy gentleman mumbled in Francina's ear. She caught a whiff of tobacco, but not what he was saying. She smiled politely anyway.

The dancing was about to begin. The quartet in the balcony stopped tuning their instruments and waited for the Bailiff and his lady to take the floor. Francina looked around for Angelo, but he was too busy talking to a group of cadets to notice that she needed rescuing. The music struck up in a great wave and to much applause. Couples glided across the polished boards and took up their positions for a quadrille.

'Francina, my dear,' said Uncle, resting his hand on her arm, 'your aunts are anxious to have a word with you. Mr Lukis will excuse you a moment, I am sure?'

She took Uncle's arm gratefully, and they wove a course across the floor, carefully avoiding the swirling couples. Depositing her before a row of sable-gowned dowagers (strategically placed so they could comment on the whole glittering spectacle), Uncle left to rescue his daughter from the clutches of Colonel McCrea.

'How becoming you look tonight, child,' smiled Aunt Marquand.

Francina kissed her frail old aunt on the cheek. She was fond of Papa's eldest sister, now quite crippled with the rheumatics. Then she kissed Aunt Sabonière (Papa's second sister), and was directed to the empty seat between them.

'Is not the room prettily got up? The roses look so enchanting draped over the balcony.'

'We are so disappointed that Angelo has not yet found the time to call on us,' Aunt Sabonière said, eyeing her nephew across the floor.

'Angelo has been much occupied since he has returned home,' Francina said, ashamed to make yet another excuse for him. These two aunts had been instrumental in fixing his passage to Ceylon. 'There are many details to finalize before he sails, but I know he is anxious to visit you as soon as possible, Aunt.'

'Is he indeed?' The jewel on Aunt Sabonière's bosom flashed sceptically.

The music had ceased. The quadrille had come to an end and dancers were returning to their places. The late arrival of the Hawtrey party distracted her aunts and they muttered disapprovingly over Mr Hawtrey's decision to attend a ball whilst his wife was still a-bed. A debate followed on how many weeks it was since Mrs Hawtrey had been taken ill. Francina listened in despair. One dance had gone, another was about to begin, and the only name pencilled in her programme was Angelo's.

Louisa and Saumarez were talking to Mr Fetherstone and the Lihous. He looked so striking in evening dress. There was an air about him . . . something irregular, irrepressible, unpredictable.

'And how did Angelo find your father, child?'

Francina turned her eyes from Gilbert Lihou to answer the question. 'Papa is still weak after his illness, Aunt, so he will not come to Guernsey after all,' she said, conscious of the row of ears straining to hear her reply.

'What a pity! It is so long since we have had the pleasure of seeing our dear brother.'

The young curate from St Andrew's was hovering. Francina smiled shyly, willing him to release her from her predicament.

'Miss Duquesne, may I have the honour of the next dance?'

Francina ignored his protruding teeth and took his arm. They took their places for the quadrille and waited for the music to start up. The curate was a bumbling dancer, more interested in making courteous observations than to follow the right steps. She tried to tell herself that it didn't matter. But it *did* matter. It mattered dreadfully. She could hardly bring herself to look at him. Still, by the nature of the dance, partners were exchanged robustly down the line, so only occasionally was she was forced to stand opposite him and cringe when he turned the wrong way. She pretended that he was not really her partner - *her* partner was the dashing cadet in the scarlet tunic at the end of the line. As she skipped and twirled along the line, she glanced surreptitiously in Gilbert Lihou's direction, but he was talking to Miss Carey.

When the dance ended, the curate handed her back to her aunts where she found the conversation continuing in the same vein as before.

Saumarez appeared and asked her to dance. She tried not to notice Gilbert Lihou waltzing with Miss Carey, but wherever she turned, there they were.

'You dance well, Sammy.'

'We have a new master at school who is a whiz with these new dances. Our old master could master the British hornpipe - but never the German waltz!'

Louisa and Mr Fetherstone brushed past them, smiling radiantly.

'I was talking to Fetherstone earlier,' Saumarez said between spins, 'He's not a bad fellow. - Do you know, Ina, I should like to join the Indian Civil Service. Would Pa agree to it, do you suppose?'

'Uncle expects you to try for Oxford.'

'I can't be doing with that stuffy old place.'

'And you might find Aunt is against the idea. She has a strong aversion to everything Indian.' She could foresee stiff opposition if Aunt thought she might lose another son to the Colonies.

'I can sweet-talk Ma.'

'Aunt has a fond wish for you to enter the Church like Grand-père,' she reminded him.

'I shall *never* contemplate the Church, however much Ma might desire it. I should like the challenge of India. Why, I should study the wildlife, and become the best shot in the district.'

She tried to listen, but the sight of Miss Carey flirting in Mr Lihou's arms was too distracting. A weight, growing in her stomach, was making it difficult to smile.

When the dance was over, Sammy escorted her to Aunt Duquesne, who was standing near the tall sash windows overlooking Market Square. Aunt welcomed her into her circle, and for a while their amusing little stories helped. Francina talked to Cousin Julia, but when she was drawn into another conversation,

Francina slipped away to the open window. The sash was up and the sweet night air drifted over her.

The rain had stopped. Roof-tops shimmered silver, and tall black chimneys stood stark against the stars. Guttering lanterns lit up the gloomy depths of Market Square and reflected in the puddles; whilst inside carriages, coachmen yawned and stretched, whiling away the hours until the ball ended.

'Miss Duquesne?'

Her heart missed a beat.

'Why are you hiding in the corner?'

The air had grown chill. But if she moved from the window she would step into his arms. Why was he here? Perhaps Miss Carey had whispered in his ear: 'Look at that little mouse hiding in the corner! Surely some kind man could spare *one* dance for poor Miss Duquesne?'

He leaned out of the window. 'What were you looking at?'

'I was wondering how I could paint the Square. The moonlight looks so bewitching on the cobblestones.'

'Only an artist could see beauty in this old familiar spot.' He returned inside. 'Miss Duquesne, I have come to request your hand for a dance.'

He was standing too close. Mrs Lihou might be watching. *Gossipmongers must have no cause to compare you to others.*

Her hand trembled as she studied her dance programme.

'The supper dance is free.'

At that moment Mrs Le Marchant came up with a young officer and hovered at their elbows. She introduced her nephew, Lieutenant Howard, who had been wounded in the war and was convalescing on the Island. Francina smiled politely and tried to focus on what the young officer was saying.

After a while, Gilbert Lihou excused himself and departed. He never glanced in her direction, but she could not stop herself from secretly watching him. She saw him sip champagne with Mr Fetherstone, and then dance with Sophie Gosselin.

The supper dance was announced. She held her breath and waited, her heart drumming against her ribs.

'Miss Duquesne?'

They began to waltz, slowly at first - then gathered speed. The room began to revolve before her eyes. Blurred images of Aunts, Uncle, then Miss Carey streaked by. Her heart flew out of the window. They were out there with it, dancing barefoot across the rooftops of St Pierre.

When the last strains of music reverberated through the air, they plunged to earth.

Supper was announced. People began to move towards the room beyond the ballroom. Her heart was still racing as he placed her hand within his arm to join them. She took little notice of the dishes on the tables. Declining champagne, she sipped cool lemonade and picked at a plate of food with a fork. Cold chicken slid down her throat, but she tasted nothing. He described an opera he had seen in Paris, while she toyed with a strawberry ice. He painted the scenes so vividly that she almost believed she was there.

Admiral de Beauvoir interrupted them with a diatribe on the Crimea. Irritation sparked in Gilbert Lihou's eyes. Perhaps the old Admiral saw it too, for he took his leave and cheerfully accosted someone else. The air was hot and close; made worse by the gas lamps that flickered and hissed above their heads. He guided her to an open window, where the sweet night air encircled them. On this side of the building, there was no view - the sheer rock face rose ink-black out of sight. The crowd had melted away. But soon the music would start up again. Leaning against the sash, she turned her head so that her profile was accentuated against the dark (it was her best feature, she had been told). She shut her eyes and imagined his eyes tracing her profile, neck and the cleft between her breasts as she had seen them do . . .

She opened her eyes and blushed. He was indeed watching her.

They were talking of poetry when Angelo appeared.

'Ina, you must try the meringues. They are quite delicious.' Hostility sparked in her brother's eyes.

Francina made introductions, and an awkward conversation followed. She tried to find a topic of common interest, but Angelo was not prepared to lower the drawbridge. After a few minutes, Gilbert Lihou made his excuses and departed.

'Don't waste your time on that likes of him,' said Angelo. 'What on earth were you thinking of, Ina?'

11

Doyle House, Pyke Yard, London

My dear son Angelo

This is the last letter you will receive on English soil. My next letter, God willing, will await your arrival in Ceylon. I remember the day when I first set foot in the East, how my heart was bursting with good intentions to succeed. I speak plainly now, Angelo: Do not let your heart rule your head. Do not be beguiled (as I was) by a pretty pair of eyes which could so easily lead to the ruination of all your plans. Set your sights high and let nothing stir you from your ambition. In an Eastern Country, where the European has his every desire attended to, it is all too easy for him to lose a sense of reality and believe that everything he touches will turn to gold with very little effort on his part. This is folly. The European of easy morals and weak convictions quickly falls by the wayside, while those who strive with the Lord's Guidance to work hard, will make the most of the opportunities that undoubtedly present themselves. Never lose sight of the fact that you are benefiting from the generosity of many kind people. Do not disappoint them, but make them proud to have helped you realise your ambitions.

Dear son, I beseech the Lord to keep you safe from harm, and deliver you safely. And I pray with all my heart that one day, with the Lord's Grace we will meet again, either in this world or the next.

Your affectionate father, Frank Duquesne

A farewell dinner was arranged in Angelo's honour. It was a family affair: the Duquesnes, Aunt Sabonière and Grand-mère Doré. Dear old Aunt Marquand had also come, accompanied as usual by Cousin Mattie. Dear Uncle, so awesome yet so mild, sat at the head and was exchanging words with Louisa. Their faces had mellowed in the candlelight. There was no mistaking it - Louisa was in love.

As little stories were swapped cheerfully around the table, emotions of gratitude overwhelmed Francina. Despite her harsh methods, Aunt meant well – she was, after all, the relative who had taken them in. She would never forget the day when she had walked into this house clutching Papa's hand . . . 'Give your Aunt a kiss, Francina,' Papa had said, pushing her towards the unsmiling woman. 'She is your mother now.'

She had suffered badly from the cold at first - no amount of blankets or shawls could ever keep her warm. Her chilblains were so painful she could hardly walk, and her nose seemed to be permanently running. It was a frightening experience to wake in the night fighting for breath. But she was granted few concessions. As far as Aunt was concerned, she was attention-seeking and was broken in like a little wild horse. But she had never encountered rules before. In India she was given the love and comfort she had craved. Here, she learned that to become civilised, one must know the pain of denial and rejection. The more she asked for, the less she was given. Losing Mamma was part of that learning process, she supposed. She came round to Aunt's way of thinking in the end, and grew cunning - showing most indifference to the things she most desired. In that way they were not taken away from her.

She learned that lesson quickly.

During that first unhappy year, she found a hide-away where no one heard her sobs. Crouching under the eaves of the coach-house, she befriended a tabby cat that had made a nest behind a heap of rags. Her little surrogate family became a great solace to her, and Baptiste would smuggle out scraps and saucers of milk for them. But Horatio discovered her secret. When Aunt found out, the cat and her kittens disappeared. She learned later that the gardener had drowned them in a bucket.

'So Angelo, you are all set to leave?'

'Indeed, Aunt Marquand. My boxes are packed. Everything is going to plan.'

'Excellent. Alex is most anxious to have you during the Cold Season. It is a busy time.'

'So I understand - but I am not sailing directly to Ceylon. I shall spend a short time in Calcutta.'

'Indeed - why so?'

Francina detected a frisson in Aunt's question.

'I have been invited to stay with the Bartons. Although I leave before them, the Bartons will travel by the Overland Route, so will arrive in India before me.'

'I need not remind you that your prime object in travelling east is to assist Alex on the Wattewelle Estate.'

'I am perfectly aware of the kindness Cousin Alex has shown me, and I intend to repay him with unstinting dedication. There will not be a coffee planter in the whole of Ceylon who shall work harder!'

'Don't exaggerate, Angelo. But it is heartening to see that London has knocked some sense into you at last.'

'I owe my change of heart entirely to you, dear Aunt.' Angelo seized her lace-covered hand. 'Aunt Marquand, I thank you from the bottom of my heart. Not a day will pass when I shall not fall on my knees and thank God for my good fortune.'

The old lady tapped him playfully on the arm. 'You're an incorrigible flatterer, Nephew. But we shall miss your cheery little visits.'

Throughout this little charade, Cousin Mattie, a pale modest woman in her early forties, sat at her mother's side. She had not said anything of significance since she had arrived. In fact Francina had never known Miss Mattie to say anything of significance or to offer an opinion on any subject (although she was always ready to agree or sympathise with others). She could not imagine Miss Mattie as a blithe young girl, full of girlish hopes and dreams, but she must have been once. She had a pleasing face and might have been pretty when she was young. Was she ever in love? Had the long empty years at her mother's side ground down a zestful disposition? Her sisters were contentedly married, each with a brood of children - did she not envy their good fortune and despair at the injustice of her own?

As expected, the conversation did not stray far from Ceylon. Now Aunt Duquesne was offering Angelo travel tips across the table. He smiled politely as he listened to cheerful anecdotes of William's adventures planting coffee, but Angelo knew (as everyone around the table knew) that Ceylon was William's nemesis. Still, it was brave of Aunt to allow Angelo to read his letters. 'Take these, Angelo,' she had whispered, handing over a black-ribboned bundle. 'Read them at your leisure, but be sure to return them before you sail. They will provide you with invaluable advice for Ceylon.'

Francina had skimmed through the letters, but between the lines she had discovered a different William from the cousin she had idolised. As she read of his daily struggles in the steaming jungles of Ceylon, of how he had trekked through twenty-six miles of mud for supplies, she discovered a vulnerable, sensitive soul, who had pined for news of Home; and all the time she had wondered: how will Angelo cope in William's place?

As he turned to answer a question, sadness crept over her. She had tried to bring up the subject of Mamma, but Angelo had only said, 'Take no notice of gossip, Ina.'

She tried to bring up the subject again, but Angelo had shrugged and walked away. It was his way of coping.

Louisa had hated her at first. She had resented the arrival of the dark-haired snivelling child who was always weeping for her Mamma, and she had begrudged sharing her bed. Every night, Francina would brace herself for the onslaught of punches and kicks. Then one night, one memorable night, Lulu left her alone and never attacked her again. She had finally come to accept that the little intruder was here to stay. They became friends after that. But who could believe that the lovely creature with the guileless eyes had once been capable of such things?

While Louisa slept, she had prayed that Mamma would come and take her away. But Mamma never came back. Eventually, she realised that she never would.

'Refresh my memory, Angelo,' Grand-mère Doré was saying across the table, 'I heard mention of the Bartons. Is that a name I should know?'

'Mrs Barton is my mother's sister from India. Father and I chanced upon her in London,' said Angelo, loud enough for his voice to carry to her silver ear trumpet. 'The Bartons are due in Guernsey soon. They will be guests of Mrs Rolichon.'

'Rolichon!' There was a note of disapproval in Grand-mère's voice. 'We never had much to do with the Rolichons. Their wealth came from privateering, which was invested in Jamaica - they were sugar planters, I believe. Mr Rolichon made a fortune at the expense of a great number of slaves, whom, it was rumoured, he treated with cruel indifference.'

Should she have expected anything else? Everything about

Mamma's family was wrong - even her friends were tainted.

'That was *old* Mr Rolichon,' Uncle Doré explained to his mother.

'When I was a young girl,' ruminated Grand-mère Doré, 'Mr Rolichon brought a little black boy from the West Indies to Guernsey. He must have been about my age, I suppose, always immaculately got up in livery, with silver buckles and a plume in his turban. He was always in attendance when Mrs Rolichon was carried through Town in her sedan chair. A sad little creature holding the lantern at the head of the procession. He died of the cold soon after his arrival, I believe.'

'We did not see a black face again on Guernsey soil again, until your mother and father arrived from India, Francina,' added Aunt Sabonière, 'attended by that servant in native dress, bare-footed and shivering with cold.'

Francina held her breath. No one around this table had ever mentioned Mamma before.

'When you were born, Francina, that servant became your nursemaid,' smiled Aunt Sabonière. 'You were never out of her arms. She seemed quite devoted to you - and to Angelo. As a small boy, you were forever clinging to her skirts!'

She was born in Grand-mère's house, the year Papa came home and introduced Mamma to the family. 'Never forget, Francina, *you* were born in Guernsey,' Papa was fond of telling her. 'That is your saving grace. No one can ever accuse you of being *country-born.*' Mamma, she knew, was country-born; she was born in India like Angelo and baby Brother, and the two older brothers who had died before she was born.

'I recall an occasion,' added Aunt Duquesne, 'when some Town boys teased that native woman mercilessly. The poor creature was so enraged that she deposited her little charge cosseted in wool and lace on the ground and gave chase; frightening the urchins so much with her foreign threats, that they never disturbed her again.'

Louisa giggled at the image of her cousin discarded like an apple core in the gutter.

'Your Papa was furious and threatened to whip her, but your Mamma was particularly attached to that native servant and managed to dissuade him.'

'I wish to propose a toast!' Uncle struck his hand so firmly on the table that that the glasses shook. 'We are gathered here this evening to say farewell to a member of our family. Twelve years ago, a young boy and his dear little sister came to live under our roof, and since that time your aunt and I have come to regard you and Francina as our own. It is therefore with the sorrow of a father saying good-bye to his son that I ask God to deliver you safely overseas to Ceylon. Angelo - we all wish you joy and contentment in your chosen course, and pray that the time will quickly pass until you return once more to our table!'

'Uncle Doré, sir!' Angelo sprang up. 'Thank you for your kind words. I know that I also speak for my sister when I say how indebted we are for the charity shown by you and Aunt Doré in taking us to your hearts. I wish I could find words enough to express our gratitude - but alas, I cannot. Someday, I shall find a way to repay your kindness. For believe me, Francina and I will be forever beholden to you.'

'Such a pity that your dear father is not with us tonight, Angelo,' whispered Aunt Marquand.

Uncle raised his glass. 'Angelo - may your journey through Life be good and righteous. Put your trust in the Lord and seek His Guidance. - Let us drink a toast to *Angelo*!'

They waved good-bye from the pier-head. He was leaning over the guard-rail waving his top hat; his hair whirled about his face. Francina fixed her eyes on him until he grew too small to distinguish from the milling crowd on deck - but still she waved her handkerchief, until the steamer had shrunk to the size of a pea; until the tenuous life-line that held Angelo to her heart was stretched taut as a violin string . . .

Then he was gone. Until that moment, she had found the courage to resist tears, but now they slide down her cheeks. She was crying not just for Angelo, but for her whole family. One by one they had all deserted her.

Uncle Doré put his hand on her shoulder as they walked back to the carriage.

She sought the sanctuary of the library on their return, and for once Aunt Doré did not seek her out for some meaningful occupation. She sat on the window seat staring across the roof-tops of St Pierre to the spot on the horizon where she had last glimpsed Angelo's steamer. She watched curls of smoke from the old part of Town meander into the sky. She watched the sea birds circling over the harbour, and a full-rigged brig glide between the islands. The daguerreotype lay in her lap. Every so often, she lowered her eyes and studied it. Clutching his likeness, she left the library.

She entered his bedroom cautiously. There was little left of him: a few screwed up balls of paper, a broken comb, a worn goose quill, the shredded remains of a snuff packet, and an empty box of cigars. She opened the box and inhaled deeply.

The collection of Grand-père's sermons that Aunt Marquand had given him lay on the bed; the same precious volume that Angelo had promised to keep by his bedside and consult every night. Clutching it to her bosom, she fell on his bed, wrapped herself in his crumpled sheets and buried her face in his pillow.

12

'Put on your bonnet, Ina. Let's walk to the Esplanade. We might meet someone.'

'I am not in the mood, Lulu.'

'Really, you are so tiresome! It's *dull* if you don't come - you know I can't divulge my secrets to Miss Hobson.'

'Go without me, Lulu.'

'We could talk scandal?'

'No, Lulu.'

'Are you still pining for Angelo?' Louisa snatched her sketchbook and threw it on the floor. 'When will you realise that most young men would *envy* Angelo's chance to travel and see the world!'

She stormed out of the library and banging the door.

Francina picked up her sketchbook. How could Louisa understand? Her life was one of agreeable awakenings with pleasant choices at every crossroads; a smooth inconsequential life, where nothing adverse had occurred. And now, thought Francina, as she studied her drawing, Louisa's head is filled with thoughts of Mr Fetherstone, and if it takes her fancy she can break his heart as easily as she can add him to her list of admirers. Everything Louisa desires eventually becomes hers. How could she empathise?

Mrs Barton's arrival was imminent. Letters had passed between Mrs Barton, Aunt Doré and Mrs Rolichon, and now all was arranged. Francina would meet her Indian aunt and uncle off the steamer and escort them to La Colline. She had arrived at the quay early. Her heart was pounding, and she had hardly slept. Unfortunately, however, Louisa had insisted on coming, and her presence was an irritation. How could she ask Mrs Barton anything intimate in Louisa's presence?

Passengers, weighed down with carpetbags, hatboxes, and bandboxes, scrambled up the pier steps in a disorderly file.

'How will you know Mrs Barton?' asked Louisa.

How would she indeed.

The arrivals streamed by: a harassed pair dragging three young sons; a nurse carrying a fat baby; two young ladies with their chaperone; a parson and his young wife; an old man leaning on the arm of a young girl; peasant women laden with cages of poultry; sweethearts; commercial travellers; a sea-captain . . . Francina eyed them all carefully - but they were either too young or too old. Then, with a sinking heart, she saw her. There could be no mistake.

'Oh, Ina,' giggled Louisa. 'That must be Mrs Barton.'

A stout figure bustled towards them. She was on the arm of a grey-haired gentleman of similar size and height, dressed in a country suit of loud brown check. The lady was about sixty years old, but that did not deter her from dressing in a most youthful manner. Over her emerald silk gown she had draped an Indian shawl, richly patterned in scarlet hues. Following them was an Indian maid-servant draped from head to foot in white muslin.

The lady caught her eye and smiled. 'Francina? There can be no doubt - you are the image of your mamma!' A black feather attached to her bonnet waved erratically in the air, emerald streamers floated in the breeze. 'I am looking into the eyes of my dear, dear sister! *Les mêmes yeux*! Theresa's nose!'

Francina curtsied.

Mrs Barton drew her to her bosom. The scent of eau de Cologne was overpowering. 'How very, very happy I am to see you, dearest Francina!'

She pronounced her words with a lilt and in a French accent. Her blue eyes sparkled with youthful energy as she surveyed her niece from head to foot, and although her hair had turned grey, her brows were still as thick and dark as her hair must once have been. Francina suspected that she was quite comely in her youth.

'You were only a child in your ayah's arms when we last saw you, *ma petite*. - How many years is it, Mr Barton?' But Mrs Barton did not wait for her husband to answer. She spun round and smiled at Louisa: 'And who is your pretty companion, Francina?'

'Mrs Barton, may I present my cousin, Miss Louisa Doré.'

Louisa curtsied.

'*Enchantée* Miss Louisa. Is it not kind of Miss Louisa to welcome us, Mr Barton? We are so looking forward to meeting your mamma.'

Mr Barton shook their hands cordially. Splendid unruly whiskers complemented his white head of hair.

'Oh, Mr Barton, we are being inconsiderate! We must move out of the way - we are holding every one up.'

Eyes watched their progress along the pier. The barefooted servant followed behind them, her face obscured by her sari.

'How obliging of Mr Doré to send his carriage. Was it not kind of Mr Doré to send his carriage, Mr Barton?'

As they waited for the luggage to be transferred from the steamer, Mrs Barton chatted on, oblivious to the surreptitious smirks around her. A crowd of urchins had gathered to point and snigger as boxes and bags arrived in a steady stream and were loaded onto a hire cart. One daredevil advanced close enough to touch the foreigner's sari, then ran away shouting triumphantly at his daring.

At last the Bartons climbed into the brougham. Francina and Louisa followed, squeezing into the spaces left by their visitors. Mrs Barton leaned out of the window and asked the driver of the hire cart to allow her servant to sit with him. After some altercation and the promise of a tip, the driver agreed.

Gesticulating heatedly, Mrs Barton babbled to her servant in a foreign tongue. The frightened woman required some persuading to climb up; but eventually she agreed and they were ready to proceed.

Mrs Barton squeezed into her seat and sighed. 'Sometimes I wonder if it is worth bringing servants from the East, they never manage to adjust.'

Then she leaned forward to pat her husband's hand.

'How are you feeling, my dear? Such a fatiguing journey!'

Mr Barton winced, then smiled. His twinkling eyes and generous proportions made him look friendly. He rested his head against the upholstery and shut his eyes. The bowler hat on his paunch rose and fell as he breathed.

Francina eyed him curiously, wondering what was wrong with him. She had noticed him leaning on his cane as he walked.

'Marseilles to Paris - London, Glasgow and Dublin! We were so touched by the kindness shown by so many dear, dear friends - were we not, Mr Barton?'

Mrs Barton fumbled in her silk reticule and unearthed a pillbox containing acid drops, which she offered to the girls. They accepted one, thrilled to succumb to the vice of eating between meals.

'What a stroke of good fortune it was to bump into your Papa and Angelo at the Covent Garden Theatre.' Mrs Barton returned the pill-box to her reticule. 'Naturally, it has been many years since we last saw Mr Duquesne, but we recognized each other immediately. Angelo was a child when we last saw him so of course he has changed greatly. Such a charming boy! *Alors,* his stories did make us chuckle - *n'est-ce pas,* Mr Barton? We are so looking forward to receiving him in Calcutta.'

The carriage jolted over the cobbles, and strained up the hill at Hauteville. It was one of the grandest streets in St Pierre, and Mrs Barton could not fail to be impressed by the handsome houses. 'What elegance and sophistication,' she cried, noting the fanlights, colonnaded porches, iron railings and intricate lantern holders. 'Such a street can surpass *any* we have seen on the mainland.'

Mrs Barton enthused on everything she saw from the window. Francina commented briefly during her pauses, but inside she was in turmoil. Was this animated lady really her aunt? Was Mamma as singular? If Mamma's arrival in St Pierre had caused as many heads to turn as the arrival of Mrs Barton, it was no wonder she was still talked about. Mrs Barton had called her: *Theresa - my dear, dear sister!* - without the faintest note of shame or embarrassment. Theresa. It was a pretty name. It conjured up images of popish saints and foreign queens: a medieval queen with braided hair and a golden aura - but no face. She could not picture Mamma's face.

Gradually the iron railings became granite walls; the spaces between the houses increased, and earth replaced the cobbles; walls became rough banks overgrown with ferns or brambles, and gnarled oaks shaded the lane. They had left St Pierre behind.

Soon they arrived at a stately entrance, each gatepost crowned with a large stone pineapple. It was the entrance to La Colline. Today the iron gates were open and attended by an old gardener who doffed his cap as the carriage turned into the grounds. Tall shrubs along the driveway screened the house –

Then a flat-roofed villa, that looked as if it had been transported brick by brick from the West Indies, came into view. The carriage drew up at the entrance, and an old footman in faded livery shuffled down the shallow fight of steps to assist the Bartons out.

Mrs Barton paused for a discourse through the carriage window on how delighted they were to see Francina again and meet dear Miss Louisa, etcetera, etcetera. Politely, the girls waited for the moment to leave. Their chance came when the hire cart rattled noisily down the drive. In the hubbub, the girls quickly said their goodbyes and signalled to the driver. Mrs Barton was still urging her servant to climb down from the cart when they sped out of the gate.

Francina leaned back against the upholstery and shut her eyes.

The following afternoon the brougham, carrying Aunt Doré, Francina and Louisa, rumbled once more through the gates of La Colline. It had been a silent journey, for Aunt had made no secret of her displeasure in coming here. 'The Rolichons are not our sort of people. We will stay the minimum time that politeness requires.'

'Cook says a *cambion*, a devil-child lives at La Colline,' Louisa announced as the house came into view.

'Cook has some strange notions, Louisa,' said Aunt. 'How many times have I told you not to listen to servants' gossip?'

The brougham pulled up at the steps, and the old footman ushered them in.

Francina's eyes looked for tell-tale signs of the *cambion*, but she saw only a square vestibule containing a stone staircase (far too grand for the size of house) which rose from the centre, divided at a half-landing and skirted the walls to a gallery above. It was a room unchanged since it was built in the last century, only now the pale green walls were flaking in places, and dust had gathered on the decorative plaster-work.

Footsteps echoed across stone floors as they followed the old man through darkened rooms with shutters drawn. Nothing in the rooms (as far as she could make out in the dim light) seemed out of the ordinary. It was just a tired old house with the furniture positioned formally against the walls.

Then she jumped as she came face-to-face with a pair of white stockings, a pale blue suit, and a gleaming white turban sprouting an audacious ostrich feather - the *cambion!*

'Don't be alarmed, miss,' muttered the footman. 'It's only Rollo.'

Francina peered into the darkness. Now she saw a smiling black boy, perfectly still, dressed in an outdated costume, proffering a tray of sweetmeats. She put out a tentative finger to touch his arm. It was cold and hard.

'Rollo,' repeated the old footman. 'He used to serve the old master. When he died, the master had his likeness fashioned in wood. He's become a sort of mascot.'

The colonnaded portico, which ran the whole length of the house, came as a surprise after the gloomy formality of the house. Bright eastern cushions were scattered on chairs and the tiled floor was strewn with Turkey rugs. Oriental swords swirled in patterns across the walls. This, Francina thought with a shiver of excitement, is how an Indian room must look.

Through windows cut in the lattice screens that enclosed the portico, she caught sight of a gardener and his boy clipping a high yew hedge.

Mrs Barton rose to greet them. Her purple plaid gown suited the gay disorder of her surroundings.

'Well, I declare, Mrs Doré, we must greet each other less formally! We are family are we not?' Mrs Barton grasped the hands of her new relative and planted a kiss on each cheek.

Aunt Doré recoiled slightly, and turned her eyes away from the crucifix glinting on her bosom. But Mrs Barton appeared not to notice. She turned to a lady a few years older than herself, seated in a high-backed chair, and introduced Mrs Rolichon.

Their hostess inclined her head graciously. 'The family of my late husband's dearest friend is welcome unreservedly in this house.'

Francina and Louisa curtsied. The fat pug sprawled at Mrs Rolichon's feet growled, but was too lazy to investigate further.

Mrs Rolichon's aquiline nose gave her an aristocratic air. She was dressed entirely in black, her ensemble enlivened only by a pearl cross hanging from a ribbon on her breast.

'May I offer you tea?'

Their hostess rang a tiny bell and directed them to sit - which they did somewhat awkwardly, in stiff chairs lavishly decorated with carvings of rampant beasts. While Francina's fingers traced the outline of a snarling bear on her armrest, she asked politely if Mr Barton had recovered from the journey?

'So kind to enquire, *ma chérie*,' smiled Mrs Barton, signalling to her servant (the same Indian maid that had walked along the pier flouting the jeers of the ragged boys). The maid slipped gracefully into the house. 'Your uncle is resting. There is nothing like *rest* to recuperate, and where better to recuperate! Such a delightful house, so comfortable. Dear Mrs Rolichon is so very attentive.'

Mrs Rolichon smiled modestly. Silver hair gleamed through her black lace mantilla.

Tea was brought out. Cups and saucers and plates of delicacies were handed round. Francina avoided Aunt Doré's eyes as she helped herself.

'You are out, Miss Doré?'

Louisa bit a corner of toast smeared with Gentlemen's Relish. 'Not yet, Mrs Rolichon. I am shortly to spend a year in Brussels.'

'Indeed? I believe there is much fashionable society in Brussels.'

'My cousin is to study music at the Conservatoire.' Francina swallowed delicately. Mrs Rolichon might have undesirable associations, but her sandwiches were very good.

'When you return, Miss Doré, you will take society by storm. Invitations will fall at your feet! There are too many salons these days that profess to be places of musical eminence, but quite frankly, I have found the standard very poor.'

'My daughter will only play for *private* amusement.'

'Naturally, Mrs Doré.'

Louisa carried a sugar cube to her cup with tiny silver tongs.

'Will you also go to Brussels, Miss Duquesne?' smiled Mrs Rolichon. It pleased her to talk to pretty young ladies.

'I do not have my cousin's musical gift, Mrs Rolichon.'

Francina looked away, her eyes drawn to a niche in the wall, a niche holding a figurine of a Madonna, an ivory crucifix and other religious keepsakes.

'My niece will be a great consolation to me when my daughter is abroad,' Aunt Doré said. 'My time is increasingly taken up with charity work. I intend to pass some of my duties into her hands.'

'Indeed, indeed.'

'What a delight it is to be on this beautiful Island amongst so many new friends, and to meet our dear niece again.' Mrs Barton helped herself to a sugary *galette*. 'I recognised her immediately, Mrs

Doré! She is the image of my youngest sister. Theresa was such a pretty child, quite her father's pet.'

'There were other sisters, Mrs Barton?' Francina asked.

'Indeed! Cecilia and Theresa were often mistaken for twins. Papa doted on them. They were known in the district as *Monsieur Savi's beautiful daughters*. It broke his heart when his little darlings were sent away.'

'Where was Mamma sent, Mrs Barton?' whispered Francina. She saw a forbidding Institution with high walls, a girl in a white flowing robe wandering along a dark corridor.

'To England.'

'*England?*'

'*Mais oui, ma petite* - Cecilia and Theresa were educated in a convent run by a French order that had sought refuge during the Revolution. But Theresa hated the English winters, and pined for her Indian way of life.'

'I can entirely sympathise,' sighed Mrs Rolichon.

'Theresa's letters broke Papa's heart. She was so unhappy. When it was time for Cecilia to leave, Theresa begged to return to India with her. Papa's plan was that she should return two years later, but Theresa announced that if she did not travel with Cecilia, she would refuse to eat.' Mrs Barton sipped her tea. 'The nuns could do nothing to change her mind. The Reverend Mother was so concerned that she gave orders for her to sail with her sister.'

The pug wheezed as Francina waited for Mrs Barton to reveal more.

'I shall never forget the look of astonishment on Papa's face when Theresa stepped off the ship at Calcutta with her sister. He had no idea she was aboard. She was not yet fourteen when she returned home.'

Francina saw it all so clearly . . . Papa blinded by her beauty, married her in all innocence. But as the years rolled by, he watched helplessly as Mamma's wilful nature grew stronger, her mood swings more violent, until, until . . .

A clock chimed. Aunt Doré coughed and glanced pointedly at her niece. The minimum time had passed. She had fulfilled her obligation to her brother. It was time to leave.

13

Miss Hobson had some errands to run in Town and the girls asked to accompany her. As they turned into the cobbled yard behind the bookbinder's shop in Bordage Street, Louise nudged Francina.

'Look who's over there!'

Mr Fetherstone was leaning against a grocer's barrow, deep in conversation with Mrs Lihou.

'Let's cross over and speak to him.'

'You go, Lulu. Meet us in the shop in a few minutes.'

'Miss Louisa seems much taken with that young man,' said Miss Hobson, as they walked across the yard. 'This is not the first time she has come across him. Yesterday he was on the Esplanade, and the day before she chanced upon him in Smith Street. It can't all be coincidence, Miss Francina. Someone is bound to notice that a young man is always seen in her company. I will lose my situation if the Mistress finds out before I inform her.'

'There is no need for that, Miss Hobson. Aunt is perfectly aware of Mr Fetherstone. He called at Elm House the other day, did he not, when I was out with my Indian aunt? Louisa will soon be installed at the Conservatoire, and then there will be no more Mr Fetherstone.'

Miss Hobson's face relaxed a little.

The door jangled as they entered the shop.

'Mademoiselle, I have just hung up a very fine watercolour,' smiled the proprietor. Placing his hammer and nails on the counter, Mess Brouard scratched his cheek and pointed it out. Francina smiled. Her attempt to paint the rooftops of St Pierre looked well in its gilt frame. It was perfect for Uncle's birthday.

'Now I must rearrange my display,' said Mess Brouard as he carefully removed the picture. 'It has been admired. A few minutes ago, a gentleman enquired if it might be for sale.'

'Goodness!'

While the picture framer wrapped it behind the counter,

Francina studied the new works on display. She was always curious to see the latest offerings, for Guernsey was the haunt of visiting artists, eager to capture her beautiful savage coastline in paint. There was a new oil painting in a style she found rather startling: wild swirling splashes of colour, unmixed and thickly spread. The artist had made little attempt to hide his brushstrokes. She studied the painting for a few minutes, trying to decide if it was the product of a disturbed mind.

Mess Brouard handed her a paper parcel tightly secured in twine. Opening her purse, Francina took out the gold sovereign Angelo had given her. Receiving her change, they bid the picture framer good day and departed.

Outside, Louisa was still talking to Mr Fetherstone and Mrs Lihou. They had been joined by Gilbert Lihou and his sister. When he saw Francina, he raised his hat and came over. Mary followed.

'Miss Duquesne, we were sorry to miss you when we called the other day.'

'Unfortunately, I was otherwise engaged.'

'You are a very gifted young lady!'

She hugged her brown paper parcel. 'It is just an amateurish watercolour, Mr Lihou.'

'I was actually referring to your drawings. Did Miss Doré not tell you? I expressed a desire to see your paintings, and Miss Doré kindly showed me your sketchbook. - I hope you do not mind?'

Her heart jumped. 'My watercolours in the green folio?'

'I distinctly recall it was a buff sketchbook of pencil drawings.'

The thought of Louisa showing her private drawings to Gilbert Lihou in her usual frivolous way filled her with indignation. How could she!

'You are displeased, Miss Duquesne?'

'That sketchbook contains silly doodles, fit for no eyes but mine.'

'I disagree. I was full of admiration. You have an enviable gift to copy anything that takes your fancy.' He turned to his sister. 'Mary, did you know of Miss Duquesne's talent for drawing?'

Before his sister could reply, Mrs Lihou had advanced towards them. 'Gilbert, we were just speaking of Miss Doré's excellent rendition at the concert. You were abroad at the time, were you not?' Her remarks were addressed entirely to him, over Francina's head.

'I was indeed, ma'am. I have not had the pleasure of hearing Miss Doré play.'

'Well, we must rectify that immediately.' Mrs Lihou clasped her gloved hands together. 'I must arrange a soirée at Belle Villa before you leave.'

'An excellent idea, Mrs Lihou.' Mr Fetherstone smiled at Louisa, who flushed at the thought of being seen to such advantage.

'I shall set my mind to it immediately. An intimate party, I think, of close dear friends.' Mrs Lihou turned to Louisa. 'It will be a pleasure to make use of our pianoforte. I am ashamed to say it tends to languish unattended in the salon.'

'Do you play, Miss Duquesne?' Gilbert Lihou asked. She was sure he had noticed his mother's rudeness in slighting her.

'A little - sadly, without Louisa's flair.'

'It would be remarkable if you were as proficient at the piano as you are at drawing.'

'Mary plays a little.' Mrs Lihou touched her daughter's sleeve. 'But who could claim to play as delightfully as Miss Doré!'

If Mrs Lihou was about to eulogise on Louisa's talents, then luckily she was distracted. Catching sight of Miss Carey passing through the gateway, she hurried over to speak to her.

Miss Hobson grasped the moment to leave. She marched up High Street with the girls trailing behind. Louisa was swinging her little embroidered reticule, singing quietly to herself.

'I feel quite mortified,' Francina announced miserably.

Louisa looked at her in surprise.

'How could you show my sketch book to Mr Lihou!'

'Ina, you weren't there to ask, and he expressed a wish to see your drawings. I can't see the harm.'

'But there's a drawing of him in the sketchbook!'

'Is there? I had no idea. Is it a caricature? Have you made him uglier than he is - given him a monstrous nose or something?'

'Of course not.'

'Why worry then? In fact, it was rather convenient - while he was studying your drawings, I was able to claim Mr Fetherstone's undivided attention.'

'Lulu, you're impossible. You think of no-one but yourself!'

Louisa stared at her in astonishment. 'Well, I really can't think what possessed you to draw Mr Lihou in the first place.' Then her eyes lit up as a thought struck her. 'Could you draw a likeness of Henry Fetherstone for me? - You must agree that his face really is worth drawing. He is so divinely handsome!'

Francina marched off in a fury. What had Gilbert Lihou seen?

At home, she discovered that the drawing she had made of him perched on the library steps was still in her sketchbook. To make matters worse, there were other drawings of him: a small portrait sketch and a full length pose. No wonder he was amused.

Louisa drew up a footstool close to her father's chair. 'Papa, guess what arrived while you were abroad?' (She had waited all evening to broach the subject, patiently sitting through Sammy's tedious account of their fishing excursion to Jersey.)

Uncle Doré looked over his spectacles.

'An invitation to Mrs Lihou's soirée! Mamma said we must not reply until you had been consulted.'

'Quite right.' Uncle returned to his newspaper. 'Nothing will induce me to attend one of Mrs Lihou's insufferable parties.'

Louisa looked mortified. Tears welled in her eyes. She lowered her head so that her curls tumbled prettily about her cheeks. 'Please, Papa. I have set my heart on going.'

'What on earth is the attraction at Belle Villa? I thought you did not care for Mary Lihou.' Uncle was oblivious to the intrigues and fancies that took place under his roof.

'But Papa, don't you see - it will be an excellent opportunity to practise, and I must practise before I go to Brussels. The French young ladies will be so talented!'

Uncle put down his newspaper. He knew he would have no peace until this matter was settled, and his resistance always melted at the sight of feminine tears.

'If it means so much to you, we shall go to the Lihous' party.'

Louisa jumped up and kissed him. 'You shall be so proud of me, Papa! - May I wear one of my new gowns, Mamma? You must see them, Papa. They have turned out so well!'

'Show me them all,' chuckled Uncle. 'Francina, do you also have a new gown for me to see?'

'Ina has no need, Papa. She is not going away.' Turning to her, Louisa added, 'I will leave you one of my old gowns, Ina. I am sure Miss Hobson can add some trimming if the hem is too short.'

Euphoria had made her bountiful.

'Papa, may I have a music lesson with Signor Bandini? He will know exactly which pieces I should play at the soirée.'

'If you must, Louisa, but from what you were inferring, I thought you were above lessons. Francina, shall you also play at the soirée? Would you like a lesson as well?'

Signor Bandini burst into Elm House the following morning with all the showy gestures and fine manners that made up the Italian maestro. 'Miss Doré, what a joy to kiss your hand! *Alors*, the Academy has lost its muse. My dear Madame - how are the young ladies of the Academy to reach such heavenly harmonies without Miss Doré to inspire them?'

'Signor Bandini, I have no answer.'

'There is no answer, Madame.'

'Signor Bandini,' said Aunt Doré, wondering if she had been wise to sanction the Italian's presence. 'My daughter is to perform at a soirée next week, and wishes advice on the pieces she should play.'

'Madame, the pleasure will be mine. What a delight to hear Miss Doré's voice again! To see her fingers fly across the keys -'

'My niece is also to have musical instruction. She too will attend the soirée.'

'Then I am doubly honoured, Madame. Shall we begin this afternoon? I am free today. Unfortunately, tomorrow my time is fully taken up.'

'Return this afternoon, Signor Bandini, the girls will be ready for instruction at two o'clock.'

'Until two o'clock, Madame. I take my leave.'

Punctually at two o'clock, a breathless Signor Bandini, his wayward locks and luxuriant whiskers looking more unruly than ever, was ushered into the drawing-room clutching a large portfolio of manuscripts. Louisa was already seated at the pianoforte practising her scales. Francina stood by the French windows despondently thumbing through a folio of Scottish airs, hoping to find a tuneful ditty that would be pleasing to the ear and disguise her lack of proficiency.

Signor Bandini stopped in the centre of the room and sighed. 'Miss Doré! How many times do I shut my eyes and conjure up that delectable singing voice!'

Flinging his portfolio onto a small table, he pulled up a stool to the pianoforte, threw out the skirt of his frock coat and sat down.

'Continue, if you please, Miss Doré, while I gather my thoughts.'

He pressed the tips of his fingers together, rested them against his chin and closed his eyes.

'Well?' smiled Louisa, when she concluded her song.

'Miss Doré, there is nothing I can teach you!'

'But Signor Bandini, was that a suitable song to play at the soirée? That is why I seek your guidance. You see, I wish to present just the right *ton*.'

The maestro pondered for a moment. Then he rummaged through his portfolio and produced a sheet of music with a triumphant flourish.

'Miss Doré, I discovered this on my recent travels. I believe the composer had *you* in mind when he committed these notes to paper! You have the flair to do this composition justice. Study the music at your leisure, and when I return again I wish you to play it to me. And now I must find a charming duet . . . Here, I have it! I shall play it through - then I wish you and Miss Duquesne to sing the accompaniment. Miss Doré, you sing the first voice, and you Miss Duquesne, the second.'

And so the afternoon progressed. Clever Signor Bandini produced some light, agreeable pieces, eminently suitable for the soirée. Francina felt her apprehensions fading under his astute coaching. He encouraged her to sing in a lower pitch and to draw deeper breaths.

'And now, Miss Duquesne, I have just the piece for you - a pretty piece, I'm sure you will agree. It has not been heard on the Island before. It is one of my lucky finds. It is not too taxing and the melody is charming. I have been saving it for a special *élève* - and you, Miss Duquesne, are that *élève*!'

Francina played the opening bars.

'No, no, Miss Duquesne! Play the melody with tenderness!

Imagine the keys are your lover's fingers. The pulse is as quick and light as the caress of a lover's fingers!'

Self-consciously Francina touched the keys again, feeling more inhibited than ever. How could she possibly play now? Everyone would assume that she was having shameful thoughts.

'Miss Duquesne, with passion, *please*!'

'Think of your lover, Ina,' giggled Louisa.

It took so little effort to conjure him up.

'Better Miss Duquesne! In the next few days you must practise this piece with as much ardour as you have done just now - and when I return, I hope to notice an improvement in your playing.'

There was a knock, and Miss Hobson entered the room.

'Miss Francina, I have come to inform you that Mrs Barton is taking tea with the Mistress on the terrace.'

Francina rose. The maestro followed suit with as much flourish as he had sat down. She stepped through the French windows to the balcony and blinked in the afternoon glare. Below on the shaded terrace, she saw that Aunt Duquesne and Cousin Julia had also called. She felt a knot of frustration. Would she ever be alone with Mrs Barton? Mamma's story was so near, yet so difficult to reach.

She returned inside. 'I must take my leave.'

'It is a timely interruption, Miss Duquesne. We have made excellent strides in a short time - and now is a good moment to draw the lesson to a conclusion.' Signor Bandini produced a notebook from the pocket of his frock-coat and thumbed through the pages. 'I must consult Mrs Doré of course, but is Monday a suitable day to continue our lesson? My time is much taken up this week. I cannot account for it, but there has been a sudden demand for musical instruction - especially from a certain young lady at the Academy.'

'Which certain young lady?' asked Louisa.

'Miss Lihou has suddenly developed an interest in music. I have been requested to devote most of tomorrow at Belle Villa instructing both Mrs and Miss Lihou. It is most gratifying to note this surge in interest.'

'Most gratifying,' smiled Louisa.

14

Mrs Barton bustled down the steps of La Colline in an abundance of flounces and startling colours. 'Am I too formally attired? I always think it a compliment to the hostess to be fittingly turned-out, and I am touched, so very touched, to be included in this auspicious family birthday.'

A line of servants emerged from the house carrying cushions, rugs and every conceivable article that might be of use on the beach. Mrs Barton craned her neck into the carriage window.

'Dear Mrs Doré, is there a *tiny* space for a few pieces of luggage in the box? I like to be prepared for any eventuality.'

After some difficulty, room was found.

Mrs Barton was assisted into Mrs Rolichon's gig. Francina climbed in and sat beside her.

'Regrettably, Mrs Rolichon will not be joining us for the picnic. The dear lady does suffer so from the rheumatics. She rarely ventures beyond the confines of La Colline these days - and poor Mr Barton is still too much of an invalid to -'

Mrs Barton broke off to lean out of the gig and address her maid in her native tongue.

The maid climbed up gingerly. Her bone bracelets tinkled as she lowered herself into the space between them. She was a slim creature and took up little room. Francina caught the scent of her hair, and an intangible memory sprang into her heart . . . of safe brown arms and a voice singing in a soft foreign tongue.

The gig rattled out of the gates of La Colline to follow the Dorés' brougham up the lane towards the southern coast of Guernsey. The sun flashed through the canopy of trees. Clouds of dust rose from the wheels of the Doré carriage and settled on their skirts.

The coachman pulled the reins and the gig fell back.

Mrs Barton settled back to enjoy the drive. '*Que c'est beau*!'

'I hope Mr Barton will soon be well enough to see something of Guernsey.'

'*Uncle* Barton, my dear. Please address him as Uncle and myself as Aunt. After all, your Uncle used to bounce you on his knee when you were an infant.'

'Fancy,' said Francina. She had no memory of that.

The horse strained up the winding lane. The coachman cracked the whip and the gig lurched forward. In sunny open spaces, the scent of flowers wafted across their path.

'Since we arrived on this delightful Island,' Aunt Barton reached across her maid's lap to pat her hand, 'I have been so taken up with society that there has not been a moment for a cosy *tête-à-tête*. I have been *so* looked forward to an intimate parley with you.'

Just then Uncle Doré rode alongside and enquired into Mr Barton's health. A conversation followed, which veered from the beneficial properties of sea air to the scenic beauties of the Island. Each time it looked as though it might draw to a close, Uncle remembered another attraction Aunt Barton must not miss. Francina bowed her head in despair. Why had Uncle chosen this moment, of all moments, to extol the beauties of Guernsey? If he started on his favourite subject - privateering - they would arrive at the beach before the American War.

At last he raised his hat, instructed the coachman to make a scenic detour to the bay, and cantered off to join Saumarez at the head of the procession.

'What an obliging gentleman! We are so very touched by the welcome shown by your family, Francina.'

'Sometimes I wonder what would have become of Angelo and me if it were not for the kindness of the Dorés.'

'*Dis-moi*, you are happy, *ma petite*?'

The question surprised her. It was the first time anyone had enquired into her well-being.

'Of course you are, my dear. *Mais je sais bien,* nothing can replace a mother's love, *n'est-ce pas*?'

Francina bit her lip and nodded.

'Although your Papa cannot speak of it himself, He wished me to tell you.' Aunt Barton lowered her voice. 'My dear, you are old enough to understand and I believe you have a right to know.'

'I know nothing, Aunt Barton,' whispered Francina. 'I do not even know if Mamma is alive.'

'My dear! *Donne-moi ta main.*'

Shyly, Francina obliged.

'She lives, she lives. Your Mamma is very much alive.'

Francina braced herself. 'Is she ill? Has she been locked up?'

'Locked up? Child, what an idea!'

On the crest of the hill they emerged beyond the canopy of trees to encounter the full force of the August sun, and drove in silence through banks of purple heather and bracken that was beginning to hint of the gold of autumn. The rugged coastline stretched out before them. The sea, which today looked so innocent and playful, had gouged the rock to form a crescent bay, sheer and precipitous, far below. Here and there, spectacular pinnacles of granite jutted defiantly out of the water.

'Your Mamma left - of her own free will.'

Her own free will? Walk away from Papa and her children? How could she!

'*Mon Dieu,* how it grieves me to say this: she lives as another man's wife, although she is still married to your Papa.' Aunt Barton fumbled in her reticule. 'Your Mamma is a kept woman.' Aunt Barton caught the words in her handkerchief and rolled them into a tight ball before the wind could carry them off to prying ears.

A kept woman? A mistress?

'Take comfort, *ma petite*. It is a secret known only within the family. My sister Cecilia is the only one of us still in communication with her. Theresa has assumed another name and lives in a part of the world where she is unlikely to encounter anyone from her past life.'

Obliterate her past life? Could a mother despise her own daughter so much?

Near the cliff edge the coachman paused, and allowed the horse to rest before the descent to the bay. Ahead, the Doré carriage snaked along the narrow lane until it turned out of sight, leaving behind a veil of dust. They alighted and strolled towards the precipice.

'You have lost a mother and I have lost a sister,' Aunt Barton said quietly. 'Theresa has disgraced our family name. She has behaved dishonourably.'

In silence they gazed across the whole amphitheatre of rock.

Beyond the far point, the black fragmented rock had weathered into grotesque shapes. Today, Francina saw a petrified head with a grimacing mouth.

'I have many fond memories of Theresa,' said Aunt Barton. 'But now, if anyone enquires after her, I reply: *Theresa is no longer with us.* They assume the worst and offer their sympathy. That is how you must regard her, *ma petite:* your Mamma is no longer with us.'

The motion of the sea was making Francina dizzy. She loved its unpredictability, its changing moods: sometimes as still as glass, sometimes black and raging with fury. The distance down did not look terrifying or intimidating today. The little white crests were fingers beckoning. It would take so little effort to lean over . . . to dive like a gull and vanish in that cool blue void.

'Take my handkerchief. Dry your eyes, *ma chérie*. It will not do to have red eyes today.'

The lane descended steeply into a deep winding gully, which followed the course of a rivulet. The ground was uneven and there was hardly room for the gig, but apart from steep flights of zigzagging steps, this was the only route down to the beach. Aunt Barton shut her eyes and clutched the upholstery as they inched down.

At the foot of the gully, the walls fanned outwards. They had arrived at a fishing hamlet and the sea stretched out before them. A scrawny dog snapped at the carriage wheels and a boy with a sunburnt face and faded smock ran alongside.

The gig pulled up and they alighted. The boy, hoping to earn a franc, asked to mind the horse.

Immediately, Aunt Barton's maid became an object of curiosity to some children playing nearby who ran up to snigger. The groom cracked his whip and cursed them. The children scattered, only to advance again when his back was turned.

Francina took Aunt's arm to guide her to the beach. The groom and maid followed, their arms weighed down with Aunt's possessions. Behind them trailed the giggling, barefoot children.

'Mind your step, Aunt Barton, it is a little slippery.'

It was hard to focus on Aunt Barton's chatter while her head whirled with thoughts of Mamma, but at last, squeezing between some large boulders, they arrived at the beach. Francina surveyed the sable line of Guernsey matrons perched by the rocks and her heart sank. They would expect her to sit by them and cheerfully answer their questions. How could she ever feel cheerful again?

She saw, also, that Gilbert Lihou and Henry Fetherstone were here, surrounded by a gaggle of girl cousins.

Eyes turned to watch them and Francina blushed. At that moment her Indian aunt's appearance seemed excruciatingly outlandish.

Aunt Duquesne, however, who never set much store by appearance and took even less interest in gossip, greeted Aunt Barton warmly, and her welcome melted the reserve of the rest of the party. The foreigner was grudgingly accepted into the circle.

'Madame, may I be of assistance?'

'So kind! Help would be most welcome, *n'est-ce pas*, Francina?'

Gilbert Lihou glanced only fleetingly in her direction when the introductions were made, for Aunt had distracted him with a volley of questions while he helped her find a suitable place amongst the rocks. Baptiste proffered a tray of refreshments, and Aunt eagerly helped herself. Her maid crouched behind her and held up a parasol to shield her face from the sun. Perched on her cushions next to Aunt Duquesne, Aunt Barton looked like some exotic eastern bird that had landed incongruously amongst a row of jackdaws. Gilbert Lihou, learning that Aunt was from Calcutta, grew so engrossed in a conversation about India that nothing else on the beach seemed of any concern to him.

'You are eating very little, Francina,' said Mrs Bonamy, emptying a spoonful of cold boiled beef into the open mouth of the small boy who sat at her feet.

'It seems too hot to eat today.'

She was sitting with the two middle-aged daughters of Aunt Marquand. She did not know these cousins well; they were both married and living abroad when she was a child. Each summer they returned to Guernsey with an ever-increasing brood of children.

'Perhaps you are thirsty.' Mrs McCrea signalled to the servant.

Bubbles tickled the roof of her mouth. The lemonade revived her. Francina let their talk drift over her head as she watched a cormorant standing transfixed on a rock, its wings stretched out like a crucifix.

'Have you had news of Angelo?'

'I do not expect to receive a letter until he arrives in Calcutta, Mrs Bonamy.'

'Calcutta is a fine city, I believe,' smiled Mrs Bonamy.

'But lacking in moral standards,' said Mrs McCrea.

Francina stared at her supercilious relative. Aunt Barton had assured her that Mamma's situation was a secret within the family circle; but how wide was the circle?

'The heat must be so debilitating!' said her sister, always ready to make allowances.

'Idleness breeds licentiousness,' sniffed the colonel's lady, brushing a crumb off the shelf of her bosom, 'particularly with such an unhealthy number of servants.'

'Indian ladies must have so little occupation. It would break my heart to send my little ones Home,' sighed Mrs Bonamy, surveying her brood bounding over the rocks.

'And such an unnatural surplus of young men,' said Mrs McCrea. 'No wonder intrigues abound!'

The children had removed their shoes and stockings and were edging cautiously towards the water's edge, their voices growing shriller as their daring increased.

'How is Mr Barton? We have not had the pleasure of making his acquaintance.' There was just a hint of condescension in Mrs McCrea's voice.

'Uncle Barton is recovering well.'

'That is good news, I am sure.' Mrs McCrea whispered an aside to her sister, and judging by their expressions it was something highly distasteful.

'Mr Barton is your aunt's third husband I believe, Francina?'

Francina looked at Mrs Bonamy in surprise. These prying ladies knew more about Mamma's relatives than she did.

The children shrieked as a wave toppled them into the shallows. Their mammas jumped up in unison and waved their arms helplessly, while nursemaids raced to scoop their bawling darlings from the water.

Francina used the moment to escape. She wandered along the

beach, examining the line of flotsam and jetsam, the detritus that the sea had thrown up. One day she might find a message in a bottle from a poor soul marooned on an island. Today she saw only a few broken shells, a crab claw, and some strands of festering seaweed covered in tiny sand flies.

'I am very angry with Mrs Barton!' said Louisa, marching towards her.

'Why, Lulu?'

'She has monopolised Henry Fetherstone all afternoon. I have hardly said two words to him. He seems more interested in talking to her than to me!'

'Understandably, Lulu. He wants to find out about India.'

'He will be living in that hateful country for at least twenty years. He will have enough time to find out about India when he is there. How can he be so insensitive and ignore me? I shall *never* speak to him again!' Louisa marched defiantly back up the beach to return to the party.

'Gentlemen! A game of cricket?' Sammy's question rang out across the sands.

The men cheered. Louisa's shoulders stiffened with rage.

The tide was still going out, and the expanse of sand, though not the size of a cricket pitch, was enough for a light-hearted game. The ladies took up their cushions and rugs to watch from the shade of the rocks. Francina returned and sat beside Aunt Barton, who appeared to have fallen asleep. Her maid was fanning her face to deter the flies.

Saumarez was sorting the men and boys into teams. Uncle Doré had agreed to play, so had a red-faced Colonel McCrea. The younger men removed their jackets.

Gilbert Lihou stood with his hands on his hips. His shirt was blowing in the wind, clinging to his arms. Perspiration had darkened his silk waistcoat.

She took out a small sketch-book and pencil from her bag. She would make a sketch of Henry Fetherstone to please Louisa. Aunt Barton was asleep, and there was no one close by who could see what she was drawing.

Henry Fetherstone's hair danced like a dishevelled halo. He had a mouth that was neither too full nor too mean. His forehead was high and his cheekbones well defined. A Greek sculptor might have admired his profile, but she found it too perfect to be interesting. But for Louisa's sake, she would try her best.

While she sketched, the sea rolled sluggishly over the hot sand. The cricket match was progressing at a slow, steady space; the elderly ladies were all dozing. Even the gulls seemed too lethargic to fly. Every so often there was a flurry as a cricketer raced between the wickets to girlish shrieks of encouragement. Louisa had forgotten her outburst. Francina watched her confer with her cousins in a giggling huddle. They would be talking of finishing schools, fashion and romance. She ought to join them, but whatever subject they might choose held little interest to her now. Mamma! She must erase Mamma from her memory. If she had her likeness now, she would stab her through the heart and gouge out her eyes with a pencil. If only Mamma had *died.*

Helena, one of Mrs Bonamy's daughters, came and sat beside her. She was an amiable thing with huge brown eyes that could express so much more than her poor mouth could, for Helena was deaf; a severe illness had left her without hearing. Yet despite or because of her affliction, Helena was the darling of her family and, thought Francina, seeing her little mouth break into a smile, it was not difficult to understand why.

Helena giggled as she recognized the portrait of Henry Fetherstone. Francina gave her a sheet of paper and a pencil and Helena settled down to scribble. Francina felt curiously comforted to feel this silent child pressed against her arm. Helena understood. For all her smiles, Helena knew that she too was different, set apart.

Finishing her likeness of Henry Fetherstone, Francina turned to a new page. Now she would try to draw Saumarez as a keepsake for Aunt and Uncle.

Henry Fetherstone was caught out. Acknowledging the young ladies' commiserations with a wave, he sauntered up the beach to join them.

Francina closed her sketchbook. The sun had slipped behind a cloud; the shade was a welcome respite. Taking Helena's hot little hand, she pulled her up. Helena smiled at her with trusting eyes. They would stroll along the beach to the far end of the bay.

The rock pools fascinated Helena. They gazed into the clear

waters to discover miniature worlds inhabited by tiny creatures. She tickled a crimson sea anemone with a twig of driftwood and watched flowery tentacles contract as silver bubbles rose to the surface.

They climbed over and round ledges of rock, and found a secluded beach surrounded by huge granite boulders covered in green weed and encrusted with colonies of limpets. They took off their shoes and stockings and placed them on a rock. Francina stretched out her toes. Granules of sand tickled the soles of her feet. She fell to her knees and scooped up handfuls. The sand was made up of tiny shells in all the colours of the rainbow, intermingled with fragments of shell, ground to a coarse powder. Sand trickled between her fingers and glinted in the sunlight.

Hitching up her skirts, she gripped Helena's hand and ran through the foam. Bubbles burst round their ankles. The sea was ice cold. Paddling through the shallows, they rounded another promontory of rock to an even more secluded bay of perpendicular cliffs, broken here and there by great fissures that formed little creeks and narrow passages. Running out of the water, Francina embraced the child in a mad impulsive moment. Raising her off the ground, she whirled her round and around, until cliffs, sea and sky had mingled into one gigantic blur. Round and around, until exhausted, they fell laughing to the ground.

Lying back in the hot sand, she watched clouds race across the skies, while all about the cliffs seemed to be falling inwards, pressing her body to the earth. Her head was still spinning; her soul whirling high above the Island. She shut her eyes and felt the sun on her face. She heard the murmur of the waves, the soft moan of the wind, the whispering sand creatures, the cries of the gulls, and felt at one with the Island.

They sat on a rock to dry their feet. Shading their eyes, they stared out across the bay and watched red-legged cahouettes, silhouetted against the sun, dive into a silver sea.

'Miss Duquesne?'

Francina quickly lowered her skirts and jumped off the rock.

'Mr Fetherstone! I was showing Helena the rock pools. They are so very beautiful in this part of the bay.'

'May I walk a little way with you, Miss Duquesne?'

'Certainly. Shall I point out landmarks or points of interest?'

She gripped Helena's hand for moral support as they edged between the rocks.

'All these rocks and caves have names,' she began in a flurry. 'Do you see that rock? Where the cormorant has just landed? - that is Le Surtait or Cradle Rock.' She repeated some of the old stories she had known since childhood; Island stories Cook had told her on dark winter evenings when Aunt and Uncle were out, stories she had known for so long, they had become part of her.

'These caves are inhabited by sarregousets -'

'*Sarregousets*?'

'Water faeries, Mr Fetherstone. They feast in these caves when the moon is full.'

He said nothing.

'Mr Fetherstone, are you quite well? You seem a little preoccupied.'

'I am distraught! The light of my life - the sole reason for my being on this Island - has forsaken me! Miss Duquesne, you know Miss Doré better than anyone. I was so sure we had an understanding. But today she has scarcely glanced at me. When I speak she looks away. What is the meaning of it?'

He looked so mortified that her heart went out to him. They ambled across the sand in silence. Helena tugged at her hand and stared up at her, mystified.

'Has Miss Doré spoken of me? Is there is any hope for me?'

'Mr Fetherstone if Louisa has spoken, it would have been in the strictest confidence.'

'Of course, forgive me. But I am at a loss to know how to proceed.'

He was not the first young man to have fallen under Louisa's spell. It was her way to tease, then heartlessly to discard suitors when she tired of them. Was Mr Fetherstone to be just another of Louisa's victims? Surely he deserved better.

'I cannot speak for my cousin, of course, but I did notice you were engaged in a long discussion with Aunt Barton. Because of the time you are spending in Mrs Barton's company, Louisa may have come to the conclusion that you are indifferent to the society of - others.'

'Miss Duquesne, nothing could be further from the truth!'

Just then, Helena pulled her hand away and splashed through the shallows. Francina picked up her skirts and waded in after her.

'I have never met a young lady who dazzles me so,' declared Henry Fetherstone, so preoccupied with his thoughts that he failed to notice that Francina had left his side.

Helena laughed when she saw Francina following and stepped into deeper water. Francina called out in panic. Helena raced out of the water and climbed onto a rock to survey her mischief, grinning impishly. Francina stood in the shallows feeling rather foolish.

Someone was watching. He stood on the beach, still as a statue. What must he think of her with her skirts hitched up like a common gypsy! Furious, she dropped her skirts and waded out towards Helena. She pulled the child off the rock and shook her. Helena burst into tears.

'A noble gesture, Miss Duquesne.' Gilbert Lihou appeared at her side. 'But a trifle foolhardy? The girl was in the shallows and not in any danger.'

'What do you know of it, Mr Lihou! How do you know any more than I what was in the child's mind?' Francina dragged the sobbing child along the beach.

Henry Fetherstone stared at them, bemused. A minute ago he was confiding to a sympathetic Miss Duquesne. Now here she was, bedraggled and angry, snapping at Lihou, who had arrived out of the blue. How had it all come about?

'Miss Duquesne!' Gilbert Lihou called, trying to keep up with her.

She quickened her pace to out-march him, but her skirts were heavy with seawater.

Mr Fetherstone followed at a discreet distance.

'I cannot express my disapproval to Helena in words - she is deaf and dumb,' she said, as he caught up with her again.

'Deaf and dumb Helena may be - but even she must be aware of your disapproval. Only a *corpse* would be inanimate enough to be oblivious to your wrath!'

'Why are you here, Mr Lihou?'

'Is this not a public beach? I am here because the tide has turned. Very soon this bay will be cut off.'

'I am well acquainted with the movement of the tides on this Island, Mr Lihou.' She eyed the foaming water fanning over the sands in front of her. The sea had almost reached the rocky promontory. In another few minutes they would indeed be stranded.

'I am only interested in Fetherstone's safety. May I remind you, Miss Duquesne, that he is a stranger on this Island.'

She bit her lip. She had not intended to speak so sharply. She rounded the promontory quickly, dragging Helena with her. The men followed.

'Steady on, Lihou,' Mr Fetherstone said breathlessly. 'You are decidedly out of order. Miss Duquesne was lending a sympathetic ear to my problem.'

At that moment, Louisa's head appeared above a rocky boulder.

'Ina, are you there? Mrs Bonamy is anxious for Helena. Is she with you? Oh, Mr Fetherstone,' she said, feigning surprise. 'I did not expect to find you here.'

Mr Fetherstone hurried towards her.

'Miss Doré, I must speak with you!'

Only a thick-skinned walrus could have come between Henry Fetherstone and Louisa at that moment. While they gazed into each other's eyes, their companions were left, awkward and lost for words. They averted their eyes from one another.

Suddenly Francina espied her shoes and stockings on the rock where she had left them. Grasping Helena firmly by the hand, she hurried over to retrieve them. To her dismay, Mr Lihou followed. To put on her stockings and shoes in his presence seemed almost indecent.

She sat Helena on the rock and brushed the sand off her feet. As discreetly as she could, she rolled up the child's white stockings to met her pantalettes under her underskirts.

He stayed close by. For some reason he picked this moment to explain about the geological structures of the rocks and the natural life found there on. At any other time she might have been interested, but at this moment she wished he would go away. She buckled up Helena's little black boots.

Now decently attired, the child ran off to survey the rock pools.

'Mr Lihou, may I have a moment's privacy to put on my shoes?'

With a courteous bow, he faced the sea while she turned towards the cliffs. As she struggled to retain her modesty, she realised in astonishment that he was reciting poetry.

'We gaze and turn away, and know not where,
  Dazzled and drunk with beauty, till the heart
Reels with its fullness; there - for ever there -
  Chain'd to the chariot of triumphal Art,
We stand as captives, and would not depart.'

She was in no mood for poetry. She was tense and confused, and it seemed to take longer than usual to put on her stockings. However much she brushed the sand from between her toes, there always seemed more to remove.

'They fear'd no eyes nor ears on that lone beach,
    They felt no terrors from the night, they were
All in all to each other: though their speech
    Was broken words, they thought a language there -'

Her stockings had become knotted. Her palms were damp, her limbs sticky with sea salt. The wind had got up and it was difficult to keep her skirts under control while she pulled her stockings above her knees. Then it gradually dawned on her that Mr Lihou had stopped reciting. He was silent. In fact, he had been silent for a long time.

She raised her eyes. He was looking at her.

Shamefully, she lowered her skirts.

Neither spoke. The air was charged, as if a thunder cloud was suspended over their heads, waiting to burst. He was looking at her with an expression she had never seen before. But this time she was not intimidated. This time she felt strangely calm.

Helena grabbed her hand and stared coldly at the man.

15

Chinese lanterns winked through the branches as the Dorés carriage rolled up the drive of Belle Villa. Francina's chest tightened. Mrs Lihou's soirée had turned into a very grand affair.

Louisa smiled. She had longed for this evening. She had practised so hard, and wanted everyone - but Henry Fetherstone especially - to be astonished by her playing.

The cacophony rose as they were ushered into the drawing room; a room, which like the rest of the house, exuded opulence and excess. Deceased Lihous hanging on the blood-red walls gazed down with contempt. They had spotted the interloper immediately.

'Fortitude, my dear,' whispered Uncle Doré. 'Let's run the gauntlet together.'

Francina took his arm. Easing around chairs, sofas, and guests contriving to be merry, they advanced towards their hostess.

Mrs Lihou stood framed in a tall, swagged window. She was dressed in black, her skirts so wide that they filled the width of the window. She surveyed her guests like a two-headed Imperial eagle, while Mary, her half-fledged chick, stood under her wing.

'So touching to see so many dear friends at our little soirée,' Mrs Lihou greeted the Dorés as though they were her dearest friends, then apologised profusely for the makeshift arrangements. Francina was at a loss to see anything makeshift.

The girls edged away as Mrs Lihou held Aunt and Uncle in conversation.

Louisa was delighted with the glitter and pomp, and there seemed little competition. Mary Lihou could be dismissed out of hand of course, and plump Jane Le Marchant was hardly the muse to inspire an artist. Miss Carey was the exception. Miss Carey had beauty, Miss Carey had charm. Fortunately, Miss Carey was dressed in an unbecoming lilac, which did little to enhance the tone of her skin. How thankful Louise was to have insisted on her new rose taffeta.

'Look, Ina, John de Beauvoir. He looks like a wet haddock, don't you think?'

He smiled from across the room but Louisa appeared not to notice. Francina gave him a friendly nod, then looked away before her gesture was misconstrued.

'Miss Duquesne, we meet again.'

It was the young officer she had met at the Assembly Rooms. Francina turned to introduce him to Louisa, but she had caught sight of someone and had slipped away.

'I hope your injuries are not troubling you so much, Mr Howard?'

But she knew the answer, for his hollow eyes betrayed his pain. If only she could think of something appropriate to say, but she knew nothing of his world - the hell that was the Crimea. Uncle had a habit of cutting articles from the newspapers that might offend innocent eyes. Once, she had found a cutting on his desk and had read of wholesale slaughter: of soldiers dying on the battlefield; hundreds more dying from their injuries in hospitals. It was a shock to learn that the English were fallible. Surely a skirmish in the Crimea was nothing compared to pursuing Napoleon's mighty armies across Europe?

'Sir, I know so little about the war. Such events are shielded from me.'

'And so they should be! War is no subject for a young lady – and certainly not tonight. I have been looking forward to this evening, Miss Duquesne, for I understand several talented ladies will be entertaining us. Might I be presumptuous and ask if you are one of them?'

'I cannot put myself in the same category as my cousin Louisa. She, I believe, is one of the talented musicians of whom you speak. - Do you play, sir?'

The words had slipped out before she could stop them. She tried to apologise, but the sentence she had composed in her mind, choked in her throat. No one could fail to notice that his left arm was severed.

It seemed an eternity before he spoke. 'I was fond of the violin. Now I must be content to let others play for me.'

Fortuitously, Mrs Lihou announced that the evening's

entertainment was about to begin. Francina followed the guests to the salon, certain that he would wish to escape from her. But to her surprise, he called after her.

'Miss Duquesne, may I escort you to your seat?'

She took his arm, grateful that he was kind enough to overlook her remarks. She sensed his discomfort. He was an outsider like herself in this glittering, brittle setting.

The salon was ablaze with light. The focus of the room was the pianoforte and around it were arranged two semi-circular rows of small gilt chairs. After some difficulty, Francina found her seat in the second row, near a pillar that would restrict her view. She sat down and nodded to her neighbour. It was the same spinster who had spurned her in the vestibule. The spinster turned to address the gentleman on her right, checking any conversation that might arise between them. Francina stared at her hands folded on her lap. Why had she come? Why had she practised so hard? She was not accepted here. These were Mrs Lihou's friends. They knew about Mamma, she was quite sure.

Louisa was flirting with John de Beauvoir. Henry Fetherstone, seated several seats away, watched in silence. Mary sat quietly beside him, waiting to be noticed.

At last Mrs Lihou interrupted the intrigues simmering about the salon to ask if Miss Carey would consent to open the soirée. Feigning surprise, Miss Carey rose to take her seat at the pianoforte. Running her fingers lightly over the keys, she fixed her eyes on Gilbert Lihou and asked if a kind gentleman would assist with her music.

The guests watched them deliberate over the pages of her music. Then Miss Carey raised her head and announced that she would play a new composition that she had discovered on a recent tour of Germany . . .

Francina caught her breath. It was the same composition that Signor Bandini had assured Louisa had never been heard on the Island. She wanted to put her hands to her ears. She had heard Louisa practise this piece so many times, and even her untutored ear could tell that Miss Carey was ruining the melody. She stared at the floor. She did not have the courage to look at Louisa.

When it was over, the salon burst into applause.

'Encore, Miss Carey!' Admiral de Beauvoir stamped his

silver-topped cane on the floor.

'Indeed,' said Mrs Lihou, 'we would be delighted if Miss Carey play again.' She glanced at her guests as if seeking their consent, then quickly said, 'See Miss Carey, we cannot dispense with your services yet!'

'Mr Lihou, will you accompany me?' smiled Miss Carey.

His voice resonated in her head and sent goose-prickles down her arms. To produce such a polished performance, they must have practised together many times.

To loud applause, Gilbert Lihou escorted Miss Carey back to her seat.

Mrs Lihou, beside herself with delight, took control of her flights of fancy and cast her eyes about the room. 'Miss Duquesne? I understand you wish to play for us?' Her smile was acrid.

Francina's ears burned as she stood up. Her skirts had caught under the chair of her neighbour, and she had to request the lady to raise the chair leg. The spinster made a great show of being inconvenienced. With difficulty, Francina eased around the pillar, through the space between the chairs, and made her way to the pianoforte. Her head was pounding as she rummaged through the portfolio. Where was her music?

Mrs Lihou flexed her talons as disquiet rippled round the room.

Oh joy! She spied her music between the leaves of another composition, and placed it on the music stand. In her haste the sheets slipped to the floor.

Lieutenant Howard sprang from his seat, marched to the piano, gathered up the sheets and returned them to the stand. 'Always ready to be of assistance,' he confided under his breath.

Francina could have wept with gratitude. Her courage returned. She took a deep breath and Signor Bandini's words flooded into her mind: *You have the ability . . . you have the technique.* She lost sight of Mrs Lihou's contemptuous looks, the malicious comments and the humiliating snubs. As her fingers touched the keys she remembered what he had taught her . . .

Mrs Lihou stood up to check the applause. 'A charming tune!'

Uncle Doré caught her eye as she returned to her seat, and smiled.

'And now,' said Mrs Lihou, 'dear Mary has been poorly and has not prepared for our little soirée like some of our guests.'

She glanced icily at Francina.

'Mr Fetherstone, would you kindly turn the music sheets?'

Murmurs of sympathy followed Mary to the pianoforte. Mrs Lihou tried not to wince when her daughter pressed the wrong key. She had hoped that under Signor Bandini's intensive coaching Mary would have made more progress. Luckily the Italian had chosen a simple piece with an agreeable refrain.

The guests clapped politely when it was over. Mary returned thankfully to her seat.

'Miss Le Marchant would you honour us next?'

Louisa had ceased listening since Miss Carey's performance. No one could suspect that the hands folded in her lap were in her head racing over the ivory keys. When it was her turn, what should she play? Bach, Mozart - or something more *à la mode*? She was flying through her repertoire at lightning speed. Should she plump for the piece she played at the concert? Could she still remember it? Her heart was thumping. Faster and faster flew her fingers . . .

'It is now Miss Doré's turn to entertain us.'

Louisa walked slowly to the pianoforte. She felt icy calm. All her anxieties were left behind on her seat. She sat on the piano stool, her mind focused and crystal-clear.

John de Beauvoir stood up. Noticing, Henry Fetherstone threw caution to the wind. Much to everyone's astonishment he appeared to catapult himself from his seat.

'Miss Doré! Allow me to turn the music for you!'

Louisa gave him one of her most endearing smiles.

When the entertainment was over, Mrs Lihou announced that a cold buffet awaited her guests in the dining room. Francina tried to catch Louisa's eye. She wanted to console her, to tell her that she had played and sung beautifully. But in the crush, she was carried along with the crowd to the dining room and lost sight of her. She made her way towards Aunt and Uncle, past a table weighed down with crystal dishes. It was a spread to be admired and talked about across St Pierre. The footman offered her some fruit cup.

Uncle Doré welcomed Francina to his circle.

'How well we have been entertained tonight,' sighed Mrs de Beauvoir. 'Some compositions, I confess, were quite new to me. The piece Miss Carey played was a delight.'

The Dorés smiled politely.

'A fine-looking gal,' added Admiral de Beauvoir.

Mrs de Beauvoir ignored her husband's comment. She picked at her lobster mousse and began a rambling discourse on the musical talents of the young ladies until, inevitably, the conversation began to gravitate towards the conflict in the East.

'I understand from naval dispatches that the bombardment of Sebastopol is being intensified,' said the Admiral. 'It can only be a matter of time before we see a change in our fortunes.'

'The sooner the better. The allies will be hard pressed to survive another winter in the Crimea as severe as last year.'

'At least the troops will be better equipped. I hear some Brigades have been supplied with the new Enfield rifle.'

'And the completion of the electric telegraph across the Black Sea must surely work to our advantage.' Uncle accepted another glass of champagne from the tray proffered by the footman. 'Messages from the Crimea can now be transmitted in six or seven hours.'

'However excellent these advancements, they do not safeguard the lives of our soldiers. More lives are being lost to disease than to Russian prowess. Sickness is an insidious enemy,' said the physician, shaking his head. 'Dysentery and fever are rife, and that confounded Miss Nightingale insists on interfering with the running of the hospitals.'

'I read in the papers that two of her nurses have died of cholera.'

'The battle front is no place for a woman. How many more well-meaning souls will have to die before Miss Nightingale comes to her senses!'

'Francina,' said Aunt Doré in a quiet aside, 'Will you find Louise and ask her to join us.'

'Please do,' exclaimed Mrs de Beauvoir, who had overheard and was weary of War Talk. 'We must congratulate her on her singing.'

Francina made her way out of the dining-room and peeped into the salon. It was vacant, but in the stillness she caught a sound.

Drawing on her shawl, she slipped outside. It was that fleeting moment just before night when the sky is cerulean blue. Only one star was visible. The moon was veiled, but it shone through a film of cloud, just enough to illuminate the path. Muffled sounds were coming from the rose garden.

Holding her skirts in close, Francina picked her way over the paving stones. Full-blown roses, pale and voluptuous, stood out like lanterns to guide her way. The path twisted and turned, then encircled a small pond. In the black water she fancied she saw darting fish. Startled, a frog hopped over a dancing moon.

Then, through a gap in the foliage, she glimpsed voluminous skirts. She was about to call out, but something made her hesitate. Louisa was not alone. She edged closer.

How could Louisa be so foolhardy! She would stand some distance away and act as chaperone. Then, if someone should come it would not seem as if Louisa really was alone in a young man's company.

She retraced her steps to the terrace and leaned over the balustrade. It was cool and damp to the touch. The sky had deepened to indigo. Now, she could see the Great Bear and the Plough and, she fancied, the hunter Orion. Perhaps at this moment Angelo was also staring up at the sky. She pictured herself standing on the deck beside him, leaning over the rail to study the stars. Waves break across the bow and sting their faces . . .

A tiny sound distracted her and she looked around. Mr Lihou was propped against the wall, shaded by a vine. A pin-prick of light told her he was smoking. She had not seen him smoke before.

She shrank away.

'Please stay.'

He advanced slowly towards her, his cheroot pulsating red and orange in the dark. 'I have been watching you. I came out here to smoke, and saw a vision gliding through the garden. I thought it was a ghost.'

She wrapped her shawl round tightly, but could not stop her tremors. He shifted his position so that he leaned over the balustrade next to her. She should edge away, increase the distance between them. But she did not.

Lifting his face to the sky, he drew deeply on the cheroot, exhaling a stream of silver vapour through his nostrils. A heady cloud enveloped her.

'You are alone?'

His question jolted her from a dream. The hobgoblins were playing their magic.

'Louisa and I – we were in the rose garden.' A cloud covered the moon as she peered into the darkness. 'She is still out there. She appears to have been delayed.'

'What on earth could possibly delay her in the garden?'

'I cannot say - but I shall look for her at once.'

She picked up her skirts and ran down the steps.

'You cannot venture into the garden unaccompanied, Miss Duquesne. You do not know the paths. You might fall into the pond.'

'Please do not concern yourself, Mr Lihou. You must return to your guests. Some of them must be wondering what has become of you!' Miss Carey for *one*, she thought icily.

She must warn Louisa before she was discovered. Cloud obscured the moon; it was hard to distinguish the path. She felt her foot sink into soft earth. Then her skirt caught on a brier. She was trying to free herself when he caught up with her.

'I have torn my skirt!' She was close to tears. It was her only ball gown.

He bent down and carefully loosened it from the thorns. 'It is only a small snag. It can be repaired, I am sure. Do not fret Miss Duquesne. Come, take my arm. I shall guide you.'

Just then Louisa and Mr Fetherstone appeared on the path. It was difficult to determine who was the more surprised.

'Aunt sent me out to look for you,' Francina said quickly, ashamed to be discovered in the dark with Mr Lihou. 'You must return indoors at once.'

'I say, Lihou - Miss Louisa is the sweetest of angels! I have -'

'Hush, Henry!' giggled Louisa, snuggling up to him. 'It's a secret. We agreed.'

'Of course, Miss Louisa, but I'm so happy!'

So saying, they departed almost as quickly as they had arrived.

Had Louisa lost her wits? If she appeared in the house draped over Mr Fetherstone, her reputation would be ruined. Francina tried to hurry after her, but Mr Lihou held her arm tight as they walked slowly back to the house.

'Your cousin has cast a spell on him,' he said. 'Fetherstone is impetuous. He is inclined to let his heart rule his head.'

'Well, luckily he has *you* as a friend, Mr Lihou, to keep his feet firmly on the ground.'

'*Here* you are, Gilbert!'

Mrs Lihou was on the terrace peering into the darkness, but her silent accusations sought their target as accurately as a poisoned dart: *shameless, wanton gypsy*.

'Gilbert, will you come inside and settle a point of disagreement? Miss Carey insists that lions reside in India. Can you put our minds at rest?'

Her voice was colder than a winter's frost.

16

The reflection in the small, pitted glass was absurd. She was dressed in a coarse blue bathing-gown buttoned to the throat, an unbecoming oilskin cap, and a huge straw hat frayed at the edges. No one could possibly recognize her. Francina peered cautiously out. The wind was fresh, the sea choppy. A young lady, half-submerged in the water, was hugging the wheel of the next bathing-machine. Francina edged down the rickety steps.

'Take my hand, Mademoiselle,' urged the bathing-woman, a large creature dressed in an unsightly brown shift.

Francina gripped the bathing attendant's hand and entrusted her life to the mercy of God. First her toes, then her limbs, torso and finally her shoulders were submerged in the water. The shift billowed around her. Francina gasped. The sea was ice-cold. She bobbed in the swell, as seawater swirled deliciously over her skin.

Miss Hobson stood on the sands. She had no desire to put even a toe in the sea, and could not understand why submerging one's self in salt water was considered beneficial to health. It was more likely to result in a cold in the head. Two unsavoury men had stopped to ogle (as they often did when young ladies emerged from bathing-machines). Miss Hobson gave them a withering look and blocked their view with her parasol.

The spaniels were racing in circles on the sand. Hearing Sammy's calls, they bounded into the sea and paddled towards him.

Francina's feet danced over the seabed . . . If she floated for long enough, the currents would carry her to Angelo's ship. Suspended in this watery domain, she might become a free spirit; a sea-mew riding the wind; a sarregouset skimming over the waves. She could fly over the bay and circle the costal defence tower. She could soar over the cliffs, land on the turrets of Castle Carey and watch Mr Fetherstone gallop up the Avenue to Elm House. She could perch on the balcony and spy in through the drawing-room window.

Lulu had begged her to leave the house early and to take

Saumarez with her. She was sworn to secrecy. Henry Fetherstone was coming to speak to Papa. 'Oh, Ina, the handsomest man in the world has asked me to marry him!'

Francina opened her eyes and cast them shoreward. Was it over? Had Uncle given his consent?

'You will catch a cold if you stay in the water much longer!'

She climbed into a bathing-machine and was rubbed dry and dressed by an attendant. When she was decent, they walked along the wide expanse of beach to a sheltered spot behind a rocky outcrop for their picnic.

Miss Hobson combed Francina's hair, and left it loose to dry in the wind. Then she opened the basket. Gulls gathered overhead.

'Why did Lulu not come with us today?' asked Saumarez biting into a sandwich. 'She usually adores a picnic on the beach.'

A gull had perched on a stump of wood behind them, waiting to steal an unguarded morsel. The spaniels barked indignantly until it flew away.

'Lulu has her reasons,' said Francina.

'Yes, but what are they? Why is everyone so secretive today?'

Saumarez marched along the beach to look for shells, kicking up sand with each step. Francina settled back to read. Apart from a couple pushing a swaddled child in an invalid carriage, the beach was deserted. Visitors had returned to their boarding houses for déjeuner, leaving behind their intricate sandcastles and forts. Footprints and messages defiled the sands. Her eyes were growing heavy. She felt the volume slip off her lap. She heard Miss Hobson repack the picnic basket . . . the click-click of needles . . . the sea rolling across the sands . . . and all the while the lament of the gulls.

When she awoke, the sea had retreated. Saumarez was a dot on the curve of the bay, throwing sticks for the dogs. The beach was busier now. Visitors had returned and were strolling at the water's edge. The bathing-machines had followed the ebbing tide and another group of ladies was experiencing the delights of sea-bathing. Their cries rang out across the sands like a far-off carillon. In the distance, someone was galloping through the shallows, throwing up spray in all directions. People moved to let him pass.

Miss Hobson glanced up from her knitting. 'Some people these days show no regard for others. They should be forbidden from riding at such speeds in a public place.'

Shading her eyes, Francina followed the rider's progress along the bay. The horse left the shallows and thundered across the sands. It galloped closer, was about to pass, when the rider pulled up and jumped down. He raised his hat and bowed.

'Miss Duquesne, may I beg a private word?'

She had never seen Mr Lihou so decisive. She stood up, conscious of being observed by everyone on the beach.

They walked across the sands, making tentative detours to examine fantastic constructions of sand. He made polite enquiries after her family, and she complimented him for the evening at Belle Villa. Then they lapsed into silence. The horse snorted and tossed his mane. Mr Lihou patted his flank.

'Miss Doré is not with you?' he said at last.

'Louisa is at home.'

'I understand that Fetherstone is to call at Elm House today? I hope everything will be resolved satisfactorily. He is a fine fellow. Upright and honest. I am fortunate to have such a true friend.'

'I am sure Mr Fetherstone speaks just as favourably of you.'

'Miss Duquesne, I have come to say goodbye. Our parting last night was not as I wished.'

She was not aware that they had parted. After seeing them together in the garden, Mrs Lihou had stuck to him like a limpet. Soon afterwards the Dorés had taken their leave.

'I shall be leaving soon - for India, I mean. Fetherstone and I return to Haileybury tomorrow. Shortly before Christmas, we catch the packet for France. It hardly seems possible but we should arrive in India by early February.' He spoke so quietly; he might have been talking to himself.

The wind blew her hair across her face. Catching it, Francina wound it into a coil and held it at the nape of her neck. It seemed so natural to be standing by his side, staring out to sea. But I shall probably never see him again, she thought, screwing her eyes against the glare.

'Loosen your hair, Miss Duquesne. I like to see it blowing free.'

She hesitated, then let it go.

'I wish to fix an image in my mind, an image of a girl with flowing hair running barefoot through the shallows. It will remind me of a very special summer in Guernsey.'

He turned to face her. 'I shall not return for a long time - ten years perhaps. I am ambitious, Miss Duquesne, very ambitious. I intend to rise to the top of my profession.'

'Mary has told me of your many prizes,' she whispered, shaking her windswept hair from her face.

He stared at her, as if she had not grasped his meaning.

'Some in India, Miss Duquesne, will put comfort and pleasure before other considerations. This will not happen to me. I shall not allow distractions to thwart my plans. No distractions - of any sort.'

She picked up a shell, an ormer half-buried in the sand. Shaking granules from its mother-of-pearl interior, she watched it shimmer from green to pink as it caught the sunlight.

'If you have set your mind on such a plan,' she said, running her finger along the silky iridescent surface, 'then I am sure you will - succeed, I mean.'

'Do you think so, Miss Duquesne?'

They walked in silence, following the fringe of foam along the water's edge.

'May I take your hand?'

Her fingers were sticky with sea salt.

'Au revoir, Miss Duquesne.'

'Good-bye, Mr Lihou.'

He mounted his horse and galloped away, almost as quickly as he had appeared.

Tossing the ormer into the sea, she returned to Miss Hobson and flopped on the rug. Screwing up her eyes, she watched a flock of seabirds fly towards the gathering clouds.

Miss Hobson frowned. Wild young gentlemen upsetting young girls. It was disgraceful.

On their return, Francina crept up to her bedroom before anyone could accost her. But as she opened the door, she found Louisa lying on the bed, sobbing into a pillow.

'Lulu, whatever is the matter? Did Henry not speak to Uncle?'

'Papa was taken by surprise. He refuses to give his consent to a young man he hardly knows. He says I am too young, and Henry is in no position to support a wife. Papa will not permit me to become engaged to someone who cannot return to Guernsey for ten years!'

'Lulu, I am sorry, so very sorry.' Tears slide down Francina's cheeks. She had tears enough for both of them.

'And Mamma will not hear of me living in India!'

'Could you live in India, Lulu? You have never shown interest in anything Indian.'

'I would live anywhere with Henry!' declared Louisa. 'Even in a mud hut in the jungle. After he left, I tried to reason with Papa. I worked on him all afternoon. I reminded him that Mamma was eighteen when she had married. But Papa retorted that he was a great deal older than Mr Fetherstone. Whatever argument I put forward, Papa pooh-poohed!'

Louisa twisted the corner of the bed-sheet until it resembled a corkscrew. 'Eventually, Papa relented a little. He will allow us to correspond - but only as friends. And we must agree to have our letters scrutinized by him or Mamma.'

She stuffed the bed sheet into her mouth and bit it savagely.

'You see,' said Francina. 'Uncle is coming round to the idea.'

'I don't think so. I have never known Papa so stubborn. He is not impressed at all with Henry. He thinks him a very - a very irresponsible young man!'

'I am sure it will only be a matter of time before Uncle -'

'But there *is* no time,' wailed Louisa, pummelling the pillow. 'Time has run out. How can I write anything of any importance if Mamma is to read our letters? I would rather not write to Henry at all!'

A feather floated in the air and landed on a tousled ringlet

'Surely you do not mean that, Lulu?'

GUERNSEY
September 1855

'Are you keeping yourself amused, Francina?' Uncle asked one day at déjeuner.

'Aunt has given me a list of tasks to complete before she returns.'

She had been left in charge of the household during Aunt's absence. She wore the chatelaine around her waist and carefully entered the daily transactions in the red accounts book as she had been shown. She was grateful for the tasks, for hard work quelled her loneliness and stopped her from brooding.

'I am sure your Aunt will be delighted with the way you have organised everything.'

Francina adjusted the flowers on the table. She had picked them that morning and arranged them in the vase herself. She was trying to make Elm House as comfortable as possible for Uncle, and had asked Cook to prepare his favourite meals. She enjoyed these times alone with him, after his interminable meetings of the Poor Law Board, and looked forward to sitting with him in the parlour while he scanned the newspapers. Without Aunt's eye upon her, she was free to read anything that took her fancy. Sometimes, she put aside her novel and read aloud some poetry or the small print in the newspaper to him.

Uncle carved himself another slice of mutton. 'I hope you are not so taken up with household duties, Francina, that you have no time for society?'

'Indeed no, Uncle. I have been showing Aunt and Uncle Barton around the Island. We intend to take a picnic to Le Gouffre this afternoon. It's such a lovely day.'

Escorting the Bartons around Guernsey and attending to Uncle's needs occupied the hours, but in bed at night, without Louisa's restless body beside her, she could not stop her thoughts from wandering. Was this a foretaste of her future: filling the daily void with household tasks? She longed for something else, for some excitement, a chance to get away from this stifling, closed society.

She offered Uncle the dish of fruit (she had plucked the pears from the garden that morning) and took a deep breath. 'Uncle?'

'Yes, child.' He selected a fat yellow pear. He enjoyed being fussed over.

'I noticed in the newspaper that a young lady had placed an advertisement requiring a situation in a private family - and it set me thinking. Perhaps I should look for a situation as governess?'

'Whatever for? No niece in my care should ever need to work. I should be failing in my duty as guardian if I agreed to such a thing. The very idea!'

'I have no fortune. I cannot expect you and Aunt to care for me indefinitely.'

'You are only seventeen, Francina. As long as you are in my care you will have a roof over your head.'

'I should like an occupation, Uncle.'

'Your aunt will not hear of it. And besides, look about the house - you have just proved how useful you are to her. That is the end of the matter, Francina.' He returned to his pear looking hurt and offended.

It was pointless to pursue the point. Uncle did not understand her frustration, her yearning to go out into the world and exercise her mind. Why had she learned so many things from the books in his library, if it was all for nothing? She pictured herself instructing a group of children, winning their confidence and affection. Watching them grow and blossom. How fulfilling it would be.

Ellie brought in the mail and newspapers

'I see your aunt has written.' Uncle Doré broke the seal and scanned the letter. 'All seems well: they are comfortably installed at Cambridge Terrace . . . Saumarez takes the train for Winchester today. On Friday they catch the steamer for Brussels.'

'How is Louisa?'

'Your aunt writes: *Louisa is finding London a pleasant distraction.*' He passed Francina the letter and opened the rest of his mail.

As she expected, Aunt's letter was brief and factual. Neither Aunt nor Louisa had thought to send her a message or make any reference to her.

'Curious,' muttered Uncle, examining a manila envelope. 'Another letter from London marked: *PRIVATE & URGENT.*'

He tore it open and read in silence, his forehead, deep furrow above his eyes.

'Nothing has happened to Aunt?'

'This does not concern your aunt. However, there is pressing business I must settle in London without delay. I must catch the morning steamer. Will you manage in my absence?'

'Certainly, Uncle. You must not concern yourself about me. Cook and Ellie are here.'

'Nevertheless, I cannot leave you in the house on your own. I shall send a note to Haute House. I am sure your aunt Duquesne and cousin Julia will agree to have you to stay. I shall not be away for long. I hope to return within the week.'

'I hope you will be comfortable here. The stairs are a trial, but we thought you might appreciate the view.' Cousin Julia raised the sash and leaned out of the window. A salty breeze stirred the net curtains. 'On a clear day you can see across the sea to Normandy.'

She kissed Francina on the cheek and turned to leave. At the door, she paused.

'Do you remember when we were children, Ina, how the boys played endlessly in the garden? Sometimes when it is quiet, I hear their voices laughing outside: William, Anthony, Charlie, Angelo and little Sammy.' She blew her nose delicately on her handkerchief. 'Now the boys have gone. Soon, only you and I shall remain -'

Francina took her hands. 'Nonsense, Julia! Soon, a dashing officer will fall madly in love with you and whisk you off the Island.'

'I think - I shall be here - for some time,' she said quietly.

Francina watched her carefully descend the stairs. She had not realised before, but Julia was as lonely as she was.

It was an odd sensation to be in cousin Anthony's room. She had never ventured in here before. Like the rest of Haute House, it was the model of neatness. The furniture was old, but had been lovingly polished. Engravings of heroic battle scenes covered the walls, and in the attic window space, a toilet glass and a vase of flowers had been placed on the mahogany chest-of-drawers. But despite Julia's touches, there was a distinctly masculine air about the room.

She unpacked her bag, disturbed by this turn of events. Even Aunt Doré was not aware that Uncle was on his way to London. How had he phrased it at the harbour? 'I shall not be meeting the family. This is business, Francina. I have no intention of spoiling your aunt's stay in London.'

A little later, she joined Aunt Duquesne and Julia in the parlour.

Julia looked up as she entered the room. She was sitting on a velvet sofa surrounded by bright cushions (all worked by her during her periodic bouts of illness). 'Have you met Blanche?' she smiled, stroking the long-haired cat with blue eyes on her lap. 'She is the most pampered cat in Town, and she knows it.'

Francina watched her cousin amongst her cushions. Why had no one, not even imperious Aunt Duquesne, managed to find Julia a husband? Was this to be her life? Languishing eternally on the sofa?

'Mamma has just been reading Anthony's letter.' Julia's eyes were wide with excitement. She seemed to gain sustenance from her brother's letters that food could not provide. Since Anthony had sailed for India, a spotty eighteen-year old cadet, and gazetted in the Bengal Artillery, Francina had been told of every adventure and misadventure that had befallen him.

'Read the letter again, Mamma, for Ina's sake.'

Aunt Duquesne required little persuading. She was proud of her son. He had turned out just as she had wished: robust, expansive, and fond of all manner of outdoor pursuits. He was in fact the male equivalent of his mother in personality and temperament. Unfolding his letter, she squeezed on her pince-nez and read in her deep resonant voice:

We rose early - at about two o'clock, so as to travel before sunrise and reach camp before the heat of the day. You would be truly astonished to see what an enormous undertaking it is to march a column of soldiers in India. For a regiment of five hundred men, there are several thousand camp-followers. I, myself, require four bullocks to carry my trunks, tent, traps and other baggage; eight men to carry my palanquin; and at least twenty servants including the horse-keeper, grass-cutter and bullock driver - to say nothing of their respective families. The column takes on the air of a travelling circus snaking off into the distance: an endless column of soldiers, bullocks, horses, camels, elephants and natives. It would not surprise me if the front of the column arrives at its destination before the rear has set off!

Exotic pictures sprang up in Francina's mind; pictures she had glimpsed in Uncle's travel books. How dull her existence seemed in comparison.

Anthony was the main topic of conversation at déjeuner. Francina heard of his latest exploit: hunting jackal with a boobery pack, which she learned was a pack of mongrel or half-bred curs. Sport, it appeared, was the prime occupation of Anthony's soldiering. While Aunt chatted, Julia picked at her food. Francina, too, found she had little appetite. The abundance in front of her only reminded her that she was not at home and not subjected to Aunt Doré's meagre portions. It shamed her to feel rootless and unsettled after the welcome she had received, but something was wrong, and her heart was heavy with foreboding.

Afterwards Julia retired to her room for a rest, and Francina slipped outside. The garden was long and narrow, surrounded by a high boundary wall that stood on the ridge above Town. The small formal garden close to the house was enclosed by a low hedge, each corner marked by an ornamental urn. A magnolia stood in the centre and waxy camellias trailed up the walls. She walked through an arch to a small orchard of apple and peach trees, and along the path to the tangle of vegetation beyond.

Here, they had all played together, chasing each other around the mulberry tree until they had fallen dizzy and laughing to the ground. Here, the boys had killed dragons, fought highwaymen, captured Napoleon or rescued fair maidens from pirates. Even in those days, Anthony's soldering instincts were in evidence. He was Admiral Nelson or the Duke of Wellington commanding his troops. But William Duquesne had been her champion: her eldest cousin, the dare-devil who had walked along the perimeter wall like a tight-rope artist, much to the consternation of his mother; William, who had died planting coffee in Ceylon.

With a pang of sadness, Francina ran her hand along the sun-soaked wall. She came upon a procession of ants, and for a moment saw Anthony's regiment marching across the Indian plain. Close by, a bee had become entangled in a web. She brushed away the gossamer strands and watched it fly free. Its liberation helped to lift her spirits.

At the small wired enclosure five brown hens were scratching in the dirt. Beyond, Aunt was attending to her bees. Aunt Duquesne was the only aunt who still clung to the old Island ways. She had been brought up in an old stalwart house in the Vale, where her grandfather and father had built up a fortune from privateering, taking advantage of the wars at the time to capture French and American shipping and earn the thanks of the Royal Navy. Aunt was educated in France after Waterloo, spoke French in the style of the *ancien régime,* and was still stubbornly speaking that language long after it fell out of fashion in Guernsey.

A row of straw skeps stood in niches in the perimeter wall. Aunt was smoking the bees out of one skep and forcing them into another. Bees were her passion. Every spare moment of her day was spent tending them. A buzzing black cloud followed her. 'Keep back, Francina,' she called from under her vast netted hat. 'The bees are angry today!'

Francina returned inside, and climbed the stairs to the drawing room. It was a high, square room with a moulded ceiling, suffocatingly comfortable. Brocade drapes, sofas, rugs and cushions muffled the sound. The walls were pasted with an acanthus-leaf paper and hung with rust-spotted engravings, while proudly displayed on a small table was the heavy silver-clasped Huguenot Bible, spirited out of France and handed down through the generations. Papa's elder brother, learned, autocratic Uncle Duquesne, dressed in his black clerical robes, stared down at her from the family portrait. Beside him stood Aunt Duquesne (looking much as she did today: sensible, stout and cheerful), and in front of them sat little Julia between her brothers William and Anthony.

Stepping through the tall windows, Francina leaned over the ironwork balcony. She gazed for a while across the rooftops to the blue islands of the Norman archipelago and watched fishing smacks plying between the islands, which at this distance appeared as white and brown specks ruffling the green waters.

Returning inside, she flopped on a sofa. Haute House was so quiet. Everyone, including the servants, tip-toed about, fearful of waking Miss Julia from her nap. For as long as Francina could remember, Julia had been sickly. While they had frolicked in the garden as children, Julia had spent much of her time languishing indoors. Francina could not help feeling, as she stared at the large family portrait, that choking kindness might have nurtured Julia's helpless dependency.

'How sad that Miss Julia does not accompany us this afternoon,' Aunt Barton said kindly. 'Her society might have cheered you up, Francina.'

The carriage halted as it met an ox-cart laden high with furze on the crest of a hill. The farmer driving the cart gesticulated angrily, exasperated by the stream of visitors constantly blocking the lanes. The coachman manoeuvred the carriage to the side and waited for the cart to squeeze past. It was a fortuitous place to stop, for they had a commanding view of the northern stretch of the Island as it undulated down to the windswept, low-lying rocky bays. Between hillocks and wind-blown copses, they glimpsed cottages nestling among the corn and pasture fields; and here and there, an ancient weathered church tower, built as much as a look-out post as to summon Islanders to prayer. Along the coastline, indomitable defence towers, batteries and forts stood as stark reminders of the Island's vulnerable past. And through a shimmering haze, she could just make out the island of Alderney rising like a pale grey whale on the horizon.

'Charming, quite charming.'

But humbling, thought Francina. For this view-point more than any other on Guernsey emphasised the smallness and isolation of her world.

The lane cleared, and the carriage rolled down the hill. For a while overhanging turkey oaks shaded the lane; leaves crackling with heat were dropping early to conserve moisture. Then once more the lane was baked in light, snaking between walls smothered in briars and ferns. Wherever they looked tiny seeds, caught in the sunlight, swirled in eddies.

''It is not like Uncle Doré to leave Guernsey in such a hurry,' Francina said eventually. The Bartons deserved an explanation for her mood. 'Something is awry, I am sure of it.'

'It is probably a simple matter that is easily settled in person than by an endless to-ing and fro-ing of letters. In business this happens all the time,' said Uncle Barton. 'I am sure you are worrying needlessly, Francina.'

They drove through a busy hamlet surrounded by creaking windmills, where cottage gardens filled with flowers were renowned as being the most beautiful on the island. Nearby, water-meadows teemed with wagtails and emerald dragonflies. Aunt Barton praised all she saw, and her enthusiasm made Francina feel more despondent than ever. She should tell the Bartons that the bay they could see glinting in the distance was once an ancient forest, haunted by the *cochon du Vazon* who foraged across its peaty bog for beech and hazel nuts - but it was hot, too hot.

The carriage skirted Rocquaine Bay, where the western sun had set the scene in silhouette. The sand glistened between the black rocky outcrops as the Atlantic waves rolled shoreward in gleaming silver sweeps. Girls in white scoops and boys in faded smocks were splashing in the shallows, whilst their elders scrabbled amongst the rocks foraging for shellfish.

Shielding his eyes, Uncle Barton gazed into the distance at Fort Grey. 'So many fortifications and towers on the Island. No wonder Napoleon was deterred from invading.'

They alighted and walked across the sands. The mollusc gatherers stopped to watch the strange little procession: a stout lady in lilac on the arm of a gentleman in a loud country suit; closely followed by a dark girl swathed in white muslin, who was holding up a parasol to shield her mistress's face. Trailing, was a young girl with downcast eyes; and in pursuit, a cloud of flies lured by the scent of eau de Cologne.

'Mr Fetherstone and Mr Lihou, they have left Guernsey?' Aunt asked when Uncle Barton stopped to examine a starfish. The purple streamers of her bonnet blew wildly in the wind.

'They have returned to Haileybury. They sail for India just before Christmas.'

'Such agreeable young gentlemen. They should do well in India.'

'Unfortunately there is a new breed of Englishman coming out to India,' remarked Uncle Barton, dropping the sea creature into a rock pool, where it settled in a whirl of bubbles amongst the sponges and rose algae. 'They expect to get rich in a short space of time, but have no intention of learning the language or of understanding native customs.'

'If I lived in India, I should try and learn the language,' mused Francina.

'*Ma petite,* if you lived in India your mind would be on dances and fancy dress balls! Oh, what a time she would have, would she not, Mr Barton?'

Francina gazed out of the attic window of Haute House. Grey clouds were amassing. Surely it must rain soon? Her eyes followed the maze of narrow cobbled streets, winding down the cliff face to the harbour. She knew the names of every one of the streets - even the unrespectable ones down which she rarely ventured. As dusk fell, lamps were lit along the principal streets. Always in the background was the sea, rolling and lapping; infusing the Islanders with her changing, unpredictable moods.

Over the darkening roofline pinpricks of light appeared, and in hazy interiors she glimpsed families gathering to eat.

Then the night noises began . . . cats wailing, sailors singing to a hurdy-gurdy, the raucous laughter of the loose women down at the harbour. The sounds echoed through the airless streets and floated up the cliff face to her window, making her feel nearer to the bustle than she really was.

Her Island. She had explored every inch of it; every hummock, crevice and moss-covered crag. She loved this place - so why was she so desperate to leave? She was like a small boat tethered to its moorings, tossing and straining to be released.

Opening her door, she peered over the banisters. A light was shining under Julia's door. Feeling her way along the landing, she crept down the stairs and knocked softly.

Julia was propped in her curtained bed, surrounded by bolsters and lace-trimmed pillowcases. Her brown hair, loose under her ruched nightcap, fanned across her shoulders. In her soft white enclosure Julia looked like a fragile ornament wrapped in tissue paper.

'Do you mind me intruding, Julia?'

'I was not asleep, Ina. I don't sleep very well.'

The small round table by her bed was crammed with pill bottles. The tumbler in her hand contained the dregs of something dark and grainy.

Francina took the tumbler, placed it amongst the decanters and pill bottles, and perched tentatively on her bed. 'Are the nights very long?' she asked.

'I try not to count the hours. I read, or daydream.'

'Do you dream of a lover, Julia? Have you ever been in love?'

Julia coloured slightly. 'There was someone a few years ago. He was an artist, a very talented artist. I did so admire his work.'

'What became of him?'

'Mamma thought him unsuitable.'

'Did you think him unsuitable, Julia?'

But she did not answer. She was far away, fingering the satin ribbons at her throat. In the silence, Francina rose to inspect a daguerreotype on the dressing table, but it was only a likeness of Anthony in his uniform.

Soon afterwards, she kissed her cousin and returned to the attic bedroom. She was never going to have an intimate conversation with her cousin. Julia was not used to baring her soul to a confidante. She lay still, listening the murmuring sea, and wishing that Louisa was with her, chattering and giggling long into the night.

2

High Street was blocked by a funeral procession. The long black line of mourners, wrapped in cloaks and wearing tall hats with streaming white crepe bands, advanced slowly up the street. The coffin borne on the shoulders of the bearers was draped in white, poignantly small. Clergy, principal mourners and bearers trudged past, followed by a straggling line of townspeople. Women in doorways dried their eyes on their aprons; men removed their hats in respect. The death of a child touched everyone.

'It's Mess Guiton's little daughter - the baker in Bordage Street. The second he has buried in two years,' an old woman explained. She placed her basket of eggs on the pavement and began to point out key members in the procession. 'Alors, penny-pinching as he is to the living, he makes up in death. *Ma foi*, Mesdemoiselles, you see no expense has been spared for the funeral. No doubt she will have a handsome memorial.'

Eventually it was clear to cross. Francina took Julia's arm and they turned into Commercial Arcade. The cheerful shop fronts with their bright signs and enticing window displays were a much needed restorative. They made their way to the chemist's shop, which was sited between the horologist's and the jeweller's. Through the new plate glass window, beyond the display of glass jars and scent bottles, they saw the chemist, Monsieur Le Feuvre, standing on a ladder inspecting a volume on a high shelf.

The bell above the door jangled loudly as they entered. Monsieur Le Feuvre returned the volume and climbed down. He was a small, earnest man, immaculately turned out in a black frock coat, high stock and spotless apron. Never idle, he was either searching in learned books or making up medicinal compounds. He rubbed his chin thoughtfully as Julia consulted him. She complained of breathlessness and palpitations of the heart.

Francina sensed a long wait, but she did not mind. The chemist's assistant, a pock-marked lad, was grinding powders behind the counter. He coloured when she approached, so to spare his blushes she inspected the row of cobalt jars on a shelf above his head. The labels were inscribed in a clear copperplate hand: *Arsenic, Fly-powder, Mercury, Opium, White Lead, Laudanum, Belladonna, Henbane, Hemlock.* How did such a noble shade of blue become associated with death?

She caught sight of the row of large glass jars shelved near the door to the laboratory. She had seen them before, but she was always moved to morbid fascination: for the jars contained foetuses, unborn children pickled in viscous alcohol, graded by size and carefully annotated with dates. The sight of those budding hands and feet, those tiny limbs criss-crossed with pale blue veins, the shadows behind closed lids, touched her deeply. But why were these unborn children displayed so heartlessly in here? Why had they not been lovingly buried? Had they no families? Had their mothers died – or were they, perhaps, fallen women? It seemed so unjust that some innocent beings were abandoned for eternity in a glass jar, while others were laid to rest with so much pomp and ceremony.

Close by were other curiosities: an unborn dog, an unborn rat, an unborn chick. In the early stages of Creation, it was impossible to tell the difference between a child and a rat.

The bell jangled, and Miss Chesterton entered the shop. Francina had not seen her English mistress since leaving the Academy, and had forgotten how much she missed her straight-forward advice. Laughing, they both spoke at once. When there was a pause, Francina broke away and took Julia's arm.

'You must meet dear Miss Chesterton. She has been an inspiration to me.'

While the three ladies chatted, Monsieur Le Feuvre ground powders to reduce palpitations.

He dropped the pills in two small blue paper packets and coughed politely. 'Miss Duquesne, I have made up your myrrh and aloe pills. 10 grains made into two pills to be taken at night, and a compound iron pill twice a day. The instructions are marked on the packets. May I also suggest you have a nourishing diet, and take frequent gentle exercise and cold baths.'

'Cold baths, Monsieur?' Julia gazed at him with guileless eyes.

'Indeed, Mademoiselle. They will lower the temperature. The

heart rate will drop if the blood is cooler.'

'And how often should I take cold baths, Monsieur?'

'At least once a day, twice if possible. Have you considered sea-bathing?'

Miserably, Julia shook her head.

'I grant that the season for sea-bathing is almost at an end, but while the weather remains hot - the hottest part of the day is most beneficial - I recommend a short sea-bathe.'

Julia managed a smile and thanked him.

Having completed their shopping, Francina and Julia took leave of Miss Chesterton, after arranging to meet her on the Esplanade in the morning.

That afternoon, while Julia rested beside her mother on the sofa, tired by her excursion to Town, Francina mulled over the questions she would put to Miss Chesterton on the Esplanade. If anyone had the power to shake Julia out of ennui, it was Miss Chesterton. She knew well enough what her English mistress thought of the submissive helplessness nurtured at the Academy, and considered attractive in young women.

A loud knock on the front door startled them. A few moments later Aunt Sabonière flew into the room, brushing aside the maid who had come to announce her.

'My dear, your face is as white as the cat's. Whatever is the matter? Sit down. May we offer you something to calm your nerves?' Aunt Duquesne nodded sharply to the maid.

Aunt Sabonière shook her head and stood grim-faced before the fireplace. When the maid had departed and closed the door behind her, she pulled out a news cutting from her reticule. 'Lottie, have you read today's *Guernsey Star*?'

'No, Sophia, not yet.'

'Oh sorry, sorry day!' Aunt Sabonière fell into a tapestry chair. She took out a lace handkerchief and dabbed her forehead.

'Is it the war, Aunt?' cried Julia in alarm. 'Have we suffered a set-back in the Crimea?'

'It's Frank,' said Aunt Sabonière.

Francina's heart leapt into her throat. Was Aunt talking of Papa?

She jumped from her chair. The ball of wool rolled off her lap and unravelled across the carpet. 'Has something happened to Papa?'

Aunt Sabonière passed her the news-cutting. 'You poor, poor child.'

Julia hurried to Francina's side. Together they read:

Mr F.W. DUQUESNE ARRESTED

Mr Francis William Duquesne was arrested on Tuesday at his lodgings in Westminster for Debt at the instigation of Mr H. Pimlott, Attorney, of Messrs Tompkins & Pimlott, Piccadilly. The contested amount is eighty guineas but other claims are outstanding. We understand that Mr Duquesne is to be detained while these matters are investigated.

Mr Duquesne, a native of this Island and a son of the late Dean of Guernsey, was for some time an indigo manufacturer in Bengal, until ill-health forced him to quit India. Mr Duquesne then commenced exporting wines and spirits to the Indies, but with only limited success. After the unfortunate loss at sea of a large cargo bound for Madras some years ago, he began to run into difficulties which time has proved insurmountable.

3

'Ina, we arranged to meet Miss Chesterton on the Esplanade this morning.'

'Go without me, Julia. I am not fit for anything today.'

Francina lay on the chaise-longue and shut her eyes. By now all the matrons of St Pierre would know of Papa's incarceration in a Debtor's Prison. She could picture the buzzing drawing-rooms as matrons huddled to discuss this latest wave of scandal.

'I shall send a note with our excuses and stay at home with you.'

'Please don't, Julia. Miss Chesterton will think it impolite if neither of us turns up.' Francina touched her forehead. 'My head does hurt so.'

Julia placed a wet flannel over Francina's eyes. 'Miss Chesterton is your friend, Ina. She has no wish to see me.'

The cool flannel was soothing. In a week or so Guernsey society might have a fresh topic of discussion, a new victim to ridicule, but now Papa's name would be on all their tongues. She was not brave enough to withstand the sneers and whispers today.

'Send her my apologies,' Francina whispered.

Julia put on her bonnet to meet Miss Chesterton alone.

Francina pictured Papa hunched in a cold, bare room. How long would he remain there? Months? Years? She longed to be with him, to comfort him. Angelo, as usual, was no help. He was on the high seas, blissfully ignorant of poor Papa's plight. Sick with anxiety, she could neither eat nor sleep. She could not even put pen to paper.

Each day the Bartons called, hoping to find her improved. In her delirium it was Mamma and not Aunt Barton who grasped her to her bosom; Mamma that rocked her in her arms and addressed her as *petit chou-chou*. She would not wake up. She would stay with Mamma forever. But Mamma disappeared again.

She heard the sea-mews circle and dive on currents of air. Above the moaning wind she heard their cries. She understood their language. They were the lost souls tapping their beaks on the panes, urging her to join them. Sometime she left her bed and soared above the clouds with them.

'Ina, there is someone to see you.' Julia touched her shoulder.

'I'm too tired.'

'I have brought Miss Chesterton.'

Francina opened her eyes and focused on the figure before her.

'Miss Francina, I am exceedingly disappointed. I did not expect this defeatism of you! This misfortune is not of your doing. It is not your place to be a *martyr*.'

Julia gasped.

'You admire Miss Nightingale, do you not?'

'Whom?'

'Miss Nightingale,' repeated the mistress firmly. 'Where would Miss Nightingale be if she had taken to her bed and capitulated under the hardships placed in her way? Certainly not in the Crimea nursing our soldiers. She would have turned out like every other woman: defeated and anonymous!'

Francina buried her face in the pillow, willing it to suffocate her.

'You have a choice: you either wallow in misfortune or you rally yourself. You are no help to your father at present. You are no use to anyone!'

Pulling up her gloves, Miss Chesterton made for the door. 'I take my leave, but remember Miss Duquesne, your future lies in your own hands.' So saying, she left the house.

Julia quickly added twenty drops of sal-volatile to a glass of water to revive her. 'Hard-hearted woman! You must have nothing more to do with her, Ina.'

Francina was not conscious of the carriage journey; yet in her delirium she knew that Uncle had returned and brought her home. She stretched like a languid cat under her own cool tight sheets, sank back against the familiar pillows and fell asleep.

Propped up in her own bed, sipping Cook's concoctions every

hour, she slowly recovered. Uncle assured her that Papa was as comfortable as could be expected. Everything was being done to secure his release as soon as possible. And he was by no means the only incarcerated gentleman: a society painter and a celebrated aristocrat were fellow inmates.

In waking moments, her eyes focused on the patchwork coverlet that she and Lulu had made one winter. She ran her fingers over the patterned hexagons. So many memories were stitched in this coverlet . . . Here was the dress she wore to the Great Exhibition - the summer Papa was at his happiest. And here, the sprigged dress she wore the day the Queen had visited Guernsey. How gay St Pierre had looked that day! The buildings were festooned in bunting. The scent was intoxicating when the Queen's carriage drove through the flower-strewn streets. They had peered through the windows of Grand-mère's tall house in the Grange Road, so close to the Royal carriage that she could have tossed a posy of flowers onto the Queen's lap if she had dared. The Queen was dumpy, not nearly as pretty as her engravings; but Prince Albert was the handsomest man she had ever seen. Charlie nearly lost an eye that day by leaning too far out of the window. A soldier standing below the window sloped arms as the Royal party passed, and grazed Charlie's cheek with his bayonet. He still carried the scar, although it was omitted from his portrait.

There was a knock on the door, and Uncle appeared.

'How are you feeling, my dear?'

'Better, Uncle'.

He handed her a letter. It was from Papa. She recognised his hand, although it was more irregular and shakier that usual. Dear Papa, his torment was plain to see. She broke the seal.

Southwark Prison

My beloved daughter,

By now you will know of my present position. Please do not be anxious on my account. Mrs Hills, my landlady is making my stay here tolerable. Every day she brings a meat pudding and her boy brings a few coals, so I eat a hot dinner. I count myself fortunate. I have my own room on the third floor. It is small and the climb up difficult, but at least it is private. The sun penetrates my window for several hours a day, and although the room is hot in the summer, it will (I hope) add to its warmth in winter. Apart from Mrs Hills and her boy I have few visitors.

Your Uncle has engaged (at his own expense) one of the best legal minds to work on my petition. Naturally, I shall repay him at the earliest opportunity. But how blessed I am to have such a Brother-in-Law! - and you to have such an Aunt and Uncle! Francina, never for one day overlook their kindness. For without their support, dear Daughter, your prospects would be nil.

I seek release under the Insolvent Debtors' Act, but until my case is put before the Court, I must remain here. When my affairs came to light, my Chief Clerk (whom I trusted absolutely) absconded. It appears on close examination of the Accounts, that for years he was drawing off the profits, which has greatly aggravated my position. There is a warrant for his arrest but I have little hope he will be caught. I should have heeded Angelo's advice. He warned me that I was placing too much trust in the hands of my clerks. But in my poor state of health there was little else I could have done at the time. I am resigned to my fate. I must be patient and let the legal process take its course. My only regret is that my imprisonment causes so much distress to my family, and especially to you, dear Francina. My poor judgement has ruined your chances. That is a lament I shall carry to my grave. But we both know a greater force is at work here. I have been cursed ever since my eyes arrested on The One who shall be Nameless. And now you, my innocent girl, are tainted by her mark.

In the court I overlook, there is not a speck of vegetation. So without consulting a calendar, I have little idea of the month or season. The noise in here is sometimes unbearable. A family lives below me with young children who find it necessary to exercise their lungs day and night without respite.

It is a blessing that you are far from this sorry place. On no account must you attempt to visit me! I have stressed this point forcibly to your Uncle. It is no place for a respectable young girl. Write often, Francina. Do not wait for my reply. I have little news to impart. Your letters are a great solace to me - indeed my only solace.

I remain, your affectionate father, Frank Duquesne

4

'You are well enough to be outside, Missie?' asked Ellie, as they stood under the apple tree. The old gardener was shaking the branches as vigorously as his advanced years would allow. The damp air was filled with the tang of ripening fruit.

'Certainly, Ellie.'

Francina had no wish to discuss her illness. She felt a little unsteady on her feet, but she could not endure to be indoors for another minute. Papa's letter was tucked into her pocket. Did Ellie know? Had she told her mother? When she walked down Glatney, would the fisherwomen propped in their doorways toss their heads and refuse to acknowledge the daughter of a Kept Woman and an Imprisoned Defaulter?

Red and green apples thumped to the ground. Ducking and weaving, they caught some in their aprons and dropped them into baskets. Barking joyfully, the spaniels joined in, burying apples in the flowerbeds.

Cook hobbled outside. The damp air was stiffening her joints.

'Monsieur asks for Missie,' she said, wiping her hands on her apron. She hobbled back to the kitchens muttering under her breath. So many interruptions since Monsieur came home. She would be pleased when Madame returned and she was left in peace to carry out her baking.

Francina removed her apron and hurried inside.

Uncle Doré was standing, silhouetted against the lace curtains of the French windows. The Bartons were also here, sitting upright on a sofa. By their solemn expressions she knew at once that this was no trifling social visit.

'Colour has returned to your cheeks, *ma chérie*,' said Aunt Barton. 'What a fright she gave us, Mr Doré! One visit she was chatting happily to us, and the next? We discover a lifeless creature on the sofa, as pale as wax. We were all very concerned!'

Uncle directed her to a chair and looked gravely down at her.

'Mr and Mrs Barton have a plan to put to you, Francina. Listen carefully, and take your time before replying. You are not expected to make up your mind immediately.'

He leaned against the chimneypiece to contemplate the empty grate.

'We understand how recent events have troubled you, Francina,' began Aunt Barton, 'and while your Papa remains detained, it will continue to be upsetting for you. So in view of all your difficulties, *ma petite*, we would like to invite you to stay with us in India.'

Francina caught her breath. Such suggestions were only put to her in dreams.

'It would be such a pleasure to have you under our roof, would it not, Mr Barton?'

'Indeed - but before we take this idea any further, my dear,' said Uncle Barton, patting his wife's hand, 'we must write to Mr Duquesne and ask his permission.'

'And we must consult my wife,' Uncle Doré added into the grate. 'In her father's absence, Mrs Doré is Francina's guardian.'

'We would not dream of advancing one step without the approval of dear Mrs Doré, *naturellement!*'

So many ifs and buts. Would Papa consent? Would Aunt? Her mind spun at the implications. In a dream she would accept without hesitation. But in her dreams Papa was not incarcerated in a Debtor's Prison. 'But it is so sudden, Aunt Barton. And you are leaving the day after tomorrow.'

'Regrettably it is too late for you to travel with us - but my sister Cecilia and her husband have just arrived in London on furlough. I know Madame Vauloué would be delighted to escort you out to India next year. I could write at once and ask her.'

Could she leave Papa to fester in a prison, alone? It seemed so cruel to abandon him.

'My dear,' said Uncle Barton to his wife, 'We must now take our leave and give Francina time to reflect on what we have said.'

'Of course! I get so carried away at times, but dear Mr Barton always puts me right.' Aunt Barton stood up. 'In view of the little time at our disposal we must act quickly. With your permission Mr Doré we will write at once to Mr Duquesne outlining our proposal. I shall also write to my sister.'

She kissed Francina affectionately on the cheeks. 'My sister Cecilia was very fond of you. When your Mamma left, you stayed with your Aunt Vauloué for a while – do you remember?'

Uncle Barton steered her towards the door while she continued: 'We understand that nothing will proceed until we have the full agreement of Mr Duquesne and Mrs Doré - but it is just as well to start putting matters in hand, *n'est-ce pas*?'

'We will return tomorrow for your answer, Francina,' Uncle Barton said quietly, as they left.

Uncle Doré opened the tall windows and stepped onto the balcony. Francina followed, running her hand along the balcony rail. Rusty flakes stuck to her palm and she brushed them off. She stood beside him and watched the smoke billowing from the brewery chimney. Uncle lit his pipe and sucked heavily until blue wisps rose into the air.

She wished he would put his arm across her shoulders. Instead they stood motionless, staring out to sea. A trading ketch was entering the harbour.

'Do you think I should go, Uncle?'

'I believe it would be best. But if you do go, it will be for a very long time. Such a journey cannot be undertaken lightly. Once there, should you find the climate or way of life disagreeable, there can be no turning back.'

He took his pipe from his mouth and stroked its bulbous casing. 'You must accept whatever situation comes your way - until, until -'

His words tumbled over the roof-tops, scattered on the wind.

Death or marriage comes to me. She understood. She had a stark choice: she could remain in Guernsey as Aunt Doré's unpaid companion, or find a husband in India. She saw herself a broken-spirited, middle-aged spinster: a Miss Mattie attending to Aunt's needs. Anything was better than that. She must go to a place far from prying eyes and vicious tongues where no one knows her.

5

Great Western Hotel, London

My dear Francina!

How fortuitous that my sister Maria Barton was in time to catch us before we depart London for Europe! I write in haste for we catch the steamer for France this very evening. Should your plans become more certain in the next month, write to me via: Mme Ledoux, 52 Rue Saint-Lazare, Paris. In time I shall write at greater length, but this brief note is just to inform you that we would be delighted to escort my dear sister Theresa's daughter out to India next year. We return to London in February to book our passage -

Your affectionate Aunt, Cecilia Vauloué

Southwark Prison, London

My Dearest Daughter,

My beloved Francina wishes to go to India? A country that has devoured my three sons - is it also to take my daughter? How can I dispute your arguments? If it is truly what you wish (and if my Sister can spare you) I must not be selfish. My shortcomings and a deceived heart have led to this predicament, a pitiful predicament in which your Father must rely on the goodwill of others to provide for his own flesh and blood. Therefore with a heavy heart I give my consent. A small amount remains in Trust for you. If the Trustees are in agreement, then use it to secure your passage. At least in this you will not be under obligation. My old complaint has returned. Yesterday I remained in bed for most of the day rising only to attend Chapel. Now I must return to bed and rest awhile. I will therefore conclude this letter. My Dear Daughter, whose welfare is the thing closest to my heart, may God guide you to do what is right. Do not forget your poor Papa. Write to me often - wherever you are.

In sadness I remain, your affectionate Father, Frank Duquesne

A few days later, Francina walked down to the harbour with Uncle Doré to meet the paddle steamer that was bringing Aunt, Miss Hobson and Baptiste home. It was a perfect day: a bright sun to temper the autumnal chill. And on this particular morning St Pierre resonated with the sound of happy people milling in the streets.

'Sebastopol!' was the word on everyone's lips. Shop windows were draped in red, white and blue bunting. One patriotic shopkeeper had added the Union Jack and French Tricolour to his display. Mess Dupuy was up a ladder, daubing GOD SAVE THE QUEEN - VIVE L'EMPEREUR on the glass of the grocer's window. Uncle Doré stopped to speak to him.

'Have you not heard, Monsieur?' smiled the old grocer. 'Sébastopol has fallen! *Che'est la volonté de Dieu.*'

'Does that mean that the war will end soon, Uncle?' she asked, taking his arm.

Uncle Doré smiled down at her. 'You may be cautiously optimistic, my dear. Our victory at Sebastopol probably marks the beginning of the end of the war.'

Celebration quivered in the air. She heard the triumphant blasts of the steamer's funnel announcing her arrival and her hopes soared. What an ideal day to tell Aunt of the Bartons' proposal.

This optimism also touched Aunt Doré, who arrived home in excellent humour. Her visit to London had been a success. Saumarez was installed at Winchester and Louisa in Brussels. The change of air had certainly improved Aunt's spirits, Francina thought, as she sat through déjeuner with clammy hands and a racing heart. She had waited so long to know her fate that these last few moments of uncertainty were almost unbearable. She glanced periodically at Uncle for the signal to tell her that he was about to usher Aunt into the parlour to break the news. Their eyes met as they rose to leave the table, and he gave a conspiratorial wink.

'Come and see the dogs' new kennel that the gardener made while you were away, Miss Hobson.' She could not bear to be alone at this moment.

Donning woollen shawls, they strolled down the garden to inspect the new kennels, picking their way through drifts of slippery leaves while the dogs zigzagged around them. A bonfire was smouldering in the grounds next door. Smoke meandered through the trees and hung in the branches, disturbing a flock of crows, who left their choking roosts and settled on the roof where they kept up a noisy protest.

'Let's sit here for a while, Miss Hobson,' said Francina, brushing leaves off the bench. 'Tell me about London.'

'It was too busy for my liking, Miss Francina. But we saw some wonderful things. We visited the Crystal Palace and Madame Tussaud's Waxworks Show. Napoleon was lying on a bed. Miss Louisa prodded him with her umbrella when the attendant was not looking, to prove that he was made of wax, for he looked so real that I cried out in fright.'

They talked of London, but all the time Francina's mind was focused on the scene in the parlour. Was Uncle telling Aunt at this moment? The more she mulled over the idea, the more desperate she was to go.

'Miss Francina, may I tell you a secret?'

'Of course, Miss Hobson.'

Miss Hobson blushed and stared at her hands. 'I am soon to be married.'

Francina looked at her in surprise. 'But to whom?'

'Monsieur Le Boutillier.'

The widower with two small boys? Surely Miss Hobson could do better than that? Francina tried to smile and mutter something appropriate, but her heart was heavy. Aunt would never agree to losing two members of her household at once.

'Does Aunt Doré know?'

'I thought it best not to concern the Mistress until we returned. She had enough on her mind - what with settling Miss Louisa into that school in Brussels. I must give the Mistress a month's notice. Then I shall leave and marry immediately. The shop is busy during the autumn, what with so many ladies requiring new outfits for the Christmas season. Now that his sister is poorly, Monsieur Le Boutillier is badly stretched.'

Baptiste interrupted them to say that La Missie was wanted in the parlour.

Francina rose from the bench and walked into the house, light-headed and timorous. As she knocked on the parlour door, the murmuring voices within fell ominously silent.

Aunt was sitting upright in her chair, studying a letter. 'Sit over there, where I can see you, Francina.'

She sat still, waiting for Aunt to finish reading.

At last Aunt looked up. 'So much has happened in my absence that I am quite overwhelmed. Your Uncle tells me that you have been ill. Are you better? Now that I have a chance to study you closely, I can see how pale you are. It is hardly surprising. The news of your Papa is heart-breaking, quite heart-breaking.'

'It was a great shock, Aunt.'

'Indeed. And scarcely have I time to absorb that distressing piece of intelligence when I am informed in the very next breath that the Bartons have invited you to Calcutta!' Aunt Doré studied the letter again. 'Your father has given his consent, I see.'

'Yes, Aunt.'

'But somewhat reluctantly, I surmise? If I know my brother's character - and I believe I do - then I deduce that he would rather you remained here. Do you not agree?'

Francina could not reply. It required all her energy to appear impassive.

'What am I to do? Comply with your whims - the whims of a young inexperienced girl, who knows nothing of India - or those of your father, my poor unfortunate brother, whose memories of India continue to torment him? And yet, against his better judgement, your father is prepared to make another sacrifice. Not only has he lost Angelo to the East but he is willing to forfeit his last remaining child.' Aunt raised her eyes. 'I consider that a selfless act, don't you?'

'Yes, Aunt.'

Uncle was standing by the fire, staring into the grate, his hands clasped behind him.

'My instincts side with my brother. You are well aware of my feelings on India. It is a country that has only brought ill-fortune and unhappiness to our family.' Aunt glanced at the letter again. 'It seems there is a condition attached. *If your Aunt can spare you*, your father writes. Well, I do not know if I can spare you, Francina. Your Uncle has told me how admirably you have managed in my absence, and that pleases me greatly - '

Words whirled above Francina's head, but she heard no more. How could she have been so naïve as to imagine Aunt would allow her to go to India? Destiny had brought her into this house as a child, and would keep her here until she died an old maid. That had been Aunt's scheme all along.

6

The storm had abated, but a strong wind was still blowing. The few remaining leaves that had stubbornly clung to branches now lay scattered across the ground. A branch from the cherry tree lay on the terrace; and the damask roses in the garden, the last remnants of summer, had been ripped from their stalks and blown away.

Francina walked the dogs along the lane between Castle Carey and Les Côtils to the high ridge above Glatney. Leaves squelched underfoot; tree-tops buffeted overhead. Clusters of yellow fungi had sprouted, adding daubs of colour to the banks of decaying vegetation. At the ridge she turned the corner and met the full force of the wind. She wrapped her cloak round tightly, leaned over the wide granite wall, and scanned the coastline for the fishing smack Ellie said had been dashed against rocks at La Salerie.

The sky was dull, the horizon hidden by cloud. Since Aunt would not permit her to go to India, she had lost heart. What was the point of aspirations, ambition, of anything? Life was more endurable if she stopped dreaming and behaved like every other dutiful young girl on the Island. This was her place. It had been a cruel trick of Aunt Barton's to suggest otherwise. Blinking, she washed her eyes clear of coal smuts which blew up the hillside from the cottage chimneys. The sea was throwing high banks of spray against the half-completed sea walls, testing their strength. One brave fisherman had set sail with as much canvas spread as he dared. She watched the vessel rise and fall on the swell - at times sinking so far from sight that she expected it never to surface again. No trucks could be seen on the gantries. It was too dangerous for men to work on the New Harbour today. Apart from the post-steamer which was leaving, there was little activity to be seen.

A solitary gull, flying seawards, remained stationary above her head, battling against the wind. After a while it swooped low and flew inland, crying piteously. She shut her eyes and surrendered to the cold; she had little desire to return home. The wind whipped round her, tugging her bonnet. Its roar suppressed thought; its power dulled anxieties.

The sky grew darker. A hailstorm erupted. Pellets cascaded down, covering everything in icy granules. The dogs pulled at their leads and dragged her homewards. The ground was wet and slippery, and it required all her concentration not to land face down in the mud.

Securing the latch, she leaned against the back door to catch her breath. The dogs shook themselves, showering the passage with water which trickled down the walls and ribboned between the flagstones, and then followed the smells in the kitchen.

'*Mon Dou*, my clean floor,' howled Cook from within. 'What imbecile let those animals in? Ellie, dry them in the scullery!'

Francina hung up her wet cloak and bonnet, and followed the paw prints into the kitchen. Cook was kneading pastry. Her sleeves were rolled up, her arms dusted with flour.

'*Oh là là* Missie. Quick, stand by the fire, dry yourself.'

Francina stretched her fingers over the range. Cook took a jug off the dresser. She poured milk into a pan, added a grating of nutmeg and a spoonful of honey and warmed the concoction on the range.

'This warm you, Missie.'

Francina cupped the drink gratefully. Clouds of steam began to rise from her clothing. She enjoyed coming in the kitchen, it was the warmest place in the house. Being below ground level, it was lit by high windows that overlooked a shaded narrow yard and the walled bank topped with iron railings. But it was not gloomy, for oil lamps and the range kept it light and warm throughout the year.

Ellie entered, holding two matted spaniels by their collars. Taking a brush from her pocket, she untangled their fur until it gleamed red with lamplight. '*Bien*, now you are good enough to go upstairs,' she said, standing back with hands on hips to admire her handiwork.

'Back to work!' scolded Cook, rolling out pastry onto a floured board. 'Always a reason to dilly-dally.'

Ellie made a face behind Cook's back: 'Miss Hobson lucky! She marry. No more listen to you!'

A noise caught Francina's attention. Beyond the railings, she saw the wheels of a carriage draw up to the house, the door emblazoned with the arms of the Dean of Guernsey. A footman jumped down, unfolded the steps and assisted two pairs of legs out. The first pair belonging to the Dean, the second to his curate.

Cook had also noted the visitors.

'Where's Baptiste? He should be home now,' she murmured crossly. Turning her head towards the scullery, she shouted: 'Ellie, the door!'

Ellie tidied her cap and raced up the stairs as the knocker rapped. At that moment the back door opened and an icy blast blew into the kitchen. Francina caught a glimpse of grey skirts in the passage.

'Come in here, Miss Hobson. You must be wet through.'

Miss Hobson stepped cautiously into the kitchen. Cook was too busy rolling pastry to acknowledge her. Miss Hobson did not often venture into Cook's domain. Cook had mistaken her reserve for aloofness and had decided that Madame's English maid was too high-and-mighty to fraternise with the kitchen servants. The two had never become friends.

'The umbrella turned inside out.' Miss Hobson shook out her skirts as she tiptoed towards the range. Francina made room for her.

Ellie returned.

'The Dean has business with Monsieur,' she announced. Seeing Miss Hobson, she giggled and ran back into the scullery.

'No tittle-tattle!' shouted Cook after her.

Cook barged between them, threw a large apple pie into the oven and closed the oven door with loud bang just as the service bell marked 'PARLOUR' clanged loudly.

'I shall see to it,' Miss Hobson said, pleased for an excuse to leave Cook's hostile realm.

Francina sipped her drink. The longer she remained here, the less time she would have to spend with Aunt Doré. She envied Miss Hobson, her chance to escape, even though Aunt was making it perfectly clear that she did not approve. It was not in Aunt's scheme of things to discover that the young woman she had rescued from a life of penury and trained to become a respectable lady's maid should repay her generosity by getting married. But humble as Miss Hobson might be, she could choose her destiny. She was not in Aunt's thrall.

Miss Hobson reappeared.

'The Mistress wishes to see you, Miss Francina.'

Aunt Doré was writing at her escritoire with a large Bible laid out before her. 'Francina, I was worried! You were gone so long.'

Since her return, Aunt had taken to addressing her in a cloying tone which Francina found unsettling.

'I was caught in the hailstorm.'

'Are you wet? Go and change at once. It will not do to catch cold - not now that I have such need of you.'

'I have been standing by the range. I am quite dry now.'

'I do not approve of you idling in the kitchen, Francina. There is a perfectly good fire in here. - And in future, if I ring the bell, I should like you to attend me, not Miss Hobson.'

'Is Miss Hobson ill, Aunt?'

'She must be. Marry a dressmaker! I have lost all faith in her judgement. I tried my best to dissuade her. I pointed out how disappointed her father - an Anglican clergyman - would have been if he could know that his daughter was marrying a *Wesleyan*. But no amount of reasoning would change her mind. That dressmaker's influence is clearly at work. It does not stand well for her future.' Aunt Doré shook her head and returned to her writing.

Francina stood by her desk. 'Was there something you required, Aunt?'

Aunt Doré looked up, distracted from her thoughts. 'Umm? Oh yes, I have written a few notes for our prison visit tomorrow. Draw up that chair, Francina. Read them aloud. I wish to absorb the full effect.'

Uncle came in. His eyes were large and troubled. 'My dear, could you step into the drawing room for a moment? The Dean is here. He has some news . . . ' There was no mistaking the apprehension in his voice.

Colour drained from Aunt's face.

'Lean on my arm, my dear,' Uncle said. 'Come, Francina. You should hear this news too.'

The two clergymen stood with their backs to the window, silhouetted against the fading afternoon light. The Very Reverend Fonnereau, Dean of Guernsey, bowed stiffly and advanced to take

Aunt's hands. Muttering soothing words, he directed her to be seated. Then his eyes fell on Francina, intimating that she should follow suit.

'Some time ago Charles wrote to me asking that should anything befall him, would I, his Godfather, inform his beloved parents,' said the Dean through a white haze. 'I agreed without hesitation, hoping that such a duty would never come to pass. But God moves in mysterious ways, dear Mrs Doré. It is not our place to question the decrees of Divine Providence. We must only submit to His Greater Wisdom.'

The Dean turned to his curate. The young man's expression was tense, the lines between his eyebrows furrowed. He had yet to learn to become impassive on such occasions. He clutched a black leather folder embossed with the Dean's crest and symbols of office and on the Dean's command, opened the folder and extracted a letter. It was black-bordered.

'And so, with great sadness, I honour the pledge I made to my dear Godson.' The Dean took the letter and began to read:

> *It is with the deepest regret that I write to inform you of the death of your son Mr Charles Daniel Doré, Midshipman of HM Steam Frigate Hawk on the 9th November 1855 at the General Hospital, Scutari. The onset of his illness was a slight fever and headache which he attributed to over-exposure. The symptoms appeared to abate, but on 26th October he had a more severe attack of fever. A rash appeared on his back and arms and he grew delirious. It was immediately suspected as being Crimean fever, and on the instructions of the Medical Officer he was transferred to a hospital ship bound for Scutari. Despite being under constant supervision and accorded the finest medical attention, he grew weaker. On the 7th November he collapsed into unconsciousness. Blisters were applied, but to no avail. He died two days later without regaining consciousness and was buried the same day. He was accorded full military honours.*

Aunt gave a choking sob. Francina reached out her hand, expecting to be brushed aside, but Aunt seized it, squeezing so tight that her nails dug into her flesh. And so they sat, motionless on the sofa, while the Dean's portentous words hung over their heads.

Uncle had slumped into a chair, his head in his hands.

The Dean brought out a small volume from his pocket, which fell open in his outstretched hands. 'Let us seek solace from the Holy Scriptures.'

Francina had ceased to listen. She was floating near the ceiling looking down. She saw herself kneeling on the turkey carpet between Aunt and Uncle, staring at the gleaming black shoes of God's Representatives, praying for Charlie's soul.

'Have another spoonful of broth, Aunt. You will make yourself ill if you do not eat.'

Aunt opened her eyes. Her face was deathly white.

'Then I shall be reunited all the sooner with my darling boys.' Aunt shut her eyes and leaned back against the pillows. 'Leave me now. Mark the place. I am tired.'

Francina placed the Bible on a side table and left the room.

She returned to the parlour. The dogs tried to jolly her by stealing skeins of silk and hiding them under cushions, then waited, shivering with expectation, for their ploy to be discovered. But she did not have the heart to indulge their little pranks, so eventually they slipped away to sulk.

She sat at the escritoire and replied to the letters that had swamped the house since Charlie's death. So many letters had arrived, and were still arriving from people she hardly knew. She was busier than she had ever been. While Aunt lay in her bed, cocooned in semi-darkness, staring at a miniature of her beloved son, she was entrusted with the day-to-day running of the house. Aunt chose not to notice the servants going about their work with reddened eyes, or to know that Uncle retreated to his library for hours at a time. Aunt was insensible to the misery of those around her, for no one could suffer as she suffered. On her better days she would issue instructions from her bedside; but on the whole it was Francina who planned the menus with Cook, and apportioned the dry stores from the great mahogany cupboard, weighing out the ingredients, scoop by scoop, on the old brass scales. It was she who paid the butcher, the baker, and other tradesmen their dues, carefully recording each transaction in the red accounts book. It was she who received, on Aunt's behalf, the stream of visitors who called to offer their condolences; and she who had instructed Monsieur Le Boutillier to measure the household for their mourning costumes. (Had he not been the best dressmaker on the Island, Aunt would have dispensed with his services, for she could not forgive him for luring Miss Hobson away.)

Miss Hobson entered the room. She sat on the window seat and set about her work, her eyes swollen with dried-up tears. She was making a mourning cap for Aunt, expending far more hours on the garment than it warranted. Surely her tears are not all for Charlie? She hardly knew him.

Uncle was pacing the library floor again. Her heart ached as each tormented tread crossed the ceiling. She glanced at the calendar. She had noted the dates of the expected position of Angelo's ship: off the West Coast of Africa, crossing the Equator, rounding The Cape of Good Hope. If the weather has been fair, he should be sailing across the Indian Ocean now . . . So much has happened since his departure, and Angelo knows none of it.

A bell rang. The pacing stopped.

Miss Hobson departed, reappearing a few minutes later.

Francina returned to her letter, but something made her turn round. Miss Hobson had covered her face with her hands and was silently sobbing.

'Whatever is the matter, Miss Hobson?'

'Miss Francina, I can do nothing to please the Mistress. And now, when she is ill and needs me, I repay her kindness by getting married. Am I so very wicked?'

Francina left her seat and took her hand. Small and cool, it fluttered like a trapped bird in her own.

'Aunt does not want to lose you. It is a shock.'

Miss Hobson shook her head.

'I am being punished for giving notice.'

7

On the morning of Charlie's Memorial Service, Francina awoke to find the window panes covered in a filigree of ice crystals. She slipped out of bed, threw on her wrap and raised the sash. A hush had fallen across the garden. In the rheumy sunlight, frost sparkled on twigs and glinted on the grass; lacy cobwebs hung over the rose bushes. Francina stood still and tried to memorise the scene before it all melted away – but it was at such moments, such moment of great beauty that she thought of Charlie. Charlie buried far away in the arid dust would never see anything so beautiful again.

Francina lowered the sash, and broke the thin layer of ice in the pitcher. Clenching her teeth to stop them from chattering, she splashed herself with water and dressed quickly. Her fingers were numb and swollen, and it was difficult to button up the thick bodice of her mourning gown, or to arrange her hair with much artistry.

Louisa showed no sign of movement. Only her nightcap was visible, nestling in the valley of the pillows. Francina had been longing to see her again, but now that she was home, she was finding her intensely irritating. A change had come over her during her three months in Brussels. She had been indulged. She was full of airs and graces.

Francina prodded her. 'Get up, Lulu.'

'Since you are plainly used to dressing in the freezing cold,' mumbled the mound, 'could you fetch me a jug of hot water? It is torture for me to dress in a room without a fire.'

Francina grabbed a shard of ice from the pitcher and shoved it under the bedclothes. Louisa shrieked, and jumped out of bed.

The tide of mourners carried Francina through the North Door. The world looked different through a black veil; it was impossible to tell if the sky was grey or blue. She stretched her fingers inside her new black muff; her chilblains were tingling remorselessly. It was so cold in Church that she had been tempted to ask Grandmother Doré if she might share her foot warmer. But it had been a moving Service. There were few dry eyes when the Dean gave his Address. He spoke at great length and with obvious fondness for his Godson.

The bell was tolling.

The long procession began to move . . . Francina watched the bowed figure of Aunt, supported on either side by Uncle and Saumarez, leading the line of mourners up the hill; a black melancholy snake winding up High Street . . .

This was the first time Aunt had ventured out since Charlie's death. She had travelled by carriage to the Memorial Service, but had wished to return home on foot. If Aunt had a body to bury, a grave to visit, it would make Charlie's passing more bearable.

'Francina?'

She allowed herself to be borne on Julia's arm. So many Islanders had turned out to honour this young sailor, this worthy son of Guernsey, hero and victim of the Crimean War. The route was lined with good souls, two or three deep, who stood with their hats pressed to their chests in silent respect: caulkers, carpenters and sail-makers from St Sampson; fishermen, rope-winders and sailors from La Salerie; shopkeepers, porters and harbour officials from St Pierre; carters, farmers and peasants from the countryside - she recognized most of them by the clothes of their trade.

She was walking in time to the tolling bell. One stroke to denote the passing of a man; one single mournful note hung in the cold still air until it was ousted by another. The line snaked up the hill ahead of her: Louisa was walking with Uncle Harry the Jurat; Grandmother Doré's sedan chair was carried by her servants in their mourning livery. The Careys, the influential de Jerseys and Le Marchants - everyone was walking in order of precedence. She was with Aunt Duquesne and Cousin Julia: the Duquesne contingent. Behind them came the servants and household attendants. Was Cook keeping up? She was so troubled with the rheumatics these days.

Turning the corner, they enter a sun-filled square and she watched her shadow contort over the cobblestones.

8

Aunt had fallen asleep. Marking the place, Francina closed the Bible and placed it on a side-table. She glanced at the clock. Eight minutes past eleven. Four minutes since she last looked. She opened her workbox, unfolded the canvas, and eyed the cabbage roses and butterflies with distaste. She had no heart for the work.

Outside, the sky was leaden, the grass wet and spattered with leaves. No one was walking. There was nothing out there, nothing at all, except a black cat prowling along the high wall of Beau Sejour. But she mustn't be gloomy, she told herself, for a small star had shone down on them: Papa was a free man. They had received the news on Christmas Eve. She had written to him immediately. But Papa's release did little to lift his spirits, which had only grown blacker during his incarceration. If only she could persuade Aunt to let her find work to help ease Papa's situation. Work might stop her from brooding, for she was beginning to fear that Papa's demon had taken up residence in her. These days she seemed to live in a state of dreamy suspension, seeing everything through a muslin curtain, unable to summon the will to do anything with much enthusiasm. It frightened her to think she might be infected with Papa's illness.

The fire was burning low. Soon she must summon Baptiste to stoke it up, but while Aunt slept, she could study her letter again.

Gresham's Hotel, Dublin

My dear Francina!

As yet we have received no line from you. It is highly likely your letters have failed to catch up with us. We are leading such a nomadic existence at present. I therefore urge you to send no letter to Ireland - the post is notoriously slack and unreliable in this part of the world - but write c/o our Agent: N. Braddon Esq., 4 Lothbury, City, London. We have booked the 28th March steamer from Southampton - so it is imperative that you write by return to our Agent confirming your intentions. Then your berth can be secured in good time. We intend taking lodgings in London for a month prior to our departure and would be delighted if you would join us. That will give us an opportunity to become acquainted with one another and to assemble your Indian wardrobe. My dear, this is not the ideal season for someone unaccustomed to the Indian climate to venture out, but we should, hopefully, return before the onset of the Rains. We are so looking forward to seeing Theresa's little girl again!

With kind regards to Mr and Mrs Doré,

I remain your affectionate Aunt, Cecilia Vauloué

Madame Vauloué required an answer by return of post. How could she possibly persuade Aunt at this moment? She was in no frame of mind to consent to anything.

Francina screwed up the letter and stuffed it into her pocket.

9

Sailing ship Queen, off Kedgeree Point, India

My dearest sweetest Sister,

As I write, I see land from the porthole. The coast is low and covered in vegetation – and what a delightful sight it is. We have made a capital run - although we are two souls fewer than when we set out. We lost a sailor overboard in a storm, and poor Mr Studd, who was ailing at the start, did not last the voyage. Also, the Captain lost a horse and two hounds (but you will read of this at length in my journal which I am dispatching separately). We are anchored off Kedgeree Point where we must stay until a tug steamer is dispatched to us - it is too dangerous for a large ship to go up-river to Calcutta without steam power. But there is much to see - so many vessels are coming and leaving. A bumboat visited us today, laden with strange fruits, and grass mats -

Francina stopped. A picture had flashed before her, a picture of herself sitting in this spot, ten or twenty years hence. Nothing would have changed. Aunt Doré, Aunt Duquesne, Julia: they were all here, listening to Angelo's letters. Only – they were older, much older. Julia had become Cousin Mattie. She had become Cousin Mattie.

'Do read us more,' urged Julia. 'Angelo writes so well.'

It had been a mistake to invite Aunt Duquesne and Julia to tea. She had little inclination for small talk. Last night she had lain awake listening to the grandfather clock strike the hour, then the half-hour, while she had tried to work out the best way to approach Aunt Doré. But as yet, she had not summoned up the courage to mention Madame Vauloué's letter. Soon it would be too late. Then at least she would not have to endure this suspense any longer.

Charlie stared down at her from his black swaged portrait, waiting to hear more. She returned to Angelo's letter.

Last night Thompson, Grant and I went ashore with the sircar and the ship's butcher to bring back provisions. We were carried across a hundred yards of mud which caused us great hilarity. – You cannot imagine the joy to step on terra firma again! It was moonlight when we landed, and were it not for the natives in white flowing drapery or the waving coconut trees, we could hardly believe we were in India. We wandered as far as the bazaar, fascinated by everything we saw. The sircar made his purchases and we returned to the beach. None of the natives would assist in putting the Sacred Bullock into the boat, so Thompson, Grant and I were obliged to strip off our boots and stockings and help the butcher. During this manoeuvre, jackals were prowling around us, and we had to shout to frighten them off. This accomplished, the bullock's legs were tied together, and we all got in and started for the ship. After a long pull against the tide we got on board, pleased with our little excursion -

She could speak no more. Her heart lay wedged in her throat. Clutching Angelo's letter, she ran to her room. She lay on her bed and stared up at a small brown patch on the ceiling . . . a brown winged creature hovering above her bed, so small, so far away. She had not noticed it before.

There was a knock on the door, and Julia tiptoed in.

'Is something wrong, Ina?' she asked, taking her hand. 'Sometimes it helps to talk.'

The dogs darted through the copse bordering Beau Sejour. Francina called them back but they took no notice, leaving her no choice but to follow. Drawing her cloak in tightly, she scrambled through the dripping undergrowth and squelched through the mulch. At the edge of the copse, she caught sight of their waggling posteriors disappearing down the lane beyond the Rope Walk. She called again, but they ignored her.

She followed testily, her thoughts wandering as aimlessly as the dogs, but always returning full circle to Madame Vauloué's letter. Forty three hours had passed since she had received it. Nothing had changed. She was no nearer going to India than she was last week - or five months ago for that matter. She had intended to mention the letter to Uncle after dinner, but he was late arriving home. Tossing in bed, unable to sleep, she had heard him creep upstairs and had thought of throwing on her wrap to meet him on the landing, but her courage had failed. A sixth sense told her that he was not in a good mood.

When she eventually caught the dogs and dragged them home, she noticed a hired gig parked before the house. This was good news. Visitors would lighten the atmosphere.

She slipped through the back door, and removed her boots in the passage. The kitchen door opened and Ellie squeezed past with a basket piled high with laundry.

'Madame asks for you,' she said, stepping into the laundry room.

Francina laced up her shoes and hurried upstairs. She caught her reflection in the glass and winced. As she tidied her hair, murmurs drifted into the hall. The door of the drawing room had been left ajar. She edged closer, trying to recognise the voices.

'But will Frank accept our help? He can be so stubborn at times,' she heard Aunt Marquand say.

'He has no choice,' said Uncle Doré. 'He is woefully behind with his rent and I understand that his landlady has made a personal sacrifice to keep his rooms vacant during his absence.'

'Then we must recompense the charitable woman immediately,' said Aunt Sabonière. 'This sorry affair must be brought to a swift conclusion. Society must have no further opportunity to debase our family name.'

'Indeed, Sophia,' said Aunt Marquand. 'I propose that we three sisters make our brother an annuity, until such time as he can support himself.'

'It is the least we can do,' sighed Aunt Sabonière. 'We must count our blessings that our noble father is not here to witness his downfall. It would have broken his heart.'

'It is a godsend at least that Angelo is out of harm's way.'

Francina dared not risk standing here any longer. Someone might appear and discover her listening at the door. She took a deep breath, knocked and entered.

'My dear,' Uncle Doré said. 'We have been waiting for you.'

She proffered kisses: Aunt Marquand, Aunt Sabonière and Miss Mattie. If she had not overheard their conversation, she could not have guessed at the anxiety behind their smiles.

Aunt Marquand patted the sofa with a crooked hand in fingerless black lace. 'Sit by me, Francina.'

She sat on the edge of the sofa, hands clasped, knees pressed tightly together. This was no accidental gathering. Aunt Marquand never ventured out in disagreeable weather.

Aunt Sabonière asked if she had heard from Angelo. Francina told them snippets from his latest letter. They listened closely, as if trying to find a crack in her account.

'I suppose Angelo has departed for Ceylon by now? Alex is in great need of the extra pair of hands on the estate.'

She had been dreading this question. 'Well, not exactly, Aunt Marquand. He has decided to take a short trip up-country, to see something of Bengal.'

'Bengal!' exclaimed Aunt Sabonière. 'What business has he in Bengal?'

'I do not know that he has any business in Bengal, Aunt.'

'When will that boy realise he is not on the *Grand Tour*.'

Francina stared at her mud-spattered skirts. Even now, with Angelo on the other side of the world, she was still the butt for his indulgent behaviour. Beside her, Aunt Marquand was trying to adjust her shawl. Miss Mattie rose to assist her mother.

When the conversation resumed, all reference to Angelo was pointedly omitted. Aunt Marquand, now encased in a black crocheted shawl, leaned over and took Francina's hand. 'Now, my dear, let us talk of something more interesting. A little birdie has told me that you have been invited to India.'

Francina glanced furtively at Aunt Doré. 'Mrs Barton did invite me to Calcutta,' she whispered, 'but of course it was only polite talk.'

'Indeed? But I believe you have received a letter?'

'A letter, Aunt Marquand?'

'A letter with a date of departure. Do you have this letter, Francina?'

Francina took the letter from her pocket, smoothed out the creases and gave it to Aunt Marquand, who read it, passed it to Uncle, who passed it around the circle.

'Why have you not mentioned this letter before, Francina?' asked Aunt Sabonière.

How could she explain that she just could not bear the rejection?

The longer she kept the letter to herself the longer she could dream that India might just possibly happen.

'Would you like to go to India, child?' Aunt Marquand asked.

Would the cage door spring open if she answered correctly? She stared at her clenched hands. She could distinguish the ridges of bone under the skin of her knuckles.

'Well, Francina?'

'Only if . . . only if Aunt Doré can spare me,' she whispered.

'I think it an excellent idea – don't you agree, Sisters?' Aunt Sabonière said, going on to give her reasons.

Aunt Marquand nodded from time to time. Despite her crippling infirmity, she had a sound head. She was the senior sister, who commanded the respect of all. 'My dear, I believe enough remains of your Grand-mère's legacy to send you to India. But before I consult my fellow trustees, I must ask if we are all in agreement?'

Uncle was first to answer. As her father had already given his consent, he saw no objections - providing Francina understood the implications. Aunt Sabonière agreed. She had found Mrs Barton a warm-hearted creature, who seemed genuinely fond of their niece. She felt sure Francina would be safe in Mrs Barton's hands.

All eyes turned to Aunt Doré. Her mouth was a thin firm line.

'I shall not stand in your way, Francina,' Aunt Doré said eventually. 'But let no one say I did not warn you: No good will come of it.'

10

The Brussels Conservatoire

My dearest Ina,

I was astonished to receive your letter. From what you imply, the idea was broached by Mrs Barton five months ago! I think it very rum that you said nothing of it to me until now. How can you think of leaving? It will be so fearfully dull when I return home. I shall have no one to confide in, and will be miserable knowing you are having a gay time in India while I sit in the glum parlour with Mamma. I am exceedingly miffed that you have kept me in the dark (especially as I have had the goodness to tell you all <u>*my*</u> *secrets) - but then it occurred to me that your going to India might work to my advantage. You must marry a wealthy Nabob and invite me out to stay with you! That way I can arrange to see Henry. Is that not a capital idea? Surely Mamma and Papa could not object to such a plan? And in the meantime, it will be so much easier to send my letters to Henry enclosed in yours (and he can do likewise). The more I think about your going to India, the more I approve! So, go for my sake, and quickly find a rich Indian to fall in love with you. (You can easily do so - there is such a shortage of the Fair Sex in India that even the* <u>*plainest*</u> *woman without fortune or family is much sought after.)*

Dear Ina, I forgive you. I shall not be sad at your departing for I know that soon I shall join you and we shall have splendid times together. Therefore Au Revoir and Bon Voyage! Keep me in your thoughts - and write to me often. I want to know <u>*everything*</u> *you do!*

I remain your affectionate and aggrieved cousin,
Louisa Doré

It had seemed so cruel to tell Louisa that she was leaving for India when Aunt and Uncle were against their own daughter going. If only she could turn round and find her sitting at the dressing table, coquettishly turning this way and that, admiring herself in the glass. There was so much she could convey by a touch of the hand or a kiss on the cheek. She tore the letter into scraps and concealed them in her pocket.

She wandered out of the bedroom, her eyes heavy from lack of sleep. She had been in this dream-like state ever since she had received the news that the trustees had released the last portion of Grand-mère's legacy. In less than a week, she would be leaving.

'*Allez en paix,*' whispered Aunt Marquand. '*Vivez en paix, et que le Dieu de Paix vous bénisse.*' The old Island blessing.

Tears welled in Francina's eyes. She would probably never see this dear old lady again. She kissed her family and all her dear friends who had braved the wind and rain to come to the harbour to wish her well.

'Go to India with our love and blessings, dear child.'

'It is time to step into the boat, Francina.'

Uncle Doré took her arm.

'I cannot leave without saying goodbye to Miss Chesterton!' she cried. For there, by the Customs House was a figure running along the quay, skirts gathered, hand pressing down her bonnet.

Breaking from Uncle's grasp, she ran to meet her. How had she managed to slip away from the Academy? Surely Madame Le Brocq would not have given her permission to leave.

Miss Chesterton took her hands. Her eyes glistened with tears.

'Goodbye, dear child. Don't forget your teacher, or all that I have taught you.'

'You understand why I must go, don't you, Miss Chesterton? We both know what will happen if I stay here - precisely *nothing*! I want to see the world -'

'Of course I understand. But do not hurry into something you might regret. Absorb and evaluate everything you see. Give yourself time to mature in that Eastern sun, for there will be much out there that will fill you with amazement and wonder. But above all, be true to yourself,' whispered her old mistress, kissing her forehead. 'Then, with God's grace, you will lead a happy and purposeful life.'

Baptiste helped her into the boat. The little rowing boat pitched and rolled as the oarsmen struggled against the incoming tide to reach the steamer. Each time the boat dipped, her stomach dipped with it. The other passengers sat huddled under their umbrellas with mouths set firm. Uncle Doré and Baptiste sat either side of her. Their pressing bodies were reassuring, but she clutched Uncle's arm, just in case.

'Look up at the sky,' coaxed Baptiste. 'Not feel so sick then.'

The steamer loomed steadily larger, until they were close enough for an oarsman to throw a rope to a sailor waiting to haul them in. They struggled up the precarious gangway and waited in a dazed group for their trunks, bedrolls and sundry packages to be hoisted up after them. Then, having counted their belongings, they stumbled about the deck, familiarizing themselves with their new surroundings, until the bad weather forced most of the passengers into the saloon.

She leaned over the guardrail to take a last look at her beloved Guernsey and the long line of well-wishers lining the harbour wall. The ship's powerful engines vibrated gently under her hands. She saw the little granite houses with their tall smoking chimneys nestling tightly under the rock. She could identify every building, every turret and every steeple. She could just make out Elm House through the bare trees of Castle Carey, and she fancied, the flat roof of Beau Sejour. Behind St Pierre the patchwork of small brown and green fields spread out like a rumpled counterpane. The sails of the old windmill perched on a hillock were turning in the wind. She saw the russet copses, the windswept purple heath, the copper bracken, the black rocky outcrops fringed in white, and her heart ached.

The siren shrieked and the steamer shuddered into life. The huge paddle-wheels began to turn, churning the sea into an angry carpet of foam. The fiery monster was champing to leave.

The dogs were running along the harbour wall, barking. Aunt Doré was dabbing her eyes with a handkerchief, a gesture so singular that it moved her to tears. Aunt Sabonière, Aunt Duquesne, Julia, Miss Chesterton, Madame Le Boutillier, they were all waving: a fluttering ruche of white. How many of these good people would she see again?

Uncle Doré rested his hand on her shoulder. 'Come into the saloon, my dear. You will catch cold if you stay out here much longer.'

'Please, Uncle - just a few more moments.'

The steamer rolled as it turned out to sea. Francina moved across the deck. Her beloved Island was shrinking before her eyes. Coal smuts and rain mingled with the tears trickling down her face. There is an old Island saying: if you keep looking, you will return one day. Narrowing her eyes against the wind and rain, she kept looking.

LONDON

March 1856

It was impossible to read. The view through the train window was too distracting. Francina shut her book and placed it the basket. Everything in England was on a larger scale: the trees taller, the hills higher, the towns busier. Church steeples soared like needles into the clouds, and the fields looked huge after Guernsey's pocket-handkerchiefs - and, she fancied, more hedgerows had been grubbed up since she was last here.

It was cold in the carriage and she was glad of the rug tucked round her knees. The sky was cold grey, darkening. It was trying to snow. Her breath misted up the window and she rubbed a patch clear to watch ice crystals cling to the glass then streak away to oblivion. She thought of Baptiste huddled in the open carriage and hoped his coat was warm.

Uncle Doré was dozing, his head wedged in an upholstered corner. The newspaper on his lap rustled as he breathed, and she leaned forward to prize it away before it slipped to the floor. As she placed it on the seat beside him, she caught the eye of the lady opposite, who smiled apologetically and looked away.

There was so much she wanted to ask Uncle. Now it was too late. They had hardly spoken since changing trains, other than to enquire into each other's comfort, for they no longer had the carriage to themselves. A fat clergyman, his pinched wife and her little dog had joined then at Basingstoke, and although he was engrossed in some religious tome and she stared vacantly out of the window as she fondled the ear of the pet on her lap, Francina felt sure they would be poised to catch snippets of conversation.

Rows of snug grey villas with narrow stripes of garden had sprung up along the railway line. She had no doubt that their façades would sport carved lintels, ornate doorways and other pretensions of grandeur, but she was seeing their backs, the unsightly, secret side containing the washing lines and coal stores. Secrets abound everywhere. She put her hand in her pocket. Her secrets were folded snugly here. While Uncle slept, she would read Angelo's letter again.

My dearest sweetest Sister –

Not in your wildest dreams could you imagine where I am staying! With our Mother*! Am I not be congratulated for discovering her whereabouts? But in case I was on a wild goose chase, I decided to say nothing until I was quite sure of finding her.*

It was that curious companion-servant residing with the Bartons who set me on the trail. She drew me aside one day and told me that she knew the whereabouts of our Mother. I thought the dark creature was demented and took no notice, but a few days later curiosity got the better of me and I broached the subject again. She told me that our Mother resides in Sooree, portraying herself as the Judge's wife. I questioned Aunt Barton, who professed to know nothing, but something in her manner made me think that there was some truth in the story, so I decided to find out.

After travelling by train to Raniganj, then embarking on a gruelling journey by dâk-gary to Sooree, I sought directions to the residence of the Civil and Sessions Judge. Imagine my apprehension when I left my card with the servant not knowing if I would be received or thrown out on my ear. After a few minutes (which seemed like an eternity), I was directed into an elegant room where I found a lady seated at a pianoforte. She held my card and looked up at me.

'Angelo?' she said shakily. 'Is it really you?'

The lady rose to her feet with tears in her eyes, and said she was my Mother. I was taken aback, for she seemed too young to be my Mother. Indeed, dearest Sister (I say this without exaggeration), she is one of the loveliest women I have ever seen. However, she pressed on me that our relationship must remain a secret, or there would be grave consequences. I promised to tell no one that I was her son, but would declare myself 'a nephew of her sister'. That went some way to alleviate her fears. We sat on the verandah and talked and talked. One of her first questions was to enquire after you, dearest Ina. When she learned that you were about to come out to India, this set her tears flowing again, for she feared she would miss you (she must quit India herself soon), and she said that she must try once more to pen another letter to you, dearest Ina.

I was introduced to her children (two girls and two boys) as a relative from Home. Immediately the elder boy began to plague me with questions: Had I seen snow? Had I ever walked on frozen water? I answered his questions as best I could and found myself an instant favourite with them. The eldest girl is about nine years old, and our Mother confessed that she should have been sent Home long ago, but was loath to part with her. I was struck by her likeness to you, Ina: the same shy smile, the same brown eyes.

I remained with this delightful family until dusk, by which time I began to detect our Mother's growing agitation, not knowing if the Judge would receive me on his return. She asked me to remain in the library while she informed him of my presence. For some fifteen minutes I waited in agonized suspense until I was ushered back into the drawing-room. But I need not have feared. The noble Judge greeted me warmly, and said that I am welcome to remain a guest in his house until they left for England. He emphasised, however, that it is imperative that my true identity remains a secret from everyone, and especially the children - they must never know that I am their half-brother. I agreed, but my heart was heavy, for I long to embrace these sweet children as a brother.

And so I shall remain here with our dear Mother as her devoted companion until they depart for England. Can you understand my joy at such a prospect? But it is only during our early morning rides when we are alone that I can speak freely, for the days are always interrupted by some passing dignitary or high Indian Official come to pay his respects. Our Mother is truly revered in these parts, as much for her beauty as for her rank.

I must now conclude if I am to catch the mails which leave tonight.

Your loving and jubilant brother, Angelo

After all Papa's attempts hide the truth, Angelo had outwitted him. He had found Mamma. But where was Mamma's letter? *Another letter*, Angelo had said. *She would try once more.* Where were her letters? She looked at Uncle sleeping peacefully. Had he deceived her for all this time? No, the mail was Aunt Doré's domain.

They were speeding through the countryside again. She saw a

man and dog crossing the frozen ridges of a ploughed field . . . crows circling over a copse of trees . . . a blacksmith hammering at an anvil . . . men unloading kindling in a yard . . .

Then fields and meadows gave way to brooding factories spewing black smoke over redbrick houses, and the train began to slow. The change in rhythm woke Uncle Doré, and he pulled out his watch to consult the railway timetable.

'We are making excellent time,' he smiled.

Her heart quickened. It hardly seemed possible, but soon she would see Papa. How young and impressionable she had been when she had last seen him; how overawed by everything. Papa had met them off the train and escorted them across London. He had shown them round his new warehouse in Blackfriars, a grimy building by the riverside piled high with casks and bottles. She had stood outside with Angelo on the decaying wharf to watch the barges plying up and down the river. The tide was out, and what she remembered particularly about that day was the number of ragged souls scavenging knee-deep in the stench at the water's edge. It was a horrible place and she could not wait to leave. Papa appeared unaffected by his surroundings, or else he had grown so accustomed to them that he ceased to notice. She remembered him proudly pointing out, on a large map in his office, the route of a shipment of wines that would make his fortune.

The factories had grown to a monstrous size, and were trampling over the villages so that they resembled no more than a motley collection of shacks and hovels. Fields had become quagmires of mud, and village ponds were fetid pools fit only for pigs.

'We must be nearly there,' Uncle Doré said.

While Uncle Doré and Baptiste went off to collect the luggage, she stood by the entrance to the Ladies Rest Room clutching her parasol, umbrella and basket. Other ladies huddled close by. Carpetbags, bonnet-boxes, a birdcage covered in a green cloth, a guitar and a camping-stool were positioned like a barricade around them. Passengers, porters and station officials dashed across the platform in front of them. Whistles blew, steam hissed and people shouted. The noise swirled and rebounded under the huge vaulted glass roof as she scanned the lines looking for Papa.

She saw a grey-haired gentleman and her heart leapt - but he was meeting the young lady standing next to her.

Gradually the crowd began to disperse. One by one, those near her were collected and disappeared out of the station. She was left alone with her belongings scattered around her.

'Carry your bags, ma'am? Will you be wanting a cab?'

'No, I am waiting for someone.' Her chest tightened. Where was Papa?

By the time Uncle and Baptiste had returned with a porter, the platform had almost cleared.

'I see no sign of Papa,' she said.

'Perhaps he is waiting outside.'

'In this weather, Uncle? Surely not.'

Clutching her parasol, umbrella and basket, she followed Uncle and the porters out of the station. The city hummed around them, and the air, thick with coal-smoke, hit them like a damp pillow. It was only three o'clock, but the light was beginning to fade and fog was descending. Flakes of snow punctured the gloom and swirled to the ground, settled for a moment then melted. Cabmen idling by their vehicles rushed forward waving arms and clamouring for attention. 'Ollo! Cab, guv'nor? Cab, sir?'

In the hubbub her eye was drawn to a person holding a black umbrella, standing apart from that animated group. He was muffled against the cold by a long grey comforter, which covered a good part of his face, and although his clothes were worn and outdated, he looked too much of a gentleman to be a cabman. She recognised those haunted eyes immediately.

'Papa! Oh, Papa!' she choked, falling into his arms.

His cheeks were ice-cold and his lips nothing more than a thin blue line.

'Darling daughter,' he whispered. 'Let me look at you.' Pride and sadness shone in his eyes as he held her at arm's length. 'What a fine young lady you have become.'

Francina smiled, but she was shocked by his stooped appearance and pinched features. Beads of moisture glinted on his greatcoat. His shoes were wet and his trousers spattered with mud. She suspected that he had walked a long way.

'How long have you been standing here in the cold, Papa? Your coat is soaked. You might have caught your death.'

He smiled. Tiredness showed in his eyes.

'Papa, you should have waited inside - on the platform. It was quite warm and dry there.'

'But I would have had to buy a ticket,' he explained quietly.

In that instant she glimpsed the truth. Lost for words, she turned to Uncle. He caught her expression and hurried forward.

Papa clutched his hand. His gesture was almost subservient. Prison had ground him down, broken his spirit. 'How obliged I am to have this opportunity to thank you in person for your kindness during my - my recent difficulties. I cannot -'

'My dear fellow!' Uncle placed a hand on his shoulder as if to put a stop to such talk. He looked so assured, so imposing next to Papa. 'I shall be staying in Town for the next few days. I have some business to attend to in the City. Will do me the honour of dining with me at my Club tomorrow evening?'

'Why I,' muttered Papa, 'it would be a pleasure.'

'Your sisters have a proposition which they have asked me to put to you. We could discuss it over a glass of port.' Uncle turned to Francina, cupped his hand under her elbow and smiled.

'Now - what do you think of your daughter? Has she not grown into a fine young lady?'

Papa, overcome with pride, could only nod.

'Her aunt will be lost without her. She was loath to part with her. We all are.'

Francina looked down, staring first at Uncle's highly polished boots, then at Papa's down-trodden ones.

'Francina has promised to write regularly and keep us informed of everything she does,' continued Uncle. 'And now, my dear, I shall take my leave. It is too cold to stand talking - and I am sure your papa is anxious to deliver you to the Vauloués.'

She stood on tiptoe and kissed him, infusing her lungs with his smell, that blend of tobacco, leather and polish, as if to take some part of him with her. His moustache tickled her cheek. She could not find the words to express her love and gratitude.

Uncle squeezed her hand so hard, she almost cried out in pain.

She turned to Baptiste and held out her hand. She wanted to tell him how much she would miss him; how much she had valued their unspoken friendship. She felt his sadness, saw it in his eyes.

'Good luck, La Missie.'

'Thank you, Baptiste.'

Three little words.

The porter placed Uncle's bags in a cab, and he and Baptiste climbed in after them. Francina watched the cab turn the corner and disappear, taking with it the two people in the world who had really cared about her.

It was easier to write letters than to say things face to face. They sat watching the bustle of London slip past the cab windows. She tried to break the silence by telling Papa news from home, passing on messages of affection from her aunts, but he just smiled. He was not listening, his thoughts were elsewhere. Their worlds had grown so much apart that only blood tied them together now.

North of the river the streets were busy, and growing busier. Buildings, so imposing, so substantial, soared into the fog around them. The last time she had been here was mid-summer. Then everything was bathed in sunlight and people had strolled in bright summer clothes. Now they were nothing more than grey shadows hunched under umbrellas, weaving through the bleak winter slush. But even so, the noise and throb of the city excited her.

The cab inched past butchers' carts, brewers' drays, wagons, trucks and omnibuses crammed with people. Every so often the cabman shouted: 'Out of the way, boy!' to a little crossing-sweeper. The crowd increased, the noise grew louder. Finally, the volume of traffic brought everything to a standstill. Shouts rang from one end of the street to the other. Someone blew a fanfare on a horn. Drivers leaned out of their vehicles and threatened one another with fists. Passers-by stopped and watched this development with interest.

'It is just as well the cabbies are paid by the mile and not by the hour.'

'How do you mean, Papa?'

'We would end up paying double in this traffic.'

A peeler blew a whistle and the bottleneck slowly cleared.

It was distressing to find Papa so preoccupied with the cost of everything. He had argued with the cab driver, fixing the fare before they had set off. But it was not his poverty that upset her as much as his demeanour, his humility. He had looked so deferential next to Uncle Doré. She had longed to see Papa again, and had envisaged their deep conversations fervently catching up on five years of separation, but it would have been easier to strike up a conversation with the cab driver.

Then he coughed, a long hacking cough.

She turned to him in alarm. 'Papa, are you not well?'

'It is nothing, my dear. Just this confounded fog. It catches at the back of my throat. I should have allowed myself more time this morning. I would not have had to walk so quickly.'

At that moment she was overcome with love for him. She remembered all he had been through; his anguish, his despair and his hurt. She remembered all Mamma had done to him and she hated herself.

'You must take better care of yourself, Papa,' she said, taking his hand. 'I wish you would move to Guernsey. Your sisters would be so pleased to see you - and I know you would find the sea air beneficial.'

'I could not live there, Francina - not now. I could not suffer the indignity of constantly being reminded of who I was or what I might have been.' He turned away. 'No one knows me here. I travel unseen and unnoticed. I am accepted for what I am. I have no past.'

His eyes had glazed over. She did not have the heart to press the matter for she knew he was right. She understood those looks and sneers only too well.

The light was fading; the lamplighter was making his rounds. A small girl, wearing boots several sizes too large and shivering with cold, was trying to coax passers-by to examine her tray of bootlaces. Everyone circled round her as if she was no more than a lamppost in the middle of the pavement.

'Have you heard from Angelo recently?' Papa asked, breaking the silence. 'His last letter was such a muddle, I could make neither head nor tail of it.'

'Angelo was leaving Calcutta when he last wrote to me.'

'At last! I was beginning to think something was keeping him there. I was not at all happy about him staying with the Bartons.'

'Why not, Papa?'

'Oh, the Bartons are well meaning enough, but Calcutta is too gay. There are too many distractions - and Angelo could easily have been swayed by the pleasure-seeking that abounds there. He is headstrong and impulsive. It will be his undoing - just as it was his mother's.' He turned his tired eyes to her. 'My dear, *you* will never be swayed by the evil influences that abound in a country where propriety is wanting. Your aunt has saved you from such a fate. She has brought you up decently and taught you sound Christian virtues. I thank my good fortune that she has checked any influence your mother might have instilled in you. Remember, Francina, the happiness of your future depends on your striving to uphold all that your aunt has taught you, for my dear, there will be little else to assist you.'

Francina stared at her lap.

'Much as I disapprove of you going to India - and believe me it breaks my heart to know that you will be beholden to your mother's relatives - I know only too well that it is your only chance to secure a reasonable future. But beware, my dear, in India men are prone to be irrational. Why that should be I do not know - perhaps it is a curse of the climate or being far from the sober influences of Home - but I speak from bitter experience. They lose their head over the first pretty face that crosses their path and throw aside all sensible considerations.'

'Do you not approve of Madame Vauloué, Papa?'

'I would rather you had as little to do with your mother's family as possible, Francina. I had my suspicions. I used to think she encouraged your mother, put ideas in her head. Cecilia Vauloué and your mother could have been twins: two indulged girls never wanting for anything with a host of admirers swooning at their feet.'

The cab entered a tree-filled square of imposing houses, and pulled up. The hubbub dropped to a hum. It was a place of quiet in the heart of the city.

'We have arrived.' Papa pulled a cloth from his pocket and rubbed the mud off his shoes.

The cab driver opened the door and unfolded the steps. Papa followed her out.

'Goodbye, my dear.'

'Are you not coming in with me? But Papa, I have hardly seen you! When shall I see you again?' It was impossible to hide the disappointment, the hurt in her voice.

'I shall send a note.'

Snow began to fall in large wet flakes around them. Papa opened his umbrella and braced himself. Then his shoulders began to sink, as if the weight building up on his umbrella was too much to withstand. She took his arm.

'Come inside for a moment, Papa. You look so cold.'

A footman ushered them in. They stood awkwardly in the hall while servants deposited trunks and bags around them. Francina caught her reflection in a tall looking glass and her heart sank. Her bombazine dress and woollen cape had never looked so dull or inappropriate. Papa squeezed her arm as the footman led them up a magnificent stone staircase, but his eyes were troubled. They passed a marble nymph posing decorously in a niche. Take heart! her smile seemed to say.

The footman showed them into the drawing room, closed the doors and left them.

The room was unoccupied. Despite its size and grandeur, it looked friendly and inviting. A fire crackled in the hearth and reflected in the polished metalwork. The walls were lined with rose silk and closely hung with paintings. Some were allegorical subjects; others engaging studies of children, but most were grand portraits of military characters. The ceiling was high and moulded, supporting from its centre a handsome chandelier. The furniture was of different styles and arranged in intimate groups, much of it protected by slipcovers of green and rose chintz. But it was the homely touches that set Francina at ease: the worktable opened to reveal skeins of coloured silks; the small baize table set up with cards and counters; and the Indian shawl draped over a chair. Of course, she knew this house did not belong to the Vauloués - for all she knew the owners' taste was very different from theirs - but the fact that the Vauloués had taken this house must indicate that there was some sympathy between the parties, and that gave her heart.

She peered out of a tall swagged window. Beyond the narrow iron balcony, through fog and swirling snow, she could just make out the dark mass of the terrace opposite, and down in the centre of the square, a formal garden arranged with benches and neat circling paths.

A faint sound caught her attention. She put her cheek to the cold pane to listen. Church clocks were striking the hour across the City. She caught the wail of a street vendor, another closer to. Then a train chugged in and out of range, and hooves clattered through the slush . . . A shiver ran down her spine. This was the music of London, and she was at the start of her Great Adventure. She wanted so much to share her excitement with someone.

She took Papa's arm. He was studying a portrait of a portly gentleman with powdered hair, wearing a scarlet coat and tartan trews. '*Colonel Adolphus Balfour,*' he read, *'was mortally wounded at the victorious battle of Assaye.'*

The doors opened and a younger, prettier version of Aunt Barton glided towards them. She was by no means slim, but certainly slimmer than Aunt Barton. Her eyes sparkled vivaciously and her hair, pulled back into a beaded chignon, was dark and glossy without a hint of grey. In her youth, Madame Vauloué must indeed have been the beauty Papa claimed her to be.

'Forgive me for being indisposed when you arrived - but Indian habits die hard. It is quite disgraceful but I cannot *exist* without my afternoon rest!' She laughed as if this failing was no disgrace at all but cause for some amusement.

A pulse of excitement raced through Francina. She had been brought up to titter, to smile with a closed mouth behind a gloved hand or a fan. But Aunt Vauloués laugh was free and fluent, flowing unchecked from the depths of her being.

'There is no need to ask who you are, my dear.'

Francina curtsied. There was something about that voice, the way it rose and fell . . . Aunt Barton had the same intonation, but Aunt Vauloué's voice was deeper. As her aunt kissed her cheek, a curious aroma of peppermint and sweet tobacco wafted over her.

'Now, let me look at you.'

Aunt Vauloué pushed her away to inspect her. As she moved, her blue silk gown rustled sensually and the crucifix on her bosom shimmered. 'How long have you been in mourning?'

'Well, I - about four months. For my cousin Charlie Doré.'

'Black does not become you.' Aunt Vauloué ran a cool finger

down her cheek. 'It does nothing for your complexion. No one follows the conventions of mourning in India. What a depressing place Calcutta would be if we did!' She laughed and turned to Papa: 'As you know only too well, Brother, we would all be turned out permanently in black!'

Papa tried to muster a smile.

'So formal, Frank? After all we have been through?' She rebuked him playfully from under half-closed lids, and held out her hand.

Papa bowed, but he could not bring himself to kiss her hand. He was being indefensibly rude.

Why had she insisted that he came in with her? He was going to spoil everything.

Aunt Vauloué smiled and pulled an embroidered bell cord. 'You will stay for tea?'

Perhaps she saw the hesitation in Papa's eyes, for she quickly added: 'Don't disappoint us, Brother. Bernard will not forgive me if I let you go before he has a chance to meet you again.'

Aunt Vauloué invit ed them to sit.

Francina sat captivated on the sofa as tea was brought in and laid out on a small table. Sipping tea, they discussed the weather and the damp London fogs. It was a stilted conversation, made all the more awkward by Papa's unsociability, but Aunt Vauloué appeared not to notice. At that moment Francina hated Papa. He was not even trying to be pleasant.

The doors opened and a foreign-looking gentleman, impeccably dressed, burst in.

Papa rose to his feet.

'My dear Duquesne, so good to see you again!' The gentleman shook his hand vigorously. Then he turned and smiled: 'Can this young lady really be the saucy little girl who used to tug at my sleeve and insist that we go out to feed the elephant?'

'Francina, this is your uncle, Bernard Vauloué.'

He kissed her hand in the flamboyant French manner, flicked out the skirt of his coat and sank into a chair. 'It is bitter outside! The snow will settle before the night is through.'

He was a small, dapper man, slightly taller than his wife but only half her weight. His eyes were dark, deep-set and languid - the eyes of someone who has lived long in the glare of an Indian sun. His small pointed beard, carefully trimmed in the style of the new French Emperor, was streaked with grey. He was some years older than Papa, but his movements were quick and energetic. It was easy to understand how Aunt Vauloué had fallen in love with him. He must have been very good-looking in his youth.

'Do you recall staying with us at Koxically, Francina?' he asked, stirring his tea.

She wished she could ask him about it, but was too conscious of Papa shifting uneasily opposite. She replied that she did not; smiling at Papa as she spoke and indicating with her eyes that she was still on his side.

'Don't you remember stepping in saucers of ice and leaving foot prints all over the verandah? What a little imp you were in those days!'

Saucers of ice? He had triggered a memory: swarms of children running along a verandah, jumping over shadows and landing in blinding squares of light . . .

'In the Cold Weather, dishes of water are placed on the verandah and sometimes, if the nights are particularly cold, a thin layer of ice will form, which in the morning the *bhisti* collects and stores in the ice-pit. But we always knew when you were the culprit, Francina,' smiled Uncle Vauloué. 'You could never resist making patterns with your footprints.'

She blushed into her teacup. She wanted so much to sparkle for her new relatives, but Papa was too inhibiting. She felt their eyes upon her, weighing her up, assessing her potential. She hoped she would not disappoint them.

'You had artistic leanings in those days.'

'She still does,' muttered Papa. 'She has made me a remarkable likeness of Angelo.'

Francina smiled encouragingly, relieved to see him join in the conversation.

'A pastime is a great asset in India, my dear,' smiled Aunt Vauloué. 'Sometimes the days can seem very long. It is as well to have an interest to while away the hours.'

'Koxically is much increased since you were there,' Uncle Vauloué was telling Papa. 'The output of indigo has almost doubled. But even so, inflation has eaten into the profits. We work harder, produce more, but hardly seem better off. These are uncertain times. Great changes are afoot - what with the war in Russia, the coming of the railways and the introduction of the electric telegraph -'

'Bernard, please! We do not wish to hear your theories on the state of India at this precise moment,' laughed Aunt Vauloué.

'But I'm sure Frank is interested to know how Koxically fares. After all, he was involved with the running of the place at one time.'

Aunt Vauloué turned to Francina: 'Your Papa was the young Assistant at Koxically when I first came to live there. The place was new to us both: he had only just arrived in India, and I was a blushing young bride. It was a delight to have a young man of refinement in our midst. One can become quite insular and uncivilised in the *mofussil*. But your father's dignified presence always pulled us up, reminding us of our manners.'

No longer, Francina thought. Papa was sitting on the edge of his seat with his knees tight together, his fingers twisting the place on his little finger that once sported a signet ring. Of course the Vauloués did not blurt out: How haggard you look! How the years have taken their toll! But she knew, just as Papa knew, that such thoughts must have crossed their minds.

'I leave the running of Koxically to Jules Savi these days. He manages it very well,' Uncle Vauloué was saying. 'He has been experimenting with jute this year. There is a great demand for it in Europe now that the war has cut off the supply from Russia.'

'Jules is my youngest brother. He was the page at our wedding,' Aunt Vauloué told Francina in an aside. She glanced coquettishly at Papa and raised her voice slightly: 'I believe it was at our wedding that your Papa first caught sight of your Mamma. She was my bridesmaid, and quite breathtaking she looked in her white gown with a garland of roses in her hair. I remember feeling quite put out by all the attention she was getting.'

'Dearest, no-one could possibly have surpassed you in beauty that day!' Her husband's voice caressed her with his words.

Inclining her head graciously, she continued with an arch smile: 'But it was your Papa's fine European ways that caught her eye. She was captivated by them - we all were.'

Francina waited for Aunt Vauloué to reveal more. Papa was staring at the patterned carpet. She wanted to catch his eye, to reassure him that she was not seduced by this talk, but he refused to look at her. Her eyes flew round the room and fell on a large portrait of two young boys in cream satin suits and frilly shirts. The elder had a bow in his hand, a quiver sprawled near his feet. The younger boy held up a dead pheasant.

Aunt's eyes followed hers to the painting. 'The small boy is Archie. This house belongs to General Balfour, Archie's father.'

'It is a very fine house.'

'Archie is Cissy's husband. He is the Magistrate at Balasore.'

Francina smiled, none the wiser. She stared at the pouting, rosy-cheeked child, copper tendrils glinting in the sunlight, and tried to imagine him as a grown man, perhaps with a wispy red moustache.

'I don't suppose you knew our daughter Cissie?'

Francina shook her head. She did not want to know about Aunt Vauloué's children.

'She was away at school when you stayed with us. I hope you meet her one day. I am sure you would like her. They have a little son now called Lionel. Each time I look at the portrait I am struck by his remarkable resemblance to Archie.'

'Is Lionel your first grandchild, Aunt Vauloué?'

'Indeed no! Lionel is our sixth grandchild. Eulalie has two children and Jacques has three.' Aunt turned to Papa: 'Do you remember Jacques, our first born? He used to follow you around like a little puppy, whining: 'Wait for me, Uncle Frank! Wait for me!' I can quite see how you lost your patience with him - but little Jacques kept coming back for more.'

Papa's mouth flickered into a faint smile. In celebration, Francina accepted another slice of gingerbread. It was a strange sensation not to have Aunt Doré's censorious eye upon her. As she bit into the moist bread, she could hear her saying: 'Young ladies must not appear greedy. Always leave a little on your plate and never accept another helping.'

'Jacques manages Moisgunge these days. He has a real flair for handling the *zaminders*,' Uncle Vauloué said proudly. 'He never negotiates over their heads. And the natives seem to respect him for it. There have been few disturbances in recent years - Mind you, he is always careful to be well protected. He has a loyal force of *lathiyals*.'

The name sounded familiar.

'Papa, did we not once live at Moisgunge?'

But it was Aunt Vauloué who answered.

'Certainly you did Francina. Dear little Albert was born at Moisgunge!'

Albert. The gingerbread stuck in her throat as her head filled with heart-rending screams. Baby Albert screaming for Mamma. She saw the expression on Papa's face. He remembered too.

'I regret - I must take my leave,' Papa stood up, 'before the weather closes in.'

'Surely you will stay to dine?' implored Aunt Vauloué. 'You must stay the night, and return home in the morning. It is far too disagreeable to venture out in this weather.'

'Indeed,' added Uncle Vauloué, 'we have hardly had a chance to talk.'

The protestations continued, but Papa would not change his mind. Aunt Vauloué pulled the bell-cord to order a cab but Papa quickly dissuaded her.

'The streets are full of passing cabs. I can easily hail one at the corner.'

Francina accompanied him down the stairs. When they were out of earshot, he turned to her and hissed: 'I could not endure that conceited nonsense for another moment!'

'Conceited nonsense, Papa?'

'All that talk of Jacques managing Moisgunge so well - and there being no trouble with the natives! It was an impertinent insult!'

'I am sure it was not meant as an insult, Papa.'

'I always suspected that the Vauloués had taken advantage of me - now I am certain!'

'Taken advantage of you, Papa?' She had no idea what he was talking about.

'They cheated me out of Moisgunge when I was weak and vulnerable. I practically gave it to them!' He was shaking with agitation. 'And now they have put that - that layabout in charge and have the audacity to boast that he is managing it better than I did!' His face was growing purple. 'Not content even with that, they are now taking away the thing most precious to me - my beloved daughter!'

In alarm Francina squeezed his arm, trying to calm him. 'No one can take me away, Papa,' she whispered. 'I shall always be your daughter, wherever I am.'

'There is something going on, I am convinced of it. Be on your guard, Francina. Promise me you will be on your guard?'

'I promise, Papa.'

'Oh, the humiliation of not being able to support my own daughter!'

The footman, waiting at the bottom of the stairs, was holding his umbrella and coat. Papa put it on and walked slowly away. She watched from the doorway until he had disappeared into the gloom. Only his footprints remained, glittering in the snow.

2

Quiet mutterings carry on the hot still air. The child slips out of bed and pads across china matting to the verandah. Peeping through the *chicks* she sees servants squatting in a shady spot just below the steps. They are watching a woman deep in thought meandering through the garden. The woman steps into a patch of light and her dress shimmers to a dazzling white. She is inspecting a shrub of scarlet blooms wilting in the heat. Plucking one, she holds it to her nose, inhaling so deeply that it seems more like a sigh.

Every part of the child aches to reach her - but her feet are pinned to the ground. She cannot move. She cannot raise the *chicks*. She tries to attract the woman's attention, but she cannot find her voice. Then, summoning supernatural strength, a tiny sound escapes - Mamma! Saying her name releases her spirits: they encircle her like a flock of sparrows, beating their wings against the *chicks* in a frenzy to escape. The commotion startles Mamma. She drops the flower. It falls on to the ground, leaving a vivid red gash down the front of her dress. She rubs at it, but the more she rubs, the more the stain spreads.

'Snowed in the night,' announced the maid, staggering into the bedroom with an enamel ewer which she set by a marble-topped washstand. 'Just a sprinklin' mind, but a right picture it looks.' She raised the blind and peered through the window. 'S'pect it'll melt soon enough, though,' she added cheerfully, her face scrubbed and wholesome as a burnished apple.

Francina stretched, and looked around the room. She had been too tired to take much notice of it last night. Papa's outburst had unsettled her and she had retired soon after dinner. But the Vauloués seemed to have understood. It was as if they all wanted to start afresh in the morning. And now, she thought, it *is* morning.

It was a pretty room, a young lady's room, comfortable and well appointed. As well as the usual bedroom furnishings, she noted an ornate writing-table, an easy chair and a slip-covered sofa. The pier-glass was draped in fine muslin and the toilette table had a lacy skirt. She watched the maid flit in front of the bed-curtains, deftly threading towels onto a clotheshorse, moving a chair, setting a screen between the door and the washstand. Grunting, she lifted the ewer and filled a china jug with water. A wisp of steam caught the light and curled to the ceiling.

'Anything else, Miss?' The maid poked the fire until flames burst into action. 'Do you wish for help with the dressing?'

Francina shook her head and yawned. 'What time is it?'

'Seven o'clock, by my reckonin', Miss.'

'Am I late?'

'Not to my knowledge, Miss.'

The maid paused in the doorway, her hand on the door knob, anxious to complete her tasks in good time: 'Madame wishes to see you in her room - when you are dressed, that is.'

'Before breakfast?'

'I believe so, Miss.'

'Francina?' called a voice from behind the screen. 'Is that you?'

'I apologise, Aunt Vauloué,' she mumbled, her face scarlet. 'I shall return later - when you are dressed.'

'Nonsense, child. I find it easier to talk in the morning, when my mind is fresh. Come in and sit down, I shall be finished directly.'

Francina smiled shyly at the maid combing a hairpiece at the toilette-table, and looked for somewhere to sit. Articles of dress were laid out on every available chair. An array of intimate under-garments of exquisite design were neatly folded and airing before the fire. Gingerly, Francina removed a stocking draped over the back of an embroidered prie-dieu, added it to undergarments folded on the clothes horse, and sat down.

'Did you sleep well?'

'Indeed, thank you, Aunt Vauloué. I was very comfortable.'

'I knew you would be happy in Miss Balfour's room. She is Archie's sister, you know.'

'Miss Balfour must be very charming,' called Francina above the trickle of water, 'if her room is any indication of her personality.'

'Speak up, child! I did not catch what you said.'

'I was just saying,' - she raised her voice - 'Miss Balfour must be a charming young lady.'

'Indeed she is. Cissie is very fortunate. She has married well - into a highly regarded and well-respected family. An *old* Indian family. There is something very particular about old Indian families, Francina. We have something of the *laisser-faire* about us. So different from those *arrivistes* who barge into the country with their fixed ideas and arrogant ways.'

A plump naked arm emerged round the screen and groped for a towel. The maid placed the hair-piece on the stand, picked up a towel and disappeared behind the screen.

'And now my dear,' called Aunt Vauloué, 'we must make it our business to see that you marry well.'

For a moment she did not recognise the face, unadorned by powder and potions that peered round the screen. She stood up and curtsied.

'Sit *down*, child! I cannot have you bobbing up and down every time I come into the room. I cannot abide formality and stiffness. We must be friends and you must call me Aunt Cecilia.'

Aunt, now encased in a flowing peignoir, sat down heavily at her toilette-table and peered at her in the glass: 'You must take me into your confidence, Francina, and regard me with as much affection as you do your own Mamma.'

The maid selected a silver brush from the table and brushed her mistress's hair with long, firm strokes. She picked up a small bottle warming before the fire, uncorked it, and poured a few drops onto her hands. With expert fingers she kneaded the solution into her mistress's scalp. A delightful scent filled the room: summer flowers, lily of the valley. Aunt Cecilia leaned back and closed her eyes.

Francina watched this ritual, enthralled. She had never in the whole time she had lived at Elm House, witnessed Aunt Doré's intimate toilette. Indeed, Aunt Doré would never subject herself to such indulgences. Plain soap and water. No fancy perfumed potions for her.

The maid knotted Aunt's hair into a small tight bun at the nape of her neck, took the hair-piece off the stand, twisted it and pinned it expertly over the bun. Then she added a beaded chignon. The effect was immediate. Aunt Cecilia looked ten years younger, serene and beautiful, with a head of luxurious black hair.

Francina caught her eye in the glass and blushed.

'*Ingénue!* Are you shocked? It is my own hair.'

'Indeed no, Aunt.' These days, falsehoods slipped easily off her tongue.

Aunt Cecilia stood before the pier-glass in a chemise and under-petticoat, put her hands on her hips, took a deep breath and braced herself.

The maid pulled hard at the stays.

'Tighter,' she gasped. 'Tighter!'

The magnificent bosom burst over the stays as the maid yanked mightily.

'The discomfort one must endure for fashion!' Aunt Cecilia sank into a chair and rested her leg on a footstool. 'I once had a waist as small as yours, Francina, but by the time it was fashionable to show it off, I seemed to be constantly *enceinte*.'

Francina blushed again. She was not supposed to know about such things.

'Stand up, child. Turn round. Let me look at you.'

Francina twirled self-consciously. Aunt Cecilia scrutinised her carefully while her maid struggled to roll up her stockings. First one leg, then the other.

'That dress will not do at all. Far too gloomy for a young girl.'

'But I am in mourning, Aunt Cecilia.'

'Then it is high time you came out of mourning. Four months for a cousin is long enough. You must change to *Indian* ways now, Francina. It would be most unfortunate if you step on board ship in mourning. Think of the fun you will miss if you cannot dance or join in the games!' Aunt Cecilia stepped into a crinoline frame. 'Besides, you must look your best when you meet Theresa.'

Her heart jumped. 'Mamma?'

Aunt Cecilia leaned forward with arms outstretched. 'There was no time to consult you. We had to act quickly. In your absence, Francina,' called her muffed voice, as petticoats and skirts obscured her head, 'I have made arrangements for you to meet Theresa in Malta.'

'Malta?'

Aunt Cecilia emerged above yards of wine brocade. 'Don't look so gormless, child. Now, do you see that letter on the window seat? It is for you.'

How Francina walked over the window without keeling over she did not know, but the distance to the letter seemed as far as a walk to India. She picked up the bulky envelope and stared at the handwriting. Her name was written across it, *Miss Francina Duquesne,* in a neat feminine hand, perfectly slanted, the capital letters executed with a small artistic flourish. Mamma's hand. She stared at her name, her mind swirling with possibilities. She could not help herself composing the words inside: *My dearest daughter, how can I possibly find the words to express my remorse at having so cruelly and deliberately cast you away? Not a day passes when I do not think of you. I curse that impulsive moment when I lost my head and abandoned you. Can you ever find it in your heart to forgive me?*

With trembling fingers, she unfolded the letter.

Beerbhoom, Sooree, Bengal

My dear Francina,

This is the first opportunity I have had since you were parted from me to write to you in the hope that this letter might reach you. I was very glad to meet Angelo, although I did not recognise him, but it was not his fault. His Father is to blame. He has ruined your prospects in life by keeping you in the dark as to my situation.

As soon as I learned that you are coming out to India, I wrote to my sister Cecilia Vauloué, enclosing £50 towards your expenses, telling her that should you wish to come to me, you would have the means and the power to do so. In truth, dear Francina, you have only to express that wish, and that wish can be fulfilled. As we are returning to England when you travel out, I am making arrangements for us to meet in Malta, where I will embrace you and keep you forever. It would take up too much time for me to write more, but as soon as you receive this, tell me what you would like to do. On calculation, I find there is scarcely time for your answer to reach me before we start (we leave India for England next March) so write to me by return, directing your letter "Mrs Havers to wait till called for" at the Post Office, Valetta, Malta.

To prevent the possibility of this letter falling into hostile hands, I will send it c/o my sister, Madame Vauloué.

Angelo will accompany us as far as Galle.

With love, your affectionate Mother, Elizabeth Theresa Havers

15 December 1855

'What will happen to me?' Francina whispered. 'Am I to live with Mamma?'

'That will be entirely up to you, but it is Theresa's wish that you should leave the ship at Malta and return to England with her. Now, Francina, we must examine your wardrobe, and if necessary shop for new outfits. One way or the other you must be properly turned out.'

3

She surveyed her bedroom like an actress contemplating a new rôle. Every available surface was piled high with packages and parcels. She ran her fingers lightly over the cool silks and muslins, the lacy trimmings, the pearl buttons, the ribbons, bows, the exquisite little bonnets . . . Louisa would be astonished to see her surrounded by so many beautiful outfits. She ought to write and tell her - but how could she do so without dropping the hint that she might never reach India? This secret was too big to tell anyone.

Could she step into this part? She ought to feel delighted to be the recipient of such generosity, but all she felt was overwhelming guilt. *Something is going on, I am convinced of it. Be on your guard.*

Papa was right. These packages are proof of a conspiracy, a conspiracy hatched by Mamma and Aunt Cecilia.

My dear, you will never be swayed by the evil influences that abound in a country where propriety is wanting. Remember, Francina, the happiness of your future depends on your striving to uphold all that your aunt has taught you.

She stared at her reflection in the pier-glass. It was reassuring to see the familiar picture: the sensible girl in her dull black bombazine, dressed in Aunt Doré's image. If she accepted these gifts was she siding with the enemy?

She re-read Mamma's letter (but by now she could almost recite it by heart) still hoping to find the words she was so sure she had overlooked: the words of remorse and sorrow. But they were not there. Yet despite her misgivings, the years of pain and the hurt, she knew she must meet Mamma. The cord was too strong, the knot too tight. Mamma had bound her up like a spider traps her prey; smothered her so tight, she was choking.

There was a knock on the door. A footman entered with a note. It was from Papa announcing that he was unwell and would not be attending the Vauloués' party after all.

Francina threw open the lid of her trunk. It was a relief to know that Papa was not coming tonight, for how could she face him with such a monumental secret hanging over her head? She unpacked her cream moiré silk, shook it out, and held it against herself as she stared into the glass. She had worn black for so long that she had forgotten how well she looked in cream. Perhaps it was time to come out of mourning. And this was not really a betrayal - it was her old gown. She pulled the bell-cord, and waited for the maid to arrive.

'You rang, Miss?'

'Is there time to have this ironed for the party this evening?'

'I'll speak to the laundry maid. Such a pretty gown! A right picture you'll look, if you don't mind me saying, Miss.'

The maid gathered up the dress and left the room.

Francina returned to her reflection. Could she do something different with her hair? Aunt Cecilia was probably having her afternoon rest, but her maid might be laying out her clothes for the evening . . . She tiptoed along the corridor to Aunt's boudoir and knocked timidly.

After a few moments the door opened a crack and the maid peered out.

'Who is it?' called a sleepy voice from the depths of the room.

'I did not mean to disturb you, Aunt, I just wanted to speak to -'

'Come *in*, child, come in.'

Francina sidled round the door. There was a strange smell in the room that clung to the back of her throat. Aunt Cecilia was wrapped in a silk peignoir, lying on a low ottoman propped up by cushions.

'Did you wish to see me, dear?'

Francina just stood there. She had sometimes seen an old gypsy woman sucking a pipe at the fair, and sometimes when she had ventured down the seamier streets of St Pierre, vulgar women had sauntered by puffing cigars. She had never seen a respectable woman smoking.

'I'm sorry, Aunt,' she whispered.

'Don't look so appalled, Francina. It's a bad habit, I know, but a harmless one.'

'I was wondering if I might have some advice on my hair.'

Aunt Cecilia smiled sleepily, and retreated into her cloud of heady vapours. 'Murphy, how should my niece dress her hair?'

Francina waited. The maid opened a drawer, pulled out a pair of white silk stockings and placed them carefully over the back of a chair. Only when she had completed this task, did she deign to turn round. She was making it quite plain that attending to the mistress's niece was not one her duties.

'Murphy, is there time to dress my niece's hair for this evening?' Aunt asked again, drawing heavily on the cheroot and exhaling a stream of scented vapour through her nostrils.

'Yes, Madam.'

'Return to your room, Francina,' Aunt said without opening her eyes. 'I shall send Murphy to you directly.'

Francina slipped away and fell onto her bed. For some incomprehensible reason she felt deceived. She had so wanted Aunt to be perfect - and not just to prove Papa wrong. Shamefaced, she stood up and stared into the pier-glass. What was happening to her? Poor Papa was ill, and she was so preoccupied with her own selfish vanity that she had not for one moment considered his predicament.

She floated down the stairs in her cream gown and new metal hoops. 'They will be a great boon in India,' Aunt Cecilia had said, 'they are so light and we can dispense with many petticoats. My only anxiety is that they might rust in the Rains.' Whether she reached India or not was beside the point, Aunt was right - her skirts belled and swayed as lightly as feather down.

It took some courage to enter the room full of chattering strangers but she was determined to make a good impression. She had left her fears in the bedroom, stuffed them under the pillow along with Papa's suspicions.

Aunt Cecilia took her arm and whispered, 'How charming you look, my dear.'

Francina smiled. She caught her reflection in a tall gilt glass, and for a second did not recognised herself. It was not just the arrangement of her glossy hair or the sheen of her cream silk gown, everything about her glowed. She glanced again, just to make sure. She had never considered herself beautiful before.

Aunt Cecilia's laugh tinkled round the room. She had recovered from her tobacco dreams, and apart from the trace of peppermint on her breath, there was nothing else to hint of her secret habit.

Francina stood by her side and curtsied each time she was presented, shivering a little when a lady remarked on her likeness to Aunt Cecilia.

There were five guests in all: a small excitable woman in her mid-thirties; her ramrod husband, whose fiery whiskers burst so startlingly from his cheeks that he might have just stepped out of a *Punch* magazine; a large overbearing woman and her opinionated husband; and a plump gentleman in his early sixties with a flushed countenance and soft fleshy jowls.

They seemed curious about her, firing questions, which she answered as evasively as possible. Then it occurred to her: no one here knew her history or anything about her. She was here simply as the Vauloués' niece. It gave her a sense of liberty, a strange new confidence.

'Will this be your first time in India, Miss Duquesne?'

'I was there as a small child but I remember very little.'

'My advice to anyone new to India is to observe three simple rules: *one,* keep out of the sun by day; *two,* avoid chills at night; and *three,* take regular doses of quinine.'

'Quinine, Mr Newbold?'

'It is a wonderful preventative. Just a few grains every other day is all that is required. I have lived in some very unhealthy districts, yet have never been afflicted by the ague, while others round about me have dropped like flies.'

'Harold,' cooed his wife, 'don't frighten the poor child.'

'I intended precisely the opposite, my dear. If Miss Duquesne follows my advice she will enjoy good health and a long untroubled life in India.'

The jowly gentleman handed her in to dinner. He seemed quiet and preoccupied, and Francina wondered if he was recovering from a recent sorrow, so whenever their eyes met, she gave him a sympathetic smile. Mr Cunningham, on her left, the husband of the overbearing woman, was dominating the conversation with talk of India. Judging by their sallow skins and deep-set eyes, they must all be on furlough from India, she decided.

Aunt Cecilia out-shone them all. Her wine-dark velvet gown set off the creamy skin of her neck and shoulders, and in the candlelight, her bare arms glowed like polished ivory. Her décolleté on any other woman of her years might have looked immodest, but on her looked magnificent (although Aunt Doré would hardly approve). Mr Moorhouse, her jowly neighbour, certainly approves, Francina thought. His eyes have hardly left Aunt for a moment. Perhaps he is not suffering from a sorrow after all.

Aunt Cecilia sipped her champagne, and gave Francina a little nod. Francina glowed with happiness. Does it really matter if Aunt smokes in her dressing-room?

'I tell you, Mr Newbold, I almost fainted with fright when the guard poked his hairy visage through our carriage window. I thought we had been invaded!'

'I cannot abide this hideous fashion for unkempt faces. It is just another affectation that our soldiers are bringing back from the war,' said Mrs Newbold.

'It is just an excuse for slovenliness as far as I am concerned,' said Mr Newbold. 'Soldiers should be properly turned out. If there are standards in dress, there will be discipline on the battlefield.'

'Discipline is a serious problem in the Crimea, I understand.'

'Indeed it is, Mrs Vauloué. If our troops can find time to smoke then they can find time to shave. It is all a question of priorities.

'I was offered a *cigarette* the other day.'

'Pray, what is a cigarette, Mr Cunningham?'

'A small thin cheroot wrapped in paper, Mrs Newbold. Can you imagine anything so ludicrous? If a man has not the stomach for a cigar, he should not indulge at all. Only a *fop* would be seen smoking such a thing!'

The conversation became bolder as glasses drained. Francina plucked up courage to sip her dessert wine. A warm sensation, not entirely disagreeable, slipped down her throat. Wine was tolerated at Elm House only when guests were present, and even then Aunt Doré never indulged. Aunt would have liked to ban liquor completely from the house but that was one sin Uncle Doré had staunchly refused to give up. Drink and smoke mingled copiously in his library - with or without the company of guests. What are they doing at home at this moment, she wondered, while I sit in this glittering dining room picking at my *charlotte russe* and sipping dessert wine? Nothing will have changed. It will all be just as I remember.

'It was the most extraordinary phenomenon I ever beheld!' said Mrs Newbold, nodding to the footman with the decanter.

'And how did this phenomenon manifest itself?'

'Oh dear, it is very difficult to explain -'

'Well then, Mrs Newbold, after dinner you must demonstrate!'

'Indeed! It would be so amusing.'

Mrs Newbold looked doubtful and glanced at her husband.

'We are only asking for a demonstration, Mrs Newbold. We do not expect you to conjure up spirits. Just show us the procedure.'

'Oh, please do!' cried Aunt Cecilia, 'I have heard so much about this vogue for table-turning, but I have never had the pleasure of attending a séance.'

Uncle Vauloué looked sharply at her, but Aunt Cecilia was in an exalted mood, so different from the languid creature Francina had discovered in the boudoir. She was growing used to her aunt's fluctuating moods: the times when her passions overflowed, and the times when she was as serene and calm as it was possible to be. But whatever his wife's humours, Uncle Vauloué, her devoted and steadfast companion, accepted them without reservation.

Francina had enjoyed their tête-à-tête on the way to hear the preachers at the Foundling Hospital, while Aunt attended Mass elsewhere. She could not believe that Uncle Vauloué was as devious as Papa implied. She had seen his compassion when confronting the mothers with their babies at the gates of the Hospital. The better she knew Uncle Vauloué, the more she liked him.

'What was Papa like, when he first came to India?' she had ventured to ask.

Uncle placed a coin into the hat of a beggar propped up against the railings while he considered the question. 'Quiet and conscientious as I recall. But the girls soon brought him out. He was no match for the girls.'

'The girls, Uncle?'

'Cecilia and Theresa. They were mischievous. Always playing tricks. But your papa was too polite to send them on their way,'

Leaving the gentlemen to their port and cigars, the ladies left the dining-room to prepare for the séance. Mrs Newbold had finally capitulated. Away from their husband's eyes, the ladies fussed about the drawing room, issuing conflicting instructions to the footmen to rearrange the furniture. Francina sat on the window seat. She wanted no part in this table-turning experiment. Cook, for all her knowledge of that kind of thing, would never lift the veil on the Spirit World. 'Folk have been struck down for tampering where they have no business,' she used to say.

By the time the gentlemen arrived, a round table covered with a green cloth and six chairs had been placed in the centre of the room. Uncle Vauloué joined her on the window seat. He seemed to share her unease.

Mrs Newbold took her seat at the table. 'It is customary to have no light in the room, I believe.'

Candles were extinguished and guests groped for their chairs.

'Now we must have complete silence during this experiment,' whispered Mrs Newbold. 'Mr Moorhouse, as you are nearest to the fire, might I ask you to open the séance with a suitable reading? *Revelations* perhaps? We will hold hands, shut our eyes and clear our minds of all irrelevant thought. Our senses must be acute, our minds passive. Should a spirit wish to contact us, we shall be susceptible to the message.'

With the aid of a flickering candle, Mr Moorhouse thumbed through the Holy Book.

Military gentlemen stared haughtily down from their portraits to the group hunched expectantly round the table, ready to strike out dissent with their sabres.

At last Mr Moorhouse cleared his throat.

'*I looked and behold a door was opened in Heaven: and the first voice which I heard as it were of a trumpet talking with me; which said, Come up hither, and I will shew thee things which must be hereafter . . .*'

In the taut silence, shadows loomed across the walls, twitching with a life of their own. Mr Newbold's shadow was taunting the stuffed owl in the glass case. Unmoved, the bird's large yellow eyes stared defiantly into space.

'Does a spirit wish to contact us?' whispered Mrs Newbold into the silence.

No one stirred.

Can't they see the shadows flickering, mocking, dancing behind the portraits? Francina's heart beat faster. Why had she come out of mourning? What if Charlie should come and see her dressed so disrespectfully? She stared into the fire, her throat tight.

'Is anyone out there?' whispered Aunt Cecilia.

She was speaking in Mamma's voice.

Is anyone out there?

The embers were crackling and spitting, spewing orange flames up the chimney. Blood pounded in Francina's head.

Mamma, Mamma! What are you doing? May I come in?

The fire was growing hotter by the second; brighter and hotter, overwhelming her with its heat. Soon the whole room was bathed in a blinding hard white light.

Go away child. Go back to bed!

Why is Baby crying so? Make him stop, Mamma. Make him stop!

4

'Would you think it an inconvenience, Aunt, if I did not accompany you to the Crystal Palace today but paid Papa a visit instead? I am rather anxious about him.'

'An excellent idea! We shall have an early tiffin and go after my rest,' smiled Aunt Cecilia, passing her a scolding cup of coffee. 'I shall use the morning to catch up with my correspondence. I have been somewhat remiss of late.'

Francina's heart fell. She had hoped to have a few private words with Papa. There were questions she wanted to ask him. She had tossed and turned last night, trying to drive them from her mind. 'That is very kind, Aunt, but there is no need to change your plans on my account. A servant could show me the way. How long do you suppose it would take me to walk?'

'Walk? The very idea! You are not in Guernsey now you know. I will accompany you and we shall take the carriage. Now, Francina, may I pass you a muffin?'

Francina picked at the handle of the basket resting on her lap. She lifted a corner of the napkin. Apples, pears, an orange and a bottle of preserve nestled on a bed of straw. But would Papa feel insulted? He could so easily think this was a gift of charity. She had reverted to her old bombazine dress and cape - she did not have the courage to face Papa any other way. Aunt had raised her eyebrows at breakfast, but said nothing. Francina knew it was unlucky to come out of mourning, and then return to it. 'Once mourning clothes are set aside they should be burnt or discarded,' Cook would say. But wasn't that just an old wives' tale? But it had been a mistake to wear her cream gown last night. She was so sure that Charlie's spirit would materialise that she had fainted, bringing the table-turning experiment to an abrupt end, Aunt had said.

The watery light exposed a bleak district of rundown foundries and shops (the pawn-broker's seemed the only lucrative business in the area, judging by the stream of people shuffling in and out with bundles under their arms). The snow had all but melted; leaving behind brown slurry - a blessing in some ways, for it filled the potholes and made for a smoother ride. Goods, pitiful goods, spilled from the second-hand clothing and furniture shops into the streets. Everything had lost its colour, smothered under layers of soot and grime. If they were driving through an artist's charcoal drawing, it could not have looked much different.

The coachman shouted something abusive and brought the coach to a juddering halt, as a bone cart tried to manoeuvre through the gates of a glue factory in front of them. It was an unfortunate place to stop. Apart from the stench of rotting carcasses, smoke billowing from the factory chimney was powdering everything in the vicinity in a fine ash. Even the finches hunched in their cages outside the bird-fancier's shop had turned white.

Aunt Cecilia banged on the carriage roof with her parasol handle. 'Do hurry, coachman!'

Searching through her reticule, she brought out a small bottle of patchouli, which she dabbed onto her handkerchief, urging Francina to do the same.

The heavy oily scent made Francina's eyes smart but at least it drowned the evil smell. Blinking, she glanced out of the window. A forlorn young creature, hardly more than a child, was sitting on a doorstep nursing a baby. The girl looked up and caught her eye.

Francina turned away, relieved to feel the carriage move again.

'Aunt, did you ever know - I mean, did you ever see Baby?'

'Baby? Do you mean Cissie's baby?'

'No, my baby brother. Albert.'

'Only once.' Aunt removed her handkerchief to test the sweetness of the air. 'It was the year you came to Koxically for Christmas. He was about four or five months old, as I recall.'

'What was he like?'

Aunt returned the handkerchief to her nose. 'A bonny baby with a halo of curls and an adorable smile. He melted all our hearts. Theresa called him her Little Treasure.'

'Do you know why he died, Aunt?'

'Not really. He grew poorly when you returned to Moisgunge -

why, none of us could understand, for he was the picture of health at Christmas. But Theresa grew increasingly anxious about him. She would write long rambling letter detailing his ailments.'

It made no sense. How could Mamma abandon a sick baby, her 'Little Treasure'? Perhaps she had misunderstood. If Albert had died before Mamma left, she could almost understand, almost forgive her. Baby's death would have made Mamma distraught, inconsolable; vulnerable to the charms of a devious man chancing his luck.

'When did Albert die, Aunt?'

'My goodness - Oh, I remember: it was when Henri had scarlet fever, or we would certainly have attended his funeral.'

'Yes, but did Albert die before or after Mamma left?'

But Aunt was distracted. The carriage had turned into a paved yard and pulled up. The coachman jumped down and opened the door. 'Doyle House, ma'am.'

Francina followed Aunt out of the carriage and peered at Doyle House. At least *Mrs Hills's Private Boarding House* possessed pretensions to respectability. It was a double fronted, three-storied house with two attic windows. Despite its shabby façade, the windows were clean and the front steps had been scrubbed. In the last century, perhaps, it had stood alone in leafy grounds, now it was squeezed in on all sides by mean redbrick buildings.

Aunt picked up her skirts, stepped round something nasty lying on the flagstones, and rapped on the front door.

The young girl who opened it seemed surprised to see a lady of fashion on the doorstep. Aunt held out her card.

'Does Mr Duquesne reside here?'

The girl wiped her hands on her apron and took the card with the tips of her fingers.

'If you please, wait in here, m'um. I'll see if he's in.'

Ushering them inside, she closed the door and scurried upstairs.

The hall was long and dark, lit only by fanlight above the front door. Francina wished she could open the door again and let out the fusty smell of boiled cabbage and rising damp. Aunt Cecilia was still holding her handkerchief to her nose. Francina stared at the basket and prayed with all her might that Papa was out and they could leave this horrid place.

Somewhere upstairs a door opened. Furtive whispers carried down the stairs, closely followed by a noise that sounded like furniture being rearranged. Skirts rustled and keys jangled. Then a woman hurried downstairs adjusting her cap.

'Hi *do* apologise! Whatever must you think? The boy is on an errand. But welcome ladies, welcome to Doyle House!'

Seeing that the two strangers in the hall looked bemused, the woman tittered. 'Oh, my goodness, hi am quite forgetting myself. Hi am Mrs Hills - the *proprietor* of Doyle House.'

Had she admitted to being the proprietor of Blenheim Palace, Mrs Hills could not have done so with more pride. She was a slim, middle-aged woman, neatly turned out, but the effect was spoilt by her loud, grating voice. She let out a gasp and clasped her hands to her bosom.

'Miss Duquesne? Miss Francina Duquesne? Your pa has told me all about you! Hi am so pleased to meet you, so pleased, to be sure!'

For an alarming second it looked as if Mrs Hills was about to peck her on the cheek. Francina took a step backwards. What had Papa told her? Had they read her letters together, smiling as they learned of her little excursions and petty anxieties?

'Mrs Hills,' she said, 'I believe I must thank you for the care you have shown my father. He has told me of the many kindnesses you have shown him.'

Mrs Hills flushed. 'Miss Francina, it is a honour to have a gentleman such as your pa residing under my roof, a rare honour, hi assure you!'

'Is Mr Duquesne at home?'

'Indeed he is, Mrs Vauloué, indeed he is. But out of sorts, and somewhat reluctant to receive callers today. But hi persuaded him,' Mrs Hills aimed a smile at Francina. 'Mr Duquesne, hi said, these ladies are no ordinary visitors. One of them is your daughter, and she has travelled a long way to see you. You cannot disappoint her!' She raised her eyes to the top of the stairs and whispered, 'Between you and me, some gentlemen want a little fussing over, if you get my meaning.'

Francina checked the bubble of indignation rising in her throat. Papa might be beholden to this uncouth woman, but there was no reason why she should be.

'In that case, Mrs Hills,' said Aunt Cecilia, 'would you kindly direct us to Mr Duquesne's rooms?'

'Certainly, ladies. Please follow me.' Mrs Hills picked up her skirts and climbed the stairs. 'Mr Duquesne's rather cramped these days since he condensed into one room, but he's cosy, very cosy.'

Papa was sitting before a small glowing fire with a rug tucked round his knees. The room was warm, the air stale. Francina tiptoed to his chair and kissed him on the cheek. His brow glistened and his breath smelled sour.

'How are you, Papa?'

He smiled, a tight-lipped smile. 'Francina, you should not have come. It's too far.'

His resentment cut through her like a knife. 'Nonsense, Papa!' she said gaily. 'We - Aunt Cecilia and I - were both so worried.'

She held up the basket of fruit as a futile offering of peace.

Mrs Hills pounced on the basket. 'Isn't that kind of Miss Francina, sir?' she said, placing the basket on a side table. 'Very thoughtful, to be sure!'

He gave her a long-suffering smile.

Taking courage from his smile, Mrs Hills bustled about the room. 'We must find chairs for the visitors, must we not Mr Duquesne?' She was about to push a chair forward, but checked herself. 'Where's that boy? Why does he always disappear when he's wanted? A good cuff round the ear hi'll give him when hi catch him!'

'Perhaps I can sit here.' Francina indicated a bed, half-hidden behind a screen decorated with yellowing lacquered engravings.

'Miss Francina, we do things proper here!' Mrs Hills leaned out of the door and called shrilly, 'Peg!'

The young girl scurried breathlessly up the stairs.

'Yes, m'um?'

'Peg, put this chair near the fire for Madame Vauloué. And fetch the stool from the parlour. You know, the one with the green padded seat - 'scuse my language.'

'Now, m'um?'

'Of course *now*, you numbskull!'

While Francina waited for the stool, Aunt Cecilia enquired about Papa's health. Illness was the one topic on which Papa could talk indefinitely. Aunt Cecilia nodded at appropriate moments, throwing in the occasional word of advice. Francina cast her eyes around the room. She had often tried to picture Papa here, writing his letters. But in her imagination his room was light and spacious. How could Papa endure to stare day after day at this gloomy swirling wallpaper? This room was crammed with furniture, and little light seeped between the heavy curtains. A small desk faced the window on which were placed a few books and writing implements. She pictured Papa sitting there staring across the dull mosaic of roofs and smoking chimneys. A half-written letter lay on the desk. Had Mrs Hills just interrupted him, glancing slyly over his shoulder as she informed him of the visitors? Had he put down his pen, taken his seat by the fire and quickly tucked the rug around his knees?

Her daguerreotype portrait stood on the mantelpiece, a reminder of her last visit to London, sitting in the photographer's studio with her hands folded in her lap, trying not to move. She looked so serious, scowling almost, but she had been anything but solemn that day. She remembered quite clearly, sitting with the head clamp pressing behind her ears, trying not to laugh when Charlie and Angelo pulled faces at her behind the photographer's back.

The maid appeared, and placed a stool between Aunt Cecilia and Papa. Francina sat down. This was not how she had envisaged her visit to Papa. She had pictured the two of them talking intimately, catching up with all those lost years - not veering cautiously from one safe topic to another while Mrs Hills fussed in the background, interrupting whenever it suited her. How could Papa allow himself to be tyrannized by that woman? Could he not see that she was a vain silly creature, who flattered herself that Papa thought something of her?

The maid reappeared with a tray of refreshments and placed it on a little table. Mrs Hills poured the tea, apologising profusely that there was no cake to offer.

'We passed much scaffolding on our way, Papa,' Francina bit into a stale scone.

'Scaffolding?'

'Many public buildings are to be illuminated. We saw workmen fixing rows of tiny lights, in preparation for the Peace Celebrations.'

'By all accounts the firework display will be quite spectacular,' added Aunt Cecilia.

'We will not see it in these parts, I dare say,' muttered Papa.

'Well, not as far as here - but Horse Guards, Whitehall and The Mall. And all the shopkeepers are decorating their windows with flags. It looks so gay, Papa!'

Papa eyed her black apparel. 'So much suffering, so many lives lost. I trust you will not be celebrating when the Treaty is signed, Francina? I expect you to spare a thought for your poor aunt and cousins in Guernsey at this time.'

'Of course, Papa.'

'Merciful heaven! So the war's finally over? Hi can hardly believe it. May hi tempt you ladies to partake of another cup? And you, sir?'

'That will be all, Mrs Hills.' There was spark of irritation in Papa's voice.

'There's nothing else you require, sir?'

'No, Mrs Hills,'

Mrs Hills pursed her lips, picked up the basket of fruit and left the room, closing the door sharply behind her.

Good riddance. Francina knew it was wrong and ungracious, in view of all she had done for Papa, but she could not help feeling that Mrs Hills was scheming to step into Mamma's shoes. The idea might have been amusing if it were not so preposterous.

But it was no easier making conversation in Mrs Hills' absence, for they had covered most topics of a trivial nature and discussed Papa's illnesses to the point of exhaustion.

'Francina has adapted well to Town life,' said Aunt Cecilia, introducing the one subject that had been overlooked. 'You must not be at all concerned for her welfare, Frank. She has become a perfect little companion. I have grown very fond of her.'

Papa stared blankly into the fire. 'It is a long time since I enjoyed my daughter's company. Now, I suppose, I never will.'

'But there is still time, Papa!'

She leaned forward and took his hand. It was as clammy as dough. 'Perhaps tomorrow - or the day after - we could spend the day together? If you are well enough, of course, and Aunt has no objection? My trunks are packed. Everything is ready.'

'I have no objection.' Aunt Cecilia looked at her and smiled. 'Tomorrow is perfect. I have a number of small tasks to complete which will occupy most of the day. But in the evening we go to

Drury Lane to see the *Il Travatore.* Would you care to join us, Frank? There is plenty of room in the box.' She brushed her skirts and stood up. 'It is time I left you both to have a quiet little talk. I shall sit in the carriage and wait. Do not hurry, Francina.'

Smiling genially, Aunt Cecilia took her leave.

Now there were no more excuses. She was alone with Papa. Now was the moment to ask all those questions that had troubled her. She took a deep breath.

'I am disappointed, grievously disappointed.'

'Why, Papa?'

'I expressly forbade you to come here, Francina. Why did you go against my wishes?'

'I am sorry, Papa, but I was worried.'

'I have told you often enough, Francina, that I am well looked after. There is no reason to worry. But to bring that *opinionated* aunt of yours to gloat over my misfortune! How could you humiliate me so? Do you think I have no feelings? Do you think I enjoy living like this? Despite my misfortunes over these long difficult years, there has always been one source of comfort: the knowledge that my beloved daughter is in Guernsey, well out of harm's way; safe from the corrupting influences of her mother and her scheming family.'

'I do not think,' Francina gulped back tears, 'that Aunt Vauloué is as scheming as you make out, Papa. I do not believe it was her intention to gloat.'

'Has she bewitched you already, Francina? Do you presume to know her better than I do? I saw her inspect this room. I saw the look of triumph in her eyes!'

Her younger self on the chimneypiece with skirts spread and ankles crossed, stared down at her, but offered no solace.

'I married her sister. They could have been twins, they were so alike. I know how she thinks. You cannot trust her. Your mother broke her word. *Till death do us part*, she said. Once before a Catholic priest and once before an Anglican priest. She broke her vows *twice*, Francina - twice before God!' Beads of sweat trickled down his temples. He bowed his head and his shoulders began to shake.

Silence rose like a wall between them. He was waiting for her to climb over; to fall on her knees, to take his hands and join him in condemning her mother. But she could not move.

'I have stayed too long, Papa,' she whispered.

'Yes, Francina. I am tired.'

'I shall go now. Will you be alright, Papa?'

'I shall rest now. Good-bye, Francina.'

She kissed his clammy brow. She should not leave him like this, spent and broken. But she could not help herself.

'Good-bye, Papa.'

She tiptoed out of the room and closed the door. She crept down the stairs like a sleepwalker.

Mrs Hills was waiting by the front door. 'You are leaving, Miss Duquesne?'

'My father is resting, Mrs Hills. He does not wish to be disturbed.'

'Will we see you again, my dear, before you sail to India?'

Francina pulled up her gloves and stared pointedly at the latch. 'Goodbye, Mrs Hills. Thank you for your hospitality.' Her smile was the epitome of correctness.

Mrs Hills opened the front door.

HEADING EAST
April 1856

Dr Guise leaned across the table. 'You have recovered from your *mal de mere*, Miss Duquesne?' he asked.

'I believe so, doctor. I heeded your advice and have taken turns on deck. I feel much better. - Have you suffered at all?'

'Dear me, no! I'm a tough old sea dog and quite used to sea travel. This will be my fourth trip to India.'

'And our last, we hope,' interjected his wife.

The steamer lurched violently. Passengers instinctively dived for glasses and decanters and held them aloft until the moment passed.

'We will soon be leaving the tempestuous Atlantic Ocean for the calmer waters of the Mediterranean,' Mrs Guise said reassuringly, between mouthfuls of boiled beef.

Francina smiled and glanced round the saloon. She did not know many of the passengers yet. There are about forty in First Class, she supposed. Most were old Indian hands by the way they talked and swaggered, but there were a few newcomers, or *griffins* as Aunt Cecilia called them. They were the wan creatures trying to find their sea legs, such as Mrs Price, the young woman sitting opposite toying with the food on her plate. She looked deathly white, and young - hardly more than seventeen. Francina gave her a sympathetic smile. If there was anyone on this ship with whom she would like to strike up a friendship, it was Mrs Price.

Captain Price was sitting next to his wife. He was some years older, fair-haired with a fine set of whiskers. Francina had overheard them whispering as they sat down: 'Why have we been placed on *this* table, Minnie? Just because Hamilton's people are acquainted with the Captain, it shouldn't give him the right to disregard Precedence. He's only a Lieutenant of four years standing. It is most irregular.'

'Please don't fuss, Edward,' whispered his wife.

'It is our duty to uphold our position, Minnie.'

Captain Price spent the meal sulking. He was the sort of person, Francina suspected, who would find fault with everything. But would he have the courage to voice his grievances to the Captain?

The sun burst through the companions like a portent of what was to come. The sea was still heaving, but the swell had lessened. The prospect of fine weather seemed to raise everyone's spirits and conversations across the table grew more animated, which, under the low saloon ceiling, reverberated at twice the volume. Most of the passengers had made an appearance today, some for the first time. Now Francina could see that besides Mrs Price, there were three young ladies of her age in First Class. Striking up a friendship with Miss Walmsley would be out of the question, so that only left Mrs Price and the dizzy Clapperton girls.

Aunt Cecilia's laugh rang out. She was talking to a bear of a man, an old family friend, Uncle had informed her. Aunt was the best dressed, most striking woman in the saloon. She glided over the ship, impervious to the weather or the looks of the other ladies. All the men, Francina suspected, must be in love with her.

'. . . it is well to improve the lot of the natives by starting schools, building hospitals and opening dispensaries,' she caught Uncle Vauloué saying, 'but to start village missions, zenana visiting or interfering in religious beliefs - that is a very dangerous course.'

'But the needs of India are not merely means or men - but *God*! India cries out for God.' Reverend Wright thumped his fist on the table. 'The Good Works, of which you speak, should not be an end in themselves but a channel through which the words of God can flow. We missionaries must not only sow the seed, but spread His Word, the living water. The seed, sir, will lie dormant until God sends the blessèd rain.'

Mrs Walmsley glanced surreptitiously from the Captain's table. Passengers at the other table, Francina noted, were also growing aware of this conversation.

'If the natives are to be won over,' said Uncle Vauloué quietly, 'it should be by example and gentle persuasion, with an understanding of their customs - not by force.'

'Surely you do not approve of the evil practices of *thuggee* or *suttee*, Mr Vauloué?'

'Such practices are totally abhorrent to me.'

'But how could we have outlawed them, if not by force?' Reverend Wright said, his voice rising as he sensed victory. 'Gentle persuasion would have got us nowhere. Thousands of innocent men and women would still be dying in the most barbaric way!'

'But I cannot sanction the imposition of alien beliefs on the very people who allowed me the freedom to practice my religion.'

Religion was another subject barred from Aunt Doré's table (and from the tables of all the memsahibs in this saloon, Francina guessed, judging by the looks darting back and forth). She wished Uncle would end this conversation before he alienated all the other passengers - but at the same time, it was rather satisfying to hear him provoke the pompous clergyman who had never set foot outside England.

'Your religion, sir? Pray what is your religion?'

'My ancestors were Huguenots,' said Uncle Vauloué quietly. 'We found refuge in India to practise our religion without hindrance, interference or persecution.'

Mrs Walmsley smiled encouragingly at the clergyman. Mrs Walmsley, Francina knew, considered herself superior to the Vauloués, and was rather put out to discover that they were occupying the second-best state-room and had struck up a friendship with the Mottrams. Colonel Mottram was a member of the Supreme Council of Calcutta and so Mrs Mottram was the Senior Lady, the *Burra-Mem*. But Aunt had no time for such nonsense. 'Planters', Aunt told her, 'do not appear in the Warrant of Precedence. We are non-officials. So I am free to speak to whomsoever I choose.'

Aunt Cecilia defied all the maxims Aunt Doré had taught her: she smoked; her glass of champagne was rarely empty, and her innocent flirtations with the cadets were making tongues wag. Yet, the better Francina knew her, the more she admired and loved her. Had Aunt Cecilia bewitched her? Had Aunt cast a spell on her as easily as Mamma had cast a spell on Papa? These days it seemed so difficult to know wrong from right.

Papa. Waves of sadness overwhelmed her every time she thought of Papa. The day before she left London they had spent the day together in the Zoological gardens. A strange eerie day -

everyone had remarked upon it. The sun had shone as bright as fool's gold. Oh, how false they were. How brittle their smiles. They had talked on silly, mundane subjects, anxious to avoid acknowledging that they might never see each other again. And all the time she had wondered: Will it break his heart if I return to Mamma?

'To impose our doctrines on the natives will only set them against us. You have only to remember Vellore,' Uncle Vauloué was saying.

'Vellore, Mr Vauloué?'

'The sepoys of Vellore were forced to cut their beards and wear European headgear and dress - a fairly innocuous decree one might assume, but it showed a complete lack of understanding of their customs and religion. It fuelled suspicion that there was a conspiracy afoot to force them to convert to Christianity. It resulted in a bloody mutiny.'

'I hope there *was* a conspiracy, Mr Vauloué. God has brought us to India for a purpose - why, the plight of your ancestors is a fitting illustration. We cannot condone false doctrines just to pander to the natives. There is a crucial flaw in your argument: their religion is false, and we have a sacred duty to spread the True Doctrine until the banner of Christ flies triumphant from one end of India to the other!'

Captain Price caught the missionary's eye across the table and smiled slyly. *He* was in agreement. The audacity of the little planter, arguing with a representative of the Church! If they had not been thrown together on this ship, he would have nothing to do with him. One might have the second-best cabins, one might have wealth, but what did that count if one was not *pukka*?

'I am so looking forward to stepping onto dry land again,' announced Mrs Guise gaily. 'Gibraltar is so picturesque. Such a profusion of flowers! And at this time of year, of course, the show will be quite spectacular.'

'There is a breathtaking view of Algeciras from the Moorish castle.' Dr Guise smiled gratefully at his wife. 'It is well worth the climb. And for those of a delicate disposition, there are always plenty of donkeys available to hire.'

Everyone around the table began to talk about the delights of

Gibraltar, until the Captain and the *Burra-Mem* rose from the table. Tiffin was over.

Francina made her way to her cabin. She squeezed past the Clapperton girls who were giggling with a group of cadets in the corridor. They gave her room to pass, but she had the impression that they were hardly aware of her existence. She was dressed in mourning, so most of the passengers were being tactfully unobtrusive, allowing her the time and space to contemplate her loss. It was as she wished. She was in no mood for socialising. The prospect of confronting Mamma in a few days was making her sick with worry. If only she could meet her in India, everything would be so straightforward. She would have time to get to know her. But within the space of a few hours of her arrival in Malta, she must decide on the future course of her life.

The sight of Miss Fuller resident as usual on the couch under the porthole was intensely irritating today. Was Miss Fuller going to spend the entire voyage cooped up in here? Would she never have the cabin to herself?

'You should take a little fresh air, Miss Fuller. I feel quite invigorated.'

Miss Fuller, a thin earnest woman in her mid-thirties, looked up from her writing. She was always scribbling in her journal. What did she find to write about, when she had not set foot outside the cabin since boarding the steamer three days ago?

2

Porpoises were leaping through the ship's wake. Francina leaned over the taffrail to watch them. If only she could behave with such abandon: leap for joy, or burst into tears as the mood took her. Her monthly cramps were bad today, ripping like needles inside. On days like this she missed Cook's warm concoctions to sooth the pain; Ellie padding into her room with a bed-warmer hidden under her apron.

Urged on by the Clapperton girls, cadets had thrown fishing lines over the side, hoping to hook something (for being Sunday, card-playing was forbidden and more young men than usual were idling on deck). If they had thrown a fishing net over this gullible group of cadets, Francina thought with admiration, the Clapperton girls could not have baited them more easily.

Esther Clapperton threw her a friendly smile. Francina smiled shyly back as she edged away. It would be nice to become her friend. But what was the point if I am quitting the ship tomorrow? She must think me a queer fish, skulking in the shadows, never joining in. Well, tomorrow I shall be gone. Miss Clapperton will never see me again.

I shall make arrangements for you to meet me . . .

Her bags were packed. She was ready to leave. Would anyone notice her absence? After a day or so, someone might ask, 'Where is your niece, Madame Vauloué, I have not seen her about lately?' And Aunt will reply, 'She met some relatives in Malta and decided to return to England with them.' The passenger will smile politely and think: I always suspected that there was something rather odd about Miss Duquesne.

A porpoise was darting alongside. Francina watched the animal (she knew he was an animal and not a fish - that much she had learned from Uncle Doré's books) weave through the water; a tireless, undulating streak of silver and black. Yesterday, perhaps, that porpoise had followed a different ship. Tomorrow he will follow another. Each day will be no different from the last . . . until he is hooked or eaten. Fate. He has no decisions to make.

The wind had dropped and the sea was a shimmering blue. Wispy clouds scratched the sky, which was almost as blue as the sea. The good weather had lured most of passengers outside - except for Aunt Cecilia who had retired as usual to her cabin for her afternoon sleep and, Francina suspected, a cheroot.

She took a deep breath. The ozone in the air was sweet, as sweet as iced mint tea. She was waiting for Uncle Vauloué. She enjoyed their brisk circuits around the deck after tiffin. For someone who had spent most of his life in India, Uncle was very knowledgeable. This morning, as they had sailed across the Bay of Tunis, she was given a graphic account of the destruction of Carthage by the Romans. Places were brought to life by his stories. She could almost hear the clash of swords ringing out across the water and see the fires glowing on the horizon. When she had asked how he knew so much about the rest of the world, Uncle had laughed and told her that when he was a boy, he had had a tutor with a passion for the Classics.

The African coast had disappeared over the horizon. Yesterday, they had been so close that it was possible to distinguish flat-roofed villages dotted between date palm groves. She had seen a camel, her first-ever sighting of one. Now, they were steaming within sight of Sicily. The sails were furled, and the funnels discharging an unbroken stream of smoke into the sky. Despite the drone of the engines turning the paddlewheels, it was unusually quiet, for few children were scampering about. Most had been ushered into the Ladies' Boudoir to attend Sabbath School under the direction of Miss Wright, giving their mammas and the sailors a break from their endless questions. There was no child older than seven years on the ship, for children above that age are sent Home, Aunt Cecilia had told her. She wondered how self-effacing Miss Wright could manage so many unruly little imps. She hardly looked the commanding type. Was Miss Wright as committed a missionary as her brother, or was she accompanying him under sufferance? There were times when Miss Wright seemed to cower when her brother addressed her.

Where was Uncle? She went in search of him. She was too restless to stand still.

I shall be delighted to embrace you and keep you forever . . .

Tomorrow, she would see Mamma. Tomorrow, the dream would become reality. Her head pounded with a rush of blood. If she thought about it too much, she might swoon.

She passed promenading couples and groups conversing by the hencoops. Friendships were forming, little cliques emerging. There were rumours of clandestine meetings. She caught a glimpse of Lieutenant Hamilton's legs firmly planted behind the lifeboat, Mrs Crawford's fluttering skirts. (It was common knowledge that Mrs Crawford was returning to India to join her husband - she had made a great show of tears for the children she was leaving behind when she had boarded the ship). Where are her tears now? Francina wondered, gathering in her skirts at the stair head.

Something was wrong. People were milling round the cabin. Murphy, Aunt's maid (who was travelling in steerage) pushed past her carrying a foot warmer wrapped in a shawl. 'It's Mr Vauloué,' she called over her shoulder, 'he's been taken ill.'

Uncle had seemed well this morning, although he had complained of a headache. A touch of sun, he had said, it was only a touch of sun. Francina squeezed into the cabin after Murphy. It was stifling, insufferably hot, the air thick with the odour of anxiety. Dr Guise's lumbering form filled the cabin. Behind him, Uncle Vauloué was lying on the couch covered with blankets, shivering violently. His chattering lips were blue, his eyes glazed, unfocused.

'Two grains of quinine in a tablespoon of milk every two hours,' Dr Guise was saying, placing his instruments back in its case. His voice was too reassuring. 'And keep a close eye on his progress. Beef-tea while he is in the cold stage. As soon as he begins to feel hot, remove the blankets. All efforts must be made to reduce the fever - but remember, Mrs Vauloué,' the doctor said, pausing at the doorway, 'it is imperative that he does not catch a chill. I shall return at intervals to check on our patient's progress - but if you are at all worried, send for me immediately.'

'Aunt, what has happened?'

Perspiration trickled down Aunt's temples.

'Ague. Your uncle has a fit of the ague.'

'It's not serious, is it Aunt? He will get better, won't he?'

Aunt did not answer. She held out a small bowl. 'Here, Francina, rub his feet with this liniment while I massage his hands. We must keep the blood warm.'

Perching on a trunk, Francina lifted a corner of the blanket and groped tentatively for one of Uncle's stiff clammy feet. Then scooping up soapy liniment with her fingers and trying not to feel inhibited, she spread it gingerly over a foot.

'Vigorously, Francina. Massage the soles of his feet vigorously!'

Francina had never been so intimate with a man before. She would have liked to have got this close to Papa, to do all the things that a daughter is supposed to do: mop his brow, feed him soup, spoon by spoon - but she had never been there when Papa was ill.

When dusk fell Murphy lit the lamp. But it was only when a steward brought in a tray of sandwiches and a carafe of wine that Francina realised that they had missed dinner.

By the time the doctor called again, Uncle's fever had broken, his saturated clothing had been changed and he was sleeping under fresh dry sheets. Aunt's fingers nervously toyed with the beads of her rosary as Dr Guise conducted his examination. She looked strained, almost ten years older, and Francina wanted to cry out: I'm here, Aunt. Let me comfort you!

'The crisis is over,' smiled the doctor. 'The patient should sleep soundly now for several hours. It is too early to tell if Mr Vauloué is suffering from quotidian or tertian ague, but the disease will strike again - perhaps tomorrow, or the day after - but rest assured, Mrs Vauloué, the attacks will become progressively less severe as the poison works its way out of his system.'

When the doctor had gone, Aunt drained her glass of port and refilled it. She had been drinking steadily all afternoon. Her cheeks was flushed, her eyes heavy with fatigue. 'We have done all we can at present,' she said, collapsing into a chair. 'Go to bed now, Francina. It's getting late and you must be tired.'

Francina kissed her goodnight. There was so much she wanted to ask, but she had left it too late. Aunt was too preoccupied to turn her mind to anything but Uncle's welfare. But all the same, a knot of panic gripped her. 'Aunt, we arrive in Malta tomorrow. What is going to happen - I mean with Mamma?'

'Is it really tomorrow, Francina? I had quite forgotten.'

Aunt lit a cheroot and clutched her jaw. 'I was looking forward to introducing you to Theresa - but that is quite out of the question now. I cannot possibly leave your uncle in his present condition. Besides, my tooth has flared up again.'

Francina could not speak. She knew already, of course. She had known the moment she had stepped into this cabin to see Uncle Vauloué writhing under a mountain of blankets. It was not a snub, she knew that. It was just one of those things. However much one plans and schemes, lives on dreams and imagines the way things will turn out - they never do.

'My absence should make no difference, Francina.' Aunt shut her eyes and kneaded her temples. 'You will still meet Theresa as planned. Murphy will go with you. I shall send a note explaining everything. You are packed?'

The curtains were swaying with the roll of the ship. Billowing and falling. Francina looked away. The motion was making her feel sick. To be dismissed so simply: You are packed? Aunt does not understand; she has more important things on her mind.

She stumbled down the corridor, following the swaying lanterns towards the saloon. As she opened the door, the voices hushed. Coffee cups hovered, and umpteen pairs of eyes followed her.

Her path to her cabin was blocked as passengers, one after the other, came up to offer their sympathy. The whole ship's company seemed to have heard of Uncle's Vauloué's illness. People she had never spoken to asked after him. His illness had brought down barriers, built bridges. Even Mrs Walmsley was prepared to spend a few moments questioning her. Francina thanked them for their concern. But behind their commiserations, she sensed other questions: *Is his illness contagious? Will the ship have to be quarantined?*

Miss Fuller was asleep, she saw with relief when she entered the cabin, for she could not bear to answer another question. Francina undressed quietly, and climbed into her bunk. Tomorrow she would see Mamma.

She lay still as an effigy, as heavy as stone.

3

It was unbearably hot. In less than two hours they would meet. *At the entrance to St John's Church*, Mamma's note said, *at the top of the Strada Santa Lucia*. Well, she had climbed the steps, found the church, and made a note of its whereabouts. She would return here in an hour's time, sit at that little shaded café opposite and wait.

The streets were crowded. Nuns, priests, and Maltese ladies enveloped in black silk faldettas tripped down the steps, peering slyly at them with dark inquisitive eyes. Brown skinned youths in loose shirts, and flowing trousers held up by bright sashes, bounded up. They stood aside to let a donkey in a colourful harness pass, his panniers overflowing with exotic fruits. Each time they stopped, the beggar children with appealing black eyes, who had followed them from the landing steps, pulled at their skirts and gestured with dirty fingers into their open mouths.

'It was a mistake to give them anything, Miss,' grumbled Murphy, lashing out at them with her hand. The children grimaced behind her back and sidled away.

Francina stopped to examine a tray of gold filigree crosses and shell cameos displayed in an open window. Instantly, a fat Maltese with a turban burst out of the shop. He bowed, gesturing grandly into the dark cavern of his shop.

'Lady, come inside, please look!'

She shook her head. Turning a corner, she found yet another shaded stair-street of stone houses with locked portals and green shuttered windows. Maltese girls in white mantillas peeped over elaborate, peeling covered balconies to watch her descend the long flight of steps.

Murphy followed moodily behind. She was making it quite obvious that she would have liked to go inside that jeweller's shop. Francina wished she would go away. She would rather wander these streets alone than have this insolent servant trailing behind. Murphy might attend Aunt well enough, but she had plainly decided that her duties did not extend to chaperoning the impoverished niece.

The steps led down to a wide promenade bounded by a thick low wall overlooking the harbour. They had reached the ramparts of Valetta, and it was a relief to find somewhere flat to walk. How quickly her legs had lost the art of climbing! A few months ago she could have tripped up and down these flights of steps without pausing for breath. Gravitating to the blocks of shade like the other European promenaders, she narrowed her eyes and stared at the dazzling fortifications, the tiers of batteries bristling with cannon snaking round the inlet. Such a grand sight, such a manifestation of British power.

The harbour was crowded with ships-of-the-line and steam frigates. Little colourful Maltese boats with high prows were ferrying passengers across the harbour. It was a scene waiting to be painted. She spotted the *Isis* towering over the small boats nibbling around her. And yet at this distance, with sails furled and her funnels cold, the paddle steamer looked oddly vulnerable. She wondered how Uncle Vauloué was faring. 'He caught the disease a few years ago,' Aunt had explained, sponging his sweating torso with a mixture of water and vinegar, 'while visiting a cousin in an unhealthy district of Bengal. The Rains were bad that year. But - Saints be praised - he pulled through. Your uncle has a strong constitution.' It had been a shock to see his thin white body, and the ridges of his backbone protruding under that saturated nightshirt. She had not realised how frail he was.

She took Angelo's letter from her purse. She was handed it soon after they had anchored, along with Mamma's note. Under a small engraving of the paddle steamer *Eastern Star* ploughing through the waves, he had written:

My Dearest Sweetest Sister –

As I scrawl this note, the palm-fringed shore of Ceylon glides closer. Tomorrow we arrive at Galle and I must turn my back on luxury, wrench myself away from the most adorable Lady in the world, and disappear into obscurity. To have been our Mother's devoted slave these past few months has been the happiest time of my life. When you read this, I shall be sitting alone in a little hut somewhere in the jungle. My only consolation is that soon you, dear Ina, will know what joy it is to be enfolded in her arms. Oh to witness the tender reunion!

How different your plans would be if I had not had the good fortune to discover our dear Mother's whereabouts. She is anxious to make up for Father's deficiencies and to give you every comfort and step up in life - and Judge Havers plainly adores her. He is highly respected and well connected, so you are sure to mix in the best Society -

'Miss Duquesne?'

Her heart sank. 'Mrs Walmsley,' she smiled, returning the letter to her purse.

'You are alone?' Mrs Walmsley asked, appalled. A servant was no substitute for a chaperone in a place where greasy foreigners abound. 'Mrs Vauloué does not accompany you?'

'No indeed. Uncle was asleep when I left, but Aunt is reluctant to leave him, for I understand the ague can strike again at any moment.'

Mrs Walmsley braced herself (for it was one's Christian duty to extend the hand of friendship at a time of illness) and said: 'Miss Duquesne, you must accompany us, I really do insist.'

'Please do, Miss Duquesne,' added Miss Walmsley, almost sounding as if she meant it. 'We have been recommended a café where the ices are particularly fine.'

'That is very kind, but I am shortly to meet someone.'

I am shortly to meet someone. The words tripped off her tongue before she had time to check them.

Mrs Walmsley's eyes lit up with interest.

'A relative,' Francina hurriedly explained, for it sounded as if she might have arranged an illicit meeting with a young man. 'A relative happens to be here in Malta.'

'Well in that case we shall take our leave, Miss Duquesne,' smiled Mrs Walmsley, relieved to be exonerated from the task of dragging this drab little creature around Valetta.

The two women gilded away, galleons in full sail.

Whether they believed her or not Francina hardly cared. Some word of this would probably filter back to the ship; amuse the other ladies for a few moments. When the ship sails and she is not found aboard, the gossip will intensify. 'Who would have thought that little mouse had it in her!' they will smirk behind their fans. 'Did anyone catch sight of him? Have all the young men on board been accounted for?' Then, after a day or so they will forget she ever existed. Even Aunt Cecilia will be too wrapped up with Uncle's welfare to think of her for long. In time, Aunt will meet Aunt Barton and say: 'I tried my best, but she was such a dull little thing.'

Her stomach contracted. *I am shortly to meet someone.* What if Mamma should not like her? What if she should be rejected for a second time? Her skin prickled. The bombazine was catching under her arms. She leaned against the wall and shut her eyes. She would rest here for a moment, regain her strength then return to the *Strada Reale* and sit at that café . . . Murphy can do what she likes. Stick her nose in every shop in Valetta for all I care.

She caught snatches of French and Italian, and languages she had never heard before. A military band was playing across the harbour. Church bells rang across the bay. She heard the shrieks of the naked boys as they dived after tokens sailors were throwing into the water . . . and all the time, the inevitable seagulls.

'Which is it?' a child's voice enquired. 'Point out the ship to me.'

'*I* not know. How I know?' replied a woman irritably. 'I no see names from here. But it should have Union Jack.'

'But they *all* have Union Jacks!'

'Not all. Look! That one has the French tricolore.'

Francina opened her eyes to see a young boy peering over the wall quite close to her, a little English gentleman in a white suit and jaunty sailor's hat.

'Master Willie, no climb up! You get very, very dirty,' said his nursemaid in alarm, a dark-skinned woman in European clothes who spoke in a sing-song accent.

Willie took no notice. He scrambled up the wall and stood on it, triumphant, his eyes sparking with glee. The nursemaid grabbed his sleeve and held tight. 'If your papa see you, you get whipping!'

Willie glanced quickly down the promenade. 'I shall get down before Papa sees me,' he promised. The nursemaid relaxed a little, but still held on tight.

'*Vul-can Fire-fly Alex-an-dria,*' Willie said, shielding his eyes and reading the names of ships. 'I can't see the *Isis* anywhere.'

The nursemaid glanced anxiously behind her. 'Master Willie, get down quick! Papa is coming.'

Francina followed their eyes. A couple had rounded the corner, a handsome couple, an English couple of refinement and taste. Three children walked with them: a girl of about nine years, a boy some years younger and dressed identically to Willie, and a perfect doll of a girl, no more than four years old and dressed in a pared down version of her sister's costume. People strolling along the promenade gave them furtive admiring glances. But it was the woman dressed in a delicate blue spotted costume with a white fichu and wide sunhat, the woman on the arm of the tall gentleman, who received most of the glances.

Francina knew immediately. She could not breathe. She looked away, gripped the wall and stared out across the harbour pretending to study the ships. The same eyes, the same straight nose, the same high cheekbones. She knew that face. She saw it every morning in the glass.

'The *Isis*!' whooped Master Willie, jumping down. He ran towards his mamma and papa, jumping up every so often to peer over the wall and point: 'There's the *Isis*!'

'Where? Where?' cried the younger boy, breaking into a run.

'*Isis, Isis!*' cried the little doll. She pulled away from her mamma's grip and tried to catch up with her brothers. The eldest child stayed close to her parents. Slim, dark haired and dainty, she was a young lady in the making, too grown-up to join her siblings.

'Don't point, Willie. You know it is not polite.'

Mamma's voice. That lovely voice that had whispered to her in dreams . . . After all this time she had not forgotten it. Instantly she was back in her dappled Indian garden sitting on her swing. *Don't push so hard, Angelo. She is only little.*

For a second, one infinitesimal second, their eyes met.

She had imagined their reunion so many times. She had imagined the tears, the laughter and the kisses. She stood across the chasm staring at her. She wanted to cry. She wanted so much to cry. She wanted to wrap her arms round Mamma's neck and unleash the tears, the pain, the bereavement that had suffocated her since she was four years old.

But she could not move. She could not speak. Hold me, Mamma. Hold me.

Mamma looked away. 'Lizzie, don't run so fast!' she called.

Nothing.

There was no spark of recognition. Not a single speck of recognition to show that she knew who she was. Surely Mamma should know her own daughter? Surely. Surely. Her heart was crushed. It crumpled to dust, melted to nothing.

She should have worn one of the pretty dresses Aunt Cecilia had bought for her. But this dress epitomized her feelings. She had wanted Mamma to see, to understand what she had been through. She wanted Mamma to love her for what she was - not for the quality of the silk or the hue of the ribbon on her dress. That was a mistake. These children, she could see, have been brought up to regard adornment and outward show as the manifestation of superiority. Here I stand, pitiful and plain, looking no better than that nursemaid. Can I blame Mamma for not knowing me?

Willie glanced fleetingly at her as he trotted past. He had already summed her up, categorised her, placed her several rungs below himself. Could she grow to love this bastard half-brother? Would he grow to respect her?

The little doll tripped and fell. Mamma hurried to reach her.

'Darling Lizzie!' She scooped her up and brushed down her pretty pink dress. 'Are you hurt, my Precious?'

Lizzie threw her arms round Mamma's neck, nuzzled her cheek and sobbed.

Where was Mamma when I fell over? I should have been that little girl clinging to Mamma's neck. I should have been Lizzie.

'My dear,' said the tall gentleman by her side, resting his hand lightly on Mamma's arm. 'You know I do not approve of you picking up the children - not in your condition. You really must take care.'

'Of course, Edmund dearest,' Mamma said in a kittenish voice, putting Lizzie down. 'I am feeling the heat today. Could we sit in the shade for a while?' She smiled up at him, beguiled him with her eyes, while her hand rested on her abdomen protruding slightly under the fichu.

Francina looked away. She saw Mamma as Miss Chesterton might see her: Judge Havers' pet, made weak by luxurious pleasures. Miss Chesterton might regard marriage as little more than slavery, but surely marriage was preferable to Mamma's position? This gentleman was at liberty to throw her into the street, should it please him to do so. So to keep a roof over her head, Mamma was prostrating herself, indulge his whims. She was indeed his mistress.

'May we go to the Public Garden, Papa?' cried Willie.

'An excellent idea, William. *We* shall go to the Public Garden. But *you,* young man, will return to the hotel with Nana and change. You look a frightful sight,' said his father. His full wispy beard gave him a dictatorial air, but he looked younger than Papa, with a demeanour that bespoke power and authority. This was the gentleman, the Pillar of the Community, the 'respectable' Englishman who had lured Mamma away and made her his slave. This was the Judge whose elevated position was founded on lies and deceit.

'Oh, Papa!' protested Willie. 'Must I?'

'Do as Papa says, Willie,' Mamma said quietly, taking the Judge's arm. She looked so young, so beautiful, so content. Francina felt strangely detached as she watched them saunter down the promenade, as if she were a figure flying across a camera obscura screen, as if she might suddenly wake up and find that this was all just a dream.

She should have made a gesture, announced who she was. Now it was too late. She could not do it. She was a coward. She had failed Angelo. She had failed Aunt Cecilia. She could not follow Mamma up to St John's Church, smiling and confident, and expect to be greeted with open arms. She had missed out. Too many vying for her attention - and soon there would be another, even more demanding. There was no room in Mamma's heart for her. There never had been. Why should it be different now? And as for that man! She loathed everything about him. She despised him from the moment she had laid eyes on him.

'Miss Duquesne, are you enjoying the sights?'

The Clapperton girls had appeared from nowhere. Loud, exuberant and friendly, they crowded round her like vultures, breathing her air, blocking her view of Mamma.

'See what I have bought,' said Miss Esther Clapperton, dangling a gold chain and filigree locket under her nose. 'Isn't it pretty?'

'Yes, but whose likeness will you put inside?' giggled her sister.

'Wouldn't you like to know!' snorted Miss Esther, dropping the locket inside her bodice.

'Mr Griffiths'. I've seen you making eyes at him.'

'Norah,' whispered her sister in alarm, 'you'll spoil everything if Ma hears you!'

Norah Clapperton smiled and tossed her head in triumph. 'See, what *I* have bought, Miss Duquesne,' she cried, holding up a pretty domed birdcage. A little canary was hopping frantically from side to side, battering his wings against the wires.

Francina caught a glimpse of Mamma behind Miss Norah's purple bonnet. She wanted to scream and push these uncouth girls away. She wanted to open the cage and let that pitiful bird escape. How long they stood in front of her talking and laughing, she did not know. She was not aware of anything but Mamma disappearing round the corner.

The Clappertons were on their way again; talking and laughing as they ran to join their mamma, swinging their purses and parasols and that wretched little birdcage.

She walks along a vaulted passage, across a dazzling courtyard where orange trees grow in pots around a silver pool, and up a marble staircase to the second floor. Mamma's suite of lofty rooms leads off an arcade shaded by cascading, sweet-scented creeper.

Mamma stretches on a chaise-longue and dabs her neck with a cambric handkerchief. 'Sit by me, Francina. Draw up that stool. We have so much to talk about.'

She cannot quite believe it. She is here, with Mamma. Just the two of them. Alone.

'I am so happy that you are here, Francina.' Mamma's hand brushes her cheek, just as it used to when she was a little girl.

She has waited for this moment, dreamed of this moment, since she was four years old. She is dancing on air. She is swimming, her feet barely touching the seabed, almost out of her depth. She is perched on the balcony, a song-bird trilling to the passers-by in the street. Is it possible to be so happy? She falls on her knees and rests her head against the folds of Mamma's skirts. The soft muslin tickles her cheek, and a delicious scent of lavender fills her head. She is too overcome to speak.

'I shall make you the *very darling* of society,' smiles Mamma, stroking her hair. 'New dresses. New bonnets. Oh, what fun we shall have. And a new hairstyle, I think. I do not like the way you have dressed your hair, Francina. It is too severe for your face - and you have a very pretty face, if you would only smile a little more.'

Her heart is bursting with happiness. She looks into Mamma's eyes, those beautiful eyes that have haunted her dreams, searching for the spark that tells her she loves her. But Mamma looks away and smiles into the distance: 'The children will soon grow as fond of you as they did Angelo. He did amuse them so with his stories and games.'

'Perhaps you have not noticed?' Mamma adds coyly, her fingers under the fichu, lightly stroking her abdomen, 'There will soon be an addition to the family . . . '

It is becoming difficult to smile; her heart is growing so heavy.

' . . . and you will be so useful to me when the baby arrives.'

The door bursts open and the children fly in. 'Mamma, Mamma! We saw a frigate being towed into the harbour with a hole in her side and her mizzenmast gone. Papa says it was blown up in the War!'

'Did he, dearest? But Willie, your trousers! What a frightful sight you look. Go and change at once,' says Mamma.

Willie gives Francina an arrogant stare as he skips out of the room. The youngest children snuggle up to Mamma on the chaise longue. She kisses them both. The older girl sits quietly at Mamma's feet, her stockinged ankles neatly crossed.

The room is shrinking, Francina slips backwards . . . Mamma is fussing over the doll, re-tying her bows, smoothing her hair. They have become so small; she might be studying a painting hanging in the National Gallery: *Mrs Edmund Havers and family at Home.* Such a good-looking family, so respectable. Mamma is saying something, but her voice has become a whisper, drowned by the sound of singing far away.

Such a melancholy tune. It drifted across the water to her porthole. Was it a song of unrequited love, of disappointment or shattered dreams? The words were unimportant. It was a song for her. She climbed out of her bunk, sat under the open port and felt a warm breeze on her cheeks. Valetta looked beautiful in the moonlight.

Lights twinkled across the harbour and shimmered over the still, black waters. Faint strains of music, then a ripple of laughter floated towards her. Mesmerised, she watched shadows flicker across a bright balcony. She might be watching little pictures spinning inside a praxinoscope.

If she had not given Murphy that scribbled note and run back to the ship she would be with Mamma now, spending the night ashore like most of the other passengers. Since she was four years old, she has felt Mamma's comforting, invisible presence. She has knelt beside her when she said her prayers, whispered words of comfort when she braced herself for Aunt Doré's whip. Mamma has been the centre of her world, circling, ever circling around her.

Now when she thought of Mamma, she would always be surrounded by children, loud demanding children, all vying for her attention. Mamma would never come to her again.

4

'Dry land agrees with you, Miss Duquesne.' Dr Guise lowered the blind and dabbed his forehead.

Francina smiled. She had felt a change come over her the moment they had stepped ashore in Alexandria. The sights and sounds and smells of the Orient had taken her breath away. She had stood in the bustling square, stared up at the huge marble obelisk and felt a glow of well-being drown the numbness; and in that instant she knew she would get over it. Life goes on. She had received too many knocks, too many disappointments not to have prepared herself. Deep down, she had known all along that it would end like that. Mamma could have contacted her, sent a message if she was determined enough. There are always ways and means.

'What a delight this new train is,' said Mrs Guise, vigorously fanning herself. 'Such a trying journey it used to be when I first came out. Trundling for hours in the searing heat on a flea-infested donkey. Then the prospect of that dreadful canal journey! Three days it used to take to reach Cairo - and the vermin in those old barges - by the time we arrived we were weak from fatigue or sickness. Naturally we were obliged to hire servants for the duration, and there is nothing more infuriating than an Egyptian servant. Even the simplest task is a mammoth undertaking.'

Uncle stirred and opened his eyes. 'Surely, that is part of this country's charm,' he said.

'Indeed, Mr Vauloué, but if one must adhere to a *timetable,* disorganisation and confusion can try the patience of a saint! Charm plays no part in catching trains or steamers.'

'How are you feeling, Uncle?' Francina passed him a flask of water. He still looked weak and gaunt, but a sparkle had returned to his eyes.

'I cannot possibly complain, my dear,' he said, between gulps of water, 'with so many good people waiting on me so admirably.'

Uncle Vauloué had suffered another attack soon after the ship sailed from Malta, which had kept them anxious for several days. During those long taxing hours sitting with Aunt Cecilia at his bedside, Francina had felt neither the desire nor the inclination to bring up the subject of Mamma, and Aunt never asked her about it, for which she was grateful. There was no point in dwelling on what might have been. Seeing Aunt's strained face, she had realised where she belonged, where she was needed. Here, at Aunt Cecilia's side.

And so she ceased to think of Mamma. It was not a conscious decision. The woman she had seen on the promenade surrounded by children bore no affinity to Mamma. She felt nothing for that woman.

Refreshed by several hours' rest in cool dark rooms at the Hotel d'Orient in Cairo and revitalised by a reasonable dinner, they were on the next stage of their journey, racing across the desert in a quaint horse-drawn vehicle to catch the steamer awaiting them at Suez. Aunt Cecilia had not only charmed the officials in the Transit Office to secure the quickest and most advantageous time to travel, but she had also persuaded the Guises to accompany them, anxious that the good doctor should be on hand should Uncle suddenly require medical attention. But so far Uncle was coping well. Regular doses of quinine had staved off another attack, and a liberal spoonful of laudanum had sent him into a deep slumber.

In fact, thought Francina, snuggling under her shawl, Uncle appeared the only occupant asleep. The others were dozing fitfully, shifting awkwardly on the hard unforgiving seats. She was too roused to sleep, for even in the dead of night there was much to see. Stars twinkled in the blackest sky she had ever seen; moonlight undulated over the barren landscape, seductively illuminating the skeletons marking the route. It was a ghostly panorama, eerier than anything her imagination might conjure up, a grisly carpet of bones glinting far into the night. Cruel testimony to the thousands of camels that had traipsed to the point of exhaustion across the desert. How long had these bones been lying here? Years? Centuries? Some of the skeletons looked different. Horses, perhaps, or donkeys. Some, presumably, were travellers that had lost their way and died of thirst.

She caught the outline of another van racing alongside, lurching precariously as it bounded over boulders and skeletons. There were six vans in the convoy - swaying lanterns in the distance pin-pointed the others. Another six would follow, then another, until all the passengers reached Suez.

Murphy grunted and stirred, squeezing her hard against the side of the van. Murphy, Francina suspected, was just pretending to be asleep. It was an excuse to spread her bulk and take up more than her fair share of the seat. Murphy was getting above herself. She was putting on airs. It had not taken her long to realise that in this wasteland she was indispensable to Aunt. So she was taking liberties. She had caught her swaggering, issuing a tirade of instructions to the hotel porters, pretending to be Aunt Cecilia.

But, thought Francina, she must not think about Murphy. Nothing must spoil the magic of this night. Travelling under this black spangled vault, she was aware of the great distance they had covered - and must still cover - before they reach India. The same moon shone over Guernsey, but over this wilderness seemed to radiate with a bewitching intensity. In her mind's eye she saw the stark white house perched on the ridge above the little grey town; Aunt Doré working in the parlour, Uncle cataloguing his books. Charlie's portrait draped in crepe. It would all be just as she remembered.

She shivered. Nothing stirred, yet she was sure there were eyes out there watching her, glinting behind the rocks. But they were too quick. She could not catch them out. Her heart quickened. She was on the threshold of a new life where everything strange would become commonplace and everything she had known would fade to a half-remembered dream. At what point does reality become the dream, and the dream reality?

5

Her chemise was wet and her waist itched, but she dared not remove the flannel band - there could be serious consequences if her kidneys became chilled, Aunt had warned. The air was suffocating. She had never known heat like this. She had hoped that once aboard the *Hindustan*, she would feel the cooling benefit of the roadsteads, but she could detect no difference. But at least in the privacy of this small dark cabin, she could dispense with most of her clothing.

Miss Fuller, she noted with disappointment, reading the labels of the luggage piled neatly on the bottom berth, was sharing the cabin with her again.

But what a joy to take off the hateful bombazine! She ripped the seams and tore off the buttons. It fell to the floor like an empty husk, a spent cocoon.

She filled the little basin with tepid salty water, and dabbed her face and neck. Hardly refreshed, she lay on her bunk and shut her eyes. She could feel the rhythmic throb of the huge engines through her horsehair mattress . . . It was a pleasurable sensation, which in different circumstances might have lulled her to sleep.

The ship's bell began to clang with increasing urgency, triggering a rolling clamour from one end of the ship to the other. It flowed like a tide along the decks, down the stairwells and along the corridors.

She climbed out of her bunk and stared at the hateful black dress. Never again would that webbing bind her into a straightjacket. Something had happened on the long journey across the Egyptian desert. She had been bewitched, seduced by the long fingers of the night. And in return, she had given up some part of herself, left it to fester and rot in the blinding desert sun. Then, she realised, a tremendous weight had lifted from her shoulders: the mantle of Mamma's shame had vanished. It lay frayed and tattered somewhere along the camel trail from Cairo to Suez.

She put on the dress that she had unpacked earlier and hung on the hook by her bunk, a powder-blue silk embroidered with a sprinkling of - of what she could only describe as shimmering dewdrops. It was not the style she would have chosen for herself, but what matter? She wanted to dance and sing and be - frivolous.

The corridor thronged with late-arrivals all demanding to be shown their cabins. So many new faces. She clutched her carpetbag to her chest and edged between two old India hands. She had learnt to distinguish them: they were full of self-importance and spoke in loud brash voices. Hurrying through the saloon she caught sight of a dark haired girl in a blue dress gliding past the tall gilt mirrors. The girl tossed her head and glanced momentarily at her.

She stepped on to the weather deck. The ferocity of the sun hit her full face, a hammer blow to the chest, but she was not deterred. The place was swarming, the din overwhelming, but she cut a path between passengers, obstacles, barrels, ropes and animals, as effortlessly as if she was flying. She passed a group of passengers she knew from the *Isis* and smiled to herself. She might as well be invisible; no one seemed to recognise her.

A young man with tawny hair was talking to the Clapperton girls. 'Well, how do I look?' he asked, trying on a palm-leafed *topee*.

The Clapperton girls looked at each other and giggled. 'It is too small,' they said in unison.

The young man leaned over the rail and threw the *topee* back into the basket. 'No good! No want!' he shouted down to the Arab in the bumboat.

The din reached a crescendo. Steam hissed through the iron plates and the funnels spewed out clouds of smoke, spattering smuts over everything. Then with a great shudder the huge paddle-wheels began to turn. Passengers rushed to lean over the guardrails to watch the *Hindustan* manoeuvre her enormous bulk towards the open sea.

She did not seek the shade. She wanted the sun to finish its task.

She leaned over the starboard rail and raised her face in submission. The sun's rays caressed her cheeks and throat and seeped hot and red through her eyelids down to the very core of her being. A warm tingle spread like a sponge through her veins, while under her fingers, layers of powder-blue silk stirred and trembled like newly emerged wings in the hot breeze.

'Have you been long in India, Mr Cowan Bell?' came a voice that could only belong to the Reverend Mr Wright.

'I followed the *Hindustan* round the Cape on her maiden voyage,' replied his companion. 'She left Southampton a week after we did and arrived at the Sandheads on Christmas Eve, four weeks before us. She was the largest paddle-steamer ever to venture up the Hoogly, and was the talk and pride of Calcutta.'

'But no longer,' said Mr Wright, indignantly. 'Fourteen years of service across the Indian Ocean has left her shamefully shoddy. Have you ventured into the library yet? I have never seen such a meagre selection of books. I counted only fifteen copies of *The Church of England Prayer Book* - every one of them torn or water damaged. How can I be expected to conduct a Service when there are not even enough books to share?'

Francina edged away to focus on the task in hand.

She stared into the churning wake. It looked cool, inviting. How could something so clear and blue turn into an angry bubbling froth? What triggers something to metamorphose? She opened the carpetbag. How she must have looked that day! A pathetic nonentity wearing her abasement as proudly as a martyr's banner. Of course Mamma did not know her.

With great ceremony, she tossed the symbols of her subjugation and misery over the side. The black dress fluttered gracefully down like some gigantic bat, looking for a moment as if it might suddenly take flight. The bonnet spun straight down, bobbed jauntily in the wake for a moment, toppled over and sank. But the hateful bombazine would not give up so easily. It billowed on the surface, arms flailing. She watched, her heart beating wildly. Anger and resentment was keeping that dress afloat. She felt sick with guilt, as though she were witness to a suicide, or was she party to a murder? The threshing arms were teasing her, beckoning her to join in a fatal *pas de deux*. It was a battle of wills: hers pitched against that demon's in the sea.

'Merciful Heaven, someone is overboard!' a woman shrieked. 'Quick, call the Captain!'

People surged from every point of the ship, pressing around her, craning their necks and pointing into the sea.

Voices, so many voices all speaking at once. The bombazine tossed and billowed coquettishly. Then, like some long suffering martyr, it rolled over in a dramatic death throw and slipped below the water.

'Ladies and gentlemen, calm yourselves!' a burly gentleman cried above the gasps. 'Nothing is amiss. What you see is nothing more than a bundle of old clothes, which I, myself, witnessed being thrown overboard only a few moments ago!'

Murmuring with disappointment, the crowd dispersed and she was left to watch the dark shape twist and turn as it tried to claw its way back to the surface. Why was it still fighting?

Then, at last, it sank from view, leaving a trail of bubbles in its wake.

The spell had broken. She was free at last and heading for India. She felt dizzy, light-headed, and her legs began to buckle.

PART TWO

I knew not but the next
Would be my final inch, -
That gave me that precarious gait
Some call experience.

Emily Dickinson (1830-1886)

GUERNSEY
April 1880

Francina caught her breath as the three-towered lighthouse loomed through the mist. She had missed Guernsey, she realised now. She had missed her music, her warm fractured light - even her cruel claustrophobic society. Five days. Was it only five days since she had received the letter? She had acted on impulse, sent off a telegraph, taken the train to London and booked her passage on the steamer. The speed of her decision had surprised everyone – including herself.

Passengers were crowding around her, buffeting her on all sides. The steamer pitched and tossed. Smuts of coal fell like rain around her. It was just as well she was dressed in black and had a veil to cover her face. A boy, muffled against the elements, was stretched on tiptoe and pointing towards the islands, which appeared as grey shadows through the mist. His pale-faced sister peered through the netting close by. Francina smiled down at her, resisting the urge to take her hand and reassure her. She had been about this child's age when she had caught her first glimpse of Guernsey. She remembered that day so distinctly. It had been a clearer day than this, and they could see the Island from a long way off. Papa had pointed it out to her. 'See, Francina, Guernsey! Your new home.' But she had caught the apprehension in his voice and stared at the pimple on the horizon with bemusement. Guernsey looked so small and cut-off – rather like the prison hulks they had seen in Portsmouth harbour. She had remembered the lush green forests they had left behind in India, stretching far, far over the horizon. Why, the Ganges was studded with countless nameless islands just like that one.

There was mayhem on the slipway. A dog had startled a donkey, which was kicking out at it, and in the confusion upturning baskets of fish being unloaded. Fishermen were shouting, trying to catch the dog. Meanwhile the gulls were gathering, shrieking and swooping at the floundering fish strewn across the slipway.

Through her veil, she caught the odour of fish and sun-baked vriac and smiled. It was good to be back in Guernsey.

'Baptiste?'

She recognised him immediately. He was leaning against a carriage with his arms folded, just as he used to do. He looked round and swept off his hat.

'Madame.' He bowed, toying nervously with the brim.

'How are you Baptiste?' Francina's smile hid a deep sadness. Until this moment, she had not appreciated the gulf that had opened between them. Good kind Baptiste, who had once risked Aunt Doré's wrath to smuggle food to her when she was being punished, now looked so abashed standing before her. Where was that devilish spark that once gleamed in his eyes? Dulled by routine, she supposed. It was wonderful to see him again and to know that he was still faithful to Uncle Doré, but she would rather have learned that he had packed his bags and was chancing his luck overseas.

'Well, Madame, very well.'

While she had travelled halfway round the world, he had remained here, in the service of the Dorés. Twenty-four years of experience had passed under her feet. In all that time, she suspected, Baptiste's horizons had hardly changed. How old was he now? Forty-seven or eight? The years had not treated him unkindly, but then trial and tribulation could hardly have taken their toll.

'Will you take the carriage, Madame?'

'I think I shall have to, Baptiste.' Hobbling up the hill to Elm House in a tight fitting skirt did not hold quite the appeal as once skipping up in a crinoline.

She was eyed surreptitiously as she climbed into the carriage, but she did not sense that anyone knew who she was. She was just one of the many English visitors who swamped the Island during the spring and summer seasons. In the short time she had returned, she was conscious of great changes. More steamers than ever were making use of the New Harbour, and visitors no longer had to suffer the inconvenience of a rowing boat to reach shore. Now passengers alighted at the Steam Packet Pier. And she was hearing English everywhere; the language dominated the hoardings and notices. Even the ragged boys, she noticed, were shouting to each other in a curious English patois.

The years seemed to melt away as she stepped into the hall, but a brief glimpse in the looking glass pulled her up sharp. Of course it was different, very different. The house was quiet, suffocatingly quiet. There were no dogs to greet her, no music seeping under the doors. She handed her cape and umbrella to a young girl, who bobbed respectfully and disappeared down to the kitchens before she had a chance to ask her name.

Baptiste picked up her bags, and she followed him up the stairs. 'We thought you would prefer your old room, Madame.'

She wondered who 'we' might be. No doubt she would find out in good time. He opened the door to the bedroom, deposited the bags quickly inside then stood in the doorway, blocking her entrance. 'The maid will see to the unpacking. Is there anything else you require, Madame?'

'No thank you, Baptiste.' She saw herself through his eyes: a trussed matron in sumptuous furs with that ridiculous feather perched on the top of her hat, looking so urbane, so out of place on this little Island. But surely he saw through the deception?

'Coffee will be served in the drawing-room in half-an-hour, Madame.'

'When may I see Uncle?'

'As soon as you are ready, Madame.'

'How is he, Baptiste?'

'I believe he has improved a little since he heard that you were coming, Madame.'

He scurried away before she could ask him anything else. She tried not to feel hurt. Her arrival must have unsettled him. She peered round the door. This had once been her room. Hers and Louisa's. It was just as she remembered: the same curtains round the bed, the same patterned rosebuds rambling up the walls – but the room seemed smaller. In fact, its smallness surprised her. And now she saw something new: a full-length painting of Louisa hanging above the chest of drawers. It was an enlargement of a *carte de visite* that Louisa had sent her shortly after she had arrived in India. Louisa, without her ringlets and with her head strategically tilted to show off her new hairstyle, looked down at her with an arch smile, so happy, so full of expectation.

Francina turned away.

Someone had placed a vase of white narcissi on the chest of drawers, but the scent could not disguise the fustiness of the room. She tiptoed to the window and pushed up the sash.

The garden looked minuscule after her rolling acres in Dumfriesshire. Why, even her kitchen garden was bigger than this garden. She pictured the grounds of Blackhill as she had left them five days ago: the expanse of lawn, dew-drenched and closely clipped, the black hedges bordering the grass walks, the angular flower beds, the croquet lawn, the tennis court, the drive sweeping around the rhododendron bushes, the swathes of daffodils under the bare trees . . . Who could have imagined that she would become mistress of so much?

She sat on the bed and the lumpy horsehair mattress puffed, resisting her weight as it used to. She ran her hand lightly over the old patchwork counterpane. So many stories were stitched into those patterns. One day there would be no one left to remember them.

The old washstand with its chipped blue and white china bowl still stood in the corner, and hanging above it, the same pitted glass. A looking glass has magical powers: it holds in its memory the face that it last reflected, until the moment that another supersedes it. Francina crept towards it and braced herself. Whose face would she see, hers or Louisa's? And for a moment as she stared into the glass and watched twenty-four years etch their telltale marks on her face, she was not sure.

She knocked quietly. There was no response, so she knocked a little louder. A woman answered softly. Steeling herself, Francina opened the door. The telltale odour of carbolic soap, ammonia and mustard told her she was entering a sickroom, and for a moment a flicker of that debilitating powerlessness returned. But now it was Uncle Doré and not Aunt who lay in the bed. His head, propped up by pillows, had slipped sideways. His mouth had fallen open. His frailty shocked her even though she had prepared herself for change. She leaned over and kissed him, catching that old familiar smell of leather and tobacco she remembered as a child.

The nurse, a capable-looking countrywoman sitting on a hard chair in the corner, packed away her knitting and left the room. Francina drew up a chair and took his dry hand, the same hand that had once clasped hers so tightly on Waterloo Station. She tried not to see an elderly man, but that imposing soldier astride a black stallion who used to turn heads on the Queen's Birthday Review. How proud she had been of dear Uncle Doré.

She sat for a while at his bedside, listening to his rasping breaths. She did not have the heart to wake him, and as he looked as though he would sleep for some time, she would take some air on the New Ground - or Cambridge Park as Baptiste now called it 'on account of His Royal Highness's visit'. Of course she must not use the back stairs. She must remember who she was. It is at times like this that she feels the relentless passing of time.

'Would you like your umbrella, Madame?'

'Do you think it will rain, Baptiste?'

She wished he would call her La Missie, like he used to. It was her special name. Now I am just plain, anonymous Madame, she thought sadly.

'It is possible, Madame.'

'Uncle is sleeping. Could you tell me when he wakes?'

'Yes, Madame.'

Baptiste opened the front door for her. She would like to ask him to accompany her, to stroll round the park on his arm. There were so many memories they shared.

She crossed the footbridge and opened the little iron gate. How popular this space was when they were children. Now, she suspected, fashionable folk probably walked their dogs along the new pier that crossed the sea to Castle Cornet.

She circled the New Ground until she reached the old bench (even more defaced with initials). Brushing leaves off the seat, she swallowed her tears and sat down. She knew this visit would be difficult, but she hadn't realised just how difficult.

It was turning chill. Clouds were building up to rain. There was hardly a soul in the park, just a solitary gentleman walking towards Castle Carey. Something about his manner caught her attention, and she watched him from her peripheral vision for a few minutes. If he followed the path then he should pass this bench, and she would take a closer look at him.

This place was full of memories, images that flickered in and out of focus. She remembered the excitement on hearing the cacophony of drums, bells and penny whistles drifting up from the harbour - the noise that heralded the Midsummer Fair. In her mind's eye, she saw herself, Louisa and Miss Hobson in their white summer dresses, squeezing between the decorated carts to read the gaudy signs of the stalls and side-shows; she saw the country women in their traditional costumes; the young men in their embroidered waistcoats; the organ-grinder's monkeys, quaintly dressed as harlequin and columbine; the tattered Russian bear performing his pathetic routine of tricks . . . then across the open space they would hear the opening bars of the old musician's *chifournie* and hurry to join the crowd watching the country dancing.

The gentleman had reached the fork in the path. He hesitated and glanced up at the sky. Spots of rain were beginning to fall. That seemed to decide it. He turned right at Castle Carey. He would not pass her after all.

She stood up and opened her umbrella. If Uncle Doré was still asleep when she returned, she would pass the time writing letters. Edith would worry until she had news of her safe arrival. Of all her children, Edith was the most reluctant to loosen the maternal strings. Why was she so insecure? She has never felt the pain of rejection, or found herself alone and fighting for her life. She blamed herself, of course. Edith was spoilt. She was born too soon. She had never loved Edith as readily as her other children. But Edith never suspected. How could she? Her father had doted on her. She was the apple of his eye, his first-born, his 'Little Rabbit'. Edith was given whatever she wanted, by a father who loved her and a mother consumed with guilt.

Some ingrained habit made her turn to call the dogs. She half-expected, half-hoped, to see them bounding through the trees towards her - but of course they were long gone.

*

The house was so still. No dogs, no voices. Just the old grandfather clock ticking on the landing. She tiptoed into the parlour. How quaint it looked with its outdated furniture. But it was comforting to see Aunt Doré's escritoire still in the same space. She perched on the hard padded chair and raised the lid cautiously, as though she might unwittingly release a multitude of secrets that were best kept undisturbed. Everything was arranged as she remembered: the cards, the notepaper, Aunt's row of red household account books neatly arranged in date order . . . For old time's sake she pulled out one entitled *1855* and flicked through the pages. Towards the end of the year, the entries changed from a bold, confident hand to a thin spidery one. Her stomach tightened as she remembered the day when Aunt, overcome at the news of Charlie's death, had taken to her bed and made her responsible for running the household. But Aunt's training had served her well. She prided herself on the efficient way she managed the Blackhill estate. She took a close interest in the farms and the welfare of her tenants. Every bill was settled on time, every payment accounted for. No underhand activity, she believed, had ever escaped her eye. How surprised her husband would have been to see his obsequious wife burgeoning into such a formidable administrator.

She opened another accounts book dated *1860* and recognised Louisa's hand. So this task became Louisa's. She scanned the entries. Every pound of butter or packet of pins was carefully recorded; every butcher's or baker's bill paid on time. She pictured Louise sitting here, gradually succumbing to Aunt Doré's indomitable authority. How different their lives became.

Something caught her attention. Crammed into the small rosewood compartments were bundles of letters tied in ribbon. She pulled out a bundle.

Her letters. All the letters she had sent from India were carefully preserved in date order (she recognised Louisa's pencil marks in the corner). It touched her to know that Louisa had saved her letters. She untied the white ribbon. This was not prying. Surely she was entitled to read her own letters?

S.S. 'Hindustan' (somewhere in the Indian Ocean)

27th April 1856

Dearest Lulu,

We are racing towards the Bay of Bengal - but even with a strong breeze it is far too hot to stir a finger, so I hope you appreciate my efforts in writing to you! Shipboard life has settled into a very Indian way now, with most of the passengers too exhausted to do anything but take a long siesta after tiffin. You would so enjoy this idle life, Lulu. The ship comes alive in the evenings with dancing or impromptu concerts. Some of the young men have formed an Amateur Theatre Company and last night gave us 'The Road to Ruin' on a makeshift stage under the stars. The moon was so bright that I could read the programme without the aid of a lamp. (The night sky is a wonderful spectacle out here, filled with marvellous, unfamiliar constellations.) Aunt Cecilia and I received dismissive looks from Reverend Wright for giggling during the serious scenes, but I do not think Lieutenant Hartwell, who played the part of the tragic heroine, was much offended.

Sadly, the heat has caused some deaths on board. A dear little monkey with an inquisitive face, that we used to see clinging to the wrist of one of the lady passengers, expired in the Red Sea. And yesterday poor Norah Clapperton found her canary dead at the bottom of its cage -

'Madame, the master is awake. He is asking for you.'

'Thank you, Baptiste.'

Francina returned the letter to the bundle. It had unnerved her to read of her former self: innocent, gullible, and so full of expectation. If she could have foreseen what would follow, would she have still gone to India? She often asked herself that question.

She closed the escritoire and left the room.

Uncle lay propped against his cushions. He opened his eyes and smiled as she came in. When the nurse had left them, Francina took his hand, hot and trembling, and pressed it to her lips. 'How are you feeling, Uncle?'

'Better, my dear. Much better now you are here.'

'Oh, Uncle, why did you not send me word?'

'I did not want to worry you. Who told you that I was unwell?'

'Madame Le Boutillier wrote to me. I came as soon as I heard.'

Uncle Doré smiled. 'She has been so kind, so thoughtful.' His eyes focused on the overflowing fruit bowl on the chest of drawers.

'I shall pay Madame Le Boutillier a visit and thank her on your behalf.'

'Would you do that for me, my dear? I have always regretted . . . your Aunt . . . she treated her badly . . . I should have said something.' Uncle Doré turned his head and gazed at a small photographic likeness of Louisa arranged amongst a group on his bedside table. 'I have had a great deal . . . of time to think -'

He began to splutter. In alarm, Francina rang the bell.

The nurse flew back into the sickroom, and picked up a spray producer off the bedside table. 'Inhale, Monsieur,' she ordered, squirting a vaporous spirit down his throat.

Uncle coughed up phlegm into a bowl that the nurse held out for him. When he had regained his breath, he lay back against the pillows, exhausted. 'There are . . . things I regret,' he whispered. 'Things I should have done things differently . . . '

The nurse tactfully left the room with the covered bowl, and closed the door behind her.

'Don't think about the past, Uncle. You must concentrate on getting better.'

'At least I did right by you, didn't I, my dear? Your Aunt would have been so proud to see you now. It was the right decision to send you to India, wasn't it?'

'Try not to talk too much, Uncle. Shall I sit here and read to you? Do you remember how I used to read the newspaper to you when Aunt Doré was abroad?'

He smiled and closed his eyes. Francina was not sure if he had fallen asleep, but she read out articles that she thought might be of interest to him, just in case he was still awake. Reading nullified the silence, stifled the memories she was not quite ready to resuscitate.

'The miscalculation by the Finance Department of the budget in which the Afghan War expenditure has been greatly under-estimated, has created considerable excitement in India and has been the subject of hostile criticism in Parliament . . . '

Eventually Nurse Bresson interrupted to announce that it was time to change Monsieur's poultice.

Francina folded the newspaper and stood up to leave.

'Don't go, my dear. Read to me while Nurse attends to her duties – unless the sight of a bare chest alarms you?'

'Of course not, Uncle.'

Over the years nursing had become a way of life to her, a lifesaving therapy. She had discovered long ago that caring for the sick or wounded helped retain her sanity.

Nurse picked up a small saucepan of water that had been quietly simmering over the fire and poured it into a pudding basin. The smell of warming linseed rose into the air. Beating the mixture vigorously, the woman quickly spread it onto a sheet of brown paper and covered it with a wad of cotton wool and a strip of flannel. Francina unbuttoned Uncle's nightshirt; helped Nurse peel the old linseed poultice off his heaving chest and replace it with the new steaming pad.

Her days evolved into a quiet, unhurried routine. It soon became her habit to sit by Uncle's bedside while Nurse Bresson took a well-earned rest from her duties. It pleased her to help this hard-working Christian woman. She learned how to change Uncle's poultice every three hours, to spray Ipecacuanha vapour down his throat, and to mix his prescription - *carbonate of ammonia (40 grains), tincture of squill (½ ounce), sulphuric ether (2 drachms), concentrated infusion of senega (1 ounce), syrup of tolu (½ ounce) mixed in 8 ounces of water. Two tablespoons to be taken every four hours.*

When Uncle was awake she would read the newspaper or a volume of poetry to him, but while he slept she found herself thinking of her Indian letters.

A gleam of light brushes across the wall. The closet door is open, and a soft, rustling sound comes from inside. Her heart stands still. She lies motionless, watching the light oscillate around the room . . . highlighting the washstand, chair, the dressing table . . . The light grows brighter. A young girl emerges slowly from the closet. She is dressed in a white flounced gown, lacy and voluminous. Candlelight plays on her golden hair that falls, loose and dishevelled down her back. Holding the candle above her head, she surveys the room then places it on the dressing table. She picks up the white veil draped over the portmanteau, holds it aloft and gazes at it for a long time. Then she throws it over her head and studies her reflection in the looking glass.

The reflection catches her eye and smiles. 'Don't I look beautiful, Ina?'

'Lulu, why are you wearing my wedding dress and veil?'

The reflection sobs. 'But how can that be? I'm the one getting married!'

Francina sat up, her temples throbbing. Moonlight had fallen across Louisa's portrait, illuminating her skin and her dress, so that she hovered in the frame, ghostly white. Her face stood out, pale and round as a perpetual moon. She turned away, brushed the damp strands of hair clinging to her neck and slipped out of bed. She eyed the black veil and dress draped over the portmanteau lying undisturbed where she had left them, lifted the silk peignoir off the hook and draped it round her shoulders. Apart from her undergarments, this was the only white item of clothing in the room.

She tiptoed barefoot to the window and pulled up the sash. The cool night air wafted over her, and she stood for a moment, listening to the murmurs of the sleeping Island and Uncle's laboured breaths echoing through the house.

Why did she feel this oppressive guilt? If she had stayed in Guernsey, would her presence have changed the outcome?

Cold was seeping through her bare feet so she returned to bed. Avoiding the portrait, she stared hard at the wallpaper. In the pallid light, the rosebuds had turned grey; the leaves and stems looked black and barbed. She hugged herself tight, remembering how she and Lulu would fall asleep, entwined in each other's arms.

But it was impossible to sleep.

She tossed restlessly as the hours ticked through the night, until she could bear it no longer. She slipped out of bed and opened the bedroom door. The house was in darkness except for a speck of light under Uncle's door. Quietly, she crept across the landing and down the stairs to the parlour.

She lit the lamp and carried it to the escritoire. She lowered the lid and pulled the bundle of Indian letters out of its compartment.

It was time to confront her demons.

CALCUTTA
May 1856

'Did you have a pleasant ride this morning, Francina?'

They were having breakfast in the Bartons' favourite corner of the verandah, the spot that overlooked the high entrance gates, which were just visible through the branches of the spreading trees in the compound. However, the loud caw-cawing of some ugly birds perched in the branches was making conversation difficult.

'We did, thank you Aunt Barton.'

She enjoyed her early morning rides with Uncle Barton. He had been showing her the sights across Town. She was particularly struck by the European parts, which were stylish and spacious. It was as though some mystical deity has plucked the buildings from a site in Ancient Rome, and deposited them out here along wide streets and boulevards. Calcutta truly deserved its name 'City of Palaces'. There are glittering pools everywhere, and plenty of open spaces for taking the air. Calcutta was the exact opposite of cramped grey little St Pierre Port. There was not one hillock or stair-street anywhere.

Now they were beginning to explore the sandy lanes of Calcutta's hinterland. Everything she saw entranced her: the temples; the sparking rice fields; the thatched mud-walled huts hidden amongst the mango groves; and the crowded, pungent bazaars where the natives eyed her curiously and grey monkeys dropped like ripened fruit from the trees.

'The guns woke me. I had a terrible fright.' Grand-mère's bony hand, encased in black, fingerless lace, trembled as she lifted her teacup.

At first Francina had found Grand-mère's mode of dress a little startling, but now she had grown used to the red gold-threaded shawl she entwined around her head instead of the customary lace cap and weepers.

'Ma Mère, I warned you last night, that it was the Queen's Birthday today,' Aunt Barton said.

'How am I expected to remember? I'm an old woman.' Grand-mère's blue eyes flashed behind her pince-nez. She looked so small perched on her cushions in her high-backed cane chair, her shoulders just visible above the tablecloth; more like a fairy godmother than a conventional grandmother. Grand-mère had proudly informed Francina that she was probably the oldest European in Calcutta. Europeans of her age were either dead or had returned years ago. 'But why should I return to France?' Grand-mère had shrugged. 'The only corner of France I know is a damp convent hidden behind high walls. India is my home. I was born here, married here, and intend to die here. All my children were born here'.

'Nonsense, ma Mère, you can remember perfectly well when it suits you.'

Netta, Grand-mère's companion, sliced papaya into a cut-glass bowl and placed it before the old lady. Grand-mère pouted at the offering like a spoilt child.

'I see that gold production is flourishing in Adelaide,' Uncle Barton mumbled from behind his newspaper. 'Prospectors are pouring in from all over Australia.'

Uncle Barton, who had changed into his loose Turkish trousers and curled slippers, had retired from the breakfast table to the far end of the verandah and was reclining in his low cane chair, one foot draped over the arm, which was the lounging fashion for gentlemen in the East. It never ceased to surprise Francina how communicative Uncle Barton was on their morning rides, whilst at home, he did little more than mumble, especially if Grand-mère was present. Uncle Barton and Grand-mère, it seemed, rarely conversed with one another. Grand-mère refused to speak English, and Uncle Barton did not speak French, so Aunt Barton generally acted as interpreter.

'In consequence, Melbourne has an acute shortage of labourers.'

His mumbled observations, drifting from time to time across the verandah, were almost drowned by din of the crows. Francina gave him an encouraging smile, for no one else seemed to take notice of anything he said. With everyone around him talking French, Uncle Barton was a foreigner in his own home.

'Ma Mère, if you do not eat that,' said Aunt Barton, 'I'll tell the *khansamah* to give it to Louis.'

'Louis, Louis Le Roi!' shrieked the parrot, lurching like a drunken sailor along his perch.

The gates ground open and a horse trotted up the drive. Uncle Barton put down his newspaper. Aunt's eyebrows flew up. She lifted the *tatties,* parted the leaves of the potted palm (carefully positioned so that she could spy on arrivals) and glanced down into the compound.

'It's Mr Cowan Bell,' she whispered, adjusting her silk peignoir over her bosom.

'Oh,' said Francina.

She was acquainted with Mr Cowan Bell. He had travelled out to India on the *Hindustan* with them. Aunt Cecilia had introduced him as an old family friend, a junior partner in Uncle Barton's mercantile firm of indigo and jute agents.

Soon, Mr Cowan Bell's head, then body materialised at the top of the stairs. Clutching his *topee* to his chest, he apologised for calling so early. His eyes fell on Francina. She nodded politely then looked away.

Uncle Barton threw down his newspaper and stood up. 'Bell, my good fellow.'

'Will you join us for *burra hazri,* Mr Cowan Bell?' beamed Aunt Barton.

Moods changed rapidly in the Barton household when a visitor arrived (even one as dull as Mr Cowan Bell). It was an observation Francina made soon after coming to live with Aunt Barton. The volatile nature of the Barton household had shocked her at first. Secretly, she would have preferred to live with Aunt Cecilia, but she had hardly seen her since arriving in Calcutta, despite living so close. The Vauloués and Bartons, it appeared, moved in different circles. Uncle Barton, being Scottish, was associated with the British mercantile and banking community, while Uncle Vauloué, a retired French indigo planter, had few connections with British society. The subtleties of Indian society were complex and confusing, indeed as confusing as the native caste system.

Mr Cowan Bell declined. Despite it being a public holiday, he had a private matter to discuss, and wondered if he might possibly intrude on Barton's time for a moment?

Uncle escorted him to the study.

'Such a nice young man,' whispered Aunt Barton.

'He is practically middle-aged, Aunt.'

'I remember when he first came out - a genial young clerk, full of enthusiasm and energy - but the climate has worn him down, as it eventually wears everyone down.'

'He did not join in society much on the *Hindustan*.'

'I expect he was just nervous of female company,' smiled Aunt Barton. 'He has lived the solitary life of an Indian bachelor for too long.'

'I nicknamed him Grizzly on the steamer,' Francina said. She did not explain that his burly physique, unruly beard, and the way he lolloped, reminded her of the dancing bears at the Town fairs.

'Not to his face, I hope?'

'Certainly not, Aunt, but it used to amuse Aunt Cecilia.'

Francina's abiding memory of Grizzly was of a crumpled individual in a deck chair studying some tome or other, while the other passengers played quoits around him. As far as she could tell, his only interest was in botany. Once to her dismay, he had blocked her entrance to the saloon to tell her of the varieties of seeds he was bringing out and hoping to germinate in his Indian garden.

'That seems a little cruel, *ma petite*. Physical appearances are not everything. Mr Cowan Bell has a kind nature. You could do a great deal worse than consider him for a husband.'

Francina choked on her tea.

'A husband! Why should I consider him as a husband? Has he said anything to you, Aunt?'

'No, not yet.' Aunt lowered her voice. 'But I think he had high hopes of bringing a wife out with him this time. Sadly, it was not to be. A kind, sympathetic young wife would do him the world of good.'

Grand-mère coughed and demanded a translation. Aunt Barton repeated the conversation in French and the old lady listened closely. Francina had a sneaking suspicion that Grand-mère could understand English perfectly well.

'Englishman, pah!' Grand-mère shook her head. 'We will find a nice Frenchman for you - like your Papa. *Alors,* how happy I was when Theresa married a Frenchman!'

'Papa is a Guernsey man, Grand-mère.'

The old lady shrugged. 'Almost a Frenchman. But why did all my daughters have to marry Protestants!'

'Ma Mère!' Aunt Barton said sharply.

Sometimes, during these fractious exchanges, Francina longed to escape to Aunt Cecilia's house. But the logistics of requesting the bearer to summon the syce to summon the buggy and all the accompanying attendants took the spontaneity out of the idea – and of course it was out of the question that she could just slip out of the house and walk the hundred yards or so by herself to Middleton Street.

'Take your time, *ma petite*. Do not accept the first offer that comes your way. Marry for love as I did,' smiled Grand-mère. 'Your grand-père and I eloped.'

'*Eloped*, Grand-mère?'

'Enough of this foolish talk!' Aunt Barton dabbed her mouth with her napkin and stood up. 'The *dhobi-wallah* will soon be here. Francina, come and help me count the *jharuns*.' Aunt always seemed agitated on *dhobi* day.

Francina stood up to follow Aunt into the house.

'After the siesta, I shall take you for a little drive to the French cemetery,' whispered Grand-mère, as she walked past her chair. 'I shall show you Grand-père's tomb.'

'I should like that very much, Grand-mère.'

The *dhobi-wallah* was squatting on the back verandah surrounded by smelly piles of soiled linen, waiting for the memsahib to give him the signal so that he could begin the weekly ritual of counting out the soiled *jharuns*.

'Here, child,' said Aunt Baron when she appeared. 'I want you to check the tablecloths and linen for holes and tears. Unfold and examine everything thoroughly. This *dhobi-wallah* is notorious for damaging my washing. He has to be watched or he will sneak in a torn tablecloth under my nose and then claim it had nothing to do with him if I should confront him about it next week. - And a word of advice, Francina,' added Aunt quietly, 'take no notice of what Grand-mère says. She has some eccentric views.'

'Why does she dislike the English so much, Aunt Barton?'

Aunt sighed. 'Grand-mère was born in the French colony of Pondichéry. Her father was Capitaine of the troops there. When she was a little girl, the English laid siege to Pondichéry, bombarding the garrison for two months, and destroying a large part of the Town - including the house in which she lived.'

'But why?'

'France and Britain were at war at the time.' Aunt Barton nodded to the butler, a tall, dignified man in a pleated turban and long white achkan, who handed her the *dhobi*-book. 'But all that happened a long time ago. The French and the English are no longer enemies. We have just fought a war in the Crimea as allies, have we not? But your grand-mère seems unable to comprehend this fact. She is old. She cannot help living in the past. So, enough of this talk, we have important work to do.'

While Francina examined the clean washing for *dhobi* damage, Aunt Barton made a note of each dishcloth and duster to be washed in the *dhobi* book, and crossed off each dishcloth and duster that had returned clean and undamaged.

The heat intensified after *burra hazri* until it was overpowering. The sun pressed relentlessly down, exhausting every creature under it, and the hum of activity around Chowringhee slowed to a whisper. Aunt Barton had no wish to make calls in the gruelling heat; neither did she feel inclined to receive any. So the *durwan* was instructed to hook up the *Not at Home* box on the gate, and without the prospect of visitors, the old ladies were safe to recline about the house in a state of demi-mode.

There was so much Francina wished to see of India, but the heat contained her like a prison. Apart from her early morning rides and the drives at sunset, she remained confined behind drawn shutters for most of the day. There was nothing to do. It was too hot to sketch in the compound, and much as she disliked practicing on the pianoforte, it was an activity that might have passed the time, but that was out of the question during the siesta. Her elderly relatives took their siestas very seriously.

Reading passed the time, but she had exhausted her supply of books and the few volumes Uncle Burton possessed were learned tomes on *Chinese Silk Production, Indian Crop Cultivation*, or *Indigo Manufacture*. Although he scoured the daily newspapers, it was chiefly the rise and fall of the commercial markets that interested him. She collapsed *déshabillé* into a cane chair, tried to ignore the irritating dirge of the brainfever bird that had adopted the tree outside her window, and decided to read *Paul et Virginie* for the second time. It was Grand-mère's cherished novel. All her daughters had loved it, Grand-mère had said, and Theresa in particular.

'What was Mamma like when she was a girl?' Francina could not help asking.

Grand-mère had turned her eyes towards the portrait of her husband, and for a moment husband and wife seemed to reflect on the trials and misdemeanours of their youngest daughter. 'Theresa was a headstrong child,' she said eventually. 'We were partly to blame. We should not have sent her away at such a young age. You see, the war prevented us from sending our children to Europe. But as soon as we heard news that the little corporal Napoleon had abdicated, and the late King's brother was instated on the throne, we made immediate preparations to send our children to France – for your grand-père was determined to give his children the best education. I tried to tell him that the girls were too young to go (Cecilia was six but Theresa was only four), but he said that it was a good time to send them, for they would be under the guardianship of their brother Gaston, who was going to the university in Paris. And it seemed sensible to send the girls together, for they were devoted to each other.'

Grand-mère returned to the portrait. Grand-père stared impassively down at her. He was thin featured with a long aquiline nose and grey hair that receded at the temples. Fish ants had channelled down one arm, but his poise overcame this indignity. He was not a man to be contradicted, even by a strong-minded wife.

'Our two little girls looked so small as they were rowed away to the ship. It was a terrible wrench to say goodbye to them – to all five of our dear children at the same time. Their departure left a grievous void at our family table, which was never properly filled again. And as it turned out, all our careful plans were overturned. When the ship neared La Manche, it was intercepted by the British. News had arrived that Napoleon had escaped from Elba and the new King had fled from France. So once again, Europe was thrown into the turmoil of war. Poor Gaston felt a great responsibility for the safety of his little sisters. One senior passenger, *bien aristocrate,* recommended that he should place the girls in a convent in the South of England run by a Holy Order that had escaped from France during the Terror. After much altercation with the British authorities, he was given leave to do so.

Francina felt Mamma's shadow on every page. Were these her tears that had smudged the print where Virginie loses her life in the hurricane? But how could someone, who had shed tears for a fictitious character, be indifferent to her own daughter?

There was so much she did not understand.

A servant raised the *tatties,* waking Francina from her siesta. Hot air seeped in, but at least it brought some light. She still could not get used to the servants, especially the male servants, wandering in and out of her room without so much as a cough to announce their presence. 'Oh, don't mind the servants,' Aunt Barton had said. 'In a few weeks you will cease to notice that they exist.' Some Europeans, she had heard, allowed servants to supervise their bathing: one to pour water over them, another to rub them dry. She would never succumb to such lazy Indian ways. 'It is just a matter of getting used to Indian customs, *ma chérie*. The more tasks they perform for you, the greater respect they have for you.'

The French Burial Ground was just at the end of Park Street, but the buggy was summoned with great ceremony. Grand-mère and Netta were assisted in. Francina climbed up and sat between them. She was not surprised to find Netta accompanying them. She was always at Grand-mère's side. This tiny, dark-skinned creature in European dress occupied a unique position in the household - not quite servant, but not quite family. And curiously, Netta had been with Grand-mère for so long that she had acquired her mannerisms and spoke French as perfectly as Grand-mère. But who was Netta? Where did she come from?

'Netta was here before I was born,' Aunt Barton had said, when she inquired. 'She grew up with us; she has always lived with us.'

It was Netta who had taken Angelo aside and revealed Mamma's whereabouts to him. Francina glanced slyly at her. What other secrets might she know?

The sun was sinking behind the trees, but the huge buggy hood raised against the slanting rays seemed only to capture the heat and contain it. It was hotter than the hottest day Francina had ever known in Guernsey; and as they travelled at a walking pace down Park Street, accompanied by the parasol attendant and the syce, nothing stirred the air.

The buggy pulled up at the gates of the Burial Ground, and they were assisted out. After a small payment to the gatekeeper, they walked slowly between the high gates and down a straight path shaded by a double row of dusty trees. The parasol attendant walked closely behind, while five paces in front, a bow-legged old man swept the path clear of leaves and other matter.

Tall obelisks, pagodas, mausoleums and tombs loomed around them like pieces on a giant chessboard. Some were the size of garden houses fashioned with pediments and classical columns; others were topped with huge stone urns. In this burial ground a person's earthly worth was indicated by the size of his tomb, each one vying to outdo its neighbour by height, mass or ornament. Francina read the names as they passed: *Xavier, De Silva, de Souza, Le Vassoult, de L'Etang, Bronzoni, Tiretta* . . . This was the Roman Catholic burial ground; the English were buried elsewhere.

A few other Europeans were strolling in the shade amongst the obelisks and pagodas, mainly women and children with their ayahs, for the high walls kept out the pariah dogs and other unwelcome animals, making this a relatively safe place for children to play.

They turned down a straight intersecting path. Halfway down, Grand-mère stopped and gazed up at a tapering column atop a stolid rectangular tomb. The column rose to a height of about ten feet - an impressive height for any burial ground, but here was dwarfed by the slim obelisk next to it and the towering one behind.

'Grand-père's tomb.'

Grand-mère gesticulated to the bow-legged old man, who swept his brush across the inscription at the base of the column.

'*GASTON ANGELO SAVI, Esquire of Elba,*' Francina read.

'When your grand-père was a young man, Elba was part of the Austrian Empire, and during the war, Franca and Austria were in alliance with Haidar Ali and his son Tipu Sultan, the great rulers of Mysore. All were united in their desire to rid the British from India.'

'So Grand-père came to India as a soldier? I thought he was an indigo manufacturer.'

'He was later, but he first came out as ship's surgeon in the massive convoy under General de Bussy's command. He was a man of peace. He wanted only to ease suffering.'

'Aunt Barton told me how much you had suffered during the war.'

'Indeed. Not only were the English content to destroy our lovely town of Pondichéry and starve us into submission, but they then rounded up all the inhabitants in the Colony, kept us prisoner for nine months, and then shipped us back to France. I was only four years old, but I remember it all so clearly. We were almost Home (having been tossed about in tempestuous seas for six months), when a large ship flying the French flag and a white pendent approached us just south of Cape St Vincent. Our Capitaine hoisted up the flag of cartel to show that we were a demilitarised ship transporting repatriated prisoners of war, and we all scrambled on deck eager to wave at a friendly face from Home. But when that ship sailed closer, it lowered the French flag, hoisted instead the English flag, and opened fire on us.'

Grand-mère covered her ears with her hands. 'I am still haunted by the sound of gunfire.'

Netta took her hand and whispered something.

'No, Netta, I will go on, the child should know,' said Grand-mère. 'My mother scooped me in her arms and hurried below to join the other women and children huddling in the cabin. Everyone was crying and praying to the Holy Mother, beseeching her to deliver us. The pounding went on and on. Then a ball burst through the ceiling and landed at our feet, injuring a child. The Capitaine and several soldiers were killed; others were gravely wounded. When the English eventually ceased firing and boarded us, they were surprised to find that we were what we claimed to be - only a cartel ship. The English escorted us to Cadiz for repairs, for our ship was badly damaged and taking in water. But the shock was too great for my mother. She lost her life soon afterwards.'

A tear trickled down Grand-mère's cheek and she brushed it away. 'My mother and her unborn child are buried in Cadiz. I have never visited their grave.'

Francina wished she had the courage to take her hand and squeeze it tight.

'When we arrived in France,' Grand-mère continued, 'there was a fervent desire in the country to free our Indian territories from English occupation. My father was immediately ordered to escort a squadron of troops back to the Indian Ocean. So I was left, a frightened, motherless orphan in a convent in Brest. Father took part in some ferocious battles against the English, and we were close to making considerable gains when news arrived that a Peace Treaty had been signed at Versailles. Our Indian territories were returned to us the following year, but Father firmly believed that if the Treaty had been delayed by a few months, France might today be the greatest power in India.'

2

'I thought it would be cooler when the Rains came, but it seems hotter than ever.' Francina said. Fanning kept the insects off her face, but it hardly cooled her down.

'Are you taking your quinine regularly, my dear?'

'Yes, Uncle, but the taste is very bitter.'

'You will get used to it, but the Rains have hardly started. What we experienced recently is a mere prelude to what will soon befall us.'

They were driving slowly round the Maidan at dusk. 'Eating the air,' as Aunt Barton called it. The shower had been a refreshing interlude, but the sun had returned with burning intensity, so that now the earth steamed and once again the vegetation looked brown and scorched.

Across Calcutta, natives were cooking their meals on open fires. Smoke seeped through the roofs of the flimsy huts built along the boundary walls of the European houses and drifted in pungent plumes across the Course. Wood smoke and coconut oil mingled with the scent of reviving grass and the stench from the river. It was a uniquely Indian combination that took Francina immediately back to her childhood.

Aunt Barton tapped her with her fan. The Governor-General's lady was approaching in her barouche, surrounded by her aides-de-camp, bodyguards and torchbearers. Starched turbans, silver emblems and staffs proceeded down the Course like two red and white glimmering caterpillars escorting a fairy queen in her silver carriage. It looked as though some grand operatic scene was about to be enacted on the Maidan. Carriages and riders edged aside and politely acknowledged the *Burra Lady Sahib* as the entourage passed.

'Poor Lady Canning, how drawn she looks these days. And Lord Canning seldom accompanies her,' whispered Aunt Barton. 'I've heard that he hardly ever leaves his desk to take a siesta.'

'Newcomers nowadays rarely make allowances for the climate,' murmured Uncle Barton. 'They think they can live as they did at Home. But whatever their rank, the climate will get to them in the end. It always does to those who do not respect it.'

Uncle Barton ordered the syce to head towards the bandstand. They joined the array of carriages, two or three deep, listening to the military band playing some popular airs. In the gathering dusk, lights began to flicker over the townscape and dance across the river. Francina was growing accustomed to the ritual of the 'evening airing' when the beau monde of Calcutta took advantage of the cooler air to congregate in their finery on the Maidan. However many times she witnessed this spectacle played under the stars and illuminated by torchlight, it would always thrill her.

Aunt Barton pointed out the Calcutta residents to her. Slipping between the British and European communities, she knew a great many people by sight, if not intimately. In the three weeks that Francina had been in India, she had come to realise how small and discriminating Indian society was. Around the bandstand, she saw the same parties coming together; the same Civilians, the same Army officers with their ladies. She would have liked to climb out of the carriage and stretch her legs, but no other woman appeared to have such a desire. It was disappointing to find that in India European women were rarely seen strolling in public places.

A carriage drew up alongside. It was Mr Crooke of the Bengal Bank and his wife.

'Have you heard, Mr Allen's fiancée was taken ill the day after she arrived in India,' whispered Mrs Crooke to Aunt Barton after the exchange of greetings. 'The wedding is postponed.'

'Let us hope poor Mr Allen's fiancée does not go the way of his last,' said Aunt Barton.

While the two ladies reflected on poor Mr Allen's predicament, Francina's eyes strayed to a group of young officers near the bandstand who were lolling against carriages and puffing cigars as they paid their respects to the *spins* of Calcutta. The spinsters were flirting in a manner that would cause acrid tongues to wag in Guernsey.

She caught the eye of one of the officers, a slim young man with fiery whiskers. He remounted and trotted towards her. Aunt and Mrs Crooke looked at Francina in surprise.

Francina blushed and introduced Lieutenant Hartwell. 'We travelled out on the *Hindustan* together. It was Mr Hartwell who taught me those Indian words.'

Aunt Barton laughed. 'You taught her well, Mr Hartwell.'

'Miss Duquesne was an attentive pupil, Mrs Barton.'

Francina lowered her eyes. She had enjoyed his company on the *Hindustan*. He had passed her after an on-board theatrical performance, flushed and sweating, and looking so absurd in his skirts and bonnet that she had giggled. Her giggles caught his attention and he had introduced himself. She knew he was one of the wild set that horsed on the decks at night, but in that curly black wig she could not tell which one. But it did not matter. She was attracted to his smiling grey eyes.

'Where are you stationed, Lieutenant?' asked Uncle Barton.

'At Fort William, sir. I am the garrison engineer.'

'Garrison engineer, eh?'

'Indeed, sir, and amongst other roles, I am responsible for the care of some of the city's ancient monuments.'

'That is commendable, most commendable,' said Uncle Barton. 'I have often mused on the sorry state of some of India's monuments.'

'In our rush to develop this country, perhaps we have overlooked them. But we are trying to rectify the situation. The preservation of India's monuments is one of many schemes we are currently undertaking to improve this country. Take the Grand Canal project, for instance. Are you aware, sir, that the Great Canal has created a course two hundred and forty-seven miles long - reviving many dead and dying villages?'

'I have heard of this excellent scheme,' smiled Mr Cooke. 'It is certain to benefit peasant and conqueror alike.'

'Surely - in the history of the world – there has never been a newly-conquered land blessed with so many rapid and remarkable changes,' added his wife proudly.

'Indeed - but unfortunately, ma'am, we sometimes encounter stiff opposition. The natives are suspicious of change.'

'I can understand their suspicions,' said Mrs Cooke, 'A chugging steam engine, spewing clouds of smoke, is an awesome sight. No wonder some of them believe we have introduced a champing monster into their midst.'

'But when the railway is extended up country, they will come to realise how advantageous it is. When I was a child, it took almost a year to receive a reply to a letter from Home,' smiled Aunt Barton. 'Now with the benefit of steam power and the new roads, people in the *moffusil* can receive a reply within three months! Soon, I understand, the telegraph will be relaying messages Home within days from all over India! We are certainly living in an age of the most extraordinary change.'

Lieutenant Hartwell turned to Francina. 'Think of the vastness and complexity of laying thousands of miles of telegraph wires across deserts, swamps and jungles, Miss Duquesne, and the multitude of obstacles that must be overcome!'

'Obstacles?'

'Indeed. If the natives have not stolen the posts for firewood, then wild beasts will use them for scratching posts or white ants will riddle them to powder. And if these are not obstacles enough, then the monkeys are sure to entangle the wires or the crows and eagles use them for roosting places!'

Francina smiled. His enthusiasm was catching.

Aunt Barton rummaged in her reticule. 'You must call on us, Mr Hartwell.'

'It would be a pleasure, ma'am.'

'We are At Home on Tuesdays and Thursdays. Here is my card.'

3

Grand-mère looked over her pince-nez as she puffed on the gold hookah mouthpiece. She was seldom without this ungainly contraption, coiled like a black and gold striped snake around her arm. She smoked, she said, to relieve her aches and pains. Francina sketched her fading eyes, the pinched nose that ran in a straight line from her forehead, and her arched eyebrows. She would try to make Grand-mère look noble and not a wizened old lady.

Grand-mère took out the mouthpiece, made a disagreeable noise at the back of her throat and aimed a ball of phlegm into the brass spittoon at her feet. Francina hoped she would not do this if Lieutenant Hartwell should call. But Grand-mère was too old and had lived too long in India to put etiquette before comfort.

A horse pulled up under the porte cochère, and someone dismounted. Footsteps hurried through the house.

Uncle Barton materialised at the top of the steps. 'The barometer is falling rapidly,' he said breathlessly. 'Look at the sky.'

He raised the *chiks*.

The sky was pewter-coloured, dark and menacing, and the wind was picking up. Suddenly a dust storm swirled across the land, blowing debris with great force across the verandah. Servants flew through the house shutting windows and doors. Coughing back the dust, Francina helped Uncle Barton escort Grand-mère from the verandah into the drawing room. Servants followed with her accoutrements. Louis was brought on his perch from the verandah and placed behind a pillar. The ladies huddled in a corner as lightning flashed across the sky. The wind howled and shook the house as though it were made of paper. The shutters burst open and the rain poured in horizontally, drenching everything before the servants could secure them again.

They remained huddled together for several hours.

*

In the morning Francina rode out with Uncle Barton to see the extent of the storm damage. Part of the stable roof had blown off, and one poor horse had broken loose and injured himself so badly that Uncle feared that he would have to be put down. The destruction across Calcutta was heart breaking. Fishing boats had been picked out of the water and scattered along the banks like fallen leaves; boats were sunk; trees uprooted; carriages upturned. The Maidan looked like a battlefield, littered with animal carcasses. Dead crows were being taken away by the cartful. Many poor natives had lost everything. And to compound everyone's distress, there were reports of extensive flooding in outlying districts.

The Rainy Season had begun.

They abandoned the steaming verandah for the green-washed drawing room, a high square room in the centre of the house, lit by a central roof lantern. Doorways, two in each wall, radiated out to the four corners of the house, so that it was rather like sitting in the transept of a church. A fire added a touch of cheerfulness to the dark room, but nothing could reduce the humidity. Insects bit and stung and swarmed in clouds around the candles, while the rain dripped into bowls placed strategically throughout the house under cracks in the ceiling.

One afternoon, Aunt Barton stood in the doorway with a young native girl at her side. 'Francina, this is Sita,' she said, coaxing the girl forward.

She hardly looked fifteen.

'Sita ran away from her late husband's family because they treated her badly and beat her when she fell behind with her duties. Her father, one of our *peons,* asked if I could help. I thought Sita might be your new ayah.'

Francina stared at the tiny trembling creature dressed in white, and wondered how it must feel to have one's dreams snuffed out at such a young age. Miss Chesterton might complain that wives in Guernsey are little more than slaves but at least when they become widows they gain their freedom. In fact, widows in Guernsey were probably the only truly emancipated women in society. For Hindu women, it seemed, the situation was reversed.

'What am I to do with her, Aunt?'

'*Do*, Francina? Take her into your room and explain her duties.'

Francina put down her pen and beckoned. Sita followed. How could she explain her duties if they did not speak the same language? She led her into the bedroom and pointed vaguely about. But Sita needed no explaining. She folded up shawls, dusted gowns, and tidied the jars on her dressing table.

Relieved, Francina returned to the drawing room.

Aunt Cecilia had just arrived, accompanied by a young gentleman with a coppery moustache and a dark-haired young woman with striking blue eyes, who looked like Aunt Cecilia.

'We have been expecting you!' Aunt Barton proffered kisses. 'But what an inclement season to travel – and in your condition, *ma chérie*. You must be quite, quite exhausted.'

Francina was introduced to Mr and Mrs Balfour. Mrs Cissie Balfour, she learned, was Aunt Cecilia's daughter.

Mrs Balfour took Francina's hands.

'I have been *burning* to meet my little Guernsey cousin ever since Mamma told me that she was bringing you out.' She kissed her affectionately on both cheeks. 'I hope Mamma behaved herself on the voyage, and did not lead you too much astray?'

'What a thing to say, Cissie,' chuckled Aunt Cecilia.

'Venez Mesdemoiselles, que je vous voie!' Grand-mère raised her pince-nez to inspect her granddaughters. 'Bon Dieu, que l'on vous prendrait pour des soeurs!'

Mrs Balfour smiled at Francina. 'As we look like sisters, you must call me Cissie for I know we will become good friends. But what shall I call you? Francina sounds *foreign* . . . I think I shall call you Fanny! The name has a nice English ring to it. What do you think of that, Cousin Fanny? A new name for a new life.'

A *new name for a new life* . . . there was a sense of adventure in the idea.

Cissie laughed. 'But I am warning you, Fanny dear; I shall take you under my wing and make it my duty to find you a suitable husband.'

Her husband's eyes twinkled. 'Be on your guard, Miss Fanny, my wife is a notorious match-maker.'

'It is just an innocent pastime, Archie.'

'Innocent? It is downright devious at times.'

'But you must admit,' Cissie flashed her husband a smile, 'I have had my successes.'

'And for how long do we have the pleasure of your company, nephew?' asked Aunt Barton, as a bearer brought refreshments.

'Dear Archie has been appointed Collector of Tirhgunj.' Cissie slipped her arm through his. 'He must leave to take up his post immediately. I shall miss him so. We have never been parted before.'

'Nevertheless, it was sensible of him to persuade you to be confined in Calcutta,' smiled Aunt Barton, 'and I can thoroughly recommend Doctor Thompson. I have always found him courteous and reliable.'

A child dressed in a grey frock with a wide lace collar bounded into the room, closely followed by his ayah. He dived behind Cissie's skirts and stared up at Francina with huge blue eyes. He was the most appealing child she had ever seen and, she suspected, much used to being admired and petted. Grand-mère removed the hookah from her mouth and muttered affectionately to the child.

'Lionel, dearest, be a good boy and kiss your Great-Grand-mère.'

Cissie nudged her son towards his elderly relative. Lionel stared suspiciously at the puffing old witch. Nothing would induce him to let go of his mother's skirts.

Cissie playfully tweaked the copper tendrils tumbling over his cheeks. 'How could any mother bring herself to cut these beautiful curls!'

'Those curls come off on his fifth birthday, even if I take the scissors to them myself,' said her husband as Lionel skipped away to torment the parrot.

'Is there any news of Murphy, Aunt Cecilia?' Francina asked, hoping to remind her of those intimate moments they had spent together on the *Hindustan*.

'Not a word. Your uncle has written to all the high officials in Madras, but he has little hope of tracing her. It transpires that she was infatuated with an Irish adventurer who was also travelling in steerage. We assume she must have eloped with him.'

'Murphy?' asked Cissie.

'My Irish maid. The scheming little madam jumped ship at Madras. Fortunately, Francina took over some of her duties, for I do not know how I would have managed otherwise.'

Francina blushed, but she had treasured those five days attending to Aunt Cecilia.

'Indian gentlemen are so unaccustomed to seeing European servants that they tend to overlook the fact that they are only servants and treat them as ladies,' Cissie said. 'Flattery goes to their heads and they develop airs and graces. But what can one expect? If one employs a *darzi* and a *chicon-wallah* there is very little work for them to *do*.'

'Do you see that gentleman walking down the aisle with the slight stoop?' whispered Cissie Balfour from behind her prayer book. 'That is Mr Jardine, one of Calcutta's most eligible bachelors. He would be an excellent catch.'

Cissie's mission to find Francina a husband seemed to occupy every moment they were together. Even in the solemn precincts of St John's, Cissie planned and schemed.

'But he is so old, Cissie.'

'Perhaps, but he is also very rich. And if you should marry someone *old*, then you might quickly become a rich young widow. Don't look so shocked, Fanny, I am only putting into words what most ladies secretly plan and hope.'

Francina wished that it was Aunt Cecilia who was sitting next to her and not Cissie. But Aunt Cecilia would never step inside this church. While she, Uncle Barton and Cissie attended the Sunday Services in St John's, Grand-mère and her aunts celebrated Mass in St Thomas's. She pictured herself kneeling next to Aunt Cecilia, intoxicated by the smell of incense; their veiled heads bowed devoutly before the statue of the Virgin Mary. . .

'Now Fanny, I am burning with curiosity: who was that young man we passed at the gate as we were leaving Aunt Barton's yesterday?'

'That must have been Lieutenant Hartwell, the garrison engineer at Fort William.'

'You can do better than a garrison engineer!'

Francina said nothing. She could not decide if she liked or hated this cousin.

'Well, how about Mr Beames, that gentleman with those splendid whiskers? He is not old.'

'But he is *fat*. You did not marry someone fat and ugly, Cissie.'

Cissie smiled, and studied the jewels glinting on her fingers. 'Archie is very good looking. But Mr Beames's looks shouldn't matter - more importantly, he is heaven-born'.

'Heaven-born?'

'A heaven-born is a Civilian of the Company. If you marry a Civilian, Fanny, you will be provided with a pension of three hundred pounds a year whether your husband is alive or dead. And for the same reason you must not marry a Queen's officer,' whispered Cissie, seeing Francina eye the scarlet tunic of cadet sauntering down the aisle.

'What reason?'

'The widow of a Queen's officer has no guarantee of a pension. The wives of officers in the Company's Service, on the other hand, can be sure of a very good pension. – Don't make that face, Fanny. Fore-warned is fore-armed. You might thank me one day, if I save you from a miserable existence as a poor widow with a dozen hungry children to feed.'

'Stop that, Lionel! You know *the great tall Tailor always comes to naughty little Suck-a-Thumbs!*' Cissie rewound the skein of silk that her son had unravelled across the floor.

Lionel peeped at his mother from behind Netta's chair. 'I shall hide when he comes.'

'If you answer back, young man, Mamma will give you a dose of castor oil.' Cissie stabbed at the tiny flannel nightdress she was smocking. 'I have told ayah often enough to stop him sucking his thumb, but the woman takes no notice of anything I say. How can I instil discipline into the child, if my orders are constantly flouted?'

'You seem out of sorts today, Cissie my dear.'

'I am sorry, Aunt Barton, but I have been trying to find a reliable wet nurse. I was expecting to engage Mrs Cameron's woman, but Mrs Douglas has hired her behind my back. It is very trying in my condition.'

Grand-mère shook her head. 'I had thirteen confinements, and nursed each one of my babies myself. Your grand-père would not allow me to send my babies out to wet nurses.'

'Forgive me, Grand-mère, but that was a long time ago. Fashions have changed. Most ladies nowadays employ a *dhood-dhye*.'

'All my babies reached adulthood, Cissie, a remarkable achievement in India. And their survival, I am convinced, was entirely due to Grand-père's ideas.'

Grand-mère signalled to the servant standing behind her. The *hookah-burdar* ran forward to replenish the *hookah* bowl with tobacco and nuggets of charcoal. Cissie watched the activity with distaste. Society ladies had given up this disgusting Indian habit long ago.

'Indeed, Grand-mère, but I don't want to spend all my time in the nursery – and Lionel suffered no consequences, did he?' Cissie glanced at her son, who was taunting the parrot with a piece of fruit. The parrot squawked and flapped his wings in frustration as the fruit was snatched, yet again, out of reach.

'Maybe not - but did you, Cissie? Your grand-père used to study the animals. If animals nurse their own young, he used to say, it must be right for us to do likewise.'

Cissie looked horrified. 'But we are not *animals*! Surely the Bible tells us that we are superior to animals?'

'Perhaps so, Cissie, but I had complete faith in my husband's methods. I only once ever questioned his judgement, and that was when he told me that he was going to take the pus from the arm of a native baby who had smallpox and scratch it into my baby's arm. I pleaded and pleaded, but he would not listen. He insisted that we should all be scratched with the pus. I was terrified, quite certain that we were all going to die - or turn black.'

'Why did you agree to such a thing, Grand-mère?'

'It was my duty to obey my husband in all things - as it will be yours, Francina.'

'As you see,' chucked Aunt Barton, 'none of us caught smallpox.'

'I never doubted him again. After a smallpox outbreak in the district, Grand-père was able to show that those who had been scratched with the pus did not develop the disease. Of course some servants refused because of their cast beliefs, but none of the Untouchable children caught smallpox. Eventually the practise caught on in the district.'

'Papa was a much-respected doctor,' said Aunt Barton. 'People came from far and wide to seek his advice.'

Grand-mère turned to Francina. 'Did you know that for a while your grand-père was surgeon to Tipu Sultan, the mighty ruler of Mysore?'

Cissie gave a little huff. 'Forgive me, Grand-mère, but you must stop talking about such people. As a Collector's wife, I have a position to uphold. It would harm Archie's standing if it became common knowledge that my grandfather had actively supported such an evil enemy. Tipu Sultan was a cruel barbaric tyrant.'

'*Alors!* Who says so, Cissie?'

'Archie says so. So does General Balfour -'

'English, English! Of course they say so, Cissie!'

A wail, following a barrage of triumphant squawks, stopped the conversation. Lionel fell weeping into the folds of his mother's skirts, cradling his finger. Cissie made sympathetic noises and pulled herself awkwardly to her feet. 'Lionel is getting fractious. He finds this weather very trying. I must take him home for his rest.'

'And I must ask the *darzi* to take in my purple silk for the ball at Government House.' Aunt Barton raised herself from her cane chair, kissed Cissie, ruffled Lionel's hair, and made her way slowly towards the back verandah, where the old tailor had been sitting cross-legged since dawn.

Blowing kisses, Cissie descended the stone staircase, closely followed by her whimpering son and his fraught ayah.

Grand-mère sucked heavily on the *hookah* as she watched her granddaughter disappear from view. 'You see what is happening to our family, Francina? The English have come between us.'

Francina hated it when Grand-mère spoke like this. Much as she found Cissie irritating, she wanted to run after her and tell her that she was only listening to Grand-mère out of politeness. She did not agree with half the things she said.

Grand-mère gazed lovingly at her husband's portrait. 'It was because of Tipu Sultan that I met your grand-père,' she said. 'He was surgeon to the entourage that escorted Tipu's Embassy from India to the Court of Louis Le Roi.'

'*Louis Le Roi, Louis Le Roi, Vive Le Roi!*' shrieked the parrot.

'Hush, Louis!' scolded Grand-mère, delighted by his patriotic intervention. 'Tipu Sultan sent a mission to France to summon Louis Le Roi's support in his attempt to drive the English from Indian soil. Tipu's Embassy was favourably received at Versailles, but his efforts all came to nothing. The Bastille was stormed the following year, and the poor King and Queen were taken prisoner.'

Grand-mère blew smoke into the air. 'When Tipu's Embassy made the return journey, my father took the opportunity to have me escorted out to India with the convoy. I was very inexperienced of the world, for I had been locked up in a convent ever since I had arrived in France, a terrified child ten years before. My chaperone and I were the only women in the convoy, and we spent the entire voyage confined to our cabin. I was very frightened, for the memory of my last sea voyage still haunted me. Before long, I fell sick with apprehension. My chaperone called the Embassy's surgeon, for she feared for my life. Grand-père was that surgeon, Francina. He was so patient and understanding - and so handsome in his uniform that I fell in love with him the moment I saw him.'

4

The *darzi* had darned the little tear on her cream ball gown so expertly that his tiny stitches were almost invisible, and after the *dhobi* ironed it, it looked almost new. Francina was delighted, and twirled for Grand-mère and Netta's inspection.

'You look charming, Mademoiselle.'

'And I have just the necklace to set that gown off to perfection,' smiled Grand-mère. 'Your grand-père gave it to me when Theresa was born. Did you know, *ma petite,* that your maman was born on the sacred river?'

Francina raised her eyebrows. 'The Ganges?'

'I was travelling alone in a houseboat on my way to join a Christmas party. Theresa made her appearance so quickly and unexpectedly, that I had to deliver the baby myself. Well, she was my thirteenth child, I knew what to expect - and of course Netta helped me.'

Netta smiled. 'And we did have that young ayah in attendance.'

'The poor woman was terrified,' chuckled Grand-mère. 'She was very young and inexperienced, hardly more than a child herself. We had to shout instructions to her.'

Francina tried not to blush at their frankness. In Guernsey, such talk was circumvented, alluded to in whispers.

'When Theresa was born, ayah insisted on dipping her in the sacred waters. I shall never forget the sight of that raging pink scrap being immersed in the *Ganga Ma.*' Netta raised her hands to her cheeks. 'She squirmed so much, I was sure ayah would drop her.'

'That probably accounts for her strong nature,' mused Grand-mère, 'for like the *Ganga Ma,* nothing will deter Theresa from her chosen course.'

'That ayah was devoted to your maman,' smiled Netta. 'She was her special charge, and when your maman left to get married, the ayah went with her.'

'So that ayah might have been my ayah?'

'Oui, bien sûr!'

'Netta - fetch the Tipu necklace from my room!'

Grand-mère unhooked a silver key from her chatelaine and gave it to her companion.

'We received news that the Queen had been guillotined the week Netta came to live with us,' she said, watching Netta glide gracefully across the matting. 'I named her Antoinette after the poor Queen, but she was such a tiny creature, so weak and feeble, that the name seemed to overwhelm her, so I shortened it to Netta.'

But that still does not explain why you took her in, thought Francina.

Netta returned some minutes later carrying a small ebony box inlaid with an intricate pattern of silver leaves, which she carefully placed in Grand-mère's lap.

'Do you see this design, Francina?' Grand-mère reverently stroked the lid. 'This was Tipu's special motif: the *bubris* or tiger scratch. Tipu Sultan was known as *The Tiger of Mysore*.'

'Tipu, Tipu, Tipu Sultan!' shrieked the parrot.

Grand-mère rewarded the bird with a grape. She selected a small key from her chatelaine and opened the box. Lying on a bed of dark velvet was a strand of golden leaves, each leaf encrusted with a jewel that glinted like a dewdrop. It was the most delicate necklace Francina had ever seen.

'Your grand-père had this made up from jewels given to him by Tipu Sultan. He had ornaments made for me after all our children were born.' Grand-mère held the necklace up to the light. 'Moonstones set in *bubris*. Your grand-père chose moonstones because they reminded him of water droplets. He called Theresa his little water nymph.'

'She wore the necklace to her first ball,' added Netta.

'She looked so beautiful.'

Grand-mère stared wistfully at the necklace. 'I planned to give this to Theresa one day - but now I think I shall give it to you. Turn round, *ma petite*. I shall fix it on for you.'

Francina studied herself in the glass, too overcome to speak. The moonstones seemed to absorb and reflect both the milky sheen of the moiré silk and the tears welling in her eyes.

'Come, come! Some ladies think moonstones are unlucky because they resemble tears, but I say: why not tears of joy?'

'But I cannot wear it, Grand-mère. It is far too good for me.'

'Nonsense, child. When I was your age my husband showered me with jewels - mostly gifts from his grateful native patients. This is India. You must get used to dressing up.'

Francina has never stepped inside so grand a place as Government House. Cissie had instructed her on her curtsy. Lady Canning's eyes fell momentarily on the moonstone necklace when she was presented, and she had blushed. In Guernsey unmarried women wore pearls or flowers, never jewels. 'Jewels are vulgar on a young girl,' Aunt Doré had sniffed. Francina hoped that the necklace did not look vulgar; she hoped that customs were just different in India. After all, Mamma had worn this necklace to her first ball. Then a thought flashed through her mind: perhaps it was Grand-mère's intention to flaunt the motif of Britain's hated enemy under the Governor-General's nose. Could Grand-mère be so devious? Hopefully Lady Canning did not know of Tipu Sultan or his motif, for the Governor-General and his lady were as new to India as she was.

Luckily she had not heeded Aunt Barton's advice and chewed *betel* to make her lips red, or rubbed a little catechu on her cheeks with a coarse towel as Grand-mère had suggested. She would have stood out like sunburned peasant amongst these pale-faced ladies.

The blazing light from the chandeliers glowed on the *chunam* pillars and reflected in the polished floor. So much light and colour. That was what had struck her most about India: the dazzling juxtaposition of so many extraordinary colours - and not only in the bazaars, but in this ballroom too. Aunt Barton's bold outfits, which had looked so excruciating in Guernsey, hardly raise an eyebrow here. She could not help comparing the military gentlemen in this glittering Indian ballroom strutting like birds of paradise in their bright dress-uniforms to the beggars and water carriers in their ragged remnants squatting in the dust outside. India was indeed a land of contrasts.

She was sharing a sofa with Aunt Barton under a *punkah* behind the row of pillars that ran the length of the great ballroom. Their section of the ballroom, comprising the merchants and bankers in their sober outfits, looked so dull compared to the colourful dress-uniforms opposite, which mingled with the occasional native prince resplendent in gold brocade and jewels. Everything in India was ruled by the Order of Precedence. Even here, places were strictly designated.

'As you see, there are no native ladies present - native ladies would not dream of attending a public function where strange men abound – but it would have been fun to see them dressed in their finery,' whispered Aunt. 'Do you see that officer in the light blue uniform leaning against the pillar? He is in the Light Cavalry. The two officers in scarlet talking to him are in the Infantry.'

Francina giggled behind her fan. 'And that curious gentleman in bright yellow, Aunt?'

'Skinner's Horse.'

From the corner of her eye, Francina saw Mr Cowan Bell sidle over and she flinched, suspecting that he might ask her to dance. He must have noticed for he changed direction and walked past her. He joined Uncle Barton and a group of Calcutta merchants (the *box-wallahs* Mrs Walmsley had sneeringly called them on the *Hindustan*) who were standing behind them.

'What do you make of these rumours regarding the new employment regulations, Barton?' she heard him ask.

'The sepoys will find such an order intolerable. Most of them would rather forgo service than cross the sea. The sepoys are a proud people.'

'To cross the sea would defile their caste, would it not?'

'Indeed. It places the sepoy in an impossible situation. To forgo enlistment is to forgo employment. It is sure to fuel rumours that the Government is scheming to undermine their caste and religion. It shows gross insensitivity on the Government's part – and at a very difficult time. There is much discontentment surrounding the annexation of Oude.'

Francina tried to block out the conversation behind her and concentrate on the glamour in front of her. Her eyes travelled the length of the ballroom to Lady Canning in a beaded white gown and sparking tiara sitting on the state chair under a canopy of crimson and gold. From this distance she looked like Queen Victoria on her throne. If only Louisa could see her now, sitting here with her hair entwined with flowers, moonstones shimmering round her neck. Cissie had helped dress her hair - of course she could not pin it as expertly as Murphy, but she was certainly cleverer than Sita, who seemed only capable of brushing it until it shone like jet.

She heard the orchestra strike up, and her heart began to race. Would anyone ask her to dance? Her hands were damp, her feet swollen and itchy inside their satin dancing pumps.

A slim young officer with fiery red whiskers in a royal blue uniform materialised before them. He clicked his heels and bowed stiffly. Francina and Aunt Barton smiled.

5

Francina stood on the verandah and watched the storks perch like statues on the parapet of the neighbouring roof. Since the storm, their numbers had increased, and now they surveyed the world from every parapet in Calcutta. Uncle Barton had told her that these gigantic bald-headed birds, with beaks as long as a man's arm, nested in the swampy regions of the Sunderbans and came to Calcutta to scavenge on the carcasses of animals that had perished during the storm.

Rain had fallen steadily all day. At first she had found the rains exhilarating. It was amusing to stand on the verandah and watch the servants' children dance naked in the puddles. But as one torrential day followed another, keeping her confined for longer and longer periods, the novelty had begun to pall. Aunt Barton rarely ventured out in a downpour, and few visitors called.

The humidity was more disagreeable than the dry heat. Sita had wrapped her gowns, bonnets and slippers in tissue paper and sealed them in her trunks, for anything left unprotected in a closet soon become stained with mildew.

She flopped into a chaise. She had taken to watching the little lizards scampering up the walls, growing fat as they preyed on the swarms of insects. Her favourite, Tik-Tik (she could distinguish him by the kink in his tail) had just emerged from behind Grand-mère's portrait. How long would it take him to swallow a fly?

Even Louis seemed affected by the weather. He sat mute on his perch with his head tucked into his green ruffled chest. A segment of his favourite fruit would not tempt him to speak today. Aunt Barton and Netta were slumped in their chairs. Grand-mère, too, had nodded off. The hookah gurgled quietly, and the old ladies snored against the raucous noise of the love-sick frogs outside.

A bearer announced a visitor. Aunt sat up and adjusted her cap just as Lieutenant Hartwell appeared at the drawing room door.

Fresh air seemed to blow through the house whenever he

arrived. These days Francina hardly noticed his carrot-coloured hair.

Mr Hartwell clicked his heels and bowed. 'The Rains have well and truly set in. Indra has set loose his arrows!'

Aunt Baron looked mystified.

'Indra - the God of Thunder and Rain, ma'am.'

'Indeed, indeed,' beamed Aunt Barton.

Grand-mère narrowed her eyes as he bowed over her hand.

'Mr Hartwell, you are quite, quite soaked! Would you like to change into something of Mr Barton's while we dry your clothes?'

'Thank you, Mrs Barton, but I am used to a few spots of rain. It is a hazard in my line of work. But perhaps I might be permitted to stand for a few moments before the fire?'

He marched to the hearth and faced his audience.

'How are your plans progressing, Mr Hartwell?'

'Slowly, Miss Duquesne, more slowly than I would wish. I left my laboratory for a few moments yesterday, when I heard an almighty crash. I raced back and found my bearer comatosed on the floor surrounded by broken glass. The stupid fellow had opened the jar of ether – quite against my orders.'

'Goodness. Will he recover?'

'He will be laid up for a few days with a sore head, but I don't expect any lasting damage.'

Mr Harwell was, of course, speaking English, so only Aunt Barton could follow their conversation. Aunt, however, looked as puzzled as Grand-mère and Netta.

'Mr Hartwell is planning to make a photographic record of the architecture of India,' Francina explained.

'Ah!' Aunt Barton said, none the wiser.

'I have brought out a portable dark-tent, Mrs Barton, and I am converting two *palkis*: one into a coating and processing room, the other as a store for the glass plates and chemicals. It is the only way to carry my equipment over rough terrain.'

'It sounds quite admirable.'

'I am also in the process of training my bearer to assist me in the mixing of the chemicals – with limited success, so far.'

Grand-mère sucked heavily on the hookah as she looked contemptuously at Lieutenant Hartwell's steaming uniform. But he was too engrossed in his subject to notice.

'But I have yet to discover how the chemicals will react in searing Indian temperatures. Ether has a tendency to boil on the surface of the plates in high temperatures - or so it was discovered in the Crimea. I shall be most disappointed if this turns out to be just a Cold Weather project.'

'Most disappointed!' said Aunt Barton.

Mr Hartwell marched towards a rust-speckled engraving hanging on the wall and studied it closely. Then he spun round.

'As you see, ladies, in India we find buildings and sculpture of the most singular complexity and design. But however admirably a painting or engraving might be executed, there will always be the suspicion lurking in the minds of those at Home that the artist could have exaggerated the splendour to impress his audience.'

'When I studied the Indian engravings in Uncle Doré's library,' said Francina, 'I used to wonder if the artist had taken liberties: altered the perspective to exaggerate the height, or discarded an eyesore to improve the composition. The buildings were so extraordinary; it was hard to believe that they really might exist.'

'You see my point exactly, Miss Duquesne. A camera makes no such artistic judgements. It records only what it sees - quickly and accurately. That is its advantage.'

Francina smiled. After their meeting on the *Hindustan*, Mr. Hartwell would seek her out, and usually find her sketching under the awning. Whilst she made sketches of the birds perched in the rigging or of the crew repairing the sails, he would loll against the railings and tell her fanciful stories, the sacred legends of India's gods and goddesses. His father was an Orientalist, a scholar and translator of ancient Indian texts, who had passed his great love of India to his son.

'You will join us for tiffin, of course, Mr Hartwell?' smiled Aunt.

'Mr Hartwell seems rather taken with you, my dear,' Aunt Barton said, when he had departed. 'We must ask Mr Barton to make a few enquiries.'

'Enquiries, Aunt?'

'Delve into Mr Hartwell's background. Find out if he is suitable.'

Francina blushed.

'Humpf!' said Grand-mère, who had sulked through the meal. 'Take heed, *ma petite*. The English are like the *peepul* tree.'

'The *peepul* tree?' Sometimes she wondered if the old lady was losing her powers of reasoning.

'Have you seen a *peepul* tree?'

'I believe so, Grand-mère. Uncle pointed one out to me growing over the stable wall. It looks rather like ivy with large heart-shaped leaves and long white twisting stems. The tree is considered sacred, is it not?'

'It is indeed – but that is partly because the tree has deceptive powers. It may look like ivy, but it is cunning, Francina. The *peepul* starts innocently enough, usually as a fig carried to the branches of another tree by a bird or a squirrel. The fig settles in a hollow and takes hold. In time it will send down roots, powerful roots that will wind round the host's trunk. When the roots reach the ground, they begin to grow upwards again, gaining in strength and abundance. In time the roots will fuse with one another and strangle the host's trunk. Eventually the host tree will wither and die, leaving behind a ghostly void. And in its place, in all its innocent glory, stands a mighty *peepul*.' Grand-mère leaned forward. 'The English are like the *peepul*, Francina. At first their arrival seems harmless. They offer gifts of friendship. They talk of peace, of building bridges and starting schools and sinking wells - now they bring the railway and the telegraph - but they will use every pretext for filling frontier towns with troops and munitions of war.'

'Ma Mère,' said Aunt Barton sharply, 'you must stop talking nonsense!'

'*Écoute bien, ma petite*. Their gifts carry a heavy price.'

6

Despite Grand-mère's misgivings, Uncle Barton's enquires revealed nothing unfavourable. In fact, Lieutenant Hartwell's father, the late Colonel, was respectfully remembered at the Asiatic Society for the authoritative papers he had published in the Society's journal. The Hartwells were an esteemed Indian family: his grandfather, father and uncle had all served the Company honorably and with distinction. As far as Uncle Barton was concerned, Mr Hartwell was welcome to call as often as he liked.

And his visits increased - Aunt Barton's warm welcomes making up for Grand-mère's hostile silences. Francina saved little stories to tell him, the kind she would relate to Angelo and Louisa in her letters. But she was finding letter-writing an exasperating task. It was hard to keep up a lively exchange when replies took so long to arrive. She had hoped that now that she and Angelo were both living in the East, she would hear more frequently from him, but she had received only one short welcoming note since she had arrived. So she saved up her little stories for Mr Hartwell. He, at least, seemed to appreciate them.

'The other day Uncle Barton opened the drawer of his desk and found a squirrel's nest amongst his papers,' Francina said, as they strolled across the compound during a break in the rain. 'The naughty little creature had mixed fur and feathers with cotton stolen from the *rasai*.'

'Do you know how the squirrel got his stripes, Miss Duquesne? The god Siva stroked his back with his sacred fingers.'

Francina smiled. She was pleased that Uncle's enquiries had revealed nothing untoward, and fortunately, Mr Hartwell was blissfully unaware that his family had been discussed at length amongst Uncle's acquaintances at the Bengal Club.

A flurry of rain made them return indoors.

To her astonishment she found Henry Fetherstone standing on the verandah talking to Aunt Barton. He had grown a moustache and looked thinner, but he greeted her with the same cheerfulness she remembered in Guernsey.

'So you *are* still in Calcutta, Mr Fetherstone. But why have you not called on us sooner? It is very amiss of you!'

'I had every intention of doing so, Miss Duquesne, but I was laid up with a fever.'

'You should have told us! I would have sent the *peon* round with a bottle of my special medicinal. It works wonders on a stomach disorder. One small teaspoon – and the pain quite vanishes!'

'That would have been most kind, Mrs Barton,' Henry Fetherstone turned his tired eyes to Francina, 'but I beg you not to tell Miss Louisa. There is no need to distress her needlessly, and as you see, I have recovered, although I remain somewhat emaciated.'

'A good Indian curry will soon set you right,' smiled Aunt Barton. 'And now, you and Mr Hartwell must both join us for tiffin, I really do insist.'

Arthur Hartwell seemed a little put out by the unexpected appearance of this wan young man, so Francina took his arm as they filed into the dining room and quietly explained that Mr Fetherstone was in love with her cousin Louisa. He cheered up after this disclosure.

'What are your impressions of India, Mr Fetherstone?' Aunt asked as the *khimutgar* served the soup.

'I have seen little of India yet. It's the fault of this absurd system of keeping new Civilians in Calcutta to "learn the languages" so to speak. It's all nonsense, considering we studied the Indian languages at Haileybury. I suspect it's just a devious ploy by the Board of Examiners to get us all into debt, for I fear, Mrs Barton, there are many temptations in Calcutta to deter us from our studies.'

Arthur Hartwell nodded sympathetically. Francina would have liked to know more about these temptations, but did not think it appropriate to ask.

'And where are you staying, Mr Fetherstone?'

'After my illness, the doctors advised us to transfer to a healthier district. Lihou and I have just moved into a chummery in Alipore.'

Francina stared into her *brinjal* soup. 'Mr Lihou is also here in Calcutta?'

'Indeed. Pressure of work has prevented him from calling, but he specifically asked me to pass on his regards to you all.' Henry Fetherstone smiled apologetically. 'I'm afraid Lihou takes his studies seriously. He has engaged the services of the best *munshi* in Town - quite unnecessarily, in my opinion - but he is determined to pass well, receive his orders, and leave Calcutta as soon as possible.'

Aunt Barton nodded to the *khitmutgar* to clear the soup plates. 'Tell Mr Lihou from an old India hand that it is extremely dangerous to overtax the brain in this climate. I have seen newcomers pay heavily for overworking.'

Francina stared at tablecloth. Pressure of work was lame excuse. The only reason he had not called was because he had no desire to see her. His mother must have written to him. *'If you want to get on in India, Gilbert, you cannot compromise. Indian society is more exacting than at Home. Steer clear of the likes of Miss Duquesne. Her mother was a bad egg – and have you heard - her father was recently imprisoned for debt. I have just written to my good friend Mrs So-and-So warning her to keep her sons away from her . . .'*

Shame and humiliation crashed down on her. She thought she was rid of Mrs Lihou's vengeful tongue, but now she realised that it had followed her out to India.

'Miss Duquesne, the *khitmutgar* is waiting to serve you.' Arthur Hartwell touched her lightly on the arm. Francina removed her hand from the table.

He, at least, does not know about my family, she thought.

During a pause in the rain, she decided to call on the Vauloués in Middleton Street. The *durwan* ushered her upstairs, but the darkened drawing room was unoccupied. Francina passed a portrait of a black-haired gentleman with sharp features dressed in a tailcoat, knee breeches and buckled shoes. He sat at a small table composing a letter. Beside him stood an ornate brass spittoon and a gold-tipped *hookah,* coiled in readiness. The painting was crudely executed, with little knowledge of perspective.

The gentleman must be one of Uncle Vauloué's forbears, Francina supposed, as she crossed the china matting.

She paused at a doorway. Peeping through the beaded curtain, she saw Aunt Cecilia kneeling over a prie-dieu in the semi-darkness gazing at an ivory crucifx. Candlelight outlined her veiled profile. She was fingering a rosary as she whispered the words of her devotions. Francina held her breath. Aunt's fusion of piety and exuberance seemed to blend so naturally with the Indian way of life.

Beautiful Saint Cecilia martyred in 177.

Francina knew it was wicked to be drawn to the rituals of the Catholic faith, but just for a moment she was a child again, spying on Mamma. She tiptoed away and found Cissie languishing on a couch in her room. She was wrapped in a silk peignoir, brightly painted with oriental birds and flowers. Her face looked bloated and flushed.

'Fanny, cheer me up. I'm bored and uncomfortable today, and the rain is making Lionel fractious.' She gestured to a servant to place a chair beside her. 'Mamma is in her room again. She spends so much time in prayer. Sometimes I wonder if she does it on purpose, just to make me feel guilty.'

It must have hurt Aunt Cecilia terribly when she discovered that her daughter had converted to the Anglican faith. Cissie, no doubt, saw her conversion as another step towards her assimilation into English society.

'Oh, I simply must tell you - Mrs Blundell just called and had some very interesting news: Lady Canning has transformed Government House. All the chairs and sofas in the sitting rooms have been covered in a pretty rose-chintz. It looks quite charming, Mrs Blundell said. That is exactly what *I* must do at Tirhgunj! I shall be the most fashionable lady in the *mofussil* with my metal hoops and chintz coverings. Would you do something for me, Fanny? Would you go to *Bordelio's* and bring me back the pattern books?'

'Of course, Cissie.'

'Then you must help me choose a pretty chintz. If we cannot find anything in Town, I shall write to Archie's sister and ask her to send out twenty yards of the prettiest chintz she can find. She will know what to send, she has very good taste. – Or do you think thirty yards would be more realistic? I shall have to consult Mamma. It is so difficult to know!'

Cissie leaned forward and whispered. 'Now - Aunt Barton told Mamma that three young bachelors will be guests at your *burra khana*. Tell me about them, Fanny, for I am burning with curiosity.'

Francina said shyly, 'I have spoken to you of one of them, Cissie.

Lieutenant Hartwell has called several times since the ball at Government House.'

Cissie threw her head back against the cushions in disgust. 'Not that garrison engineer, Fanny! It is bad form to encourage him, especially as you have no intention of marrying him. You must have nothing more to do with him.'

Francina flushed. 'But I enjoy his company, Cissie. He has become a good friend.'

'Unmarried girls do not have bachelors as good friends in India - you should know that Fanny. You must quietly, but firmly, deter him. It is the kindest thing you can do. Now, tell me about the other gentlemen. Aunt Barton said one was very handsome.'

'That must be Henry Fetherstone. I knew him in Guernsey. He came out this year. He is new to the Civil Service -'

'A *griffin!*' Cissie sighed. 'How many times must I tell you? Griffins are in no position to marry. They practically live in the saddle, and are actively discouraged from taking a wife until they have been in India for at least five years - and even then it is frowned upon. You have only to ask Archie. He was thirty when we married, and that was considered young -'

Francina stamped her foot. 'Enough of this, Cissie! Why must you see every man I meet as a potential husband?'

Cissie's eyes opened wide. 'Well I *do,* and so should you. It is not how *I* see it, but how society sees it. Do you realise, Fanny, that if it becomes known that you are coquetting with young men whom you have no intention of marrying, you will quickly get a reputation as a flirt, especially as your mother -'

Cissie stopped, and bit her lip.

'My mother? What about my mother, Cissie?'

'Fanny, I swear on the Bible that I have not told a *soul.*'

'What do you know, Cissie?'

'Mamma told me in the strictest confidence. I have not breathed a word to anyone, not even Archie. I would not dare! Archie is a highly principled Being.'

'What do you *know*?'

'Well, a married woman who renounces her husband and children and *chooses* to live as another man's *mistress* is - in Archie's eyes - worthy of all reprobation,' said Cissie haughtily. 'If Archie ever found out, he would forbid me from associating with such a creature - even with such a creature's daughter. It grieves me to say this, Fanny, but should your mother's situation become common knowledge in Calcutta, it will *ruin* your chances. So you see, it is *imperative* that you marry as soon as possible, before any of this surfaces.'

Francina stared at the hands clenched in her lap. 'Does Aunt Cecilia think as you?'

'How Mamma thinks is of no consequence. Mamma is oblivious to the codes that rule Calcutta. She lives in the past. In her day it was not considered improper to keep company with the natives. Sometimes Mamma's Indian habits make me cringe with embarrassment.' Cissie put her head in her hands. 'I keep begging her not to associate with those Portuguese half-castes from St Thomas's. As a Collector's wife, she places me in a very awkward position. Sometimes, Fanny, I wish with all my heart that she had not married -'

Cissie stopped and bit her lip.

Francina stared at her. She knew that it shamed Cissie that her father, a Frenchman, could never be part of the Establishment, or that his status as an indigo planter was so lowly that it did not even warrant a mention in the Order of Precedence, but . . .

Cissie smiled self-consciously. 'You see, we all have a cross to bear. You do not know what agonies I go through when I see the ladies eyeing me up and down. I know what they are thinking. And I die of embarrassment every time Grand-mère takes that brown creature out with her. I have seen the way the ladies look at her, and wonder who she is.'

'Netta? Who is she, Cissie?'

'It is better that you don't know.'

'Please tell me.'

Cissie started at the ceiling, her lips pressed firmly together.

'Please, Cissie. You said we were sisters, don't you remember?'

Cissie gestured to the ayah to leave the room. When she had gone, Cissie whispered: 'Netta is not Grand-mère's companion as most people assume. Netta is Grand-mère's sister.'

'Her *sister*!'

'Well, her half-sister. But things were different when Grand-mère was young. In her day it was the custom for a French gentleman to keep a *bibi*.'

'A *bibi*?'

'A *bibi* is a native mistress. When Grand-mère's father, the colonel in Pondichéry, was ordered back to France, he left his *bibi* behind. She died soon afterwards - of grief, Mamma said, leaving a half-cast infant child. Grand-mère was married to Grand-père then, and expecting her first child. She took pity on the little creature and decided to bring her up with her own children. But Grand-mère does not realise how customs have changed. She does not see the *harm* she is inflicting on us all when she goes out with Netta.'

At that moment Lionel raced into the room, shrieking with glee at having broken from his ayah's grasp. He burrowed amongst the folds of Cissie's peignoir and tried to scramble onto her lap. His ayah hovered anxiously in the doorway.

'No, Lionel, dearest. Mamma is too hot and tired.'

Lionel, half-submerged in yards of painted silk, stood between his mamma's knees and rested his cheek on her swollen abdomen.

'Lionel made such a sweet observation during the thunderstorm. He described it as a *bhisti* pouring water from his bag. I do declare, Fanny, the little darling is going to be as clever as his dear papa!'

Lionel thrust a thumb into his mouth and sucked contentedly.

'If only dear Archie were here to listen to his clever boy. I have not yet received word that he has reached Tirhgunj safely. I fear he might have got caught in the storms.'

'I am sure you will have news very soon, Cissie.'

'Oh Fanny, think of poor me tomorrow. While you are enjoying yourself at the *burra khana,* I shall be suffering an evening of Grand-mère's idiosyncrasies. All that nonsense about Tipu Sultan, and her ridiculous insistence on speaking French! The British are the rulers here now. Why can't Grand-mère understand that if one wants to succeed in this country one has to conform, and that means speaking English? Archie is English and so am I - now. I cannot allow her or Mamma to jeopardize my position, or Archie's position, which amounts to the same thing. India is an imperious place. One ill-placed remark or murmur of a suspicion could be enough to push one outside society.'

Francina watched Cissie stroking Lionel's head. By marrying

Archie Balfour, one of a heaven-born of the British ruling class, Cissie had catapulted herself from the British equivalent of the Indian Untouchables to the topmost Brahmin caste, and she was revelling in her exalted position. Cissie had become more English than the English.

'I pray with all my heart that this baby will have fair hair like Lionel's,' whispered Cissie, winding her son's golden curls around her fingers. 'Archie and I have never discussed it, of course, but you do not know how privileged you are, Fanny. *You* are not country-born.'

7

The embroidered gown was an inspired choice. She smiled at her reflection. The powder-blue silk glowed with an incandescent radiance in the damp twilight. Despite the insect bites, she was pleased with her appearance. She caught Sita's eye in the glass and smiled. She had arranged her hair exactly as Cissie had done for the ball at Government House. She learned quickly.

Francina turned away from the cheval glass and took a deep breath. Now she must push all anxieties aside. A servant came in carrying an aromatic coil smoldering in a small dish, which he wafted round the room, whilst another servant drove the insects out from under her bed with a long grass switch. She left them to their work, and rustled like a newly emerging butterfly through the fragrant rooms to join the Bartons and their guests on the front verandah for the *burra khana*.

Arthur Hartwell arrived punctually at seven, spruced and spirited in his dress uniform, and was warmly greeted by the Bartons. They had grown so used to his visits that they were beginning to treat him with a familiarity normally reserved for relatives. He bounded smartly to Francina's side and showered her with compliments. Mr Cowan Bell appeared soon afterwards. He had made an effort and tidied himself, but his red perspiring face spoiled the effect. Despite having lived for so long in India, he seemed unable to master the climate. But she was feeling happy tonight, so for once she graciously acknowledged him. He bowed gratefully, and hovered close by as though waiting for a suitable moment to corner her.

Aunt Barton, cheerful and chatty in her purple silk, was trying hard to please her guests. The streamers on her new lace cap swung saucily as she guided Colonel Denning across the room to meet Mr Moran, the indigo broker. Francina looked at the vases overflowing with flowers, the sparkling ornaments, the array of servants in their crisp white uniforms holding brass trays of drinks and delicacies, and a warm glow of gratitude flowed over her. Aunt had worked hard to make this evening a success and Francina knew that it was primarily for her sake. Yet, despite her smiles, Aunt looked tired. She would never say it of course, but Francina felt sure that she would like to see her settled.

She glanced at the clock. Arthur Hartwell was explaining the wet collodion process to Mr Cowan Bell. 'Its great advantage is its ability to produce high-quality plates away from the studio, thus giving me the freedom to travel . . . '

She vaguely listened (she had heard it all before). Her eyes kept darting to the corner of the verandah, where she had a clear view of the top of the stairs. But Arthur Hartwell had the annoying habit of blocking her view, as if determined to engage her full attention, for whenever she stepped aside to keep the stairs in sight, he would shift his position so that she ended up no better off. In this manner they would gradually work their way around the room.

Mr and Mrs Cooke arrived next. The room abounded with genial affection as guests greeted friends. Francina raised her glass to her cheek and shivered, enjoying it delicious coldness. Aunt had ordered a box of ice especially for party, which was being preserved for as long as possible in a tank of saltpetre.

'Mort à la Republique! Vive le Roi!' screeched the parrot periodically from Uncle's study, where he had been banished for the evening. His indignant protests were for the most part drowned by the rumble of thunder and the sound of rain battering the roof, and it was testament to the Bartons' popularity that so many guests had braved the storms. A damp mist was seeping through the venetians, bringing with it clouds of tiny biting insects seeking shelter in the house. Guests began to gravitate to the drawing room, in the hope that a fire might reduce the humidity. Francina was carried along with them and lost sight of the stairs.

Arthur Hartwell continued his eulogy beside a large blue and white Chinese water jar sprouting a potted palm. 'One of the most difficult problems in India is the dust,' he said.

'Dust?' inquired Mr Cowan Bell.

'Mr Fetherstone, how delightful to see you,' she heard Aunt Barton cry. 'So kind of you to venture out in this weather!'

Francina stood on tiptoe to catch a glimpse of him, but Mr

Cowan Bell's large bulk stood in the way.

'Because of its sticky nature, wet collodion attracts dust.'

'How was the problem overcome in the Crimea?' asked Mr Cowan Bell.

'Mr Lihou!' came Aunt Barton's voice, 'so kind of you to join us as well this evening, especially as a little birdie has told us how hard you have been studying.'

She caught sight of him through the crowd and held her breath. The thought had crossed her mind that over time she might have improved his image: straightened his nose, chiselled away his flaws - but seeing his face again with its mass of imperfections, it was infinitely more fascinating than the one she remembered.

'There are so many people I would like you to meet,' came Aunt Barton's voice. 'Do you know our dear friends Mr Cooke of the Bengal Bank and his wife?'

He drifted away with Aunt Barton. She could neither see nor hear him now. All she heard was a long discourse on photogenic paper. She had never regarded Arthur Hartwell as a bore before (Mr Cowan Bell certainly, but never Arthur). While he revealed the secrets of preparing photogenic paper, her eyes scanned the room for another glimpse of him. The air was unbearably hot. The insects were stinging and her prickly heat had flared up again.

'The paper must first be pinned to a board, and one side coated with silver nitrate.'

Goose pimples prickled her arms as she sensed him looking at her from across the room.

'How does one coat the paper?' she asked, with a bright smile.

'With a brush especially prepared for the purpose,' Arthur Hartwell said, tuning to her. 'But one must take care to distribute the fluid evenly.'

'Miss Duquesne.'

She feigned surprise. 'Mr Lihou, you have come. We were so sure that the rains would deter you this evening.'

It was hard to take her eyes away from his face. His new black whiskers suited him so well.

'When we said goodbye in Guernsey, I had no idea that we would meet again so soon.'

'It was a great surprise when Aunt Barton invited me out.'

'How is your family? Your brother?'

'They are all exceedingly well. And Mrs Lihou?'

'Mother worries that I am not taking proper care of myself, and insists on sending me instructions on what I must eat and wear. All nonsense, I'm afraid.'

'Perhaps if you had followed her advice, you might not have taken ill like poor Mr Fetherstone.' She flashed a smile. 'You were taken ill, were you not, Mr Lihou? Otherwise I am sure you would have called on us sooner.'

Gilbert Lihou sipped his glass of punch. His dark eyes studied her closely. They were as fiery as she remembered, but deeper set. 'I do not have to ask if you are happy, Miss Duquesne,' he said eventually. 'I have never seen your eyes sparkle so.'

'Indeed!' laughed Arthur Hartwell. 'You should have seen her on the *Hindustan*, sir – a sober little thing, hiding in a corner, scribbling away in her sketchbook – eh, Miss Duquesne?'

Gilbert Lihou seemed a little surprised by this interruption.

Francina blushed. Arthur had been shuffling beside her ever since Gilbert Lihou had arrived. She could not ignore him any longer, so she made introductions.

'Lihou? I fagged for a Lihou at Charterhouse.'

'That was my cousin George. He is now the Sessions Judge at Purneah.'

'Is he indeed? Fancy hearing of old Stinger. We used to call him Stinger, don't ask me why. When you next write, ask him if he remembers Hartwell Minor.'

Arthur began to reminisce about his school days. Francina stared at her hands in despair. She could feel Gilbert Lihou's eyes burning into her face. She wanted only to focus on them, but politeness made her transfer her gaze from time to time to Arthur's.

His eyes began to wander, as though looking for an excuse to leave. 'Is Mary well?' she asked to keep him here.

But there were many other things she would have preferred to ask. She could not stop thinking of the last time they had met. How differently they had behaved on the beach that day, and how estranged they seemed now.

'Indeed. She will be very interested to know that I have seen you. I shall write and tell her in my next letter.'

Francina smiled as she imagined Mrs Lihou's face when she heard that her beloved son had been entertained by the likes of Miss Duquesne.

'Mother wants Mary to finish in Switzerland.'

'Switzerland!'

They had travelled halfway across the globe; raced across hostile deserts in bone-shaking carriages; braved storms and tempests in rat-infested steamers to arrive in the City of Palaces, one of the most exotic places in the world, and here they were talking about the two most boring people on earth. It was almost a relief to be interrupted.

'I say, Mr Lihou, did you see the Great Exhibition?' asked Arthur Hartwell. 'Regretfully I did not - but on my recent furlough, I made several visits to Sydenham. In my opinion, the Crystal Palace is one of the great wonders of the modern world. Did you know that Mr Paxton found his inspiration to build that amazing edifice by studying the structure of the giant water lily?'

'Ah, the *Victoria regia!*' Mr Cowan Bell burst into the conversation. 'I was privileged to observe that giant *nymphaea* when I passed through Chatsworth last year.'

Francina groaned inwardly. He could spout on for hours if he was not stopped. But Arthur Hartwell smiled encouragingly. 'Did you study the leaves - particularly the undersides?'

'It was too dark to make a very close inspection,' said Mr Cowan Bell. 'I had specifically requested to see its nocturnal flower. I saw the magnificent *Victoria regia* unfold by lamplight. It was a delight: a luxuriant white flower, flushed with pink. But the leaves, I understand, can grow to eight feet in diameter and are strong enough to support the weight of a child.'

'A child as old as Lionel?' Francina was determined to be included in this conversation.

'Lionel?' Gilbert Lihou looked directly at her.

'Mrs Balfour's son,' Arthur Hartwell said, before she could reply. 'Little scamp. He hid my notebook when I was last here. We were in turmoil looking for it, were we not, Miss Duquesne?'

Arthur Hartwell was standing too close, so she stepped away from him. This was not going well. But how could it go otherwise? Mr Hartwell would not leave her alone.

'That notebook was of great importance to me. It contained some vital measurements of lintels, arches and so forth. We eventually found it hidden behind some cushions in Mr Barton's study. I was rather short-tempered that day, was I not, Miss Duquesne?' laughed Mr Hartwell, inching towards her.

She moved away again, irritated by his constant interruptions, but he only stepped closer. He was being presumptuous and Gilbert Lihou was watching. She understood the look in his eyes and her heart sank, for he seemed to believe that she was spoken for.

'I have studied drawings of the giant water lily,' said Mr Hartwell, flushed with the excitement of his subject. 'The secret of the leaf's strength lies in its structure. The ribs are an inch deep and radiate from the centre. These principle ribs have in turn multiple branches that are crossed by a rigid membrane, which give the appearance of a spider's web. It was this very structure that provided Mr Paxton with the inspiration for the Crystal Palace.'

'Paxton's observations must surely serve as a lesson,' said Gilbert Lihou. 'We must learn to study nature with his scientific eye.'

Gilbert Lihou had capitulated. Mr Hartwell had captured his attention where she had failed miserably. She accepted a nut off the tray proffered by the bearer and bit it savagely.

'How many more inventions are waiting to be inspired by nature? I tell you, Mr Lihou, we are living in exciting times.' Arthur rubbed his chin enthusiastically. 'I have pondered over the dilemma for many hours: how might we utilise Paxton's invention in India?'

'Surely, this country is too hot to erect buildings of glass?'

'Indeed it is, Mr Lihou, but think of the advantage of constructing buildings in the pre-fabricated form. If we could only transfer Paxton's principles to materials more sympathetic to the Indian climate - why, our improvements in this country would increase at a phenomenal pace!'

Now Gilbert Lihou hardly looked at her, for a heated discussion ensued on Paxton and his inventions. Francina turned away to see Henry Fetherstone edging towards her.

'At last, Miss Duquesne,' he whispered, 'I would have come over sooner, but I was waylaid by that gaggle of Indian matrons.'

Francina smiled. 'You must excuse Aunt's friends. It is a treat for them to meet a new face from Home. Were they grilling you mercilessly?'

'Most certainly! Society, opera – fashion. In fact on every subject I know nothing about. Now if I had been interrogated on political economics, law – even the Salt tax - I might not have looked such an ignoramus, but for some reason those subjects were not brought up.'

Francina laughed gaily. They talked of Louisa, then of her voyage out. Mr Cowan Bell joined them and could not refrain from relating his usual anecdote of her tossing clothes over the rail of the *Hindustan,* causing such confusion, he said, that a life-ring was hurled overboard to aid the drowning passenger. They laughed, and so did she.

At last they were summoned to dine. Arthur Hartwell quickly offered her his arm. Francina put on her brightest smile and followed the married ladies down to the dining room.

Aunt Barton had taken great pains over the table plan. As she had explained to Francina, nothing in India can so quickly terminate a friendship than for a guest memsahib to discover that she been designated a place that demeans her status. 'It is all nonsense, as far as I am concerned,' shrugged Aunt, 'but the British take the order of precedence very seriously.'

Gilbert Lihou and Henry Fetherstone, being the most junior newcomers to India, were placed at the ends of the table. Francina's status as an unmarried woman placed her next to Gilbert Lihou. Arthur Hartwell sat opposite, and Mr Cowan Bell sat next to her. She felt slightly uneasy at being the only unmarried woman here tonight, but at least Cissie was not here to criticise Aunt's guest list or sneer at her old fashioned habit of placing all the dishes on the table at once, so that the fish, joints of meat and fowls jostled with the curries, desserts and sweetmeats.

The table was decorated as brightly and as spectacularly as possible. Vines intertwined amongst the finger bowls. The rice was rainbow-coloured; the table napkins arranged like drifting swans, and the coconut ice was stained pink. The *malis* had gathered all the remaining flowers that had not been decimated by the rain, and Francina had arranged them in crystal vases between the sago puddings, gulabs and brandied mangoes. Hopefully they might last the evening before all the petals dropped. Flying insects swarmed round the lamps and shed their wings over the white damask tablecloth.

Conversations started around the table as the *khansamah* removed the silver covers from the glasses to fill them with wine.

'Have you heard that the *Orientalist* broke her shaft in a gale off Ceylon?' someone said. 'It nearly drifted ashore. They managed to get it to safety, but all the passengers have been held up in Galle.'

'Mrs Harley was travelling on the *Orientalist*,' came Mrs Cooke's voice. 'She was hoping to get Home to see her little boy, who has been poorly. She must be very anxious.'

Arthur Hartwell and Mr Cowan Bell were discussing the difficulties of extending the railway line beyond Raniganj. 'The terrain is mostly mangrove and very hostile in character - disease, tigers, alligators, and so forth.'

'I understand that Mr Jenkins has died of jungle fever?'

'His demise will set the scheme back many months.'

Francina turned to Gilbert Lihou. With Arthur distracted, perhaps she could now engage his attention.

'Do you ride much out here, Mr Lihou?' she asked, in a manner she hoped sounded sophisticated. She was determined to astonish him with her new confidence.

'Ride? Certainly. Fetherstone and I go for long scrambles in the country when the weather permits. He's a first rate horseman. I have a job keeping up with him sometimes. My steed is rather temperamental. He's supposed to be a half-Arab but I'm beginning to think there's a smattering of mountain goat in his veins.'

Francina sipped her almond soup. 'You are being modest, Mr Lihou,' she smiled, remembering how he had thundered across the sands in Guernsey. 'But it is strange that we haven't come across one another, for I often ride out with Uncle Barton when it's fine. Calcutta can be quite delightful in the early mornings.'

'But as you well know, Miss Duquesne, riding in slippery mud during the Rainy Season can be very disagreeable,' laughed Arthur Hartwell. 'Why, only this evening, my long-suffering mount had to negotiate a fallen tree and yet *another* flooded lane.'

The *khitmutgars* removed the soup plates, and offered platters of fish. Arthur continued his discourse on the trials of travelling in the Rains as he helped himself. When he was distracted again, Francina tried once more to engage Gilbert Lihou in conversation.

'Riding is primarily a dry-weather activity, I suppose, but

walking has no seasonal limitations - for men at least. Unfortunately, ladies in India do not have that licence. What I really miss out here is the freedom to walk where I wish. Beyond the perimeter of the compound we ladies must either be carried in hateful *palkis* or confined to carriages.'

'I am afraid that is because we British have a penchant for mimicking native customs,' came Mr Hartwell again, as he tucked into his fish pilau, brightly coloured in turmeric.

She ignored him. 'Sometimes I pretend to be taking an exhilarating walk along the cliffs –' (She jumped, as a servant launched himself from behind her chair to swat a hairy moth that had landed at her elbow.) 'That is what I miss about Guernsey: the turbulent sea and the wind. Do you not sometimes long for an icy wind to cut you to the quick, Mr Lihou?'

'In this sweltering heat, I can think of nothing more agreeable.'

At last she had his full attention. 'Indian customs are so restricting - for a woman, I mean. It distresses me to be followed everywhere, unable to raise a finger to do anything for myself. Why, even if I drop a handkerchief, a servant will come scurrying from nowhere to pick it up.'

'Vive le Roi! Mort aux Anglais!'

She glanced round the table, but no one else seemed aware of the feathered agitator in the study. 'How I long to have the freedom to roam where I please – as I used to walk the dogs along the beach - do you remember, Mr Lihou? But here, it seems, even dog-walking is considered inappropriate for a woman.'

'But the dog-walker in this country is regarded as no better than an Untouchable!' came Arthur again.

Francina was beside herself with despair. What was the matter with Mr Lihou? Why did he let Arthur Hartwell keep interrupting? And where was that spark she remembered in Guernsey?

'The native already considers the European lady wanting in morals because she socialises in mixed company,' continued Arthur Hartwell cheerfully. 'Do you not see the predicament, Miss Duquesne? How could a native respect a *sahib* who allows his woman to be reduced to the status of a dog-walker? Women in this country are regarded as chattels, gilded and preened to show off their master's worth.'

'Native women might be considered as chattels by their men folk,' said Francina, 'but surely *you* do not see us as chattels, Mr Lihou, objects to be displayed?'

'How I see you is of no consequence.'

She flushed, wounded by his remark. A beetle flew in and crashed to the table. She crushed it angrily under the base of her glass. It left a brown stain on the tablecloth. She knew that she was conducting herself badly, but she could not help herself.

'But *we* are not chattels. We have a soul - as much of an inner life as you!'

'That I do not deny but, as Lieutenant Hartwell so rightly pointed out, in India, a man's greatness is manifest by outward show and ceremony. Natives are impressed by greatness. It is a characteristic that we have learned to cultivate to gain their respect.' He scooped an insect out of his wine glass and placed it, gasping, on the tablecloth. 'That is the paradox of this country. Status and privilege go hand in hand, like a pair of scales. The more the privileges: the greater the restrictions. That is the nature of India.'

'For a woman certainly, but not for a man!'

She hated this cool indifference of his. She felt an urge to gouge her nails across his cheek. She saw herself doing so, leaving bleeding ridges down his flesh. He would be left with a permanent scar, a reminder of her that he would carry to his dying day.

'You told me once in Guernsey, that to gain the natives' respect in the colonies we must stand above them. Now you contradict yourself by saying that we must conform to their customs. You cannot have it both ways, Mr Lihou,' she said stiffly. 'If European women follow native customs we should be no better than slaves!' She saw Miss Chesterton striking the blackboard with her pointer, urging her on. 'We are not mannequins, automatons without feelings!'

'Miss Duquesne, please calm yourself,' Arthur Hartwell said in alarm.

But she could not calm herself, however much she wanted to. The conversation was not going as she wished, but she had no idea how to turn it. The insect wriggled helplessly on its back, and she watched its death throes with sadistic satisfaction.

'Sometimes I feel as if I'm in purdah,' she said. 'We may sneer at the natives' custom for imprisoning their women in zenanas, but is there really much difference between their customs and ours?'

'I am sorry that you find the Indian way of life constricting, Miss Duquesne. I have this abiding memory of you wading barefoot through the sea in Guernsey –.'

'A child of nature?'

He nodded.

'Surely that is a contradiction in terms, Mr Lihou? A child is a dependant. A creature of nature (the very word *nature* implies a degree of freedom) is independent. I have no freedom – *women* have no freedom. We have no opinions, no redress, we just submit.'

'I fear India might have captured that free spirit of yours.'

'Not India, Mr Lihou, society has captured it!'

'Would you be so kind as to carve the joint, Mr Lihou?' called Aunt Barton from the centre of the table.

'Certainly, Mrs Barton.' He looked rather relieved to be assigned this task and not to have to continue the conversation any longer. Francina stared at the tablecloth. She watched him slice the haunch of mutton in silence, wishing she could think of something to say to cancel her outburst. The *khitmutgar* hovered at his side, waiting to pass the plates of meat to the guests.

The insect hardly moved now. It lay on its back, resigned to its fate.

'You should not have come to India, Miss Duquesne,' Mr Lihou said eventually. 'One loses a sense of perspective out here. This is a dangerous, unpredictable place.'

'Oh, I am perfectly safe,' she said, trying to control the emotion in her voice. 'The walls of the compound are high. There is no danger of me being mauled by a wild animal.'

'That is not the sort of danger I was referring to.'

The wind picks up. The shutters bang. She jumps out of bed to secure them, and discovers that the windows are barred. A man on the verandah is leering at her, a burly man with a full brown beard. 'At last I have you, savage beautiful creature!' he sneers, seizing her arm through the bars. 'Now I shall tame the wild thing.'

'Sir, you may bend my body as easily as a reed in your hand,' she cries defiantly, 'but you will never capture my soul. My spirit rides free and lucid as the wind!'

'Don't torture me so with that look of cold indifference! It is *you*, spirit with will and energy, virtue and purity that I want - not just your delicate frame!' He releases his grip, and hides his face in his hands. 'Oh, my hope - my love- my life,' he sobs with such pathos in his voice, 'if I cannot have all of you, then I must let you go!'

When she looks around, the walls and roof of her chamber have melted away. The man has disappeared. Clouds race above her head and the moon gleams like a lantern in the firmament. With a leap she is free, bounding with the swiftness of a doe over fields and ditches. Briars and thorns tear at her nightgown. She runs aimlessly through clumps of heather. Stones cut her feet. The wind whistles through her hair. Where is she? Where should she go? She blunders over heath land, and wades knee-deep through undergrowth.

Hunger gnaws at her. How much time has passed? Days? Weeks? A force compels her onwards. She will not give up; she cannot give up. Crossing the moor, she follows a track ribboning towards a light blinking on the hill. It is a lantern swinging above a doorway of a bleak stone house. Rain stings her shoulders, and soaks her nightgown. Unable to unfasten the garden gate, she half-climbs, half-falls over it and staggers towards the huge oak door set in a stone recess. Carved grotesques snarl down at her. With one desperate throe she raps on the knocker.

Eventually a servant opens the door a crack.

'Please, may I speak to your master?'

'Vagabond! Be off with you. We have no gypsies here,' barks the servant, slamming the door in her face.

She collapses on the doorstep. She will surely die if she sleeps out here. 'Let me in,' she whispers to the locked door. 'Let me speak to your master.'

Gathering all her strength, she edges round the building, looking for a side door, an open window, anything that might afford her shelter. The ground is a quagmire. She slips, stumbles. Her feet are caked in mud. She can hardly lift them. The wind is building to a tempest. The rain is horizontal slapping her hair in long wet snakes across her face. At last she sees a chink of light, and taps frantically at the lattice.

'Let me in, let me in!'

'Who are you?'

'I'm come home. I'd lost my way on the moor!'

The lattice opens. Strong arms reach out and haul her in.

She slips effortlessly inside, as if she has left her mortal body, but that cannot be for his rough face is nuzzling her neck.

'Come, warm yourself. Stand by the fire.'

He guides her gently towards the hearth. There is no light in the room save the glow of the embers. She is a mannequin, void of voluntary movement. As if in a trance she watches him kneel before her and place her feet in a bowl of warm water. Now he is sponging them, so very gently. First one foot, then the other. Rivulets of warm muddy water streaked with blood trickle down her legs and dissipate into the bowl.

His face is close, his granite-hewn features awesome in the firelight. 'You will catch your death if you do not take that wet thing off,' he whispers, unbuttoning her nightgown.

She steps out of it and views it dispassionately, a discarded cocoon at her feet.

Now he is rubbing her dry with a rough linen cloth. Her arms and legs glow pink as peach bloom. She could be five years old, standing before the nursery fire being patted dry by Nurse, but she cannot be for her breasts are quivering with painful fullness. Waves of pleasure begin to envelope her. She wants to swoon, to capitulate in a languorous heap on the rug.

8

Will he call today? Will the rain hold off? She had spent the morning trying on outfits, and then flinging them across her bed in exasperation. What impression did she want to make? She could not think clearly, for her mind kept returning to their conversation. Why was she so outspoken last night?

Eventually she resorted to a simple oyster silk, which she hoped would show her in a quiet, decorous light.

She was writing a letter when a servant entered her room to announce that a sahib wished to see her. Glancing quickly in the glass, she pinched her cheeks and raced to the verandah. He had come! He wasn't put off by her senseless prattle about slaves and chattel. No, he had admired her boldness. Of course he had. That was what he had implied in Guernsey, wasn't it? He liked to see her running barefoot through the shallows with loose-flowing hair. But she must be careful to watch her tongue. She must not appear too opinionated in future. Better keep her views to herself from now on -

But it was not Gilbert Lihou.

'How kind of Mr Hartwell to call in such disagreeable weather,' beamed Aunt Barton. 'Did you see much destruction on your way, Mr Hartwell? We heard that poor Mr Inman took a tumble when his pony took fright in the high winds - broke his collarbone, so Dr Thompson said. And I fear our flowers, poor things, will have taken a battering. Such a pity! Mr Barton takes a great pride in his plants. We have some very unusual specimens of - oh dear, I forget the *botanical* name - but we certainly have some very fine *roses,* or so I've been told. Are you interested in horticulture, Mr Hartwell?'

'I know little about plants, ma'am - but I would very much like to see Mr Barton's roses.'

'Why, of course! As it has stopped raining, perhaps you would like to show Mr Hartwell the rose garden, *ma cherie*?' Aunt Barton gestured impatiently towards the compound. 'I am sure the fallen branches will have been cleared away by now,'

Francina stared at Aunt in dismay. Why was she so animated?

A swarm of crickets, dazed and battered, lay on the steps. Francina kicked them out of the way. The *malis* were clearing up the storm debris, but the compound could not look sadder.

The noise of lovesick frogs rose to a cacophony as they walked along the sodden, steaming path. The arbour was a sorry, wind-blown sight, bereft of blooms.

'I am afraid we are too late,' she said crossly, picking her way across a carpet of fallen rose petals. It was a ridiculous idea of Aunt's to venture out on a day like this. The wet was seeping through her slippers. She certainly had not chosen this oyster silk to traipse through the mud.

But Arthur Hartwell was not interested in the roses. He stopped abruptly and faced her, flushed and agitated. 'Miss Duquesne, I was unable to sleep last night.'

'The storm was very bad.'

'It was not the storm that kept me awake, - but you.'

'*Me*, Mr Hartwell?'

'Arthur. Please call me Arthur.'

'Arthur,' she repeated, brushing her skirts. She had to be careful, for greenfly could leave a nasty smear.

'I have been thinking about you all night.'

She felt ashamed. Since Gilbert Lihou had re-appeared, she had not thought about Arthur Hartwell for a single moment. He was looking at her so earnestly that her heart sank, for she had an inkling of what he was about to say, and she wished with all her heart that she could prevent him from saying it.

'Miss Francina - may I call you Miss Francina?' he asked breathlessly. 'I have been appointed Assistant to the Chief Engineer in Oude, and the appointment, I believe, will quickly pave the way for further promotion.'

Perhaps she was mistaken, perhaps that was all he had come to tell her. She relaxed and smiled. 'That is good news. I am very happy for you.'

'Are you really, Miss Francina?'

'Why, yes indeed.' She must say something profound about Oude. Oude? What does she know about Oude? She heard some talk recently . . .

'Oude is a poor lawless state, but now that that despot King is safely ensconced in Calcutta, the Company plans far-reaching improvements - metalled roads, bridges, the sinking of wells and such like. Do you realise, Miss Francina, that at present hardly any public works exist in Oude!'

'Is that so?'

'I consider myself privileged to be amongst those who will be responsible for bringing great changes to Oude. And while I am there - conducting a survey of the country - I intend to make a photographic record of everything I see. The monuments, tombs, forts, palaces -'

'You must! It is the perfect opportunity.'

His smile faded. 'But there is a cloud -'

'A cloud?'

He seized her hand. 'You have it in your power, dear Miss Francina, to disperse that cloud. Put me out of my misery! I leave Calcutta for Lucknow at the end of the week. I cannot say how long I shall be away - a year, perhaps two. Before I go, may I put a question to you? May I have an assurance, a slight inkling that your future might possibly weld with mine in Oude?'

She had day-dreamed, visualised herself on an expedition with Arthur Hartwell, imagined the two of them camping in some remote valley in Central India; seen herself mixing his photographic chemicals, and helping him write up a detailed record of all the curios they might come across. It could have been so exciting, so enthralling . . .

'Miss Francina?'

But it was too late.

'Miss Francina, my future happiness depends on your answer.'

The cook, squatting at the cavernous entrance of the kitchen, was eyeing them curiously. He was plucking a chicken, which he held firmly between his toes. Feathers were flying everywhere.

Francina pulled her hand away. 'I am truly sorry, Mr Hartwell, but at present I cannot consider such a question.'

'When might you consider such a question? Time is running out.'

'On your return, Mr Hartwell. Put the question to me on your return.'

She looked away. She could not bear to see him close to tears.

*

The rain returned, and became a deluge after Arthur Hartwell left. They could not take a drive that evening - or the next day. Francina paced the floor while the wind shook the walls and rainwater dripped into bowls placed strategically around the house. The servants stoked the fires in the grates, but nothing could reduce the humidity. Damp clung to her hair and clothes, weighing her down with exhaustion. This was an even more hateful season than the Hot Weather. Mould was spreading across the walls and mildew spotting the furnishings. Every species of insect that crawled and stung had taken refuge in the house; while the ubiquitous white ants marched relentlessly from room to room looking for a leg of furniture that had not been obstructed by a saucer of water. Would the rain never stop?

Sick with anticipation, her ears pricked for the telltale sounds of a visitor coming through the gate. Surely the rain would not deter him? It had not deterred Arthur Hartwell.

'Sit down and compose yourself, *ma cherie*. It is very trying for us to watch you.'

Francina knew that Aunt Barton was disappointed and puzzled by her behaviour. She had not asked about the conversation in the garden with Arthur Hartwell. There was no need - his downcast face and abrupt departure had said it all. She knew that she had behaved illogically after encouraging him. But now was not the time to think about Arthur Hartwell.

Why does he not come?

'Perhaps it is not too late,' Aunt Barton said kindly. 'I am sure Mr Barton could convey a hint in the right direction. After all, Mr Hartwell does not leave until the end of the week. These days, I believe it is almost *de rigueur* to reject one's first proposal - although, it would have been quite beyond my understanding. I accepted all mine without hesitation.'

Abdul appeared, with a *chit* on the silver salver. Her heart leapt.

But it was note from Aunt Cecilia.

'Cissie has had her baby!'

9

Cissie lay in bed, propped up by pillows. There was a hush in the room that seemed to stifle the sound of rain lashing against the shutters. A fire burned in the grate, airing the little nightdresses and flannels arranged neatly on the clotheshorse, but there was no sign of the baby.

Cissie smiled weakly as Francina kissed a feverish cheek.

'Oh, Fanny, how I suffered!' Cissie looked exhausted. Black hair crossed her forehead in matted strands.

Francina took her hand. 'Poor Cissie. Aunt Cecilia did tell me.'

A shrill little cry drifted into the bedroom.

Cissie covered her ears. 'Every time I hear that noise, my milk flows. Oh, Fanny, it's so uncomfortable, and I don't think these bindings can be tied any tighter.'

The cries developed into a series of sharp little hiccoughs.

Francina followed the sound into the dressing room. A wicker-cradle stood in the corner. She tiptoed towards it. The ayah gently parted the muslin curtains for her. Peeping above the folds of a lacy shawl, Francina saw the shock of black down covering the baby's head, her mottled lids fringed with silky lashes, the faint blue veins pulsating at her temples, her tiny hand resting on the pillow. The fragility of this tiny, perfectly formed being took her breath away.

The ayah scooped the baby up in her lace shawls.

Francina took the baby from her arms and kissed her warm forehead. 'One day, little Maud, you will grow up to be as beautiful as your mamma,' she whispered.

The baby stopped whimpering, stuffed a clenched fist into her mouth, and began to suck lustily. Francina carried the bundle into the bedroom.

'She looks like you, Cissie,' she murmured, leaning over the bed.

Cissie glanced briefly at her newborn daughter, but made no attempt to take her.

A small, comely woman bustled into the room, carrying a

steaming bowl wrapped in a hot flannel. A comforting aroma of cinnamon and heated almond oil wafted through the air.

'Mrs Balfour,' said the nurse, 'it is time for your poultice.' She stared at Francina, as if to indicate that her presence was not required. Francina tiptoed back to the dressing room and returned the baby to her ayah.

The next day there was a break in the cloud. For a full hour the sun shone without a drop of rain. The garden, with its new green flush, shimmered and sparkled in the sunshine, and the hot air steamed with the smell of drying earth. Francina's spirits soared. Surely he must come today. She heard the gates grind open and someone ride up the drive. Quickly smoothing her hair, she raced through the house to the verandah.

'Mr Fetherstone,' cried Aunt Barton. 'So brave of you to venture out in this dreadful weather! Are the roads flooded? We have heard very bad reports of flooding in Baranagar.'

'Is Mr Lihou not with you?'

'Lihou asked me to give you this, Miss Duquesne. He has gone up-country. He left by the early morning train'

'He has left Calcutta?'

Why did he not say goodbye? Francina tore open the envelope.

My dear Miss Duquesne –

It was a pleasure to meet you again and to find you looking so well and spirited. I write soon to my sister Mary and will certainly tell her of our encounter, for I know she will be pleased to have news of you. I found Lieutenant Hartwell a gentleman of much enthusiasm and sound opinions. Please send him my hearty greetings.

Unfortunately, our reunion will be cut short, for I have been appointed Assistant Collector of Kandria. I leave immediately, and go armed with a surfeit of letters of introduction from the good people of Calcutta. Please convey my kind regards to Mr and Mrs Barton and to your Grandmother, whom, regretfully, I did not meet.

I send my heartfelt prayers for your future happiness, and will always remain your affectionate friend and well-wisher,

Gilbert Lihou

No forwarding address, no promise to write. Did she displease him so much? No, all this nonsense about Lieutenant Hartwell, he must have believed that she was spoken for.

'How curious! Lieutenant Hartwell has also received a posting. He has gone to Oude and will be there for a very long time,' she said brightly, willing him to relay this message to Gilbert Lihou. 'Is Oude anywhere near Kandria?'

'*Ma chérie* did you say *Kandria*?'

'Mr Lihou has been appointed Assistant Collector of Kandria.'

'What a coincidence! My granddaughter lives near Kandria.'

Aunt Barton gestured to the servant for her walking stick.

'I am a rusty old engine these days. My joints seize up dreadfully if I sit for too long.'

Francina took her arm. 'May I fetch something for you, Aunt?'

'The walk will do me good. Amuse Mr Fetherstone for a minute would you, *ma chérie*?'

'It is so sudden,' Francina whispered when Aunt had left the room. 'When did Mr Lihou know of this appointment? Why did he not mention it at the *burra khana*?'

Henry Fetherstone shrugged. 'Who can tell what goes on in Lihou's head? He keeps things close to his chest when he has the inclination.' He turned to her in an agitated fashion. 'Miss Duquesne, while we are alone, may I take this opportunity to give you my address - so you can forward my letters to Miss Louisa and hers to me? I do not know what I would do if I could not rely on your kindness to act as intermediary.'

'It is no kindness, Mr Fetherstone. It is my great wish that one day you and Louisa will find true happiness together.'

He handed her a card. '*Assistant Collector of Mhorabad*,' she read.

'You see, Miss Duquesne, my orders have also come through. I too must leave Calcutta.'

'Where is Mhorabad?'

Everyone was leaving. In her mind's eye she saw the dusty plains of India stretching on and on into infinity; everyone she knew, scattered like tiny pebbles across an endless plain . . .

'Between Meerut and Delhi.'

'Delhi is a fine old city, I believe.'

Aunt Barton reappeared. 'Here is my card, Mr Fetherstone. Send it immediately to Mr Lihou. He must promise to call on my granddaughter. He will be warmly received. The Bulpitts of Nudinapur are renowned in the district for their hospitality.'

'Aunt, Mr Fetherstone is also leaving us. He has a posting to Mhorabad.'

'You too? And just as we are getting to know you!'

When he had gone, Francina stepped into the compound. The green saturated world steamed in the humid heat. She dabbed her face and neck, hardly conscious of the biting insects. Who was there left to notice - or care - if her face was covered in red blotches? She clutched her stomach. She felt dead inside. She took Henry Fetherstone's card out of her pocket and stared at it closely. She was, at least, grateful to keep this tenuous link.

You should not have come out to India, Miss Duquesne.

How right he was.

The vultures were gathering, wheeling in the sky in increasing numbers as they did after rain. She stared up at them with a mixture of fascination and revulsion. Uncle had told her that the Parsees placed their dead in *dakhmas,* roofless towers where the vultures transmute the bodies to eternity.

'All alone, Miss Duquesne?'

Why did he always appear when he was least wanted? She had a vision of Mr Cowan Bell's hairy bulk splayed out in a *dakhma,* being devoured by vultures.

He cleared his throat. 'Miss Duquesne, you seem a little melancholy.'

'I am exceedingly melancholy.'

Aunt Barton had put him up to this. 'Go into the garden, Mr Cowan Bell,' she must have whispered, 'Francina's out there. She needs cheering up.'

Well, it would not work.

He coughed. 'As the rains look as though it might hold off for a while, may I be permitted to take you for a drive? Have you visited the Ochterlony Monument? It is a strenuous climb, but the panorama of Calcutta from the top is well worth the effort.'

Why not? It would be a distraction.

✸

The Hoogly was rising, threatening to burst its banks. But the showers were lessening, and now the sun burned for hours at a time. But there was no respite from the insects. At dusk, they rose in clouds from every tank and pool to bite and irritate, while incense coils burned in every room in a futile attempt to deter them from entering the house.

She visited Cissie's baby as often as she could. She loved the hushed industry of the nursery, the smell of baby clothes airing over the brazier, but most of all she loved to watch the *dhood-dhye* sit cross-legged on the floor as she nursed the infant. Francina would listen spellbound as the ayah sang Indian lullabies to her tiny white charge. Neither Francina nor little Maud understood a word, but they were both mesmerised by her soft, expressive voice. As she suckled, little Maud would stare wide-eyed into her foster mother's benevolent face, her tiny pink hand caressing her brown breast. Bengali was destined to be Maud's first language, the language she would inherently associate with loving and giving. It would imbed into her unconscious memory long after she had grown up and forgotten it. It would always be there, like the murmur of the wind, to haunt her dreams.

Cissie did not often venture into the nursery, and rarely stayed to watch her baby suckle. She was more interested in regaining her figure than following her daughter's progress. Perhaps it was for this reason that Francina was drawn to the child. She felt an irresistible urge to protect her; to drown her with love enough to buffer her against the setbacks she sensed might lie ahead.

While the baby slept, satiated with milk, she would cradle her in her arms. Sometimes Lionel would sidle up, sucking his thumb, lean his head against her arm and listen as she sang to her. Where the lullabies came from she had no idea, but she knew them instinctively. Birds, she had been told, have an inherent compass that leads them directly back to their ancestral feeding grounds, just as the salmon has an inborn memory to find the place where it was spawned. Perhaps human memories are inherited in much the same way. She wanted so much to believe that these songs, just like the colour of her hair or the shape of her nose, passed from mother to daughter.

10

'The *dhoby* and ironer are being exceedingly troublesome,' announced Aunt Barton as they sat down to *burra hazri*. 'The ironer is ill, and so the clothes are not done.'

'I am sure Abdul can find a replacement.' Uncle Barton helped himself to kedgeree.

Aunt shook her head in despair. 'But he says a new one wants *twenty-two* rupees a month. It's extortionate! And all the fault of newcomers like Mrs Elliot, who gives her ironer *twenty-nine* rupees a month. Have you heard of anything so ridiculous? Of course the servants hear of it, and think they can all demand higher wages -'

A young man with a light brown beard burst into the room.

They stared at him in astonishment.

'Angelo?'

Francina jumped and pulled him towards the table.

'It's Angelo!'

'But your beard!' said Grand-mère. 'No wonder we did not recognise you, *mon cher petit-fils*.'

'It makes you look older – discerning almost,' observed Netta as he flew round the table proffering kisses.

'As if Angelo could *ever* look discerning,' smiled Uncle Barton, shaking his hand. 'Abdul quickly bring a chair! Sit down, dear boy. Sit down.'

'Why on earth did you not write to tell us you were coming?'

'Letter-writing is such a bore, Aunt Barton. I prefer the element of surprise.'

'Well, you certainly surprised us, wicked boy! How long will you be staying – as long as possible, I hope?'

'It is difficult to say. Three days, perhaps four. I have some sensitive negotiations to conduct in Town.' Angelo helped himself to kedgeree. 'One of our agents has been causing us problems. Mr Marquand is anxious that I see him in person - to nip any misunderstandings in the bud, so to speak.'

'Mr Marquand must have a high regard for your abilities, Angelo' said Uncle Barton.

Angelo smiled as he shovelled food into his mouth. 'I am not used to such exotic fare. My cook is an imbecile. A hard-boiled egg is the limit of his culinary expertise. I am afraid Ceylon is very primitive when it comes to the civilised refinements of life.'

As everyone laughed and plied him with questions, the house pulsed with a new lease of life.

'Did you have a good coffee harvest at Wattewalle this year?'

Angelo shook his head. 'Unfortunately, we have been beset with problems, Uncle. Soon after I arrived, Wattewalle was invaded by rats. The estate looked as if it had been ravaged by a hurricane. Young branches were gnawed, tree buds ripped off. The coolies killed as many as a thousand rats in a single day.'

His audience murmured sympathetically.

'The ayah even found one climbing into the infant's cot.' Angelo nodded to the *khitmutgar* to refill his cup. 'Mrs Marquand, who was lying-in at the time, took it very badly.'

'We had a similar experience on the *Hindustan*,' said Francina. 'Miss Fuller woke up one night to find a rat nibbling her toe. She screamed for the steward, but it scurried away before he arrived. After that we set traps, but neither of us dared climb into our bunks until we had made a thorough inspection of our cabin.'

'We are always bracing ourselves for some new calamity. If it is not an invasion of squirrels, it will be monkeys or a herd of elephants.' Angelo gave a dry laugh. 'And believe me, there is nothing more frightening than trying to deter a herd of elephants from taking a short cut. '

'Mr Drummond told us that one year his coffee crop was infested by a plague of insects.'

'Mr Drummond?' Angelo sipped his tea.

'He travelled out on the *Hindustan* with us,' said Francina. 'I believe he manages an estate close to Wattewalle. Did I not mention him in my letter? He is acquainted with Alex Marquand. It is strange that you have not come into contact with him yet.'

'I have heard of him. But you forget, Ina, how isolated we are.' Angelo stood up. 'Now, will you all forgive me if I take my leave? I have some difficult negotiations to set in motion. Mr Marquand is anxious to have me back at Wattewalle as soon as possible.'

'Come and go just as you please, dear boy. Treat this house as if it were your own.'

He departed almost as abruptly as he had arrived.

Angelo did not return for dinner. He had not returned by the time the household retired for the night. He appeared the next morning on the verandah dishevelled and disorganised, as though his negotiations had lasted long into the night. His appearance startled Francina, but as no one else around the breakfast table seemed to notice, she said nothing.

After breakfast, Angelo took his sister for some air in the buggy.

'Syce, drive slowly!'

It was a futile remark, for progress through the Lal Bazaar was always slow. The street bustled with natives of all castes and religions milling between the overloaded bullock carts and the packed *cranchees* pulled by tired puny horses. Coolies balancing enormous loads on their heads, weaved between the carts. She was beginning to recognise the different nationalities: the Chinese with their straw conical hats and long plaits down their backs; the Africans in their loose gaudy gowns, and the Armenians with their baggy trousers and up-turned shoes. Colourful displays of spices, fruits and bright native toys spilled out of open shop fronts. Shopkeepers squatted beside their brass and earthen pots, the inlaid boxes, the embroidered shoes, caps and cotton saris. Crimsons, hot orange and sizzling pinks vyed with lime green, blues, purples and mauves.

Angelo scanned the ornate façades of the native houses rising behind the hotchpotch of booths and stalls lining the street, as though he was looking for someone. Francina sensed kohl-lined eyes spying on them through lattice-screened balconies.

'What a delectable sight to see a woman, unencumbered by stays, gracefully undulating her hips,' he muttered as a woman, balancing a water jar on her head, glided by.

Francina stared at him in astonishment.

He eyed her closely. 'Are you spoken for, Ina?

She blushed and shook her head.

'Why ever not? A pretty girl like you must have had an offer by now.' He looked offended, almost ashamed, as though her unmarried state reflected badly on him.

'I haven't fallen in love yet.'

A beggar with hideous red-stained teeth was running alongside.

'Love! What has love to do with anything?'

'Could you marry someone you do not love, Angelo?'

'Yes,' he said without a moment's hesitation. 'It is our duty to restore this family to its rightful social position - by whatever means at our disposal.'

'But Aunt Barton does not seem unduly concerned.'

'I hope Aunt is advising you properly? Sometimes I think she is just an empty-headed old woman. That was one reason why I wanted you to return with Mother. No one could have your interests more at heart than your own mother.'

'Why should Mamma have my interests at heart? They never concerned her before.'

'Frankly, Ina, your coldness towards Mother is difficult to understand. I was incensed when I received Mother's letter with the news that you did not even have the courtesy to meet her in Malta!'

Was this his reason for coming to Calcutta? Was he on a mission to return her to Mamma? Indignation swelled in her chest.

'Why, Ina? Mother could have given you an *entrée* to the best London circles. But after all our careful plans, you did not even deign to meet her!'

She turned away, sick inside. She knew he could insist that she leave India. That was his prerogative as her brother. In Papa's absence, he had complete authority over her. Why, because she was a woman, should she be at the whim of someone whose judgement she questioned? Miss Chesterton was right. Women *are* no better than slaves.

The gig lurched to a halt as a cow and her calf sauntered into the middle of the street. The syce shouted and waved his stick, but the cow stood her ground and gazed at him with languid eyes. Dusky children, taking advantage of the captive travellers, encircled the gig, their arms laden with curiosities. A small girl with kohl-rimmed eyes and a huge red flower pinned in her oiled hair, held out armfuls of exotic fruits. Francina examined a half-open peach-like fruit.

'Whatever is it?'

'Mace,' said Angelo, indifferently.

'I'm sorry that I have offended you, Angelo, but I do not think you see Mamma in her true light. You seem to have forgotten the pain and misery she put us all through. Why should I trust her?'

She saw Papa huddled in a shawl in his dreary little room, Mamma preening in glittering circles. Had Angelo forgotten that she was the cause of Papa's downfall? She would not be disloyal to Papa. She watched a street-seller preparing *pan* in the street. He picked up a wet green leaf, smeared it with lime and betel nut, and folded it into a triangle.

'Grand-mère advised me to take my time, and not to accept the first offer that comes my way. I'm sure Grand-mère has my interests at heart.'

'What does that mad old trout know!'

'You must not talk like that, Angelo. Grand-mère has been very kind to me. She gave me a necklace. I wore it to the ball at Government House -'

'What was it like?'

'It was a magnificent spectacle. The dresses were so beautiful. From a distance Lady Canning looked like Queen Victoria -'

'Not the ball, Ina - the necklace!'

'It is made of moonstones and so delicate that I was afraid to wear it.'

The man handed the tiny parcel of *pan supari* to a customer clad in a dirty dhoti with thin bowed legs.

Angelo's eyes followed hers to the pan-seller. 'Chloral is more civilised. It does not stain the teeth or lips red.' he said dismissively.

She looked at him closely. She has never known him to talk like this before.

At last the cow, bored by shouts and gesticulations, sauntered off with her calf to examine a vegetable stall. The gig jerked forward.

'Moonstones, eh? Will you show me the necklace, Ina? I should like to see it.' He leaned back and re-crossed his legs.

'Some weeks ago, when I was in Galle waiting for a shipment of supplies which was delayed by bad weather, I got talking to some fellows over a game of cards. They were on their way to join their brother in Australia, who is in the Blue Mountains prospecting for gold - and earning as much as ten pounds a day!'

He turned to her, his eyes gleaming. 'That is more than an Indian Collector can hope to earn in *three years*. Men are flocking to Australia from all over the world - Ireland, Germany, California, even China - and new seams are being discovered all the time. When the shipment eventually arrived, I took leave of the fellows, and traipsed back to Wattewalle with my train of coolies through the mud and mire, only to discover that the bridge we had negotiated on the way down had been washed away in a storm, and now we had to find another means of crossing. And all the time I was mulling over what those fellows had told me. The prospect of returning to my dank hut with only Marquand and his prim little wife for company held less and less appeal.'

Francina fixed her eyes on the red splats stippling the ground.

'When I finally returned to Wattewalle,' he continued, 'Marquand immediately accused me of procrastinating, of prolonging my stay in Galle. In his experience none of his other assistants managed to make a week's trip last two weeks. I was very fatigued, Ina, having travelled for three days with little sleep. I could have retorted that it is because I am cautious that I am still here while poor William lies in a jungle grave, but I bit my tongue. The next day, Marquand called me in to the office to tell me of his latest scheme: experimenting with tea-growing and shipping over artisans from China to train the coolies - as if we don't have enough to contend with just keeping the coffee free of pests and blight! It was the final straw. And then I thought: I don't have to put up with this any longer. I am not suited for a planter's life - and apart from anything else, I don't think I could endure another season of rain and hurricanes.'

Francina turned away. She would do nothing to encourage this talk. She caught sight of a fearsome black creature with bared fangs and a red dripping tongue framed in an ornate temple doorway. A garland of human skulls hung around her neck, and in her multiple arms she carried the severed heads and hands of her victims.

'*Qui ne risque rien n'aura rien.* So here I am: on my way to make a fortune in Australia.'

'How could you, Angelo, after all the sacrifices the family have made to help you! How did Cousin Alex take the news?'

He shrugged. 'Quite frankly, I think Marquand was rather relieved. We did not see eye to eye on many things. He will be far better off with an assistant who does not keep questioning his mad-brain schemes.'

'But what about your debts, the advances from Aunt Marquand and Aunt Sabonière?'

He laughed. 'By the time the aunts come to know of it, Ina, I shall be wallowing in gold! I shall be able to repay them sooner than they think. All in all, everyone will benefit from this plan - even Father. Just think, Ina, I will soon be in a position to help Father! That would not have happened for years if I had stayed at Wattewalle.'

'*Baksheesh*! *Baksheesh*!' shouted a ragged boy running alongside.

Angelo leaned out of the carriage and raised his cane. 'Filthy little beggar. Be off!'

The boy pulled a face and turned away.

'Naturally, I have had to settle my affairs and pay off my outstanding debts more quickly than I would have liked, which has made me, temporarily, short of funds.'

Francina braced herself.

'Do you have any funds you could possibly lend me - just for a short time, Ina?'

'I have nothing, Angelo.'

'Nothing at all?'

She shook her head.

'But did you not mention a bank bond that Uncle Doré had given you?'

'Yes - but that was on the strict understanding that I only use it in an emergency.'

'But this *is* an emergency, Ina. This is very much an emergency.'

'I think Uncle meant me to use it - if I should need - to return Home that is.'

She would never forget her last day in Guernsey. 'Come in here for a moment, Francina,' Uncle Doré had whispered, ushering her into the library. 'We shall be leaving early tomorrow, and this is the last chance I shall have for a private word.' He opened the drawer of his desk and brought out a buff envelope. 'Take this and keep it safe, my dear. I want you to promise me that if - for whatever reason - you should decide that India does not live up to your expectations, you will use it to secure your passage Home.' She did not want to accept the envelope but she knew he would have been hurt if she refused. 'As long as I live, my dear, there will be a bed waiting for you in this house.'

'Are you planning to return Home in the next few months?'

'No, of course not.'

'So, what is the problem? I shall only be *borrowing* it. Very soon I shall refund the money with interest. Believe me, Ina; you will not notice that it is missing!'

'Is Angelo still out?' Grand-mère enquired at tiffin.

'He has business in Town, Grand-mère.'

'Such a conscientious boy,' smiled Aunt Barton. 'It is delightful to see him again, of course, but he should have told us that he was coming to Calcutta. Surely no business is so urgent that there is no time to send a *chit*! We could have made him so much more comfortable if we were prepared.'

'He is his mother's son,' Grand-mère said quietly. 'Impetuous and unpredictable.'

In the silence that followed, Francina toyed with her *murghi pilau*, but she had no desire to eat. Where was he? And why on earth was she colluding in this reckless adventure?

On their return, Angelo had urged her to fetch the bank bond. With a heavy heart, she had found the packet in her trunk and handed it over to him. She was too tired and upset for arguments. She just wanted him out of her life as quickly as possible. He had changed, and she did not understand this new aggressive manifestation, and she was fearful that if she did not comply with his wishes, he could easily decide that the Bartons were not looking after her interests properly and insist that she be sent to Mamma.

Angelo had frowned at the bank bond. 'Only fifty pounds? Do you have anything else - any jewellery, perhaps, that I could use as collateral?'

Her chest had grown tight. 'Only my pearl earrings and locket.'

'Nothing else? Did you not mention a necklace?'

'*No*, Angelo!'

'May I just see it, Ina? You did promise to show it to me.'

Angelo took the necklace out of its box, held it up to the light and examined it closely.

'It's fine craftsmanship for an Indian piece. Moonstones, eh?'

'Moonstones set in *bubris*.'

'May I take it to have it valued? I have been given the name of a broker who is very discreet.'

'*No*, Angelo! What would Grand-mère say?'

'But she need not know, Ina. You ought to have it valued. Surely you would like to know its worth? Let me, at least, just ask his advice.' He tucked the box under his jacket, kissed her, and slipped out of the house.

Francina glanced at the clock. Three hours ago. Heaviness lay like a lump of suet in her stomach. What was he doing? When he returned, she would pull him aside and demand that he give up this hare-brained plan. He was not cut out to be a gold prospector. He must return to Wattewalle immediately and tell Alex Marquand that he has made a terrible mistake.

To pass the time, she decided to call on the Vauloués in Middleton Street.

The house was in chaos, half-packed boxes were everywhere.

'We have just received a letter from Archie,' said Cissie, bustling about. 'He wishes us to join him immediately. And the *dhood-dhye* has finally agreed to travel with us, but she took some persuading. I have had to increase her wages to twenty rupees a month. It is daylight robbery! But what could I do? I'm at her mercy and she knows it, wretched woman.'

Francina burst into tears. 'Oh Cissie, I shall miss you and the children so much!'

Cissie looked at her in surprise. 'Fanny dear, I shall miss you too, of course. But you will be my spy. You must write and tell me everything that happens in Calcutta. I want every piece of scandal - and don't forget to notice the new fashions.'

'When are you leaving?'

'On the morning train. Archie has arranged for *palkis* to await us at the end of the line.'

'But you haven't met Angelo. May I bring him round this evening?'

'That's impossible. We have so much to do, and we're so pressed for time. Come and see us off at the station tomorrow, Fanny - and bring Angelo with you. And when we have settled in, you must promise to visit us, for I have a feeling that life is going to be rather dull in Tirhgunj.'

Francina returned home in worse spirits than when she had left. Events were moving out of her control. To make matters worse, Abdul informed her that Angelo-Sahib had not yet returned.

She lay in a heap on her bed, unable to do anything but count the minutes on the clock and hope that at any moment she would hear the gates grind open and footsteps bound up the steps.

He had not arrived when they sat down to dine. What was keeping him? She had hardly seen him since he had arrived in Calcutta, but in that short time he had turned her life into a tumult. The older he became, the less she understood him. And as for his infatuation with Mamma! Could he not see that she was the cause of the family's misfortunes? The more she thought about it, the more indignant she became. He had always been dazzled by appearance and position - but what a tenuous position! It would only take a whisper to circulate that Mamma was not what she claimed to be, and all her sparkling connections would vanish like quicksilver. And where would that leave her daughter? A pariah in London society. How could Angelo be so irresponsible to suggest that she should return to Mamma.

'Are you feeling unwell, Francina? You've hardly eaten a mouthful. And, my dear, I could not help noticing that you ate very little at tiffin.'

At that moment Angelo burst into the room, almost knocking over the *khansamah*, who was standing to attention in the doorway.

'What a very taxing and frustrating day!'

He flopped into a chair, wiped his forehead with a handkerchief, and held out his glass to the *khitmutgar*. 'But I am delighted to say that everything has worked out satisfactorily. My business is complete. I have secured a deal!'

Aunt Barton clasped her hands together. 'Excellent news, my dear boy!'

Angelo jumped up and raised his glass. 'And so I wish to toast you all: Grand-mère, Aunt Barton, Uncle Barton, my sweet little sister, Netta. - Thank you, thank you all for making my stay so enjoyable and fruitful!'

'Angelo, you sound as if you are about to leave us,' chuckled Aunt Barton.

'Indeed I am, Aunt. I leave Calcutta tomorrow.'

'So soon?'

'What ship are you sailing on?' asked Uncle Barton.

Angelo shrugged. 'Oh, some humble country boat that stops at obscure little ports - I forget the name - but I have written it down somewhere. I had great difficulty in finding a passage. Everything was booked. I had little choice. I was just happy to take the first berth available.' He laughed. 'But frankly, I am not concerned about luxury. I'm just anxious to leave as quickly as possible.'

'Marquand will be delighted to know that you have concluded your business so promptly and successfully.'

'He will certainly be surprised.'

'Come outside, Ina,' whispered Angelo, catching her arm as they rose from the table after dinner. 'I have so much to tell you.'

'Angelo, what's happened? I was sick with worry.'

'I've had such a depressing time. Every vessel to Australia was taken; every clipper, every country boat - there was not even a rowing boat to be had! Nothing. I tell you, Ina, I was feeling pretty low.'

'It was meant to be, Angelo,' she smiled, weak with relief. 'Australia was a wild idea -'

'But wait! I then had the most amazing stroke of luck. As I was leaving the booking office, news arrived that some poor devil due to sail tomorrow had passed away in the night. So I have taken his place!' Grinning, Angelo took the letter out of his pocket. 'I have booked my passage on the *Lady Adelaide* which leaves for Australia at dawn tomorrow!'

He threw his arms round her waist, lifted her up and whirled her down the path. 'I feel in my bones that this is meant to be. Everything will turn out fine. And I have you to thank. I could not have done it without you, dear Ina – and it isn't a miserable hammock in steerage, but a first-class cabin all to myself.'

'A first-class cabin? Isn't that a little extravagant?'

'Ina, Ina! It will be perfect. Just think of the people I shall meet, think of the connections I shall make! By the time I reach Melbourne, I shall be weighed down with introductions to the highest circles of Australian society.'

'And did you - did you enquire about the necklace?'

'What a stroke of good fortune. A fellow in Galle put me on to him. Swore by him. Very discreet, and a low rate of interest. A rare being who spurns unscrupulous dealings.'

'So, what did he say?'

'He has taken it as collateral, for a very favourable advance.'

She could hardly breathe. 'He has taken the necklace?'

'It is only a temporary measure. In a few months' time, I will post you back the money *with interest* and you can retrieve it. Soon, little sister, I shall be in a position to give you a necklace five times more magnificent!'

'But you said that you were only taking it to have it valued, Angelo. You were just going to ask his advice. You said nothing about leaving it with him.' She was choking with indignation. How could he have tricked her like this?

'Don't look so worried, little sister, everything is in order.' He took her hand. 'I was assured that he is a highly principled individual. His offer was just too good to refuse - and you would be truly astonished to know how many distinguished folk use his services.'

'Is it - is it too late to have the necklace back?'

'Of course it is! I had to use it to secure my passage. And there will be other expenses until I strike lucky. I must set myself up with some good equipment, and I shall have to buy shares in a mining company.' Angelo kissed her on the forehead. 'If I am going to embark on this enterprise, Ina, I must do it properly. There's no point in doing anything half-heartedly. I shall slip away before dawn, long before anyone is awake. I don't want to have to answer awkward questions.'

'But I have arranged for us to say goodbye to Cissie Balfour at the station in the morning. She is looking forward to meeting you!'

'Unfortunately, that pleasure will have to be postponed. Keep my plans a secret - at least until I strike gold. I rather fancy surprising everyone.'

✱

The hours ticked through the night. She heard Angelo snoring in the next room, and she hated him; hated him for destroying her peace of mind, for interfering in her life, for colluding with Mamma - but most of all she hated herself for being duped. Mother and son: two indulgent, self-centred profiteers cast in the same mould. Her best friend and sympathiser, protector and confident, the person she had loved most in the world, had died the day he had allied himself to the enemy. Why had it taken her so long to realise this?

She could not wait to wave him out of her life.

She forced herself to rise when she heard him stirring in the early hours. Putting on her wrap, she entered his room, kissed him goodbye and watched him slip silently and efficiently away, as though he made a habit of night time adventuring.

She returned to bed and, for the few remaining hours until the household stirred, mourned for her lost family.

11

Wattewalle Coffee Estate, Ambgamona, Ceylon

My dear Cousin Francina,

Unfortunately this letter brings some disturbing news. It seems that Angelo has left Wattewalle without a word to anyone. I have made enquiries and it appears that he was last seen at Galle boarding a country boat bound for Madras or Calcutta. This is not the first time he has disappeared without leave, but it is certainly the most serious as he has taken all his possessions with him.

After making extensive enquiries, I have discovered that he was mixing in bad company in Galle and fear that he may have absconded leaving a trail of debt behind him. I sincerely hope this is not the case. If he is in difficulties, then I am sure we could come to an arrangement to resolve this swiftly and satisfactorily for all parties concerned. If Angelo should visit you in Calcutta, could you please stress upon him the seriousness of his actions and persuade him to return at once? In the meantime, if Angelo appears at Wattewalle then I shall send you word immediately, and I apologise in advance for worrying you needlessly.

I remain your affectionate cousin, Alex Marquand

Everything he had told her was a lie. He had deceived her and everyone who had tried to help him. But to lie to his own *sister*? Poor Papa! This news would surely destroy him. How could she keep it from him? Cousin Alex was sure to write a long angry letter to him. The repercussions would go on and on. . . . And what if Uncle Doré should find out about the bank note?

She collapsed into a chair and put her head in her hands.

'Miss Duquesne?'

She jumped. The room was so dark, that she had not noticed anyone coming in.

'Mr Cowan Bell, I did not see you there.'

'You were engrossed in your letter. It's not bad news, I hope?'

For a wild moment she felt tempted to tell him the whole story. But what would happen if she did? Could Angelo be arrested in Australia? She stuffed the letter into her pocket.

'Just my cousin playing silly games.'

She must be strong. Why jeopardise this chance for Angelo to set things right? Perhaps he will find gold in Australia. Then he can pay off his debts and she can retrieve the necklace. In time, everyone will forget this dreadful episode.

Aunt Barton appeared in the doorway of her room, leaning on her stick. 'Francina, Grand-mère thinks that you are spending too much time in your room. We know that you are missing the company of your friends, but you must not languish about feeling mournful. Now, cheer up, for I have some good news.'

Francina raised her head from the pillow.

'Follow me, *ma cherie*. I have something agreeable to show you.'

Francina slipped off the bed and quickly tidied her hair in the glass. He had come in person! My dear Miss Francina, she heard him say, I have been unable to continue my journey without seeing you for just one more time. I implore you, Miss Francina, please, please reconsider my offer . . . Oh yes, Arthur, yes, yes!

But Aunt Barton led her to the back verandah, to the old *darzi*, sitting cross-legged on his mat surrounded by paper patterns and materials.

'Grand-mère asked the *darzi* to make you a new ball-gown. Do try it on and see if it fits.'

Gathering up the ball-gown, Francina ran to her room. She remembered this fabric. She and Aunt had discovered it in *Taylor's Emporium*: an exquisite iridescent silk that had just arrived from China . . .

She stared at herself in the glass. The gown had three flounces edged in pale blue ribbon. The skirts were more voluminous than any she had ever worn before, and accentuated the extraordinary quality of the silk, which oscillated from pale pink to pale blue. She was touched that Aunt Barton and Grand-mère should have secretly designed this wonderful ball-gown for her. The froth of lace between her breasts and below the short wide sleeves set off the silk beautifully. She had metamorphosed into an exotic insect, and glided flightless back to Aunt Barton.

'Quite charming! It will be perfect for the ball at Belvedere.'

The *darzi* proudly shook his head. The pins and needles jabbed into his scull-cap glinted like a pincushion.

'Now run along, my dear, and show Grand-mère. She has been longing to see you in it.'

Grand-mère was sitting on the front verandah in her usual chair smoking her hookah. Netta was feeding nuts to the parrot. Francina twirled for their inspection. Aunt Barton admired the spectacle from the doorway.

'Grand-mère, it is loveliest gown I have ever seen.' Francina kissed her on the cheek.

'The colour suits you very well, Mademoiselle,' smiled Netta.

'And how your necklace will set off that décolletage!' said Grand-mère. 'Go and fetch it, *ma petite*.'

The demon had come out of the sea. It stood before her, black, headless and mocking; triumphant in its moment of reckoning.

'Francina?'

The ground began to tremble. The potted-palm was swaying. She at the epicentre of an earthquake. But Grand-mère, Netta, Aunt Barton just smiled, unaware of the catastrophe that was unfolding around them.

'Francina, fetch your necklace.'

By the time she reached her room, her skin had erupted into a hot rash. She fell on the bed, her new gown billowing softly around her. Her forehead, palms - every part of her - was oozing through the silk. What could she do? What should she say?

She heard the sweeper attending to her duties in the bathroom so she sat up, smoothed out the ball gown and pretended to search for something. Feverishly she opened drawers, unlocked her trunk, opened her jewel case - seeing nothing through a film of tears. But what was there to see? There was nothing to find. She repeated this farcical exercise three times before the *mata-rani* emerged from the bathroom and salaamed as she manoeuvred that hateful basket out of the room.

Dizzy with fear, Francina sidled back to the verandah. This was the worst moment in her life: worse than anticipating a whipping from Aunt Doré, worse that learning that Papa has gone to prison or that Mamma had disappeared. Worse, worse, worse.

'I am sorry, Grand-mère, but the necklace is not there.'

'What do you mean, Francina?'

'It is not in my chest-of-drawers, my trunk, or my jewel case - not anywhere.'

Grand-mère's face drained of colour. The hookah gurgled in the silence. '*Mon Dieu.* You are quite sure? You have checked everything?'

'Yes, Grand-mère. I have searched everywhere - several times.'

'But where did you keep it, Francina?'

'Locked in my trunk.'

'Are you quite sure it was locked?'

Francina burst into tears. 'I should have been more careful -'

'Nonsense, child, we shall get to the bottom of this. Nothing like this has ever happened before. I have always trusted the servants. Some of them have been with us for over twenty years.'

Abdul the butler was summoned. He, in turn, called the house servants: the bearers, *peon, khitmutgars,* the cook and the *musolchi,* the *chaprassi,* the *hookah-burdar, punkah-wallahs,* the *ayahs,* under-women and the sweepers. They stood in a semi-circle according to rank, before the *Burra-Mem* and the Memsahib, looking puzzled and apprehensive. Grand-mère solemnly asked Abdul to ask each servant in turn if they know where Miss-Sahib's necklace was.

Shocked and offended, each vehemently denied any knowledge of the necklace.

'One of them must know,' said Aunt Barton. 'Abdul, tell the servants that I shall only pay half wages until the culprit confesses. Now we must ask the outside servants. Abdul, tell them to assemble by the back steps.'

The servants salaamed and filed out in silence.

Francina slipped back to her room, shaking with apprehension. She never expected to see the servants humiliated like this.

An eerie hush descended. There was no swish of brushes, no tinkling of curtains, no jingling bangles, no coughing, spitting or earnest chatter. No sound of any activity. For once the cook was not berating the *musolchi* boy in the kitchen, or the *bhisti* clearing his throat. The *punkahs* were still. The sweeper's children were not playing in the compound. Even the parrot was quiet . . .

The whole household was stunned to silence.

She sat on the bed, her head in her hands. This nightmare would go on and on until she put a stop to it.

Still in her new ball-gown, she retraced her steps to the verandah, her heart as tight as a hangman's knot. It was the longest walk of her life. 'Grand-mère, may I have a private word?'

When she was told, Grand-mère rang the silver bell.

'If Angelo had only come to me, I could have helped him,' she said quietly. Her voice was as cold as a shard of ice.

The butler entered the room.

'Abdul, will you inform the servants that there has been a misunderstanding. Miss-Sahib has found the necklace.'

Giving Francina a look of contempt, he salaamed and walked away.

'How could I have doubted my good and loyal servants? Will I ever regain their trust?' Grand-mère stared into the distance as though her granddaughter was too despicable to look at. 'For over forty years I have treasured that necklace. Now it now lies in the clutches of a greasy moneylender. Nothing like this has ever happened before. You, your brother and your mother - you have all brought nothing but disgrace to our family. Now go.'

Francina hung her head. She wanted so much to fall at her feet to beg her forgiveness, to make Grand-mère love her again. She could try to explain how Angelo had tricked her out of the necklace - but why should Grand-mère believe her? Excuses would not bring the necklace back. Of course she was to blame. She understood Angelo better than anyone. She should have seen though his tricks.

She fell on the bed and shut her eyes; her head was thumping like a hammer.

Daylight faded. Darkness descended. A servant came in to light the lamp, but she sent him away. She woke in the dark, shaking violently. No one had summoned her to dinner. She had become a pariah.

No amount of blankets could warm her. Waking, she found her bedclothes wet and threw them off. A charcoal brazier had been set up in her room to dry her sheets and towels. The air was so humid, she could hardly breathe. How long has she been lying here? The pain behind her eyes was excruciating, her skin red-raw, on fire. The demon had entered her body. It shook her bones and rattled her teeth. Let it reap its revenge. The pain, the sleepless nights and the raging fever. Nothing was punishment enough.

'Make up a draft: 12 grains sulphate of quinine, 2 drachms hydrobromic acid and ½ oz syrup of orange peel, mixed in 8 oz water. I suggest Miss Duquesne takes two tablespoons, three times a day. I shall return tomorrow morning to check on her progress. Dengue fever, Mrs Barton. There is much of it about.'

But it was not the weather that had made her ill, but a cancer growing in her heart. Her body was weeping. Her hopes were dead. *Where was the girl of yesterday? - Where her life? - Where were her prospects?*

'Her mind is wandering, Doctor.'

I wish I were a girl again, half-savage and hardy and free . . . Why am I so changed?

'Keep her calm and tranquil, Mrs Barton. Nothing must tax her mind. No novels or pens, no visitors. Nothing.'

In the crushing heat, she wanders across a barren rocky landscape, climbing ridge after ridge. Every time she clambers to the top, another ridge rises in the distance. She scrabbles up stony escarpments, her feet raw and bleeding. She slides down sandbanks to cross sandy nullahs, deftly avoiding the muggers . . . Then at last she sees a dot on the horizon, a figure photographing an ancient temple . . . But as she tries to reach him, another mound of sand rises between them. The harder she tries, the more difficult it becomes. She will never reach him.

Someone rubbed warm scented oils across her forehead, and stroked her temples with gentle expert fingers. She opened her eyes and smiled gratefully. Sita, at least, had not deserted her. She knew what it meant to be an outcast.

12

'I shall get up today,' she said in faltering Hindustani. The air was cooler. That wretched brazier had been taken away.

Sita helped her on with her wrap. Dressed in a cheerful day gown and with her hair neatly arranged, she stepped unsteadily out of her room for the first time since she had been taken ill. Servants at their posts salaamed stiffly as she walked through the silent reception rooms. Did they know the truth behind the missing necklace? Indian servants had an uncanny knack for discovering secrets.

She heard voices. Giddy with apprehension she stepped out to the verandah and curtsied deferentially. For a moment Grand-mère stared at her in surprise, then her eyes narrowed and she looked away.

Francina turned to Netta. 'I was looking for Aunt Barton. Where might she be?'

'Your aunt is in her room. She is not well,' Netta said.

Francina curtsied again and made a hasty retreat.

Her throat was dry, her eyes stinging. How could she survive in this house if Grand-mère refused to talk to her? She stumbled through the darkened rooms, avoiding the huge japonica pots spouting palms, the little ebony tables set up like altars with miniatures and likenesses of Grand-mère's descendants (not daring to check of her own was still amongst them), and called softly at Aunt Barton's bedroom door. The bearer stood aside as she parted the bead curtain.

'Why did you not tell me you were poorly, Aunt?'

Aunt Barton, wrapped in a silk peignoir, was resting on her bed in her cavernous room. The punkah hung limply above her head. Francina knelt at her pillow and took her hand. Aunt smiled but her face looked drawn.

'It's my old trouble again. Indigestion. The discomfort seems particularly sharp today.'

Francina kissed her damp forehead. 'I would have come sooner if I had known.' She had wondered why Aunt Barton had not called on her recently. Grand-mère, of course, had never visited her sickroom once.

'I had no intention of troubling you with my petty problems while you were ill, my dear. But it is heartening to see you up and about at last. How are you feeling?'

'Better, Aunt. How long was I lying in bed?'

'About three weeks. We were very concerned.'

'May I fetch something to ease the pain?'

'I've just had some bicarbonate of soda, but could you fetch me the gum lozenges? If I suck one at regular intervals, Dr Thompson said it will help to neutralize the acidity in my stomach.'

Francina went to the small table beside Aunt's huge netted bed to fetch the gum lozenges.

'You have just missed your aunt Cecilia. If you had come earlier, you could have heard her proposition.'

'Oh?'

'The Vauloués are planning a trip up-river to visit a sick relative in Murshidabad. They will be stopping en route to see their son Jacques and his wife in Moisgunge, and wondered if you would like to accompany them? It might amuse you to see your old home again.'

Francina held her breath. 'Could I go, Aunt?'

'The change would do you good, my dear. It might put some colour back into your cheeks. You could spend Christmas at Moisgunge with your cousins, while your aunt and uncle continue their journey up-river to Murshidabad. They could collect you on their return.'

'But I ought to stay here and look after you.'

'Nonsense, Francina. Plenty of people here can do that. It would make me happy to know that you are away from this gloomy house. And it would be a treat for Evangelina to have some female company. She rarely sees a new face at Moisgunge.'

It seemed the perfect solution but she was weeping inside, for she was sure that Grand-mère had concocted this plan to be rid of her.

'Your grand-mère is a stubborn old stick,' said Aunt Barton.

'When she gets an idea in her head, it is very difficult to shake it out of her. I am sure that a few months absence will soften her again.'

Francina tried to smile. She wished she shared Aunt's optimism.

'I should very much like to see my childhood home again.'

Her heart lightened at the thought of it.

'It's settled then,' said Aunt. 'I shall send a *chit* to my sister to tell her. The Vauloués are leaving at the end of the week, so you must pack everything you might need for the next two months. They have chartered a pinnace, so you will travel up-river in some style.'

Overcome with sadness, Francina kissed her, hoping with all her heart that she had not become a hindrance to this kind old lady.

'The doctor will be here soon. He will give me one of his marvellous medicinals, as he always does, and I shall feel better in no time. I have great faith in Dr Thompson. - Fetch that cap off the stand for me, my dear. I must be properly dressed to receive him.'

13

The wind had dropped, so the pinnace was towed by a dozen half-naked boatmen, who trudged along the bank. It was a miracle how much energy the boatmen could expend from their thin, sinewy bodies while existing on one meal a day. Occasionally, one would lose his footing and slip into the water where he would flounder like a porpoise, clinging to the ropes, while the *manji* taunted him with playful banter until he regained control.

No one seemed concerned that muggers might lurk amongst the tangle of floating hyacinth, so Francina was keeping an unofficial vigil. But perhaps predators were attracted to easier prey, like that half-burnt body she had seen bobbing downstream – or the corpse of a tiny baby on that small wreathed raft.

Following the pinnace was a country boat packed with servants and their families, a travelling kitchen, and a larder full of bleating goats and fowls. It was hardly a quiet journey: the shouting *manji,* chanting crew, babbling servants and bleating animals. It was probably the noise that was keeping the muggers away.

Exotic temples and villages, half-hidden amongst the trees, slid past. Rich merchant houses jostled precariously with ancient palaces . . . children frolicked in the water with their elephants or water-buffalo . . . Each bend in the river was a view asking to be sketched, if only she could work quickly enough. Somewhere out there, Arthur Hartwell was setting up his photographic equipment to record scenes as picturesque as these.

They passed former Danish, Dutch and Portuguese outposts, now all ceded to the British. Chandernagar had returned to the French, but nearly one hundred years ago, Uncle Vauloué told her, the little settlement was attacked by General Clive. The inhabitants had fled to the safety of the fort, but it was bombarded by Admiral Watson, who had sailed up the Hooghly with three of his largest ships. It was one of the most ferocious battles ever fought between the British and the French in Bengal, and Fort d'Orléans had never fully recovered from the ravages. Now the solvency of the town was secured by the British on condition that neither opium nor salt was manufactured within its two miles radius.

They had stepped ashore briefly for déjeuner, and she was struck by the cleanliness and order of the place. The roads were swept and well-watered so there was little dust. Aunt Cecilia had pointed out a flat roofed house with arched venetian windows opposite Government House. It was the house where Grand-père had spent his final years, sitting under the cork tree in the garden that sloped down to the river.

While Uncle Vauloué went off to pay his respects to the Governor, Aunt had hired a *tonjon,* and they were carried across town on the shoulders of four men to the boundary ditch that divided this little French settlement from the rest of British India. They saw the stone boundary columns proudly inscribed *Liberté, Egalité, Fraternité* and peeped over the walls of the European houses to admire the gardens and courtyards laid out in the French style. With its tree-lined avenues, fluttering tricolores and French-speaking inhabitants, Chandernagar was a French provincial town transported to Bengal. Aunt showed her the church of St Louis with its pink walls and green shuttered windows. When she and Mamma were girls, they had celebrated mass here. Stepping inside, they lit candles and knelt together before the statue of the Virgin Mary.

Sunlight sparkled like scattered jewels across the muddy waters. The journey was acting as a palliative. Each mile travelled, increased the distance from Grand-mère and the necklace. But even so, distance would never completely erase the necklace from her mind - it returned, intermittently, to haunt her days and nights.

The pinnace hit a sandbank, lurched and shuddered; the pastels rolled off her lap and across the deck, and a young attendant ran to pick them up. But she had grown used to these thumps and jolts. Towed at this irregular pace or tacking from one side of the river to the other, they were making about twenty miles a day. In two days they had travelled nearly forty miles . . .

Uncle Vauloué climbed up to join her on the deck above the cabins. He watched as she drew a small boat with a bamboo mast and ragged sail silhouetted against the sun. Francina smiled up at him. She enjoyed his company and listened to his stories about the

Mogul Emperors. Uncle knew about the necklace - of course he did - but neither he nor Aunt Cecilia ever brought up the subject, and for that she was grateful.

'I am sorry to disturb you, my dear, but your aunt asks for you.'

Francina handed her pastels to the attendant, who followed her down the companionway. It pleased her to be useful to Aunt Cecilia.

She knocked on the cabin door and entered, blinking until her eyes became accustomed to the gloom. Aunt Cecilia stood by a travelling chest, holding a small decanter of ruby-coloured liquid. She was dressed in an embroidered peignoir and her hair was piled loosely under a lace cap.

'Could you help me prepare my draught, Francina? I cannot sleep with all the commotion outside. And the boat is lurching so much, I am afraid of spilling it.'

Francina recognised the ruby-coloured liquid. It dismayed her to see that Aunt was still dependent on it. 'Don't look so alarmed, my dear. It's just a healthy restorative.'

'Are you still troubled by toothache? Did you not see a dentist?'

'The tooth was pulled long ago. But I experienced such an elevation of spirits, that I have acquired a taste for it.'

Aunt had suffered from toothache on the *Hindustan* but had refused to have the tooth drawn until she consulted her dentist in Calcutta, so Dr Guise had prescribed laudanum to ease the pain. It became one of Francina's duties to prepare Aunt's daily physic after Murphy jumped ship. She filled a glass with water from the carafe and added some sugar.

'The dose has increased to thirty drops,' Aunt said, warming the sugared water over a candle.

Francina inserted a pipette into the tincture of opium. Was it really so wrong to administer to Aunt Cecilia that which she craved? Aunt Doré's opinions hardly seemed relevant on this busy Indian waterway.

'The panacea for all human woes,' smiled Aunt Cecilia, as she watched thirty drops of laudanum dissolve in the water.

Aunt sipped the rosy liquid. Then she kissed her niece, leaving a faint trace of jasmine and patchouli on her cheek.

''Thank you, my dear. Now, leave me to take my siesta.'

Francina returned to the upper deck and found Uncle Vauloué

dozing in a deck chair. A breeze tugged at the awnings, carrying with it the stench from a smouldering funeral pyre. She held her breath and looked away. The *manji* shouted a tirade of instructions, and the boatmen scrambled back on board to unfurl the sails. For a while, there would be a respite from the chanting.

She found a clean sheet in her sketchbook and opened her box of pastels.

Now the pinnace was tacking steadily against the wind, her sails taut and lightly reefed. The sky was an exquisite blue: a perfect background for the soaring birds that were plunging, swift as arrows, into the murky waters to emerge triumphant with a quivering fish in their beak. A gull with black wing tips landed on the railing to survey the river, and she quickly included him in the foreground of her drawing.

The river traffic was steadily increasing. Earlier, they had passed the Company paddle-steamer towing a large flat boat packed with cabins on her regular eight hundred mile route from Allahabad to Calcutta. Now, the waters teamed with fishing craft. Nets rose and fell like fluttering insect wings as fishermen cast them from their crescent boats and hauled in shoals of jumping, silver fish.

She glanced at the sky. Dusk came early during the Cold Weather, bringing with it a mist that would creep over the river. Devotees were gathering on the steps of the *ghats* with their little lighted terracotta pots, their garlands and flowers, waiting to immerse themselves in the holy waters and perform their pujas as the sun cast its dying rays over the land.

Soon, the pinnace would moor for the evening; they would dine early and then stroll along the riverbank until the light faded, leaving the boatmen and their families to light fires and prepare their own meals. This was her favourite time of the day: the air would be cool enough to wrap a soft *pashmina* across her shoulders; Aunt Cecilia would be in an expansive mood after her siesta, and Uncle would point out the signs of animal activity to her.

'See, Francina, fresh elephant droppings. Elephants are creatures of habit. They have probably used this path for centuries in their search for food. Villagers must be mindful when building or cultivating new fields that they do not obstruct their migratory routes, or they might find their huts or crops trampled to a pulp.'

MOISGUNGE
November 1855

Jacques's wife was bustling amongst the exotic orchids and potted palms at the far end of the verandah, whispering and cooing as she scattered seed into the beautiful ornamental cage of her tiny fluttering *lals.* A black and white bird flew in from the garden and perched on her shoulder. It was her pet *dhyal.*

'Are you hungry, my pet?' murmured Evangelina. She spoke French with an Indian lilt.

'Sultan was brought to me as a fledgling, and learned to fly indoors before I released him,' she said to Francina. 'He's so tame that he flies into the house when he hears me playing the pianoforte, and accompanies my singing – don't you, my sweet?'

The cockatoo, chained to its green bamboo perch, squawked and flapped its wings.

'Now, Mirana, don't be jealous,' chided Evangelina, stroking the cockatoo's feathers.

Evangelina was devoted to her pets. She appeared to see life as it might have existed in the Garden of Eden: different species cohabiting peacefully together. She expected the retinue of pets she brought into her household to tolerate each other, just as she expected the servants of her household (the Mohammedan and Hindu house servants, the Nepalese gate-keeper, the Goanese cook, the Brahmin gardeners, the Untouchable sweepers and Buddhist bearers) to live peacefully together. They were all God's creatures, and all to be nurtured and cared for like children.

Francina returned to her letter. While she wrote, she was conscious of the children's shrieks rising from the garden. Victor the eldest was five years old, closely followed by Aurelia. Philippe had just learned to walk. Their upbringing was a revelation: they had never known rules, regulations or punishment. They had the entire run of the bungalow and their toys were scattered everywhere. If she had behaved with such untamed abandon when she had first arrived in Guernsey, it was no wonder Aunt Doré had taken her so swiftly in hand. *Plus de discipline . . .*

A boy in a ragged dhoti was staggering across the grass carrying a goat's bladder bloated with water. Francina leaned over the balustrade and watched him empty the bladder into a curious bamboo contraption that held three earthenware vessels, placed one on top of the other. 'What is he doing?' she asked.

Evangelina glanced down into the garden. 'Replenishing the drinking water supply.'

She shouted to the boy, who sauntered off, leaving the bladder to trickle wastefully across the path. 'Lazy good-for-nothing! I told him to change the rags yesterday.'

Despite her childlike appearance, Evangelina was a resolute housekeeper who tolerated no nonsense. Francina had attended one of her morning 'kitchen inspections', which she conducted with great solemnity. The scrubbed utensils were examined to make sure they had been properly cleaned, and the room checked to make sure there was no trace of garbage festering in the corners. Having lived in Bengal all her life, she understood the wily ways of her servants as no English memsahib could. She was particularly careful of her family's health, and everything that her family ate or drank. Every day the cow was brought to the verandah steps; the brass vessel was ritually turned upside down to check that there was no water in it to dilute the milk, and the *guala's* hands were inspected for cleanliness. Only then was the *guala* allowed to milk the cow and always in the memsahib's presence.

'Where does the water come from?'

'The river.'

Evangelina giggled when she saw her expression. 'It's perfectly drinkable, Mademoiselle. The water drips through the vessels and rags, passes through a bed of charcoal and then a bed of sand. It seeps out of the bottom, crystal clear. I would rather drink river water than stagnant green tank water.' She held out her hand. 'Finish your letter later, Mademoiselle. It is cool this afternoon. Come. We will stroll around the garden.'

Protected from the sun by their *solar topees* and parasols, they walked arm in arm down the steps, between the lines of potted marigolds, through an arch of nodding palm trees, and along the path that would lead eventually to the river. The garden pulsed with colour: the purple bougainvillea and red hibiscus vied for attention with the pink oleander.

Francina turned back to gaze at Moisgunge. She had felt an immediate affinity with this bungalow and its rambling capacious garden. It stood on pillars about four feet above the ground, built to no particular plan: it just seemed to evolve out of the landscape and the magnificent trees that surrounded it. A huge shaggy overhanging roof, supported on white pillars, which were smothered in honeysuckle and jasmine, shaded the verandah. The bungalow contained just four rooms (plus bathing and dressing rooms) but they were vast and partitioned into smaller areas by cane screens. There was no front door to speak of - all the rooms opened onto the verandah which skirted three sides. She remembered much of the furniture from her childhood, in particular the towering almirah which Evangelina, with the cook in attendance (and Mamma in her time), would unlock each morning to weigh out and distribute the daily dry stores.

'Moisgunge looks her best at this time of year,' Evangelina said, proudly pointing out the cornflowers, phlox, zinnias and the poinsettias. 'I think they are like the flowers you have at Home, *n'est-ce pas?* - Tell me, Mademoiselle Francina, what is Europe like?'

Francina took a deep breath. Where to begin?

'I only know a tiny corner of it, a small island off France. It would not surprise me if the Moisgunge estate is larger than the island of Guernsey.'

Evangelina gasped. 'And you never left this island?'

Once, Francina explained, when she had visited the Great Exhibition in London.

'And they speak French on this little island?'

'We used to - now we speak English. But the peasants still speak French: Guernsey French.'

'You see! It is just like this in India! Now we must *all* learn to speak English. And does it snow on your little island, Mademoiselle? It snows in the Himalayas, but I have never seen it. I cannot imagine what it must be like.'

'It is delicious. You tingle all over with cold.'

'I would be very happy on your little island,' smiled Evangelina.

Francina stared at the pretty, dark-eyed *jeunesse*. Should she tell her how miserable her life would be? How the likes of Mrs Lihou would sneer at the little planter's daughter, *born and bred in the jungle,* laugh at her *chi-chi* accent and bar her from Guernsey society?

'I think it is more beautiful and peaceful here.'

Evangelina tittered in the shy way of the native ladies.

'You are being kind – but one day, one day Jacques has promised to take me to Europe.'

'Maman, Maman, regardez-moi!' cried Aurelia. She was playing on a swing that was lashed to a swooping branch of the great banyan tree. Thrusting out her white-stockinged ankles, she ordered the bearer to push harder.

'Hold on tight, *mére jani!'*

'I'll be careful, Maman.'

The children spoke in a hybrid language of French and Bengali, and knew few words of English. Francina watched the old man submit to Missy-Baba's demands without a murmur. She had never seen the children without a servant in attendance. They were always inventing games to keep them amused. Spoilt and indulged, it was no wonder Indian children grew up to believe themselves special – especially the *chota-sahibs* who were revered by the servants as little gods.

'Victor, don't climb so high! You might fall.'

'I shall lament the day when the children are sent away,' whispered Evangelina. 'I have begged Jacques to keep the boys here and engage a tutor for them, but he says that the world has changed since we were children. We are in British territory now, and under this new administration, the children must learn English ways, for the English are not inclined to adopt Indian ones. But the thought of little Victor going so far away, and for so long . . . He will be a man when I see him again.'

They stood in silence, watching the children playing, as if trying to imagine Moisgunge without its wild young heart. Then, leaving her children in the care of the old bearer, Evangelina led Francina towards a gate set into a high overgrown wall.

Something made Francina hesitate. She recognised the high crumbling arch rising above these tall ornate gateposts. 'I used to play here when I was a child,' she explained when Evangelina turned to see why she had stopped. But why should she feel the tight knot in her stomach? Something had happened when she had played amongst these old guava and pomegranate trees.

'Come, Mademoiselle, let us find Père Auguste.' Evangelina stretched out her hand.

Francina took it, and followed her through the old secluded orchard with her head down, trying not to remember.

The old priest, a short, shrewd-eyed Franciscan, was sitting outside the chapel on a bench in the shade smoking a cigar. He had a bloated countenance and fat clammy hands (having no doubt grown stout on Evangelina's generous portions and lazy on Jacques's fine imported cigars). His piebald pony was tethered to a tree. His syce was asleep in the shade beside a battered *ekka* with a fringed canopy. The fly-whisk balancing on his abdomen, rose and fell with his snores. The priest was a frequent visitor to Moisgunge. He was supposed to be preparing Victor for his schooling in Europe, but Francina had seen little evidence of serious lessons. The *chota-sahib* was an unruly little monkey, who wriggled out of anything he did not like. His maman, however, made up for her son's irreverence by doting on every word Père Auguste uttered.

Rarely, it seemed, would Evangelina do anything without the advice of her priest and confessor.

2

One afternoon, Jacques asked if she would like to accompany him on his inspection of the indigo lines. The elephant was waiting for them outside her hut; her tethered leg swinging gracefully as she picked at a mound of leafy branches. The *mahout* was adjusting the *howdar*.

Francina ran her hand gingerly down the animal's rough flank. It was like stroking an old fissured tree trunk. A pungent, but not disagreeable, animal smell filled her nostrils.

'Her name is Tara. It means *Good Fortune* in Hindustani.'

Tara twisted her trunk to investigate the stranger. Spraying misty breath down Francina's cheek, she picked at the seed buttons on her bodice and delved delicately into the folds of her skirts. The floral pattern seemed to fascinate her. Francina was more amused than frightened. Despite her huge size, Tara had more grace than many of the overblown matrons she had seen dancing at Government House.

Jacques helped Francina mount the steps and arrange herself on the padded seat, then he clambered up after her. The *mahout* scrambled up Tara's trunk with the agility of a monkey, and positioned himself behind her head. Muttering softly, he tickled her ears with his feet and the great beast shuffled off at a steady, lumbering pace.

Francina clung to the corner post of the *howdar*. The swaying motion did not make her feel queasy, but induced a feeling of drowsy relaxation. Whenever the *mahout* addressed her, Tara grunted softly in reply. Animal and keeper had developed their own private language.

They lumbered past the assorted outbuildings of the indigo factory: the boiler house with its squat chimney, the waterwheel, the graded steeping vats and the flaking godowns, where, Francina was told, the indigo would be stored until it was transported down to the auction houses in Calcutta. Coolies were sealing up fissures in the indigo-stained walls of the huge steeping vats.

Although the vats were empty at this time of year, a whiff of fermented indigo still impregnated the air, and flakes of indigo fluttered in the breeze like tiny blue insects.

Shambling high above the ground on this wonderful benign animal, Francina had an unbroken view of the indigo fields that stretched far, far to the horizon. She felt extraordinarily safe and secure. They rode past village women with naked babies strapped to their sides, who were desilting the ditches. The women salaamed and threw their washed-out saris demurely over their heads. Jacques pointed to the ripening crop stretching waist-high all around them.

'Indigo - as far as the river. Moisgunge indigo is cultivated over an area of about fifty square miles. There are small cultivations of rice, *pán* or vegetables interspersed amongst the indigo, which the villagers grow for their own use, but indigo is the primary crop.'

The *mahout* tapped his cane on Tara's shoulder and she sank slowly to her knees.

Jacques jumped down and helped Francina to the ground. The *mahout* rooted in his shoulder sack and produced a ball of *gur,* which he broke into pieces and fed to his huge charge while he waited to continue their journey.

Jacques scooped up a handful of earth and let it crumble between his fingers. 'Indigo grows well on this soil. It is deposited as a rich mud when the river overflows, and because the course of the river is changing – it is shifting eastwards – we gain more silt each year on which to plant. But it is not all good news. When Grand-père first cultivated indigo in this area, a high proportion of Ganges water flowed down the Bhagirathi through the Hooghly and out into the Bay of Bengal. Now the Bhagirathi River has become so silted that a greater proportion of Ganges water flows into rivers on the eastern border, and we are left with an increasing number of dead rivers. It is a problem that one day will become acute, for indigo factories require an abundant source of clear fresh water.'

Francina broke off a stalk of the spidery plant and studied its pinnate leaves, marvelling at how this insignificant plant could be responsible for her family's fortunes and misfortunes.

'We sow twice a year, and harvest the crop three months later. This crop was sown in October, after the rains had softened the ground. We harvest next month, before the indigo flowers,' Jacques said. 'But so many factors must come together for us to make a good profit. The rivers may or may not flood, cyclones or a plague of insects might decimate the young crop, and, most importantly, the *ryots* may or may not cooperate in sewing the seed –'

'*Ryots*?'

'The peasant smallholders. They are responsible for the indigo in the outlying districts. They undertake to grow, cut and pack the crop at their own expense. We buy it from them and convert it into indigo dye at the factory.'

As they rode across the countryside, Jacques's keen eyes surveyed the ground.

'Look, Francina, the prints of wild boar in the mud over there. A family, I should think, of about three adults and a few young. Can you see their scratches on this tree trunk? Boar can be more dangerous than tigers if they are protecting their young.'

Jacques had an inexhaustible knowledge of the country, and appeared to know the telltale signs of every creature that roamed in his district. Francina felt safe in his presence. India was in his bones, he told her. One day his bones would enrich Indian soil, just as the bones of his ancestors had done generations before him. This was Jacques's world. He wanted nothing else. He was at peace.

'Do you see that blue bird with the heavy black bill sitting on that old tree trunk? The sighting of a blue jay is auspicious. He represents the god Shiva, whose neck turned blue when he swallowed the poison of the world.'

Tara attracted attention wherever they went. Village children emerged shyly from doorways to watch her pass. The more daring ran up to tempt her with branches of leaves or *chapattis*. Tara accepted all offerings graciously and diplomatically, like the grand old lady that she was.

They skirted a bazaar, and passed a young boy driving his goats back to his village for the night. His animals kicked up a cloud of dust that danced like molten gold in the sun's dying rays. 'It is *godhula*, the hour of cowdust,' murmured Jacques. 'All over India, animals are returning to their villages at this moment.'

The light was fading, so they quickened their pace and returned home along the river bank.

Men were planting melons in the silt. Gulls circled lazily over the long stretches of silver sand as country boats moored for the night.

In the gathering mist, they watched a group of men cooking their meal on the bank. The smell of spicy food hung in the air, reminding her of a time long ago . . . when she had travelled on an elephant just like this, wrapped in Papa's arms and listening to his heart beating steadily against his chest as they had lumbered along. She had never forgotten that moment of sublime contentment.

During dinner, a tiny barefooted figure, dressed in a white nightgown and lacy cap, padded into the room. She pulled at her father's sleeve and stared up at him with huge, tear-filled eyes. Jacques scooped her up in his arms and set her on his lap.

'Can't you sleep, *mére jani*? Would you like a little soup?'

The child pouted prettily, but refused the soup. At the tender age of three, Mademoiselle Aurelia was a mistress of artfulness. Everyone, from her papa down to the *bhisti,* went out of their way to cajole and humour her.

'Even Aurelia, Jacques insists, must be sent away to school,' murmured Evangelina, watching the *khitmutgar* tempt Missy Baba with a morsel. 'This house will be like the Towers of Silence without the sound of little voices.'

'We will be blessed with lots more children, Evangelina,' smiled her husband, kissing his daughter on her forehead. 'Children's voices will always be heard at Moisgunge.'

When she had had her titbits, been petted and kissed, Mademoiselle Aurelia allowed the ayah to carry her back to bed.

'What am I to do?' lamented Evangelina. 'It is so hard to be cross with the little monkeys. If I am firm, the servants undo everything. They cannot bear to see a child cry. If I say to Victor, "No pudding today because you are naughty," the servants will give him pudding when my back is turned. They spoil the children.' She tried to look aggrieved, but she was really delighted to see her children indulged by the servants.

After dinner they sipped long cool drinks on the verandah and listened to the distant murmur of the bazaar wafting towards them on a faint breeze. Fireflies, tiny pinpricks of dancing light, flittered against the darkening vegetation.

Calcutta and all her associations seemed far, far away.

✸

Sometimes Francina accompanied Evangelina to say goodnight to the children. She would sit on the edge of their cots and listen to the sing-song language of their prayers, while incense burned in the mosquito coil on the small table. She was inexplicably drawn to the children's evening rituals. It reminded her of her own bedtimes when she had shared this cavernous nursery with Angelo. It amused her to see the ayah's little reed mat rolled up in a corner, where it had always been. She saw herself propped up in her cot under the mosquito net just like little Aurelia, quivering with expectation as she waited for the rustle of silk along the verandah . . .

The bead curtain would tinkle and slowly divide. Mamma would stand framed in the doorway in her shimmering green gown. She would lean over the bed, smelling deliciously of jasmine and camellia, her emerald earrings glinting in the candlelight.

'Have you said your prayers, my darling?'

'Yes, Mamma.'

'Did you pray that tomorrow you would be a good girl and do as ayah says?'

'Yes, Mamma.'

'Kiss me goodnight then, my darling.'

One evening, while Evangelina listened to the children's bedtime prayers, Francina slipped into the little chapel before the priest sounded the bell for Benediction. It was tiny, just large enough to accommodate an altar and six pews. She used to follow Mamma in here, crouch on the cool mud floor behind the pews, and watch her light a candle.

She sat in the pew nearest the altar, hardly daring to breathe. Behind the altar the angel in the peeling fresco smiled benevolently down at her, while the golden-haired cherub nestling on a cloud stared quizzically into the firmament.

Francina placed her fingers on the yellowing stone toes of the Virgin Mary and closed her eyes. Blood sluiced through her veins as she heard Mamma's voice, remote and dispirited, echo back through time. *Bless me, Holy Mother, for I have sinned.*

3

A group of dusty coolies were squatting under the tamarind tree, listening to one of them reading from a book which he held open in his arms. Evangelina smiled and urged Francina to stop and listen.

'Père Auguste has been writing simple Bible stories in Bengali. Nearly ten years of painstaking work. One of his native assistants, for a small sum, comes each afternoon and reads the Bible to our servants in their own language. It would be my greatest wish, Mademoiselle, to convert at least one of our servants to Christianity. So far they seem happy to sit for an hour in the shade, but I have never seen any of them show more than a passing interest in what they hear. Their heathen ways run very deep. And of course they do not understand the concept that all are welcome in God's House. If the Untouchables are permitted into God's House, then those in the caste system do not think very highly of joining. Native customs and prejudices run very strong -'

Evangelina watched in disbelief as her son raced across the garden, shrieking at a languor monkey that was sitting in the middle of the path. 'Victor, where's your *solar topee*?'

Victor jumped up and down in frustration as the monkey skimmed up a tree. 'Ganesh asked me to look out for him. He's been stealing vegetables.'

'I don't care what Ganesh says. You mustn't go outside bareheaded. Marieji, bring out Victor's *topee*!'

Eventually, the old ayah hobbled out of the house, muttering and shaking her head. She was so tiny and small-boned, that Victor's *topee* looked like a weighty lump of clay in her hands.

'At least Marieji is a Christian,' Evangelina said proudly, 'a Thomist Catholic from Pondichéry. She has been invaluable to me. I don't think I could have managed without her. She has had so much experience of babies. She was living at Moisgunge long before my husband's parents came here.'

'Then - she must have been here when *I* lived here.'

'Do you think so, Mademoiselle? Shall we ask her? *Ayah-ji!*'

Marieji turned her head. Evangelina addressed her in the children's hybrid language. The old ayah self-consciously pulled her white scarlet-edged sari to half-cover her face. Her skin was darker than the other servants, and her white hair was tied in a low chignon. Her silver earrings were so heavy that they had weighed down her earlobes. It was difficult to tell how old she was – somewhere between forty and seventy, Francina guessed. She had seen this old servant standing discreetly at the back of family prayers, muttering the Lord's Prayer in her native language.

'Marieji, do you remember long ago delivering a baby into this world?' Francina asked slowly in French. 'A baby who was born on the *Ganga Ma?* Her name was Theresa.'

'Tesa-Baba? She was born in a houseboat.'

'Tesa-Baba was my mother.'

'Thou art *chota* Tesa-Baba?' Ayah let out a sob and clutched Francina to her tiny frame. The keys, tied in a knot that hung from her shoulder, dug into her waist.

'Marieji, did you once travel with Tesa-baba across the sea?' Francina asked, moved by the old woman's display of affection.

The old ayah nodded. 'Tesa-Baba's daughter born in cold, bad place.'

'A bad place?'

'Boys throw stones. See, I have mark on forehead.'

Marieji's soft melodious voice; the scent of her oiled hair; the jingle of her glass bangles . . . It was Marieji who had slept on the floor beside her cot, curled up on her thin grass mat; Marieji who had cradled her during those hot nights to quell her nightmares with gentle Indian lullabies; Marieji who had poured warm oil into her ear to sooth her earache; Marieji who had coated her neck with blue flour paste when she had mumps. Marieji was the steadfast angel who had haunted her dreams for so long.

Now it was Marieji who tiptoed into her screened-off portion of the nursery each morning to wake her with a cup of *palangki char*. '*Chota* Tesa-baba,' she would smile as she pressed her knuckles against Francina's temples and lavished blessings upon her.

Francina found herself irresistibly drawn to this old servant. She had cared for many children in her long life but every one of them, it seemed, held a special place in her heart. Sometimes Francina would slip into the dining room when the children were having their early déjeuner. She would pull up a chair to the low nursery table and make up stories while they ate. Although Evangelina had urged her to speak English to the children, she found herself unconsciously adopting their hybrid language. Victor and Aurelia would listen wide-eyed, toying with their *pish-pash,* as she told them stories of faeries, sarregousets and of the *King of Auxcriniers* – in fact all the Guernsey stories Cook had told her on the dark winter nights when Aunt and Uncle Doré were out.

The days passed slowly and uneventfully. Moisgunge had its own particular rhythm that was tempered by the landscape. Moisgunge was surrounded by water, smaller tributaries of the mighty *Ganga Ma,* and sometimes on some misty days it was impossible to see the opposite bank. They might have been marooned on an island, for that was what it felt like on mornings and evenings when gathering cloud crept over the waters.

Visitors were rare, so that even dour Père Auguste's appearances were welcome. He brought news of the outside world, his own particular little world that extended down to the French colony of Chandernagar, some thirty miles away. Francina tried to imagine Mamma living in this beautiful marooned place with only three small children for company. Papa like Jacques, no doubt, had spent hours away from home inspecting the indigo lines.

Every morning, Moisgunge 'runners' from the factory would collect the post from the nearest *dak* bungalow some five miles away, and bring it to the house. Their arrival was announced by a fanfare of jangling brasses that could be heard a long way off. The noise was supposed to scare wild animals away as the runners passed through jungle. Each morning as the fanfare grew louder, Jacques and Evangelina would smile as Francina's heart sank. Would this be the day she received that irate letter from Papa asking if she knew of Angelo's whereabouts?

The mail brought her no pleasure these days.

✸

Coolies from the outlying districts were making their way to the Moisgunge factory in growing numbers, bringing with them their wives and children. The indigo crop was nearly five feet tall and about to flower; it was almost ready to harvest. A makeshift village of mud huts was springing up on the waste ground around the Moisgunge; while in the factory complex itself, life took on a heightened urgency, as everything was being made ready for the manufacturing process to begin. The machinery was cleaned, oiled and repaired; the pumps were tested; and the godowns swept clean in preparation for the new harvest of indigo.

Jacques announced that he had business to attend to in Kishnaghur, and Evangelina and Francina agreed to accompany him. Their journey began in the afternoon after the fiercest heat of the day. The ladies were packed into *palkis* and carried by bearers to the *ghat*. Jacques rode alongside, with his syce trotting beside him. A pair of *banghy-bearers* carried their overnight bedding and luggage in bundles suspended from a long bamboo pole which they slung on their shoulders and carried between them.

At the *ghat,* villagers chewing *pán,* were also waiting for the ferry. They salaamed and stood aside, for the sahib and his party took precedence. When they had boarded, the villagers weighed down with their bundles climbed the sagging gangplank and stood in a huddled group, a discreet distance from the sahib's party. The sail was hoisted, and the boatmen, clad only in their loincloths, shipped their oars and sat in the bows. The sail filled and the ferry pitched alarmingly it was swept up in the current and headed towards the opposite bank. Francina was glad to have left her *palki* behind. The ferry was little better than an oversized flat-bottomed *dinghy,* and if it should sink, she would rather chance her luck in the open river, than drown, trapped in that coffin-like box. She joined Jacques who was leaning against the side, staring at the vast expanse of brown flowing water.

'Long, long ago,' said Jacques dreamily, 'when the earth was dry, the river goddess Ganga - a kind of heavenly Milky Way - consented to come down to earth. Bhaginatha, the Hindu sage was so afraid that the weight of her fall might shatter the world that he prevailed upon the great god Siva, the destroyer and creator, to carry Ganga on his head. The river became entangled in Siva's matted hair, and descended like heavenly droplets in the Himalayan Mountains. And that is how that the river goddess Ganga entered the world, bringing in her sacred waters her blessings and fertility.'

'It is a beautiful story,' said Francina. Jacques almost believed it. He saw no conflict between his Christian religion and the telling of this sacred Hindu myth.

He laughed when she remarked on this. 'Perhaps I am a follower of Akbar.'

'Akbar?'

'Jacques!' scolded Evangelina. She hated it when her husband exposed his heathen sympathies.

'Akbar was a great enlightened Mogul emperor who had a Christian wife and a Hindu wife. He tried to unite all the peoples of his empire by founding a new religion that combined Hinduism, Mohammedanism and Christianity.'

'So now you want to take a Hindu wife as well as a Christian one?' pouted Evangelina.

'Perhaps – for I am sure a Hindu wife will not answer me back so readily!'

'What became of Akbar's religion?' Francina asked.

'It died with him. He was its only convert. But just think what would have happened if it had succeeded - there would be no more religious wars -'

'Take no notice of what Jacques says. He has lived too long in the jungle,' Evangelina said. 'He is in danger of going native.'

A *gharry*, a two-wheeled springless carriage pulled by two bullocks, was waiting for them on the opposite bank. Francina and Evangelina climbed in and tried to make themselves comfortable with the cushions they had brought from the *palkis*, while their overnight luggage was tied onto the roof. A fresh horse and syce awaited Jacques. When the luggage was secure, they set off at a steady pace with the bearers jogging ahead to make sure the road was clear of animals or fallen vegetation. The *gharry* jolted along deeply rutted cart tracks or along the high *bunds* that divided the indigo and paddy fields, whilst Jacques rode alongside.

Sometimes the track led through mango groves or scrub;

sometimes through a belt of forest where mimosa and *sāl,* draped with creepers, formed graceful arches above their heads. As dusk fell, the bearers lit lanterns to guide the way. After about two hours of steady jogging they arrived at a Government *dak*-bungalow, where a simple dinner of chicken curry awaited them. Their rooms were basic, containing a pair of string beds, a table and two hard chairs, with douching rooms beyond. The *chapoys* were made slightly more comfortable with the bedding they had brought with them. Francina was so tired, that neither her surroundings nor the high-pitched whine of the insects trying to find a hole in her mosquito net mattered, she fell asleep instantly.

They were woken before sunrise with a welcome cup of *palangki char, and* set off again with a fresh pair of bullocks and a new set of bearers. After several hours, they found themselves travelling along a wide sandy road shaded by a beautiful avenue of teak trees – it was the approach to Kishnaghur.

In the bustling bazaar beyond the native town, the driver flailed his whip as he manoeuvred the *gharry* between the *ekkas,* bullock carts, food peddlers, water carriers, beggars, hungry dogs, children – and the ubiquitous bull resting in the middle of the road. Colourful goods of every description spilled out of the booths and stalls. It all looked so enticing from the *gharry* windows – shoes, sandals, bolts of cloth of the most dazzling hues . . . gold and silver filigree ornaments . . . intricate brass, enamel pots and bells . . . basket ware, wooden boxes that fitted into one another… vast platters of breads, pastries, sweets and fruits (swarming with flies and yellow wasps) . . . little clay toys, gaudy statues . . .

An ornate, but dilapidated, stone gateway marked the end of the native town and the entrance to the Civil Station of Kishnaghur. They had left the colourful hubbub of the bazaar behind - but more agreeably, the black fêted pools, the smells, vermin, and the emaciated animals scavenging through the slimy mounds of refuse. Here was order and civilisation: wide straight roads and avenues shaded by overhanging trees; *pukka* Company bungalows set in well-watered square compounds; the new gothic church; the sun-baked maidan; the club; the emporium and shops, and the *cutcherry* – the courts and offices of the British Government of India, built to administer civil and criminal laws and to regulate revenue.

While Jacques left them to speak to the Deputy Commissioner at the *cutcherry*, Evangelina and Francina went off to inspect the 'British improvements'- as Evangelina called the dull regimented buildings.

The Civil Station seemed small and enclosed after the sprawling native town they had just passed through. Would she be living in similar cantonments if she had married Arthur Hartwell? Francina could not quite imagine herself confined to half-an-acre of compound and surviving on the limited gossip of a military station. By now she would probably be heavy with child, and enduring a lonely existence in a thatched bungalow while he was on a mission to persuade the Oude natives to dig a new well for their village.

In the emporium, Evangelina held up the cup of a newly imported English tea service and sighed with delight. The new little bonnets, dressed with flowers, ribbons and coquettish feathers entranced her - as did the new gowns, hoops and undergarments. While Evangelina examined every article with awe and longing, the other memsahibs in the emporium eyed her disdainfully. Evangelina, luckily, was too preoccupied to notice.

They joined Jacques for *burra hazri* at Madame D'Almeida's hotel, a lofty old native house on the edge of the Civil Station. Madame D'Almeida was the fat, cheerful widow of an indigo planter, who had known Jacques since he was a boy. She welcomed them warmly and gave them her best table. After the meal Jacques returned to the *cutcherry* to finish his business and the ladies were urged to take advantage of one of Madame D'Almeida's many 'cool bedrooms'.

Later, refreshed and bathed, Francina and Evangelina drove to the Burial Ground where they had arranged to meet Jacques. They sat in the dappled shade beside an old tomb (whose inscription told them that under these stones lay the *Mortal Remains of a Distinguished & Zealous Collector of the Revenue*.

Evangelina leaned back against the blackened plinth, surrounded by her cache of precious parcels, and fell asleep.

Francina left her stone seat to inspect the tombs. Why did she feel an affinity with burial grounds, and this one in particular? She was sure that she had been here before. She used to play hide-and-seek with Angelo amongst these tombs, whilst Marieji dozed under these spindly trees and Mamma wandered off to meet an acquaintance.

The trees were taller now, some had been cut down. Many of the tombs looked neglected, but others were recent, impressive editions. She read the long flowery epitaph on one of the grandest tombs. This Resident's long life – *a brave and sincere soul, who fulfilled his life with zeal, energy & impartiality* - was an exception. Most of the poor souls buried here had their short lives ruthlessly snuffed out by cholera or some other cruel Indian disease . . . countless infants buried before their first birthday . . .

Black mould obscured the inscription on this tiny tomb, so she peered closer to read it:

Albert Duquesne
died 18 February 1842
aged 1 year 4 months

Her stomach contracted. Was this Baby Albert's grave? It looked so small and pitiful; the inscription chillingly brief. Where were the tender sentiments - *Sacred to the Memory of our Dear Beloved Son* - that appeared on the other tombs? There was no mention of his parents, no sense at all that this child had been lovingly interned. It shamed her to think that Papa could have sanctioned such an ignominious memorial. She tried to remove the black stained mould with her handkerchief, but it was too ingrained. She touched the carved recesses of his name. Soon it would be impossible to read, and little Albert's grave would become an anonymous pile of stone, smothered by weeds and ivy.

Surely Mamma's little 'Treasure' deserved better?

She hurried back to the child with kohl-marked eyes, who had accosted them at the gate, and pointed to her strings of wilting marigolds. The child murmured '*Baksheesh*!' Francina gave her the handful of *annas* and *pice* she found in her purse and chose a garland. Returning to Albert's grave, she draped it across his tomb and recited a prayer.

If only she could remember what he had looked like.

On their return to Moisgunge, she went in search of the old ayah, and found her trying to calm a fractious Philippe for his afternoon sleep.

'Marieji, do you remember my little brother – Albert-Baba?'

Marie shrugged and threw her sari over her head, as if she had no wish to talk about him. Her snub upset Francina. She crept to her corner of the nursery, lay on her bed and stared at the taut ceiling cloths that caught the snakes and vermin nesting in the thatch. Even Marieji, who had cared for so many children, could not find a place in her heart for little Albert. What had the poor child done to deserve such indifference?

She must have fallen asleep, for Marieji was leaning over her bed, shaking her by the shoulder. '*Chota* Tesa-Baba, come, come!' She was gesturing towards the garden.

Francina threw on her clothes and followed her outside. The afternoon sun was blinding. Nothing stirred. Even the birds, it seemed, were having a siesta.

Marieji led her to the huge tamarind tree, which cast a dense circle of shade across the drive every day. At present, there was no one to be seen, but towards evening, two or three coolies or their families would inevitably squat under its mass of feathery leaves waiting to consult the memsahib on medical matters or to ask the sahib to arbitrate in their quarrels.

Balancing on an upturned flowerpot, Ayah inserted a stick into a fissured hollow in the trunk, and prodded about cautiously. When she was sure that nothing nasty lurked in wait, she wrapped her sari round her hand and forearm, and gingerly felt inside. She brought out a small brass box inlaid with silver.

'Many seasons I hide this box,' she said, wiping it clean. 'I wait for Tesa-Baba. But she no come. Now I give it to her daughter.'

Francina recognised the box immediately, and ran her fingers over the inlaid silver initials: *T E D*

Theresa Elizabeth Duquesne

She used to creep into Mamma's room while she was resting, and try on the jewels from this very box. How she had preened like a princess in the looking-glass, bedecked in Mamma's jewels! She shook the box gently. Something rattled inside.

'The key, Marieji. Where is the key?'

Ayah looked troubled and shook her head.

Francina inserted her hand into the hollow, but there was nothing else down there.

4

Dearest Lulu –

How unhappy I was to receive your letter and read that Aunt and Uncle Doré have taken the news of Angelo's disappearance so badly. But despite my brother's faults I do not believe he is at heart a wicked person. You must trust me, dearest Lulu, when I say I know that his disappearance has an honourable motive. Angelo believes that he has found a solution to his plight, and if everything works out as he hopes, he will soon be in a position to repay his debts. I owe it to my brother – and to all our dear aggrieved relatives – to give him this chance to put things right. I have written to Alex Marquand, assuring him that Angelo is determined to atone for his mistakes and to compensate fully everyone he unintentionally wronged.

I enclose a letter from You-Know-Who, which I hope will go some way towards softening your heart towards me. The note with my forwarding address to him went astray, so that his letters were sent down to Calcutta, and had to be forwarded up to Moisgunge. The delay must be very distressing for you.

Your affectionate and loving cousin, Francina Duquesne

She sealed the letter with a wafer, exhausted and angry. Why should she always take the blame for Angelo's misdemeanours? She pictured him lounging in his cabin while she was left to placate everyone in his wake.

Victor was protesting as usual over his lessons, and Philippe had taken a tumble. It was difficult to think clearly in this riot of noise, and she always found the sound of a crying baby unsettling. She shut her writing box. Her head was aching.

She did not have the strength to reply to Papa's tirade today.

She put on her *solar topee* and stepped outside. Everything in the garden was drenched in a hard white light, and from this distance, the hibiscus flowers looked like dripping red hearts. Screwing up her eyes against the glare, she opened her parasol and walked down the bungalow steps. Two coolie women were squatting on the path, picking out weeds with their fingers. They stopped chatting and salaamed as she passed.

She hurried across the newly-watered grass to seek the shade of a copse of trees, disturbing a flock of parrots that screeched through the treetops. Squirrels scampered away; while high in the branches, weaver birds were diving in and out of their bottle-shaped nests, too busy to notice her. She had come to love the informal tangle of Moisgunge's garden with its trees and wild life.

Avoiding the shortcut through the old orchard, she followed the shaded overgrown wall that skirted the stables and Tara's hut, and led eventually to the tall pillars marking the perimeter of the grounds.

The *durwan* at the gate watched as she stepped out into the sun-baked lane. The traffic caught her by surprise. It was teaming with overflowing bullock carts that moved like a slow undulating snake towards the factory. Beyond the lane, the fields lay like a flat washed-out quilt under a hard colourless sky. The last lines of indigo were being cut, gathered into large bundles and piled high onto bullock carts. Everyone was involved - coolies, women with babies strapped to their backs, and children - all weighed down by the oppressive heat and crawling like insects.

Despite the heat and the weight of her skirts, she quickened her pace and stared ahead so she would not notice the curious glances of the shuffling multitude. It unnerved her to walk beside these dusty, tick-ridden bullocks, for they could become aggressive if they smelled a beefeater in their midst. She had hardly eaten beef since arriving in India, but how long would it take for the smell on her skin to subside? She dabbed at her face and neck with a sodden handkerchief. She felt so confused and lonely. If only there was someone she could confide in. Evangelina would not understand; she was as innocent as one of her pampered pets, living out her life in this enchanted jungle wilderness.

She seemed to be drifting further and further away from everything she had depended upon, and closer and closer to . . . what?

'Mademoiselle, I do not advise you to walk a great distance at this time of day. May I drive you somewhere?' Père Auguste pulled up in his *ekka*, forcing the bullock carts to manoeuvre precariously close to the ditch.

'Thank you, mon Père, but I am only walking to the factory.'

'Nevertheless, Mademoiselle, I insist on taking you. The syce can walk. He is used to the heat.'

Père Auguste shouted to the syce, who handed over the reins and climbed down. Too fatigued to protest, Francina took his place on the hard bench beside the old priest. His fat cigar enveloped her in a cloud of strong-smelling smoke (a similar brand of tobacco she remembered Uncle Doré smoking, and she was suddenly overcome with homesickness). Inhaling deeply, she shut her eyes and wished she could fly magically back to Uncle's library, and find that it was Uncle Doré's arm she was pressing against, and not the arm of this dishevelled old priest .

'You are not a Catholic like your mother, Mademoiselle?' he asked, jerking the reins.

Francina looked at him in surprise.

Père Auguste smiled. 'You see, I was very fond of your mother. It is in honour of her memory that I still conduct the services here. Moisgunge was the first indigo concern in this area to build a chapel. Your mother was very proud of that fact. Did you know that the chapel is dedicated to Sainte Thérèse?'

Francina shook her head.

'The chapel was built for your mother as a wedding present from her father. I believe he was the first European to own land in this part of Bengal.' The old priest brushed ash off his white summer robes. 'Her father, Monsieur Savi, persuaded the Maharajah to give him a long lease on the group of villages adjoining his land, making his *dihat* - which is the Persian word for 'villages' - one of the largest in the Kishnaghur district. Moisgunge is one of the four out-factories in the *dihat*, and all four are managed to this day by his descendants.'

Was this the person she remembered whispering to Mamma behind the pews? Taking a deep breath, she asked in a small voice, 'Père Auguste, do you remember my baby brother Albert?'

The old priest smiled wistfully. 'Whenever I see the cherub in the fresco, I am reminded of that poor innocent babe.'

'The fresco in the little chapel?'

The old priest nodded, and looked solemnly at her. 'And now, as

I look at you I am reminded of his mother. Tell me, my child, do you ever see your mother?'

Francina shook her head and stared at his dusty toes straining through his leather sandals.

Père Auguste puffed on his cigar thoughtfully as he surveyed the long procession of bullock carts laden high with indigo. 'Monsieur Jacques has transformed this concern,' he said eventually. 'When I first came out here as a young Franciscan, Moisgunge had just come under the management of a proud, headstrong young man, new to India, who used to intimidate the villagers if they refused to grow indigo. So an air of suspicion and mistrust grew up: the *ryots* mistrusted the *zeminders*, and the *zeminders* mistrusted the overseers. This impasse continued until a new Collector was appointed to the district, an enthusiastic young man, anxious to demonstrate the new English powers of John Company law. When the Collector came to hear of the manager's bullying tactics to oust a man from his home because he refused to grow indigo, he issued a summons against him. The manager capitulated and agreed to pay a large sum to pacify the worker. Word of this quickly spread through the *dihat* of the manager's loss of face and as a result, the *ryots* grew courageous and began to demand higher wages to grow and process the indigo.

But that is all in the past. Monsieur Jacques has transformed Moisgunge into one of the most well-maintained concerns in the district.'

'I was in Kishnaghur a few weeks ago, and I saw the grave of my baby brother,' Francina whispered. 'Mon Père, did you bury my baby brother Albert?'

The old priest took the cigar out of his mouth and flicked it into the dust, narrowly missing the syce that walking alongside. 'I wish I had, I wish I had.'

Francina's heart banged in her chest. 'Why didn't you?'

'Because I was not here.'

Père Auguste pulled a large handkerchief out of his pocket, tilted back his straw hat and mopped his bow. 'Your father dismissed me from my duties at Moisgunge. He was suspicious of the Catholic Church. He believed I was a bad influence on your mother. But your mother was a tender flower, as innocent as the day she was born.'

Bless me, Holy Mother, for I have sinned.

The smell of fermenting indigo, which for the last few days had begun to impregnate the air, was growing stronger as they neared the factory. Francina caught sight of the muddy river, glinting lazily in the distance, and the crowded *ghat,* where further shipments of indigo were being unloaded from outlying districts to be transported to the factory by cart.

'We have arrived. I must say goodbye now. I take the steamer down to Chandernagar and will not return to Moisgunge for several weeks.' The old priest raised his hand and made the sign of the Cross. 'God bless you, child.'

Francina watched the syce drive Père Auguste down to the *ghat.* She had already decided that she would not mention this conversation in her letter to Papa, just as she would not mention stumbling over baby Albert's grave.

She followed the slow procession of bullock carts carrying the indigo plant to the steeping vats, where it was unloaded into the largest of the vats. Coolies were adding water to encourage the fermentation process. Francina pressed her handkerchief to her nostrils. The stench was overpowering; even her hair seemed to reek of fermenting indigo.

In a second set of tanks nearby, the plugs of the largest vat had been opened and an evil-looking liquid was emptying into a second, shallower vat. As the liquid spread across the floor, it turned from yellow-orange to a bright frothy green. Coolie women were removing the dead obnoxious plant from the upper vat, and carrying it in foul-smelling dripping bundles on their heads to an area of open ground where they were spreading it out to dry in the sun. Their clothes and skin were saturated in indigo dye.

She eventually found Jacques sitting at a big table on the factory *chabutra* under the trees outside the office. She hardly saw Jacques these days; he was up before dawn, and appeared exhausted and ravenous at sundown. *Burra hazri,* he had told her, was a simple, hasty affair taken either in the saddle or at his office desk. If there were time, he would snatch a quick siesta in the shade wherever he happened to find himself.

Barefooted coolies, women and children, their skin and shabby remnants stained with the yellow, green and blue stages of the indigo process, were making their way towards the *chabutra.*

Francina had a strong sense that these workers did not feel intimidated or coerced by their sahib, and she could understand why they had made him their unofficial magistrate. 'I have told them many times that they must take their grievances to the Court at Kishnaghur,' Jacques had told her one evening, 'but they trust my judgement. So I fine them if I think them in the wrong and distribute the money to the beggars. They seem satisfied with the arrangement. But the authorities would not like it if they knew.'

Beside the *Burra Sahib* stood his foreman, a dark-skinned man in European dress, who was arranging ledgers on the table. The coolies and their families began to squat on their haunches in a semi-circle, their eyes fixed on the bulging jute sacks of *rupees*, *annas* and *pice*, which the foreman was ostentatiously tipping out and arranging into varying heights of towered rows that spanned the length of the table. Some of the women had newborn infants slung in strips of cloth across their backs, or were balancing older naked babies with bloated stomachs across their hips. They were all silent, transfixed by the sight of so much coin positioned like a disciplined regiment on the table in front of them.

Jacques saw her and beckoned. One of the factory *lathiyals*, a tall fearsome-looking Sikh in Moisgunge livery, placed a chair for her beside his. She climbed onto the elevated platform and sat next to Jacques. It was a relief to be out of the sun.

'Evangelina is so taken up with the preparations for Mrs Bulpitt's visit, that I thought it best to keep out of her way,' she explained, when he asked why she was here.

Jacques chuckled. 'It is so rare for Evangelina to receive visitors. She likes to make sure everything is in order.'

Evangelina had existed in a state of anxiety ever since the bearer had brought the *chit* informing her of Mrs Bulpitt's impending visit. She had immediately instructed her servants to turn the dressing room into a guest room. Beds from the storeroom were hurriedly assembled. All day, bare feet had pattered across the matting, dusting, sweeping and polishing. 'Mrs Bulpitt is a cousin of Jacques,' Evangelina explained as she arranged canna lilies in a cracked yellow and blue vase. 'I have never met her, but Jacques speaks fondly of her.'

The foreman, having arranged his piles of coin, now consulted one of the ledgers. He ran a slim finger down the closely inscribed lists, raised his head and barked in a high-pitched voice. One by one, the peasants rose as their names were called and made their way to the *chabutra.* The foreman consulted his ledger again, counted out the correct amount of *rupees,* and dropped them disdainfully into the cupped hands of the workers standing expectantly below the platform.

The line of men, women and children shuffled past. As everything seemed to be progressing smoothly, Jacques asked if she would like to look around the factory. His foreman was quite capable of being left in charge for a while. If a problem should arise, one of the *lathiyals* could easily come and look for him.

Francina conducted the factory inspection on her cousin's arm. A servant followed, carrying a huge umbrella to protect them from the sun. Coolies salaamed as they stopped by a group of vats.

'Doesn't it bother the coolies to have blue skins?' Francina asked, pressing her handkerchief to her nose, as she watched coolies standing in rows, knee-deep, in the evil-smelling fermenting liquid, and vigorously swishing it with flat pieces of bamboo to encourage it to turn from green to blue.

'No more than it bothers a chimney sweep at Home to have a black skin, I suppose,' chuckled Jacques. 'Perhaps the coolies believe themselves to be closer to Vishnu.'

'Vishnu?'

'The god Vishnu, in his incarnation as Krishna, is often depicted with a bright blue skin. Krishna is a favourite god of the coolies. He was raised by peasants and renowned for his exploits with the shepherdesses,' he added mischievously.

Jacques showed her briefly around the furnaces, where the indigo was conveyed down channels to be boiled for several hours. 'We use *cetee,* last season's dried indigo plant as fuel. It is very economical,' said Jacques. 'The steaming glutinous liquid is strained through vast sheets of cloth to cleanse it of impurities. It is then dried and pressed into *leel* - cakes of pure indigo colour.

In the *palki* on her return to the bungalow, Francina studied the small cake of *leel* that Jacques had given her, stamped with the

Moisgunge factory mark and wrapped in thin yellow paper. Were the two preoccupations so very different - her family's obsession with these vibrant blocks of blue and Angelo's desire to seek his fortune from brilliant nuggets of gold?

The dog barked as the bearers jogged through the gate, and chased them down the drive, sending the Moisgunge household into turmoil. Servants appeared like magic to welcome her.

'Oh, we thought you must be Mrs Bulpitt!' Evangelina said, running down the bungalow steps. 'Where have you been, Mademoiselle? We were so worried. Salim saw you walking down the lane. We were about to send out a search party!'

Francina climbed out of the *palki* and apologised. She held up the cake of *leel*. 'Jacques has been showing me around the factory.'

Evangelina took her arm. 'Never mind, Mademoiselle. Come, let us sit in the garden and wait for Mrs Bulpitt. I am so nervous. You must help me entertain her.'

They sat under the great banyan tree drinking lemonade while they waited. A feast of welcome was being prepared A kid had been especially slaughtered, Evangelina told her excitedly, as appetising smells drifted across the garden from the cookhouse.

Both Aurelia and Victor were in high spirits at the prospect of having European children to play with. While they sat and waited, Aurelia entertained them with nursery songs, which she sang in a lusty high-pitched voice as the bearer pushed her on the swing. Evangelina clapped her hands in delight. 'How much English Aurelia speaks since you came to stay! Tell me, Mademoiselle, what is *Pop goes le weasel*?'

Victor was playing with the sweepers' children. They had constructed a kind of ball out of taut rags which they were throwing to each other. The rules of the game were incomprehensible to Francina, but the children seemed to understand them perfectly. Of all the children on the Moisgunge estate, the sweepers' children looked the most robust. They survived on the leftovers from the table, which in Guernsey would normally have been fed to the pigs. None of the other Moisgunge servants, of course, would ever touch European food – fresh or leftovers - but caste taboos did not apply to the Untouchables.

The dog pricked up his ears and barked loudly. Victor threw

down his bat and chased the dog to the gate. Evangelina stood up.

'Mrs Bulpitt has arrived,' she said, adjusting the tortoiseshell comb in her hair.

Francina followed her to the bungalow steps as two *palkis* and an entourage of *banghy-bearers* jogged round the corner.

The *palkis* were lowered to the ground and the slatted panels pushed back.

Mrs Bulpitt emerged as Britannia might emerge to survey a newly conquered land. She was probably in her late twenties, of medium height, but big boned and imposing. She towered over the line of servants who had gathered to welcome her.

'What an excruciating journey!' she said, launching into a long description of how the Company steamer had been delayed by the volume of river traffic, and how they were held up by an incident at the *ghat*, etc, etc . . . She addressed her monologue to Francina as though assuming her to be the Mistress of Moisgunge and Evangelina nothing more than her companion - or worse, her servant.

Francina quickly announced that she was merely a houseguest, staying at Moisgunge at the kind invitation of her cousin Jacques and dear Madame Vauloué. She emphasised the name 'Madame Vauloué' with reverence as she touched the arm of their petite hostess.

Evangelina remained strangely mute, with a faint social smile fixed on her face. The English words of welcome she had practised all afternoon did not materialise.

Mrs Bulpitt did not seem perturbed by her *faux-pas*. She bent down to kiss her tiny hostess with the beguiling charm she might greet a pretty child or a favourite pet. Polite formalities exchanged, Mrs Bulpitt now seemed much more interested in finding out about her English-speaking cousin than to indulge in stilted French small talk with their country-born hostess.

A scuffle distracted her. Two pink-faced children and their ayah climbed out of the *palkis* and huddled behind Mrs Bulpitt's voluminous skirts.

'My children.'

Mrs Bulpitt placed loving hands on their golden heads. Alice was six years old, with eyes as colourless as the sky and skin as pale as an elephant's tusk. She was a perfect miniature of her Mamma. Freddie, a year younger, towered over his sister.

Evangelina smiled, and kissed them affectionately on their foreheads (it is so much easier to deal with children than a worldly Englishwoman. Children, after all, are the same the world over regardless of race or creed). But Victor sloped away. He could not contain his disappointment at the sight of this pasty-faced intruder, who was so much taller than himself.

'Victor, come back here and shake hands with your cousin!' Evangelina called in her best French. But Victor stuck out his tongue, and raced off to continue his game with the sweeper's boys. Evangelina was mortified.

Undaunted, Freddie sauntered off to commandeer the swing, where from his swinging vantage point he watched his savage little cousin whooping with the native children.

'Grandmamma Barton has told me so much about you, Miss Duquesne,' smiled Mrs Bulpitt as Evangelina led the way up the bungalow steps. 'That was why I was determined to stop off at Moisgunge. I simply had to meet my cousin from Guernsey before returning home.'

'How is Aunt Barton?'

'She finds the house very quiet these days. She has taken up the hubble-bubble. It helps to settle the niggle in her stomach, she says. Honestly, it was like visiting a *zenana*,' Mrs Bulpitt said, shaking her head, 'watching those three old ladies puffing hookahs all day long.'

Francina listened politely and answered Mrs Bulpitt's questions as briefly as possible, but she was aware that Evangelina's smile had fixed into a grimace. Evangelina could not understand a word they were saying.

The atmosphere at Moisgunge had changed now that Mrs Bulpitt (or Jane as she insisted Francina should call her) had arrived. It was as though Evangelina had introduced a mongoose into her menagerie and discovered that the creature's natural instincts had upset the equilibrium of the place. Jane Bulpitt was pleasant enough, but she made little effort to converse in French so that Evangelina was left out of their conversations unless Francina acted as interpreter.

'Aunt and Uncle are still in Murshidabad? I'm sorry to have missed them. Strictly speaking, Aunt Cecilia is my Great Aunt, but she seems far too young to be called Great Aunt, don't you think?' Jane Bulpitt said, the next day at *burra hazri*. 'When Mamma died, I lived with Aunt Cecilia until I was sent Home to school. She was like a mother to me, and Jacques, as dear as a brother - sometimes, I regret to say, a very irksome brother. Do you remember tying my pigtails to the bedpost, Jacques?'

Jacques laughed. It was a treat to see him presiding over the table in the middle of the day. For once Evangelina had persuaded him to leave the workings of the factory to his foreman and join them. But despite Jacques's presence, the meal was a fraught affair. The boy cousins would not become friends; they eyed each other across the table with suspicion and hostility.

The girl cousins were faring better. Alice had decided that tiny Aurelia, with her dark silky ringlets and lustrous brown eyes, was to be her own special pet. Aurelia, in awe of this older fair-haired girl, submitted willingly. She had sat obediently on the bungalow steps all morning with her ankles neatly crossed, while Alice had arranged her hair into exotic styles entwined with flowers. Now they sat as close as Siamese twins, communicating in sign language and a scattering of Indian words.

'I am sorry Mr Bulpitt not come too. You miss him much, *n'est–ce pas,* Madame?' Evangelina asked shyly in her halting English.

Jane Bulpitt looked grave. 'It is difficult to persuade my husband to leave his fields for any activity other than hunting, Madame Vauloué.'

'Boy, boy!' Freddie shouted to the *khitmutgar* as he thumped his empty glass aggressively on the table. 'More milk!'

Evangelina flushed. 'Poor child. There is no more milk until the morning. The cow cannot keep up with your healthy appetite!'

She consulted the *khitmutgar* who left the room. He returned a few minutes later to inform the memsahib that the *guala* could supply a little goat milk, but it would have to be boiled. Evangelina relayed this information to Jane Bulpitt, who relayed it to her son.

Freddie stamped his foot with rage. 'But Mamma, you know I *hate* goat milk!' Tears slid down his fat cheeks to his pouting milk-stained mouth. 'I hate it here. I want to go home!'

Jane Bulpitt flew from her seat to console her fraught son, and for the first time since his cousin had arrived, Victor smiled.

A few days later *chota hazri* was interrupted, as usual, by the jangling bells of the Moisgunge runners delivering a large packet of mail. This morning there was a letter for Francina with a strange postmark. Recognising Angelo's scrawl, she quickly broke the seal.

S.S. Lady Adelaide,
near Port Philip Heads, Melbourne, Australia

My dearest sweetest Sister

We have been in a state of great excitement all day, waiting to hear those longed-for words 'Land ahoy!' And at noon, just as we were rising from table, the welcome cry came from the masthead. In the rush to clamber onto the deck, I missed my footing and slipped down the companionway, badly twisting my ankle. But I managed to hobble to the rail, where I saw with my own eyes that unmistakable sight of land -- the distant shores of Australia! Oh dearest Ina, I felt an immediate rapport with this green mass on the horizon. I know in my bones that this country will be kind and generous to me.

Unfortunately as the day progressed, my ankle swelled so much that I was obliged to cut off my boot. I am now resting in the saloon with my leg propped up. The Doctor thinks I may have broken it. The other passengers have been most sympathetic, and Mrs Finch has <u>*insisted*</u> *that I must stay under her roof until my ankle mends.*

It is most frustrating, for I was hoping to spend the next few weeks assessing the goldfields in the Melbourne district. I have discovered that there are several goldfields within a hundred mile radius of the town - Ballarat, Bendigo, and Castlemaine being the three principal ones. But I must just be patient and wait until my ankle mends. I have become acquainted with some very kind and influential people on the voyage, who have given me introductions to all the leading Melbourne Residents - now do you see how my scheme for travelling First Class has paid off? Most of the steerage passengers have come out as prospectors. Unfortunately, they will now have a head start, for I fear that my ankle may set me back several months -

It was hopeless. She would never see the necklace again, and she would never have the means to return to Guernsey. She had been ensnared in this Indian wilderness like one of Evangelina's birds.

'Fanny, you look troubled. Is it bad news?'

'My brother has broken his ankle. He will be laid up for several weeks.'

'How irksome.' Jane held up her letter. 'I have some disagreeable news too. Frederick insists that I return home immediately with the children. Isn't that a nuisance? And just when we were getting to know each other.'

For once Jane Bulpitt lapsed into silence, lost in her own private thoughts. The silence propelled Francina back to Russel Street, where she was explaining to Grand-mère that she could not retrieve the necklace yet because Angelo's plans had suffered a setback. Her chest constricted as the old lady's eyes narrowed with contempt. She would rather drown herself in the river than live with Grand-mère's cold antipathy again.

'I've just had a marvellous idea,' cried Jane. 'Why don't you come up to Nudinapur with me, Fanny? We have plenty of room – and little Alice would be delighted. She has grown so fond of you.'

Francina stared at her.

'It is a relatively easy journey. We travel upriver to Allahabad by Company streamer. From there *palkis* will take us to Nudinapur.'

'But how shall I return to Calcutta?' She had absolutely no wish to do so, but it seemed only polite to ask the question.

'Oh, don't worry! There is always someone passing, who could escort you down.'

Why not? It was the perfect excuse not to face Grand-mère yet. She screwed up Angelo's letter into a tight ball so that his lies and fantasies were imprisoned in her fist. She would throw it into the river. Perhaps the goddess Ganga would take pity on him and grant his wishes. Then she could return to Calcutta with her head high and reclaim the necklace.

'I would like that very much.'

She felt elated by her impetuous answer. For the first time in her life there was no one behind her who could over-rule or undermine her decision. It gave her a wonderful feeling of liberty and independence.

Evangelina rose from the table and made her way to the far end of the verandah. A pang of guilt flowed over Francina as she watched her billing and cooing to her fluttering *lals*, and wished she could think of a way to entice her back to the breakfast table. She felt like a traitor who had sided with the enemy.

Jane Bulpitt's eyes followed hers down the verandah.

'I am sure you are aware that there is more than a hint of black blood in her veins,' she said in a low voice. 'It was most unfortunate that Cousin Jacques should marry into such a family. He really should have been more particular. And the way she brings up her children! The boy is nothing more than a savage. Jacques should have stamped his authority on him long ago. The girl is harmless enough. In time, I dare say some neighbouring planter or colour-blind sergeant in a British regiment will marry her and overlook her *chi-chi* accent, but I can't see either of them coping with the discipline of an English school – or even a French school for that matter. The boy is a bad influence on poor Freddie. Even if my husband had not summoned us home, I would feel it my duty to make my excuses and leave. Freddie really is not happy here.'

Had she been too hasty in agreeing to go with Jane Bulpitt? If only she could stay at Moisgunge and not go anywhere. But it was too late. Evangelina would not want her now. As far as she was concerned, Francina had revealed her true colours.

NUDINAPUR
February 1857

Francina peered through the slats of her *palki*. The house loomed before her, glistening like a wedding cake in the moonlight. The flat roof was decorated with an ornate parapet and small ornamental towers rose from the corners. The ground floor was raised on an arched plinth about five feet above the ground and reached by a wide flight of steps. Jane had warned her that Nudinapur was large, but she had not expected a house the size of an English country mansion.

She followed Alice out of the swinging bed, which had served as their coffin-like home for the last two days and nights, relieved to stand on terra-firma once more.

A black spaniel bounded down the steps, barking joyfully. Freddie scrabbled out of his mother's *palki* and threw his arms round the little dog. 'Scamp, I have missed you!'

The servants had been warned and were lined by the steps to welcome the memsahib home. The head servant, a dignified man dressed in a crisp white tunic, red cummerbund and exotic headdress, stepped forward and solemnly addressed Jane, who translated his news to Francina. The sahib was away. A tiger was seen near the village worrying the cattle, so Frederick had gone with a few houseguests to hunt it down.

'Are there many tigers round here?'

'There used to be a great many. We are generally aware when a tiger is on the prowl for the deer and monkeys sound the alarm. But it is rare for one to venture close to the house, although they have been known to skirt the native village and carry off a calf or pariah dog. Once, one carried off a baby.'

'A baby!'

'It was a very hot night. Apparently the family was sleeping outside their hut; relying on a fire to keep predators away (the villagers can be notoriously slack about their safety sometimes). Unfortunately, the fire burned itself out during the night and the tiger seized the opportunity to carry off their infant. After that, the beast acquired a taste for human flesh and began to terrorise the village. Frederick eventually set out to kill it.'

The servants salaamed as they climbed the steps. Bearers followed, carrying boxes on their heads.

'And did he?'

'Naturally. Frederick would never let a four-legged creature get the better of him. I believe its head now graces a wall in the hunting-gallery - or is it the billiard-room?' Jane gestured vaguely into the depths of the house. 'I am not sure exactly where it hangs. One tiger's head look very much like another. I dare say I could probably find a date engraved on the plaque underneath. But I find all those snarling heads rather gruesome, don't you? I would rather be surrounded by paintings of homely country scenes.'

They crossed the verandah and stepped into an ornate pillared vestibule, almost bereft of furniture. Candlelight from the wall sconces reflected pools of light on the shinning stone floor. At one end a mighty wooden staircase, heavily carved, rose majestically to the first floor. Jane took her arm. 'Tomorrow I will show you the house. Nudinapur was once the hunting lodge of a native prince, which accounts for some of its quaint decorations. I would have preferred something more homely, but Frederick is delighted to live here and keep up its hunting traditions.'

Alice skipped up and pulled at her skirts. 'I am so glad you've come, Miss Fanny.'

Francina woke in her enormous tented bed to hear a peacock announce his haunting presence in the garden. She stretched languidly, drinking in her surroundings. Although it was delightful to sleep in this luxurious fashion, she missed her corner of the Moisgunge nursery, with the children calling her from behind the bamboo screen. She listened to the familiar sounds of a household waking up: the swish-swish of the sweepers' brushes across the floors, then the sharper sound of brushes on the paths outside . . .

Similar sounds would be waking the inhabitants of Moisgunge.

A pang swept over her as she remembered the tears in old Marieji's eyes, and the expression on Evangelina's face when she had said goodbye. If only she could have explained that her reasons for leaving had nothing to do with them or Moisgunge.

A cock crowed. It seemed a good moment to get up. She slipped out of bed, pulled on her wrap and opened the venetians. A glimmer of light outlined a vast, misty plain.

She could just make out the vegetable garden, the water tank and wells, the stable-block and a collection of thatched huts partly hidden by clumps of trees, which she took to be the servants' quarters. Beyond Nudinapur's sloping grounds, about a quarter of a mile away, was the indigo factory with its now-familiar collection of outbuildings and steeping vats clustered on the bank of a meandering river. Around and beyond the factory, silvery irrigation channels criss-crossed the newly planted indigo fields.

She walked through the house in search of Jane. An attendant directed her along the first floor verandah on the opposite side of the house, where she found the Mistress of Nudinapur sitting outside her bedroom surrounded by potted ferns and flowers. The *chits* were still rolled up to allow the last breath of night air to waft through the rooms. Beside her, a small cane table covered by a crisp white cloth was spread with tea things, and in the centre, a crimson rose drooped in a crystal vase.

'Draw up that chair,' smiled Jane. She was wrapped in a flowing white gown and her hair was loosely pinned under a small lace cap. Relaxed and at ease, she looked younger, softer, than Francina remembered her at Moisgunge. It had not struck her before, how close they were in age. There was hardly five years between them.

'After *chota hazri* I will take you for a ride and show you the countryside.' Jane swept her hand proudly across the landscape. 'What do you think? Frederick has had every palm tree removed, so that when we look across the grounds we can pretend we are in England. We have imported roses and all manner of plants from Home. Doesn't it look exactly like an English garden?'

Jane passed her a cup of lukewarm tea. The sky was lightening; the mists had almost disappeared. It was easy to distinguish the grounds of Nudinapur (with its geometrically shaped flower beds and straight lines of flowerpots) from the land beyond the cactus hedge, but only a person with poor eyesight could see this as an English garden. Beyond the cactus hedge, the land looked nondescript and colourless. And apart from the clumps surrounding the native village in the distance, the small white temple and the few struggling specimens marking the *bund*, there were few trees - certainly no palm trees - to be seen.

'Don't you feel isolated out here?'

'Not at all,' Jane said, almost too emphatically. 'With good horses, Cawnpore is only about three days northwest of us. It is a very fine town, which I have been told rivals Cheltenham or Brighton in sophistication, and positively bristles with society and amusements. We often make an excursion to Cawnpore during the Cold Weather. There is such an air of gaiety during the Racing Season. I do not care much for the races, but Frederick likes to test his Arab in the hack races. The Assembly Rooms have fine boarded floors (it is so much more agreeable to dance on boards, don't you think?) and there are several European shops and a theatre. – Now of course, we have a smart new church, but more importantly, preparations are underway to bring the railway up from Calcutta.'

They watched a pair of sandy-coloured mongooses play a rough-and-tumble game on the newly watered grass.

'The only slight blemish of Cawnpore society is the *Burra Mem* - Lady Wheeler,' Jane reflected.

'But why?'

A dog barked somewhere in the house. The mongooses froze; then darted away like slippery eels through the flower beds.

'Well, she is hardly one of us. It is common knowledge that her mother was the native mistress of an Irish officer. And Lady Wheeler, herself, was General Sir Hugh Wheeler's mistress, and mother of several of his children, before he married her. But luckily for us, the *Burra-Mem* keeps very much to herself – rather like the native ladies in purdah - so we have little to do with her.' Jane waved her hand in the opposite direction. 'Kandria is nearer, but it is a small dull Station, with only two ladies. The Deputy Commissioner's wife Mrs Fraser is pleasant enough, but has little conversation. Major Campbell's wife is a half-cast and quite ignorant of English customs - particularly of dress. I do not encourage Alice and Freddie to play with her children.'

When Francina had changed, she found Jane dressed in a cream riding habit, waiting for her on the gallery landing between two enormous majolica pots sprouting umbrella palms. A bearer hovered nearby carrying her white pith *topee* and a riding crop.

'There are two other staircases, besides this one. A side one painted white, and a rickety outside one which the servants use,' Jane told her, as they gathered up their looped skirts to descend. 'Two further flights, a lighthouse stair from the east and west verandahs, on the first floor leads to the roof.'

Jane led her through a labyrinth of lofty rooms, each nearly thirty feet high and guarded by snarling tigers or leopards skins with huge yellow teeth, who lay spread-eagled across the polished *chunam* floors as though waiting to snare an unsuspecting foot. Severed heads of other beasts lined the walls, and glass cases of moth-eaten birds and reptiles, dotted amongst the furniture, were annotated with brass plaques recording the date and place of the kill.

'The house contains about twelve apartments, besides bathing and dressing rooms, set on two floors,' Jane said. 'There are also two Hot Weather underground apartments.'

The rooms were sparsely furnished. Tired damask sofas and chairs stood in isolated splendour between the display-cases of stuffed beasts or oriental weaponry. Jane had tried to prettify the rooms with chintzy covers and worked cushions, but the effect looked incongruous amidst the snarling beasts, hunting trophies and weaponry. In an antechamber (which seemed to serve as a small library) paintings of English hunting scenes dominated – all showing evidence of being attacked by silver fish. Francina glanced hopefully at the titles on one of the bookshelves, but the volumes appeared to reflect Mr Bulpitt's interests: *The Craft of Pig Sticking, Plain Tales of a Shikari, Horse-Breaking Illustrated*. Only the well-thumbed copy of *The Lady's Home Doctor* and a volume on *Indian Household Management* could belong to the Mistress of Nudinapur.

'Neither Frederick nor I are avid readers,' Jane said with an apologetic smile, 'but I am sure we could have volumes sent down for you from the library in Cawnpore. And my dear friend Mrs Mackenzie would be only too delighted to lend you some of her reading matter. If you like, I could send her a *chit* this morning.'

'Where does Mrs Mackenzie live?'

'In Umritpur - about ten miles from Cawnpore.'

They made their way across the drive to the stable block, a long low flat-roofed crumbling building set behind a row of trees. 'The elephant houses,' Jane told her, pointing to the two octagonal towers flanking the stable block. 'If Frederick is hunting tiger, he will have taken the elephants.'

Some of the stalls were empty, but there was stabling for at least two dozen horses and there were several grooms milling around. Francina had learned that in India each animal would have its own syce and possibly its own *pūrbeah*, grass-cutter. A bandy-legged old man clad in a shabby *dhoty* was filling a trough with water.

Jane stroked the muzzle of a buff stallion, while his syce fanned flies away from his eyes with a hair switch. 'This is Caesar, Frederick's half-bred Arab. My husband is devoted to him. Sometimes I think he takes more interest in his horses than he does his children, but I suppose that is typical of most fathers.'

Jane selected a sturdy piebald mare with a sweet temperament for Francina. When the ponies were saddled and bridled, the syces led them into the courtyard and helped the Memsahib and Miss-Sahib to mount. The sun was now a dazzling semi-sphere on the horizon, and the temperature was rising. Francina lowered her veil to protect her face from flies.

Soon they were trotting besides newly-sown fields and jumping the narrow irrigation channels. Salim, their armed attendant, followed on a scruffy up-country pony.

Men watering the fields took no notice of them; neither did the skein of honking geese flying to the nearest *jheel*. They came to a field sprouting lines of indigo, veered away and followed the crumbling bank of an irrigation channel, in need of repair, to a dirt road leading to a village.

'Avert your eyes, Fanny.' Jane wrinkled her nose. 'It's that *saddhu* again. The fellow's quite mad. Frederick has tried umpteen times to have him removed, but it's impossible when the natives treat him as some sort of living deity.'

But Francina could not divert her eyes. They had become transfixed on the deathly white creature walking along the road towards her, his long matted hair plastered with cow dung. He was naked - but he had rubbed ash over his body so that he looked like an emaciated ghost. A brass pot, tied to his loins by a piece of twine, clanked eerily against the brass bowl in his hand. He stood aside to let her pony pass, and she blushed uncomfortably as his red drugged eyes stared defiantly into hers. It was the look on his face that disturbed her more than his nakedness – a look that was both arrogantly lewd and bewitchingly seductive.

'Who was that,' she whispered when they were out of sight. An obnoxious smell lingered in the air.

'The natives regard him as a holy man, a follower of Siva, but Frederick says he is nothing more than a drug-ridden beggar who travels from village to village beguiling the natives.'

Crows cawed noisily from the trees as they approached the village, and an assortment of half-starved pariah dogs rushed forth, growling and barking. The little mare stiffened and Francina patted her neck to reassure her. Salim lashed out with his whip, and the dogs fled barking.

An uneasy silence followed that initial commotion as they rode through the village, modified by the clatter of horses' hooves. An old woman kneading cow dung into flat cakes outside her hut, glanced, but did not acknowledge them; Children peered from shadowy doorways, but did not smile or wave; women collecting water at a well, a group of village elders huddled under an ancient tree, stall keepers and vegetable sellers muttered amongst themselves and watched them pass; There was no chatter, no laughter . . . They had just travelled across a vast tract of Indian wilderness: two defenceless white women travelling alone with their children and ayahs, escorted as they were by umpteen scantily clad natives, and never once had she felt in any kind of danger. Yet out here, in this nondescript village set in the middle of nowhere . . .

'Do those villagers work on the Nudinapur estate?' Francina asked when they were once more in open country, riding along a raised dirt road, shaded at intervals by stunted thorn and eucalyptus trees. The land stretched out either side of the *bund,* flat and parched, like a vast dried up riverbed.

'Mostly. The ones left in the village are probably the old, young or infirm,' Jane said. 'The able-bodied are employed in some capacity or other. Look, there are some in the fields over there.' She pointed to a group of men in the distance, bent over primitive hoes, who were scraping the earth between the sprouting lines of indigo. Vultures, on the lookout for a meal, circled high above them. 'Some of them are employed as *lathiyals*.'

'*Lathiyals?*'

'Nudinapur's private police force.'

'Does Nudinapur need a private police force?'

Jane laughed. 'Sometimes a *ryot* would rather plant rice or vegetables. He has to be persuaded to fulfil his contract and plant indigo. - Oh, look! There's Mr Hopkirk, our Assistant.'

Jane's face broke into a smile at a figure in the distance wearing a huge conical hat, and riding a small native pony. He was trotting along the *bund*, overseeing a team of men with bullocks drawing an antiquated plough across the hard stony earth. 'Let's ride over. I'll introduce you to him.'

Mr Hopkirk was a conscientious young man in his early twenties, new to India, Francina learned as they cantered over to speak to him. Nudinapur was his first placement.

Mr Hopkirk raised his hat, and smiled in a manner that made Francina think he was unused to female company.

'I hope my husband has not been working you too hard in my absence?' teased Jane. 'He's on a *shikar*. Tiger, I understand. Do you know when he is due to return?'

Mr Hopkirk shut his black notebook and placed it in his jacket pocket. He was usually the last to know about Mr Bulpitt's plans, he confessed with an embarrassed smile.

Francina pointed in the direction they had just come. 'Has something happened in that village?'

'What do you mean, Miss Duquesne?'

'I can't quite explain it . . . Perhaps that wandering *saddhu* has cast a spell over the village, or the people are expecting some calamity, like an outbreak of cholera –'

Jane laughed. 'Fanny, you do have a futile imagination!'

'Who is Siva?'

'The god of destruction and reproduction; a particularly unpleasant character with unspeakable desires that I would rather not tell you about.'

'His consort, the goddess Kali, is an even more unsavoury character. I'm sure you must have come across representations of her,' added Mr Hopkirk. 'She's usually depicted as a fierce black creature with multiple arms carrying sculls and weapons.'

'With a long red tongue?'

'Indeed. She is one of the most terrifying gods in the Hindu pantheon, and has an unquenchable thirst for blood and sacrifice.'

'Why the natives should choose to idolise such a gruesome creature is beyond my comprehension,' sniffed Jane.

After a pause, Mr Hopkirk plucked up courage to raise a problem that had come to his attention since his employer's absence. Jane interrupted him with a laugh. 'It is far too hot to stand in the sun and discuss something as dull as indigo! Come over to the Big House this evening, and tell us over dinner.'

'Of course, Mrs Bulpitt.' Mr Hopkirk raised his *topee* and bowed deferentially.

Jane giggled as they rode away. 'Poor Mr Hopkirk, I'm afraid he still has a lot to learn about life on the Indian plains.'

'How long has he been here?'

'This is his second season. He came out with such noble ideas of improving the lot of the natives. He used to spend hours studying the local language in his spare time, and trying to understand the wily ways of the workers. But my husband soon showed him the error of his ways.'

'Does he write poetry?' With his delicate frame and fly-away hair he reminded her of an engraving she had seen of a consumptive poet, who had died young.

'Goodness, Fanny, I have absolutely no idea.'

But Francina knew that he was not calculating the length of an indigo line in his little black notebook, but fervently composing long ardent poems to quell his loneliness: *Thou still unravishe'd bride of quietness, thou foster-child of silence and slow time . . .*

Afternoon tea was served on the shaded verandah outside the drawing room. The verandah was about twelve feet deep. Lofty oriental arches unfurled gracefully above Francina's head. It was like sitting in an orchard under a canopy of beautiful stone trees; and if it had not been for the snarling heads and antlers, the cane furniture and the oriental rugs scattered across the polished floor, she might have imagined herself in the haloed nave of a cathedral. Beyond the verandah, the garden shimmered under tides of heat.

Alice sidled up, swinging her loops of string. 'Shall we play cat's cradle again?'

'Really, Alice. Let Miss Fanny drink her tea in peace.'

There was a commotion at the gates: shouts, barks and blowing horns. The spaniel sleeping peacefully at Jane's feet, pricked up its ears and slunk into the house. Jane smoothed her skirts and stood up. 'Frederick is back.'

'Children, children,' she called softly, 'Papa is home. Now you must be good and as quiet as little mice. Remember to give Papa a kiss, and don't annoy him with silly questions. You know how tired he is after a hunting trip.'

They sat in silence, following the sound as it headed towards the stables. Neither child felt the urge to run across the grass to greet their father. After a while the sounds approached the house. Three men in hunting costume with wide pith helmets crunched round the corner, guns slung over their shoulders. Behind them the corpse of a tiger, tied by its paws to a pole, was borne on the shoulders of four bearers.

'Thank goodness he has killed something,' whispered Jane. 'He should be in a good mood.'

The magnificent beast was carried across the grass to a fanfare of bugles and hunting horns, and dumped unceremoniously at the foot of the steps. A cloud of red dust rose then settled. The *mali's* children, who had heard the commotion, were watching from behind the plumbago bushes. One was brave enough to skirt the canna lily beds. Freddie and Alice shrieked when they saw the tiger. They raced down the steps to examine it, each daring the other to kick it. They took no notice of the men.

The men watched the children for a moment, and then strode up the steps, puffing cigars.

'You're back, my dear - and about time too!' boomed a red-faced man with enormous whiskers. 'I shall have to think seriously before letting you stay with those disreputable relatives again.' His huge bulk filled the verandah as he paced up and down, shouting for chairs. Jane proffered her cheek.

'Frederick, dear,' she said in a small voice, 'how are you?'

Mr Bulpitt kissed his wife then smiled down at Francina. 'And where did you find this charming little filly?'

'Frederick, this is my cousin, Miss Duquesne. Dear Fanny was staying with Jacques Vauloué at Moisgunge, and kindly agreed to accompany me back to Nudinapur. It is such a pleasure to have her here.'

'Cousin, eh? Well, Miss Fanny, you are welcome to stay as long as you like! A pretty young filly to liven up the proceedings is just the tonic we need - eh gentlemen?'

His two companions greeted Jane then crowded round Francina's chair. The gentle fragrance of flowers that has been wafting up from the garden was lost under heavy draughts of sweat, gun smoke and tobacco. She was introduced to Mr Wilson, a neighbouring planter, and Mr Mackenzie, the Government Opium Agent.

'May I offer you something to drink, gentlemen?' Jane asked, her hand poised on the teapot.

'Tea?' roared Mr Bulpitt. 'My dear, you have been away a long time! Is that what they drink at Moisgunge, those lily-livered relatives of yours? *Koi hai!* Cold brandy-pegs! *Jeldi, jeldi!*'

The men slumped into chairs and brayed about their hunting expedition – each escapade becoming more daring and exaggerated as it passed from one hunter to the other. While on the wall behind them, the head of a sloth bear bared its teeth, oakum oozing from its seams.

The women put aside their work to listen, while servants padded silently across the verandah with trays of drinks and refreshments. No one enquired into Jane's six week excursion to Bengal, or the health of the children. The tiger *shikar* was the sole topic of conversation on the verandah.

Mr Mackenzie puffed at his cigar as he rustled through an old newspaper. Mr Wilson drew his chair close to Francina's.

'You must come when we next go hunting, Miss Duquesne.'

'I have no desire to see animals slaughtered for sport.'

'I read in the *Central Star* that Mr Boileau has been barbarously murdered,' Mr Mackenzie said from behind the newspaper.

'How did it happen?'

'He was riding with a guard of sowars, apparently. They were all cut to pieces by that notorious *dacoit* Fuzzil Ali. He escaped to Nepal, so they say.'

'I doubt if you would have seen anything to offend you, Miss Duquesne,' said Mr Wilson, wiping his receding hairline with a large handkerchief. 'The grass was high and there was such a stampede of elephants, beaters and dogs that I for one did not realise it was all over until the bugle sounded.'

She smiled politely, but there is something about Mr Wilson she did not like. He was sitting too close, and staring at her in a manner she found uncomfortable.

Mr Bulpitt drained his glass and held it up for a refill.

'If the Oude Commission is not safe, what hope is there for us?'

'He will have to be hunted down like a wild beast in his lair. We cannot allow villains like him to escape. He must be caught, and severely punished to set an example.'

'Enough of this talk, gentlemen, with ladies in our midst!'

Mr Wilson winked at Francina and she flinched. Only butchers' boys had ever winked at her before. No one of consequence would ever do anything so ill-bred.

The children were prodding the tiger with sticks. Freddie whooped, and jumped on the tiger's back, sitting astride as though he was riding a horse. Using his stick as a whip, Freddie struck the carcase violently on the rump. Alice shrieked with admiration, and the men roared their approval.

'That's the spirit, young man,' shouted Mr Bulpitt. 'Show 'm whose master!'

'Freddie, come away from the animal. It must be riddled with fleas,' called Jane. She did not seem to find her son's antics as amusing as his father did. 'And Alice, please come out of the sun!' She gestured to the bearers. 'I think it is high time that animal was taken away.'

'What will happen to the tiger, Papa? Will its head be cut off and hung on the wall?'

'This time, young man, I think we'll have it skinned and made into a fine rug.'

'May I watch it being skinned?'

'Certainly not, Freddie!' Jane said aghast.

'If my boy wants to see the animal skinned, he'll see it skinned! It might toughen 'm up! I don't want my son growing into a spineless pansy.'

Jane bit her lip. 'Children, it is time for Salim to take you for your ride. Get them ready, ayah - and wash their hands thoroughly.'

Protesting loudly, the children were dragged away by their ayah.

'Well, my dear,' Mr Bulpitt pulled his whiskers so they stood proud and erect, 'after that delightful little interlude, I think it is time for us all to sojourn until dinner.'

He took Jane's hand and assisted her to her feet. This, it turned out, was the signal for the party to break up, for the hunters to wend their way back to their rooms and tents, and to fill the remaining hours of the day with fitful sleep, letter-writing or other languid pursuits until sundown when they would re-assemble for the evening's entertainment.

The pillared dining hall looked even more impressive at night. By day the candelabras and wall sconces had looked dusty and rather sad (with the odd crystal pendant or ornamental branch missing), but in candlelight these blemishes were hardly noticeable. The silver tureens, glassware and gold-rimmed porcelain laid out on the white tablecloth were replicated *ad infinitum* in the tall Venetian wall-mirrors - as were the scantily-clad figures cavorting in the bacchanalian paintings. Still, it was better to be surrounded by crude copies of classical myths than the severed heads of spitting cats.

Mr Wilson escorted her to her seat.

She spread her skirts out - not so much to form a perfect bell, but a safety barrier about her. This was the first time she had worn this gown since that fateful day in Calcutta (and now, seeing the effect it was having on her escort, it might have been wiser to have worn her cream moiré silk). But Jane had insisted that she dress up to dine – and at least evening dress had the effect of making the gentlemen look slightly more agreeable. 'I like to think that formalities remain as high in Nudinapur as they do in Calcutta,' Jane had said.

Indeed, if the Governor General and his lady should arrive unexpectedly to join them, the Bulpitts could do little more to impress them.

The table, resting on clusters of heavy brass paws, was

generously laid for six, but could expand to seat many more (judging by the number of chairs lining the walls). *Khitmutgars,* in white turbans and uniforms, stood smartly to attention. She had not been at Nudinapur long enough to recognise the servants that belonged to the house, but she knew that in India servants travelled with their masters. So the ones standing behind the guests, presumably, were also visitors to Nudinapur.

She nodded shyly at Mr Hopkirk, who was sitting at the other end of the table, pleased to see that he had joined them. But small and wiry, he looked quite out of place, rather like a gamekeeper's little terrier that had come across, not a field of gambolling rabbits, but a den of snarling wolves.

Mr Bulpitt slurped his soup noisily.

'Any news from Cawnpore, Hopkirk?'

'There seems to be much discontentment in Oude, sir.'

'Discontentment?'

The wolves pricked up their ears. They had targeted a victim.

'Against the Company's Government.'

The pack closed ranks and circled round. 'Why so?'

'The people do not like the changes. Apparently they prefer the old system, corrupt and tyrannical as it was, to anything we might wish to impose on them.'

'Why the natives are even more senseless than I thought!' exclaimed Mr Bulpitt.

'I have heard that they have a deep and growing suspicion that we are colluding with the missionaries to eradicate their caste system and convert them all to Christianity.' The little terrier was bravely fighting his corner. 'These new laws and taxes only seem to have increased their suspicions – suspicions that are now causing ructions in the native town of Cawnpore.'

'I blame the number of ruffians from Oude flooding into Cawnpore,' said Mr Mackenzie.

'Why on earth should anyone want to flood into the native town? It is an evil, sprawling rabbit-warren of a place without any architectural beauty.' Jane signalled to the *khansamah* to remove the soup bowls.

'To seek anonymity in British territory.'

'Can't the natives see the great benefits coming to Oude? Why, the moment one crosses the river from Cawnpore into Oude one is struck by the crumbling disorder of the country.'

Mr Bulpitt was shouting at Mr Hopkirk as though it was his fault that the natives of Oude were ungrateful. Mr Hopkirk shifted uncomfortably in his seat.

Mr Wilson lost interest in this conversation and leaned towards her, wafting tobacco breath across her face. 'You must come and see Wilsonghur, Miss Duquesne.' He grinned, exposing a row of yellow teeth.

'Wilsonghur?' Francina leaned away as much as she could without appearing impolite. She had no desire to talk to him. She wanted to listen to the exchange across the table.

'Wilsonghur is my indigo concern. It lies about ten miles from here on the road between Kandria and Cawnpore.'

'It seems to me that indigo looks the same wherever it is planted,' she said turning away.

'Ah, Miss Duquesne, but I was really referring to the house in which I live.' Mr Wilson smiled smugly and moved his chair closer. 'Nudinapur is a - ' he waved his hand dismissively in the air, 'a mere *pimple* compared to Wilsonghur.'

'It is not *buildings* that are important, but the people that inhabit them,' she said coolly, turning away.

'Quite so, Miss Duquesne, quite so.'

To her astonishment, she felt a finger trace the bare flesh of her arm. She pressed her arm to her side as a trail of goose pimples crept up her flesh. How dare he touch her like that! She thought of saying something cutting, but decided that cool indifference was a better policy.

The heated exchange across the table continued into the next course, but it was hard to follow because Mr Wilson was distracting her with his incessant questions. 'What do you think of the quail, Miss Duquesne? I shot it myself this very morning.'

The quail, even drowned in *shikari* sauce, had suddenly lost its piquancy.

'Miss Duquesne, it is so unfair, so unjust,' Mr Wilson murmured as he leaned towards her again. 'Why should Nudinapur - of all places - be blessed with such a divine visitation?'

He was trying a different approach, trying to capture her

attention with what he believed was beguiling talk. Well, it would not work.

She felt a foot creeping towards her own. She wanted to kick it out of the way, but that might only encourage him. In any case soft satin would make little impression on heavy leather. She moved her feet out of his reach and glanced helplessly in Jane's direction, as his shoe trampled indiscriminately over the hem of her oscillating pink-blue silk while it searched in vain for a satin pump.

'Miss Duquesne, you are the loveliest creature I ever saw.'

Jane was too busy playing the part of a sparkling hostess to notice that she was being molested. The *khitmutgar* opposite had noticed. He gave her a look of arrogant disdain which placed her on a rung far below the *nautch* girls. Hot and confused, she watched Mr Hopkirk dissect the saddle of mutton, and wished with all her heart that it was Mr Wilson trussed under his carving knife.

'I, for one, would never dream of travelling to Lucknow without an armed escort,' Jane was saying. 'One hears so many alarming stories of *dacoits*.'

'Lucknow is a lawless barbaric city!' Mr Wilson burst into the conversation with great force. If he could not capture Miss Duquesne's attention physically he would do so orally.

'Indeed. *Thuggees* are still coming to the attention of the Government.'

'*Thuggees*?' mouthed Francina to Mr Hopkirk.

'Bands of robbers who murder their victims along lonely highways. They profess to commit their crimes under the patronage of the goddess Kali,' whispered Mr Hopkirk.

'Do not alarm yourself, Miss Duquesne,' smiled Mr Mackenzie, reassuringly. 'The Government is making tremendous strides to have that evil cult eradicated.'

'That ruler was an imbecile! Incompetent and unjust!' Mr Wilson drained his glass and held it up for a refill.

'But great changes are in the air,' said Mr Mackenzie. 'It was the best thing that could have happened when the king was hauled down to Calcutta.'

'But in his wake lies a cauldron of disaffected men ruined by the annexation,' Mr Hopkirk said from his corner.

'Why can't they realise that we only want to improve their lot?'

Jane added, bemused. 'Surely they must prefer *us* to those cruel Moguls with their barbaric laws?'

'Hear, hear!' shouted Mr Bulpitt.

Encouraged, Jane continued. 'Why are they being so tiresome? *We* are the rulers now. Throughout history peoples have been conquered by someone or another. Why, *we* benefited greatly when we were conquered by the Romans, didn't we?'

Mr Bulpitt raised his glass to his wife, surprised by her little outburst.

While meats, stews and curries were passed back and forth across the table, and were eventually followed by the desserts and crystallised fruits, the tussle between leather and satin continued under the table without respite.

Mr Mackenzie stood up. 'Gentlemen, it is almost one hundred years since Mr Clive won his decisive victory at Plassey. I wish to propose a toast that the Union Jack will fly over India until the day that the sun ceases to rise!'

'I have heard it prophesied that our presence in India will only last for a hundred years,' muttered Mr Hopkirk during the toast. No one else appeared to hear his remarks, or if they did they took no notice. Francina leaned across the table to speak to him.

'What do you mean?' she whispered. 'When is the hundredth anniversary?'

'In four months' time - on the twenty third of June.'

'Take no notice, Miss Duquesne,' said Mr Mackenzie, seeing the look of alarm on her face. 'It's just talk. They're all excitable and spineless – frightened of their own shadows, most of them. Mohammedans and Hindus - why they hate each other! They'd rather cut the other's throat than turn on us.'

'That,' smiled Mr Wilson, 'is our trump card.'

'And inertia,' added Jane.

Mr Wilson scraped back his chair noisily and stood up.

'I wish to propose a toast. Please raise your glasses, gentlemen, to the two lovely ladies of Nudinapur.'

He looked hard at Francina. She lowered her eyes and vowed never to wear anything décolleté in Mr Wilson's presence again.

'To the two lovely ladies of Nudinapur!'

The men were getting drunk. Mr Bulpitt began to aim little balls of bread across the table to snuff out the candles. Roaring with laughter, the others joined in. There were guffaws of approval when a pellet landed in the glass sconce – and even louder guffaws when the candle was snuffed out. One pellet misfired and hit the *khitmutgar* standing beyond the table. For a moment there was silence - then Mr Bulpitt laughed louder and aimed a bread pellet straight at the man. The others roared their approval and joined in, beleaguering the poor servant with pellets of bread, which they aimed with considerable force. The gamekeeper's terrier had been bypassed; a new victim had been selected. The *khitmutgar* stood motionless beside the sideboard as the onslaught continued. His dignified passivity seemed only to antagonise his predators, and they brayed as though they were on a hunting expedition, taunting the kill before allowing it the solace of death.

Mr Hopkirk, Francina noticed, did not join in this childish pastime. He looked uneasy, out of place amongst these vulgar uncouth planters. She could not bring herself to witness the *khitmutgar*'s humiliation, but she could feel his silent outrage unify the other servants into a deadly barricade around the room. In Guernsey she had known the parameters - they were laid out in black and white like the columns in a rule book: good behaviour or bad behaviour. In Guernsey she had only herself to blame when she had breached the rules and suffered one of Aunt Doré's whippings. Everything was different here. In Nudinapur there were no rules – at least none she understood.

A cold sensation trickled down her spine. How many servants were there at Nudinapur? Twenty? Thirty? Forty? Out in this wilderness the Europeans must be outnumbered by a ratio of least ten to one . . . and that did not include the vast populations in the surrounding villages . . .

'Fanny,' whispered Jane, 'I think we should leave the gentlemen to their port and brandies. Come. Let's see if the children are asleep.'

2

The tiger kill signalled the end of the *shikar*, and the hunting fraternity left Nudinapur early the next morning with their stinking trophies, which would be sent post-haste to the overworked taxidermists in Cawnpore.

Francina soon grew attuned to the daily routine, for each day passed very much like another. She would rise before dawn and ride out with Jane to explore the countryside until the sun rose too high. Then they would return home, discard their riding habits and have a cold bathe. Refreshed and dressed in a light morning gown, she would join Jane and the children for *burra hazri* on the verandah. Afterwards the cook would be summoned. He would appear on the verandah clutching his book to plan the day's meals and discuss the accounts with the memsahib. Jane would unlock the store cupboard and weigh out the dry stores for the day's meals. Whatever else was needed, the *khansamah* would buy in the bazaar. 'I know he cheats me, but that is his *dastur*,' shrugged Jane. 'It would cost me a great deal more if I had to do the shopping. I just have to make sure that he does not cheat me too blatantly.'

Apart from planning the meals and overseeing the accounts, Jane made a daily cookhouse inspection to see that the pots and pans and kitchen utensils were properly cleaned. Otherwise, she never stepped inside the cookhouse and never interfered with the cooking. Her other household duties were minimal. She left the running of Nudinapur very much to her head butler, the *khansamah*. 'He seems to do nothing at all,' she complained, 'but if I dispensed with his services, the household would collapse overnight.'

It required ingenuity to fill the long yawning hours that stretched out after *burra hazri*. The day divided itself into bouts of sewing, sketching, letter-writing or thinking up ways to amuse the children. If they were lucky, they would not see Mr Bulpitt until tiffin – and if they were exceptionally lucky, they would not see him all day. He spent his days out with his syce, either overseeing the sprouting indigo crop, or shooting something for the pot. On these occasions he was usually accompanied by two fierce-looking *lathiyals,* tall bearded men with elaborate turbans, who wore crimson sashes and carried lead-tipped sticks.

Not only did the house sigh with relief when the master was out, but it also burst into song. Francina could hear Jane trilling in the drawing room as she descended the stairs. Music was Jane's solace, a pastime that totally absorbed her. But Jane, Francina had discovered, only played when her husband was out. 'Confounded racket,' he would bark if he returned unexpectedly to discover her at the pianoforte. So music became synonymous with the sahib's absence. It was the signal for the household to relax. The Mistress of Nudinapur bloomed and her children stopped bickering. Even the man sweeping dust down the stairs tackled his duties with renewed vigour. Everyone rejoiced when Mr Bulpitt was out.

Francina walked through the hunting gallery on her way to the day nursery, and as usual, a creeping paralysis came over her, for this room, more than any other in Nudinapur, oozed with Mr Bulpitt's brooding presence. All the creatures displayed in these cases (such as the mongoose wrestling with the cobra, or the piglet pinioned between a vulture's talons) were locked in a perpetual struggle between life and death, and all were displayed here as testimony to his bloodthirsty inclinations. She had the feeling that if she stayed in this room for very long, she too might find herself imprisoned in a glass case.

Alice and Freddie were sitting at their low table in the corner of the verandah waiting to start their lessons. To pass the time and keep ennui at bay, she had become their self-appointed governess. It was a plan that delighted Jane, for it gave her a chance to practise her music. The children, Jane confessed on an early morning ride, had had governesses, but none had stayed for more than six months. So Francina had volunteered to fill the role until a new one was appointed. She was enjoying the challenge – and so were the children.

'Good morning Miss Fanny,' they said in unison.

She asked if they had slept well, and then clapped her hands. 'Now we must begin our lessons. And if you both work very hard - I shall give you a special treat this afternoon.'

'What treat?' said Freddie.

'I shall tell you a story about the faeries that live on the Island of Guernsey.'

'Didn't you live there once, Miss Fanny?'

'I did indeed, Alice. But we can discuss that later. For the moment I would like you, Freddie, to finish the exercise that you started yesterday while I give Alice a history lesson.'

Miss Alice made her customary grimace (as she did for every subject). Master Freddie took out a crayon from his box and set to work. It had come as a revelation to discover how eager Freddie was to learn. The petulant boy that she had met at Moisgunge had turned into a surprisingly obedient disciple. His sister, however, was more difficult to manage, so Francina had written to Miss Chesterton to ask her to send out (or recommend) some suitable exercises. In the meantime she improvised; tried to remember all those little rhymes that had made her own lessons so much more agreeable.

'*Willie, Willie, Harry, Stee, Harry, Dick, John, Harry Three . . .* What comes next, Alice?'

Alice screwed up her eyes, as though she was trying to think.

Music drifted out to the verandah. Alice's fingers began to tap out the rhythm. It was more fun to listen to the music than to remember the names of the Kings and Queens of England.

'*Willie, Willie, Harry, Stee, Harry, Dick, John Harry Three,*' repeated Francina. '*One, two three . . .?*

'*Neds! Richard Two*!' shouted Freddie, from his end of the table.

'Don't shout, Freddie.'

'Is a King of England like a Maharajah?'

'No, Alice. He is much more important.'

'Why?'

'Because he wears a crown!' shouted Freddie. 'And carries a sword covered in jewels!'

'If you interrupt again, I shall make you stand in the corner.'

Freddie meekly bowed his head, and continued to copy the letters that she had drawn out for him on a sheet of a paper. His tongue followed the letter-forms as carefully as his crayon.

'Have you ever seen the King of England, Miss Fanny?'

'Not the King of England, Alice – but I have seen the *Queen* of England.'

Alice's eyes grew wide with admiration. 'Was she wearing a crown?'

'No, she was wearing a bonnet – but it was a very pretty bonnet.'

'Oh!' said Alice, crestfallen. 'But why was she not wearing a crown?'

'Because Queen Victoria is a modern queen'

'What does *modern* mean?'

'It means she is living now – not a long, long time ago, before there were steam engines or the electric telegraph -'

'What is the *electric telegraph*?'

The art of being a good teacher is to have a limitless amount of patience. This morning, however, patience was in short supply. 'I think we have studied enough history for today, Alice. Find that sheet of paper, and try to copy out the letters as well as you can.'

In the silence that followed, Francina began a letter to Louisa. These letters were getting harder to write, for it was difficult to keep up the illusion that she was happy out here. Oh, she would be the first to admit that her motives were purely selfish. She did not want to tell Louisa anything that might make her change her mind about coming out – although that did not seem at all likely. Louisa's letters were full of Henry Fetherstone and very little else. He seemed to occupy every facet of her waking being (and probably her sleeping being as well). She tried to picture Louisa sitting quietly in the parlour, dreaming of the day when Aunt and Uncle would finally agree to her engagement to Henry Fetherstone. In the meantime, all she had to look forward to were these monthly letters, which hopefully (depending on the reliability of the *dâk-ghari*) would also include a secret note from him. It was a huge responsibility to act as intermediary.

3

'Hunting boar is a very risky business,' explained Mr Bulpitt as he sank into a cane chair. His bearer passed him a long hog spear and a sharpening stone. 'It requires cool nerves and a great degree of horsemanship to charge through the long grass after him.'

Jane and Francina raised their heads and tried to look interested, but they had heard this subject umpteen times before. Francina handed Alice the paper gown she had just cut out for her costume doll.

'Why isn't she wearing a crinoline?' frowned Alice, folding the tabs over the paper doll.

'Ladies did not wear crinolines in those days. Your Great-Grandmamma was dressed like this when she was a young lady.'

Alice stared at her in disbelief.

'Have you been to a bull fight, Miss Fanny?' Mr Bulpitt asked,

Francina looked up from her paper cutting and watched him sharpen the tip of the spear with the stone. Sweat glistened on his temples. 'No, I have not.'

'Regretfully, neither have I. But the pig-sticker, like the matador, must aim the hog spear between the shoulder blades to kill at the first attempt. Timing is everything. You only have one chance. A wounded hog can be extremely dangerous. If you don't get the boar, he'll charge straight at you, and cut your horse to pieces.'

Mr Bulpitt had been honing his hog-spearing techniques for the last few days. His long-suffering syce had been ordered to gallop at full speed across the scrub trailing a bloated goat's bladder from a rope while the Sahib followed, brandishing a long hog-spear. Now, on the eve of the most important event in Nudinapur's sporting calendar, Mr Bulpitt was prepared and in fighting mood.

'Razor-sharp. That should do the trick.' Mr Bulpitt smiled as he tested the glinting tip of his hog spear. 'Major Campbell has won the Nudinapur Cup for the last two years, but this year I am determined to snatch it back from him.'

'I'm killing the pig, killing the pig!' Freddie was running across the grass brandishing a stick which he aimed like a spear at the spaniel. The dog yelped, jumped over a flowerpot and raced across the drive kicking up a cloud of red dust.

'Young man, hold the spear in the tent-pegging manner!' Mr Bulpitt sprang out of his chair and thrust the spear under his arm. 'Like this!'

Freddie ignored his father. He picked up the stick and ran after the dog, whooping gleefully. A man, squatting on his haunches to pull weeds out of the lawn, shuffled out of his way.

Mr Bulpitt shook his head and slumped back into his chair. 'That boy will never make a pig-sticker if he doesn't listen to instructions.'

'I am thinking of putting the Frasers in the Chinese room and the Mackenzies in the Clive room,' Jane said, taking advantage of her husband's genial mood. 'Do you think the Campbells will be comfortable in the Red Room, Frederick? It is rather small, I know, but the antechamber would be very suitable for their children –'

Mr Bulpitt sprang out of his chair.

'Don't trouble me with irrelevancies, woman!' he shouted. 'I don't give a cuss where they sleep - put 'em all in tents, for all I care!' He stormed down the verandah brandishing his hog spear, with his bearer hurrying behind.

Jane bit her lip. 'Frederick is always nervous before the Pig-Sticking Competition. I just hope he wins. He'll be in a frightful mood if he doesn't.'

'I'm afraid you must find our society a little dull after Calcutta, Miss Duquesne, but we try our best to keep ourselves amused,' Mrs Mackenzie said in a high, irritating voice. 'We always play croquet during the Nudinapur Cup. It has become a tradition for us ladies.'

She swung her mallet and hit the black ball. It rolled across the hard, uneven ground, hit the hoop and bounced off.

The wives and children of the pig sticking fraternity had been keeping themselves amused since dawn, when their husbands had kissed them goodbye and ridden off with their hog spears and attendants. Bait had been laid, boar had been spotted. For a few blissful hours, their families would be spared 'pig talk'.

Mrs Campbell positioned herself for her shot. She was a petite, bird-like woman with olive skin and raven-black hair, which she wore neatly coiled under a fetching chip bonnet. She was accompanied by a servant, whose sole duty, it seemed, was to carry a huge umbrella to protect her face from the sun. She was exquisitely (but perhaps a little over) dressed for a game of croquet, but nevertheless, she had beautiful eyes and a quiet graceful manner. Francina was not at all surprised that a handsome cavalry officer should have fallen in love with her. She was the epitome of delicate feminine beauty. Beside her, Mrs Fraser looked almost manly.

Mrs Campbell swung her mallet. To her surprise the red ball shot through the first hoop.

Francina gave her a friendly smile. She sensed her discomfort amongst these self-assured Englishwomen. Of all the women here present, she liked Mrs Campbell best, but she knew it would be impossible to strike up an intimate friendship with her. She was a timid thing with little conversation, whose life seemed to revolve around her husband and children.

'Have you heard? A friend of Mrs Woods had a bad experience while stopping over in the Old Cawnpore Hotel,' said Mrs Mackenzie in an aside while Mrs Campbell positioned herself for her second stroke.

'Mrs Woods? The wife of Captain Woods of the Fifty Third?' asked Jane.

'There isn't another Mrs Woods in Cawnpore, is there?' There was a spark of irritation in Mrs Mackenzie's voice.

Mrs Campbell looked up. 'I've heard that Mrs Wood's little boy has measles.' She glanced anxiously at her three darlings, who were huddled under a tree with their ayah watching the other children playing a game of quoits. 'I do hope your boys were not in contact with him? Mine have only just got over the chicken pox. It would not do at all for them to catch measles while they are so delicate.'

She was assured that Mrs Mackenzie's twins (the boisterous copper-haired boys throwing quoits) had not seen Master Woods for several weeks. Relieved, Mrs Campbell swung her mallet. The red ball bounced off a clump of earth and rolled sideways.

'Anyway, to carry on with my story . . . The lady in question was told that all the hotel rooms were occupied by a party of native princes,' continued Mrs Mackenzie, as Jane positioned herself for her shot. 'She was offered two very unseemly verandah rooms.'

Mrs Mackenzie appeared to be Nudinapur's chief source of tittle-tattle from the cantonments of Cawnpore. She was a dumpy woman in her early thirties. In Guernsey, society would have scorned her coarse manners, and her plain features would have deterred most suitors, but out here on the Indian plains, she had found her métier as wife of the Government Opium Agent, and was mistress (no doubt) of a household much larger than one she could ever know in England.

'Why on earth did she not stay with Mrs Woods?' asked Jane. She hit the blue ball with such force that it knocked the red ball sideways.

'Because Mrs Woods' boy has measles,' said Mrs Campbell.

'Of course,' giggled Jane, placing her ball next to the red one.

The croquet players reflected on the trials and tribulations of childhood illnesses as they watched Jane's ball knock the red ball out of the way, then shoot through the second hoop.

A group of attendants was watching the game from the boundary in mystified silence, trying to understand why some memsahibs were hitting balls through hoops, while others were knocking balls as far away from the hoops as possible.

'As I was saying,' continued Mrs Mackenzie, 'the lady in question was made very uncomfortable by the insolent behaviour of a group of sepoys who were loitering in front of her apartments. She felt so insulted that she decided not to stay another minute, but to continue her journey through the night to Meerut.'

'Meerut?' said Francina. At last she felt qualified to contribute something to this conversation. 'I have just received a letter from a friend in Meerut. He speaks very favourably of the place. He tells me that the strawberries are just coming into season.'

'I was not aware that you are acquainted with a gentleman in Meerut, Fanny.'

Francina blushed. 'This particular gentleman is betrothed to my cousin. He was just visiting Meerut. He resides in Mhorabad. He is the new Assistant Collector there.'

'Is he indeed,' said Jane with disappointment. She positioned herself for her continuation shot. 'I hear that a new Assistant Sahib has moved into Mr Massey's bungalow. Presumably you have met him, Mrs Fraser?'

Jane's luck had run out. The blue ball hit the third hoop and bounced pitifully away.

'He seems a pleasant young man – rather earnest, I thought. But I have seen very little of him. If he is not at the *cutcherry*, then he is on tour. He takes his duties very seriously.' The Deputy Commissioner's wife swung her mallet and hit the yellow ball.

'I am sorry that he has not called on us yet,' frowned Jane. 'It would have been amusing to see a new face at Nudinapur.'

'Memsahib, Memsahib!' Salim was galloping down the drive at great speed. He swerved onto the grass towards them, and came to an abrupt halt, gabbling excitedly.

The memsahibs gasped at his news. The children left their quoits and ran over. 'What has happened?' they asked at once.

'There has been an accident.'

Jane dropped her mallet and shouted, 'Salim, ride to Kandria. Quick! Fetch Doctor Brown!'

4

'More coffee, Mr Wilson?' Jane smiled sweetly.

'That would be most kind,' said Mr Wilson, trying to scoop up a forkful of egg curry and rice with his left hand. His right arm was strapped close to his chest.

Francina frowned. Why was Jane being so nauseatingly charming? The more she fussed over Mr Wilson the longer he would prolong his stay. There was no earthly reason why he could not return to his beloved Wilsonghur by *palki*, if he was not fit to ride. She had no sympathy for him. He might fool Jane but he did not fool her. She was in a bad mood and she had a headache, made worse by the incessant cacophony pounding from the native village.

'It is the festival of Holi,' Jane had explained at *chota hazri*. 'It would not be wise to venture beyond the gates today. Emotions run high. The lower castes love this festival because it gives them the excuse to attack their elders and betters without redress. It is supposed to be harmless fun, but it can become boisterous and get out of hand.'

'Attack?' Francina had asked in alarm

'They throw coloured water and powder over everyone.'

Mr Wilson dropped his fork in exasperation. 'It is no good, Mrs Bulpitt, I cannot do it. I shall just have to starve until my shoulder mends!'

'Nonsense, Mr Wilson. You must build up your strength. Fanny will help you eat, won't you, my dear?'

Francina did not return Jane's sugary smile; instead she gave her a pleading stare, which anyone with the smallest degree of intelligence could interpret. It was all very well for Jane - she was safely wedged between her children, too far away to spoon feed Mr Wilson.

She scooped up some rice with his fork and waved it petulantly under his nose. Mr Wilson grunted with pleasure as he opened his mouth to accept her forkful, and chewed noisily, like an overgrown extremely ugly baby. It offended her to do something for him that he might enjoy.

Jane watched him devour a second forkful. 'You had a very nasty fall, Mr Wilson. Luckily Major Campbell had the presence of mind to finish the animal off, or I dread to think what might have happened.'

'What might have happened?' Freddie stared with interest at a grain of yellow rice dancing on Mr Wilson's moustache.

Jane ignored her son. She clasped her hands to her ears. 'I shall be so relieved when this festival is over!'

The noise was growing louder. A lively procession of drums, bells and pipes was moving along the road towards Nudinapur. The excitement was too much for Freddie. He slipped down from the table and raced across the verandah with his four-legged companion in joyous pursuit.

'Do not go out of the gate!' His mother sighed helplessly as she watched them head straight in that direction, followed by a hobbling old attendant.

'What is the festival in aid of?' Francina asked.

Mr Wilson grinned, exposing a row of tobacco-stained teeth. 'It is the Hindu festival of fertility, Miss Duquesne, in honour of Krishna and the milkmaids.'

He leered, as though waiting for her to pursue this subject so that he could embarrass her further, and she raised her hand to hide her reddening throat. Why did she always have the feeling that he was undressing her with his eyes?

After *burra hazri*, she escaped to her makeshift schoolroom at the far end of the verandah to prepare the lessons for the day, while Jane set off on her cookhouse inspection. She heard the children's laughter ring out across the garden as she rubbed their slates clean and laid out fresh pieces of chalk. In all this excitement, it was going to be difficult to persuade them to sit down and concentrate. Should she use the occasion to talk about English festivals? What did she know of such things? Did the burning of an effigy of Guy Fawkes count as a festival? But was it right to encourage the children to think that such an action was cause for celebration? She could anticipate the awkward questions that might follow.

'Freddie, what have you done!'

An imp, splattered from head to foot in red paint, was peering at her from behind a pillar. He held up a paper bag as his father might hold up a brace of pheasants.

'Suvla gave me this,' he grinned.

Alice held out her hands. 'May I have some?'

Freddie showered her in red powder, and she shrieked with glee.

'Naughty children! Tell ayah to find you some clean clothes before your mamma catches you looking like that.'

The children ran off screaming with mischief. The fat *darzi,* sitting cross-legged on his mat, grinned, so did the old *punkah-wallah.* Francina shook her head in mock exasperation and returned their smiles. Everyone forgave children.

How long would it be before she received a reply from Miss Chesterton? It was difficult to think of new ways to teach the children without the appropriate books to guide her. She could feel her mind beginning to stagnate without proper stimulation. Perhaps she could regurgitate something she had read in Uncle Doré's library. She shut her eyes and rubbed her temples to encourage dormant memories to surface . . . but nothing materialised. Her past life had become nothing more than a few faded images pasted into a scrapbook.

She set out the paints and crayons on the table. As this was the first day of the Indian spring it might be appropriate to learn about nature and the budding flowers. But what did she know about Indian plants?

She had a strange feeling that she was being watched. Out of the corner of her eye saw a figure standing by a pillar. She backed away and pretended to search for something in the toy box. After a few moments she heard footsteps creeping towards her and her stomach tightened. She spun around and eyed him coldly. Attack was the best form of defence.

'Do you want something, Mr Wilson?'

'I do, Miss Duquesne, I certainly do.'

'I am sure Mrs Bulpitt can help you. I am about to start the children's lessons.'

'But they are not here yet.' He stepped forward and seized her wrist with his good hand.

Francina gasped. 'Let go, Mr Wilson! The servants are watching.'

'Damn the servants.' His calloused hand encircled her wrist. The more she struggled, the tighter he gripped. The *darzi* and the *punkah-wallah* sat with their heads bowed, but she felt their sympathy swirl like a warm tide and transport her to a place of safety, while it drowned this bully in a sea of hatred.

Mr Wilson's right arm slipped out of his sling and into the pocket of his jacket where his fingers rustled in a paper bag. She watched, breathless with rage, as he smeared red powder across the palm of her captured hand.

'How dare you!' If her eyes could have thrown daggers they would have pinned him, writhing to the floor.

'Fanny, don't take it so to heart. It is only a harmless little game.'

Jane was shaking with silent laughter in the doorway. She had been watching all along and had done nothing to help her. She had probably encouraged this prank.

Grinning like a hyena, Mr Wilson dropped her hand.

Francina fled though the house, cradling her hand as though it had been slashed with a blade. In her mind's eye she saw drops of blood splattering the stairs to her room. She flew into her bathing room and plunged it into the *chatti* to remove every greasy trace of him from her skin.

The children were having a Bible lesson. She drew a large boat. 'Now children, we must draw all the animals that took shelter in the Ark. Two of each species. A male and a female – that is a boy and a girl animal,' she said, hoping the conversation would not become indelicate.

'Can I draw a snake?'

'Of course, Freddie.'

'What does a girl snake look like?'

'Exactly like a boy snake. You will probably find,' she added, as a flash of inspiration struck her, 'that like many bird species, the male snake is more brightly marked that the female. She is probably also smaller.'

Freddie settled down to draw his snakes.

Francina smiled. They had not seen Mr Wilson for several days, but this was the first time she had felt at ease since his accident, for she could not get over the sensation that he might be lurking in a doorway waiting to pounce on her. After his pathetic deception was uncovered, he had left Nudinapur with his arm un-bandaged and in working order. His ploy to smear paint over her hand had misfired.

'Alice, what will you draw?'

Alice was staring dreamily across the garden while her hands conducted the tune that her mamma was playing on the pianoforte. Her timing was perfect. She was a very musical child. 'I don't like drawing animals.'

'Draw Mr Noah and his wife then.'

Alice picked up a crayon. Francina's chest swelled with satisfaction. The more she taught the children the more pleasure it gave her. Perhaps she should quietly ask Mrs Mackenzie if she might knew of a memsahib in Cawnpore that required a governess. It could place her in a town where there was a library and get her away from this house and all its connotations. It might be the answer to her predicament. She unlocked her writing box and took out paper and an inkwell.

There was a commotion at the gate. A raucous noise like a loud bird-scarer accompanied by drums, clapping and chanting, clattered down the drive towards the stable block. Scamp, who was sleeping under the table, raced off to investigate.

'The monkey-man!' shrieked Alice, flinging down her crayon, and jumping up.

'Alice, come back! You must not get down till I give you permission.'

'Monkey-man, monkey-man!' shouted Freddie, chasing his sister down the steps.

What on earth made her follow them? It was hardly dignified to run across the grass after the children. Rounding the corner of the stable block, she almost ran into a tight circle of men gathering to see the monkey-man. Umpteen pairs of eyes turned on her. She wanted to apologise and run away, but that would make her look even more ridiculous.

'Children, come back at once. You haven't finished your lesson.'

The children took no notice. They pushed through the huddle of men for a ringside view of the wizened monkey man, who was chanting in a nasal whine and rattling his small drum. The men smirked as she pushed through the throng after them.

Two brown monkeys, the species that she habitually saw scavenging outside the temples, were dancing on the end of their strings. They twirled, somersaulted and walked on their hands, so that their tattered remnants swirled about their little bodies and faces. The children giggled and clapped their hands. The men jeered. On cue, the little female lifted up her patchwork skirt and wriggled provocatively around the circle. The drumming increased. The bawdy roars grew louder. Suddenly the male monkey jumped on the little female. She screeched in terror. Her tiny cries pierced Francina's heart. The spectators bellowed with approval as they witnessed the tiny creature's abuse and humiliation. Blood rushed into her head. She was not sure what she was witnessing, but it was wrong, dreadfully wrong. The cacophony of noise and laughter banged against her eardrums, and she felt sick - ashamed that her species should train these innocent creatures to perform such degrading acts to order.

'Freddie! Alice! Come away at once.' Shaking with shock, she pulled them screaming out of the crowd. The men sniggered as she pushed through them. She had never experienced such blatant derision before.

The mustard fields approaching the village were in flower, adding bright patches of colour to the muted washed out landscape. The signs of renewal should have cheered Francina up, but they only made her more depressed. The Hot Weather would follow the short Indian Spring; then there would be months of debilitating heat to endure. She tried to shake herself out of her mood, but it was difficult. She had slept badly, and in a restless dream had found herself metamorphosed into a female monkey grappling with a hairy brute that looked uncannily like Mr Wilson.

'What is the meaning of that monkey dance?'

'What monkey dance?' murmured Jane.

Francina looked at her curiously. She had only just told her how the children had run off to see the monkey-man, but Jane had not been listening. She repeated the story.

'Some Hindu ritual concerning the monkey god, I suppose,' Jane said eventually. 'But what is of more interest to me was your account of the children. I shall tell them sternly that if they disobey you again, I will inform their father and he will certainly punish them.'

They lapsed into silence. Francina had been trying to start up a conversation ever since they had set out on their ride, but Jane had made little effort to respond. She had lost the desire to try again. She glanced slyly at Jane. Her eyes were darting furtively across the fields, as though she was searching for something. She did not seem at all herself today.

They skirted the village to Francina's relief (she had never got over her antipathy to the place) and turned into a nondescript lane that looked little more than a rough goat track.

'Have I shown you where Mr Hopkirk lives? This is a short cut. I discovered it some months ago. We will have to jump a few ditches, but they won't be too much of an obstacle.'

Jane had found her tongue. All the way to Mr Hopkirk's, she chatted about anything that came into her head. But Francina listened with only half an ear. She had to concentrate. She was an adequate rider, but not a natural one. She braced herself (and shut her eyes occasionally) as they jumped a series of narrow man-made ditches, watched by an astonished group of coolies who were tilling the fields of sprouting indigo.

At last they joined a white dusty lane and cantered along level ground. Francina slowed down to regain her composure. The sun was growing fiercer, making her dizzy, and her clothes were clinging uncomfortably under her arms. It was difficult to understand how Jane could have found this shortcut by accident.

'Almost there!' Jane called, as she began to fall behind.

'I must have a drink soon,' said Francina weakly, eyeing a group of children filling water jars at a well.

'Look!' Jane pointed to a quaint little building with a shaggy pyramidical roof in the distance. It looked like a giant beehive sprouting in the indigo fields. 'There it is.'

They cantered over the hard earth between the indigo lines towards a ragged but formidable cactus hedge, thick enough to keep all but the most determined predator out, and peered over. Mr Hopkirk was sitting on the verandah, studiously writing at a table. Jane called and waved. He jumped up and shuffled his papers, as though embarrassed by this unexpected intrusion.

A grey dog with a corkscrew tail, sleeping at his feet, barked indignantly as they trotted through a broken gateway. Mr Hopkirk threw a boot at it. The animal yelped and bolted through a scrubby vegetable patch.

'We could not see you working in the fields this morning, Mr Hopkirk, and wondered if you were unwell.' Jane said, as he hurried down the steps to meet them.

Assuring her that he was in perfectly health, he held out his hands. 'I was just catching up with some paperwork.'

Jane smiled, freed her feet from the stirrups and allowed herself to slip gracefully into his arms. It seemed to Francina (as she dismounted unaided) that the Mistress of Nudinapur and Mr Bulpitt's Assistant were locked in that position for a fraction longer than propriety dictated.

Mr Hopkirk shouted to his servant to take away the empty soda bottles and bring coffee. He removed the riding-crop off the table, dusted down the bamboo chairs, and urged his guests to sit. Francina patted her face with a damp handkerchief, and stared wistfully at the *punkah* hanging limply above their heads. But there did not seem to be a *punkah-wallah* in Mr Hopkirk's meagre household that could set it in motion. She picked up a pamphlet lying at the floor beside her chair. *Little Dorrit*, the title read.

'My sister sends out instalments to me,' smiled Mr Hopkirk. 'She likes me to keep up with reading from Home. Are you acquainted with Mr Dickens's current work, Miss Duquesne?'

Francina shook her head.

'It is not as amusing as some of his earlier writings - Miss Dorrit's father is incarcerated in a debtor's prison, and there seems no way out of his predicament. You are very welcome to borrow earlier instalments, if you wish.'

'Thank you, Mr Hopkirk, but I think I should find that particular story rather depressing.'

'But probably true to life, don't you think? Mr Dickens is a master at showing us life as it really is.' Mr Hopkirk seemed anxious to talk about anything other than indigo.

'But why must we confront such disagreeable things out here?' pouted Jane. 'When I remember Home, I wish to think of tranquil villages, a steepl'd church by the village green, rosy-cheeked children skipping to school, fat sheep grazing in lush fields - I do not care to read about misery.'

'You're quite right of course, Mrs Bulpitt.'

'When you next write to your sister,' smiled Jane, 'you must tell her that from now on she must only send you agreeable stories. Tell her that is an order. Mrs Bulpitt i*nsists*. We cannot allow you to become melancholy, Mr Hopkirk. Who else is there around here to cheer us up at the Big House in the evenings?'

Jane flashed her eyes and Mr Hopkirk blushed.

Francina was a little taken aback by Jane's familiarity, but it was impossible not to feel sorry for Mr Hopkirk, eking out a lonely, overworked existence in this odd little bungalow with only a couple of servants and a scraggy dog for company. Glancing briefly into the darkness, she saw his simple living quarters - two rooms at the most, and both opening off the verandah. She wondered if Papa's bungalow had looked like this. Papa, when he had first come out to India and found himself Assistant on the Vauloués' indigo concern. Did Mamma, the pretty younger sister, slip away from the Big House and visit the shy young Assistant in his bungalow, just as Jane was doing? She imagined Mamma teasing and coquetting, sending poor Papa into raptures of embarrassment.

'Perhaps there is something on my bookshelf more to your liking, Mrs Bulpitt?'

Jane waved her hand dismissively. 'I don't have time to read - but Fanny does. She always has her nose in a book.

'Miss Duquesne, please borrow anything off my shelf that takes your fancy.' Mr Hopkirk motioned into the depths of the bungalow.

Francina thanked him and tiptoed self-consciously into Mr Hopkirk's bedroom. She did not like to pry, but she was desperate for something to read (she had re-read *Jane Eyre* and *Wuthering Heights* so many times that she could practically recite them off by heart), and apart from past editions of *The Cawnpore Racing Calendar,* Mr Bulpitt's library was almost non-existent. She tried not to let her eyes linger too long, and but she could not help noticing how simple and austere his room was: a narrow, unmade bed enclosed within a looped-up mosquito net, a wardrobe, a dressing table with a spotted mirror, and an easy chair. A riding-crop and shot gun stood propped in the corner. That was all. His clothes were hung on pegs around the walls, and his boots and shoes paired neatly below. There was a silver-framed *carte de visite* on the dressing-table of two unsmiling, stiffly corseted women in mourning – his mother and sister perhaps?

'Have you heard the rumour coming from Berhampore, Mrs Bulpitt?' she heard Mr Hopkirk ask.

'Berhampore was mentioned some days ago, I believe.'

Mr Hopkirk appeared to be a civilised, learned man, but to Francina's disappointment, his small library contained little light reading. There were a few poetry books, some medical and reference books, and one or two classical works written in Greek. There were no novels. She returned to the verandah a few minutes later carrying a well-thumbed copy of *Punch* and a volume of John Keats' poetry. Nothing else had caught her fancy.

'What is the rumour, Mr Hopkirk?' she asked. Jane and Mr Hopkirk stepped abruptly away from each other, like children caught raiding the pantry. Francina blushed. She had intruded.

'It seems that the sepoys of the Nineteenth have taken it into their heads that the cartridges for the new Enfield rifles have been with greased with cow and pig fat,' said Mr Hopkirk, regaining his composure.

'Is that such a bad thing?'

'The sepoys are required to break the cartridge with their teeth, and if Muslims or Hindus should become contaminated by the fat, they would immediately lose caste. The rumour has unleashed suspicions amongst the sepoys that the Company is conspiring to force them to become Christians.'

'Surely that is absurd?'

'Indeed, but any rumour that suggests that the cartridges are defiled with both beef fat and hog's lard in one fell swoop offends both Mohammedans and Hindus. It could be enough to unite them.' While he was talking, he picked up a scrap of paper from the table and slipped it into his pocket.

'Don't look so worried, Mr Hopkirk,' Jane laughed. 'It all happened a long way away.'

'But news travels fast these days. India has shrunk dramatically since the electric telegraph was installed.'

'Mr Hopkirk, you are too much of a pessimist! Take no notice, Fanny. India abounds with silly rumours. When you have lived in this country for as long as I have, you will see how unfounded all these rumours are. Why, only yesterday I heard a story of a sahib being refused water in the bazaar. - Shoo, go away!' shrieked Jane. The pariah dog had returned, and was skulking at the bottom step. 'Why don't you shoot it? Horrid, mangy thing.'

'He means no harm.' Mr Hopkirk poured some water into a saucer and placed it on the bottom step for him. 'He seems to have adopted me. I fed him the odd scrap and he decided to stay. He was pitifully thin when he first arrived, but he's fattening up nicely.'

Jane stared at him. 'Supposing he has rabies?'

'He doesn't have rabies. He's a loyal companion and a very reliable guard dog.'

'What fun it is to have you here, Fanny,' Jane said, as they rode back to Nudinapur at a more sedate pace. 'It's the little things – like riding over to see Mr Hopkirk. Everything is so much easier now . . . ' Her voice trailed dreamily away.

Had she been invited to Nudinapur - to act as ruse?

'Tell me,' smiled Jane, 'what do you think of Mr Wilson? I am sure you are aware that he is showing more than a passing interest in you. Indeed, I have it on good authority that he has fallen head over heels in love with you.'

Not Mr Wilson. Not that bumbling, overweight drunkard.

'Please don't encourage him, Jane, I beseech you! I really do not think we are at all suited.'

'You mustn't mind his style, Fanny. He is brusque, I admit, and his manners unpolished, but he has just lived on his own for too long. He is like a gruff old bulldog, I always think. His bark is worse than his bite - indeed, where ladies are concerned, I do not believe he *has* a bite. It would not take much effort on your part to become Mrs Wilson, if you had a mind to. Think seriously about it, Fanny dear. He is a rich man with a fine house. And it would be so nice to have you established close by.'

It would never come to that. He sickened and revolted her.

'Don't dismiss him out of hand, Fanny. I'm sure in time you will come to appreciate his good qualities,' smiled Jane.

5

A nagging doubt had begun to germinate during the hot interminable nights: had she been tricked into coming here? Was this just an elaborate plot to remove her as far as possible from Calcutta, so that she had no alternative but to accept the likes of Mr Wilson? She saw it all so clearly now. Aunt Barton must have written to her granddaughter, begging her to take Francina to Nudinapur:

Dearest Jane - Find someone up there willing to take her off our hands! Marry her off as quickly as possible. Grand-mère will not have her back in Calcutta - not any more.

Letters were probably flying down to Calcutta:

Dear Grandmamma Barton - I have no good news to report yet. I am trying my best, but Fanny is a very exacting young lady. When she has a mind she can be Miss Charming herself, but recently a change has come over her and, I am sorry to say, it is not for the better. She can be tetchy and sullen at times - she is certainly not the sweet young lady I discovered at Moisgunge. And what is more, she looks set on refusing an excellent offer from one of the most respected planters in the district, a gentleman who would make an excellent husband and who is obviously devoted to her. I fear that if she turns him down it will serve her very ill. I am at my wits end!

She mulled over this possibility on their morning ride, and it was making her sick with worry. Yet the evidence seemed to speak for itself. Jane knew of her antipathy towards Mr Wilson, yet despite her hints and protestations, refused to do anything to discourage his attentions towards her. Now, whenever he appeared at Nudinapur, she would scurry out of his way. But, like a seasoned alley cat, the more she rebuffed him, the more interested he seemed to become. She glanced slyly at Jane, who had ridden ahead and was studying a tree spilling over the wall of the old white temple. Could she really be so devious? Perhaps the heat was playing tricks in her head. *One can lose a sense of perspective out here,* someone had said once.

'Fanny, come over here.'

Jane pointed into the branches with her riding crop. The tree was covered in clusters of tiny star-shaped cream flowers. The cloying sweet scent had attracted clouds of tiny black flies.

'Nim flowers,' said Jane. 'The Hot Weather has begun.'

'Stop rocking your chair, Freddie. You know what happened to *Fidgety Phil who wouldn't sit still.*'

'What happened?'

'He over balanced, pulled the tablecloth and all the hot dishes fell on top of him.'

'But that won't happen, Miss Fanny, 'cause we're not eating anything!' said Fre ddie cheekily.

The *punkah-wallah* was doing his best to stir the air, but the children were growing fractious. Soon it would be too hot to have lessons on the verandah, even with the *chits* rolled down.

'Why have you brought that pistol, Freddie? I do not like to see pistols on the table when I am giving you a lesson.'

'Papa always carries a pistol with him.'

'Papa is not having a lesson. When you go to school in England, Freddie, you will not be allowed to carry a pistol.'

'What will happen if I do?'

'You will be whipped severely.'

'I don't think I want to go to school,' pouted Freddie.

'Of course you do. There will be lots of boys to play with. You will play cricket - and all sorts of other games. You will like school very much. Now, we are getting side-tracked. I want you to lay out three rows of buttons. Each row must have five buttons. Can you do that for me?'

'I think so.' Freddie wrinkled his forehead in concentration.

Francina hid a smile. It was rewarding to watch the spoilt little terror she had encountered in Moisgunge turn into this studious child who was so eager to learn. It was the want of mental stimulation that had caused his aggressive behaviour, and his father's bad influence, of course. The sooner Freddie was sent away to school the better.

Hooves thundered down the drive. The spaniel barked and ran off to investigate. Freddie looked up in interest.

But it was Mr Wilson who trotted round the corner on an exhausted-looking horse, having doubtless just ridden over from his beloved Wilsonghur. His syce followed on an equally exhausted rumpled pony.

'It's *him* again,' whispered Freddie. 'Why does he keep coming?'

'I don't know, Freddie, but I wish he wouldn't.'

Mr Wilson dismounted. The dog, sensing his young master's hostility, snapped at his ankles. Mr Wilson kicked out at it, and in his anger, loosened his grip of the reigns. The horse bolted, hotly pursued by the dog. Mr Wilson shouted to his syce to catch the confounded animal and take him to the stables. His weary syce wheeled his pony round, dug his heels in, and set off after the terrified animal that was bolting through the garden. Men ran from the stables to help him.

Mr Wilson stormed up the steps. Dark patches of sweat had stained his jacket. Hot and dishevelled, he looked even more disagreeable than usual.

'Miss Duquesne, may I have a private word?'

Stirruped boots clipped purposefully across the stone floor towards her. Freddie stopped counting buttons and eyed him aggressively.

'Miss Duquesne, may I speak to you?'

A reek of sweat wafted towards her. She glanced into the depths of the house, hoping that Jane would have heard the rumpus and come out to investigate, but the piano lesson she was giving Alice continued unabated.

Mr Wilson's eyes followed hers into the dark cavern of the house. 'Mrs Bulpitt knows I am here. She is perfectly happy for me to interrupt you.'

'It is not convenient. I am giving Freddie a lesson.'

Mr Wilson flicked dust defiantly off his *solar topee*.

'Miss Duquesne, I have been trying to speak with you privately for some time, but I have never managed to catch you on your own. Would you care to step into the gallery with me for a moment?'

'Will you walk into my parlour?' said the Spider to the Fly.
'Tis the prettiest little parlour that ever you did spy;'

'Mr Wilson, nothing you have to say to me cannot be said here - in front of this child.'

Freddie was watching with hostile suspicion, ready to defend her honour. His toy pistol lay cocked on the table.

'The way into my parlour is up a winding stair,
And I've many curious things to show you when you're there.'

Mr Wilson cleared his throat. 'Miss Duquesne, I have been mulling over something you said. You told me once – very perceptively I thought - that it is the *people* who inhabit the buildings that are important, not the buildings themselves. Your words wounded me at the time, but now I understand! Now I see what has been missing from my life. *You,* Miss Duquesne! You have been missing from my life. Wilsonghur cries out for a mistress. I cry out for a wife!'

'Oh no, no,' said the little Fly, 'to ask me is in vain,
For who goes up your winding stair can ne'er come down again.'

'Mr Wilson, please let go of my hand.'

'You would want for nothing. I am a rich man. I would give you every luxury. Please, Miss Duquesne, say that you will be mistress of Wilsonghur.'

'Mr Wilson, let go of me.'

'Let go of her, sir!' Freddie pulled at Mr Wilson's trousers and fired his toy pistol into his huge posterior.

'Miss Duquesne, I implore you to consider my offer. I am nothing more than a . . . a discarded snakeskin without you!'

'Let go of her. Let go of her!'

'Go away, you snivelling brat!'

Mr Wilson lashed out at her brave little champion, throwing him against a chair. The toy pistol spun across the polished floor. Freddie howled with humiliation and rage.

The singing stopped. Jane flew out to the verandah and threw her arms round her bawling child. 'My poor darling! What on earth happened?'

The dog, hearing the cries, lost interest in the bolting horse and raced back to the verandah to defend his young master.

'I have called at an inconvenient moment. I shall leave at once. Good day, ladies!' Mr Wilson stormed down the steps.

He kicked the dog off, who was wrestling with the toe of his boot, and shouted for his horse which was still creating havoc in the garden.

'My roses!' wailed Jane, as it crashed through a newly-erected arbour.

Mr Wilson stomped up and down the drive, shouting obscenities until the terrified animal was brought under control and dragged neighing back to his master. His syce followed on a tired-looking pony.

'Useless good-for-nothing!' shouted Mr Wilson, raising his whip.

'Don't you *dare* strike that man!'

Francina hitched up her skirts and ran down the steps. She stood defiantly between Mr Wilson and his cowering servant and narrowed her eyes. 'It wasn't his fault that the horse bolted. A *gentleman* would never blame his own shortcomings on his servants!'

Mr Wilson stared at her in astonishment. His whip fell helplessly to his side. He had encountered headstrong fillies before, but never the two legged variety.

Francina bent down to examine the horse's quivering flanks, which were lacerated with rose thorns. 'And before you leave, Mr Wilson,' she hissed, brushing flies away from the seeping wounds, 'I suggest you have these cuts treated or they will become infected.'

6

The sky was a white-hot vault, suffocating everything in its path. Francina lay in her darkened room and willed the *punkah-wallah* to move the stifling air, but she was too fatigued to ask him to pull faster. She had been at Nudinapur for more than six weeks, and she was beginning to have the uncomfortable feeling that she might never leave. During the last few days she had hinted to Jane that she might have outstayed her welcome. 'You must not think of it, Fanny dear. I should be mortified if you left – and the children would miss you terribly.'

But if she did decide to leave, could she do so without an escort? Where would she go?

'Throw water, damn you!' boomed a voice through the depths of the house.

Her heart sank. The Master of Nudinapur had returned. For all his boastful trumpeting, even Mr Bulpitt could not subdue the power of the Indian sun. These days they had to endure his company for longer and longer spells. Like the brain-fever bird, he was another unwelcome consequence of the Hot Weather. At least they had not heard a whisper from Mr Wilson since his preposterous outburst. But like flies: you swat one, and another buzzes obnoxiously in its place.

She heaved herself up. She must take control, or she would become like every other European woman out here: a listless body on a couch.

In the bathroom, she threw cupfuls of brown water over her salt-encrusted shoulders and watched rivulets trickle down between her breasts and cross the tiled floor, taking with them flakes of skin and the odd hair.

Mr Bulpitt's voice resonated periodically through the house like a rumble of thunder – rebuking some poor servant, no doubt. But why don't the servants leave? She was quite certain they all despised him, and she could not believe that he paid them well. If he did, he certainly demanded his pound of flesh.

Some days ago she had come upon him thrashing a syce with a horsewhip. The man did not even raise an arm to defend himself - he just cowered like a wounded animal. That was what she had found so shocking. 'What on earth do you think you are doing, Mr Bulpitt!' she had shouted. Her boldness had astonished herself as much as it had him. He had stopped; his arm poised in the air, and stared shamefully at her, like a child caught in some forbidden act by his nurse. Then the hard glint returned to his eyes. 'I caught this ape stealing a sack of grain!' Giving the syce a kick in the ribs, he stormed away. She had stood her ground and watched him go, seething with anger. Another syce, who had been watching from the stable block, ran to help her pull him out of the sun. The poor man was very nearly unconscious. They propped him against the wall in the shade and gave him a drink of water. Flies gathered immediately, buzzing round the lacerations on his back and arms. She had run into the house, shouting to Jane to fetch the medical box, and had flinched when she saw Mr Bulpitt lounging on the verandah in a cane chair with his feet up, puffing a cigar. He raised his glass to her. She eyed him coldly as she waited for Jane, but he had only winked at her. She heard him chuckle as he watched them run outside with the medical box, as though he found this little display of feminine defiance rather entertaining.

A servant was letting down the mosquito net when she returned to the bedroom and she adjusted her robe. But he seemed unaware of her. He stepped outside onto the balcony and climbed the steep spiral staircase to the roof. In a few moments he would, like Mohammedans all over India, spread out his prayer mat towards the west, and prostrate himself before the setting sun.

Francina sat at the dressing table and shut her eyes as Sita brushed her hair. When she opened them again, Sita was staring quizzically at her in the glass. Francina touched her temples. 'I have a pain,' she explained in her limited Hindustani.

Sita put down the hairbrush and left the room. Francina watched her glide gracefully away, and a pang of guilt flowed over her. She was so preoccupied with her own misfortunes that it had not occurred to her until now that Sita probably felt as out of place here as she did. Although they could only communicate in simple language, she felt in a curious way they were kindred spirits. How did Sita feel coming to this part of the world, where (presumably) few of the other servants spoke her language? Had she made any friends? Where did she sleep? She was supposed to have a room in the servants' quarters (one of those little windowless rooms beyond the stable block) but Francina had never seen it.

Sita appeared some minutes later carrying a sweet-smelling substance in a small brass bowl. Setting it down, she scooped up some in her fingers and began to gently massage it into her temples. Francina shut her eyes.

She had kept a watch on the poor syce. She had cleansed his wounds with iodine and opium plasters (as she had seen Evangelina dress the rat bite of a servant at Moisgunge) and had tried to reduce his fever with wafers of willow bark. She learned, after a fashion, that his name was Sanjit, and that he came from a village nearby. Now she made a point of seeking him out as he groomed the horses in the stable block. Mr Bulpitt appeared to have forgotten about him, but even so, she was careful to make sure that he knew nothing about these charitable visits. As far as the *Burra Sahib* was concerned, the *soor* could have disappeared – or dropped dead.

Sita buttoned up her new taffeta gown. Little did Francina guess that this lovely gown that she had noticed the *darzi* quietly stitching over the last few weeks was for her. Her heart swelled with shame. She had misjudged Jane. The heat was weaving mischief in her head.

She turned to the cheval glass and caught her breath. For a fleeting moment she thought she had come face to face with Mamma - Mamma in her viridian gown and emerald earrings, leaning over her cot to kiss her goodnight and smelling so deliciously of jasmine. *Have you said your prayers, my darling?*

She bowed her head sheepishly. No, Mamma, not for several months. It did not seem appropriate to bring God into this house.

She gathered up her rustling skirts to make her way down to the drawing room. The attendant at the top of the stairs salaamed. She had the distinct feeling that all the servants of Nudinapur had heard of her act of compassion, for these days they seemed to make a point of acknowledging her.

Cold indifference had melted into warm accord.

The drawing room, like the rest of the house, was muffled in darkness, for the setting sun still carried a blistering potency. Jane was sitting on the sofa under the *punkah*, working by the light of an oil lamp. She looked up. 'Fanny, green suits you extraordinarily well.'

Francina smiled and twirled for her. 'It is a colour I have never worn before, although I remember that Mamma was very fond of it. Thank you, Jane. It is delightful. See how it glows in the lamplight!'

'Charming, quite charming!'

Her stomach contracted. Only now did she notice Mr Wilson playing chess with Mr Bulpitt in a dim corner beyond the pianoforte. They scraped back their chairs and stood up. Two *shikaris* announcing their presence from the *machan*.

Mr Wilson bowed stiffly, as though trying to remember long-forgotten manners. He had flattened his hair with pomade, and was wearing a white evening jacket. She had never seen him so clean. Perhaps Jane had hinted that a smarter approach might be more effective, for he had waxed his moustache to points that protruded either side of his face, giving him the illusion of a permanent grin. He obviously imagined that this spruced variation would have her swooning at his feet.

But how did he sneak into the house without her knowing? She glanced from Jane to Mr Bulpitt as it slowly dawned on her: this was no fleeting visit, but one that had been carefully planned. Was this why Jane was so insistent that she should wear this new gown tonight? She fell, stunned and betrayed, into an armchair to consider her next move.

The men returned to their game of chess and Jane returned to her needlework. Francina opened her workbasket and looked surreptitiously from one man to the other as they moved chess pieces across the board. She had never known either of them engaged in a thought-provoking activity before.

'Do you realise, Fanny, the barometer recorded 100° on the verandah this afternoon,' said Jane brightly. 'We ought to start up the thermantidote, but it is such a noisy contraption.'

Francina made an appropriate comment as she threaded a needle with pink silk for the jacket she was embroidering for Alice.

Soon servants began to pad across the verandah to roll up the *chiks* and light the sconces. The sun had set at last, and a warm current of air crept into the drawing room. Francina put down her work and stepped out to the verandah. She leaned against a pillar to stare at the deepening sky. At least she could trust the stars. They pulsed like constant friends in the firmament. She listened for a while to the high-pitched drone of the cicadas . . . but the sound of hooves kicking dust along the drive distracted her. Peering into the darkness, she followed a speck of light as it moved towards the stable block, and wondered who it was.

The spaniel growled aggressively, shot down the steps and bounded into the night.

Suddenly a terrifying noise filled the blackness – animals fighting to the death. Mr Bulpitt flew across the verandah and down the steps, waving his pistol above his head and shouting for his men. Servants, carrying lamps and brandishing sticks, eventually emerged from all corners of the house to help him.

Jane ran out to join Francina behind the pillar. 'Scamp,' she called, her voice quaking with fright. 'Scamp, come back here!'

The loud rapport of a pistol silenced the commotion.

'Scamp?' whispered Jane. 'Pray God nothing has happened to him.'

Suddenly a little black dog burst out of the darkness and shot up the steps, yelping pitifully. He rushed into the drawing room and dived under the floral shawl draped over the pianoforte. Only his quivering nose was visible. Jane ran after him.

'Are you hurt, my pet?' she asked, lifting up the shawl.

Mr Bulpitt stormed back into the house with his pistol cocked. 'Where's that dog!'

Jane leaned back against the pianoforte using her voluminous skirts as a protective shield. 'Do you mean Scamp?' she whispered.

The children ran into the room in their nightclothes. 'Mamma, Mamma, what's happened?' Francina took hold of their hands.

'Keep out of the way, children,' she said, keeping her voice calm.

'Scamp, yes Scamp!' spluttered Mr Bulpitt. 'He's been attacked by a rabid dog!'

Jane gasped. Alice burst into tears.

Freddie wrenched his hand away and dived under the pianoforte. 'Please don't shoot him, Papa!' he howled, throwing his arms round the whimpering dog.

'Come away from that animal before he infects you, young man!' shouted his father.

Mr Hopkirk burst into the room. Blood spattered his buff-coloured breeches. 'Sir! That dog you shot belonged to me. I can assure you he did *not* have rabies.'

'*Your* dog! Confound it, man, you know you must never bring dogs into the grounds!'

'I tied him up, but he slipped his rope and followed me,' said Mr Hopkirk. 'But he didn't have rabies – I'd swear my life on it.'

'Perhaps it was for the best,' smiled Jane, trying to restore some equilibrium to the evening. 'He was a scruffy thing you must admit, Mr Hopkirk. Children, stop crying! Scamp will not have to be put down after all. He was very brave to protect us from that horrid pariah dog.'

Alice crawled under the pianoforte to help her brother console their gallant little pet.

'Sit down, Mr Hopkirk. You look quite exhausted.' Jane unfolded a large ivory fan to cool her flushed face.

'Something strong to drink, old boy? I think we all deserve something strong after that.' Mr Bulpitt sank into a comfortable chair and signalled to the bearer. '*Raja's pegs! Jeldi, jeldi!*'

'Scamp's ear is bleeding, Mamma!' sobbed Alice from under the pianoforte.

'Is it?' said Jane wearily. 'Fanny, would you be a dear and fetch the medical box?'

A bearer helped her carry the medical box from the hunting gallery.

Sipping their drinks, the men watched her crouch down in her voluminous taffeta to coax Scamp out from under the pianoforte.

'Anyway,' said Mr Bulpitt, his voice tempered by a generous gulp of Spanish brandy and French champagne, 'what the deuce brought you over here at this hour, Hopkirk?'

The children held the trembling dog while Francina dabbed iodine on his torn ear.

'I thought you should hear the news at once, sir. Mungul Pandy has been hanged.'

'Excellent news!'

'Mungul Pandy?' asked Jane, looking at her husband.

'That drugged sepoy of the Thirty-Fourth. He incited the sepoys to mutiny at Barrackpore.'

'Not that cartridge nonsense again?'

'I'm afraid so, my dear.'

'Now children,' whispered Francina. 'Take Scamp away and give him lots of love. He has had a nasty fright tonight.'

The children scurried away with their reprieved pet before anyone could have a change of heart. Francina returned to her embroidery. It was a miracle she had not stained her new gown.

'I heard it from Mr Fraser, who has just returned from Cawnpore.' Mr Hopkirk sipped his drink with shaking hands.

'Let's hope this hanging teaches Jack Sepoy a lesson once and for all.' Mr Bulpitt stood up, stretched, and turned to Mr Wilson. 'After that little interruption, I think it's time we returned to our game of chess, don't you, old boy?'

Grunting approval, Mr Wilson joined him at the chess table.

'We've been far too lenient on 'em - that's the problem,' Mr Bulpitt said after a few moments of concentration. 'We've given in to their every little whim.' He moved a chess piece aggressively, as though he was sending a sepoy to the gallows.

'Too much time on their hands in my opinion,' observed Mr Wilson. 'Boredom, that's the trouble. Not enough wars to keep Jack Sepoy occupied. - Knight to castle!'

Mr Bulpitt stared at the chessboard in disbelief.

'You will dine with us, of course, Mr Hopkirk?' smiled Jane from the sofa.

Mr Hopkirk glanced down at his bloodstained clothes and across to Francina's shimmering taffeta.

'At the moment, I would not be good company. I hope you understand, Mrs Bulpitt?' He muttered something about having to dispose of the carcass before the jackals did . . . His voice trailed miserably away as he stood up to take his leave.

'Of course we understand, Mr Hopkirk,' smiled Jane generously.

'Ridiculous business,' muttered Mr Bulpitt when his assistant had scurried away. 'He deserved to have that animal shot. We're not living in some namby English shire. He knows how careful we have to be of rabies at this time of the year.'

'Checkmate!' shouted Mr Wilson, triumphantly.

Francina tied a knot and cut the silk thread, sensing that he would be glancing over to make sure that she was aware of his victory. She remained unmoved and unimpressed. In any case, she did not believe he had won fairly: this was all part of the plan to impress her with his mental prowess.

The *khansamah* announced dinner and Francina packed away her work.

Mr Wilson materialised like a powdered peacock before her. 'I'm pleased you like the gown, Miss Duquesne,' he said, exposing his blunt yellow teeth. 'I knew green would suit you. It's my favourite colour.'

7

She left the children playing dominoes in their underground schoolroom and stole though the darkened house, carefully avoiding the drawing room where she could hear Jane playing the piano (the less Jane knew of her movements, the better). She crossed the verandah, now screened by cotton-lined *chiks* that hung from ceiling to floor between the pillars, and tripped down the steps. The glare bounced off the iron-hard ground and hit her in the face. She narrowed her eyes and quickly crossed the drive before the sun had a chance to burn holes in the soles of her pumps.

Unlike the brooding atmosphere of the house, there was an air of tranquillity about the stable block. She shyly acknowledged the stable-*wallahs,* who led her to Sanjit who was dozing on some jute sacking in one of the stalls. One of them kicked him playfully, and he jumped up apologetically.

'How are you today, Sanjit?' Although she had learned a few words of the local language, their conversation was generally accompanied on both sides with a great deal of sign language.

'Good now, Miss-Sahib.' His dark eyes had lost their dull feverish look. Today they sparkled with wellbeing.

As usual, a row of grinning faces quickly gathered at the stall to follow the Miss-Sahib's daily medical inspection. Sanjit did not seem to mind this lack of privacy. He had become the celebrity of the stable block.

'No more fever?'

'Gone.'

'Show me,' she said indicating his wounds.

Sanjit lifted up his white shirt and turned his back towards her. She stepped forward to examine it. The pattern criss-crossing his backbone had over the days gradually turned from weeping lurid pink to black encrusted scars. She took out the bottle of liniment from her pocket, uncorked it and delicately swabbed the cuts with a clean pad of cotton lint. He had stopped wincing with pain now.

'Are you rubbing in the ointment as I showed you?'

He rolled up his sleeves and stretched out brown sinewy arms. 'Good, Miss-Sahib.'

She returned his smile. 'Yes, very good.'

She truly believed that if she had not cleaned up his wounds and reduced his fever, he would have contracted lockjaw or some other deadly infection. The medical inspection over, Francina edged back through the crowd of stable-*wallahs*. She had not noticed before that Mr Hopkirk's pony was tethered in one of the stalls. She hurried into the house, following the sound of a much-practised Chopin Nocturne, to the dim drawing room.

Why was she surprised to find Mr Hopkirk standing by the pianoforte turning Jane's sheet music? Her first instinct was to leave, but that might look as though she suspected something, so she sat under the punkah and took up her sewing.

Shortly afterwards, Mr Bulpitt burst into the room, hot and covered in dust.

'Have you heard the latest, Hopkirk?' He sank heavily into a chair. A cloud of dust rose from his jacket and settled on the floor. His hair was matted, and a line of dust marked the line across his forehead where his *topee* had lodged. 'There's to be a court martial in Meerut. Some native regiments are refusing to take the cartridge.'

Mr Hopkirk shuffled uncomfortably. He looked like a rabbit caught in a snare. 'But I understood that the paper wrapping need no longer be bitten off, but can be torn off by hand?' he said as loudly as he dared. It was not in his nature to shout during a piano recital. (The Mistress of Nudinapur played on. She was used to her husband's interruptions.)

'They now believe that there is something wrong with the paper - that its glazed appearance is a result of greasing.' Mr Bulpitt wiped his face with a large handkerchief, smearing red dust across his forehead. 'I met Wilson by the canal. He told me the news. I tell you, someone is spreading malicious rumours.'

'Unfortunately, once these suspicions spread, they take on a momentum of their own –'

'The page, Mr Hopkirk, please turn the page!' called Jane.

Mr Hopkirk quickly complied, and continued, 'Any incident that offends religion - and in this case both the Mohammedan and the

Hindu religions – must be treated with the utmost sensitivity and tact.'

Mr Bulpitt snorted. 'Sensitivity and tact! My dear young fellow, forgive me for being blunt - but *you* are a newcomer to this country. I know these natives. I know their wily ways. We have fallen over backwards to accommodate their idiosyncrasies. Fewer troops in the world are more indulged than these native armies! (The louder her husband shouted, the more passionately Jane struck the keys.) They are lauded in general orders and - without any application on their part - have their pay and allowances increased. It is no wonder they have such an inflated opinion of themselves. *Stop* that confounded racket, woman! I can't hear myself think!'

Jane stopped mid-note and stared at the piano keys with her head bowed, saying nothing. Mr Hopkirk stood limply at her side, as though hit over the head with a cricket bat.

Francina rolled up her work and stood up. Staring icily at Mr Bulpitt, she professed a headache and left the room. She did not know how else to register her disapproval. Jane remained motionless at the piano, a picture of crumpled despair.

The heat and lack of exercise was making her fall into a stupor. She stared at herself in the glass. Her skin looked sallow and pasty; there were deep shadows under her eyes. She had pulled her hair back rather severely, but these days she took little interest in dressing up. It would only encourage Mr Wilson if she prettified herself. He had spoiled one of her few remaining pleasures.

She sat under the punkah, having discarded as many clothes as was decently possible (there was nothing more she could do to keep cool), and dipped her pen into the inkwell. It was so hard to write letters these days; each day melted indistinguishably into another, so that it was difficult to remember what had happened yesterday, because nothing had happened yesterday. But she must write a few lines to Louisa, however dull, if she was to catch the *dâk-ghari* that would leave Cawnpore in a few days' time. She had waited as long as possible, in the hope of receiving a letter from Henry Fetherstone, but the *dâk* from Delhi was late, so this mail there was nothing to forward to Louisa. And she must be careful not to say anything that might make her anxious, but rumours were circulating. Something had happened at Meerut. The telegraph wires had been cut so it was impossible to ascertain exactly what. And now, it was feared, a similar disturbance had occurred in Delhi. But what kind of a disturbance? 'It is too far away to trouble your pretty little head about,' Mr Bulpitt had said, cleaning his pistols.

There was a rush of wheels on the drive. The dog barked. She tied up her peignoir and stepped on to her verandah. Shielding her eyes against the sun, she hid behind a pillar and pulled the *chits* to one side. A carriage and carts and the usual entourage of banghy-bearers weighed down with luggage were snaking round the drive and congregating under the porte cochère. Judging by the number of attendants and the amount of baggage, whoever had arrived planned to stay for more than a few days.

She heard boys' voices whooping through the house, and recognised the Mackenzie twins. Why had Jane not warned her that the Mackenzies were expected today? She returned to her room and dressed quickly. At least with the Mackenzies and their attendants filling up the house, there would be less opportunity for Mr Wilson to ambush her in a secluded corner.

To her surprise, the company in the drawing room was unusually subdued. Mr Wilson bowed from across the floor, but made no attempt to harass her. He was behaving with unexpected civility these days, but she trusted this new, spruced version even less than she did the old one.

'Have you not heard, Miss Duquesne?' Mrs Mackenzie whispered breathlessly as they filed into the dining room. 'All the principal military stations in the North West have been in open mutiny. The sepoys of more than thirty regiments have risen against their European officers.'

'What do you mean, Mrs Mackenzie?'

'Delhi has been sacked, and every European murdered in cold blood. Churches have been burnt down, the Treasury broken into –'

'Every European?'

'As far as we can tell. Every man, woman and child. Communications have been cut –'

Mrs Mackenzie stopped talking as a *khitmutgar* came between them with a platter of chicken curry. She helped herself in silence. Francina glanced round the room. She knew by their expressions that the Nudinapur servants had heard this news. Mrs Mackenzie's servants were the latest link in the mysterious Indian grapevine. But *everyone?* The Clapperton girls were joining their father in Delhi . . . was it really possible that those two innocent girls could have had their lives snuffed out by a group of mutinous sepoys? And what of the other passengers from the *Hindustan*? So many were heading for the Northern Provinces . . .

'And Meerut?' Francina asked, when there was no risk of them being overheard. Blood pounded in her ears.

'We believe that several British officers, their wives and children have been slaughtered –'

'But are there not European troops stationed up there?'

'Not enough to overcome the sepoys, apparently.'

Francina sat rigid with fear. In her mind's eye she saw Henry Fetherstone felled from behind in one stroke by a blood-crazed sepoy as he sat at his desk; his smiling head bouncing across the stone floor like a red croquet ball. But wait! Henry was not stationed in either of those places. Mhorabad was half way between the two – and it was not a military station, but a civil station. She clasped her hands tightly together so that no one (but especially the servants) would see them shaking as she recited a silent prayer.

'What about the civil stations?' she whispered.

'What do you mean, Miss Duquesne?'

'Have the civil stations escaped the massacre? You see, I have a friend . . .' She bit her lip, unable to say more, in case she broke down and exposed her vulnerability to the servants.

Mr Mackenzie leaned across and said kindly, 'Miss Duquesne, do not alarm yourself. We can contain this outbreak. It is, admittedly, the most disturbing outbreak there has been, but communications are being restored. The best thing we can do is to behave as though nothing has happened. We must not show the natives that we are in any way alarmed. We must not show fear, Miss Duquesne. And we certainly have nothing to fear in Cawnpore. General Wheeler is quite adamant on that score. He trusts his men implicitly. And he has always been on excellent terms with the Maharajah of Bithur.'

'Do you mean Nana Sahib?' whispered Jane.

'He prefers the more flattering title of Maharajah. I always address him as Maharajah. Flattery is a small price to pay to keep him on our side.' Mr Mackenzie gave a small, superior smile. 'I have always found him extremely courteous – as is his spokesman Azimullah Kahn.'

'Yes, he is charming, quite charming,' added his wife, cheering up a little, 'with an excellent command of French and English.'

'The Maharajah has always shown a lively interest in the proceedings of our Government and in our arts and customs, and he always has a kind word for every sahib he meets in the station.'

Everyone around the table let out a collective sigh of relief. No one so cultured, so familiar with the British way of life and the British code of justice, could possibly be a turncoat.

'And he entertains most lavishly,' said Mrs Mackenzie, 'although his idea of good taste is quite amusing. Did you know that at one of his grand dinners, his guests were served soup in a *trifle* dish!'

Everyone laughed heartily. It would demonstrate to those standing in silence that they were not afraid of a few sepoys in the Upper Provinces who had lost their heads and gone berserk.

'Unfortunately, he has always refused to be entertained in return – so he has never seen how it should be properly done. Apparently it is because the Government will not allow him the compliment of a salute.'

'But why not?' asked Francina, breathing more easily now.

'Well, he's hardly a royal personage,' said Mr Mackenzie. 'He's only the adopted son of the last Peshawar of Poona – the son of an impoverished corn merchant, so they say.'

'I've heard that Lady Wheeler is of the same caste as the Maharajah,' added Mr Wilson.

'That at least is in her favour,' sniffed Mrs Mackenzie.

'According to the Collector (and he probably knows the Maharajah better than any other European in Cawnpore), the Maharajah regards the outbreaks as *most regrettable*. The Maharajah even offered his home as a refuge for his Collector's wife and children.' (Mr Mackenzie was always ready to show his superior connections.) 'No, Mrs Bulpitt. We can safely say that the worst of the storm is past. We have nothing to fear in Cawnpore.'

'But those disturbances in the city? The fires in the infantry lines? There are thousands of sepoys stationed in Cawnpore and only a handful of European troops and officers -'

'Nothing more than isolated outbreaks, Mrs Bulpitt,' Mr Mackenzie waved his hand dismissively, 'which have been quickly brought under control. Sir Henry Lawrence has sent down a few European troops from Lucknow, but it is merely window dressing. Rest assured, General Wheeler is qualified to deal with any local trouble. Remember, he is a soldier of fifty years' experience, liked and respected by all his men. We are fortunate to have such an experienced leader in our midst.'

Mr Mackenzie's words of reassurance began to put everyone at their ease, and the conversation gradually shifted from the military and political to the social and economic – until his wife burst out, 'But to see all those vehicles discharging that multitude into the entrenchment - it was so degrading.' Mrs Mackenzie was struggling to keep her composure.

Francina glanced at the servants to see if they might understand what she was saying. It only needed one of them to have a vague grasp of English to relay this conversation to the others.

'What entrenchment?' she could not help asking. Why did everyone around this table know so much more than she did? Why was she always kept in the dark?

'An earth wall has been thrown up around the barracks at Cawnpore, enclosing an area of about nine acres – which can be defended by cannon and pounders in the unlikely event of a sepoy attack. But I stress, Miss Duquesne, it is extremely unlikely.'

'However, I do question General Wheeler's judgement in fortifying the barracks,' said Mr Bulpitt, shaking his head. 'It would have been wiser to have fortified the magazine.'

'General Wheeler clearly does not expect danger,' Mr Mackenzie gave Francina an encouraging smile, 'if he believed otherwise, he would have moved his wife and family into the entrenchment.'

Mr Wilson leaned towards her and whispered. 'You must come and stay at Wilsonghur, Miss Duquesne. It is as solid as a fortress. You could not be safer in Windsor Castle.'

For a wild moment she wanted desperately to believe him. She toyed with her food, shifting it from one side of her plate to the other, but she had no appetite. Perhaps no one else did either; they were just making a show of being unconcerned.

After tiffin, she joined Jane and Mrs Mackenzie on the settee under the swaying *punkah*. She felt the need to be close to her own kind. The *kus-kus tatties* were down, and the drawing room lighted by candles. The men stood by the piano, conversing in low tones as they puffed on their cigars. Their conspiratorial postures unnerved her and she was pleased to hear the children playing in the nursery – their boisterous voices restored a sense of normality to the atmosphere.

Mrs Mackenzie whispered behind her fan, 'You cannot imagine how degrading it looked – the vulgarity of having to live in full view of society. Families grouped together all day long; working and eating at long tables . . . a soldier's family sleeping next to an officer's family. I would rather chance my luck in Umritpur than live in that entrenchment. Why, oh why did I not take my children to England before the Hot Weather!'

'My dear Mrs Mackenzie,' Jane said, patting her hand. 'You must stay with us. We would not hear of you returning to Umritpur, would we, Frederick?'

'Would we - what, my dear?'

'I was telling Mrs Mackenzie that she must stay with us until the trouble dies down.'

'Indeed. Stay – all of you!' Mr Bulpitt stretched out his arms to encompass everyone. 'There is plenty of room.'

'You are so kind, so kind.' Mrs Mackenzie fingered the cameo at her neck. She was shaking with relief. 'It is not for me, of course, but my dear boys . . . I could not bear -'

'Hush, Mrs Mackenzie,' smiled Jane. 'We must not let our imaginations run wild. No one will bother us in this backwater. In a few weeks' time, when this horrid crisis is over, we shall look back and wonder why we were all so anxious.'

Later in her room, Francina finished her letter. There was so much she wanted to write, so much she wanted to tell Louisa, but she must not say anything that could frighten her.

Adieu, adieu, dearest Lulu. How I long to see you again. I pray that one day my wish will be granted. Please give my love and affection to Uncle and Aunt Doré, Sammy, all my Aunts and Cousins – and of course Cook, Baptiste and Ellie - and everyone else who remembers me!

I remain as always, your affectionate and loving cousin, Ina

8

The scent of flowers and of newly watered earth drifted in though her open windows. The evening seemed unexpectedly cool after the crushing heat of the day. Her bathe had refreshed her. For a short while at least that stab of anxiety would be subdued.

Voices floated up. People were beginning to congregate on the verandah below her room. Perhaps it was not so disagreeable to have a full house: Mr Wilson might be distracted by requests to play billiards and Jane could ramble on to her heart's content about the problems of her servants to a more sympathetic pair of ears. She sat at her dressing table and let Sita brush her hair in long even strokes. This evening she would allow her to braid and twist it as she liked. Why fight the inevitable?

'Not this dress, Sita,' she said, throwing the green taffeta off her bed. 'That one!' She pointed to her oscillating pink and blue gown hanging on the hook. She would challenge fate, laugh in her face. Whatever Providence had prescribed would happen, whether she wore her most uninspiring or her most provocative outfit.

She heard Mr Bulpitt's hearty laugh as she descended the stairs to the drawing room. Someone, no doubt, had cracked a joke at the expense of the ruled illiterate. Well, at least that was one joke she had managed to avoid.

'More *simkin* for the ladies! And brandy for our guests!' she heard him shout.

Jane must have heard her approaching, for she burst through the bead curtain to meet her in the drawing room, her eyes shining.

'Come out quickly, Fanny. Come and meet our new visitor!'

New visitor? Francina caught her excitement. New visitors brought fresh air, novelty; anecdotes on the outside world to enliven the flagging conversation. And this visitor was obviously not the harbinger of bad news. She followed Jane out to the verandah.

Was she dreaming?

He was leaning against a pillar smoking a cheroot, deep in

conversation with Mr Bulpitt. Silhouetted against the last rosy glow of daylight, he looked so fine, so vital next to the bloated older man. She clutched the back of a chair to steady herself.

'Fanny, my dear, let me introduce you to the new Assistant Collector of Kandria.' Mr Bulpitt drained his glass, as his wife coaxed her forward.

'Mr Lihou has heard of my husband's reputation,' laughed Jane, taking her arm. 'No one is permitted to pass within ten miles of Nudinapur without calling on us. Frederick would be very offended if anyone tried such a thing!'

Gilbert Lihou's eyes opened wide with incredulity. 'What are you doing here?'

'Mrs Bulpitt is my cousin,' she said, catching her breath. There was no denying it: life on the Indian plains suited him very well.

'Fetherstone told me when he sent me Mrs Barton's card, but never for a moment expected -'

'Neither did I.'

'Are you two acquainted with one another?' Jane asked in astonishment.

'We knew each other in Guernsey.'

Jane clapped her hands together. 'How perfectly delightful!'

All other conversations ceased. Mr Wilson watched closely.

'And which of these gentlemen is your betrothed, Miss Duquesne?'

The question reverberated down the verandah. Eventually the reply came back like an answering peel of bells. 'I am not attached to any of them.'

'But I thought -'

Mr Wilson was advancing like a bull elephant eyeing up a rival: trunk raised, ears flapping. This time there would be no misunderstanding. 'I have *never* been attached - to anyone,' she said.

'Not through want of anyone trying!' snorted Mr Bulpitt. 'She's a fiery little filly! Keeps 'm all at arm's length.'

Everyone laughed – everyone except Mr Wilson.

'Have you heard from Mr Fetherstone recently,' Francina asked, her ears burning, 'in view of these dreadful reports coming out of Meerut and Delhi?'

The young bull took no notice of the rogue elephant rearing in the background. 'I received a *chit* from him a few weeks ago. He was working in the *mofussil,* well away from any trouble. He's probably sleeping under a tree blissfully unaware of what is going on around him. As soon as the telegraph is restored, we shall have news of him.'

She smiled with relief. 'Yes, I am sure we shall.'

She was about to ask why he had been so secretive about his appointment at Aunt Barton's *burra khana,* when Jane pushed her aside to ply him with questions of her own. Soon everyone, including Mr Wilson, had gathered to besiege the new Assistant Collector of Kandria with questions.

Francina slipped away. She would save her questions for a quieter moment. She leaned against a pillar and stared into the gathering darkness while Jane led the questions in her beguiling way. She heard that he was discovered camping some five miles away, acquainting himself with his new responsibilities, and had been persuaded by Mr Bulpitt to erect his tent in Nudinapur's grounds. She also learned that his district was small in comparison to others, but nevertheless, it was an area of well over eight hundred square miles.

The *khansamah* announced dinner.

'Now, Mr Lihou, you must sit by me, and tell me all about yourself!' said Jane.

Gilbert Lihou bowed. Smiling coquettishly, Jane accepted his arm, and led her guests into the dining room.

'May I escort you, Miss Duquesne?' Against his white jacket, Mr Wilson's teeth looked even more stained than usual. Yesterday she hated him. Today she despised him.

'I understand you have taken over Mr Massey's bungalow, Mr Lihou - the one close to the *cutcherry* and jailhouse,' said Jane brightly when the guests were seated and the soup handed round. Much to Francina's disappointment, Jane had placed her between Mr Wilson and Mr Mackenzie. 'I remember Mr Massey as a quiet little man, quite unsuited to life on the Indian plains. I was not at all surprised to learn that he had retired early through ill health. Is his bungalow comfortable?'

Gilbert Lihou shrugged. 'Comfort – or the lack of comfort - is of no importance to me, Mrs Bulpitt. The bungalow is just a place where I occasionally rest my head. I am generally in the saddle by five and on the move until nightfall. I sleep under canvas wherever I find myself.'

Francina studied the jewels of fat lapping the gold rim of her soup bowl while she listened to Jane beleaguering him with her silly questions. She loved Jane, of course she did, but at this moment she saw her though his eyes and she saw a woman dulled by domesticity, a mind stupefied by isolation. She saw them all - the whole miserable uncouth lot of them - through Gilbert Lihou's eyes.

'Personal government is the only form of rule the people understand, so I must present myself constantly to them, deciding cases either sitting on horseback at the village gate, or under a tree outside the village walls,' he was saying to his hostess. Work completed, he would remount his horse and repeat the process in the next village. 'Sun, rain – the weather is a matter of indifference to me.'

'It is just as well that you are constantly on the move, Mr Lihou,' laughed Jane. 'There are so few amusements to be found in Kandria. It's such a dull little station.'

Mr Wilson's breathy words were brushing across her cheek. Francina leaned away as far she dared. She was sick of listening to his clumsy prostrations. Why did Jane always place her next to him at dinner? Tonight of all nights. His hand was creeping under the table. She gave him a savage nip, digging her nails into his flesh as hard as she could. He sucked in his breath and withdrew his hand to examine the red marks on his knuckles.

'Little vixen,' he smiled. 'I like vixens with spirit.'

She screamed silently. Was there nothing she could do to deter this oaf? His coarse manners, his musty smell, his bloated red face – he had never looked more repulsive than he did tonight. If Gilbert Lihou's presence served nothing else, then it had pulled her up sharp. She would *never* accept Mr Wilson – even if he were the last man on earth.

She glanced up. Gilbert was watching their silent skirmish across the table. She pushed her chair away, turned her back on Mr Wilson and leaned forward to listen to the conversation across the table. Let everyone in this room know that Miss Duquesne was being harassed by the Cockroach of Wilsonghur.

She threw in a question now and then to turn Gilbert Lihou's attention towards her, but whenever she did, Jane intercepted with another. She was beginning to realise that it was going to be impossible to speak to him in private. Jane would always be present, always ready to monopolise the unattached or interesting man. As Mistress of Nudinapur that was her prerogative. Francina's only purpose was to add a degree of respectability to her flirtations.

'We must be partly to blame for these incidents. We have become too detached from our subjects. In such a climate, mistrust and dissent festers,' he was saying. 'We must encourage more communication, more interaction between the ruled and the rulers – and I speak of both sexes - so that rumours can be quelled before they grow out of hand.'

On the wall behind him, the bacchanalian revellers cavorted unperturbed in their woodland glade

'But it is impossible to have closer communications when native ladies are kept apart,' sighed Mrs Mackenzie. 'It places us ladies in a difficult position, for if we attend feasts or *nautches,* we are automatically seen by the natives as - how can I phrase it - *loose*. And as for *zenana* visiting! What a nonsense that is, trying to conduct a conversation in sign language.'

'Perhaps we should learn their language?' suggested Francina.

'Learn their language!' roared Mr Bulpitt. 'Which language? My dear girl, do you realise how many languages exist in this country?'

'It would be more sensible for them to learn *our* language,' trumpeted the rogue elephant behind her back. 'English should become the universal language of India.'

'I instruct my servants in English. I would never trouble myself to learn a native language,' sniffed Mrs Mackenzie. 'I am told that the Hindustani language is particularly rich in terms of abuse. I have no desire to hear or understand their profanities.'

She was fond of demonstrating her refinements to all and sundry.

'Then you are at the mercy of your servants. How do you know if they are speaking disrespectfully to you?' said Gilbert Lihou.

'I would know,' Mrs Mackenzie said coldly. 'One does not have to understand their language to know when one's servants are being insubordinate.'

'Besides, was it not Mr Macaulay who said that modern Indian languages are not worth learning, that they are all just rude dialects of Sanskrit?' said Mr Mackenzie.

'And was it not Macaulay who also said that if all the historical information were collected from all the books written in the Sanskrit language, it would hardly equate to the value found in the most paltry abridgements found in any English preparatory school today?' Mr Wilson smiled smugly. He would show that conceited cub that he was no ignoramus.

'Here, here!' boomed Mr Bulpitt.

Mr Wilson raised his glass. 'I put it to you, ladies and gentlemen, that one single shelf of a good pupil's library is worth more the whole native literature of India and Arabia put together!'

'Do you read Sanskrit?' asked Gilbert Lihou.

'Do I - what?' said Mr Wilson.

'Do you read Sanskrit, sir?'

'No, of course not.' The impudent puppy.

'Well, I do, sir. I have studied the language closely for several years, and from my experience, I suggest that Mr Macaulay is badly informed. Sanskrit is one of the oldest, most beautiful languages in the world. It was carved in stone long before the English had the merest hint of a written language.'

Mr Wilson's face turn purple with indignation.

'And as for the native literature of India and Arabia being of no value,' continued Gilbert Lihou, 'I suggest it is of immeasurable value. Since ancient times, far reaching philosophical writings have passed from India and Arabia to Greece, which in turn, some thinkers believe, have provided the basic foundations of our own philosophical ideas. In other words, our cultural heritage owes its very existence to the native literature of India.'

No one said a word. The air had become very close.

Mrs Mackenzie was vigorously fanning herself.

'No wonder,' she exclaimed. 'The *punkah* has stopped.'

Everyone looked up. The *punkah* was as still as a sheet of glass.

'*Koi hai*!' shouted Mr Bulpitt. '*Punkah-wallah*!'

The punkah remained motionless.

Mr Bulpitt drained his glass and rose unsteadily to his feet.

'It's about time that brute was taught a lesson!'

'Frederick,' whimpered Jane, 'please send the *khansamah*. It really isn't worth -'

'Hold your tongue, woman! If you want something done in this house, you have to kick it into the lazy devils!'

There was a rush of conversation as everyone tried to divert attention from the embarrassing sight of Mr Bulpitt stumbling across the room and launching himself into the blackness of the verandah. The sound of thumps and whimpers, interspersed with the roar of abusive epithets, rose above the conversation. Mrs Mackenzie glanced around uneasily and burst into a fit of nervous giggles. Francina grew sick with anger and shame. The *khitmutgars* remained motionless behind the chairs, but she could sense their hatred rising like a deadly barricade around them. Not for the first time did she see herself – and the whole Albion race - from their point of view.

Gilbert Lihou rose from his seat.

'I advise you not to interfere in another man's affairs,' said Mr Wilson.

Gilbert Lihou ignored him. He burst into the blackness. 'That's quite enough, sir!' she heard him say.

'What confounded business is it of yours?'

'I assure you, sir, it is very much my business.' Gilbert Lihou thrust his head back into the dining room. 'Miss Duquesne, fetch a lamp quickly!'

Francina picked a candelabrum off the table and ran outside with it. She knelt beside him and held up the lamp so he could inspect the *punkah-wallah's* injuries. The old man was clutching his stomach, whimpering. The gash across his forehead was bleeding profusely.

'Puh! Learn their language? That's the only language they understand!' roared Mr Bulpitt, swaying drunkenly from one leg to the other.

'He's been badly cut,' said Gilbert Lihou. 'Quick, fetch the medical box!'

She dashed through the dining room to the hunting gallery and returned with the medical box. The diners sat around the table, mute. Mrs Mackenzie was nervously twisting the rings on her fingers. Everyone could see that the box was difficult to manage, but it was the young *khitmutgar* who helped her carry it out to the verandah.

Francina moistened her table napkin with iodine and gently dabbed at the old man's injuries until they had stopped bleeding. The old man winced and whimpered. He was pitifully thin. He could have put up little defence against his master's boot.

'You're a guest in my house!' spluttered Mr Bulpitt, propping up a pillar. 'How dare you tell me how I should treat my servants!'

'I am the Assistant Magistrate. It is my duty to administer the laws in this district. If you harm this man again, sir, I shall have no option but to arrest you for assault.'

The Master of Nudinapur sneered.

'My dear young fellow, there is no need for that. You will soon discover that business is conducted differently in this part of the world. *Baksheesh*? Is that what you want? Something to make life more comfortable in that drab little bungalow of yours?'

'While I am stationed here, no one in my district will be above the law - I repeat, *no one*. And I will never condone bribery from any quarter.'

Muttering profanities, Mr Bulpitt staggered back into the dining room. 'Boy, more brandy!'

They were alone on the verandah, kneeling beside the *punkah-wallah*.

He looked at her. 'Thank you, Miss Duquesne. You did well.'

She smiled and lowered her eyes. Only now did she notice that her beautiful gown was stained with blood.

'I'm sorry,' he said.

Mr Wilson was silhouetted in the doorway watching them. Gilbert Lihou helped her to her feet. Squeezing past Mr Wilson, they returned to the dining room.

After a few minutes the *punkah* flapped back to life like a huge menacing vulture.

'Will you excuse me,' Francina said to Jane. 'The excitement has given me a headache . . .'

'Of course, my dear,' smiled Jane. 'Would you like the *khitmutgar* to bring you up a nightcap?'

She lay fully dressed on her bed in the darkness. Gilbert Lihou's presence had made her doubly ashamed of her relatives. During Mr

Bulpitt's outburst, she had caught him eyeing them as a visitor might scrutinise animals in a zoo. *Miss Duquesne's relatives are nothing more than a troupe of wild savages,* he will write in his next letter to Mrs Lihou. *Living out here, divorced from civilisation, they have lost all sense of decent behaviour. If Mrs Doré had the slightest inkling of the sort of influences her niece would be subjected to in India, she would never have allowed her to leave Guernsey.*

She could picture the smirk on Mrs Lihou's face when she receives his letter. By nightfall, everyone in St Pierre would know that Miss Duquesne had turned into a savage.

There was a flurry of movement downstairs. Footsteps were gravitating towards the drawing room. Presently, musical notes floated up to her balcony as someone ran their fingers along the piano keys. Amid drunken guffaws, Jane begin to sing:

How sweet I roam'd from field to field,
And tasted all the summer's pride,
Till I the prince of love beheld,
Who in the sunny beams did glide!

He shew'd me lilies for my hair,
And blushing roses for my brow;
He led me through his gardens fair,
Where all his golden pleasures grow.

With sweet May dews my wings were wet,
And Phoebus fir'd my vocal rage;
He caught me in his silken net,
And shut me in his golden cage.

He loves to sit and hear me sing,
Then, laughing, sports and plays with me;
Then stretches out my golden wing,
And mocks my loss of liberty.

She held the pillow over her ears to muffle the sound. But how could she sleep, knowing that he was downstairs? The music had stopped; the noises from the drawing room had become murmurs.

She stepped onto the balcony and watched stars explode across the firmament. The constellations were dazzling. She ran her fingers over the rough stone, still warm from the day's heat, and tried to make sense of the dark swirling shapes, the bushes, paths and flowerbeds that had been swallowed by the Indian night. Darkness wrapped itself round her, hot and heavy with the scent of flowers, but offered no solace.

She listened to the drone of the cicadas; then the long, plaintive note of a pariah dog scavenging somewhere down by the nullah - each soulful cry hung and quivered in the darkness, and pierced her caged soul. She wished he had not come. She wanted him to remember her as she was in Calcutta, vivacious and sparking and free. She wiped away a tear, but she was too numb to cry. She just wanted to be left alone to bury herself in this wilderness.

A strange little wail, coming from the direction of the servants' quarters, seemed to capture her mood. Of course, it was the *mali*'s new infant. Was it hungry? Perhaps she should find some food to give to its mother. But then she remembered: the *mali* was a Brahmin, the highest caste of Hindu. His family would rather the baby died than let its mother eat food contaminated by her hand. She put her head in her hands. She was of no consequence to anyone – not even the gardener's family.

She heard another sound . . . Someone was crossing the flat roof above her head. She stood still, alert as a wild cat. This was no servant. This trespasser was wearing shoes.

The footsteps stopped. Someone was leaning over the parapet wall, directly above her head, smoking. A white sleeve loomed through the darkness and wiped the star-studded canopy. Red embers glowed, fell like shooting stars and disappeared.

The footsteps started again, turned direction, and began to descend the winding flight to her balcony. She slipped into her room and silently barred the *jilmils*. The last thing she wanted at this hour was to fight off the drunken affirmations of Mr Wilson.

Hairs rose on the back of her neck as the footsteps came closer . . . They were just outside her window. She caught the smell of tobacco, a familiar mollifying smell that once -

Her heart leapt into her mouth. Could it be? She lay on her bed drenched in sweat, and tried to think rationally. A moonlit shadow brushed across the *jilmils*. He was pacing outside her windows just six feet away, only separated from her by thin slivers of wood.

She removed her slippers, padded across the floor, unlatched the venetians and - oh, so silently - peeped out. He was leaning over the balcony staring into the darkness; his head and shoulders steeped in moonlight, his body flexed as a coiled spring. He could be a leopard stalking an animal that was foraging in the garden - except -

Except that she was watching him.

Keeping the *jilmils* ajar, she tiptoed to the dressing table and lit the lamp. The light would catch his eye; lure him to her window . . . .

She was a spider, artful and focused, spinning a web in a dream where time stood still. She unbuttoned her bodice, stepped out of her skirts and unhooked her stays. *Loosening her fragrant bodice by degrees, her rich attire creeps rustling to her knees.*

In dreams hooks and buttons would fall effortlessly away, but now each action seemed to take as long as an hour for her fingers trembled so much . . . But she must behave as calmly and as naturally as possible, without the faintest hint of inhibition. He must believe that she had absolutely no inkling that he was out there.

Her heart was racing; her breath coming in short, fast starts - she listened, her senses acute and finely tuned; listened for the slightest sound that would tell her that he was out there, watching her.

The trap was set, the air so thick she could hardly wade through it. Crossing the floor, she caught sight of herself in the cheval glass and stopped to undo her hair. Half-closing her eyes, she played provocatively to her reflection, raised her arms to feel for hairpins which she stuffed, one by one, into her mouth. The band of sweat-crumpled cotton across her torso had left the imprint of her stays and she shivered, for the sweat was turning chill. She saw herself as he must see her: dishevelled, déshabillé. The image was not disagreeable. She could be a woodland sprite - but she was more like a sea-nymph, damp and encrusted with sun-dried salt. *A mermaid in sea-weed.*

She waited, poised at the centre of her web.

The gossamer vibrated. Her heart was racing. His presence was palpable. The aroma of tobacco grew stronger. It seeped through the venetians - a silent, seductive palliative sent to give her courage. Shutting her eyes, she shook her hair loose and a hairpin dropped lightly to the floor. But she would not to stoop to pick it up, for she must move with the grace of a dancer, each step carefully choreographed. She positioned her foot on a stool, directly in his line of vision and slowly began to roll down a stocking. First one then the other -

The curtains parted and Sita burst into her room carrying a tray.

All her courage and resolve, enmeshed in those silken strands, vanished into the night, and she collapsed on to her bed in shame.

9

The air was still, the afternoon sun merciless. Even in her darkened room everything seemed weighed down by the heat. Shards of light found their way through the *jilmils,* scattering violent gashes across the floor. There was not a sound to be heard - beyond the creaks of the *punkah* and screams of the brain-fever bird. It was stifling, unbearably hot. Her skin was on fire. She had sponged herself in brown filtered water, but felt no cooler. Sweat was seeping through her skin again. Her sheet was soaked. It was impossible to sleep. Each time she was about to doze off, that infuriating bird would wake her with its monotonous elegy. Perhaps she should suggest that Mr Bulpitt set his guns on it . . .

'*Brain-fever! Brain-fever! Brain-fever!*' screamed the bird.

She rose from her siesta as restlessly as she had retired. What was he doing at this moment? Had he returned to his tent? If only the walls of her room could fall away, if only she could see beyond the trees and through the canvas of his tent. She had seen inside his tent. She had gone with Jane and Mrs Mackenzie to inspect it on their early morning ride, although she had tried to dissuade them from the idea. 'But he is a guest on Nudinapur soil. It is my duty to see that he is comfortable,' Jane had said. Thankfully, he had left to attend to his duties, but they had peeped through the canvas opening, much to the astonishment of his servant. It was small, just large enough to take a *charpoy,* a table and camp chair; the kitchen was assembled under a tree. This was how he lived from week to week, ready to move at a moment's notice.

She put on her coolest printed muslin, picked up a sketchbook and her pastels and made her way downstairs. She had taken to arming herself with her drawing equipment – it gave her an occupation, an excuse to distance herself from everyone without appearing overtly rude (reading was impossible in a room full of loud, inconsequential chatter).

After tea, Jane and Mrs Mackenzie returned to their game of

cards, and the men retreated to an underground room to play billiards. For a short while at least, she would not be pestered.

'Sketch in here, Fanny,' Jane called from the drawing room. 'Then we can talk to you while we play. It is far too hot to sit on the verandah.'

'But the light is better out here, and there is a slight breeze.'

This was almost true: the sun had left this side of the house so the *chicks* were partly rolled up, but it was still very hot. However she had chosen her position carefully. It was opposite the rose garden, in view of the gate that he would have to open when he returned to his tent. Alice was acting as stooge.

'Keep still, Alice.'

'There's a fly on my nose!'

Despite the heat and the irritations, Alice sat in a cane chair with her ankles crossed, as quietly as any six year old was capable. But she was not an easy subject: her features were too regular. Oh, she had the appealing charm of most little girls of her age, but she would never grow into a beauty. She was too much like her mother in that respect. Francina outlined her oval chin, her pale eyes and her pouting little mouth in soft ivory - while in the nursery behind her, the din continued as the boys felled lines of lead soldiers with their marbles.

The dog barked. Footsteps crunched along the drive towards the stable block . . .

She followed the progress of the noise as she drew a pair of fair brows arched over inquisitive eyes. Her fingers were sticky; it was difficult to hold the pastel.

He was sauntering towards the rose garden with a gun slung over his shoulder, closely followed by a bearer who was carrying a large box on his head. He stopped at the gate and glanced back at Nudinapur House. Then he issued instructions to his servant and handed over his rifle. The bearer opened the gate and vanished from view. Gilbert Lihou turned and walked across the grass towards the house. From her peripheral vision she watched him sprint up the steps, two by two. The grueling heat had clearly not exhausted him.

The prickly heat on her arms and neck had flared up. Her pastel was beginning to flounder. If she lost concentration now, she would ruin this sketch. Footsteps clipped along the stone floor towards her.

She did not have to look up to know how well he looked in breeches and riding boots. How should she greet him after last night's charade? With a modest smile or a witty *bon mot*? Could she think of one?

But Jane intercepted him as he passed the drawing room arches.

'Mr Lihou!' she called out in her sweetest voice, 'have you had a fruitful day?'

He thrust himself through the bead curtain into the drawing room. 'Tolerably, ma'am,' she heard him say. He added something in a lower voice, which must have been humorous, for it was immediately followed by a burst of shrill laughter. Snatches of conversation drifted out to the verandah, but Francina could not catch what was said, it sufficed to show that Jane and Mrs Mackenzie were doing their best to flatter the Assistant Collector.

Eventually she heard him say, 'Well, ladies, I bid you adieu, I have a report to write up.'

'You are dining with us later, are you not, Mr Lihou?' called Jane.

'Certainly, Mrs Bulpitt.'

He was in sight once more. It would be rude not to notice him now. Francina looked up and acknowledged him politely.

'Ah, I had forgotten how good you were at drawing.'

He planted himself in front of her with his back against the glare, his legs slightly apart, and tapped his *solar topee* impatiently against his thigh. His hair was matted and he looked tired. Dark patches of sweat had seeped through his jacket.

He walked up and leaned over her shoulder.

'You don't mind, do you? As I recall, you were rather sensitive about showing your work.'

It was difficult to concentrate while he stood so close.

He peered at her drawing. She could feel his breath fluttering across her cheek as she lightly shaded the side of Alice's nose. His smell was not like Mr Wilson's sour odour, drowned in attar of roses – his scent filled her head with cumin, wood resin and musk.

'It is quite remarkable! I would never have thought of adding green to a skin tone.'

'It is a well-known trick.'

'Is it indeed? – There, you see, Miss Duquesne, you have taught me something today.'

He flicked open his gold cigar case. She noticed a crest engraved on the lid: a phoenix rising from the ashes. 'Do you mind if I smoke?'

She shook her head. She had over-rouged Alice's cheeks. She had spoilt her drawing.

He struck a lucifer on the heel of his boot.

As it flared, Jane appeared at the drawing room arches. 'What are you two whispering so conspiratorially about?'

'Miss Duquesne is giving me an art lesson.' He sucked on his cheroot until it glowed red. Then he exhaled – those same tobacco vapours that had seeped through the *jilmils*.

'Are you, Fanny? May I see?'

'Certainly, when it is finished.'

'Mr Lihou, I must apologise for my husband's behaviour last night. I am afraid it was the wine talking.'

Gilbert bowed and turned away. 'We shall say no more about it, Mrs Bulpitt.'

He clipped along the verandah, bowing smartly to his hostess and her companion as he passed the drawing room arches again. He put on his *solar topee* and bounded down the steps, drawing on his cheroot. Sauntering across the grass, he raised his face to the sun and exhaled a stream of smoke, a gesture reminiscent of an elephant trumpeting. Then he opened the gate beyond the rose garden and disappeared.

The hour until dinner seemed as long as a year – she had no recollection of how she had filled the time other than by daydreaming. When she was ready, she gathered up her skirts and floated down the stairs in her cream gown of antique moiré (the gown she was wearing when Gilbert had whirled her across the boards at the Assembly Rooms). This gown, at least, had only brought good luck. Taking a deep breath, she parted the bead curtain and stepped out to the verandah.

'Ah, Miss Fanny, come and join us!'

Mr Bulpitt cupped his hand under her elbow and guided her into his circle, which comprised of Mr Wilson and the Mackenzies. It was impossible to exchange more than a brief nod with him, for he was too far away. Jane, as usual, had gathered the unattached men to flutter round her candle.

'Poor Edgar has been very fretful, the little pet,' said Mrs

Mackenzie, fingering the garnets around her throat. 'Ayah said that he hardly ate any supper. I do hope he is not ailing from something.'

Mr Mackenzie asked Francina a question, which she answered, but she had little interest in what anyone in this group was saying.

A servant offered her a glass of champagne and this evening she accepted. Were her hopes like the bubbles in this glass, rising expectantly only to dissipate across the surface?

She sensed him behind her.

'Could you spare Miss Duquesne for a few moments?' he called to Mr Bulpitt. 'There is something she really must see.'

Six pairs of eyes followed them down the verandah as he led her to a spot far beyond Jane and Mr Hopkirk.

'Look interested,' he whispered, pointing to a fat brown moth, encircling a lighted wall sconce. 'This is just an excuse to get you away from those dreadful people.'

Francina stared intently at a hairy moth that was launching itself mindlessly against the glass.

'I know they are relatives of yours,' he whispered, 'but why on earth did you come here?'

'It's a very long story -'

'Miss Francina – may I call you Miss Francina? - I beg you to return to Calcutta as soon as possible.'

How could he say that! At this particular moment, she had no desire to be anywhere else.

'What are you two looking at?' called Jane.

'A very unusual moth, Mrs Bulpitt – the *Blatta fusca lepidoptera*.'

Francina was impressed. 'Is that really its name?'

'Of course not,' he whispered. 'I've just made that up.'

She smiled, conscious of something igniting between them.

'But I recently caught a glimpse of a *Pulcher papilio lepidoptera*. I have never seen such a fine specimen. It is illusive and unpredictable, but a sheer delight to the eye.'

'I should like to see one.'

'The best time to catch sight of one is late at night. Just before you go to bed tonight, Miss Francina, glimpse in the looking glass and you will see a *Pulcher papilio*: a beautiful butterfly.'

She blushed. He leaned close, so close she thought she saw herself reflected in his eyes.

'What time do you ride tomorrow?'

'Just before dawn.'

'Lihou!' called Mr Wilson, 'Could you come over here and settle a point of argument?'

'Why on earth should I give a second of my time to that old reprobate?' he muttered.

'I call him the Cockroach of Wilsonghur.'

He smiled; then turned to the Cockroach enquiringly.

'With so much knowledge,' sneered Mr Wilson, 'we were wondering if you might be one of those new *competition wallahs*.'

'I am indeed.'

'A *competition wallah*?' she whispered.

'I'll explain some other time. Which direction will you go?'

'Along the lane that forks to Kandria.'

'Beyond the old white temple?'

She nodded.

'I'll wait for you at the temple. Now, I think we had better return to the others before that oily miscreant challenges me to a duel.'

At dinner she found herself seated between Mr Hopkirk and Mr Wilson. Gilbert sat opposite, between Jane and Mrs Mackenzie. Did she dream it? Did he really suggest that they should meet at the old temple? For the first time since arriving at Nudinapur, she saw a world beyond her prison walls and caught a glimpse of a lush green land where birds sing in the pomegranate trees and fountains shimmer with sparking water . . .

He smiled at her across the table and her heart leapt, but she quickly lowered her eyes as a trickle of fear ran through her. Mr Wilson could spoil everything if he suspected something. There was no knowing what an old bull elephant might do if he perceived a rival – however imagined or unfounded.

She had no desire to eat, but picked at morsels so as not to arouse suspicion, while Mr Bulpitt ranted on about something and Jane played her usual beguiling tricks. Nothing bothered her tonight (not even when Mr Wilson's foot periodically nudged her own), for she was not really confined to this sweltering room; she had transformed into a beautiful moth that was flitting breathlessly in and out of the night jasmine, her wings satiated with its perfume . . .

A musky aroma entices her to the verandah where she spies a Blatta fusca *dancing circles around the sconces . . .*

'An odd thing happened yesterday,' Mr Hopkirk said between mouthfuls of curry. 'My bearer brought me a chapatti given to him by a man from the village, who instructed him to bake four more and distribute them to the next village -' he broke into a fit of coughing and Jane signalled to a servant to replenish his glass. 'No reflection on the food, Mrs Bulpitt. This duck is excellent!'

Hovering in the cool air, she beats her wings to waft her scent towards him. Bewitched, he turns and follows her out into the balmy night . . .

'I broke the chapatti open, but there was no message concealed inside, but still being suspicious, I gave it to a scavenging pye, who devoured it without harmful effects. What do you make of it?' Mr Hopkirk gulped his wine.

The enchanted insects weave and tumble through a tangle of honeysuckle. Pollen falls from their wings like fairy dust.

'I have heard that the natives regard the chapatti as a talisman against disease,' said Mr Mackenzie.

The time on the mantelpiece clock was notoriously unreliable, but in about eight hours she would see him. She must plan her movements carefully . . .

At last dinner was over. Jane rose from the table to lead the ladies into the drawing room. Satiated, Mr Bulpitt leaned back and called for brandy and cigars.

Gilbert pushed back his chair and stood up. 'Ladies, gentlemen, I must rise early tomorrow. Would you excuse me if I bid you all a good night?'

'Don't you ever let up, Lihou? It can't be good for you to be constantly scribbling in those ledgers of yours. We're shooting partridge by the *jheel* at dawn. Do you care to join us?'

'Regrettably, Mr Bulpitt, there is something I must attend to.'

'Perhaps you would rather ride with us ladies tomorrow, Mr Lihou, if sport does not take your fancy?' Jane said over her shoulder at the doorway.

'As a matter of fact, I'm hoping to catch sight of a rare *lepidoptera* - the *Pulcher papilio*. Have you ever come across one, Mr Wilson?' Gilbert asked, looking directly him.

Mr Wilson shook his head. He knew he was being duped and his face turned purple. In a fury he lashed out at a pair of moths circling above the table. The *Blatta fusca* fell stunned to the floor.

'Plain English, Lihou!' barked Mr Bulpitt. 'What in God's name is that? Some kind of snake?'

'I believe it's a species of butterfly,' said Mr Hopkirk.

'A butterfly!' exclaimed Mr Bulpitt. 'Why the deuce should anyone want to waste time on something so *namby-pamby*. What are you going to do if you find one, Lihou? Drown it in ether and keep it in a specimen case?'

'I don't believe in confining creatures to glass cases for my own gratification. I prefer to watch them roaming free in their natural habitat.' He bowed, turned, and disappeared into the night, closely followed by his bearer.

'Confound the fellow's impudence!' muttered Mr Wilson, squashing the moth under his boot. 'If that's an example of the new sort of Civilian they're sending out these days - God help us all!'

10

She reins in her pony and listens to the dawn chorus. The stars have vanished, only the morning star remains. It blinks in the grey light, a beacon to guide her to the old Hindu temple.

She feels light-headed. She wants to fly to that stunted tree and sing a full-throated duet with that *dhyal.* Instead, she takes a deep breath to steady her nerves. Women filling pitchers at a well converse in muted voices, as though this was an auspicious day to be observed with reverence and humility. She smiles to herself. But this *is* an auspicious day. She wants to dance and sing and proclaim it to the world.

She rides along a narrow embanked roadway that ribbons across the plain. The mist is clearing to reveal the thin silvery channels dividing the parched fields that fall away on either side. Shadowy figures are watering the lines of indigo.

Soon the old temple looms through a swathe of mist before her. Silhouetted against the dawn light, it looks rather like a flattened onion flanked by two squat cucumbers. Above it, the morning star shivers with expectation.

The temple bell is ringing. At the open gateway, she catches sight of an old priest wrapped in a cloak, climbing the steep steps to call devotees to prayer.

'*Om, Om, Om!*' chants the priest.

He is leaning against the wall of the courtyard, waiting for her.

He smiles, grinds his cheroot under his shoe and shouts to his servant to unhitch the horses. They ride abreast, barely three feet apart, with only the clip-clop of hooves to rout the silence.

'When I was riding here the other day,' he says, breaking the silence, 'I came across a forgotten garden beyond that clump of trees. Would you like to see it?'

She clutches the reins with white knuckles and follows as he canters along a narrow track dividing the indigo fields. Soon they break into a gallop, and wheel through thorn-scrub and over tussocks of grass. A herd of black buck grazing nearby, raise their heads and bound away. Beyond the trees she sees the tumbling walls of the garden, overgrown with vegetation.

He dismounts and instructs the servant to tether the animals.

She loosens her feet from the stirrups. He holds out his hands and grasps her waist to brace her fall. For a moment they stand motionless, his hands encircling her waist.

Then he takes her hand and guides her through the ancient gateway. The huge wooden doors have disappeared, scavenged long ago for firewood, only the rusty hinges remain. They find themselves in a ruined colonnaded courtyard. A pair of doves takes flight.

This was where a Maharajah once entertained, she thinks, as they pick their way over the fallen masonry to inspect the remains of a fountain. Dancing girls in gold-embroidered crimson might have whirled across this marble floor, while their master reclined on silken bolsters and smoked his hookah.

'I found this place by accident, when I was chasing a butterfly.'

He leads her across the courtyard. She is in a dream, watching herself from a great height: a girl in a blue riding habit being led through a tangle of crackling vegetation. Every so often the girl bends low to avoid overhanging ivy.

They reach a dilapidated arch in the far wall and enter another enclosed garden, much larger than the first. In the centre, stands a crumbling tomb encircled by trees. Perhaps in this dappled shade, songbirds fluttered in cages suspended from the branches, whilst underneath, concubines played with leopard cubs, orphaned when their mother was killed in a *shikar*.

The vegetation envelopes them in a muffling cloak. The sounds beyond this place have faded away. Here, time stands still. Here, everything is on fire.

He kicks a circle of smouldering ashes, and picks up a burnt chapatti. 'Someone was here not very long ago,' he says, 'but I'm sure it is nothing to worry about.'

Bemused, she returns his smile.

Silence falls around them again. The air is heating up, but the sky is hard and pallid without a hint of rain. Soon it will be too hot even to stand in the shade. She tries to show some interest in the tomb, but it resembles little more than a crumbling pile of masonry.

'Whose grave is it?' she asks.

He takes off his *solar topee* and wipes his brow. Surely he has brought her here to tell her something important? She peels off her gloves and shuts her eyes as she fans her cheeks with the gloves.

The tension is unbearable.

She takes off her riding *topee* and lifts the matted tendrils at the nape of her neck. Her throat is dry. She has left her flask tied to her saddle, but nothing will induce her to break this moment to fetch it. Nothing. Not even if she should look down and find a cobra at her feet, hooded and poised to strike.

He must say something soon.

You - you strange and obscure unearthly thing! - I love you as my own flesh. You - poor and obscure, and small and plain as you are - I entreat you to accept me as a husband. I must have you for my own - entirely my own. Will you be mine? Say yes, quickly.

His silence is excruciating.

She sweeps aside the white frangipani flowers scattered over the tomb. Perhaps they hid an inscription –

'Owh!'

Something nips her. She drops her *topee* to nurse her finger. Now she notices the trail of ants scurrying across the tomb transporting morsels down a crack in the stone. 'I've been bitten,' she whimpers. She holds out her finger.

'You poor girl,' he murmurs, taking her hand. The scent of frangipani rises up between them, pungent and cloying. He presses her finger to his lips.

Come to me - come to me entirely now, he said. Make my happiness - I will make yours.

Are you in earnest? - Do you truly love me? - Do you sincerely wish me to be your wife?

Behind him, the fissure across the tomb opens ... The demon is clawing its way out. It leaps into the air, ashen-white, cadaverous, with long matted hair and hollow eyes. It dances around them, mocking, odorous, grunting and snarling. Emaciated white legs bend and curl with the dexterity of an India rubber ring, and a long pink tongue flickers obscenely, tasting the air like a snake.

✸

She lay drenched in sweat, her pillow wet. It must be past midnight. She looked around as her eyes grew accustomed to the dark. Something was different . . . that awful monotonous creaking had stopped. The *punkah* was still. The *punkah-wallah* must have dozed off, or perhaps he was nursing his injuries, poor man. Mr Bulpitt had struck him very hard.

Then she saw him.

A ghostly figure beyond the web. Quite still.

She lay motionless, trembling and damp, seeing herself as he must see her: hands folded across her breasts, hair fanning out across the pillow, toes just visible below her nightgown.

Silken, hush'd and chaste.

She closed her eyes and waited to be woken with a kiss . . .

In a drowsy half-sleep she dreamed of lovers fleeing from Bluebeard's castle, gliding like phantoms through the night past sleeping dogs and dragons . . .

She opened her eyes in time to see him creeping noiselessly towards the verandah.

'Please don't go,' she whispered.

He stopped. 'How long have you been awake?'

But it was a jackal that answered, howling for her mate.

He groped along the mosquito net, looking for the secret entrance to her chamber. Loosening the threads, he climbed inside; head first, then shoulders. He had slashed his way through the briars, killed tigers, fought off wolves, bears and hot-blooded ogres –

Now at last, he winds himself into her dream . . .

In her head she heard the brush of caught wings as he sat tentatively on the edge of her bed, and she almost swooned at her cunning.

Neither spoke, neither moved. She stared through the darkness trying to read his eyes, his smouldering coal-black eyes, while all around the air closed in, pressed down on them like a great weight.

He took her hand and kissed her fingers, one by one.

This is meant to happen, she wanted to whisper. But all the same, she knew that she was about to step into an abyss from which there would be no turning back.

'I must go,' he whispered. 'Someone might come in.'

'Don't leave me!'

But he breaks away and wrestles with netting. In his attempt to escape, he discards his battered wings. A necktie shoots across the floor. Then a waistcoat . . .

But it was too late. She had him.

She grasped his hand. 'I hate it here. Please, take me away!'

'But it's impossible.'

'You can find a way. There is always a way.'

'You stupid, foolish girl!'

His voice trembled in her ear. He was holding her as a lover holds his love; his rough cheek grazing hers, his fingers running through her hair, pulling so hard that it hurt. He kissed her softly on the mouth. She stopped breathing, in fact, she had stopped breathing so long ago she would probably soon die.

She shut her eyes and heard his laboured breath as his fingers toyed with the buttons of her nightgown . . . His lips were on her neck and in her hair. She felt helpless, excited, utterly overwhelmed.

She has never felt a man's bare skin before. She has an urge to dig her nails into his flesh, to sink her teeth into his shoulder.

Adonis, my Adonis.

He buried his face in her hair. His heart pounded in her ear. She tasted the sweat on his cheek and her reserve melted to nothing. Her heart could not contain the love that had welled inside.

She was that little doe, free and flighty as the wind. She was not confined to a gilded cage; had not been bought, or married off against her will. She was no one's mistress. She was free. Free to choose her lover. And she wanted him. That deep chronic ache had stifled all rationale. She no longer cared about propriety or logic or what tomorrow might bring.

Nothing mattered but to keep him here.

He kissed her face; traced her skin with light feathery strokes . . . She gripped his arm, dug her nails into his flesh and braced herself.

'I won't hurt you,' he whispered. 'I just want to love you.'

She never expected this, never imagined this. How could she? This was the dark, secret world from which she had been excluded.

His touch was so exacting, so pleasurable. This was not a dream. This could not be a dream. She could never have imagined this. She lay back, oblivious of everything but his touch and the sensations sweeping through her body.

She has waited for this moment all her life: two halves fused together, two halves making one. Madeline and Porphyro. Paul and Virginie. Catherine and Heathcliff - united beyond the grave.

11

The peacock's haunting cry woke her. She opened her eyes, and found herself alone. She brushed her hand across the sheet . . . and smiled. He really was here last night. His smell was over her, strong and pungent. He had marked her with his scent, staked his claim on her. She belonged to him. She stretched like a satiated cat, buried her face in the pillow where his head had lain, and shut her eyes to dream the dream again.

But – there was a glimmer of light through the crack in the venetians. How could she have overslept! He would be waiting for her at the old white temple. She jumped out of bed and shouted to Sita who was hanging fresh towels in the bathing room to help hook up her riding habit. She would not bathe this morning. She could not bring herself to wash him off her skin. She would carry his smell like a tight embrace all day.

She ran through the house and found Jane and Mrs Mackenzie, dressed for their morning ride, pacing the verandah with their riding *topees* in their hands.

'At last! We were beginning to think you might have fallen ill,' frowned Jane, tapping her riding crop against her looped skirts. 'We were just about to set off. The tea has been cleared away, but I could call the -'

'Please don't, Jane. I don't want anything.'

The world looked different this morning. Brighter. Sharper. Focused. She knew the secret. She had stepped over the threshold.

'But you must have a drink.' Jane signalled to a servant.

'We thought you might be suffering from the same complaint as poor Edgar,' said Mrs Mackenzie, while they waited for the bearer to bring Miss-Sahib's tea. 'The little pet kept his ayah awake all night. He has a slight fever. I have given him some rhubarb powder, but he's still fretful. If he has not perked up after our ride, I shall have to summon the doctor.'

'Incidentally, Fanny, *you* look a little flushed this morning.'

Francina touched her hot cheeks. If she looked feverish, so much the better.

They rode three-abreast through the gates of Nudinapur. She reigned in her pony and fell behind. She would not sully her mind with talk of Mrs Mackenzie's boy. She wanted to think only of last night. Besides, it was difficult to keep a straight face when she felt so ecstatically happy. A joyous refrain seemed to be playing over and over in her head. But why should she keep a straight face? Soon everyone – Jane, Mr Bulpitt, Mr Wilson – would know that she and the Assistant Collector of Kandria were in love. She wanted to proclaim it to the world, to wear a red mark on her forehead or paint a bright gash across her palm. For all his schemes and plans, she had outwitted that old cockroach.

How wonderful the countryside looked this morning. White egrets flying overhead were heading towards the old Hindu temple as if to say, 'Follow us, child! Your destination lies in this direction.'

As she trailed behind, she planned their future life together. She would take a close interest in his work and accompany him on his travels – she would *insist* on it – and she would never allow herself to sink into a state of apathy. They would live like carefree gypsys, pitching camp wherever they found themselves. Whilst he set up his table under the trees to listen to the petitions and grievances of those living within his jurisdiction, she would encourage the wives and children to consult her on health matters. She would write to Calcutta for appropriate manuals and set up her consulting table opposite his. Later, they would mull over the day's events as their simple meal cooked on the campfire. Then they would tumble into bed under a star-studded canopy, tired but fulfilled, and fall asleep in each other's arms.

'Eyes straight ahead, ladies,' called Jane. 'That *saddhu* is back.'

He was sitting in the lotus pose under a thorn tree near the entrance to the village. She would not have noticed him if Jane had not pointed him out (he blended so well with his surroundings). As they rode past, he raised a skinny arm and raged abusively. Villagers, squatting in the dust around him, glanced at the *mem-log* and smirked.

The village was unusually noisy. Tom-toms pounded, conches blasted. The racket had set the pariah dogs into a frenzy of barking which lasted until they had left the village and bazaar behind.

They were riding through open countryside once more. The barking was now a faint, intermittent fracas in the distance - but the tom-toms were still pounding relentlessly.

'Oh, by the way, Fanny,' Jane said, turning round, 'your friend Mr Lihou has gone away.'

'Gone away?' She whipped her pony's flank and caught up with them. 'Jane, what do you mean – gone away?'

'The *peon* brought me a *chit* this morning while I was dressing.'

'Could I see the *chit*? Do you have it with you?'

Her hands shook as she unfolded the scrap of paper:

My dear Mrs Bulpitt, she read, *I write in haste to inform you that I have received notice of some unexpected matter that requires my attention. I must leave immediately. It is with the deepest regret that I find myself unable to thank you and Mr Bulpitt in person for your kind and generous hospitality. I beg you, Mrs Bulpitt, to say goodbye on my behalf to Mr and Mrs Mackenzie, Mr Wilson, - and of course, Miss Duquesne. I hope in due course to . . .*

And of course Miss Duquesne. Was that all she meant to him? An afterthought, a postscript written on a scribbled note? She almost laughed at her foolishness. Of course! This *chit* was designed to put Jane off the scent. She would find Gilbert waiting for her behind the wall of the old Hindu temple, just as they had arranged. Her dreams and hopes, which for a catastrophic moment were about to sucked into a bottomless whirlpool, were miraculously retrieved. In her mind's eye, she saw them bob away to be washed up on a beautiful fertile island.

They had almost reached the temple.

Jane was talking. Regardless of the risks, she could wait no longer. She must see him now, just for a moment, just to make sure.

She slipped through the open gate and into the courtyard.

Apart from an old woman who was sweeping the steps, the courtyard was deserted. Rhesus monkeys fell like rain from the branches of the tree, bared their teeth and formed a threatening circle around her, jumping and whooping aggressively. The pony neighed. Francina pulled hard at the reins to keep her under control.

'What on earth are you doing in here, Fanny?'

Jane and Mrs Mackenzie had followed her into the courtyard.

'I thought I might rest under the tree.' She would lie on the ground. If the monkeys ripped her to pieces so much the better.

'I feel unwell.'

There was no need to pretend. She could hardly speak. A lump in her throat had grown to the size of a croquet ball.

'I would not advise it – not *here*. The natives would not like it.'

The woman had stopped sweeping. A crowd had mysteriously appeared and was eyeing them with hostile suspicion. Some of the elders were carrying long sticks.

'I should turn back,' whispered Mrs Mackenzie. 'I ought to see how little Edgar fares.'

'We will all turn back. Besides, it is getting far too hot to be out at this time of day.' Jane looked coldly at Francina. 'And in future we must insure that we set off *well before* sunrise.'

She lay on her bed, curled into a tight ball, too stunned to cry. She had known the risks – Aunt Doré had warned her often enough. 'Do not stray from what you know to be right, Francina. Every man – from the highest to the lowest - will test a young girl's resolve. If she wavers, or in any way succumbs, he will despise her and discard her. Be especially cautious of men with silver tongues, who beguile and flatter.'

I don't want to hurt you. I just want to love you.

Were they just empty words? Those looks, that seductive smile - she thought he loved her, she really thought he had loved her. She thought she had found a safe pair of hands to carry her into a calmer current, but those hands had thrown her into the whirl and tumult; dashed her mercilessly against the rocks. How did she misjudged him so badly?

But she did not blame him. How could she? She had encouraged him, lured him into her bedroom; used her sex as a weapon, played on his weaknesses like a courtesan. If she had not succumbed, he would have waited for her at the old Hindu temple. If she had been worthy of him, he would still be here. He had tested her resolve and found her deficient. She was no better than a fallen woman.

A fallen woman!

She buried her face in her pillow. I am just like you, Mamma: *the true daughter of an infamous mother*. We stem from the same contaminated branch. Soiled, intemperate, unchaste. We are both flawed, despicable creatures.

'*Strumpet! Strumpet! Strumpet!*' screamed the brain-fever bird.

Sita moistened a flannel in a bowl of water and placed it gently across her forehead. Francina shut her eyes and breathed in the comforting odours of this silent girl's flesh . . .

Mamma used to do this. 'My poor sick darling,' she would murmur as she ran her fingers through her hair. 'Mamma will make you better,' she would say as she leaned over the cot to kiss her flushed forehead. Then she would sink back into her pillows, delirious with happiness and fever. She clutched herself tight. If only she could be that little girl again, curled in Mamma's arms.

Safe from all the bad.

She threw off the flannel and jumped out of bed. The bowl tipped over, spilling water across the floor. Sita watched in silence as Miss-Sahib threw open the lid of her trunk and rummaged inside, throwing out sketchbooks - bundles of letters – leather cases of daguerreotypes – Cold Weather clothes - satin dancing pumps wrapped in tissue paper -

She found Mamma's jewellery box wrapped in a cashmere shawl, and carried it carefully back to bed. It made quiet noises like a newborn baby as she rocked it in her arms. Something inside was asking to be released. She tried to prise the box open with her fingers, but it remained locked. She ransacked her room until she found the small ivory-handled paper knife in a drawer. The blade snapped in two as she tried to lever the lid open, but the box remained stubbornly locked. She threw it to the floor. The corner chipped, but the box would not open.

Sita stood in the doorway and watched, open-mouthed, as she raised it above her head and dashed it to the floor again. One of the silver inlaid initials fell out, but it did not open. She raised it up again, but Sita seized it before she could throw it and ran out of the room clutching it tightly to her chest.

Francina fell across her bed. 'Why did you take it, Sita? I must open it, I must!'

*

'Your ayah asked me to come and see you, Fanny. She is worried.'

Jane was standing at the end of her bed. She had changed out of her riding habit into a cream day gown. Sita stood behind her, cradling the jewellery box in the folds of her sari.

'How are you feeling? Can ayah get something for you? Cool lemonade, perhaps?'

Jane paced impatiently up and down the room, fanning herself. 'Edgar's no better. He has a fever and a sore throat. We have sent to Kandria for the doctor, but I don't expect him to arrive until tomorrow - but quite frankly, Fanny, I have little faith in him. The man's a fool, and never offers advice unless he's primed. But what can we do? There is no one else. Do you have a sore throat? Fever?'

Francina shook her head.

'Well, that's a relief. Still, just to be safe we shall ask the doctor to examine you when he arrives. Let's hope it is not contagious. It would not do for me to catch anything in my condition. It's trying enough coping with a house full of guests – and goodness only knows how long they'll be staying - without having to contend with sickness as well. And on top of everything else that wretched *punkah-wallah* has disappeared. Frederick will be furious when he finds out.'

So saying, Jane rustled imperiously out of the room.

Francina held out her arms for Mamma's jewellery box. 'Give it to me, Sita.'

Sita hesitated, then sidled up and handed it to her. Wrapping it tenderly in the cashmere shawl, Francina held it in her arms and rocked herself to sleep.

She awoke cocooned in her sheets with the jewellery box still cradled in her arms. Flies buzzed round a plate of refreshments on a side table. She had no recollection of anyone putting it there. The air was stifling. 'Throw water! Pull the *punkah*!' someone called from the depths of the house. Her head throbbed with the same relentless persistence as the tom-toms down in the village. Why so much drumming - today of all days?

She sat up. Of course! There was still a vestige of hope. Why did she not think of it before? She dressed quickly; picked up her skirts, ran through the house and down the steps. She had forgotten her *solar topee,* but no matter.

She raced to the rose garden, unlatched the gate and ran though the vegetable garden, the orchard – on and on until she came to the place where he had pitched his tent.

In a dappled clearing, a patch of disturbed earth bordering a square of brown grass marked the place where his tent had stood; nearby, charred cinders remained where a fire had heated his water. Nothing else was there. She fell to her knees and pounded the hard earth. How could he do this to her? She grabbed handfuls of stones and threw them into the scrub.

When there were no more tears to shed, she stood up, brushed the cinders off her skirts and walked stiffly back to the house, gliding through the rooms like a phantom, unaware of the servants standing sentinel in the doorways.

Mamma's box was still wrapped in the shawl on her bed. Like an automaton, she scooped it up in her arms and climbed the spiral staircase to the roof. The light was fading, but the stone burned underfoot. A hot suffocating wind was blowing. The sky was blood-red. Black shapes swirled high above her head, crucifixes in the firmament. The scavengers were waiting. Soon she would fly with them. She would become one of them, a soiled despised creature, loved by no one.

She leaned across the parapet with the box cradled in her arms and stared down at the path encircling the house. Would it work? Was it high enough?

The *mali* was watering the plants. Dark patches seeped from the pots and spread like black talons across the red earth. There was just enough room to place her foot in the latticework and hoist herself up a few inches.

Now the other foot.

You loved me – then what right had you to leave me?

She was high enough to lean over. She would wait until the *mali* disappeared around the corner.

Does he always take this long to water the plants? She never noticed before. How rational she is! So calm, so strangely composed. She never thought it would feel like this. No fear, no fear at all.

In a few minutes it would all be over. No more Gilbert. No more

Mr Wilson. Just a long, blissful sleep . . .

'Miss Fanny! Miss Fanny!'

Alice was running across the garden waving her arms, looking up to the roof. At this height she looked no bigger than a peg doll. Sita tottered behind her. They stared up at her open-mouthed.

'What are you doing up there?'

She slid down behind the parapet and hugged her knees. Tears rolled down her cheeks. She was so useless. She could not do this - not with Alice and Sita watching.

12

'Miss-Sahib! Jow! Jow!'

Francina opened her eyes. The stench of burning filled her nostrils. Sita was beckoning frantically from the doorway. Jumping out of bed, she threw a shawl over her nightdress and swept the contents on her dressing table into a carpetbag. It was night, but an eerie glow lit up the room. Clutching the bag, she followed Sita out to the landing. The main staircase was engulfed in smoke. Flames licked the crackling fronds of the potted palms. Soon sparks would ignite the curtains and turkey carpets. Holding their breath, they ran, coughing and spluttering, back through the bedroom and out to the verandah. It was impossible to lean over the balustrade for more than a few seconds -smoke was billowing up from the floor below. Sparks had set the *chiks* alight along the far end of the verandah. The *chiks,* like the china matting, were tinder dry. Soon the whole verandah would ignite as easily as brushwood.

'Quickly, Sita.' Francina pointed to the narrow spiral staircase to the roof. *'Jeldi, jeldi!'*

The roof offered only a brief respite. The heat of the fire was spiralling up from the floors below. The stone was hot to walk upon. They ran to one of the small ornate observation towers set in the corner of the roof. The servants' staircase, thankfully, had not yet caught fire, although someone had tried to block it off with a sack of straw. Nearby, an upturned oil lamp had blown itself out. Throwing the sacks out of the way, they scampered down the narrow wooden staircase as quickly as they dared.

There was pandemonium outside. Everyone was running in all directions like a colony of angry ants whose nest had been disturbed. Braver servants were carrying small items of furniture or paintings out of rooms that were not yet alight. Mr Bulpitt was beside himself with rage. Wrapped in his dressing gown and wielding his pistol above his head, he stomped across the drive cursing and bellowing, threatening his servants with their lives unless they brought out more furniture. For their part, they watched the growing inferno with a kind of fatalistic wonder, pretending not to understand him. Some of the more obliging were passing buckets along a human chain, but it was a futile, half-hearted gesture - much of the water spilt in the process. They were being deliberately slow and uncooperative.

'Miss Duquesne, thank goodness you're safe. I've been looking for you everywhere!'

Mr Wilson loomed out of the darkness towards her, dressed in a ridiculous Chinese purple dressing gown, nightcap and riding boots. Only now was she conscious of her state of undress. She clasped the carpetbag like a talisman in front of her and backed away. She felt doubly afraid of him now that Gilbert Lihou had gone. He seemed to gain height as he swaggering before her, preening like a peacock that had beaten off a rival.

'My soldiers, I want my lead soldiers!' howled Freddie, as his mother dragged him aimlessly across the grass.

'Hush, dearest. We'll find you more soldiers – better, more magnificent soldiers. Just stop that noise, there's a good boy. Where's Alice? Has anyone seen Alice?'

Francina saw her chance to escape. 'I must help Mrs Bulpitt look for her,' she called, running from him into the darkness. 'Alice! Alice, where are you?'

'I'm here, Miss Fanny!'

A small girl sprang out from behind a flowerbed, hugging her favourite doll, her eyes wide with fear, her face streaked with smuts. In the firelight, her white nightgown and cap glowed red and orange. She fell sobbing into her arms. Francina scooped her up and carried her to her distraught mother.

Jane burst into tears as she kissed her little daughter. 'At least everyone has been accounted for - but what shall we do? Where shall we go!'

She was on the verge of hysterics. Francina took her trembling hand and led her to one of the sofas that had been rescued from the house and placed incongruously under the rose arbour. 'Sit here, Jane, and calm yourself. You must look after yourself in your condition.'

Jane covered her face with her hands and sobbed.

Freddie put his arms around her neck. 'I'll look after you, Mamma,' he whispered.

Mrs Mackenzie was sitting on an upright chair in the middle of the drive with an assortment of baggage around her. Her feverish son sat limply on her lap. Her other son sat huddled on the ground by her feet, too bemused to cry. Her husband, retaining a modicum of dignity in a brocade smoking jacket thrown over a flowing nightshirt, stood over his family and tried to reassure them.

'Why?' whimpered Mrs Mackenzie. 'Why is this happening to us?'

The two women stared blankly at each other from their points of the garden, but neither had the strength to offer the other comfort.

A hot gust sprang up, fanned the flames and carried them to parts of the house that had so far escaped the inferno. Fire took hold in most of the downstairs rooms. Now it would take much more than a few bucketfuls of water to quell the flames.

Alice thrust her hand into Francina's. Her closeness comforted them both. They stood on the drive in silence and watched the magnificent wooden staircase cave in with a gush of fire through the gaping vestibule. Beyond the blackened drawing room arches, flames were leaping from one stuffed head to the next. Mr Bulpitt's prized trophies fell off their brackets, one after the other. Oakum cascaded from snarling heads in burning chunks onto the glass cases, shattering the panes. The stuffed creatures, frozen for eternity in their agonizing death throes, burst into flames.

Suddenly a series of explosions lit up the sky. Everyone ran for cover. Mr Bulpitt's hoard of cartridges had ignited into a spectacular firework display.

'I shall not rest until I find the culprits responsible! Hanging, drawing and quartering will be too good a punishment,' he roared. No one took any notice of him. Deprived of his stronghold, he was no more than a spoilt child having a tantrum. The servants stood like a menacing pack of hyenas waiting to see who would be first to turn on their master.

Carriages began to rumble along the drive in slow succession. Every wheeled vehicle that could be mustered had been harnessed with horses from the Nudinapur stables. The animals, terrified of the noise and the smell of fire, were difficult to control.

Now that the Master of Nudinapur had fallen, Mr Wilson assumed command. He strutted up and down on his mount, his purple dressing gown flowing dramatically in the hot breeze, bellowing instructions as boldly as Napoleon retreating from Russia.

'You must all stay at Wilsonghur. There is plenty of room for everyone!'

The Mackenzies needed no further inducement. They ran towards the vehicles before Mr Wilson had finished his sentence (Mr Mackenzie weighed down with his sick son in his arms). 'Edgar is so poorly,' explained Mrs Mackenzie, as she climbed into the most luxurious carriage and ordered her servants to pile on all the baggage they had managed to salvage. 'We must put him to bed as soon as possible!'

The carriage and carts carrying the Mackenzie family, their attendants and baggage, sped off into the night.

'But we can't go without Scamp,' howled Freddie as his mother lifted him into the second carriage. 'Where is he?'

'I'm sure he's just hiding under a bush,' said his mother wearily. 'We'll come back and look for him another day.' She called to Alice to join them.

'I want to go with Miss Fanny!'

'Get into the *ekka* then and follow us,' said her mother, weak with fatigue. Servants were stuffing rescued belongings in the spaces around her. 'But hurry, we must stay in convoy.'

Carriages and carts sped away with dazed adults and children, loyal servants and salvaged baggage. Only the old *ekka* remained forlornly on the drive.

Mr Bulpitt lifted his sobbing daughter into it. 'I'm staying to restore order into this mayhem!' He turned to survey his ravaged empire. 'Whoever is responsible still has *me* to contend with. I shall never let those miserable scoundrels get away with this - not until my last dying breath!'

Francina and Sita clambered into the *ekka* after Alice. It was a tight squeeze, but Sita took up little space. Alice sat on Francina's lap. Sanjit jerked the reins and the *ekka* rumbled slowly down the drive.

'My doll's face has melted!' wailed Alice.

Francina hugged her tight as she glanced back to see the Master of Nudinapur gallop defiantly towards the inferno. Ahead of him the house loomed like a huge charred skeleton of stone. Every doorway and window space glowed red, as the fire hungrily consumed everything combustible inside. She saw a black-haired girl in a blood-spattered ball gown dancing on the parapet, laughing as Angelo's lies, Papa's tirades rose as orange embers into the night sky; she saw all her belongings, the sketchbooks, the children's schoolwork, her cream moiré gown rise into the night sky. She stared at Nudinapur until the house had become a faint red glow on the horizon. She felt no emotion, just a numbing sense of release.

She turned to face the direction in which they were heading. A figure on horseback was thundering towards them. Her heart leapt as she peered closely into the darkness . . .

13

'*Jor se challo!* Keep up with the convoy!' Mr Wilson's boomed out as he materialised on horseback through of the night.

Francina shut her eyes. This must be a bad dream. She would sleep until cockcrow; then jump out of bed to meet Gilbert at the old Hindu temple just as they had planned.

She dozed intermittently while Alice whimpered in her arms . . . The fracas of barking dogs told her that they were driving through the village; then hooves over hollow planks pinpointed the little bridge -

The pony reared. Alice shrieked as the *ekka* swerved violently from side to side.

'Keep that animal under control, you blithering idiot!'

Sanjit struggled manfully to calm the pony, but it was impossible while Mr Wilson bellowed, scaring the poor animal out of her wits. Mr Wilson dug in his spurs, and galloped forward to seize the bridle. The pony darted erratically, like a terrified little monkey trying to shake off a debauched suitor. The passengers shut their eyes and gripped each other in silence as the *ekka* tottered precariously from side to side. The pony lost her footing, stumbled and slid down the embankment, taking the *ekka* and everyone inside down with her. Alice screamed hysterically.

'Are you harmed, Miss Duquesne?' shouted Mr Wilson. He dismounted and staggered down the embankment as quickly as an ungainly bulk in a purple dressing gown could.

She shook her head, crawled out of the toppled *ekka* and stood up before he had a chance to touch her. She was trembling from shock, but would rather die in the ditch than be aided by him. Sita helped Alice out, took the child in her arms and rocked her until her screams subsided. Luckily, no one had suffered anything more serious than a few bruises.

Sanjit released the pony from her bindings and pulled her gently to her feet. He stroked her neck and spoke reassuringly while he examined her carefully all over.

Mr Wilson found a lucifer in his pocket and relit the candle in the lantern that had fallen into the ditch. 'Hold this, Miss Duquesne,' he shouted, 'while we try to right the vehicle.'

She held the lantern while Sanjit scrabbled underneath the *ekka*. He emerged a few minutes later, muttering and shaking his head.

Mr Wilson cursed under his breath.

'Now what are we going to do? The fool says the shaft's cracked. It cannot carry the weight of a passenger - let alone a driver.'

Sanjit muttered again and pointed into the darkness.

'The syce says there's a *machan* in that field where the *mem-log* can take shelter while he walks to the next village to fetch a carpenter,' translated Mr Wilson, 'but the dratted pony's lame, so even if he manages to fix the shaft – which he very much doubts - we shall still be without an animal to pull the confounded vehicle!' He raised his face and bayed to the moon. 'Why was the imbecile driving so slowly? A *snail* could have travelled more quickly. The convoy must be at least an hour ahead of us by now!'

He paced back and forth along the embankment.

'Miss Duquesne, would you care to ride with me? My horse can carry the weight of us both. The child can wait in the *machan* with the ayah until I return from Wilsonghur with fresh horses and a reliable carriage. It would give her a chance to catch up on her sleep.'

Francina shrank in horror at the thought of riding pillion in her state of undress. Knowing the old cockroach, he would ravish her before they turned the first corner.

'It would be a better idea if Alice rode with you. I shall wait in the *machan* with ayah until you return.'

'But I won't go without you, Miss Fanny, I won't!' howled Alice.

'Well, I'm not taking that child unless she quietens down.'

'Hush, Alice. I shan't abandon you. Now, let us walk to the *machan* and wait for Mr Wilson to bring us back a nice carriage. Sanjit, lead the way!'

Mr Wilson watched her setting off after the syce into the wilderness, dragging a wailing brat and a timid servant. He mounted with difficulty (he had strained his back with all that twisting and turning) as the odd little party disappeared into the darkness. It hardly seemed *gallant* to leave an innocent girl with just that imbecile to protect her. But what was the alternative? Nothing he suggested had met with her approval. She was a most perplexing creature.

'Miss Duquesne, please wait a moment!'

Would she never be rid of him. 'What is it, Mr Wilson?'

Master and horse trampled indiscriminately through a field of tobacco towards her. His raised pistol glinted menacingly in the moonlight. She backed away, her talons exposed. The ogre had come to claim her by force. She would be whisked away and imprisoned in an attic like Bertha Mason, never to be seen again.

Sanjit's eyes widened like a cornered leopard.

'Miss Duquesne, take my revolver. I cannot leave you out here unprotected.' He winced as he dismounted. 'Do you know how to use it? Look, let me show you.'

She tried to concentrate as he explained the principals of its mechanism, but in her mind's eye all she saw was a purple mound splayed amongst the tobacco crop. How long would it take for the vultures to dispose of the body?

'*No*, Miss Duquesne! *Never* point a loaded weapon at anyone unless you mean business! As a safety precaution, I suggest you carry it out of harm's way in that bag of yours.'

Is anyone out there? She is speaking in Mamma's voice. There is no sound to be heard. She steals down the wooden staircase to the hunting gallery. Her friends are waiting. She taps gently on the glass. They stiffen: the owl, mongoose, wild piglet and the mugger's chick. She taps again. Is anyone there? This time the glass shatters into a thousand pieces and falls like droplets to her feet. She holds her breath . . . and hears a distant rumble: the ogre is snoring, lying insensible in a drunken stupor. Her friends blink; shake themselves from their long entranced sleep and bound out of their cases. Wait for me! But they are too quick for her. They scurry out of the hunting gallery and out of the house, their joyous shrieks echoing through the night. She glides into the dining room and lights all the candles. The room grows brighter and hotter, until it is bathed in a blinding hard white light. Laughing, she picks up the candelabrum and steers swiftly from room to room, pulling grimacing heads off the walls and piling them in a long train behind her. She climbs the stairs. The drunken snores beckon her like fingers to the ogre's bedchamber. She creeps inside. She watches the huge purple mound rise and fall as he snores, and chuckles softly as flames lick the bed hangings and start a merry dance. She is the Pied Piper leading a line of dancing children to the roof. Flames crackle and spit, spewing orange embers high into the night sky.

She woke, shivering with cold. She could hear animals skulking around the *machan*. The lame pony, tethered below, neighed and tried to kick out at them. Sanjit had not walked to the village to fetch a carpenter after all; he had positioned himself halfway up the rickety ladder where he could keep watch over them. He shouted and threw stones until the jackals scurried off across the fields, their manic shrieks echoing into the night.

She snuggled close to Alice, wrapping her shawl tightly around them both, while Sita slept huddled in a *chuddah* at their feet.

Fruit bats were flying over; dawn was a faint glimmer along the horizon when Sanjit's head appeared above the platform.

'No good stay here, Miss-Sahib.' He pointed to a white track, barely visible through the ground mist, snaking between the fields. 'We go my village. Better.'

He stared at her with dark anxious eyes. But she trusted this abused servant more than she ever would Mr Wilson.

She kissed the sleeping child awake. 'Alice, ask Sanjit how far his village is from here.'

He held up two fingers.

'Two *koss*,' yawned Alice, rubbing her eyes.

Francina delved into her carpetbag for paper and a crayon and tore a sheet out of her sketchbook.

'Alice, ask Sanjit the name of his village.'

He told her, and she wrote the name down phonetically:

Mr Wilson - We are going to the village, which is about four miles along the track that forks from here to the east – It is the village where the syce comes from. We will wait for you there.

Francina Duquesne & Alice Bulpitt. 2 June 1857.

She tucked the note in a gap between two planks in the wall of the *machan* where Mr Wilson would easily find it.

'Do you think you could walk a little, Alice? My arms are tired.'

Francina lowered the child gently to the ground. They must have been trudging along this path, which was little more than a disused goat track, for several hours now. The sun was burning - it scorched her shoulders through the fine lawn of her nightgown. And the piercing glare had encouraged a thumping headache to build behind her eyes.

'But my feet hurt – and the ground's hot!' wailed Alice.

'I know, dearest,' said Francina, wiping perspiration from her eyes. She looked down at her own dusty gold-embroidered slippers, designed to slide over cool marble floors and wondered how much longer they would last. The soles were rapidly disintegrating on this unforgiving terrain.

Sanjit handed Francina the pony's reins and lifted the little girl onto his shoulders. Alice put her arms around his neck and smiled.

'What a pity you left your *solar topee* behind, Alice.'

Francina folded up her shawl and placed it like a flat cushion on Alice's head to protect her from the sun.

'Will it have burnt in the fire?'

'I'm afraid so, Alice.'

She was too tired to prolong the conversation. Her throat was parched, she was dizzy with fatigue. All around them, fields of poppy, pulse and indigo trembled in the searing heat.

They trudged on again in silence, their pace dictated by the pony who was limping badly. Francina stroked her muzzle to encourage her, but she wondered how much longer the poor creature was destined for this world. Mr Bulpitt would take one look at her and shoot her cleanly through the head.

'*Pani, pani,*' whimpered Alice.

'Hush, Alice. When we get to Sanjit's village, you can have a drink of water, I promise.'

'How much further is it?'

'Not far now.'

They disturbed a flock of parrots grazing in a poppy field. The birds rose sluggishly into the air, drowsy on an overdose of opium. Men working nearby looked up when they heard the commotion and smirked at the strange little procession. One of them shouted to Sanjit, who grunted curtly in reply. Their incivility unsettled Francina and her hand crept for reassurance to the carpet bag balanced on the pony's back.

Soon the track joined a wider, badly rutted path.

'*Pani.*'

Sanjit pointed in the distance to an old acacia tree growing by the path, where they could just make out the stonework of a well. They quickened their pace. The pony, sensing water, also found a renewed burst of energy to reach the well.

'My mother thank you, Miss-Sahib,' said Sanjit slowly, pointing to his healed wounds.

A frail weather-beaten woman dressed in a widow's sari, nodded shyly from a dark corner of her hut, too overwhelmed to address her guest directly. She had probably never seen a white woman before, let alone found one sitting on the floor of her hut. It was difficult to tell how old she was, but a life of hard physical drudge on the Indian plains had probably aged her beyond her years. Francina wanted to say that it was she who should thank Sanjit for bringing them to this place of safety, but she did not speak their language. Instead, she nodded and smiled in frustration.

A crowd had gathered at the open doorway, to ogle and gape at the *mem-log* as though they were nothing more than caged curiosities in the Zoological Gardens. Francina caught the words '*feringhi*' and '*Angrezi-log*', and although the crowd seemed largely benign, she detected mocking undertones to their whispers. Sanjit shouted abusively and the crowd dispersed. Then he lowered the *chits* and untied the bamboo curtain at the door opening to give them a modicum of privacy.

Sanjit's sister, a slender girl of about twelve years old, placed small palm-leaf bowls of nuts, seeds and plantains on the ground in front of them and backed away, her almond-shaped eyes fixed on Alice, mesmerised by her golden curls.

'Eat, eat!' urged Sanjit's mother, through her son.

She felt embarrassed to accept food from these poor people, but she knew it would be impolite not to do so. She suspected that Sanjit's mother and sister probably existed on one meagre meal a day. While she sipped water and nibbled nuts, Sanjit took his mother and sister aside and began to whisper in their language. She caught the words 'Sahib Bulpitt' and 'Nudinapur' as she sank to the mud floor and fell asleep beside Alice and Sita.

Furtive whispering outside the hut woke her, and she sat up. Mr Wilson must have arrived to escort them to Wilsonghur. Her eyes darted round the hut. Alice and Sita were still asleep. Could she escape through the window and hide in the scrub? But she could never get far in bare feet (out of politeness, she had left her threadbare slippers at the entrance). He would follow her on horseback, and flail her to the ground with his whip.

She crept towards the opening and peeped through the bamboo curtain. Sanjit was conferring with a group of village elders on the mud platform. His mother and sister were squatting at a discrete distance from them, shaping pancakes of cow dung and slapping them onto the wall to dry. Shadows were swinging to the east. It must be early afternoon. Reassured, that Mr Wilson had not appeared, she sipped some tepid water and fell asleep again.

She spent the rest of the day in a half-waking, half-sleeping trance, until Sanjit's sister touched her gently and offered her a portion of their precious evening meal. A scrawny hen ran into the hut after her, searching for morsels.

Alice frowned at the mound of rice and dhal. 'I don't like this!'

'Just be a good girl and eat it.'

Francina scooped up dhal with her fingers as Sita was doing, and smiled to herself. She had discarded her past life as easily as a snake sloughs off a skin and - despite her present discomforts - felt more liberated than she had ever felt before.

Sanjit and his family ate their meal outside. When he had finished, he came into the hut and began to gesticulate with troubled urgency.

'Sanjit says bad time for *Angrezi-log,*' translated Alice. 'We must stay inside, out of sight.' She threw grains of rice across the clean floor and chuckled as a hen darted after them. 'Sanjit says if Sahib Wilson not come tonight, *ekka* will take us to Wilsonghur in the morning.'

Mr Wilson had not appeared by the time they were preparing to spend their second night away from Nudinapur. Sanjit's mother and sister chose to sleep outside, huddled close to the embers of the dung fire, while their guests appropriated the hut. Sanjit slept in the doorway, carefully positioned to protect both the females outside and those inside.

While Alice murmured in her arms and the jackals howled like banshees, Francina lay awake, staring at the crescent moon glinting through the bamboo curtain. A refrain from a nursery song kept repeating over and over in her head . . .

For who goes up your winding stair can ne'er come down again . . .

Was this to be her last night of freedom? She knew in her bones that if she went to Wilsonghur, she would never leave. This surely was the work of Providence, her chance to break free and get as far away from Mr Wilson as possible. Could she persuade the *ekka* driver to take her to Cissie Balfour at Tirhgunj? It was a long way, and no doubt dangerous, but what had she to lose? She was living on borrowed time.

By cockcrow she had formulated her plan.

JUNGLI
June 1857

Sanjit had looked puzzled when she announced that she was not going to Wilsonghur. 'Sahib Wilson – bad man,' she had explained. Reluctantly, he helped her prepare for a journey in the opposite direction. At her request, he had forced the lock of Mamma's jewellery box with a twisted piece of wire and, as she hoped, they discovered several items of jewellery inside. Sanjit had taken a heavy gold necklace to the moneylender, and from the proceeds had procured bowls, dry food stores and native clothing from the bazaar. She had kept the remaining handful of *rupees* for emergencies, but had given Sanjit a smaller gold necklace as a gift. And to make sure he would not be accused of theft or abduction, she had written a long note *To Whom It May Concern* explaining what she had done.

By late morning they had packed the hired *ekka* with provisions for the journey and had left before Mr Wilson had time to make his appearance. Sanjit had travelled with them to his uncle's village, a day's drive away. Disguised in native clothes, they had entered the village unnoticed, and were quickly ushered into the uncle's hut. There they crouched in the semi-darkness in a stifling hut, between the potter's wheel and stacked earthenware pots, while Sanjit and his uncle conferred on the mud platform outside.

Eventually, the two men stepped inside. Their faces were drawn and unsmiling.

'I beg you, Miss-Sahib, go back,' Sanjit's uncle said through Alice. 'Not good for *mem-log* to travel in oxcart.'

'Then I stay here. I will never go back.'

Alice translated. Silence followed. An animated argument ensued. Francina glanced from Sanjit's troubled face to the old man's pock-marked one. Were they deciding how best to get rid of the *mem-log*? They could so easily hit them over the head and throw their bodies into the river. They would be devoured in a flash by the muggers and disappear without a trace. Who would admit to having seen a white woman and child in this hut? (Certainly not the uncle's wife, who was standing in the doorway glowering at them.) Sanjit could take the remaining jewels and sell them for an exorbitant price. No one would question him. He had a letter to prove they were a gift. Had she mentioned specific items in the letter - or jewellery in general? What a stupid oversight.

Eventually Sanjit's uncle raised his hands in a gesture of weary resignation. 'Oxcart slow. Many days to reach Tirhgunj,' he said through Alice.

Trembling with relief, Francina offered him a small down payment and the promise of a large payment when they arrived, but she wished that it were Sanjit who was taking them to Tirhgunj. She had little confidence in this sullen, pockmarked old man.

They had been travelling in this old bullock cart for three days now, and she knew little more about Sanjit's uncle than she did at the beginning of the journey. She had learned only that his name was Krishna. The cart was carrying a selection of his pots, stacked in varying shapes and sizes. It was a clever deception. A passer-by would see nothing unusual: just an old potter travelling with his family to sell their wares in the bazaar.

Three days . . . at little more than walking pace . . . It was a slow, painful journey, for the bullocks required regular stops for food, water and rest.

A camel train, led by angry-looking men with large turbans, black beards and curled knives thrust into their cummerbunds, was approaching. Francina quickly pulled the sari over her face and hid her sunburnt toes under the folds of her sari. Alice did the same. Through the fine weave of her disguise, she watched the line of haughty camels and their drivers plod past, kicking up a cloud of dust that caught in her throat and made her eyes smart. A youth, at the rear of the train, glanced curiously at them and she held her breath, hoping he would not realise that they were *feringhi*. A camel wandered off course and distracted the youth. He ran after it, shouting and waving his stick.

'Good girl, Alice,' Francina whispered, when the danger had

passed. The child's fair hair was a pressing concern, and Alice was instructed to keep it covered and to hide herself in the presence of strangers. It was a difficult task for a lively, inquisitive child.

She had not planned to take Alice with her. She had hoped that the child would have travelled to Wilsonghur while she made her escape in the opposite direction. But Alice had thrown such a tantrum that there seemed no option. 'You may come with me on the condition that you do exactly as you are told,' she had said. 'This is going to be a long, uncomfortable and dangerous journey.' Alice had raised liquid eyes and promised.

Sanjit would have delivered the note to Jane by now, explaining that Alice was on her way to Tirhgunj. Poor Jane must be frantic with worry.

Sita pointed to a blue bird with a big head and a heavy black bill sitting in the branches of a nim tree. The bird eyed them warily but did not fly away. Francina smiled. It was the first blue jay she had seen since Jacques had pointed one out at Moisgunge. Perhaps – like the earrings - it was a good omen. It had been an unexpected thrill to discover Mamma's emerald earrings in the jewellery box. The earrings had sparkled in her cupped hands with as much vitality as they had once sparkled in her dreams. She had held the earrings up to the light and remembered how she used to tiptoe into Mamma's room and find her at her dressing table. Mamma would catch her eye in the glass as she hooked the shimmering jewels into her lobes and smile, 'Is that you, my darling?'

She would nod and sidle up.

'Can't you sleep, my darling?'

She would shake her head and wait for Mamma to reach for the crystal perfume bottle with its blue silk tassel. It was a little game they used to play.

'Hold out your wrists, my darling.'

Mamma would spray a cool concoction over her, and she would scamper back to bed and fall asleep drenched in Mamma's scent.

But why did Mamma leave the earrings behind?

Providence. Her daughter was meant to find them. They were her gift, a talisman to protect her on this difficult journey. When this ordeal is over, she will take the earrings to the moneylender in Calcutta and exchange them for the moonstone necklace. Then

Grand-mère will take her in again, and everything will be as it was before.

There was another surprise in the jewellery box: a small square of tissue on which was penned the name *Albert.* Unfolding it, she had discovered a coil of fair baby hair, as soft and fine as chick's down.

Sita reached up and broke twigs off an overhanging tree. She peeled the bark off the twigs, and handed them around as eagerly as she would a plate of cakes.

'For cleaning your teeth,' Alice explained, rubbing the twig across her teeth as Sita was doing. Francina copied, grateful for anything that might make her feel fresher.

How many drab dusty miles have they covered in this creaking bullock cart? How many temples and mud-walled villages have they passed? How many *nullahs* have they crossed? How many nights have they spent under straw in the bullock cart? It was difficult to think clearly in this heat - and dust . . . so much dust . . . It clung to her hair, to the perspiration trickling down her body, and rubbed between her toes. How she longed to bathe. But only once had it been safe enough to wallow in a stream with the bullocks. Oh, to submerge in cool, cool water with her clothes billowing around her.

They were approaching habitation. Francina pulled the sari over her face. Alice did the same. They had become chrysalises, pupae; worms burrowing in the dark.

A woman, enveloped in a *burqa* and balancing a huge earthenware pot on her head, ambled past and glanced at the cowering forms in the bullock cart through her eye grille. Francina eyed *burqa* woman through the weave of her sari, and tried to imagine who she was. Perhaps the eyes behind the embroidered grille were doing the same. Two faceless shapes inspecting each other . . . She sensed empathy in the eyes behind the grille. They were sisters. Shapeless nonentities; suspended in time and waiting for the moment to transmogrify.

Suddenly a noise, like the distant rumble of thunder, filled the silence. *Burqa* woman stepped out of the way. Old Krishna shouted and twisted the tails of the bullocks. The cart stopped precariously close to the ditch.

'Quick, Alice, under the *bhossa*!'

Sensing her fear, Alice dived amongst the sacks of straw without a murmur of protest. Francina threw sacking over her. In her haste, the sari slipped off her head, and she qucikly covered herself again. Her heart pounding, she glanced at *burqa* woman. Had she noticed?

The rumble grew louder; it was accompanied by aggressive chanting. What she had feared most came galloping towards them: a group of mutinous sowars, about twelve in number, in a mismatched assortment of dirty uniforms, were riding hard towards them waving curved swords above their heads. Several were brandishing muskets.

'Deen! Deen!' they roared defiantly. *'Fatteh Mohammed!'*

One young rebel carried a tattered green flag. As he galloped past, he glanced at the bullock cart and halted abruptly. Francina shut her eyes. It was about to happen. He would tear the sari off her head, discover that she was an impostor and kill her – or worse . . .

Old Krishna began to gabble excitedly.

It was all over. The old man was denouncing them to save his skin. She had never trusted him. Those shifty eyes, that sullen expression -

The rebel shouted back at him. She caught the words: *Allahabad - feringhi – kuttle – Cawnpore -*

The rebel came closer, mesmerised by the anonymous shape cowering besides the old driver. He pointed aggressively and shouted again.

Suddenly there was a shrieking tirade of abuse from *burqa* woman. She had put her pot on the ground and was waving two plump hands in the air, pointing angrily up and down the lane. The young sowar was caught by surprise. Perhaps the veiled woman reminded him of his mother or his grandmother for he answered her sheepishly, full of apology. But *burqa* woman was not satisfied. She continued her harangue until the sepoy bolted off in a cloud of dust to join his fellows, shouting, *'Deen! Deen!'*

Old Krishna muttered under his breath and spat in the dust. Grunting at *burqa* woman, he tugged the bullocks' tails, and they shuffled off again.

*

Only the bullocks seem unaffected by the encounter with the sowars. They crawl at their usual pace, responding eventually to a tug on the tail or a whack across the rump. Crawling . . . to the next water stop. Old Krishna sits hunched beside her, silently masticating *pān*. She reads anxiety in his posture as he spits a stream of red liquid into the dust. Why he is risking his life for this *feringhi?* Why doesn't he just abandon them in the middle of nowhere and return to his village? How would Sanjit ever know that he had not delivered them to Tirhgunj?

Everything dances in the shimmering heat . . . What is real, what a mirage? A hot wind blows, throws up dust and desiccated matter. High above, vultures follow like sinister portents. Thunder rumbles. Lightning flashes in bursts across the sky. But no rain. When will the Rains come? The native food is beginning to take its toll. Nothing but rice, chapattis, dhal . . . And the niggle in her head has grown to a thumping pain that stops her from sleeping. Even with her eyes shut, the glare seeps through her lids and burns the backs of her eyes. She is so weary, so tired of this blistering heat. If only she could pull down *chiks* . . . shut venetians, fall asleep in a dark room . . . dream of a cool, cool stream . . . wake up when this is over.

'My skin itches,' whimpered Alice.

'Try not to scratch, dearest.' Francina looked in alarm at the pink rash that had erupted on her face and arms. She filled a bowl with water from the *surahi* and held it out for her to drink.

Sita dipped a strip of nightdress (which now served as essential rags) in the water and placed it over the child's flushed forehead. Alice fell back onto the straw between the earthenware pots, under the makeshift awning of sacking and shut her eyes.

'It's so hot!' she said in a small muffled voice.

Sita leaned over to fan the flies off her face, as she had done for most of the day. Francina returned to her huddled position under the sari, too fatigued to cajole the child. She should have insisted on leaving Alice behind.

The sun was sinking; shadows were lengthening. Refreshed from their siestas birds sang in the thickets, and a jungle fowl darted audaciously in front of the cart, as if to say: 'Catch me if you can!'

The landscape was changing . . . stony ground and thorn scrub were giving way to high grass and choking bamboo. Tiger country. A troop of monkeys whooped and screeched through the trees like a band of disaffected sepoys. The birds took flight. Had something frightened them? The tall grass beside the lane had recently been trampled, and there was a strong smell of wild boar in the vicinity.

She unclasped the carpetbag at her feet and felt inside for the pistol. It was just as well to have it within reach. Something might be lurking in the grass, waiting to pounce.

There was a lifeless bundle on the lane ahead of them - possibly a deer savaged by a tiger or a leopard. As they drew nearer, she leaned across old Krishna to take a closer look.

It was the body of a man. A beggar perhaps – his clothes were nothing more than tattered remnants, his body just skin and bone. There was no sign of a struggle, no gaping wounds, no indication that he might have died fending off a savage beast. Was he bitten by a cobra? Did he starve to death, poor man?

A blood-curdling shriek filled the silence. *'Miss-Sahib*!'

Before she registered what was happening, a man had sprung out of the undergrowth and was running towards her brandishing a knife. He snatched the carpetbag, and began to run. She stared at the space between her feet in disbelief. Everything she treasured - gone. She sprang from her cowering position, a thing possessed.

'No!' she screamed. 'Bring it back, you filthy robber!'

Picking up an earthenware pot, she threw it at him with all the strength she could muster. To her surprise, it caught him on the back of his head. He gasped and stumbled, dropping the carpetbag. The contents spewed out across the ground.

Armed with another pot, Francina jumped out of the cart as the man was staggering to his feet. She threw the pot hard at him. This pot missed, shattering everywhere. Seeing her coming like a deranged beast towards her, he grabbed the jewellery box.

'Drop it!' she screamed, diving for the pistol which he had not noticed lying in the grass.

The man froze when he saw the pistol, his eyes large and white with terror. He began to gabble in his language, pleading for his life she supposed, while he backed away with the box still clasped to his chest.

'Drop it or I fire!'

He showed no inclination to drop the box. Holding the pistol in two hands, she fired.

He stood paralysed, expecting to keel over writhing in pain.

But - he was unharmed. In that instant, they both realised that the pistol was unloaded. Now, Francina was afraid. She saw his eyes narrow and his mouth fix into a terrifying grimace as he bellowed, raised his knife and lunged at her. She jumped out of the way. The knife grazed her arm, and a searing pain shot through her body. At that moment, another pot crashed down on his head. Sita was standing in the cart, pelting the man with pots. The man tottered and fell again, dropping the knife and the box, which spilled open. Francina saw the earrings sparkling in the dust, but she dived for the knife before the man could stagger to his feet. Ducking and weaving to avoid the knife and the pots crashing around him, the man grabbed what treasures he could and limped off into the undergrowth, issuing a torrent of deadly threats.

His accomplice, meanwhile, had transmogrified from an inanimate being into a prancing demon that was threatening old Krishna with a knife. The old man lashed out at him with his stick. Sita turned her attention to this villain, and a barrage of earthenware pots now crashed down on him. Screaming, Francina rushed at him with the knife. The man stared at her in horror. Outnumbered, and no match for a raving white woman, he turned tail and ran off to join his fellow in the thicket.

Francina watched him go. She picked up the damaged box. There was nothing left inside - just the square of paper containing baby Albert's hair.

'*Jeldi, Miss-Sahib, jeldi*!' cried Sita, urging her to return to the cart.

Francina glanced at the thicket. The rascals might be spying on them, licking their wounds, planning another assault. She stuffed the box into the carpetbag and climbed stiffly back into the cart. Her legs and arms were bleeding, lacerated by thorn and sharp-edged grasses. Only now, did she realise what danger she had put herself through, and she shook and wept like a baby in Sita's arms.

Old Krishna muttered under his breath, twisted the tails of the bullocks and they set off once more at an agonisingly slow pace.

2

Francina watched Krishna and Sita disappear into the crowded bazaar. She felt frightened and vulnerable without them. The sari concealed her face but she would have a coughing fit if anyone should come too close. But she did not believe anyone (not even the Untouchables sweeping slimy refuse into piles) would approach her. She must be a repellent sight, and probably smelled like a well-seasoned *saddhu*. Her sari, soiled with grime and sweat from umpteen days of travelling, was now splattered with blood. Only the pariah dogs, sniffing around the cart, were finding her remotely interesting. No one else would give this filthy creature in a bullock cart a second look - unless of course those *budmarshes* should arrive in the village and spread a story that an *Angrezi* disguised as a poor native was travelling in a potter's cart.

Sita had rubbed ash dampened by her own spittle into the lacerations on her legs, and had had tied a tourniquet above the wound to stem the blood trickling down her arm. By a stroke of good fortune, the bottle of liniment she had used to clean Sanjit's wounds had found its way into her carpetbag and was not lost during the robbery. They had cleaned the cut and covered it with a clean strip of rag to deter the flies. Her bandaged arm and the bloody sari were now hidden from prying eyes under a *chuddah*.

There was a murmur from the shrouded bundle under the awning. She glanced furtively towards the back of the cart. Alice had slept all day and was losing interest in food. But there was little she could do while they were parked on the edge of the bazaar under the gaze of so many dark suspicious eyes.

'Alice, how are you feeling, dearest?' she whispered.

'I want my mamma,' whimpered Alice.

Villagers were beginning to cook their evening meals. The smell of *ghee*, dung fires, and sandalwood mixed with the occasional whiff of an aromatic spice, floated over the stench of sewage, urine and rotting garbage. It was the amalgam of smells that characterised every Indian bazaar they had travelled through. To distract herself from the smells that made her feel hungry and nauseous, Francina ran her finger along the red velvet interior of the battered jewellery box. She had kept Mamma's box close to her since the robbery, terrified of losing it again. The velvet lining was coming loose, and she prised it gently away from the side. Something was concealed behind the lining. Holding her breath, she extracted three small scraps of paper, tightly folded. She unfolded the first scrap. It was a note, written in a bold hand – quite unlike Mamma's artistic hand. The ink had smudged, whether by raindrops or tears, she could not tell, but it was still legible:

3rd April 1841

Dear Mrs Duquesne

I lie here, fighting to restrain myself from riding over and knocking him senseless. But I know that would only aggravate the situation. You will never convince him that his suspicions are groundless. Your husband is a jealous man. It is only natural - you are a very beautiful woman. I must leave at once and resolve never to see you again, for I cannot bear to be the cause of all your pain and suffering.

I remain your most devoted friend and admirer, Edmund Havers

She tried to put the date of the note into context. Mamma and Papa were living in Moisgunge then . . . she was three - almost four years old. Angelo was five, and baby Albert must have been . . .

She shut her eyes and tried to recall the date on the tombstone . . . about six months old.

The other notes were written some nine months later:

15th January 1842

Darling Angel

You cannot bring the children with us! In the eyes of the Law they are his. You have no claim on them. The Law will pursue us mercilessly. We would find no resting place. Think hard of the implications, my Darling. What would be their future? What would be ours? To make this venture succeed, you must be prepared never to see them again - and that is a sacrifice I cannot ask you to make.

Yours devotedly, Edmund

28th January 1842

Sweet, sweet Angel –

The only way to convince him that Albert is his - is to leave the child behind. There is no other way. But can you take that risk, my Darling? Might he not inflict his revenge still further on the poor innocent babe?

Your own Edmund

Francina clutched herself. Mamma did take the risk. Three weeks later Albert was dead.

She is that little girl again, curled up under her mosquito net, almost asleep . . . Something disturbs her. Rubbing her eyes, she scrabbles out of bed and peeps though the *jilmils* . . . Two silhouetted figures, a man and a woman with their heads close together are whispering at the far end of the verandah. But this time she does not race across the matting towards them, anticipating that delicious moment when Papa will turn around, scoop her up and pretend to scold: 'Why is my naughty little imp not sleeping?' as he whirls her round, and she will giggle and throw back her head to watch the starry canopy transform into a gigantic Catherine wheel. This time she hesitates, shrinks into the shadows and keeps her presence hidden. Something is wrong. Their voices are tight, constrained. Mamma's head is cowed. Papa's posture is stiff, menacing. He slaps her across the face with such force that Mamma reels back against the chair. The sound reports through the night, like gunshot. Once. Twice. Thrice. Mamma sinks slowly to her knees, cradling her head in her arms. It is her silence, her complete submissiveness that is so shocking. Paralysed with fear, the little girl cowers behind the pillar, too stunned to cry. The commotion wakes baby who sleeps in a cot by Mamma's bed. He wails at the top of his lungs, the spokesman for their terror. Papa turns his head towards the noise, his fists clenched in rage. He steps over Mamma, kicks her aside and makes for the bedroom. Mamma is roused into action. Leaning against the upturned chair, she drags herself up. A dark red gash stains the front of her dress.

She stumbles after Papa. 'Frank, for pity's sake! Leave him be!'

Mamma's cries echo through the night like the howl of a wounded animal. Baby senses Mamma's fear. His cries become shriller. How can such a little being produce such a big noise? Baby's screams are accompanied by other sounds; muffled, thumping sounds that the little girl has heard in her sleep. She runs into the nursery and jumps back into her cot. She pulls the pillow over her head to block out the noise. But it is loud, so loud. It goes on and on and on. She cannot drown it out.

Angelo has heard it too. He tugs at the mosquito net, and climbs into the cot beside her.

'It's only a game. Cover your ears, Ina.' He strokes her hair like Mamma does. 'It is only the jackal attacking a deer down by the nullah.'

3

The evening meal was a mute affair of stale chapattis and over-ripe plantains, for they had run out of dried stores. The spare rupees she had kept in Mamma's box were lost during the scuffle, and now there was nothing left to buy food.

As daylight faded, they settled down for an uneasy night in the cart on the edge of a village. Old Krishna slept slumped in his driving position, as though ready to leave at a moment's notice. Earlier, she had seen him conferring with some village elders outside the temple. What had they discussed? What had he heard? She hated being at the mercy of this old silent man.

The bullocks were tethered near a small fire to keep predators away. She lay beside Alice's hot shivering body. Her arm was stiff and throbbed with pain. The encounter with the robbers had left her mentally and physically exhausted; the mosquitoes droned and bit, and the hot wind that had swirled dust and debris all day showed no sign of abating. It was going to be a long, oppressive and uncomfortable night. She stared at the waning moon, listened to the owls hooting and the dogs howling - but more importantly, she was listening for barking deer to sound the alarm of a tiger in the vicinity. (But if one attacked, what should she do? The pistol would be as useful as a piece of driftwood.) She kissed Alice's feverish forehead. She owed it to this child to stay alive.

Something crashed through the undergrowth. She held her breath. But it was probably wild boar or *nilghai* – a tiger would not announce his presence so crassly.

It is still dark when old Krishna harnesses the animals to set off again. He walks beside the bullocks holding a lamp to light the way. She is too exhausted to open her eyes, but knows the road is badly rutted. Each jolt of the cart sends a shooting pain up her arm.

She is floating, floating on a soft white cloud, high in the firmament, watching a miserable group of people struggle through the undergrowth. At times the bullock cart seems to disappear under choking elephant grass. This cannot be the road to Tirhgunj. Is it a short cut? Why don't you take the *pukka* road! she shouts at the top of her voice, but they are too far away to hear. In any case that old man does not understand a word she says . . .

Every bone in her body aches. She feels light-headed, whether from heat or hunger or fever, she cannot tell. Her throat is parched. Her arm throbs. The flies buzz incessantly, attracted by the smell of dried blood. They land on her face, crawl across her cheeks. But she is too tired to brush them off . . . When will the sun show mercy?

Sita helped her sit up, poured water into a bowl and urged her to drink. She opened her dry lids and tried to focus. The landscape had changed. Neat square fields and thin irrigation channels as far as the eye could see. She recognised the crop. Indigo – almost ready to harvest. Ahead, an avenue of trees led to a large white pillared house with a high thatched roof.

'Tirhgunj?' she whispered.

At that moment, two official-looking Sikhs riding country ponies and brandishing lead clubs, sprang out from nowhere and postured menacingly. Old Krishna gabbled to them. She caught the words: *budmarsh - Angrezi-log.* Still gabbling, he climbed down, hobbled to the back of the cart and threw the covering off little Alice with a dramatic flourish. The child whimpered in terror and hid her face under her arm. Her hair was splayed like molten gold across the sacking.

'Don't be frightened, Alice!'

Somehow, Francina found the strength to climb to the back of the cart. The Sikhs stared at the filthy apparition, the shameful specimen of white womanhood crawling over the sacks of straw. She scooped the child up and cradled her to her bosom to shield her face from their assassins. The pain in her arm was excruciating, but no matter. It would soon be over. She shut her eyes and waited for the blows to knock them both senseless.

But nothing happened.

The Sikhs shouted at old Krishna, waved their clubs and

indicated that he must follow them. The old man climbed obediently back into the cart, whacked the bullocks, and they shuffled down the avenue like condemned prisoners going to the gallows. Dogs accompanied them – not mangy pariah dogs with corkscrew tails, but sleek, well-fed hunting dogs. Hearing the noise, dusky children, neatly shod and dressed in European clothes, poured out of the white house all shouting at once; they were followed by attendants in crisp white uniforms. The children circled around the cart, pointing and giggling. Francina cowed under her sari and covered her ears to block out their jeers.

Somewhere, a man boomed in an authoritative voice. The children stopped laughing and fell silent as a horse trotted briskly down the drive.

'*Pourquoi tout ce bruit, les enfants*?'

'*Ce sont des pauvres, Papa. Des pauvres blancs.*'

A hand touched her gently on the arm. 'Madame?'

Madame? Such a respectful, courteous word. She peeped out of the sari to see a bespectacled gentleman peering anxiously into her face. It was difficult to focus for spots were dancing before her eyes, but for a moment she though it was Uncle Vauloué.

'*Vous êtes anglaise, Madame*? You Eenglish?'

She tried to answer - but darkness swallowed her up.

4

Russel Street, Chowringhee, Calcutta, India

3 September 1857

My dear Mrs Doré,

It is with great joy that I am able to tell you that after three months of anxiety, we are able to report that Francina has been found safe and well. She and my great-granddaughter Alice were taken in by some kind planters who kept them under their roof and are nursing them back to health. They appeared one day at their door in a bullock cart, bedraggled and in a poor way. At first Francina was too ill to tell them who she was or where they had come from, so it is only now that the story of their astonishing escape from the burning house at Nudinapur has come to light. We are beside ourselves with happiness at the news of their safe delivery, having feared that they must have perished in the terrible Insurrections.

When the Rains subside, & the roads are safe, my niece's husband Mr Balfour will collect them and take them back to Tirhgunj. My niece is adamant that Francina and Alice must stay under her roof for as long as it takes for them to recover their strength. Luckily, all seems quiet at Tirhgunj. It appears to be one of the few Civil Stations that escaped the Troubles. As yet we have had no news of my granddaughter Mrs Bulpitt, or the rest of the party that fled from Nudinapur that night, but this miraculous news of Alice & Francina has raised our hopes that we will soon hear the joyous news of their deliverance as well. I understand that on the night of the fire, most of the party fled westwards, but Francina and Alice became separated & travelled eastwards. We can only thank Providence for sparing them.

Calcutta is in state of turmoil, overwhelmed with dazed and frightened fugitives, the majority of them women & children, who are arriving by the boatload from the Upper Provinces, each bringing their own woeful tale of atrocities. Daily, we scour the lists of arrivals, searching for the names of our loved ones - one day, God Willing, we will learn of their safe delivery.

We are plunged into the deepest grief by the melancholy tale of the poor women & children who were massacred in the bibighar. The horror of the story can scarcely be surpassed. All over Town the cry of vengeance is rising. We are holding our breath that Lucknow does not prove to be another Cawnpore, but these constant delays for reinforcements are most provoking. With the telegraph wires cut & the dâks disrupted, news reaches Calcutta only spasmodically. Troops arrive daily from abroad, but in this vast country it takes so long for them to reach their destination.

I must also report that Mr Barton and I will be leaving India next month. My ailments continue to trouble me, and my dear husband says I must delay no longer but seek expert medical advice in London. It has been difficult to book a passage while so many others are also trying to leave, and it distresses me to think that I might be taking the berth of a refugee whose needs are so much greater than mine, but I cannot argue with Mr Barton. He insists that we must go. I beg however to assure you my dear Mrs Doré, that I shall be leaving Francina in very capable hands.

Mr Barton joins me in sending you and Mr Doré our best regards. God bless you both.

I remain yours affectionately, Maria Barton

TIRHGUNJ
October 1857

'Your arm is healing nicely. That planter's bizarre treatment seems to have stopped the infection from spreading. He probably saved both your arm and your life.'

'Maggots,' whispered Francina, rolling down the sleeve of her peignoir to hide the bandage, 'Monsieur Martine cleaned the wound with maggots.'

Cissie Balfour held a handkerchief to her mouth and tried not to retch. 'Fanny dear, it must have been perfectly frightful. Now, thank goodness, you are in the safe hands of a respectable English doctor.'

The doctor inclined his head modestly.

'I believe Monsieur Martine was a surgeon before he became an indigo planter,' Francina said curtly. English, this doctor may be, but she did not like his supercilious attitude or the smell of liqueur on is breath. 'And it would not be an exaggeration to say that he probably saved Alice's life as well. He treated her with his own special medicinal, which cured her dysentery.'

'Did he indeed?' The doctor snapped his bag shut. 'Well, Miss Duquesne, I must take my leave. Other patients, etcetera, demand my attention.'

Cissie signalled to the bearer to show the doctor out. 'So good of you to come in this inclement weather, Doctor.'

The doctor raised his hat and departed.

'Now, Fanny dear,' said Cissie, as his buggy rumbled out of the drive, 'will you receive visitors this morning? The ladies of the Station are so anxious to meet you.'

'Of course, Cissie. Everyone has been so generous . . . I must write to thank them. Mrs Smythe for the dress and undergarments, Miss Nye for the bonnet. But my arm -'

'Hush, Fanny! Everyone understands - although why Mrs Smythe should have thought it fitting to palm you off with her old clothes, I find rather insulting. Does she imagine that *we* cannot provide for our own flesh and blood? I expressly *forbid* you to wear any of Mrs Smythe's cast-offs, Fanny. It would make *me* – the Collector's wife - look particularly mean and uncaring.'

Cissie stopped to adjust her lace cap in the looking glass. 'I shall put her garments in a box and send them down to Calcutta. Mamma tells me that Lady Canning has a team of ladies collecting old clothes for the destitute refugees.'

'I know why Miss Fanny has a bad arm,' cried Alice. 'A nasty man cut her with a knife!'

'Alice, you must never tell *anyone* that horrid story. It must remain our little secret. It makes Miss Fanny sad to be reminded of it - and we don't want to make Miss Fanny sad, do we?'

'No Aunt Cissie,' pouted Alice, tickling baby Maud's nose with a feather. The baby chuckled with delight.

'Now, Fanny dear, it is time to get ready to meet the ladies of the Station. I suggest you wear your new striped gown. A shawl should conceal the bandage. - Alice, you must change too. Put on you new dress and clean white stockings. Ask ayah to comb your hair and tie it up with ribbons. And do *not* bring that filthy old doll into the drawing room. If I see it again, I shall throw it on the fire!'

Cissie arranged her protégé artistically on the chaise longue, teased a hair back into place, and spread her skirts carefully, so that the blue striped skirts fanned out like a peacock's tail. When she was satisfied with the picture, she arranged herself on the chair beside Francina and took up her work.

The clock ticked quietly as they waited.

While she had been confined to bed for most of the time at Monsieur Martine's, Francina had grown used to – and was comforted by - the constant buzz of his twelve children chattering joyfully in the background. The noise had reminded her of Evangelina's twittering *lals*. She was finding the quiet, controlled order in Cissie's household a little disarming. The new white and rose-chintz covers had gone some way to livening up this dull Company drawing room, but nothing here was out of place, nothing left to chance. Everything was designed to impress.

Whispers were heard on the verandah.

Cissie presented the ladies of Tirhgunj as they tiptoed reverently into the drawing room and filed past the chaise longue. Mrs Robinson held out a bouquet of red rosebuds. 'I picked them myself. The first roses of the season.'

Cissie thanked her on her cousin's behalf, and handed the bouquet to a bearer.

'It is so very good of you to see us, Miss Duquesne,' said Mrs Smythe. 'We shall not impose on your time for too long. We know you are still recovering from your dreadful ordeal.'

Francina smiled and inclined her head, resisting the urge to thank Mrs Smythe publicly for the clothes.

'Miss Duquesne, we are so honoured,' gushed her sister Miss Nye, curtsying deeply.

'We heard of your daring escape from the burning house -' Mrs Allen said breathlessly.

'- and how you rescued the dear child from the jaws of death!' added Mrs Low.

Chairs were found for the ladies of Tirhgunj and placed in a semi-circle around the chaise longue. The ladies sat, hands neatly folded in their laps, and stared politely. It slowly dawned on Francina that they were waiting for her to speak. In some strange way, her ignominious adventure in a bullock cart had elevated her to the status of Royalty.

'Thank you for your - gifts,' she began, trying hard to imagine what Lady Canning might say in similar circumstances, 'and for venturing out in this inclement weather.'

'But it has stopped raining,' gushed Miss Nye. 'It stopped raining several hours ago.'

Francina blushed. Lady Canning would have noticed that it had stopped raining.

Silence fell again. Then Mrs Robinson burst out, 'Did it rain much on your journey down to Tirhgunj, Miss Duquesne?'

'I don't believe so – but then I spent most of the time drifting in and out of sleep.'

Her memory of the journey down the Grand Trunk Road to Tirhgunj was little more than a few disjoined fragments . . . She was aware that they were escorted by a small band of well-armed Sikh attendants loyal to Mr Balfour . . . and that the road had thronged with reinforcements - troops newly arrived from the China expedition - the Fusiliers, Highlanders, Foot and Royal Artillery, all weighed down with guns, ammunition, tents and supplies, and all heading for the Upper Provinces on a never-ending bullock train. The soldiers had informed Mr Balfour (to much hearty bravura), that they were on their way to relieve Lucknow. 'Remember Cawnpore!' was the battle cry she heard along the route.

'My cousin was still very weak when my husband brought her home, but we were so anxious to have her safely under our roof.' Cissie gave a small superior smile. 'Of course, it was very kind of the planter to take her in, but when one is ill, only *family* can really provide the proper care and attention.'

'Indeed,' said Mrs Smythe. 'But do tell us, Miss Duquesne, what happened after you escaped from the burning house.'

'And how did you manage to avoid detection?' added her sister. 'The countryside must have been swarming with blood-thirsty murderers.'

'I was in disguise. I was dressed as a native woman.'

The ladies of Tirhgunj held their breath. 'Fancy! And was the child also in disguise?'

'Indeed she was.'

'Coffee, ladies?' interposed Cissie. It was a good moment to divert this line of questioning. She signalled to the bearer.

Coffee was poured. Little refreshments were handed around.

'Where is the child?' whispered Mrs Low, nibbling a Savoy biscuit.

'Playing in the nursery, I believe,' smiled Cissie. 'Sugar, Mrs Smythe?'

'Thank you. Do you think we might possibly . . ?'

'Of course.' Cissie was revelling in her rôle as benefactress. She signalled to the bearer to fetch Missie-Baba.

Mrs Low leaned forward and whispered, 'Tell me, Mrs Balfour, have you had any news of you-know-who?'

'Not a whisper. Of course, we have not given up hope – we must *never* give up hope.'

'No, indeed. We must not give up hope.' Mrs Low said, just audibly.

'Miracles do happen.' Cissie leaned across and patted Francina's hand. 'Who would have thought that after ten weeks of silence we should have received that extraordinary letter telling us that our dear Fanny and little Alice were safe and recovering at a planter's house? Their deliverance is truly a miracle.'

'A miracle,' sighed the ladies of Tirhgunj.

At that moment Alice skipped into the drawing room in a fetching white embroidered organdie dress. The pink satin ribbons in her hair matched the large sash around her waist.

'The little angel!' gasped Mrs Smythe.

'Did you wish to see me, Aunt Cissie?' the little angel asked in her sweetest voice. Who could believe that this innocent little creature framed in the archway was once the filthy urchin asleep in a bullock cart?

Smiling, Cissie held out her hand. 'Come here, dear child.'

Alice ran to her. They understood each other completely. They were both playing the same artful game. Alice had inherited not only her mother's looks but her beguiling charms. She would disarm and propitiate, and make her way in life. And why not? She was learning to survive in a savage, unpredictable world.

'Alice and Lionel play so happily together,' whispered Cissie, running her fingers through Alice's golden tresses. 'If our worst fears should materialise, then we shall bring her up as one of our own. There is no question about it. We have grown so fond of her.'

'And to think she might have been . . .' whispered Mrs Low into her handkerchief. 'Oh, Mrs Balfour, why is there so much senseless cruelty in this world? Seeing this innocent child standing before us - how could anyone . . ? Oh the treachery and merciless barbarity of the ruffians! How can it be that after one hundred years of wise rule and teaching, three months of madness has brought us to this present deplorable state?'

'Hush, Mrs Low, we must not frighten the child.'

Mr Balfour said Grace - as he did before all the meals he presided over. After enduring months of near savagery at Nudinapur, it had come as a shock to Francina to find God again - not the easy, benevolent God she had encountered at Cousin Jacques's or at

Monsieur Martine's, but a commanding, controlling God. Mr Balfour was a gentleman of principle who took his duties seriously. If he was not riding across the town with his Overseer, making sure that his orders for the improvements were being carried out, attending court, or galloping across his district to settle a heated dispute, he was at his desk writing up a learned report. Time was at a premium. So it came as a surprise to find the Magistrate and Collector of Tirhgunj still sitting at the breakfast table. There was, however, a particularly large budget of letters in front of him this morning.

Cissie looked up from her own letter and smiled. 'Mamma is organising a fancy fair to raise funds for the wounded troops that are being brought downriver to the Fever Hospital. Oh, Fanny - we must do the same! *We* must organise a fancy fair, here in Tirhgunj. Don't you think that would be an excellent idea, Archie?'

Mr Balfour appeared not to have heard.

'Archie, dearest, is something wrong?'

His eyes darted from one face to the other. 'I am afraid I have some rather bad news.'

'Oh, Archie,' whispered Cissie. 'What is it?'

'Some time ago I wrote to Kandria asking for information about the Bulpitts. At long last I have received a reply – not from Fraser, the Deputy Commissioner - but from a Lieutenant Hibbert, who appears to be temporarily in charge of the Station. Hibbert questioned some of the Wilsonghur servants and according to them, Mrs Bulpitt, her son and the Mackenzies *did* indeed arrive at the house – but I am afraid Mr Bulpitt did not. A witness states that Mr Bulpitt died at Nudinapur, crushed by falling masonry shortly after the rest of the party left for Wilsonghur.'

'The poor fatherless child!'

And Mr Wilson?' Francina asked. The name that had once caused so much anguish, now tripped easily off her tongue.

Mr Balfour removed his spectacles and wiped the lenses with a large handkerchief. 'Mr Wilson never arrived at Wilsonghur. His body was found on the Kandria road.'

'So – he never returned to find the note,' whispered Francina. 'Jane must have assumed that Alice and I had perished with him.'

'And what news of dear Jane and little Freddie?' Cissie said behind her handkerchief.

'According to the servants, a few days after the party arrived at Wilsonghur (the accounts are not very clear on which day exactly), they awoke to find the house in flames. Understandably (after all the distress they had been through) they decided to flee to Cawnpore and seek refuge in General Wheeler's entrenchment.'

'And did they?'

'Unbeknown to them, that evil scoundrel Nana Sahib had ordered groups of sowars to hunt and murder all Christians, and any Indian found harbouring Christians, in outposts around Cawnpore - in fact, any Christian who had not already taken refuge in the entrenchment.' Mr Balfour put his head in his hands. 'My dears, there is no record of Jane or little Freddie or anyone in their party ever reaching Cawnpore.'

Cissie sobbed into her handkerchief.

'And what of the residents of Kandria, Mr Balfour?' whispered Francina. 'Why did the Deputy Commissioner, Major Fraser not answer to your letter?'

'I am afraid Kandria did not escape the slaughter. Sometime on the 6th June the bungalows of the Europeans and the Christian half casts were razed to the ground by a party of mutinous rebels passing between Delhi and Cawnpore. The jail was sprung open and the prisoners released. Major Fraser and his wife tried to escape in a buggy, but were killed along the Cawnpore road. An eyewitness stated that Major Campbell appeared on the verandah of his bungalow and valiantly kept the rebels at bay for at least an hour with his pistols, but when the villains set the roof alight, the flames drove him and his family into the compound where they were hacked to death. The two clerks, their wives and families died in similar circumstances.'

Blood pounded in her head.

'And what news of Mr Lihou, the Assistant Collector?'

'No trace has been found of the Assistant Collector, or the Doctor.'

No trace . . . She suddenly felt cold and nauseous. The room was spinning. Her tea spilled into her lap, drenched her thighs in hot liquid, but she was powerless to -

'Look to her, Archie, she has fainted!'

2

'Mrs Balfour, may I have a word in private?'

The blinds are down. It is so quiet. Shadows flit in and out of focus . . . Whispers drift round the foot of her bed.

'Are you sure, Doctor? There can be no mistake?'

'I had my suspicions for the last few days - but now I am quite certain.'

'How long?'

'About five months.'

'How appalling! How could it possibly . . ?'

'Open the window, I'm burning!'

'Be quiet, Fanny. I cannot open the window. No one must have the slightest inkling of your condition. Do you quite realise how *difficult* this is for me? As wife of the Collector of Tirhgunj, I have a position to uphold. I think it is best for all concerned if you keep confined to this room for the duration. I shall simply explain to visitors that you have had a relapse and are unfit to receive anyone. Archie must *not* know of this (although how we are going to keep it from him, I have absolutely no idea). Luckily he is so busy at present worrying about the Uprisings that he little time for me or his children - and hardly seems to notice what goes on under his nose. I just *pray* that we can keep this *dreadful* business a secret. Servants are notorious for spreading gossip. That ayah of yours is the only servant who will attend you, Fanny. She seems trustworthy, and unusually devoted to you – why, I cannot quite understand.'

Cissie paced the room in her rustling black silk, beside herself with indignation. How could Fanny do this to her! The heroine she had brought into her home had turned into a pariah. 'As soon as it is born and sent to an orphanage, and you are fit to travel -'

'An orphanage?'

'Naturally! You can't possibly keep it. And I would have thought you would *want* to be rid of that black thing as soon as possible.'

'*Black* thing?'

'Surely you must realise that the *thing* you are carrying is black?'

Francina stared at her.

'Try to think rationally, Fanny. I know that sepoy . . .' Cissie shuddered, driving unspeakable images from her mind. 'Quite frankly, if *I* have been in your place I would have . . .'

Killed myself.

I should have done the honourable thing like those poor women of Cawnpore; noble, brave Englishwomen who took their own lives rather than suffer a fate worse than death. Pure, unsullied heroines of Albion. Cissie would have liked that. She would have honoured me nobly in death. No expense would have been spared to make me a fitting memorial. She would have brandished my name as a saint. 'I had a dear, dear cousin,' she could have confided in a low, anguished voice, 'who suffered dreadfully in the Troubles. She took her life, you know - well, of course, she had no choice.' And the good ladies of Tirhgunj would have shaken their heads in sympathy. Instead, here I am, unclean, violated, an embarrassment. Cissie despises me now.

'As soon as you are fit to travel, you must return to Calcutta. There will be less chance of scandal breaking there. We must be thankful that whilst these dreadful events continue, society's mind is on far greater topics. Perhaps in Calcutta you might find -.' Cissie tossed her head and stormed out of the room. 'Frankly, Fanny, I *fear* for your future!'

How long have I been shut up in here? Only Sita and Cissie come to see me now. That kind lady who gave me the flowers, or Miss Nye who lent me the journal - why don't they come any more? Cissie keeps reading snippets from the newspaper.

'*A single bomb killed and maimed seven married women who were seated in the ditch*'. Her voice has changed. It is hard and brittle. She never talks to me now . . . just reads the newspapers. '*To the imagination of our countrymen, oppressed and bewildered by the infernal tumult, it seemed that the land was live with a hundred cannon and a myriad of sharpshooters . . .*'

The walls of the room are dark, closing in, pressing down . . . My unborn child is stirring, nudging me to notice its existence. But I mustn't notice, mustn't love it. It is nothing to me.

'Day and night the fire never ceased . . . the round-shot crashed and spun through the windows, raked the earthwork . . .'

'How is Alice? Why does she not visit me any more?'

'It would not be fitting for her to see you in your condition.'

My condition is concealed under umpteen shawls. This poor child, sleeping peacefully in its dark warm world, will never know its mother's breast. What a cruel future awaits it - thrown into an orphanage for half cast children because its mother is too cowardly to admit the truth.

'Never in European warfare has the sword been deliberately pointed at a female breast. If the Nana knew the valour and strength of our officers too well, how came it that he did not respect the weakness of our ladies?'

'Cousin Jane. Mr Hopkirk. Little Freddie?

'We have had no news of them. No one has.' Cissie's eyes narrowed with contempt, as though she was thinking: Why you? Why were you spared?

'When the Nana exhorted his followers to slay and spare not, he spoke to willing ears. He believed our power to be a chimera, and he discovered it to be a hydra . . .'

She buried her face in her pillow.

Why was I spared? I should have died with my child in the *bibighar*. This living hell would be over. If only I could just fall asleep and never wake up. My child and I.

Convulsive, cramping pains wake her. She is shivering - from cold or heat? She can hardly breathe. Her unborn child is ripping at her insides. She doubles over, clutching her stomach. *I won't hurt you. I just want to love you.* A ghostly figure stands at the foot of her bed, a miserable spectre, ragged and bloodied by war. It grips her in his arms. *I wish I could hold you until we are both dead!*

Yes, you may kiss me, and cry: and ring out my kisses and tears. You loved me - then what right had you to leave me? What right - answer me?

'Memsahib, memsahib, come!'

Forgive me. If I've done wrong, I've died for it.

'What is it, ayah?'

'Miss-Sahib very sick.'

I have not broken your heart - you have broken it - and in breaking it, you have broken mine. Do I want to live? What kind of living will it be when you - oh, God! would you like to live with your soul in the grave?

'I will give her another vial.'

Are you possessed by a devil to talk in that manner to me when you are dying? Is it not sufficient that while you are at peace I shall writhe in the torments of hell?

'Fanny, can you hear me?'

I shall never be in peace - I am not wishing you greater torment than I have. I only wish we had never parted.

'Fanny, will you sit up and take this? It will help you to sleep.'

The spectre is fading. *You must not go! You must not, I tell you.*

But the spectre vanishes.

She lies in bed, shivering, drenched in sweat. Her body is dissolving. Her unborn child is clawing its way out . . .

'This is most inconvenient, Mrs Balfour. I was asleep.'

'I am sorry, doctor, but she seems to be convulsing.'

Hot breath wafts across her face, reeking of whiskey and stale tobacco. Rough fingers prod and kneed her abdomen. *And where did you find this charming little filly?*

'Get away this moment! How dare you touch me!'

'Fanny, it's the doctor. You must let him examine you.'

I won't hurt you. I just want to love you.

'Just a false alarm, Mrs Balfour. I shall give her a few drops of laudanum. That should settle her till morning.'

'But I have just given her a vial, doctor.'

'Have you? Oh well, one more shouldn't hurt. She will have a good night's sleep. That's what we all deserve - eh, Mrs Balfour? A good night's sleep.'

She is leaning over the rail watching a bird skimming over the waves - up and over, up and over, tumbling and falling . . . But a tiny wail distracts her and she is drawn to the sound like a magnet. Where is it coming from? She follows it down stairwells, along endless corridors that twist and turn back on themselves . . . She begins to run. Where is it coming from? So many false trails, so many locked doors. But here! Deep in the bowels of the throbbing ship she finds it. Pink and soft and warm. Tears stream down her face. For a moment I thought I had lost you, she laughs, scooping it up and cradling it in her arms . . . I shall never let you go, never, never . . . She presses it to her breast, and it suckles hungrily. All the love she has held back gushes out in a hot flood . . . So much love. How can a body contain so much love? Forgive me, forgive me. I shall never let you go, never, never . . . But it gives her a savage nip and latches on tight like a limpet. This is not right. This is not right at all. It is turning black. It wraps itself round her, squeezing so tight she cannot breathe. She runs up stairs, turns left and right - but it is still there, clinging tight and hard as a cancer. Sick with revulsion, she pulls and pulls. Finally she prises the thing off. With one great heave, she throws it over the side. At last she is rid of it. She leans over the rails, weeping with relief, and watches it sink, twisting and turning beneath the water. She feels dizzy, light-headed. Nothing is amiss, ladies and gentlemen. Nothing is amiss. Merciful Heaven, a baby! Quick, call the Captain. People are pressing all around her, pointing into the sea. Voices, so many voices, all speaking at once. Nothing is amiss, ladies and gentlemen. Nothing is amiss . . .

'It's quite pale, Doctor. How can that be?'

They are in a corner, huddled together. Whispering.

'Who can comprehend the mind of Satan, Mrs Balfour.'

'Mercifully it is dead.'

He leans over, fanning whiskey breath across her face, and peers at the husk in the bed. Lifts her eyelids, one by one. You won't find anything. She's not in there. She wants to push him away, but she can't because she's not there. She's over here. His red mottled nose fills her vision like a giant bruised apple. There are grey hair tufts inside his nostrils and his nose whistles as he breathes. Wheeee-wheeee-whee. He is saying something but she cannot hear because she's not there. She's over here, nursing Gilbert's baby. I shall never let you go, never, never . . .

'She is losing a lot of blood. Ask the woman to fetch more towels – and hot water!'

She never saw it. She was delirious, insensible to its arrival. It was whisked away, smuggled out of the house in bloody rags. She did not even know its sex. Was it fed to the crows? Thrown in the river without ceremony, food for the muggers? No one will tell her what happened to her baby. Hers and Gilbert's. For all these months she has carried Gilbert's baby safely inside her, close to her heart . . . Now, there is nothing left of him to cherish. *I gave him my heart, and he took it and pinched it to death; and flung it back to me.* Her breasts weep tears, hot gushing tears run in white rivulets down her stomach to join the red tears of her womb. Sita binds her up tight, painfully tight. She is swaddled so tight, she cannot weep.

'He's in the bottle! I saw him. His little fists clenched - who put him there? He can't breathe! Take him out! Take him out!'

'Hush, Fanny! - She's delirious, Doctor. She has been muttering like this for days.'

'What terrible secrets must be eating her mind, Mrs Balfour.'

3

'Fanny, a gentleman is here. Will you see him on the verandah? Ayah will help you dress.'

Her heart leapt. He has come! She knew he would come. He was not killed at Cawnpore after all. She is crying and laughing . . . It is just as well that Sita is helping . . . She cannot do up her bodice, her fingers are trembling so much.

She looked at herself in the glass. So thin and pale! Will he notice these dark rings under her eyes? Still, no matter. Everything will be better now. Everything will be better.

A burly man with a red face and a full brown beard was pacing up and down the verandah, clutching his *topee* and perspiring profusely.

'Miss Duquesne?'

It was not -

She fell into a chair. The dam burst; she could not stem the flood. All the tears she had stored poured out. She could not stop.

'I am so sorry, Mr Cowan Bell, but Fanny is still very delicate. It is her nerves, you see - the smallest thing seems to set them off.'

He wiped his glistening face with a large handkerchief.

'I understand, of course I understand, Mrs Balfour. What a trial she must have gone through.'

'We will probably never know the full story.'

'Poor defenceless child.'

'And so now do you understand my reasons for writing to Mamma? She can receive far better council in Calcutta. There is nothing more we can do for her here. Quite frankly, the doctor here is an imbecile!'

'You have my complete assurance that I shall deliver Miss Duquesne quickly and safely into Mrs Vauloué's hands.'

He leaned towards her. Warm breath wafted across her face. 'Miss Duquesne, can you hear me? You must not be afraid. I have come to take you back with me to Calcutta. We shall travel slowly by *palki*. The Grand Trunk Road is safer now. It is being manned by the Queen's soldiers.'

He was talking to her as though she were a child . . . but she heard nothing. She was only conscious of his hot trembling hand, pawing her fingers. She was his little *poupée,* his fragile bisque ornament. *He caught me in his silken net, and shut me in his golden cage.*

He outwitted her. It is always the quiet ones you least suspect. She will rest quietly in her cage. She is too weary to fight. No doubt it will be a pretty cage, velvet lined, comfortable . . .

She'll not want for anything . . . be fed on dainty morsels, and asked to play and sing.

4

Middleton Street, Chowringhee, Calcutta, India

2 March 1858

My dear Mrs Doré,

Francina has returned to Calcutta and is safely under our roof. As you know, for the past few months she has been nursed by my daughter Mrs Cissie Balfour at Tirhgunj, but my daughter was so troubled by her slow recovery, that she decided that Francina must return to Calcutta as soon as it was practicable to consult the doctors here. Our esteemed friend Mr James Cowan Bell escorted her down to us last week. We were delighted to see her again, but I confess to having been deeply shocked by her appearance. The poor girl was unable to walk up the steps unaided, and is still prone to tears at the least opportunity.

Although we were looking forward to having our dear niece with us for many months, that pleasure will be cut short, for I am delighted to inform you that Francina is engaged to be married. (No doubt, she will give you a much fuller account of her prospective husband, but for the present I wish to assure you, dear Mrs Doré, that my husband & I fully approve of the match. Mr James Cowan Bell is highly suitable in family & for a man in the prime of life has excellent prospects. In addition to which he is good, amiable & much respected, so that we think our dear niece has made a good choice. (Even in these melancholy times, golden beams of happiness do occasionally gleam between the dark clouds.) The marriage will take place shortly at St John's, & we all hope that this happy prospect will do much to restore Francina to perfect health, for I fear it will take many months of tender nursing before she recovers from her terrible ordeal. But Mr Cowan Bell is a patient, understanding man. It is his greatest desire to see his beloved Francina fully restored to her former health.

Forgive me, for I have more melancholy news to impart. My sister Maria's condition is causing us great concern. Mr Barton writes that the doctors in London say it is too late to remove the tumour. My poor sister left us in very low spirits. With her uncertain health and age, she knows that her chances of returning to India are slim, and it grieved her very much to desert her mother and family during these terrible, uncertain times. And now the news that we all dreaded - that her beloved granddaughter Jane Bulpitt & family did indeed lose their lives in the Uprising - can only compound her distress.

Calcutta continues in a state of turmoil, with every boarding house over-flowing with fugitive women and children from the Upper Provinces who have escaped with their lives & little else. A temporary hospital has been set up for the reception of the wounded officers, & we are all doing what we can to help. We are sheltering two poor ladies & their children under our roof at this moment. Both have lost their men folk; & the ladies, themselves, escaped a harrowing death by the very narrowest of circumstances. These are indeed dark days in India's history.

My husband joins me in sending you & Mr Doré our best wishes.

I remain, affectionately yours, Cecilia Vauloué.

PART THREE

Each that we lose takes part of us;
A crescent still abides,
Which like the moon, some turbid night,
Is summoned by the tides.

Emily Dickinson (1830-1886) *Time and Eternity*

GUERNSEY

May 1880

She leaned over the wall of the Esplanade. A trading ketch was cutting through the water; her brown sails billowed taut in the breeze. The *Sea Sprite* from Portsmouth, the name on the stern informed her. The captain's voice boomed out and deft sailors scurried about adjusting sails. The vessel changed tack and headed towards France.

France . . .

For a brief moment she saw herself standing on the deck. How perfect that would be. . . Why did she have this constant yearning to be somewhere else - to be someone else? She had never felt comfortable with the appellation 'Mrs Cowan Bell', any more than she felt comfortable as this creature trussed in its expensive ebony casing.

The rhododendrons would be flowering at Blackhill soon . . . such vivid pinks and mauves. They were James's pride and joy. Seventeen years. Is it really seventeen years since the seedlings were brought back from India? It was a miracle so many survived.

No, she cannot return to Blackhill yet. No one can deny that Scotland is beautiful, but so cold and damp. And that heavy opaque light choked her at times. She felt no empathy with the place. She never has. She has never truly *belonged.* Oh, she ought to be grateful. Why, some probably envy her, mistress of that great baronial mansion. But the house is like a mausoleum when the children are away. She rattles around those dreary rooms like a pea in a drum - lonely, but not alone. No, she is never alone, when every move she makes is monitored, watched, scrutinised. The house is full of spies.

James never suspected, of course. He loved the place. Blackhill was the manifestation of all his dreams. Even now, two years after his death, she feels his haunting presence checking her out. Whenever she strolls in the garden, she half-expects to come across him striding down the path, prodding the seedlings with his cane or chatting to the gardeners by the greenhouses.

No, she cannot return to Blackhill yet.

He told her that he had loved her from the moment he saw her throwing those clothes into the sea. He stifled her with his love.

She made only one stipulation when they married: that he must retrieve the necklace from the moneylender's and return it to Grand-mère. He did so, and asked no questions, and for that she was grateful. Would he have married her if he had known? She never found the courage to tell him. But she tried to make up for it. She was *Mrs James Cowan Bell: the charming hostess, renowned in the district for her grace and hospitality* - the perfect wife and mother.

'Madame, Madame, wake up.'

Nurse Bresson peered into her face. 'Madame, it is three o'clock in the morning. Time you were in bed. I shall sit by Mr Doré for a while.'

'How is Uncle?' she asked, suppressing a yawn.

'As you see, he sleeps soundly. His breathing is more regular. The treatment is working. But if you do not take care of yourself, Madame, we shall soon have another patient on our hands,' whispered the nurse kindly.

Francina stretched her back. 'Tomorrow, perhaps, I shall make some calls. There are so many people I must see before I leave.'

'That would be a good idea, Madame.'

Francina leaned over the sleeping old man and kissed his dry, leathery forehead. His face twitched into a smile, but he did not open his eyes.

She folded the letter, dragged her tired body to the parlour and returned it to the bundle of letters in the escritoire.

A cool wind cut through her clothing as she stepped out of the hired gig. She rapped the knocker of Haute House loudly, and took a deep breath. A maid opened the door and ushered her into the drawing room.

It took a few moments for her to realise that the crumpled old lady on the chesterfield smothered in a shawl with a yarn of blue wool stretched over her hands was Aunt Duquesne, and that the middle-aged woman sitting beside her, winding it into a tight ball was Cousin Julia.

'Ina, dear! We have been so looking forward to seeing you again!' Julia held out her face to receive Francina's kisses. She looked painfully thin.

'What a fine lady you have turned into – hasn't she Mamma?'

'What did you say, dear?' Aunt Duquesne blinked through thick spectacles, as an urbane stranger kissed her awkwardly on the cheek.

'Mamma, this is Francina – dear Frank's daughter,' Julia said in a loud voice.' You remember Francina, don't you?' Julia leaned forward and whispered, 'Mamma's hearing is not what it used to be.'

'Frank's daughter?' muttered Aunt Duquesne. Her face broke into a smile.

'Please sit down, Ina. No, do sit nearer the fire. Your cheek is cold. Is it very cold outside? I'm afraid we haven't ventured outside today, have we Mamma?' Julia rolled up the wool, while Francina chose a seat as far from the fire as possible. The room was very close. She should have handed her fur cape to the maid after all.

Julia nodded to the maid hovering in the doorway. 'Martha, bring some coffee – and that special cake.'

The maid looked mystified. 'The Dundee cake, Miss?'

'Yes, yes, the Dundee cake! – And the best china. This is a special occasion, Martha. '

'Very good, Miss.'

While the maid set up a small table in the centre of the room and carefully unpacked the best service from the corner cupboard, they exchanged family trifles.

Soon the air became infused with the aroma of brewing coffee. Francina sipped her drink. The room was just as she remembered – only a little more threadbare: the acanthus-leaved wallpaper; Aunt's collection of French china; the brocade drapes, faded where they had caught the sun. The great Huguenot Bible, marked with the daily reading lay open on the table where it had always lain; but now a sleek black cat curled before the fire where once a white one had slept, and more embroidered cushions than ever covered the chairs.

Nothing else had changed in twenty-four years.

'How do you like this coffee, Ina? It comes from the Wattewalle Estate. Alex sent us a box for Christmas. He sends us a box every Christmas - and a box of tea. Tea production at Wattewalle has now outstripped coffee production.'

It would have been impolite not to inquire after Cousin Alex.

It was the cue for Julia to relate all the stories she knew about Alex Marquand and his family. She probably knew as much about Alex's family as she did her own - but then what else was there for her to do? Julia lived her life through everyone else's.

'Anthony writes regularly, of course, but his letters are predominantly about military campaigns and expeditions. And all those strange names! *Mohumrah, Jemadar, Jampon* - sometimes we have no idea what he is writing about, do we Mamma?

'What did you say, dear?'

'I was saying that Anthony's letters are full of strange names, Mamma; we have no idea what he is writing about! - That was why we used to appreciate your letters so much, Ina. You always gave us a quiet *domestic* view of India.'

'How is Anthony? Is he still in Afghanistan?'

'Indeed. His eyesight is troublesome. The glare of the sun is taking its toll. We will be very glad when these skirmishes are over. The surgeon has warned him that if his eyesight shows no sign of improvement, he may be compelled to go before the Medical Board and considered for early retirement. We should be delighted to have him home, but Anthony would be devastated. Soldiering is his life.'

Anecdotes were exchanged until every member of the family, from the oldest to the very youngest had been discussed, but there was one person whom they both pointedly omitted - Angelo.

'More coffee, Mamma?'

Did Julia keep this cheerful pretence all the time? Were there ever moments when she raged and tore at her hair? Of course not. Julia was the perfect daughter: chaste, obedient and dutiful.

'We treasure all your letters - don't we, Mamma? But we especially enjoyed your *Indian* letters. You wrote so vividly that we could picture the country and the people as clearly as if we were living there. Would you like to read them, Ina?' Julia stood up and opened the drawer of the bureau. She held up a bundle of letters, tied in faded pink ribbon. 'See. I have kept them all.'

Francina declined. She had no wish to resurrect any more falsehoods. 'Sometimes it feels as though India was nothing more than a (she was about to say *bad* but checked herself) dream.'

Julia laughed. 'How can you say that, Ina? You would not have met your dear husband if it had been a *dream*!'

Francina nibbled the cake. She was told that Madame Le Boutillier had sent it over as a little pick-me-up when Aunt Duquesne was colded.

Francina promised to call on her very soon. 'And are you still in touch with Miss Chesterton?' She had made various attempts over the years to contact her old mistress, but her letters were all returned unopened. Miss Chesterton appeared to have vanished off the Island.

Julia glanced furtively at her mother. Then she leaned forward and whispered, 'How could I, Ina? I realised from the start that there was something highly suspect about her.'

'Highly suspect? What do you mean, Julia?'

'Miss Chesterton had some very strange notions. She was one of those Women's Rights fanatics. Did you not hear of the scandal? It came to light not long after you left. It appears that she was inciting the girls at the Academy. One poor girl, a Miss Lefevre, took her preaching to heart and ran away to London. She joined a group of dissenters who were provoking unrest amongst the working classes with their radical publications. Miss Chesterton, apparently, had encouraged her, not only immorally but financially as well. It caused terrible ructions when the truth came out. Parents were in uproar. Miss Chesterton was dismissed and left the Island in disgrace. The Academy never fully recovered from the scandal.'

'What happened to Miss Lefevre?'

'Oh, she was eventually tracked down. She was discovered distributing leaflets to fallen women in a very disreputable part of London. Her brothers brought her home and had her committed to a private asylum.'

'Wasn't it rather drastic to lock the poor girl up?'

'Well, she must have been unbalanced to have behaved so irrationally. And restraining her in an asylum is perhaps the best course for her. God willing, with corrective treatment, her excesses will be tempered and one day Miss Lefevre will return to the fold, a fitting member of society.'

'Bowed and chastened.'

'Indeed. But Miss Chesterton is the real villain in this drama. She infected the girl's mind with her un-Christian ways. She ruined that poor girl's life. Women like that deserve to be put away themselves!'

Were Miss Chesterton's ideas misplaced? She had such high hopes that one of her girls would carry the flag, Champion the Cause. But she was thwarted in the end, like poor Miss Lefevre (like we all were) by the overpowering forces of convention. In the end we all found the obstacles too great. It was easier to submit than to fight. . . .

'I used to dream of running away and doing something highly irrational - like becoming one of Miss Nightingale's nurses.'

'Just think, Ina. If you had not been so level-headed, you might have ended up like poor Miss Lefevre - paying the price for Miss Chesterton's dangerous ideas!'

'I used to find some of her ideas truly inspiring.'

'Perhaps you did, Ina, but you were rational enough to realise that there is a vast difference between dreams and reality. We all have dreams, but most of us realise they are only dreams. It is the sensitive and the vulnerable who cannot distinguish between dreams and reality - and those are the poor girls that must be protected from menacing women like Miss Chesterton.' Julia's cheeks flushed pink with indignation.

Francina looked at her. Julia must have had her share of dreams. More dreams than most, she suspected. Poor Julia. She stayed behind like an obedient daughter, and played the role that had been mapped out for her from the day she was born.

'What a beautiful piece of embroidery,' she said, to change the subject.

'It's a new prayer cushion for the Church,' smiled Julia, holding it up her to examine. 'But sometimes I wonder if I have not made St Peter's head too small?'

Francina admired the flowing waves and the leaping silver fish and assured her that St Peter was in perfect proportions. Religion was the substitute for Julia's dreams.

'By the way, Ina, did you ever receive that letter?' Julia asked, when Francina stood up to take her leave.

'The letter?'

'The letter found in that bag of loot on that dead sepoy, which eventually found its way to Anthony after the Mutiny? Some thoughtful person must have deduced that Miss Duquesne might be a relative of Captain Anthony Duquesne and sent it to him. Anthony knew at once that it was for you. There could only be *one* Miss Francina Duquesne living in India.'

'Yes, I did receive it.'

The letter had travelled across India and taken over a year to find her. She was newly married and heavy with child. She still had it, and could recite every word of it. It was her most treasured possession.

2

'Your presence has worked wonders on our patient, Madam,' smiled the doctor, returning his stethoscope to its black case. 'I think Mr Doré is well enough to spend a few hours a day sitting in an armchair – and if the weather is particularly mild, I might even suggest a short spell in a sunny corner of the garden, as long as he is well wrapped up, of course.'

'The credit must go to Nurse Bresson, Doctor. I was only obeying instructions,' Francina said at the front door.

'Indeed.' The doctor marched to the little gate, raised his hat and smiled. 'Good morning, Madam.'

She walked into the parlour with the bundle of letters tied up in their white ribbon, stuffed them back into the rosewood compartment and locked the escritoire. She would keep her memories concealed inside - alongside the letters from Angelo that she could not bring herself to read. She would leave them all safely stored amongst Aunt's account books.

'Shall I light your pipe for you, Uncle?'

'Would you, my dear.'

Francina selected a pipe from the rack on the bureau, pulled out sinewy strands from the old tobacco jar and pressed them into the pipe bowl. It was so long since she had done this. She had never lit her husband's pipe. She struck a lucifer, sucked heavily on the pipe until sparks caught hold and a wisp of smoke spiralled to the ceiling, and placed it gently between Uncle's lips.

'You see, Uncle, I have not forgotten.'

Uncle drew on the pipe with a grunt of pleasure, leaned against the pillows and shut his eyes. Tobacco smoke wrapped its protective arms around them both. She smiled and inhaled deeply.

'How long have you been looking after me, my dear?'

'Nearly three weeks.'

'And will you be returning directly to Scotland?'

'As the weather looks settled, I thought I might take a short trip to France. Explore the countryside around Carteret.'

'Carteret? Your aunt Sabonière had some property near Carteret.'

'A cottage, Uncle, which she left to me when she died. I expect it is just a ruin, but it might be fun to seek it out. I thought I would take my sketchbook. It is so long since I tried my hand at drawing.'

In truth, she had never felt the urge while James was alive.

'You see, Francina,' Uncle pointed to the drawing hanging on the wall. 'I still have your sketch of the rooftops of St Pierre. It is the first thing I see when I wake up in the morning.'

She made a detour to the New Cemetery. It was the visit she had been putting off since her arrival. She had intended to come to Guernsey to pay her respects when they had left India, but events had played against her. Walter was poorly, then little Marie had the first of her seizures; she was so ill, it was impossible to leave her. Then the boys caught scarlet fever . . .

She bought some tulips from the old woman sitting near the steps. A scruffy boy raced ahead to open the gates for her. She smiled and gave him a farthing. In earlier times she would have known his father and his grandfather. The cemetery was fuller than she remembered, and the tombs looked surprisingly plain after the huge monuments with over-flowing epitaphs she had come to know in India. Here the dead were recorded with a blunt simplicity.

She made her way to the corner of the burial ground, to the spot where she and Lulu used to while away the hours dreaming of their future. The cypress tree had been cut down. A new tomb now occupied the spot. She approached on tiptoe and glanced at the inscription. It contained the remains of dear old Mrs Doré . . . and her son, Harry the Jurat. She approached the old Doré tomb cautiously.

Sacred to the memory of
LOUISA
died 24 February 1863 aged 26
Beloved daughter of . . .

She never envisaged herself coming here to pay her respects to Louisa - Aunt Doré, perhaps - but never Louisa. But who reading those lines could have any inkling of her sunny disposition or her zest for life? She placed the tulips on the tomb, and ran her fingers along its lichen-spattered lid. It was a constant source of regret that she was unable to attend her funeral. But they were still in India, and by the time they had received the news, Louisa lay cold in her tomb. Was she in some way responsible for her death? If Louisa had gone to India in her place, would she be standing here, looking down at her name carved on this tomb? No. Louisa would have died anyway. She would have died with her beloved Henry in the Mutiny . . . Louisa was destined to die in her prime. But for a few brief months she would have experienced the exquisite joy of sleeping in the arms of the one she loved.

She made her way slowly out of the New Cemetery, reading remembered and forgotten names. *Aunt Marquand . . . old Monsieur Priaulx . . . Sophie Gosselin* - Surely not Sophie Gosselin? Was it the same wasting disease that carried off Louisa?

The *Dressmaker and Haberdasher's* sign with its fancy ironwork fastenings was visible some distance away, for it was the most elaborate sign in High Street. Francina crossed the street and studied the facade. The establishment had expanded to incorporate the old tea dealer's business next door. Most of the shops in High Street now sported large plate windows, but *Madame Le Boutillier's* windows displayed a refinement more akin to a large provincial town than a small Island capital.

She glanced in the window, and for a fleeting moment saw a cloaked figure reflected in the glass . . . The figure faded, and in its place she saw the slim silhouette of an urbane sophisticate, a creature quite out of place in this busy Island street. At what point did the artless girl turn into the elegant woman? Beyond the reflection, four sylph gowns of exquisite workmanship occupied a space that once contained, at most, two voluminous crinolines.

The interior of *Madame Le Boutillier's* caught her by surprise. The shop radiated a new graceful opulence (clearly the work of an aesthetic feminine eye). The fashionable flocked wallpaper was the perfect backdrop for the sumptuous new gas chandeliers.

A pleasant faced young girl, neatly attired, came up and curtsied.

'Is Madame Le Boutillier in?'

'May I ask who is calling, Madame?'

Francina handed her a card. The girl directed her to a seat and disappeared through an inner door marked: PRIVATE. Francina sat down, her pulse quickening at the prospect of seeing Miss Hobson again.

A few minutes later, the girl returned and directed her up a narrow flight of stairs.

Francina felt surprisingly at home in Madame Le Boutillier's sunny parlour overlooking the little harbour. The room was airy, comfortable, exquisitely tasteful. Silver-framed photographs, displayed on every gleaming surface, lovingly recorded the history of the Le Boutillier family. She glanced at the formal tinted wedding portrait (Miss Hobson looking rather stiff in a brown silk crinoline) to the most recent: a smiling Madame Le Boutillier seated on a rustic studio bench between her two fetching daughters. (Miss Lydia was the charming young girl who had taken her card. Miss Katie was downstairs working behind the haberdashery counter.)

'My stepsons are abroad,' Madame Le Boutillier was saying. 'It is my deepest regret that my dear husband did not live long enough to see how well his sons have fared. Édouard is a lawyer, and Grégoire is a shrewd business man - just like his father.'

Miss Hobson has not stopped smiling since I came into this room, thought Francina, accepting a morsel of *gâche* from the plate proffered by Miss Lydia. She radiates confidence, a peaceful serenity - so different from the timid mouse that once cowered under Aunt Doré's barks. Aunt, who had sneered at her decision to marry a shopkeeper - well, Miss Hobson surprised us all. She followed the dictates of her heart and found true happiness.

'And how is Mr Doré?'

'Uncle has made a remarkable recovery. I left him sitting in an armchair reading the newspaper. When he heard that I intended to call on you, he was most anxious that I should thank you for recommending Nurse Bresson. I do not think Uncle would have pulled through without her fastidious care.'

'She is the best nurse in Guernsey in my opinion. No one could have made my poor husband's last days more peaceful or more comfortable.' Madame Le Boutillier stared fondly at the large painting of her husband dominating the room. He looked more imposing in his portrait than Francina remembered him in real life.

'It is a pity they could not summon the likes of Nurse Bresson when Louisa fell ill.'

'Whenever Miss Louisa came into the shop, she was so eager to tell me of your doings in India,' Madame Le Boutillier said quietly. 'She was always talking of the day when she would follow you out to India.'

Francina sipped her coffee as she reflected on those years, long ago when she and Louisa had huddled under the counterpane, discussing their plans and dreams.

Outside, the scream of gulls reached fervour pitch. One flew past the window, trailing sinew from its beak with a shrieking crow in hot pursuit. The fisherwomen down at the harbour must be gutting the morning's catch. So much had happed to her since she was last here, but the same daily dramas in Guernsey were still re-enacted.

'And how is your brother, Mr Angelo Duquesne?'

Of course she would ask. 'He is well. He is in Canada.'

What he was doing there, she had no idea, and had no desire to know. Hatching another of his hair-brained schemes, no doubt. She paid him a small allowance. Well, she could afford it, and it kept him out of the way – and hopefully out of the country. But sooner or later, like a bad penny, he would turn up again.

Strange, she should always think of Mamma whenever Angelo's name came up. She saw her now, walking along the ramparts, her blue-spotted dress shimmering in the sunlight. Always at a hazy distance, always accompanied by him. Sometimes in a crowded street, she would brush past someone of a similar height and colouring. But after she had recovered her composure, she knew of course that it was not Mamma. The woman in the street was too young, always much too young. She had fixed the image of Mamma in her mind at the age she had last seen her on that afternoon in Valetta. The same age that I am now, she thought incredulously. Here I sit, trussed in black, just as I did on that fateful day. As far as she knew Mamma was not wearing widow's weeds. As far as she knew Judge Havers was still wielding his influence over her. She had heard from Angelo (it must have been a year or so afterwards) that they had married as soon as Mamma had received the news of Papa's passing.

'Canada! He is certainly a well-travelled gentleman. He must have many interesting stories to tell of all his adventures. Did he marry?'

'Sadly he is on his own.'

She refrained from mention Angelo's poor wife, who had returned home, deluded and dejected, to live with her family in Ireland. Of course Madame Le Boutillier would have no idea of the constant irritation he was to his relatives with his abortive schemes and begging letters. No doubt he plagued Mamma as much as he did everyone else, and she, no doubt, pandered to his demands, terrified that he might divulge her secret.

'And your children, Mrs Cowan Bell, they are well?'

Francina spoke briefly of her children: Edith who was expecting her second child; Alicia, who had recently married; James, who was at Addiscombe. He was so like his father, serious and conscientious, a credit to his mother. (She secretly hoped - although she had never asked him – that Angelo passed on news of the children to Mamma. It was one reason, perhaps the only reason, why she tolerated his reappearances. Sometimes in her imagination she would fabricate a meeting with Mamma and imagine their conversation . . . but really, it was too late, much too late to make amends. But it was her deepest regret that Mamma did not know her grandchildren.)

'Just like my boys!' smiled Madame Le Boutillier. 'They have been good to me, and so protective towards their sisters. No suitor will ever be good enough for them.' She laughed. 'But their brothers mean well. They are ambitious for their sisters. I am very blessed.'

They talked pleasantly of friends and children until the Town clock struck twelve. Francina stood up to take her leave. 'You will keep a close eye on Uncle for me, won't you Madame Le Boutillier?' she said as they made their way downstairs. 'And write to me immediately if he shows signs of a relapse?'

'It would be a pleasure, Mrs Cowan Bell. – But before you go, I would like you to meet my younger daughter Katie.'

Miss Katie was handing a parcel to a grey-bearded gentleman, who raised his hat and stepped smartly out of the shop as they approached the haberdashery counter.

'Your mamma has told me all about you, Katie,' smiled Francina. 'She is especially proud of your silk work. Have you anything here to show me?'

Blushing, Katie opened a drawer and brought out a shawl, exquisitely embroidered. Francina had no need to feign compliments; the work was as fine as anything she had seen in London or Edinburgh. She held out her hand and took her leave of Madame Le Boutillier and her daughters. It had been a delight to meet her charming family.

'By the way,' said Madame Le Boutillier at the door, 'did you recognise that gentleman who was leaving as we came downstairs?'

'Should I know him?'

'That was Mr Lihou.'

'Mr Gilbert Lihou?'

'Did you not recognise him? Well, I suppose it must be some - some twenty-five years since you last saw him.'

'He was not killed in the Mutiny?'

'Why, dear me, no!' said Madame Le Boutillier. 'Perhaps you are thinking of the other gentleman, poor Mr Fetherstone? He died in the Troubles, God rest his soul. I am surprised you have not come across Mr Lihou. He usually takes a daily stroll across Town.'

'Mr Lihou lives in Guernsey?'

'Why yes - for most of the year. He returned from India a few years ago. He had a distinguished career there, I believe. He often comes into the shop on errands for his wife.'

'His wife?'

'We have never seen her, the poor lady. It is rumoured that she does not leave her room. They say she never got over the death of their only child. The poor little thing did not survive her third birthday.'

'And does old Mrs Lihou of Belle Villa live with them?'

'Oh no! Mrs Lihou lives with her daughter in England.'

She completed her transactions as if sleepwalking.

Gilbert Lihou. Here. On the Island.

Her heart was a re-wound clock, ticking again.

High Street was crowded with folk coming to and from the markets. She lowered her veil. She had no wish to be recognised or intercepted. She studied the notices at the Post Office: *the Daily Packet lists; the times of High & Low Tides; the Hours of Sunrise & Sunset; the Customs House Regulations.* But she took in nothing. She left the Post Office and followed the crowds like an automaton.

A bare-footed gypsy in a floral headscarf edged in coins blocked her passage. 'To bring you luck, lady?' she smiled, shoving a small bunch of white heather under her nose.

Luck? Luck? Francina fumbled in her purse.

The gypsy gasped at the florin. 'I've no change, ma'am,' she said.

'Just take it!'

The gypsy woman snatched the coin and bit it between her teeth. 'This is your lucky day. Believe me, lady, your lucky day!'

Francina took the heather and pushed the old woman aside.

The crowds led her to Market Square, busier, noisier than the surrounding streets. A barrel organ was playing near the steps. Loud tinny refrains compounded the babble.

'Feel, Madame,' grinned a toothless old woman wearing sabots. 'Soft white wool. Fine English wool.'

Francina flinched at her garlic breath, and sidled away.

Then she saw him. His top hat was clearly visible above the crowd, his distinctive profile silhouetted against the sunlight. She could have been that girl again, experiencing all the pain and anguish of first love. She returned to the stall to regain her composure. Flustered, she fingered the array of knitted garments. Was it wise to confront him after all this time? What should she say? Twenty four years is a long time - it was a lifetime for Louisa.

The old woman smiled hopefully, exposing a line of blackened teeth. 'See, I have others. Please look! I have shawls, gloves, stockings - which does the lady prefer? Point out the colour. This one? Only five francs.'

The shawl resembled fine Brussels lace. A perfect present for her new grandchild.

'Madame, you like? Please give me a price.' The old woman thrust her face close to her own. '*Foi*, Madame, you will find no finer in Town. See, I sell it to you for only four francs!'

'Yes, yes, I will have it. But wrap it quickly! I am in a hurry.'

The old woman rummaged with painful slowness in a basket she kept under the stall for newspaper and string. Panic choked Francina. She glanced around, straining on tiptoe to keep him in sight. His presence had awakened feelings she thought long dead. But feelings of what? elation? euphoria? No, this time they were different. This time they erupted like an earthquake, and overwhelmed her to bursting point.

At last she had her parcel. Slipping her wrist through the loop of string, she raised her veil and left the stall.

They were walking towards each other. She must have taken ten paces without breathing. She had no particular plan in mind. She had no idea of what she would say when she reached him, but something was drawing her to him as surely as water to a sponge . . .

I have found you out – I am come back to you.

Now she had reached him she was lost for words, terrified of making a blunder, of exposing her feelings.

He nodded briefly as she passed and raised his hat. He did not recognise her.

She turned away. Her heart was close to collapse. She should say something. Once before she said nothing and ran away. She regretted that mistake all her life. She dug her nails into her palms and took a deep breath. Her courage had almost run out.

'It *is* Mr Lihou, isn't it?'

He stopped and turned. The colour drained from his face. 'Can it really be . . ?'

She almost cried with relief. 'Yes, yes, it is!'

'But I thought . . . in the Mutiny, you - you -'

'No - it's a long story. But, but I thought the same of you.'

'No, I didn't. I am - I'm still here.'

They began an exchange of polite enquiries, the usual courtesies that take up so much time and have so little meaning, which they conducted in strained voices against the cacophony of noise: polite, stilted words to cushion the awkwardness. There was so much she wanted to say, so much she wanted to ask.

'Did you know that Fetherstone -?'

'Poor Louisa never got over it. I believe she died of a broken heart.'

'I misunderstood her,' he murmured. 'I never quite realised -'

'None of us did, Mr Lihou.'

'I am married, you know,' he said after a pause.

'Yes,' she whispered, 'I did hear.'

The fire had gone from his eyes. That special gleam, that burning spark of fire she had once so admired. Where was it now? Worn down by his ambition to rise to the top of his profession, she supposed.

'My wife - my wife . . .'

'I know.'

'And you?'

'My husband is - my husband died.'

'I'm sorry.'

'He was a good man,' she whispered. It seemed immoral to bring him into the conversation and to condense the last twenty four years into a few cold sentences: *I was married. My husband died. He gave me seven lovely children.* He belonged to another world, another time.

No more words were forthcoming. The barrel organ was playing a tune she vaguely recognised. She could hardly bring herself to meet his eyes and not stare at his brown silk stock or his fur collar. But this was not the time to be overcome with girlish ineptitude.

His eyes were the same intense blue . . . but Indian eyes now: deep-set and encased in lines of weariness. And the furrows across his forehead express a sadness that marked his whole demeanour. Time had ground him down. His vulnerability touched her as she has never been touched before.

'I am leaving tomorrow.'

'Forgive me,' he said, his voice straining, 'but it is difficult to hear above this noise. What did you say?'

'I said, I am leaving tomorrow for France. I shall spend a few weeks in Carteret. I am taking my sketchbook. I am hoping to - to make a few sketches . . .'

'You were good at sketching. I remember . . . Carteret is a charming place.'

'So I have been told.'

Carteret. Is this all they could talk about? When there are so many things unsaid? She might as well be talking to her dressmaker or the apothecary, for the conversation would be no different. What a fool she has been. What a deluded imbecile. It was a mistake to confront him. She should have lived with her dreams.

There was nothing left. They said good-bye. She turned and walked away.

But this was wrong. She should have said something. If she does not say it now, it will be too late.

'Mr Lihou? Mr Lihou, I did receive the letter.'

He turned. 'The letter?'

'The letter you sent to Nudinapur . . . after you - after you left.'

'I tried to find out what had happened . . . I made enquiries.' He could hardly speak. 'The house burnt down - so I thought. . . '

'I received it eventually - in Calcutta. It was discovered, by chance in a hoard of loot abandoned by a sepoy on the Cawnpore Road. It took a year to find me. But it arrived too late. By the time I received it, I was - '

She looked away. It was all too long ago.

LETTERS

May 1984

Blackhill, Dumfriesshire, Scotland

23 May 1984

My dear Mrs Corfield,

I reply to your letter seeking information about my Grandmother Francina Cowan Bell. She died when I was four years old so I hardly knew her. What I do know is as follows:

Grandmother was born in Guernsey in 1838 and died in this house in 1912. My Grandparents married in Calcutta during the Sepoy Mutiny. Grandfather was a partner in firm of indigo and jute agents out there. They had seven children. Edith, Alicia, James, Marie and Walter were born in India. Connie (who died young) and my father William (their youngest child) were born in Dumfriesshire. Although he was only seven years old when Grandfather died, Father had fond memories of him. He was a great shot, a first-class fisherman and quite devoted to Grandmother.

When Grandfather died, Grandmother took up painting (so the story goes) and turned out to be rather an accomplished artist. She was left a small cottage near Carteret in Normandy by a relative in Guernsey. The cottage became her private retreat and no one was encouraged to visit her there. She usually planned her trips when her children were at school, so they were not inconvenienced. In later life, she spent most of the year over there.

We have some of Grandmother's paintings hanging here at Blackhill. There is a particularly fine one of the cottage (looking rather quaint with a thatched roof, roses over the door, and hens running in the yard). It hangs above her desk - in what was once her private sitting room - and is painted in a free Impressionist style. When Grandmother died, she left the cottage to a young Frenchman living near Carteret, a gifted artist whom she seemed to have taken under her *wing. (She was fond of collecting waifs and strays, and was a generous benefactress - as this enclosed news cutting of her Obituary shows.) I was in Paris a few years ago and by chance came across an exhibition of his work. He painted in bold sweeps of colour - rather like the artist Matisse. Had he not been killed in the Great War, I am sure his work would be better known outside France. (The Tate Gallery holds some of his work in their Reserve Collection. If you are there, ask to see the paintings of <u>René Henri Lihou</u> 1882-1917.)*

I especially liked his paintings of a woman reclining on a couch in a loose floral robe with hair twined casually on her shoulders. The sitter reminded me of a portrait we have of Grandmother, but it could not have been her for she was always elegantly turned out and only wore black after Grandfather died.

Your letter inspired us to open Grandmother's strong box which has been languishing under a layer of dust in the attic - something we have been meaning to do for a long time. We were rather disappointed when we broke it open (having procured the services of local locksmith at great expense). It was full of the usual personal mementoes: children's letters, locks of hair - nothing of any great value. We found a few letters kept in a very battered jewellery box. Perhaps you can make sense of them? I enclose copies of them for you to read.

Grandmother had a brother, I believe, who spent his remaining years in the Dumfries Asylum. In her will, she requested her children to continue the weekly payments for his upkeep, which I believe they did until his death in 1921.

I am sorry I cannot be more help. It was so long ago and my memory is not what it used to be. Father used to refer to Grandmother as 'a dark horse' for she was reluctant to talk about her past or her family. So it came as a great surprise to learn that she saved your Great-Grandmother's life during the Indian Mutiny. Could you give me more details?

Please return the notes and Obituary to me in due course. The photograph you may keep.

Yours sincerely, George Cowan Bell

Enclosure: Letter found in Mrs Cowan Bell's strongbox. The envelope is addressed:

~~*To Miss Francina Duquesne, c/o Mr F. Bulpitt, Nudinapur Indigo Concern, near Kandria*~~

The address is crossed out and over this is scrawled:
REDIRECT TO:
CAPTAIN ANTHONY DUQUESNE, BENGAL ARTILLERY

Written in camp – in haste –
on the Muttput road, twenty miles from Kandria
2 June 1857

My dear Miss Francina,

Forgive my abrupt departure, but I was called away early this morning to settle a dispute, which threatens to escalate if it is not quickly resolved. There was only time to write a brief note to Mrs Bulpitt, but I made up my mind that as soon as I pitched camp, I would pen a long letter to you to explain my feelings.

Now, as I sit in this sweltering tent, I can think only of you. You are the sweetest, most beautiful creature that has ever – or will ever - cross my path. When we met again in Calcutta, I knew it would not be long before some fortunate fellow secured your hand (indeed, naïve as I was, I thought this was already the case), and I left Calcutta with a heavy heart – for I truly believed that you had already decided on your future plans.

But on that fateful day when Providence threw us together again, I realised that my earlier assumptions might have been unfounded. During these last few days at Nudinapur, as we renewed our friendship, I discovered to my joy that you did not seem indifferent to my presence (as I had sometimes sensed you were in the past). Just knowing that you were in the same room would set my heart in turmoil, and I found myself asking: what is success without happiness? For until that moment, marriage had played no part in my ruthless ambition to succeed.

Now I know I shall never be truly happy if you are not by my side. So with trepidation I take up my pen and pray with all my heart that it is not too late - dearest Miss Francina, could you contemplate life as the wife of a poor Assistant Collector? On my present salary I can offer you very little. But with prudent management we might scrape by.

If I am not too late, if there is any hope of my securing your affections, please send word to me at Kandria and I shall return immediately to claim your hand.

I am in torment. I love you to distraction.

Gilbert L.

END

Glossary of Anglo-Indian Words

from *Hobson-Jobson: A Glossary of Colloquial Anglo-Indian Words and Phrases etc,* (first published 1886)

Angrezi-log – British people
ayah – Indian nanny or maidservant
baksheesh – tipping, charity giving, bribery
bhang – cannabis plant consumed as a beverage
bhisti – water carrier
bhossa – straw
bibi – European's native mistress or a Muslim wife
box-wallah – itinerant peddler selling (chiefly European) knick-knacks
bubris – stylised tiger stripes
budmarshes – rascals, bad fellows
bund – embanked road
burqa – one piece cloak covering the body with small netted square to see through
burra hazri - big, or main breakfast taken at about 9 or 10 am.
burra khana – grand dinner
Burra Mem – senior lady
chabutra – elevated structure or platform
chatti – large earthenware water pot
chicks – finely–split bamboo blind
chicon-wallah – a man who embroiders
chit – note (usually delivered by the *peon*)
chuddah – a sheet or shawl
chunam – a fine polished plaster made of lime
chuprassi – messenger or attendant
chapatti – small, thin cake of coarse unleavened bread
chota hazri –'little breakfast' consisted of tea, coffee, fruit or biscuits taken at about 5 am before the early morning gallop
chota-sahib – little master
competition-wallah – East India Company official selected by examination
cutcherry – court of justice, office of a magistrate or other civil official
dacoits - robbers

dâk-ghari – post cart or carriage
darzi – tailor
Deen! – for the faith!
dhobi-wallah – laundry man
dhood-dhye – wet nurse
dhoty – loose loin cloth
durwan – gatekeeper or porter
ekka – bullock cart
feringhi – a derogatory term for foreigner
guala – milkman
hookah-burder – servant who looks after hookah
hookah – Indian hubble-bubble pipe
howdar – elephant seat or saddle
Jeldi, jeldi!'- hurry, hurry!
jheel – shallow, marshy lake
jharuns – cloths, napkins
jilmils – venetian blinds or shutters
Jor se challo! – Get on with it!
khansamah - head butler
khitmutgar – table waiter
Koi–hai! - 'is anyone there!' a call to summon a servant
Koi hai! kuttle - massacre
lathiyals – guards which carry a *lathi*, a thick iron-bound club
machan – hunting look-out platform
mahout – elephant driver
mali – gardener
mata-rani – sweeper queen
mére jani – my darling
mem-log – white women
moffusil – up country, countryside
munshi – language teacher or translator
musolchi – cook's boy
nautch – erotic entertainment by Indian dancers
nullah – dried up river bed
palki – palanquin
pani – water
pan supari – betel nut (a stimulant)
peon – messenger
pish-pash – child's meal of mashed chicken and rice
pukka – top rate, best

punkah – large frame of wood covered with cloth to stir the air
punkah-wallah – servant who moves punkah
rasai – cotton quilt
ryot – cultivator or farmer
saddhu – ascetic holy man
sahib – master
suttee – Hindu custom requiring the self-immolation, of a widow on her husband's funeral pyre (abolished by the British in 1829)
shikar – hunting sport, shooting
shikari – hunter
sower – cavalry trooper
syce – groom
tatties (kus-kus tatties)- woven grass roller blinds
thuggee – a secret society of robbers and murderers devoted to the goddess Kali
tiffin – luncheon
tonjon – an open sedan chair carried on the shoulders of four men.
zemindar – landholder, person recognised by British law as the proprietor of land
zenana – native women's quarters

POEMS CITED

30 *Tis melancholy, and a fearful sign…* Lord Byron, *Don Juan* c III 5
63 *I met a Lady in the Meads…* John Keats, *La Belle Dame Sans Merci*
130 *We gaze and turn…* Lord Byron, *Childe Harold's Pilgrimage* c IV 50
130 *They feared no eyes…* Lord Byron, *Don Juan* c II 189
444 *Will you walk into my parlour…* Mary Howitt, *The Spider and the Fly*
472 *How sweet I roam'd from field to field…* William Blake, *Song* (1783)

QUOTATIONS FROM

Charlotte Brontë, *Jane Eyre* (1847)
Emily Brontë, *Wuthering Heights* (1847)
John Keats, *The Eve of St Agnes* (1820)
Heinrich Hoffmann, *The English Strewwelpeter,* (Leipzig, 1848)
Sir George Trevelyan, *Cawnpore*, (Macmillan & Co, 1910)

Acknowledgements

I am deeply grateful to the following for their help in the research and writing of this book. Firstly, the late Major-General James Scott Elliot for allowing me full access to his family archives - without his generosity and kindness this book would never have been written.

I also acknowledge the invaluable help given to me by the staffs of the Indian Record Office & Library, the Priaulx Library in Guernsey, the British Library, the National Archives of Scotland and the National Library of Scotland, the National Library of Wales and the Birmingham Reference Library.

Ros Riley of Warwick University for her initial encouragement and Dr Carole Angier for her valuable advice; Joy Neal for pointing me in the right direction; Megan Thomas, Olivia Lybbe-Simms, Dr Rex Valentine, Gwen Ritter and Lara Sturge for reading parts or all of the manuscript; Tim Burt for his editing skills, and Ruth Mannion-Daniels for the final push.

Finally, special thanks to my son Adam for escorting me around Calcutta and across Bengal; to my son Toby for his excellent suggestions, and to my partner Martin for his help, understanding and unfailing support.

I dedicate this book to them.